REACTION TO THE VICTIM

An Uptown Chicago Mystery

J M Grant

DEDICATION

This novel is dedicated to my beautiful city of Chicago, to my friends and colleagues at the Chicago Public Library and to librarians everywhere.

ACKNOWLEDGEMENTS

Special thanks to my first readers, Lisa Manzari and Cynthia White; to my sister Jude and brother-in-law, John for the encouragement; and to my partner Jacqueline for putting up with me. A very special thank you to Mary T. Boyle, retired sergeant of the Chicago Police Department for your invaluable suggestions and comments; thanks also to my safety net, Adriana, Jacqueline and furry friends, Joey, Milo, Eleanor, Harris and Stevie – you keep me courageous and together in my artistic obsessions. Thanks also to KEG.

Note to the reader

The story takes place around 2006-2008. You will notice no one is texting, using Smart phones, IPads and other technologies.

Reaction to the Victim is a work of fiction. All characters in this publication are entirely fictitious and any resemblance to real persons, living or dead is purely coincidental. The actions of real people, organizations and government entities mentioned in this book are also fictional. I took liberties with police protocol and procedures, intellectual property law, and psychiatric therapies and drugs. My reason for choosing Northwestern Memorial Hospital and the Evanston Police Department for the story was strictly for locale and convenience, in no way do the incidents in the narrative reflect on the fine work these organizations do.

REACTION TO THE VICTIM

CHAPTER 1

The black unmarked police car cruised through Chicago's Uptown neighborhood and headed west on Lawrence Avenue. The city was in the midst of its second heat wave of the summer with no relief in sight. Most residents stayed indoors or sought refuge in the cool waters of Lake Michigan while Uptown's notorious homeless population huddled in the shade of alleyways, on the cool concrete steps of churches, and under trees in local parks. To most people living here, this was another typical summer.

Detective Jim Ballard and his partner, Detective Monica Falco, turned south on Sheridan Road. "Sometimes I don't even recognize this neighborhood," said Ballard under his breath. "I grew up around here, you know, went to Lakeview High School down the street."

"You've told me that a half dozen times," Falco said, vaguely looking out the window of the vehicle.

"It wasn't a great place to grow up. The city was a stinkin' rundown rat hole back then. I remember when I was taking classes at Truman College waiting for the bus one night. These guys came outta nowhere and tried to jump me. Man, did I run!" Ballard laughed and rubbed his chin.

"Did you get beat up?" Falco asked, humoring him. She'd heard the story before.

He paused as he let a pretty girl cross the street. "Uh, no. I was pretty fast back then."

Ballard headed up a side street as Falco checked addresses. The North Side had been hit by a string of car thefts that pointed to a local auto repair shop. Ballard had a hunch the repair shop was actually a chop shop that funneled stolen parts to other shops in the city. They cruised past a grungy storefront and garage.

"The place doesn't look suspicious to me. Normal-looking customers out front," Falco said, squinting.

Ballard shook his head. "Yeah, well, I have my doubts about this guy. The owner's got a rap sheet. I can't believe he's gone legit."

They headed west back to Sheridan and stopped for a red light at Montrose. Falco eyed the painted windows of Jake's Chicken, a neighbor-hood dive that attracted mostly curious types. She smiled and read comically from the store's window, "Only a rooster can get a better piece of chicken!"

"Hey, that place is an institution," said Ballard, pointing his finger. "Maybe one day we'll go there for lunch, cuz I know they're good to cops."

"Noooo, thanks," laughed Falco. "That's the path to a coronary, plus I wonder if the health department's been there lately." She squinted at the storefront as the light turned green.

"I used to hang out at a lot of these places, the Rainbow Roller Rink as a kid, Jimmy's Sub Shop, the Green Mill. Boy, that was great music…great music," he recalled wistfully.

"The Green Mill's still around."

"Yeah, but I never have time to go. Plus my wife…well…"

Falco watched traffic move north on Broadway as they headed west toward Clark Street. Uptown had changed. Monique's Afro-Centric Braids just south of the Tattoo Factory had been replaced by an upscale red-lac-quered sushi place. Across the street, just north of the grungy Aldi discount grocery store, stood a tiny dress boutique and a spacious specialty food store that featured imported cheeses and wines.

Ballard leaned in toward his partner. "Hey, Justin over at booking said he saw Sam and your ex at some soccer clinic over the weekend."

"Oh, really? That's nice," she said, gritting her teeth. "Sam has really taken to soccer. It was my weekend to have him, but Jeffery wanted to take him somewhere. Guess it was a guy thing."

"Been to any games lately?"

"A few," Falco said with a sigh as she looked out the car window and tried not to let sadness overwhelm her.

Ballard sensed her discomfort. "It ain't easy. Divorce, that is. I've been through it once too. It ain't easy." Falco bit her lip and stared ahead. "Hey, let me ask you something," Ballard continued, changing the subject. "Are you on track for one of those profiler positions they're talking about adding?"

Falco looked a bit surprised for a moment; no one was supposed to know about the new positions. "Uh…well, I was approached to apply," she said, not wanting to say too much.

"Well, you got that female intuition goin' for you. I ain't cut out for that shit. I heard the training is tough, like goin' back to school."

Their radios broke in. "2306 Lassiter wants you back at the station ASAP. Do you read?"

"Got it – on our way," said Falco.

"Shit. Now what?" mumbled Ballard. He pulled the Crown Victoria into an empty parking place and squealed it into a U-turn.

Falco tried to suppress her gasp and muttered loud enough for Ballard to hear, "Jesus, you know sometimes…"

"Yeah, what?" belched Ballard.

"Nothing, nothing," muttered Falco. Ballard was politically connected; his cavalier attitude grated on Falco. *When Ballard screws up he just makes a little phone call and it all goes away,* Falco thought.

She gripped the handle on the car door. They careened south down Ashland and headed toward Addison to the twenty-third district headquarters of the Chicago Police Department.

CHAPTER 2

A crowd of uniformed cops gathered in the dingy conference room, taking seats in the odd assortment of folding gray-blue vinyl office chairs that surrounded the rectangular conference table. It was ten forty-five a.m.

"All right, everyone. We're just waiting for a few more people," shouted Chief Edward Lassiter, district commander of the twenty-third police district.

There was a rumble of voices and chairs being dragged around the table. Ballard and Falco, arriving late, sat in the back on a large marble windowsill. A dozen uniformed cops sat around the table. Falco and Ballard were the only ones wearing street clothes. Outside the glass-enclosed room was a buzz of activity.

Chief Lassiter was thick waisted and burly for a man near retirement age. His hair was curly around his ears and thinning, a mixture of brownish red and gray. Rarely was the chief seen without his reading glasses worn low on his nose or without one of his dated ties. He always dragged his tie loose from his collar and rolled up his sleeves upon entering the station for the day.

He positioned a stack of files on the conference table and moved his coffee cup out of spilling range. "Okay, folks, we've got a situation here," Lassiter began, his voice booming. "At Roll Call this morning you all heard the alert about the prison break down state. We've got some new info on this guy.

He's a convicted murderer and bank robber by the name of Brian McCaffery. He escaped from maximum security in Marion. Based on what we know about him, we think he'll be making his way to the city, unless we can get to him first. This guy is a real maggot. Does anyone remember him from a few years back?"

The uniformed cops looked at one another, then someone from the back of the room broke the silence. "Wasn't he the guy whose bank heist was busted by some woman and then he went after her?"

"That's the guy," said Lassiter, piquing everyone's interest.

"I remember that case. It was a real media circus once it went to trial," Ballard whispered to his partner. "We had a whole team of cops on duty just to keep the reporters in line."

Falco glanced at Ballard, "Gosh, yeah, I remember that. It was all over the news."

"A little background on Mr. McCaffery and how his escape affects us," Lassiter continued, rubbing his hands together. "McCaffery had a long rap sheet of petty crimes: home invasions, assault with a weapon, car theft—the usual crap. Somewhere along the way, he gets the brainy idea to hold up a bank in Evanston and crack their vault." The chief looked around the room then at an open file on the table. "So McCaffery and his partner—I forget the guy's name—borrow some books from the local library on locks and safe-cracking. Believe it or not, some libraries actually have these kinds of books on their shelves."

Lassiter paused and shook his head then twisted a bottle of water open.

"McCaffery and his accomplice do their research. They figure out the kind of vault the bank has and find the mechanicals in the books they borrowed from the library. They case the place—the floor plan and escape routes. They put the whole scheme on paper: location, date, time; the whole who, what, when, and how. But here's the kicker," Lassiter said, eyeing the group, "when McCaffery returns the books to the library, he leaves a copy of the planned heist in one of the books."

"Brainiacs," Falco sniffed.

"Enter librarian, Andrea Fulbright," Lassiter said. "McCaffery goes to the library to return the books. He runs into Ms. Fulbright, who's opening the library for the day. She does the guy a favor and offers to take the books from him. Nice lady. Fatal mistake. Later on, Ms. Fulbright finds the papers in one of the books. Being the good citizen she is, she goes to the Evanston police and shows them the plans, but they basically blow her off."

The room shuffled with whispers and commentary.

"When Ms. Fulbright returns to the library, a staff member tells her some guy came in looking for some books he returned earlier, saying he left something in one of them. Ms. Fulbright immediately knows it's McCaffery looking for his plans."

Falco listened closely as she chewed the end of her pen.

"Well, she didn't hear again from the Evanston police until after the heist that following week," Lassiter said. "Lucky for them, they had officers in the vicinity and screwed the job, killing McCaffery's accomplice but allowing McCaffery to get away. Egg on their faces; they bring Miss Librarian in for questioning. She supplies them with a detailed description of McCaffery and reiterates her story—probably with some big-time attitude, I would guess. So McCaffery's bank heist is foiled, his accomplice is dead, and he's wanted all over the state. Ms. Fulbright demands protection from the Evanston police, but they refuse, saying he's probably over state lines by now. The reality was McCaffery was after her. We now know he quietly stalked her at the library and at her home for a week before he made his move."

Ballard's stomach growled. He shifted in his seat and rattled a box of Tic Tacs, pouring a dozen or so into his mouth. Annoyed by the noise, Falco gave him a dirty look. He glared at her then loudly chewed the candy.

Lassiter continued the story as he swept around the room, "Then one night, just as the library is closing, McCaffery slips inside and hides. He comes upon an eighty-year-old female staff member and slashes her throat with an eight-inch hunting knife, virtually taking off her head. Then he goes after Ms. Fulbright. She manages to fend him off long enough to hit a panic button. They struggle and then he drags her outside, stabs her in the back and arms, then flees the scene. He's later caught just over the Indiana state line."

Chief Lassiter paused, took a swig of coffee, and proceeded in a steady tone. "Ms. Fulbright survived the attack and the murder trial and media circus. The jury threw the book at him. McCaffery was convicted of first-degree murder, attempted murder, and bank robbery. He was sentenced to life in the federal pen in Marion."

Monica took feverish notes. "You writing a book there, Falco?" Ballard teased.

Lassiter took a deep breath and paused, letting the story settle. "Unfortunately Miss Fulbright was severely traumatized by the ordeal and was hospitalized before the jury came to the guilty verdict. The subsequent civil case months later found the City of Evanston and its police department liable for Ms. Fulbright's injuries. She settled for an undisclosed sum. Interestingly, when we requested information about the case from Evanston PD, their response was that their files were archived and they couldn't retrieve them right away. They said they'd get back to us." Lassiter chuckled and shook his head in frustration as faces hardened around the room. "We've gathered what we can from our databases, but copies of their files would be helpful for what we're dealing with now."

The chief looked around the room and changed his tone. "Okay. Two things need to go on here, people. One, the entire department has been put on alert for this guy. Actually the alert is statewide. Amanda will be passing out packets of information and copies of McCaffery's mug shot. Two, we'll be providing protection for Ms. Fulbright twenty-four seven until McCaffery is apprehended."

Voices in the room rose with questions and comments. Chief Lassiter raised his hands to quell the noise. "Okay, okay. You're all wondering why *we* are providing protection for the victim. That's because Ms. Fulbright lives in *our* jurisdiction now."

"Lucky us," sneered Ballard as he looked at his watch. "Looks like our chop shop case is officially on the back burner."

Lassiter glanced toward the back of the room and made eye contact with the two detectives. Raising his voice over the rumble, he said with a smile, "Heading up our team protecting Ms. Fulbright will be our tactical team, Ballard and Falco."

The room of uniformed officers turned to them. Falco kept her annoyance to herself and nodded to Lassiter. "Great," she said under her breath. *Twenty-four seven. I've got Sam this weekend*, she thought.

The noise in the room grew louder. "Uh, people, I'm not finished here!" Lassiter shouted, trying to maintain control. There was a shuffle of papers as the officers pulled apart the packets of materials the chief's assistant was passing out. "There's one other thing I want to make you all aware of," Lassiter said, and the room quieted. "Ms. Fulbright isn't a big fan of the law enforcement family, in light of her experience with the Evanston PD and the fact that her emotional state was at one point compromised. So please, *please*, treat her with kid gloves. That means kindly and with sensitivity and respect. We don't need a civil case on *our* hands."

Dan Riley, a beat cop, leaned over to Ballard and said, "I heard Fulbright's kind of a weirdo."

Falco leaned back. "Now how would you know that?" she asked him, knowing she really didn't want an answer.

"She lives in my beat, Montrose, Buena…right by the El tracks."

"What does she do, walk her dogs naked or something?" asked Ballard.

"Don't be cute," said Falco as she got up from the windowsill.

"Ballard and Falco will have your assignments. And I have the information on Ms. Fulbright for you two," Lassiter said as he eyed the detectives. He motioned for them to come forward to the front of the room. The detectives made their way through the maze of chairs and feet. "Here's a photo and her address," Lassiter said, shoving papers into a manila file. "If she's smart, she won't balk at the twenty-four seven." The chief looked up. "One other thing. The media will be on this in no time, so make sure Ms. Fulbright has some privacy even if it means blocking off the street and the alley. And keep the TV cameras away from her home."

"How about a fucking miracle while we're at it?" Ballard whispered to himself. He took an empty seat at the conference table.

Lassiter met Falco's eyes. "Sorry, Falco," he said, leaning his head to one side, "but I think we need a woman on board here. You know?"

Falco flattened her lips together and nodded. She put her hand out for the file then looked at the photo and the list of officers and their assignments. "Some of these folks need to be shifted around," she said, looking at Lassiter and taking out her pen. She circled some names, drew arrows up and down the pages, and made notes in the margins. "Can someone make these changes?" She handed the paper to the chief's assistant, Amanda, who obliged with a scowl. Falco gathered the rest of the files. A few minutes later, Amanda returned with the revised assignments. "Ballard, get off the can already. We've got to do this," Falco said. She looked at him with irritation, and he got up with a grunt.

"Once we get settled over there and look over Fulbright's place, we'll figure out who'll do what shift," Falco said. "I don't think we both need to be there staring at each other, so figure out if you want day or night."

"I'll do nights so I can go home after we give the vic the news," Ballard said quickly.

"Fine with me." Falco scanned the revised list then looked around the room. "Riley, Strickland, Torres, and Langer, let's go!"

Falco and Ballard made their way out of the station and got in their vehicle. The others followed, paired up in their squad cars.

"What have we got on this Fulbright woman?" Ballard asked as he started the car.

Falco looked through the file. "Hm. Well, she's forty-six, one disorderly conduct in '96 and a DUI in '99."

"DUI? Hm… Okay," Ballard said as they pulled onto the street.

CHAPTER 3

The black Crown Victoria headed north on Sheridan and turned left onto Buena. "This is a one-way street with speed bumps. That's good," Falco said, scanning the neighborhood.

They went through the alley underneath the El tracks, turned right, and then turned onto Andrea Fulbright's street. Ballard parked the vehicle across the street. They found the address and buzzed the speaker on the wrought iron gate.

"Hello?" said a man's voice.

"Is this the residence of Andrea Fulbright?" asked Ballard.

"Yes, it is, but she's not home right now. Can I help you?" responded the cheery voice on the other end.

"Well, we really need to talk with her. Can we come in?" asked Ballard.

"Who are you?"

"We're from Chicago Police, Detectives Bal—"

The gate buzzed, and the detectives went through the heavy entrance door. It led to a marble interior space with silver mailboxes and a twisting staircase that led to two units upstairs.

"Second floor north," came a voice from two flights up. "I hope you're not going to try to sell me raffle tickets to some policemen's ball or whatever," said the voice from above.

Falco and Ballard made their way up the stairs, eyeing details—windows, stairs, and basement access.

Falco presented her ID to the man, who stood in front of the apartment door waiting for them. The man was roughly six foot one and more slender than muscular. He sported a cropped blue T-shirt embroidered with the letters "HRC" and slim dark jeans. Handsome with an angular face embellished by a meticulously trimmed goatee, he had the stance of a dancer with broad shoulders. His cheery voice hardly matched his face, which clouded over with concern. He met the detectives with piercing eyes.

"Oh, so you *are* the real police. I didn't think…" He gasped, and shrugged his shoulders.

Falco smiled briefly and started, "I'm Detective Falco and this is my partner, Jim Ballard, from the Chicago Police Department. We need to speak with Ms. Fulbright. Can you tell us where she is or when she might be back?"

The man leaned against the closed door and eyed them suspiciously. After a pause he said, "She's working at her studio right now. I could try her cell phone, but I can tell you right now that she doesn't have it on. She doesn't like to be disturbed while she's working," he said in a snippy tone.

"Can we come in please?" asked Falco, making a pleading face.

"Oh, uh…I guess. Sure. Excuse me for being rude. I don't get to visit with the cops that much. Please…come in. I suppose it's better for us to talk inside instead of where everyone can hear us." He motioned them to enter. Music blared inside the apartment. "Sorry. I had to get my Cher fix," he said as he turned the music down to nearly a hum.

"Nice digs," muttered Ballard in Falco's ear.

She gave him a dirty look. They scanned the expansive place. *Most likely a gut rehab*, Falco thought. *Gut rehab,* she repeated to herself. *I sound like Jeffery.* Jeffery was Falco's ex-husband and owner of a construction business in the suburb of Park Ridge.

Falco looked up as they entered the hallway that led to the living room and was struck by a large, intricately colored painting on the wall. She let out a small gasp and knew exactly where she had seen work like that before. *That amazing gallery in South Beach*, she thought. *Our last vacation before the split.* She stared at it some more, taking in its wispy brushwork and energetic colors.

Ballard brushed close to her, pushing her sideways and out of the foyer. The man led them into the living room, a large and open space with tall windows, gleaming hardwood floors, and sparse furniture. "Palatial," Ballard said.

"Are you Ms. Fulbright's husband or significant other?" Falco asked the man.

He looked at them both with surprise and said, "Oh, no…no, no!" He waved his hand and laughed.

"Then would you mind telling us your name and your relationship to Ms. Fulbright?" Falco asked.

"I'm Michael Hansen," he said, initiating a handshake from each of them. "I used to be Andie's personal nurse, and as it evolved, other things too. Actually I'm a registered nurse, but currently I'm finishing up my research for a doctorate in psych. Andie had some serious problems in the past, and I took care of her." He paused, clearly not wanting to say too much. "But she's better now, and I'm just a friend who sometimes fixes her computer and does laundry at her place." He smiled broadly and playfully kicked at the basket of clean laundry. "I live in a high-rise and doing laundry there with other people around is a real pain," he confided. "I live on the fourteenth floor and the laundry room is on the third floor. It's so boring waiting for your stuff to finish, and you never know whether you should ride the elevator all the way up between cycles or whether you should bring a book and stay down there, waiting for each cycle to finish. Unfortunately it's so noisy down there that you can't really read. Yet it's risky to leave your clothes there because things have been known to get stolen, especially if you have nice things."

"So you're here doing laundry?" Ballard asked dryly, looking up from his notepad and wishing this Michael person would shut up already.

"And I'm fixing Andie's computer," added Michael with a smile. He pulled a brightly colored polo shirt from his laundry basket and began to meticulously fold it. "I'm upgrading some graphics software. Would you two like to sit down?"

Ballard's radio squawked, and he silenced it. "This is going to take longer than I thought," he mumbled to Falco.

"So what do you need to talk with Andie about?" asked Michael. "Does she need to go to traffic school or something?"

Ballard and Falco looked at each other. Falco leaned forward and said, "Can you try her cell phone or is there a phone at her studio? How far is her studio from here?" She was getting impatient and looking for other options.

Just then a car door thumped closed below in the back alley, and everyone looked in the direction of the noise. A flash of hope rose in Ballard. He glanced at Falco with a little smile. They heard footsteps trudge up the outdoor wooden stairs.

"Oh, you may be in luck. That might be her now," Michael said melodically. He hummed to himself as he went to one of the living room windows. He looked down and pressed his forehead to the glass.

Andie Fulbright, looking distracted and annoyed, appeared at the bottom of the first landing of stairs. She was talking to herself and gripping her cell phone. "She's not in a good mood," Michael said lightly as he glanced at the detectives.

She's going to be in an even worse mood when we finish talking with her, Falco thought.

Michael, muttering something to himself, opened the kitchen door and started down the stairs to meet Andie. When she saw Michael, she raged, "Don't tell me Kat is on the phone. If she calls me one more time, I'm going to fucking lose my mind! How much work do you think I got done over there with her calling every fucking second? I'm under a serious deadline and every aspect, every aspect of my life—questions, questions! Nine messages on my voice mail! God, I just…" she sputtered. "I threw my fucking cell phone, and now it's busted!"

Andie paid no attention to Michael and what he was trying to say to her. Finally Michael put up his hands and said, "Whoa. Whoa there," stopping her noisy ascent. He bent down to meet her eyes and put his hands on her shoulders.

Andrea was pissed off. She stopped and looked at him, confused and annoyed, and shouted, "What! What! *What* is it, Michael?"

Quietly and composed, Michael said, "Two cops are here to talk to you… detectives."

Andie stopped and thought for a moment. Her eyes darted around, and she said, "What? Police?" Her heart began to race. She looked at Michael and searched his face, his eyes for something, some kind of answer. "What could they want with *me*?" she said with hardly a breath. She pushed Michael softly out of the way with a hand on his chest and stomped up the stairs and through the door.

Andie entered the kitchen area and walked into the living room where the two detectives stood. She anxiously looked at them. Ballard, a stocky man with brown-and-gray wavy hair, wore a brown sports jacket, a blue denim shirt, and a silk tie. His khaki pants were pressed, and his wing-tip shoes looked newly shined. He gave Andie his proverbial detective smile—short, detached, and official. Andie gazed at Falco with expectant eyes. Her olive skin and wiry hair gave away her Italian ancestry. Her features were angular, her eyes more black than brown. She was slightly taller than average, thin—almost bony—and dressed in a tan linen blazer, black pants, and a crisp white blouse.

Andie's anger hid the fear on her face. She nodded to both and said in a tiny voice, "What do you want?" Distrustful and distracted, she moved farther into the room, out of place among the gleam and artfulness of her furnishings. Her hair, light brown, shoulder length, and disheveled, was host to a dusting of sawdust and what appeared to be spray paint. She was small and thin but wiry, and her forearms and hands were those of an artist or carpenter. She wore a black, clingy tank top peppered with a variety of paint colors from previous projects. Sweat streaked a clean line through a thin layer of dirt and sawdust on her chest, making its way between her breasts. Over the tank top she wore a hopelessly dingy Western shirt with pearl buttons. It covered only slightly the bulge of a well-worn leather tool belt, which hung low on her hips and held a hammer and a pair of battered work gloves. Her steel-toed boots were scuffed, and she smelled of some kind of solvent or paint. She shook her head, looked at her hands, and wiped them on her pants. "Sorry," she said, distracted. "I left in a hurry. I forgot something. What…what do you want?" she asked again, searching their faces. Falco and Ballard introduced themselves and showed their IDs.

"Ms. Fulbright," Falco started with a polite smile, "a few years back were you involved in a case with a Brian McCaffery."

Instantly, as if struck by a jolt of static electricity, Andie winced and stepped back. She gasped and shot Falco a fearful look. She clutched herself in defense. Michael's eyes darted between the detectives and Andie. He wasn't sure he wanted to hear the rest.

"You knew him? Mr. McCaffery?" Falco asked, tentatively, almost kindly.

CHAPTER 5

Three hours dragged by as Falco tried to stay awake. *I should have taken Michael up on the coffee*, she thought. Her peanut butter and jelly sandwich hardly satisfied her hunger. She rolled the kinks out of her neck and looked at her watch. *God, it's quiet. Everyone must be asleep.*

Strickland, Torres, and Riley were radioing in their replacements. *At least it's not cold outside*, she thought. *I'd feel bad if those guys had to keep warm.* She sighed as she glanced out the window across the room. *What a way to spend a summer night*, she thought. A black cat meandered into the room. "Hello, kitty," Falco said in a soft voice. "And who are you?" The cat, a big Maine Coon named Leo, jumped onto the table and headed for Falco.

"Hi there," she cooed. He jutted his head into her hand and purred. "You are huge!" Falco said, smiling. Leo made his way around the other end of the table, leapt off, and headed toward the water dish where he sat and stared at Falco. "I could use a drink too," she said in a whisper. She went to the sink, refilled the water bowl, and set it down for the cat. Just then, Ballard radioed to let her know he was on his way up. "Small miracles," she said out loud. "Ten twenty. He's actually early. Thank God."

When Ballard entered, Falco briefed him. Illinois state police had set up road blocks that bordered the south side of the city as well as east at the Indiana border and west from Oak Park to Skokie. Law enforcement had nothing to go on—no vehicle description, no witnesses in the vicinity of the prison, and no information from any of McCaffery's fellow inmates. The FBI e-mails indicated McCaffery might be heading to Mexico, but no one knew for sure. Falco told Ballard to be ready for a long night; she'd see him in the morning around nine-thirty.

As Falco headed down the stairs, it dawned on her. She had forgotten to call Jeffery about taking Sam this weekend. She couldn't believe she'd let that slip. She climbed into the Crown Victoria and put her head on the steering wheel, angry with herself that she had forgotten it was Friday.

"Shit! Shit! Shit!" she said, banging her head on the steering wheel. She shuffled through her purse, looking for her cell phone. "Damn it!" she cursed. She started the car and pulled onto Irving Park Road and headed west. She stopped for a red light and searched her purse again. This time she found the phone and dialed Jeffery.

"Hello?" came a relaxed voice on the other end.

"Hi, Jeffery. It's me,"

"What's up, M?" he said. "Are you okay? It's a little late."

"Yes, I know and I'm fine. I'm just getting off work."

Jeffery let out a loud sigh. She knew what that meant. When she and Jeffery were married, she had been a street cop. Within their first year of marriage, Sam was born. Elaine Falco, her mother, quickly took to the role of grandmother and took care of Sam until he was old enough for preschool. In the meantime, Falco went back to work. Like her father, she quickly moved up the ranks at the Chicago Police Department. Each new position demanded more and more of her time. Jeffery complained that she would bring her job home with her, and Falco, not wanting to be like her father, made a conscious effort to separate her home life from her career. Before long Jeffery began to resent both her and her job. Once she made detective, the situation grew worse.

Sam was in second grade when Falco and Jim Ballard were caught in an altercation between rival street gangs while doing routine surveillance with the narcotics unit. Two officers were killed during the clash. After that, Jeffery's resentment and worry grew. Elaine Falco stood by Jeffery, fueled by her own resentment of the Chicago Police Department and what it had done to her own husband.

Falco found herself wrestling with wanting to be a good mother to Sam, her responsibilities to her job and the department, and her constant need to make things right with Jeffery. Both she and Jeffery knew the dangers of her being a cop; Jeffery threw them up in her face every chance he got, especially when news of violence on the street hit anywhere in the city.

"Listen, Jeffery," she said, ignoring his irritating response. "Can you keep Sam this weekend? We've got a big deal going down. This inmate from—"

"Sure, sure, sure," Jeffery broke in. "No big deal. It's fine, M," he said in a patronizing tone.

"I'm sorry. Tell Sam I'll make it up to him next weekend, okay?"

"I'll let him know," Jeffery said flatly.

"Tell him I'll call him tomorrow, all right?" There was a pause, then Falco said in a weak voice, "Thanks, Jeff." She hung up the phone feeling pangs of sadness and guilt. "I'm sorry, Sammy," she said with a sigh as she shook her head and gripped the steering wheel.

CHAPTER 6

Andie woke up with a start. She looked at her watch; it was 2:44 am. Was it a dream? Was McCaffery out there? She looked for evidence around her room, some kind of note or newspaper headline. Nothing. Hmm. Maybe it *was* all a bad dream. Cool air shifted in the room as the air conditioning blew on. The ceiling fan cast shadows on the walls, breaking across the lines of the window blinds. Andie paced around the room, her head aching. The room seemed to spin along with the blades of the fan. Then she spotted her broken cell phone. Reality pulled her back like a vacuum, and fear pierced her heart. She continued to pace. She looked at her hands; they were shaking.

"I can't stay here," she whispered. "I'm a sitting duck, bait for the cops. He'll find me." She opened her medicine cabinet and saw her trusty meds, Xanax and Zyprexa. She took the Xanax off the shelf, almost dropping the bottle and knocking another into the sink. "No, no," she told herself. "What I need is a knife, a weapon—*something*. No, what I need is to hide somewhere, to run away," she whispered as she paced the room. She knocked her fists against her head. She spun around and looked out the window; it was a clear, humid night.

She looked across the street to the other houses; all the windows were dark. Everyone in the city was asleep with no worries, she thought. She shook her head and whispered to herself, "I can't stay here and wait for him to come." She thought for a long moment, but her mind was blank. She sat on the bed and stared into the darkness.

Then the word "Nigel" surfaced as just a thought.

Nigel, the word came again, cloudy in her mind.

The word came to her lips. "Nigel."

Andie got up from the bed and went to the window. She breathed onto the glass; her breath appeared briefly on its surface.

"Nigel, yes, yes. *Nigel*," she whispered slowly, smiling. Tears came to her eyes. She moved toward the dresser and picked up a large framed photo of herself in front of the *Nigel T.* "Sometimes the answer is right in front of you," she whispered.

Hands shaking, she opened her closet door and packed a small duffle bag. *I'll need some food too*, she thought, *and some ice, a jacket, a long-sleeved shirt, shorts, and my gloves.* She found her gloves on a top shelf and kissed them before stuffing them into her bag. She packed underwear, suntan lotion, and her boat shoes. "Keep it simple," she told herself.

She filled her cats' bowls with fresh water then kissed them as they lay on the bed. She put on her Tevas and a light T-shirt and ripstop cropped pants. "Don't worry, boys. I'll be back. I just have to get out of here," she whispered to the cats, who blinked sleepily.

As she cracked open the door of her bedroom, she heard someone typing on a keyboard. Michael was asleep in the next room. *It must be one of the detectives*, she thought.

Andie crept down the hallway to the door that led to the stairs and the front door. The alarm system was activated; she'd have to put in her code to disengage it. She breathed deeply, trying to calm herself. Her hands were shaking, but she knew this was her only chance. "You're not going to get me motherfucker," she whispered as she grit her teeth.

Slowly and deliberately, she pressed her hand over the tiny speaker on the alarm box in an effort to muffle the beep that would result from her entering the code. She entered the numbers as the LED display flashed. It emitted a tiny beep, hardly audible. Smiling, she mouthed the words "Okey dokey." She quietly opened the door of the apartment and looked up and around; no one was there. Cool. She closed the door and looked down the stairwell—no one. She thought of the cops out there in their cars, Detective Ballard surfing the net in her living room or clicking away at some mindless computer game. "Idiots," she whispered.

Andie took a deep breath and descended the stairs, her bag slung over her shoulder. The big door leading out would be the next challenge. *It's heavy and the entrance is well lit. If I'm going to get caught, it'll be there*, she thought. It was after three a.m. and still dark; the birds were beginning to wake up and sing. Andie grabbed the handle of the heavy entry door and slowly squeezed the lever; it made a squeak and a clunk. She clenched her teeth. The door opened with a strong push. *Humidity*, she thought. *Everything swells up in this heat.* The rush of hot air blew through her hair; for a moment it soothed her, a welcome change from the adulterated coolness of the air conditioning.

She squeezed herself out and helped the door to slowly close. She took a deep breath and backed into a tall privet hedge next to the doorway as she hugged the duffle bag close to her chest. Just then one of the night duty officers appeared in the doorway, having heard the noise. He opened the door and looked around; Andie was right next to him but hidden deep in the hedge. She held her breath.

The officer backed into the entryway and let the door shut. He stayed there for a while, looking out into the front yard, left then right. He waited, studying the stairs, the street. "Go away already," Andie whispered. She didn't move a muscle. After a few minutes, the cop, apparently satisfied that everything was okay, ran up the stairs and returned to his post.

Andie crept out of the privet hedge, ducked low, and made a run for the cyclone fence on the right side of the yard. She put her right hand on the bar and jumped over it, duffle bag flying, and dashed down the sidewalk toward Montrose Avenue. A smile surfaced on her face as she headed inside the Jewel grocery store on Sheridan for ice, water, bagels, and apples. Running out onto the street, her grocery bag in tow, she snagged a cab that took her as far as the gates to Lake Michigan's Montrose Harbor. She jogged the rest of the way to the boat slips.

Out of breath and feeling paranoid, she ran down the pier to the large wrought iron security gate that, once open, would lead to the expanse of boats docked at the harbor. She felt shaky and exhilarated at the thought that she was going to pull off her escape.

"Oh, God," she said to herself, out of breath and stopping short at the locked security gate. She looked at the white buttons with numbers that were barely visible, worn smooth by the many summer boaters who kept their sailboats and motorboats at Montrose Harbor. She knew the code but was blanking out. "Take it easy," she told herself. She closed her eyes and breathed and saw the pattern of the numbers in her head, a kind of a T shape. She tried the numbers that corresponded with the pattern in her mind. Her hand shook as she twisted the doorknob. No luck. She looked around. No one was anywhere in sight. She took another deep breath and tried the numbers again. This time when she turned the knob the lock released with a tired clink. She pushed the gate open; it let out a groan as she gasped in relief. "Oh, thank the universe," she whispered.

Smiling, Andie slipped through the iron gate. She walked quickly down the pier as she spotted the boat. "There you are, my love," she said. "I bet you didn't expect me today and at this time of the night! God, I need you."

The *Nigel T*, a thirty-two-foot Catalina sailboat, was named after Nigel Tetley, a British engineer who, in 1968, had raced Robin Knox Johnson along with a few other brave sailors in the first singlehanded race around the world. Tetley had pushed his boat, the multi-hulled plywood *Victress* too hard, thinking he was being chased by another multi-hulled boat piloted by Donald

Crowhurst. The *Victress* broke up after having completed more than four thousand miles of the five-thousand-mile journey. Tragically, Tetley had no reason to push the *Victress*. It turned out Donald Crowhurst had faked his round-the-world trip, sailing only in the Atlantic and radioing in false position reports. Years later Nigel Tetley tried to build another multi-hull in hopes of racing again but couldn't secure the sponsorships needed to finish the boat. He died by his own hand not long after that. Andie thought he was a noble soul.

She fumbled with her key to enter the cabin. It was stuffy inside, but it cooled down quickly once she popped open the windows. A gentle breeze floated in as the *Nigel* creaked. She unpacked her bag of food and emptied the ice into the icebox. Then she dashed up the stairs to the cockpit and put on her gloves and shoes.

She inspected the lines, untied the mainsail, and readied the sheets. She checked the unfurling mechanism on the jib; it was ready to go. Walking around the port side of the boat, she checked the wind direction and arranged the lines, tossing the excess rope down below. She made her way to the stern and outboard motor. "We don't have much gas," she said out loud, "but I think we'll be okay."

She made sure the motor was in neutral and pumped the choke then pulled the cord. The engine started with a gust of blue smoke. She gunned it, and it quieted down. "Thanks, baby," she said to *Nigel*. "I hate doing this by myself." She jumped to the pier and untied the bowline then walked the boat slowly out of its slip. "Just a little momentum," she said. She loosened the other lines and gave the boat an even push, which rotated it out of the slip. Then she untied the lines completely, threw them on deck, and pushed off with her leg to set *Nigel* off straight and toward the mouth of the harbor. She dashed to the motor and put it in forward; it sputtered. She caressed the tiller and steered the boat toward open waters.

The breeze was steady and pleasant past the harbor. She pointed the *Nigel T* into the wind and went about the task of hoisting the mainsail. That was the hardest part of setting off, and it took a lot of her strength. She grunted and grunted as she pulled up the mainsail.

"Jesus!" she cried out. "Come on, girl!" Finally, after Andie had worked up a sweat, the sail was full; it caught the wind and bellowed out. She looked up at the telltales and the compass, adjusted their direction from the helm, and they were off heading east. "Maybe Michigan City!" she laughed. She looked at the sky; a hint of a sunrise burned somewhere off in the darkness. "I hope you can swim, McCaffery, you bastard!" she said with a laugh.

CHAPTER 7

It was close to ten a.m. when Falco drove up and parked behind Andie's blue Volvo Cross Country. It was a hot morning already, and if she had to work today, it might as well be inside. The morning shift was soon to start. Robby Torres was moving his unmarked vehicle farther up the alley, and Tim Strickland was heading up the back stairs with a cup of steaming Starbucks.

Falco sighed and said, "Day two." She hoped today would be calmer and she might get a chance to speak with Andie about what had happened four years ago with Brian McCaffery. She thought of Sam at Jeffery's, playing with his Xbox or the dog. She missed him.

She climbed up the stairs and, once inside the apartment, saw Michael talking with Officer Strickland. They were smiling and having a friendly conversation. From the bits of the conversation she heard, it seemed they had some mutual friends. Torres was talking with Ballard, who looked more than ready to leave.

"Hi, guys," said Falco. "How is everything? Anything I need to know?"

"I was just filling Torres and Langer in," said Ballard, looking annoyed at Strickland and Michael, who were chewing the fat. He cleared his throat loud enough for the two to stop talking. Michael smiled, embarrassed, and backed out of the room toward Andie's bedroom.

Sergeant Riley slipped in late and joined Falco, Ballard, Torres, and Strickland for a briefing. McCaffery had been sighted at a gas station in the south suburbs, some thirty miles away. Falco felt hopeful that this might be over soon. The feds thought McCaffery might be traveling with another man, an insider in the prison system. FBI agents were frantically checking all leads and talking with witnesses.

Chief Lassiter had told Falco to question Andie about what had happened in an effort to get inside McCaffery's head. She assumed that meant the Evanston police were still scouring their archives for the files—or maybe not.

Falco and Officers Torres, Langer, Strickland, and Riley were in place for the morning shift. Ballard, antsy to get home, gathered his belongings and headed toward the door.

"Excuse me," Michael said as he entered the living room. Pale and looking shook up, he said, "I think we have a problem."

Falco, seeing the look on his face, immediately became concerned and got up from her chair. "What's wrong?" she asked. Ballard moved toward the two of them, his hand on his gun.

"I can't find Andie," Michael said.

Both detectives ran down the hallway in a clatter. Michael followed. The two cats, which were lounging on Andie's bed, scattered in a flurry of blankets and pillows. Ballard dashed into Andie's studio, opposite her bedroom, and checked the closet and under her worktables. Falco looked in Andie's bedroom and checked under the bed, in the closet. and the bathroom. Neither room showed evidence of a break-in or a struggle.

"None of the windows look like they've been tampered with or even opened," said Falco, her voice tense.

"There's no use looking in my room. I spent the night there. She's not there," Michael said, bewildered and trying to stay out of the way.

Ballard and Falco, confused and concerned, shook their heads. "Where the hell is she?" Ballard yelled, looking at Michael for answers and feeling responsible. Ballard had Strickland and Langer check the stairwells. Riley scoured the front and back of the building, and Torres circled the block. No sign of Andie.

Falco got on her radio and requested an APB with a description of Andie and McCaffery. Michael, biting his lower lip, paced the hallway. "Could this McCaffery guy have gotten in overnight? Maybe through a window?"

"That's impossible," growled Ballard. "I was here and I heard nothing. Neither did the uniforms outside."

"I don't see any evidence that anyone went in or out of a window," assured Falco, who held up her hands to calm Ballard down. "What about the front door?" She focused her attention down the hall toward the door. Something caught her eye. She walked down the hallway, stopped by the door, and studied the security alarm display. "It's been disarmed," she said and turned toward Ballard. "Did you know the security system was disarmed?"

Ballard clomped down the hallway with a desperate look. He squinted at the box as if staring at it would somehow give him the answer.

"Can we find out what access code was used to disarm it?" Falco asked no one in particular. She turned her attention again to her partner, who was still looking at the security box. "Did you hear anything at all last night?" she asked Ballard, who looked pale.

"Detectives? I think I know where she is," Michael said as he peered through the bedroom doorway. "I looked inside her closet. She left in a hurry, it seems. Her duffle bag is gone and so are her gloves and boat shoes."

"Boat shoes?" Falco and Ballard said in unison as they entered the bedroom.

"Boat shoes?" Falco said again. "What could she need boat shoes for?"

Michael leaned forward and said quickly, "I can almost guarantee that's where she is."

"Wait a minute. Wait a minute!" said Falco. "What are you talking about?"

"She's on her boat, her sailboat. It's docked at Montrose Harbor."

"Shit!" snapped Falco, turning in a half spin. "Ballard, get on the phone to the marine unit!"

Ballard looked at her with annoyance and sheepishly took out his radio.

"What kind of boat… Uh, does it have a tag number or something we can use to ID it?" Falco asked Michael.

"I've been trying to think of the name," he said. "Wait a minute." He picked up a large photo from Andie's dresser. "Here's the boat." He squinted at the letters that half appeared on the boat's bow. Falco looked closely over Michael's shoulder. She shook her head, not being able to work out the name.

"The *Nigel T*!" said Michael, all of a sudden. He poked at the photo. "That's it, Detective. The *Nigel T*."

Falco's radio was buzzing, and that meant Ballard was tracking down the necessary reinforcements to find Andie. She gave Ballard the boat's name and repeated its location. Suddenly it occurred to her—what if McCaffery was on that boat? *God, this is bad, really bad*, she thought. *I hate boats.*

CHAPTER 8

Andie took the *Nigel T* out about six miles. The sun was high above, and despite the gorgeous weather, her thoughts were heavy with fear and dread. Thirsty and hungry, she put the boat in irons, set the sails, and jumped down the stairs to the cabin. She pulled the rest of her clothes out of her duffle bag. Something clunked deep down in her bag. She felt down blindly, wondering what she had left in there. A shiny flask reflected daylight as she pulled it out of her bag. "Whoa!" she said with a smile. She shook the flask; it was almost full. "Single malt scotch!" she proclaimed, raising the flask above her head. "The gods are with us, Nigel!"

She opened and raised the flask and inhaled the sweet scent of the liquor. She took a swig, then another; the scotch was a bit warm. She sighed deeply, looking up at the ceiling and then down at her hands. She was still shaky. She fished through her duffle bag again, found Fauré's *Requiem*, inserted it into the CD player, and turned up the volume. The music filled the cabin. She sank into one of the cushions in the dining booth, put her face in her hands, and wept.

* * *

Chief Lassiter was pacing and spouting off on the radio. "What the fuck happened over there? How the fuck did this happen?" he bellowed. "I got you two and four uniforms over there and Fulbright disappears!"

Falco imagined the huge vein in Lassiter's forehead bulging as he yelled at her and Ballard. They could only take the heat and stare down at the floor.

The Marine Unit radioed that they would meet the detectives outside the mouth of Montrose Harbor. Falco took Michael's cell phone number, then she and Ballard piled into their vehicle. Blue lights flashing and sirens sounding, they made their way through the beach traffic as they drove to the lake via Montrose Avenue. Within minutes they were parked and heading to Pier 7-B.

Falco was getting a sick feeling in the pit of her stomach. Ballard was having trouble keeping up with her as she jogged up the path to the pier. Seeing the Marine Unit boat moored in the deep water, she looked back for Ballard, who was wheezing and working up a sweat. His shirt was sticking to his back, and his silk tie was loose around his neck.

The unit officer radioed Ballard and confirmed that the *Nigel T* was no longer moored in its slip and that a Marine Unit helicopter was searching the waters. Ballard's radio squawked. It was Lieutenant Paul Lorenzo. "If she's got GPS, finding her will be easy," he said. Ballard, having done this once before, pointed toward a small Chicago police motorboat that would take them to the awaiting 25-foot motor lifeboat outside the harbor.

"Oh, God, Ballard. I can't go on that tiny thing," Falco groaned, squinting at the boat.

"Which thing—the big one or the little one?" he said with an impish laugh.

"Neither," she said weakly.

"You're gonna have to."

Falco felt panicky and hoped Ballard would decide to go alone. She looked out at the water and considered her options. Ballard continued to walk and then looked back at her. She looked at the waiting boat again.

"Okay, all right," she said, throwing her hands down in resolve. "I hope I don't lose my breakfast," she muttered. She didn't want to duck out on JB. It would be all over the department. She set her jaw and walked fast toward Ballard, who was on the radio again with Lieutenant Lorenzo talking and laughing.

"They're hitting it off," she snipped. "This isn't a fucking fishing trip!" She felt a headache coming on. "If he'd just do his damn job, we wouldn't be in this fucking mess," she said as she hurried to catch up.

* * *

Andie stared off as Fauré's "Requiem" swelled. She closed her eyes.
Libera me, Domine,
de morte aeterna,
in die illa tremenda
quando coeli movendi sunt et terra,
dum veneris judicare
saeculum per ignem.
(Free me, Lord,
from eternal death,
on that day of dread,
when the heavens and earth shall move,
when you shall come to judge the world by fire.)

She looked at her hands; they were shaking. She thought some food might make her feel better. Looking for a knife, she rooted around the kitchen drawers. Finding her offshore folding knife, she opened it and sliced a bagel and an apple. She was feeling dizzy and figured she was dehydrated, so she guzzled some water and put some ice on her forehead. The boat was bobbing happily; it was quiet for a summer day on the lake, not too many motorboats—just the sound of a helicopter now and then. *I wonder what that's about? I hope no one's hurt or something,* she thought.

Andie poured some scotch into a plastic cup over some melting ice. She settled into the music once again and felt a sense of peace coming on. *I can stay here until it's over*, she thought. *Maybe I should turn on the radio. Maybe they caught McCaffery and I don't even know it.* She drifted off with the music, losing herself in the rhythm of the boat and the warmth of the scotch. The sun was fading, but it was still hot outside. Time drifted as two hours passed.

Andie had fallen asleep but awoke with a start. In the distance came a rumble and the swish of waves. It was a motorboat approaching quickly. The *Nigel T* began to rock and sway. She gained her bearings but was feeling the scotch. As she turned down the music, she heard someone yelling somewhere out on the water. She listened but couldn't make out the words. *It must be some partiers fighting or something in the distance,* she thought. She looked out one of the cabin windows but saw nothing.

Fear and paranoia overtook her. *What if it's McCaffery?* she thought. *What if he found me?* She dashed toward the kitchen and retrieved her offshore knife. She unfolded it and gripped it tight and listened.

"*Nigel T, Nigel T!*" came an amplified voice. "Andrea Fulbright. *Nigel T.* Identify yourself. Is anyone on board, *Nigel T?*"

"Jesus Christ! What the fuck! It's McCaffery," Andie hissed. She scampered toward the rear of the cabin and flattened herself against the wall next to the stairs. "I'll get you before you get me, motherfucker," she shouted. Her whole body was shaking.

"*Nigel T,* this is the Marine Unit of the Chicago Police Department requesting permission to come aboard. *Nigel T,* this is the Chicago Police." Lieutenant Lorenzo tried again, "Andrea Fulbright, if you are on board the vessel, please come on deck. Do you read, Ms. Fulbright? Do you read, *Nigel T?*"

"Fuck you," she whispered, swallowing hard. The knife rattled in her hand. "Take it easy," she told herself.

The voice boomed louder, "*Nigel T,* this is the Chicago Police Marine Unit! We are requesting permission to come aboard. Do you read?" There was a pause, then the voice bellowed, "*Nigel T,* we're coming on board."

There was silence, then a bump and a jerk and a grinding noise. Andie held fast next to the stairs. She held her breath, expecting the worst. A loud clump, clump, clump sounded above. She heard voices—two men, maybe three. She looked up at the ceiling as tears welled in her eyes.

Falco watched Ballard, Officer Dennis Shepard, and Sargent Randy Hillenbrand straddle the rails of the motor lifeboat and climb on board the *Nigel T*. She bit her lip. She was glad Ballard was doing the rescue with his marine-unit buddies. Moving about the cabin and deck of the twenty-five foot motor lifeboat, she felt more comfortable now and was able to focus on doing her job instead of obsessing about being on a boat in all this water. Her thoughts turned to Andie. She wondered if she was okay, if somehow this whole scenario could have been prevented. She feared that McCaffery might be on the boat or that Andie had done something to harm to herself.

Ballard, Sheppard, and Hillenbrand boarded the *Nigel T*. Ballard, the first on deck, had his gun drawn. The two marine officers followed behind as Falco joined three other Marine Unit officers on the deck of the motor life-boat. She gripped the handrail, her eyes on the three men.

Ballard yelled, "Ms. Fulbright, this is Detective Ballard. Are you down there? Are you all right?"

No sound.

Ballard yelled again, "Ms. Fulbright, are you down there?" He waited. "Okay, I'm coming down." He lowered himself down the stairs, fumbling with his gun in his right hand and gripping the rail with the other. He reached the bottom stair, and a flash of metal twisted up and cut through his silk tie. Startled, he jerked to the right and saw Andie with the offshore knife; her hand and the knife flew past him. In a swift motion, he grabbed her arm and, using her own momentum, threw her to the left and onto the cabin floor.

The knife flew. Ballard grabbed her by the collar of her shirt and threw her face first into the map table and then to the floor. She screamed as she hit the floor and then grew silent, stunned and breathing fast. He straddled her, and she gasped in surprise. "Get the fuck off me, you bastard!" she screamed.

Ballard yelled, "You almost cut my throat, you crazy bitch!" His tie was sliced almost in half and hung by a twist of shiny threads.

Andie struggled against the weight of the detective. She cursed at him, screaming, "Get off me, you bastard, you motherfucker!" Ballard stretched out her arms and cuffed her from behind, taking some of his wrath out on her in the process. She shouted even more belligerently, "Get those off me! You can't do this. You can't do this. This is private property, goddamn it! Get those off me!"

Ballard smiled as he yanked Andie up from the floor. Her head jerked back and then swung forward. She was bleeding and dizzy, trying to get her bearings. Ballard yanked her up again, holding her steady as she struggled to find her balance. "Let go of me, you asshole! Let me go!" she yelled.

Ballard pulled her cuffed hands back as she winced in pain. He leaned in close and whispered in her ear, "Behave yourself, little girl. We're taking you home."

The two officers heard the commotion but kept their distance, staying on the deck. The boat rocked from the ruckus. Hearing the noise and profanity, Falco figured Andie was alone on the boat and was okay.

Ballard set Andie on the bottom stair of the cabin and gave her a push up. She resisted, but the two officers took their cue and gently hoisted Andie up by each arm until her feet rested safely on the cockpit floor. Shepard held her tightly; she was shaking with rage and trying to wrestle free.

Ballard emerged from the *Nigel T's* cabin with Andie's duffle bag, with the flask and offshore knife in evidence bags. "Okay, guys, I'm done here," he said. "She's all yours!"

Andie leapt forward. "No! No! What do you mean?" she shouted. She looked at Ballard and then at the two Marine Unit officers, her face full of panic. "Wait…wait…no. You're not going to take my boat! You can't take my boat!" she repeated, searching the faces of Shepard and Hillenbrand.

"Oh, yes, we can," said Ballard in an instigating tone. "These two seamen are going to sail her back to the harbor."

"No! No, this is *my* boat!" She rushed toward Ballard, still furious at how he had treated her.

"That's the deal, Ms. Fulbright. Plus I hardly think you're in any shape to do anything, let alone sail this fine vessel," Ballard said, waving the evidence bag that contained the flask. "There are laws about operating a marine vessel under the influence. I'm sure you're aware of them."

Shepard chimed in, "Ms. Fulbright, Hillenbrand and I are lifelong sailors. We'll get her back safe and sound."

Andie grew more agitated. "You can't take my boat. You can't," she said desperately, as tears streamed down her face. She was breathing hard, and her eyes darted as if to find an escape route.

Shepard steadied her, holding fast, making sure she didn't try to jump off the boat handcuffs and all. Ballard stuffed the knife and flask into Andie's duffle bag, slung it over his shoulder, and grabbed Andie's arm. "Look, honey," he said. "You're gonna get on that cruiser nice and easy."

She struggled against him, but it was no use. He was twice her size.

Shepard and Hillenbrand took their places on the *Nigel T*, Hillenbrand at the helm and Shepard with the mainsail sheet in his hands. They loosened some lines and let the boat drift away from the motor lifeboat. "Prepare to tack," Hillenbrand said.

The *Nigel T* blew forward, catching the wind. Shepard released the starboard sheet of the mainsail; it blew over across the boat. Then he released the starboard jib sheet and wrapped the port sheet around the wench, cranking, cranking. The sails billowed, rattled, and swung over to the port side, sending the *Nigel T* in a northerly direction.

"Ms. Fulbright," Hillenbrand yelled from the stern, "she's a beauty. We'll take care of her and lock her up tight. Don't worry!" They both waved as the *Nigel T* picked up speed and headed toward the skyline.

CHAPTER 9

Lieutenant Lorenzo entered the cabin and assured Andie that her boat was in good hands. Falco, seeing that Andie was cuffed, helped her to a seat in the cabin. Noticing the cut on her head, she brushed her hair from Andie's forehead and asked, "Are you okay, Ms. Fulbright?" She smelled alcohol on her breath. "Have you been drinking?"

"I had *a* drink, yes," she said, trembling and still angry.

"Can I look at your head?" she asked Andie, who didn't seem aware that her head was bleeding and that blood was dripping down the side of her face.

Andie avoided Falco's eyes and turned away. She was shutting down and Falco knew it. Her father had done that after he'd had his stroke—too many questions, too many people looking and staring. Andie's shaking was getting worse.

"You're trembling. Are you cold?" asked Falco,

"I'm okay," Andie said abruptly. "Can you take these off me?" she asked, referring to the handcuffs. Her eyes were bloodshot, and she looked scared.

Falco paused then said, "I don't think that's a good idea right now, but I can do this." She unlocked the cuffs in the back and re-cuffed Andie's hands in front. Andie looked at her hands and at the cuffs, then wiped the tears from her face. "Sorry," Falco whispered.

Andie's forehead was bruised and bleeding. Falco did her best to clean the two-inch cut and dress it with a butterfly bandage. Lieutenant Lorenzo gave her a cup of water and a blanket. Andie sat sullenly and scanned the skyline; the long shadows of the Sears Tower and John Hancock stretched across the shimmering lake. Trying not to cry, she fought off waves of tremors.

With Andie quiet, Falco walked gingerly around the boat and found Ballard talking on his cell phone; it sounded like he was speaking with someone back at the station. Chuckling and looking satisfied with himself, he held the plastic evidence bags with the flask and knife inside. They flopped around as he gestured. Falco glared at him, her jaw set and her arms crossed in front of her. Ballard looked over at her, and his smile faded. He put up his finger, meaning he'd be done in a minute.

Falco barely waited for him to hang up his cell phone. "What the fuck were you thinking, JB? We were instructed to treat Ms. Fulbright with respect and sensitivity and what do you do? You tackle her then cuff her and drag her off her boat."

Ballard glared back. "I didn't drag her off the boat, and I didn't tackle her," he said. "She's drunk, or didn't you notice? And did you see what she did to my tie? That's aggravated battery! She came at me as soon as I stepped on that last stair. She could have slit my throat with that knife. I just disarmed her. And don't blame me for that cut on her head," he added, avoiding Falco's eyes. "She could've fallen over and banged it way before we got there."

Falco glared at him. "It just doesn't look good, Ballard. She's really upset."

Ballard countered, shouting, "She's drunk, Falco. Drunk! You can't reason with a drunk. You know that as well as anyone."

Falco's body jolted from her partner's words. She felt a rush of emotion and tried to hide the dull hurt that quickly consumed her. She looked out to the water then turned and walked away.

Ballard looked down and changed his tone. "Hey, Falco...Falco!" he shouted after her. "Come on. I didn't mean that. Oh, come on. I didn't... Shit!" he said, throwing down his hands and dropping the evidence bags.

Falco entered the cabin to check on Andie then dialed Michael's number.

Michael answered the phone out of breath. "Detective Falco?" he asked excitedly.

"Hi, Michael. We're on our way back. We've got Andie here on a CPD marine unit cruiser, and we're heading back right now."

"Oh, thank God," Michael said with a sigh. "Is she okay?"

Falco turned, out of earshot of Ballard. "No, not really. She's been drinking and she's pretty shaky. Can you meet us at Lakeshore Hospital? We have to take her there first." Falco gripped her radio, "Hey zone 2, can you have a crisis intervention team meet us at Lakeshore?"

CHAPTER 10

The transfer from the boat to the dock to the detectives' vehicle was a blur to Andie. She found herself slumped in the back of the car, handcuffed and staring out the window. Falco and Ballard were silent. Ballard pouted and mumbled to himself as he drove; Falco clenched her jaw while replaying the interchange with her partner in her head. Michael met them at Lakeshore Hospital where Andie was to be evaluated. He explained the situation to the attending physician who agreed to release Andie into the care of Michael and the two police officers. Just after dusk the car came to a halt behind Andie's place. Traffic noise and the rumble of the El train let Andie know they were home. A rustle of movement and voices came toward her.

The car door opened to Michael's voice. "Come on, let's get inside."

She was still handcuffed, her body racked with tremors, as Michael helped her up the back stairs, a jacket hiding her cuffs. Once everyone had entered the apartment, and the back door was securely closed, Falco gently unlocked the handcuffs. Michael led Andie to her bedroom, where he closed the door.

"I'm sorry, Michael," Andie said in a small voice. "I...I guess I panicked. I couldn't see straight."

"Panicked?" Michael asked loudly. He grabbed her by her arms, twisted her around, and pulled her in front of him. Then he steered her to the bathroom mirror. "Get a good look," he said. "Go on!" He pushed her into the vanity, closer to the mirror, and she jerked violently.

She looked at this person in the mirror, hair full of wind and sweat, her body twisting from the tremors. She met her own eyes in the mirror, her hair stringy, her body spastic. "Please!" she whined, looking away and trying to break free of Michael's angry grip. "I'm a mess, I know it. I can't think straight. I should have thought this out."

"Sorry?" Michael scoffed and pushed her on to the bed. Venting his anger, he told her how much he had worried, how he had feared that Brian McCaffery was behind her disappearance, how he had blamed himself for her disappearance. Andie looked at the floor, unable to defend herself.

* * *

Ballard hung around long enough to hear some of the fireworks between Michael and Andie. He and Falco rearranged their schedules, and he agreed to come back to cover the night shift at two a.m. Falco sat down at the laptop and rearranged a notebook and files on the dining room table. Ballard fumbled with his things, finding the two evidence bags with the flask and offshore knife. He set them on the dining room table. Falco glanced at them, taking her eyes off the laptop screen for a second.

Ballard hesitated, leaned forward, and quietly spoke, "Listen, Falco—"

"Forget it," she snapped.

Ballard waited, eyeing her, then quietly opened the door and left. He walked down the stairs heavily.

Falco made contact with the officers scheduled for the night shift. Everyone was in their places, the building was secure, and the street was quiet. She rubbed her eyes and reflected on the day's events. The fear in Andie's eyes haunted her. She thought about Brian McCaffery and what it would be like to be hunted.

The dispatcher on the radio broke in and reported that McCaffery had been spotted at a gas station on the West Side. Within hours a van had been stolen and a man was dead. *He's still in the city*, Falco thought. The FBI and Chicago Police had set up roadblocks around the perimeter of the city. How had McCaffery managed to give them the slip? Why hadn't he left the state?

Falco's radio cracked. Dr. Forrest was on his way up, reported one of the uniform cops in the stairwell. "Dr. Forrest," she said softly to herself.

A muffled knock came at the door, and Falco opened it. "Hello?" Falco said.

Dr. Forrest was tall and slender, fiftyish, with dark eyes and hair. "Oh, hello," he said in a charming tone. Falco stepped back to let him in. He looked at her ID badge then looked ahead into the living room. "Where's the patient?" he said as he made his way past Falco and toward Andie's bedroom. She followed him with her eyes as he entered the hallway. He looked back at Falco. "Dr. Alan Forrest," he said with a smile. "Andie's psychiatrist." Michael met him halfway to the bedroom, and the two spoke in hushed tones.

Andie continued to work through the unrelenting tremors, clutching herself and rocking forward and back. Dr. Forrest appeared in her room, faintly smiling and looking concerned. "Andie? What's going on?" he asked, kneeling in front of her on the floor.

"Alan. Oh, hi," she said weakly. She put her arms around him, and he returned the embrace.

"How are you? Not doing too well, I see."

"No, I'm not," she admitted.

"Tell me what's going on," he said. "How did you get that cut on your head? And whatever possessed you…" He pulled out a small flashlight and, cupping Andie's chin in his hand, lifted her head to get a better look at the bandage and check her pupil response. She squinted at the light as he looked at her squarely. "When was the last time you ate something?" He didn't wait for an answer and immediately asked, "How long has it been since you took your meds?" He took Andie's wrist to check her pulse.

"I had…" she started.

"How much alcohol did you have today? How many drinks?" Dr. Forrest asked with greater impatience. "You know we've had this conversation before, about mixing your meds with alcohol."

Michael stepped in. "From the number of pills left in each bottle in her medicine cabinet, I figure it's been five days since she took her meds, except for the two Valiums I gave her on… What…was it yesterday when this all came down?" He looked at Andie.

"So technically you stopped taking your meds on Monday. Sound right?" Dr. Forrest asked.

She looked down and shook her head. "I just forgot, I guess, with the show and all and Kat on my back. I don't know, really. And then I took Nigel out. You know, I needed… I didn't see any other…" she stammered.

The doctor turned to his black bag, checked a small pad of paper, and unwrapped a syringe. Andie caught sight of the needle and balked. "Oh, no, no. No needles, please. Come on, Alan. *Please!*"

She moved to get up from the bed, but Michael stopped her. He leaned down so Andie could hear him and said in her ear, "Sorry, girl. You slip up on the meds, and the needle is what you get."

"Fuck you, Michael," Andie said, pulling away from him and putting an elbow to his chest.

"All right, you two," Dr. Forrest said. "Andie, sorry. All bets are off today."

He motioned to Michael to hold Andie still. Her body rattled, shaking the bed. He wiped the crook of her elbow with an alcohol swab and tightened the tourniquet around her lower bicep. He gently inserted the needle into Andie's bulging vein then loosened the strap, which released the medication into her bloodstream. Within seconds her body quieted.

"I'm going to call in an IV from Weiss," Dr. Forrest told Michael. "They'll get someone to drop it by. The fluids will help. She'll be better in the morning."

"Okay," said Michael.

The doctor headed out of the bedroom as Michael followed, closing the door behind them.

"Is Ms. Fulbright going to be all right?" Falco asked, looking up at Dr. Forrest.

"I think so," he said as he took a seat at the table. "She's exhausted and dehydrated, and the alcohol didn't help." He looked at her with a smile and added, "I didn't get your name, Detective."

"Detective Falco," she said.

He held her gaze. "You look awfully familiar to me. I've seen you at the courthouse maybe?"

"Possibly. I'm there pretty frequently." She nodded with a nervous smile and suddenly felt uneasy. *Is this guy coming on to me?* She wondered.

Still smiling, Dr. Forrest glanced at his watch. "Oops, now I've really gotta run." He got up from the chair and turned to Michael in the kitchen. "I'll call in that IV, Michael. It'll be here within the hour. Nice meeting you, Detective," he said, extending his hand. He grabbed his bag and winked at Michael. "Keep me posted," he said with a smile and left.

"Hot date, I guess," Michael mused. It was nearly eight thirty, and the night was still young.

CHAPTER 11

The apartment was quiet. Despite the calmness after the day's events, Michael felt out of sorts. Andie's phone rang incessantly. Michael switched the ringer to mute. *Kat can call later, and so can everyone else*, he thought. It seemed the word was out around town and in the art community that Andie's ordeal with Brian McCaffery wasn't over. His escape from Marion had made its way to the local news, and TV news trucks would soon find their way back into Andie's life. Michael dreaded that more than anything.

"You hungry?" he asked Falco.

"Me? Uh…" Falco thought for a minute and realized she hadn't eaten anything since about seven that morning. "I'm starving," she admitted.

"I've got just the thing," Michael said. He opened the refrigerator and pulled out a container of pasta sauce. "Homemade, fresh, and from scratch." He raised the container for her to see. "Just heat and add pasta."

"I don't want you to go to any trouble."

"No trouble! Andie made a huge—and I mean *huge*—batch of sauce a few days ago. She was putting off going to her studio to finish whatever she had to do there, so she decided to make this pasta sauce instead. It's fab, really. She's a great cook."

"Okay, twist my arm," Falco said, appreciating Michael's gesture.

Before long, Michael put the steaming dish of pasta and sauce at the opposite end of the dining room table, away from the clutter of police equipment. He set the place setting with a napkin and silverware and tossed some fresh chopped basil on top of the dish.

"Wow," Falco said. The fragrance of the sauce and the basil filled her head. She moved to the other end of the table.

"One more thing," Michael said, as he grated some fresh pecorino cheese on top. "Enjoy."

"This is wonderful," she said, sitting down and taking the fork. She couldn't remember the last time someone had prepared a meal for her. She tasted the pasta and sauce. "Oh, this is terrific. Is this a puttanesca sauce?"

Michael nodded. "The basil's from the back deck. Andie grows tons of it and oregano too."

"My grandmother used to make a sauce like this, and she grew basil in her backyard," Falco said, reminiscing. "This takes me back to when I was a kid."

"Well, I'll leave you to your memories," Michael said. "I've got some work I need to do in the other room. I'll get the door when the IV comes." He shuffled down the hall to the office.

Falco finished the pasta; the food energized her. She rinsed her plate and silverware and put them in the dishwasher. She scanned the kitchen and studied the spice bottles, lined up on racks on the wall, which contained herbs, seeds, and powders she'd never heard of. She glanced at the variety of knives on the knife rack near the stove and perused the large collection of pots, pans, and kitchen implements that hung from a massive pot rack. *With stuff like this, you can't help being a great cook*, she thought.

Her thoughts returned to her grandmother. She remembered her getting up before the crack of dawn to make Italian bread for the week. She could see her working the dough over a large butcher block dusted with flour, her gray curly hair pulled back, stubborn strands falling low over her forehead. She remembered walking into her grandmother's house and smelling fresh basil and freshly picked vegetables from the yard. She felt a sense of disappointment not only in herself but also in her mother, who had rejected the lifestyle of "Italian mama." *It's not Mom's fault that she didn't choose to be like Grandma,* she thought. *Times change, and she had Dad to contend with, and me and Peter. Maybe I should start cooking more.* Her thoughts then turned to her father. She could see him talking happily to her grandmother. They both appreciated good food. Sadness filled her as she thought of her father. She hoped he had been proud of her. She couldn't cook worth a damn, but she was a good cop just like he'd been.

Several hours later, Falco looked at her watch. It was one a.m. No news. She quietly made her way through the space and checked on Michael, who had fallen asleep watching a movie, his laptop dark and on the floor. She peered into Andie's room; the IV was connected and hanging from a nail where a picture had hung earlier. Her breathing was deep and rhythmic. The cats guarded her on the bed; they looked up when she nudged open the door.

CHAPTER 12

Ballard reported in at two a.m. Falco was drained and barely said a word to him. Anticipating another long night, he'd brought a thermos of coffee with him. He offered her a cup for the road, but she mumbled something about needing to get some sleep and that she'd hitch a ride with a squad car and leave the Crown Victoria out back. Falco had trashed the evidence bags and given Michael the knife and flask to put away.

Ballard cupped his chin in his hand and opened up the solitaire game on the laptop. Late-night traffic hissed outside. It was a humid night, and Uptown was quiet. Officer Langer knocked on the door quietly, saying he needed to take a leak. Ballard let him in and reminded him not to leave the seat up. Langer gave him a smirk.

"No news, eh?" Langer asked after exiting the bathroom.

"Nope," said Ballard. "McCaffery got somebody on the West Side, they think, but nothing since then. No sightings of the stolen vehicle either."

"Bet he knows somebody and is hiding out," sniffed Langer.

"He killed a guy and stole a van on the West Side," Ballard said, then stared at the computer screen and went quiet.

Langer sat at the table and eyed Ballard. "How ya like working with Falco?"

"She's okay. She's a good cop, very thorough. Lots of smarts," he said, not looking up from his solitaire game.

"I heard she gives you a lot of shit," Langer said, looking at him with a wide grin.

"Who'd you hear that from?" Ballard chuckled. "Yeah, well, I think she gives a lot of people a lot of shit." He gritted his teeth and avoided Langer's grin.

Langer leaned in and eyed Ballard. "A lot of people think she's hot—I mean, for an older woman, ya know."

Ballard shrugged. "Don't think she's dating anybody yet."

"What do you mean? She ain't married anymore? What happened to her husband—uh, Jeffery something—the guy with the construction business?"

"The divorce was final a long time ago. But you're a little young for her," Ballard cracked with a smile.

"Her dad was a good cop. That's what I heard."

"He had a great rep on the West Side," said Ballard. "He broke some big cases but then started hittin' the bottle. The story goes that his wife hated the force and wanted him to do something else, but he wouldn't budge. I guess she made him pretty miserable most of his career."

"Makes you wonder why Falco ended up a cop," Langer said thoughtfully. "Must drive her mother crazy."

"Maybe that's the point."

CHAPTER 13

The Sunday *Tribune* thumped on Falco's doorstep, awakening her suddenly. Her neck was killing her as she opened her eyes and stared at the TV that was chirping some cartoon show. She'd fallen asleep on the sofa with an unfinished glass of red wine still on the coffee table. Her shoulder holster was wrapped around her Glock 22 next to her wineglass. *At least I took my weapon off*, she thought.

It was already eight-thirty and she had to get moving. She dragged the paper from the front step and waved to her neighbor, who was already mowing the lawn. She made some coffee, stuffed a stale bagel in the toaster, and headed for the shower. *Day three*, she thought.

Falco dressed quickly and put on her shoulder holster. Her back was stiff. She looked in the mirror as she walked out the door. Her hair was a mass of curls; she scowled at the sight of herself. Coffee and bagel in hand, she opened the door of her gold Camry; it was steamy inside. *Should have put it in the garage*, she thought as she drove.

* * *

The morning sun shone brightly into Andie's living room. Ballard stretched and drained the last of his coffee from his thermos. "Time to go soon," he said with a yawn.

"Good morning, Detective," sung Michael as he walked into the kitchen.

"Oh. Hi, Mike," said Ballard.

"Want some fresh coffee?" Michael asked as he took a bottle of milk out of the refrigerator.

"No, thanks. I think I've had enough. I'm just waiting for Falco."

"Anything new with McCaffery? God, this is really dragging on. I may have to move in permanently. Maybe you and Falco—uh, Detective Falco—too," Michael said in a dry tone.

"How's Ms. Fulbright?" asked Ballard, as he packed up his things and straightened up the work area.

Michael glanced down the hallway toward Andie's room. "She's okay. Still sleeping." The cats romped into the kitchen upon hearing Michael's racket. "Okay, sweeties!" He turned to Ballard and confided, "I call them sweeties even though they're boys."

Ballard gave him a detached look and peered at his watch.

* * *

Devon Avenue was moving along, but Falco cut south on Pulaski. Her radio chirped; it was Chief Lassiter. He explained that the FBI was taking heat about not having apprehended McCaffery. "Turns out the feds are also dealing with a string of child abductions in the north suburbs, young kids. We may be losing some muscle, Falco," Lassiter warned. "Let's hope McCaffery surfaces somewhere. I want you to try to pull some information from Ms. Fulbright. The FBI hasn't given us anything yet. This'll be good experience for you with your app in for the profiler team."

"I'm working on it, sir. She's been a mess," said Falco. "I'll try to talk with her today."

She continued south on Ashland. Traffic was slowing and tempers were rising. She felt perspiration drip down her chest. "Why do I bother to shower in this weather?" she said out loud. She cranked the AC higher.

Falco parked on the street and radioed Ballard that she was on her way up. Officer Torres, who was already on duty, smiled broadly and let her in the building's entry door. *Nice teeth*, she thought as she climbed the stairs.

"Hey," she said breathlessly as Ballard let her in. She relayed the conversation she'd had with Lassiter in hushed tones, not wanting to stress out Michael with the prospect that the FBI might be pulling agents off the case. Michael waved at Falco, who returned a nod while she spoke to Ballard.

"That's just great," Ballard said, pissed off.

"Keep it to yourself, okay?" she whispered.

"You look tired," Michael said as Falco closed the door behind Ballard.

"I'm a little stiff today. It must be from all those lake breezes and fresh water from yesterday." She smiled. *Or maybe it's from sleeping on the sofa*, she thought. "How's Ms. Fulbright?"

"Still asleep."

Falco looked concerned and nodded her head in acknowledgement. "Hey, thanks for dinner last night. It brought back a lot of memories."

"Thank Andie. She's the cook!" Michael said jovially.

"I'll do that." Falco took a seat at her now familiar post. She sighed and rubbed her eyes.

CHAPTER 14

Michael was awaiting the delivery of some much-needed groceries from Treasure Island. He pulled some pans out of the cupboard and assessed the contents of Andie's refrigerator. He sighed and said, "Good thing I ordered eggs." The phone rang softly. Falco looked up from the laptop at Michael. "Yes, I hear the phone ringing, Detective, and we're not answering it," he said, singing.

"Are you getting crank phone calls or hang-ups?" Falco asked.

"Oh, no. Nothing like that. It's Kat—Katherine Cohen to be exact. She owns the Cohen Sloan Gallery on Huron. That's where Andie's show is supposed to be—if it happens. Kat's a royal pain in the ass." He moved toward the dining room table. "When she finds out Andie hasn't finished the work, she's going to be spitting fire."

"What kind of artwork does Andie do?"

"Mostly two-dimensional works lately, but she's also done a lot of sculpture." Michael gazed up at the painting in the foyer and was about to say something when the phone rang again.

Falco turned to her laptop and began to read her e-mail: "RE: McCaffery Files from EPD." It was from Lassiter. He finally had received a file on McCaffery from the Evanston police. "Skimpy at best," read the e-mail. The file contained mostly newspaper clippings from the bank job and the trial and some brief records on McCaffery, booking photos, fingerprints, etc. Lassiter said he'd send the folder over that afternoon.

Michael glanced at his watch impatiently. He looked out the front windows then returned to the kitchen and sighed as he thumped his fingers on the granite countertop. Falco looked up from the laptop and asked, "Waiting for something?"

"The groceries," he said with a smile.

"Gotcha."

He sat down in a huff on the sofa near the dining room table where Falco was sitting. "How far do you come to get here?" he asked.

"I live north and way west, in Sauganash."

"Oh, that's nice, very quiet. Far from the beaten path, so to speak," Michael said, rubbing the back of his neck.

"Yes, it is. I grew up in Edgebrook, and then my parents bought the house in Sauganash, which really is the same neighborhood. The Sauganash house is my house now."

Michael looked at her in surprise. "You mean you live in the house you grew up in?"

"Well, my parents bought it when my brother and I were in middle school, so I didn't spend my entire childhood there," she said a bit defensively.

"What made you buy your childhood house?"

Falco sighed. "It's a long story, but in a nutshell, my father died rather young, and my mother grew tired of the responsibility of a house, so she sold it to me and my husband for next to nothing not long after we were married. I more or less inherited it. When we got divorced, I bought him out of his share. It's a nice house, really. I have nice neighbors, a park nearby, and a yard. I won't tell you what I pay in property taxes, though. It's not like living here in Uptown, and it's a bit of a drive now that I work at the twenty-third district. On a good day it takes me thirty minutes."

Falco's cell phone rang. She looked at the number and quickly answered. "Hi, sweetie," she said.

Michael took a cue and went searching for his groceries, looking out the front and back windows. He ended up back in the kitchen, where he took out some muffin pans from the cupboard.

"I know, Sam. I'm really sorry about this," Falco said in a pleading tone. "Can Dad help you with that? I'm not sure who *François Viète* is. Let me think. This is for math camp?" she asked, feeling helpless and a bit stupid. She could tell Sam was frustrated, but she could hardly help him with his home-work on the phone.

"You can't use the Internet? Can Dad take you to the library? Yeah, maybe try that… Okay," she said. "No, of course I won't forget. We'll do something really great for your birthday," she said, changing her tone. "No, not Disney World," she said flatly. "Okay, I'll talk to you later. I love you. Bye, kiddo."

Falco closed her phone and slid it into her purse. She stared off, thinking of Sam and wishing they were together in his room at her house doing his homework. She struggled to fight off the familiar feelings of guilt and emptiness.

"You have kids?" Michael asked from the kitchen.

"I have a son, and I should helping him with his homework. He's taking an accelerated math class at school this summer—actually it's math camp—but math isn't my thing, and obviously I can't be there now anyway."

"Doesn't he live with you?"

Falco was getting a little tired of the personal questions, especially when it came to her son. "He lives in Park Ridge with his father. Better schools," she said. "I have him on most weekends, except for this weekend." Falco sighed, feeling self-conscious. "My husband—my ex-husband—and I felt Sam would do better with his father this summer. My schedule is so crazy and, well, Jeffery, my ex, owns his own business, so his schedule is much more flexible for a kid in school." Falco looked away for a moment, lost in her thoughts. "His birthday's coming up," she continued. "He wants this game for his Xbox that's almost impossible to get. With this McCaffery thing, I hope I can get my hands on one. It's not like it's Christmas or anything like that. This shouldn't be so difficult."

Michael thought for a moment. "I have a friend who works at the university bookstore. She orders all the books, music, and media stuff. I can ask her if she can get a copy of the game if you like."

"Really?" Falco chirped.

"Sure."

"I'd hate for you to go through any trouble, but you'd be up for sainthood in my book, if you could get it."

"I'll call her on Monday and let you know," Michael said with a smile.

Falco pulled a piece of paper out of her purse that had the name of the game Sam wanted and gave it to Michael. Her radio squawked; Michael's groceries had arrived.

"Great!" he said with a clap of his hands. A few minutes later, he brought in three bags of groceries containing coffee, sugar, milk, cheese, orange juice, olives, tomatoes, eggs, and other items Andie had on a list from last week. "Talk about being out of stuff," he said to himself as he put the perishables in the refrigerator. Hearing something, he stood up suddenly from bending down in front of the refrigerator and said, "There's life! I think there's life!" He heard water running. "Time to make the doughnuts."

He went down the hall, peered into the bedroom, saw the bed had been stripped, and heard the water running. *She's okay*, he thought.

Michael now had the ingredients for blueberry muffins, one of Andie's favorites. He washed and picked through a colander full of blueberries and tossed out the smashed or green ones. He heard Andie's studio door close and then the rhythmic thump, thump of dance music. *Hm*, he thought. *She must be feeling pretty good.* The thump, thump, thump continued.

Falco asked, "Do I hear music or something?"

"It's Andie. She's on her bike trainer in her studio. She's working out."

"Oh, well that's…positive," Falco said, staring into her computer screen.

Forty-five minutes later, the muffins were almost brown. Michael peeked into Andie's studio. The door was now ajar, the music soft. Andie was glassy-eyed from her workout, sweating and smiling almost dreamily. She had a pair of bright-red Everlast boxing gloves on, and from the size of her now bulging arms it looked like she had beaten the crap out of her punching bag. Still swinging in agony from its hook on the ceiling, the bag bore a ripped and wrinkled mug shot of Brian McCaffery.

Andie was bent over, hands on her knees, when Michael entered the room. "Hey," he said, smiling. "You look good."

Andie looked at him through her dangling hair and smiled broadly, breathing hard. She began to untie her gloves. She was dripping wet with sweat; her hair carried little droplets of moisture that fell onto her face.

"That bandage on your head makes you look like Rocky Balboa," said Michael.

Still out of breath, Andie stood squarely in front of him. "Listen," she said, looking sad, "I'm really sorry about yesterday…about my—"

"Not another word. You know that," Michael cut in. "I'm sorry too. I wasn't very nice to you." He turned and headed out of the room. "Hey, I ordered some groceries, and I'm making blueberry muffins for you. Don't forget your meds, girl. We need to get you back on track." He scurried down the hall back to the kitchen.

Falco was feeling drained. It was only one thirty. "Maybe I'll try to talk with Andie a little," she muttered. She looked up and across the living room to the adjoining kitchen and saw a strange figure enter the room—a small person, built like a teenage boy with scruffy hair, broad shoulders, and sinewy arms stemming from a sweaty gray tank top. She thought for a moment that maybe the delivery boy had forgotten something and Michael had let him back in. The figure had his back to her and was pulling out a bottle of Gatorade from the refrigerator. Confused, Falco rose to her feet and put her hand on her gun.

Michael was joking around, talking nonstop as he filled the second batch of muffin cups. Andie's music flowed from down the hall—thump, thump. Michael moved to the beat, and the figure moved toward him. They did the bump to the music and laughed. The figure turned to Michael, smiling, and to Falco's surprise it was Andie.

Veins bulged from Andie's arms, and sweat dripped from her hair, darkening her shirt. She could have passed for a friend of Sam's. Andie looked like an entirely different person than the helpless, trembling being Falco had seen over the last few days. Of course she had a lot less clothes on now, Falco thought. Andie wiped her face with a paper towel; she was still pumped from her workout. Her hand was shaking as she held the bottle of Gatorade to her lips.

Andie turned and went into the living room, where she looked out the back door and squinted in the bright sunlight. She wore baggy red shorts and gray cross trainers. Her legs were wiry, tanned, and bruised. She turned around and said, "Hi, Detective Falco." She came closer. "Sorry about my sweat." She pulled absent-mindedly at the front of her tank top.

Falco smiled broadly. "It's nice to see you up and around."

"You mean not a basket case?" Andie said, mocking herself. She leaned against the dining room table; its metal felt cool against her hot thigh. She paused, looked down at her shoes, and then at Falco. "Hey, um… I want to apologize for my behavior yesterday. I did a really stupid—well, a really dangerous—thing, and I'm sorry," she stammered.

Falco smiled. "You were trying to save yourself and didn't realize that staying here is the best thing. It's okay. Apology accepted."

"Thanks," said Andie quickly.

"Oh, the Marine Unit officers brought this back for you." It was the recording of Faure's *Requiem* she had in the CD player and the key to the *Nigel T's* cockpit.

"Oh, great," Andie said weakly, taking them in one hand. She took a swig from her bottle of Gatorade as fear surfaced in her face. "Any word…any news about *him*?"

"Well, the FBI thinks someone is hiding him. We're pretty sure he stole a van in Humboldt Park yesterday and killed someone."

Andie grimaced as a wave of fear swept through her. Falco paused and continued to look at Andie. She marveled at her level of fitness and her form. Intrigued, she studied her. So many contradictions, she thought— physically strong but mentally unstable; a woman who at first glance could pass for a teenage boy. Her heart skipped as she found it hard to take her eyes off her.

The phone rang again. "Kat's back in town, sweetie," Michael said. "She's called numerous times since early this morning. Why don't you get it over with and talk to her?"

Andie's face turned to annoyance. "I'm gonna go hide." She turned and gave a little wave to Falco and left the room.

* * *

Andie lowered herself into her studio desk chair and stared at a sketch she was working on. *It wasn't right*, she thought. Something wasn't right. Sighing, she crumpled up the paper and let it fall to the floor. She looked at the *Requiem* CD as Detective Falco's face surfaced in her head. She closed her eyes for a moment, then sighed again and spun around in her chair. "God, she's beautiful, but she's a fucking cop." She smiled and shook her head. *Let's not even go there*, she thought.

The phone rang two more times over the next thirty minutes. Each time it shattered the calm of the apartment and made Andie cringe. Michael knew not to answer it without Andie's permission. Fifteen minutes later the calm was broken again by the sound of loud footsteps rising from the alley. A woman's voice grew louder, as did the footsteps. Someone was climbing the wooden back stairs. On the ground floor, Officer Torres radioed to Falco that he'd just had a run-in with an obnoxious blond who insisted on seeing Andie. "She won't show any ID, and she's really pissed off," Torres told Falco.

Michael overheard the conversation. "That's Kat," he said. Through the living room windows came a flash of color. A woman with short, spiky hair and wearing a linen suit and large, noisy jewelry brushed past. Kat was in her mid-forties, five foot five, and big boned. Her hair was a loud blonde; her chunky earrings and bracelets were white gold and platinum. At the landing of Andie's space, she made a clatter as she tried the doorknob. Seeing Michael at the kitchen sink, she glared at him through the glass door as if that would make him open it.

"Hi, Kat," said Michael, letting her in.

She dragged off her sunglasses and looked around and into the living room. She made eye contact with Falco, who entered the kitchen to ensure Kat was who she was.

"I have called *twenty-three times* in the last few days and eight times just this morning. I have left countless messages on the voicemail and with you Michael!" Her voice grew progressively louder. "Why hasn't Andie returned my calls?" Kat demanded, stomping her feet. "And what is going on here? Why are there all these police around here and on the street? I had to park illegally in the fucking alley!"

She looked around the room again, and her eyes met Falco's. "And *who* are you?" she said in a condescending tone, looking Falco up and down.

Michael broke in, "This is Detective Falco of the Chicago Police Department. Detective Falco, this is Katherine Cohen."

Kat didn't bother to acknowledge Falco. She turned and brushed past her and out of the room. "Where is she? Where is she? We've got a fucking deadline!"

Michael's face contorted. "Sparks are gonna fly."

CHAPTER 15

Andie had showered and was gazing at her computer screen in her studio. Her hair was damp, and she wore a skimpy white T-shirt, blue jeans, and leather flip-flops. Mozart was playing on the stereo. Kat stormed into the room, startling her. "Jesus!" Andie said as Kat burst in.

She pushed Andie and the wheeled office chair she was sitting in away from her drawing table and hit her with a barrage of accusations and finger pointing. "Goddamn you, Andie. I have called you two dozen fucking times, and you don't have the decency to talk to me? I spent a small fortune calling you from Belize, and all I got was your whiney, fucking voicemail! Where the fuck have you been? Do you realize we have a show this weekend? Twenty-seven of your paintings need to be inventoried, moved, and hung by Friday. I don't hear from you for four fucking days, and I find you at home, sketching here like you don't give a fuck. Do you have any idea what your little games can do to me and my reputation?" Andie tried to explain, but Kat put an angry finger to her lips. "Shut up! Don't you say a goddamn word until I've finished." Andie took a deep breath and looked away.

Hearing the noise from down the hall, Falco said, "Is she okay in there?" She tilted her body to look down the hall.

"Andie can take care of herself," Michael said nonchalantly. He thought for a moment, and added, "Well, most of the time." Falco had a look of concern and surprise on her face. Michael leaned over the counter. "Never a dull moment around here, eh?"

Kat continued to yell over the Mozart. Andie's eyes drifted toward the music as if to tune Kat out. Kat turned to the stereo and angrily pushed at the silver buttons, attempting to turn off the music. Andie got up from her chair. "Leave that alone! Can you lighten up? There's more going on here than the show."

Kat's nostrils flared as she pushed Andie aside and reached under the desk and pulled the plug from the outlet. "Now you'll listen to me!" she yelled.

A knock came at the apartment door; Michael answered it. Officer Strickland had a thick folder for Falco. Michael took it, smiling at the uniformed cop. He closed the door, half singing, "I do love a man in uniform." He put the file on the dining room table near Falco's laptop.

Andie broke the news to Kat that she hadn't finished most of the work she had hoped to complete by Friday. Kat responded with more yelling and stomping. Her back was against the wall with this show, and Andie was entirely to blame. Kat said she would have to make some key decisions about this show, like it or not.

"There's no way the show is going to happen on Friday," Andie said, almost pleading.

Kat raged, saying the invitations were already in the mail. She poked her finger into Andie's chest. "And thanks to you the catalog isn't going to happen either. No photographer is going to shoot un-mounted canvas."

"I don't even want a catalog!" Andie shouted. "It's not a good idea and it's an unnecessary expense. It serves *your* ego not mine."

"Well, we don't have time for it!" Kat yelled back.

The arguing continued for another ten minutes. Then things quieted down, and before long the studio door opened. Michael acted like he hadn't heard any of the arguing, but of course he and Falco had heard most of it. During the confrontation in the studio, Falco had gotten up from her chair and was leaning on the dining room table, measuring the tone and tempo of the conversation.

After a few minutes, Kat and Andie walked down the hallway and stopped just outside the living room and kitchen. It was apparent the two had reached an agreement about the show and that Kat was on her way out. She slung her bag over the shoulder and turned to Andie. "Okay, so I need the key," Kat said, putting out her hand.

"The key?" Andie asked.

"Yes, the key, Andie. The key to your studio. I'm going to get Mario to pick up the canvases," she said matter-of-factly. "He'll finish the stretcher frames and mount the canvases."

Andie looked surprised. "No, no, I didn't agree to that. I'll finish them myself. I can get over there, and I'll stay until I finish."

"That's impossible. We don't have time, and I can hardly trust that you'll be able to finish them, considering you're virtually under house arrest," snapped Kat.

Andie looked at the floor and shook her head. "No, Kat. I can't have some-one else messing with my work."

Kat stepped close to Andie, her anger returning. "Mario is a master crafts-man. He's very good at what he does. Your work will be fine, and it'll be fin-ished and ready to hang."

"I can't let you do that," Andie said. Kat glared at Andie, her fists clenched. "It's *my* work, Kat."

"It's your work in *my* gallery!" Kat shouted.

Falco heard the scuffle of feet. Kat grabbed hold of Andie's arms and pushed her against the wall, her face full of rage. "Let go of me," Andie warned through her teeth. "Kat, let go of me!"

Falco quickly appeared from around the corner. "Let go of her, Ms. Cohen…please," she said firmly, glaring at her. The blood drained from Kat's face. Falco stepped closer. "It's my job to ensure Ms. Fulbright's safety, and right now you appear to be a real threat."

Kat looked up at Falco, glanced at her leather shoulder holster and gun, and let go of Andie. "Okay, sorry," she said tersely, trying to hide her uneasiness.

Andie looked up at the ceiling, embarrassed about the entire scene. Falco stood by, waiting and making sure Kat didn't touch her again.

After all the shouting, Andie relented and handed Kat the key to her studio. She felt a sickening ache and a loss of control. The idea of someone touching and handling her work made her stomach churn. Unfortunately McCaffery was still out there, and it was highly unlikely the cops would allow her to leave her place to finish the work in her studio. Kat left satisfied, having won the battle; the show would go on.

Andie watched out the window as Kat trotted down the back stairs and drove away. She rested her forehead on the glass door and stared down long after Kat had driven off.

Michael came up to her from behind and put his arms around her. Resting his chin on her shoulder, he said, "God, what a bitch. How 'bout a muffin?"

CHAPTER 16

Michael flicked on the mini CD player that was mounted under the kitchen cabinet. It was the Cher CD he was listening to when the detectives first came three days ago. He skipped to the tenth track; the music swirled and thumped. Andie was still looking out the glass door. Michael danced to the beat then held Andie from behind and made her sway to the music with him. She scowled and shirked back, not cooperating. She took a deep breath and mouthed the words to the Cher tune, "Do you hear me? Do you want me?"

Michael sang the chorus, "Baby, it's all or nothing now. Don't wanna run, and I can't walk out. Breaking my heart if you leave me now..."

Andie stood back and shook her head at Michael pretended to swish his long Cher hair off his shoulders. She smiled as he danced around the kitchen and glanced at the timer on the oven as the music waned. Putting his fingers to his chin, Michael looked philosophical. "The problem with lesbians is that they're control freaks—all of them. You put them in a relationship and it's a constant tug-of-war."

"I'm not a control freak," Andie said. Michael rolled his eyes. "Okay, I'm not a control freak like *Kat* is a control freak," she said defensively.

"Kat is a control freak and a manipulative bitch," Michael snarled.

"Well, I think any time you have a relationship, gay or straight, there are control issues," Falco offered out of nowhere. "So you've got to have some give-and-take."

"In Kat's case it's *take, take, take*," Michael said. He pulled the last batch of muffins out of the oven. They were steaming hot, and the smell of blueberries hung in the air. "Ah, don't you just love blueberries muffins?" he said as he pulled a cooled one apart.

"God, you made enough for an army," Andie said, looking at the overflowing tray.

"Well, we have the army here, or maybe it's the cavalry," Michael said.

Fresh coffee gurgled in the coffee maker. Michael motioned to Falco to join them, and the three stood around eating muffins. Falco let the other officers know Michael had made enough for them too. They didn't hesitate to come in for a few and some fresh coffee. "Leave some for Detective Ballard," Michael told them as they ate.

"No way!" said Andie, smiling. Her mood was lifting despite the drama.

The uniformed officers left, and Andie and Michael sat in the living room. Falco's radio was hissing with static and lost voices. She took her seat at the table and adjusted the frequency. She eyed the file on McCaffery and strategized her approach with Andie. *I've got to make some progress on this*, she thought.

"How long have you known Ms. Cohen?" asked Falco.

"Too long," Andie said with a sigh. "She gets a little wound up sometimes."

"A little?" Michael asked sarcastically.

Andie got up to change the CD to Mozart's *Piano Concerto Number 23*. She sighed as the music filled the room. Falco watched Andie as the music seemed to calm her and take her someplace else.

"This is nice," Falco said.

"It's Mozart. He's God as far as I'm concerned," Andie said.

Michael laughed. "And the only man you'd ever fuck." He glanced at Falco. "Andie told me that."

"True," Andie said. "I'd fuck Mozart in a minute and bear his children too."

Falco gave Andie a confused look. The music swelled. Andie looked pensive. She turned to Falco and Michael and asked, "Do you think I should replace Detective Ballard's tie?"

"No, that's all in the line of duty," Falco said.

"Michael, what do you think?"

"Well, I'm always into nice gestures."

"It would have to look similar to the one I ruined," Andie surmised, leaning forward on the sofa. "I wouldn't want to get him something he would hate."

"Don't worry about it," said Falco firmly.

"I could go to Bloomingdales or Saks or Burberry. They have some beautiful ties there."

"I'd go to Sears on Lawrence for Ballard," Michael blurted out.

Andie gave Michael a playful shove then fell back on the sofa laughing. Falco laughed and shook her head at the two of them.

The phone rang; it was from the gallery. Andie hesitated before she picked it up. It was Aisha, Kat's assistant, saying she needed an inventory list of all the works that were to be included in the show. Andie had the canvases numbered, but she'd have to get the inventory list from her computer. She offered to e-mail it to Kat once she located the file, but Aisha said she would just drive over. After hanging up the phone, Andie let Falco know that Aisha was on her way and to let her come up.

CHAPTER 17

Falco looked at her watch and wondered how Sam's homework assignment was going. It was three o'clock. *He's at soccer practice*, she thought. She sighed thinking of him. *He's so motivated. He loves math and reading and doesn't get into much trouble. I've got to make some time for him next week.*

Falco picked up the file that Lassiter had sent over. It was thicker than what he had indicated. She pulled it toward her and flipped through it. At the top of the stack of papers was a mug shot of Brian McCaffery. From his booking record, she saw he was thirty-six years old, six foot one, and 180 pounds. He had blondish red hair, freckles on his arms, and a large tattoo of a Celtic cross on his chest. He looked mean in the photo. She flipped through the file and was struck by the huge stack of newspaper clippings and copies of articles clipped together. Ballard was right about the media circus. She looked through the clippings. The headlines read:

"Woman Fatally Stabbed at Local Library"

"Murder Revenge Plot Revealed"

"Librarian Helps Foil Bank Heist"

"Library Murder Trial Begins"

"Librarian to Take the Stand"

"Guilty Verdict for Brian McCaffery"

Andie's picture was everywhere. In every shot she looked terrified. A longer article outlined the trial coverage and included pictures of the botched bank heist and the crime scene at the library. It also featured a photo of the eighty-year-old library worker McCaffery had killed.

A tiny knock came at the back door just as Falco's radio squawked. Aisha was on her way up. Michael let her in, smiling and calling to Andie; she carried a dozen roses. "From Kat, for Andie—not you!" Aisha laughed.

Aisha was taller than average, thin, and African American with delicate dreadlocks that tumbled onto her face and neck. She wore a coral-colored shell top with slim jeans and a thick black leather belt. Michael joked with her about Kat and called again for Andie. "You know where her studio is," Michael said, waving his hand. "Just go on in."

"Michael, put those in water, please," Aisha said. She glanced at Falco and made her way down the hall.

Andie was focused on her computer, trying to find the inventory file. Her stereo played Sibelius. Aisha slipped in. "Kat had me bring you a dozen roses," she said, smiling.

Andie looked up and smiled warmly then leaned back in her chair and turned the music down. "This won't take long. I think I know where it's filed. The trouble is, I can't remember the name I gave it."

Aisha, appearing bored, looked at the screen. She glanced around the studio then out the window.

"Hey, do you still need that letter for grad school?" asked Andie, not taking her eyes from the computer screen.

"Yes, but I'll let you know when," Aisha told her. She paused, then said, "I heard that man escaped from prison. I'm sorry you have to deal with that all over again. You look really stressed out, baby, and really distracted."

Andie wasn't paying attention. Aisha came around to the back of her chair, put her hands on Andie's shoulders, and gently squeezed. Andie stopped looking at the computer screen, and her head dropped. "Oh, god, don't do that. I won't get this done."

Aisha moved closer and said in her ear, "Baby, you are so tight." Andie rolled her head back, enjoying her touch. Aisha cooed, "Relax. I'm gonna make you feel better." She made her way around the chair, knelt down, and pushed the chair and Andie away from the desk. Andie smiled.

Aisha pulled Andie's knees apart and fit her slender body between them. She looked deep into her eyes and said, "I want to kiss you, make love to you." Andie took a breath and bit her lip then smiled and tilted her head. She hesitated and moved her chair back just a bit and shook her head meaning, *we'd better not.*

Aisha moved close, still looking for an answer, her eyes darting around and searching Andie's face. "Come on," she cooed. Andie wavered and smiled as Aisha leaned closer and closed her eyes. Her lips brushed against Andie's. They kissed, their lips warm and soft. They kissed again.

Their eyes met for a moment as their lips parted. Aisha touched Andie's face and ran her fingers to her jaw and then behind her neck, squeezing. Andie caressed Aisha's bare shoulders and then her upper back, bringing her in closer. They kissed deeply, their tongues touching and sucking, their teeth gently biting. Their breasts touched softly then squeezed together closely. Aisha pulled Andie's shirt up and ran her hands up her ribs, stopping at her breasts. She cupped them and squeezed. Andie moaned, and her head fell back.

Aisha pulled Andie's top off over her head. She kissed her neck, moving down her chest to her breasts. She sucked and nibbled one of her nipples as Andie tried to break free in ecstasy. Gently Aisha pinched her nipples and pulled her up. "Come on. Let's finish this, baby," she said.

They both stood now as Aisha backed Andie into the studio door, using her weight to close it. Andie submitted. "Oh, god," she whispered, looking deep into Aisha's eyes. Aisha looked at Andie, who was now half naked and smiling breathlessly.

Aisha unbuckled the belt of Andie's jeans and pulled them to the floor. She knelt before Andie and maneuvered the jeans and sandals off. She spread Andie's legs and ran her fingertips between her legs and slipped them inside her. Andie jerked and moaned; she was so wet. Aisha pulled her down to the bare floor, kissing her mouth and nipples, sucking them, making them hard and red. Her hands moved slowly up and between her legs. She caressed her labium then found the hard bead of her clit. "You are so wet," she whispered.

She moved around to Andie's bent knees, caressed her inner thighs, and slid her thumb into her warmth, thrusting it in and out. "Oh, god. Oh, god," Andie moaned, her pelvis rocking. Aisha bent down, flattened her tongue, and licked Andie's soft petals and sucked her clit, slowly and sensuously at first, then faster, teasing her.

Andie's body swelled with a glowing heat. She moaned deeply, her back arched in ecstasy. Aisha thrust her fingers deep inside her, rhythmically moving them in and out until Andie's muscles tightened around them and she came with a cathartic cry. "Oh, god! Oh, god!" she called out.

Aisha clapped her hand over Andie's mouth to silence her. She moved on top of her, laughing and kissing her sweetly. They both gasped for breath. Andie's body was racked with the tremors as the orgasm faded. Tears ran down her eyes, and she began to weep.

"Oh, baby," Aisha cooed. "It's okay. It's okay." She stroked Andie's hair and kissed her tears.

Andie looked up at her and pulled her close. "Oh, fuck that was nice." Aisha smiled.

The two slipped across the hall to the bathroom, where Aisha washed up and put on lipstick and Andie got dressed. Aisha smiled again, eyeing Andie as she left the bathroom. She was sitting on her bare mattress. "I have to do laundry sometime," Andie said apologetically. She pulled Aisha on top of her on the bare mattress and kissed her. "I don't want to think about your leaving, about your going off to grad school," she said as she got up and moved on her side.

"I know. I don't want to think about it either, at least not right now," Aisha said just as her phone began to vibrate.

"Oh, fuck. That's Kat. You're in trouble." Andie sat up and gave her a sly look.

"We're both in trouble!" Aisha said, smiling.

"I don't care," Andie said as she caressed Aisha's arm.

Andie smoothed the wrinkles from her clothes and ran a brush through her hair. "I'll walk you out."

They hung against each other down the hall. Michael was putting away the clean dishes from the dishwasher and gave the two a naughty look.

"See you, my love," Andie said softly.

Aisha turned to Andie as she opened the door to leave. Andie pulled her close by her leather belt and kissed her. Aisha returned the kiss and gave her a long look. "Take care of yourself, baby."

Andie looked down from the door with her hand on the glass and watched Aisha get into her car. She turned around and saw Michael looking at her. Falco kept her eyes away. She leaned against the door and whispered, "Desire makes me weak." Andie left the kitchen and headed down the hall back to her studio, smiling to herself.

Michael mused out loud, "I wonder if she found that inventory list."

CHAPTER 18

Andie hid out in her studio for the rest of the night, listening to music and sketching. Falco heard classical music from down the hall. Michael had disappeared into the small bedroom with his laptop. After a while, Andie felt sleepy; she made the bed with clean sheets and settled in with the cats. "You guys always love your mommy even though sometimes she's not around for you, right?" she asked Leo and Curry. She opened a book from her side table and adjusted the reading lamp over her shoulder. She put on her reading glasses and immersed herself in *The House of Mirth*.

Ballard should be here, Falco thought. *I hope he's not running late.* She had a sinking suspicion that the FBI was going to pull agents from the case. *Tomorrow is Monday, day four. I bet they'll do it then.* She sighed and wondered how long all this would go on.

"Second shift not here yet?" Michael asked. It was nearly ten thirty.

Falco eyed Michael wearily. "I may be here a while." She stood up slowly and stretched, then said, "Michael, can I ask you something?"

Michael came closer and leaned on one of the dining room chairs. "Sure."

"I've been asked to get some more information about Brian McCaffery. The file we got from the Evanston police was incomplete, and the FBI files aren't available yet. I'm going to need to get some detailed information about McCaffery from Andie. Will she talk about him and what happened? Any info I can get from her would really help us figure out what he's thinking or who might be hiding him."

Michael hesitated then gave her a direct look; his tone was very different now. "She has never, ever spoken to me about McCaffery or the case. All I know about it came from talking with Dr. Forrest and reading newspaper articles."

"Well, that's what I have here." Falco pointed to the file. "But there's nothing here that'll help us get inside his head. Andie may remember something, maybe give us some bit of information that can lead us on a different path—a path that can help us track him down. Do you think she'll talk with me about him?"

Michael crossed his arms in front of him and shifted his weight to his right leg. "Like I just said, Detective, she's never spoken to me about it. At one point I remember bringing him up almost by accident and she just got quiet or said something like, 'Don't talk about rope in a hanged man's house.' I doubt she'll talk with you about it, especially with all this happening all over again."

Falco thought for a moment and looked at the file. She wasn't getting anywhere. "I just thought—"

"Look," Michael interrupted, looking annoyed, "if you're looking to get my permission to approach Andie about the subject, to get her to talk about her ordeal with you, I'd have to say no. You don't have my permission. I'm afraid of what it might stir up in her. She's been teetering for the last few days, as you know. Talking about it might push her over the edge."

"She seems to be doing okay," Falco countered.

"That's the meds," he said quickly, "and you hardly know her to make that kind of assessment. She's dealing with posttraumatic stress and a panic disorder. Sometimes she loses touch with reality, especially when she gets really stressed. These are all very serious conditions, Detective, and…well, the risk is too great. It's my job to make sure she's safe and calm."

"Okay," Falco relented, leaning on the table, her head dropping down. "Okay."

Michael left the room with a quick turn. Falco put her fist to her head and whispered, "Shit, now what?"

Michael peeked into Andie's room after seeing her light was on. She'd fallen asleep with her reading glasses on and her book tented open on her chest. The cats, also fast asleep, were a fortress around her. "Edith Wharton, no wonder…" Michael sniffed. Leo barely opened his eyes. Michael turned off the light, closed Andie's door, and went to bed.

CHAPTER 19

Every room in the apartment was quiet. The rumble of the El across the street came at ten-minute intervals. It was twelve thirty a.m., and Falco was tired and cranky. She was stewing in her own anger at how she'd handled the conversation with Michael. *Play by the rules and get screwed*, she thought. On top of everything, Ballard was having car trouble. *Why doesn't he just get a squad and get his ass over here?* she thought irritably and looked at her watch again.

Out of the quiet darkness of the hallway came a whispering voice. Andie appeared carrying her big cat Leo. She was wearing a light cotton tunic over a white silky undershirt and baggy printed pajama bottoms. "Oh, let's see what we can find, mister," she whispered. She turned up the dimmer slightly on the kitchen light and glanced over to the living room, where Falco sat.

"Oh, hi. How come you're still here? I thought I'd see Detective Ballard," Andie said, pulling at the hem of her shirt.

"Ballard is having…transportation issues," Falco told her.

"Oh…hm." Andie scrunched up her face, as if feeling Falco's pain. She put some food in Leo's bowl. Curry, hearing the noise, came running. "Everybody's hungry," Andie said, watching them eat. She rustled her hair. "I can't sleep." She rubbed her forehead. She turned and glided a wineglass from the mounted rack under the cabinets and uncorked a bottle of red wine. She poured it evenly, swirled it in the glass, and held the glass to her nose. "Nothing like a nice Cabernet for a sleepless summer night," she said, entering the living room and sitting on the sofa. Leo came over and jumped on Andie's lap. "How's my big guy?" she said in baby talk. She took a sip of the wine, taking in its aroma. "I hope you don't mind the company. I had one of my nasty dreams, so I'm wide awake and a bit shaky." She looked at her trembling hands.

Falco gave her a concerned look. "What kind of dream?"

"Oh, the usual. I'm being chased by someone…scary stuff. Usually he's got this huge knife, and his eyes are red like a rodent's." She looked up and scanned the ceiling. "They're bound to get worse as long as this is going on," she mumbled. She swirled the wine again and took another sip then looked down at Leo. She smiled and glanced at Falco.

"You're really attached to those cats, aren't you?"

"They're my saving grace. Leo is my favorite, actually." She looked over at Curry, who was still eating. "We're soul mates." She rubbed her forehead again and sighed. "I've got this nasty headache on top of it all, but that's what happens when I have one of those dreams. Plus I really screwed up my meds." She looked at her shaking hands again.

"Should you be drinking that, Ms. Fulbright?"

"No, I shouldn't," Andie said flatly. "But your mommy is as stubborn as you," she said to Leo. "I could take some more pills. I used to take Xanax and a variety of sleeping pills, including Ambien, but that got to be another problem, along with other things…painkillers, what have you. So it's wine or sometimes something stronger. But only when Michael's not around. Actually, this is a very nice Cab," she said thoughtfully, swirling the glass again and looking at the color. She put Leo on her chest and whispered something to him, then kissed him on the head.

Falco smiled. "He sure is a big cat."

"Oh, yeah, and he's very friendly. I don't know if he's made friends with you yet."

"He's come by to say hello," Falco said with a grin.

"Do you have any pets?"

"No, but my son has a dog, which he's very attached to," Falco said, "but Sam lives with his father."

Andie smiled and scratched Leo's neck then set him next to her on the sofa. She got up and looked out the back window and glanced at Robby Torres, the officer on duty. He smiled at her. She pointed to the glass of wine and he laughed.

"He has a nice smile," Andie said, turning back to Falco.

"Yes, he does."

"They're probably all getting sick of this business...and of me," Andie said with a chuckle. She was feeling the wine.

"I'm sure it'll be over soon. The feds have some leads, and McCaffery's been spotted in a few places," Falco said reassuringly. She eyed Andie's glass of wine; it was already half empty. "Do you still work as a librarian?" she asked her, hoping to continue the conversation.

"Not really. I mean, I no longer work as a librarian in the classic sense—working in a library, doing reference and readers' advisory and stuff—though I sometimes do workshops. I haven't done them in a while, though. I've managed to support myself with my artwork for a few years now, along with stocks and other investments, that sort of thing."

"Do you miss it?"

"Library work? Sometimes. I miss the reference work, especially children's reference, and I liked doing story times with little kids." Andie smiled, reminiscing. "They used to get so excited when they'd come to the library. Their sweet faces—they would see me and wave and smile." Falco nodded as Andie continued, "I miss some of the patrons too, the regulars who came by every week to pick up books and return others. Reading was a big part of their lives. You'd really get to know them, what they liked to read and all. I remember this guy who was into all this obscure scholarly stuff. He'd come in and request these out-of-print books and hard-to-find journal articles. He had some weird mathematical theory he was trying to prove. He'd come and talk to me about it. I didn't get most of what he told me, but he was sweet and appreciative when we got his stuff in," Andie said with a wistful smile. She took another swallow of wine. "I don't miss the bullshit, though… and the crazy stuff, the crazy patrons. I could tell you some stories."

"I can imagine," Falco said.

"Well, you work with the public. I bet you've got some too." Andie leaned back into the sofa, looked up at the ceiling, then put a gentle hand on Leo. "I remember this one woman came in wanting these crazy books about healing and detoxifying the body. She stopped coming in for a few months, then one day out of the blue she showed up again. She smelled weird, and her skin was this funny color. She told me she was on a new health regimen. Guess what it was?"

Falco shook her head. "I have no idea."

"She was drinking her own urine!" Andie laughed, almost falling off the sofa.

"No!" Falco said in disbelief. "Oh, that is really sick!" She put her hand over her mouth.

Andie continued to laugh at her story and said, "You know, when I went to school to become a librarian, I thought that meant helping people access information from the Internet, books, and databases—you know, do book discussions, help kids with homework assignments and research papers, or help seniors find their favorite mystery writer or the best washing machine in

Consumer Reports. The reality is you're actually a babysitter, a referee, a social worker, a cop, a lawyer, an IRS agent, a nurse, and an entertainer," she said with a laugh. "I'm sure I left some other jobs out." She continued, "I've had to deal with the homeless taking paper-towel baths in the restroom, fights over computer usage, vandalism. Let's see…attempted child abductions, drugs, hypodermic needles and vodka bottles in the restroom trash, folks peeing on the furniture or worse, lots of porn, irate mothers whose kids owe hundreds of dollars in fines. It goes on," she said, shaking her head. Falco shook her head and smiled curiously. "I don't miss any of that, let me tell you."

Falco leaned forward, "I guess I had no idea the kind of stuff that goes on in nice quiet libraries."

"But those were the bad days. Most of the time you go home feeling pretty good about the work. It's the kids looking for science fair information or the latest Harry Potter book or the regulars who really know how to use the library and all its resources that make librarianship satisfying and fun," Andie said with a little smile. She started to say something then stopped short. "Oh, god, I'm blabbing. Sorry."

"That's okay," Falco said with a laugh. "It's interesting to hear that side of library work…beyond the stereotypes."

"You mean beyond the support hose and the cranky old ladies?" Andie asked, laughing. "Seriously though, it's a great second career if you ever get sick of all that crime." She flashed Falco a wry smile. "Hey, and I hear prison libraries pay really well."

Falco gave her a pensive look as her radio squawked; it was Ballard coming up.

"Oh, good for you," Andie sighed. "I'm gonna make myself scarce." She stood up from the sofa and grabbed her glass.

"Goodnight, Ms. Fulbright," Falco said with smile. "Thanks for the company."

"Please, it's Andie, okay?" She smiled at Falco and left the room.

What a lovely smile, Falco thought.

"Hi, Falco. Sorry I'm late," said Ballard in a small voice. The armpits of his shirt were dark with sweat, and his face was beaded and flushed.

"You gonna be able to get home tomorrow morning?" Falco asked, gathering her things.

"Yeah, the wife's picking me up."

"Nothing's new here," Falco grumbled, brushing past him. She headed out the door, down the stairs, and out to the street. The streetlights were hazy with humidity as she walked heavily to her car.

"Okay, where the hell did I park?" she whispered to herself. She heard the dull clink of something metal off to her right and saw a man sitting under the glow of a streetlight drinking a can of beer. He was hunched over doing something; his left arm was extended. "Oh, great. He's shooting up," Falco muttered. She walked closer as the man looked up from what he was doing. "Are you okay, sir?" she asked.

He caught the glint of her badge then eyed the six-pack of beer at his feet. "Yeah…yeah, Officer," said the man. "You want one?"

Falco gave him a closer look. He was taking his blood pressure with a portable blood pressure machine. "No, thanks," she said, shaking her head and walking off. The man shrugged and squinted at the machine. "Only in Uptown," she said with a sigh.

CHAPTER 20

Falco got into her car and slammed the door. She was exhausted. She sat in the silence and recalled her conversation with Michael. It settled there, gnawing at her mind like bad news. "You blew it," she whispered. She started the car and pulled out of the parking space and onto the street. She gripped the steering wheel and bit her lip. *I shouldn't have even asked him,* she thought. *I could have just started an innocent conversation with Andie. Shit! Now what am I going to do?*

She went over the scenario again in her mind. Her eyes darted across the road as she drove. "Don't kid yourself. The issue is dead," she said out loud as she made her way west on Irving Park Road.

It was nearly two in the morning by the time she got home. Her neighborhood was deathly quiet as she walked up the sidewalk and climbed the steps to her front door. She heard the echo of her footsteps off the awnings. As she pushed open the front door, she suddenly felt terribly alone. She turned on the lights, changed clothes, and stashed her weapon in its locking drawer. She eyed a bottle of Chardonnay on the countertop in her kitchen; it was warm. She uncorked it and splashed it over a handful of ice cubes and took a long sip.

Day four, she thought, *but it'll be nice to see Andie again.*

"Andie," she said out loud. "Why am I thinking about her?" Andie's face appeared in Falco's mind, and she smiled. *She's very sweet,* she thought. *She'd be a nice friend, never a dull moment knowing someone like her. She's different, offbeat, flaky in a nice way. Most of her friends are gay, though, and she hates cops. She doesn't seem to hate me, though. At least I don't think she hates me.*

* * *

Ballard's radio went off. He jerked awake from dozing in the chair at the dining room table. "Jeez," he hissed, looking around and hoping no one had seen him. He adjusted his tie and holster; it was five fifteen a.m. He said into the radio, "Ballard here. What's up?" It was Lassiter informing him that the FBI had pulled half its agents from the McCaffery case just as Falco had suspected they would. The feds were stretched thin, and political pressure from the rich folks in the north suburbs where the child abductions were taking place took priority. Ballard sighed. "Great."

The chief told him Falco would be stopping at the station for an FBI briefing before relieving him for his shift. The feds would outline their revised strategy on the McCaffery case in light of the reduction of manpower. Ballard looked annoyed and prepared himself to stay longer. *Gotta call Sylvia and tell her I'll be late,* he thought. *By the time I get home, the sun will be high in the sky.* He scowled. *If she thinks I'm mowing the lawn, she's got another thing comin'.*

Andie got up and did her usual workout. Despite a good sweat, she was feeling anxious. After four days of being confined to her space, she was beginning to feel like a caged animal. Michael was on the phone with someone, talking loudly in the office next to Andie's bedroom. He seemed angry about something and was talking fast.

Ballard kept looking at his watch, antsy to leave. Andie appeared in the kitchen and was surprised to find Ballard sitting at the dining room table instead of Falco. "Where's Detective Falco?" she asked.

"She's at an FBI briefing at the station," he mumbled, not wanting to elaborate.

"Did they get him? Is there something new on the case?" Andie asked, quickly moving closer to where Ballard was sitting.

Ballard gave Andie an up-and-down glance, not expecting to see her with so little clothes on, sweaty and hot. "I don't know anything right now, but I'm sure once Falco gets here she'll give me an update." He wasn't about to reveal what he already knew.

Michael came out of the office in a fury. Andie looked at him with wide eyes, wondering what was wrong. Before she could speak he said, "I can't believe this. I can't believe he'd do this!" Michael grabbed his wallet and shoved it in his back pants pocket. He clutched his keys and headed toward the door; he looked angry and worried. "I've got to run out," he said, looking at Andie and letting Ballard know with a glance. "Josh told me he was going to stay with Roxie, and he hasn't been there in two days. My neighbors called saying she was crying and barking. I don't know what happened to him. How could he forget about Roxie? I have to go, Andie. I'll be back as soon as I can."

"Okay," Andie said in a hallow tone. "I hope everything's okay."

She followed him as he headed toward the door. Michael grabbed at his pants pockets checking again for his keys; he swung open the door and ran down the front stairs and out to the street.

Andie suddenly felt lost: no Michael, no Falco. She decided to take a long shower. Maybe that would settle her. She took her meds and stepped into the hot, steaming stream. It felt good on her tingling muscles; she breathed deeply and rolled her head from side to side.

CHAPTER 21

The FBI briefing took longer than Falco had expected. A convenience store was held up overnight on the far northwest side near Harlem Avenue. Video cameras revealed a man matching McCaffery's description but with a beard. He had used a high-powered rifle in the robbery and made away with close to $1,000. Falco was concerned for a number of reasons, but what alarmed her most was that the convenience store wasn't far from her home. *He's really making the rounds, and he needs money*, she thought. She wondered whether someone was hiding him. *Why is he robbing a convenience store, and where the hell did he get the high-powered rifle?* she thought. She looked closely at a still of the video footage. The man definitely fit McCaffery's description. *Maybe this is the break we needed*, she thought. The FBI had farmed out the leads to the remaining agents, and Lassiter had recruited more uniformed cops to fill the holes in manpower.

In her head, Falco rewound her conversation with Michael from the night before. She was still kicking herself for having talked with him about getting more information from Andie. *I'm always playing by the rules*, she thought. *I should know better by now. God, I really fucked this up.* She gritted her teeth.

"Hey, girl!" whispered a fortyish stocky woman with an FBI badge clipped to her blouse. Falco looked up, surprised. It was Brenda Salerno, a woman who had joined the force at the same time Falco had. Brenda slipped into the empty seat next to her.

"Oh, my god, Brenda. How *are* you?" Falco smiled, happy to see her after so long.

"It's been ages!" said Brenda, touching her arm lightly.

Brenda Salerno was a street-smart cop who had joined the narcotics squad not long after she and Falco had graduated from the police academy. They became fast friends, being two female rookies in the department. Big-boned and busty, Brenda used her body and snarky personality to get information out of suspects, especially male suspects. During interrogations she would charm and sweet-talk them then turn up the heat. Before long the guys would be telling her their life stories.

Brenda's contentious interrogation techniques and reputation with the other officers off the field had resulted in her nickname "Butter" Salerno. When Falco had regularly worked with her, the men around the department cooed, "Butter Salerno, sweet and salty." Brenda didn't really mind, but Falco always called her by her proper first name.

"I haven't seen you around," said Falco. "Looks like you transitioned to the FBI. Congratulations!"

Brenda smiled. "Yes, and I really like it." She bent down low so no one else could hear and whispered, "Hey, I heard you were one of the three picked for CPD's new profiling team. Congrats yourself!"

Falco looked surprised. "I haven't heard a thing, but I've been consumed with this McCaffery case." Her heart lightened with the news, but she wondered how Brenda could have found out. Falco reasoned that Brenda still had friends on the force; maybe that's how she knew.

The briefing ended after an hour, and the agents and police packed up their notes and left with leads to follow and locations to report to. The two women said goodbye and promised to meet for lunch sometime soon.

Falco got in her car and headed toward Uptown, feeling better about herself after hearing the news about her application. She dreaded seeing Michael after their last conversation. *Maybe this'll all be over soon,* she thought. She cut west to Clark Street and quickly knew she'd made a mistake. "Shit! A fucking Cubs game, I should have known." She made a quick right on Waveland then a left, north up Sheffield. Hoards of Cubs fans were walking down the sidewalk and street to Wrigley Field. Just ahead, a crowd of young men congregated in the street near the 7-Eleven on the corner. Falco politely honked her horn so she could get past, but they ignored her, smiling. "Okay guys, move out of the street," she said to herself, moving the car closer. They didn't move.

"Get the hint, boys," she said opening her car window. They still weren't moving. Finally she blew her horn loud and long and pumped the gas, making the car jerk forward. "Come on! I'm trying to get through here!" she yelled, exasperated.

"Hey, lady, fuck you!" said one of the guys.

She stopped the car with a jerk and flashed her badge, "Move out of the way and off the street, assholes!" she yelled.

Seeing her badge, the crowd parted, and she drove past them, pissed off. "Fucking self-absorbed frat boys," she muttered. "It's going to be one of those days."

CHAPTER 22

It was nearly noon when Falco entered Andie's apartment. She heard choral music from down the hall. Ballard was looking beat and stressed out. She gave him an update on McCaffery and the FBI's scaled-down plans. "Where is everybody?" she asked.

Ballard smirked as he told her that Michael had gone out on an "emergency" and Andie was working in her studio. "Mike left to deal with his dog, and Andrea's been talking to herself in her studio with that crazy church music playing. If ya ask me, Falco, both of them are nutty."

Falco didn't respond to Ballard's remarks and closed the door behind him as he trudged down the stairs. She took the file on McCaffery out of her canvas briefcase and placed it down. She shook her head, still disappointed with herself.

Violin music came from down the hall. Andie appeared in the living room looking stressed and distracted. "Oh, hi, I thought Detective Ballard was still here," she said. "He sure doesn't say much. I don't think he likes me." She looked out the back door. "I don't think he likes my music either," she said, laughing. She leaned against the kitchen countertop and swayed to the music from down the hall.

"Ballard doesn't like anyone or anything," said Falco, half smiling. "How's your head, by the way?"

"It's fine. I heal pretty fast. As for the bruises, well…" she said, shrugging.

"Where's Michael?"

"Oh, uh…" Andie, pinched the skin between her eyebrows and paused as if to concentrate on what she was about to say. "He had to go home and check on Roxie, his dog." She came closer into the living room where Falco sat. "Josh, Michael's boyfriend, was supposed to take care of Roxie, but Michael's neighbors called this morning saying Roxie had been crying and barking most of the night. Turns out the neighbors only saw Josh there twice since Friday. She probably hasn't eaten or been taken out since then."

"That's not good," Falco said.

"Josh is party boy. He's so irresponsible. I can't believe Michael puts up with him. He needs to get rid of him. He's just a leach," Andie said, catching herself and stopping short. She was pacing, rubbing her hands on her jeans. She sat on the sofa and closed her eyes.

"Are you okay?" Falco asked.

Andie smiled as the music swelled in the other room. "I'm a bit out of sorts today," she said, almost apologetically. "I'm feeling really confined and a little anxious, and my hands seem to be going numb. This Beethoven is helping a little, though," she said, closing her eyes. She got up suddenly and started to pace again, clenching and unclenching her fists. She looked at her watch; it was nearly two thirty. "This adagio from Opus 127 is so amazing," she said, gazing at Falco. "The longing… Oh, my god," she whispered, putting her hand to her chest.

Falco's cell phone rang; it was Sam. "Sorry," she whispered to Andie.

Andie continued to pace. Falco had a brief conversation with her son, mostly about plans for his birthday after camp. He had come up with an idea of something special to do. She smiled as she spoke, her head down, talking privately. "Okay, that sounds like a plan," she said. She asked about his summer class and his math homework and then said goodbye. She sighed and slipped her cell phone into her purse. Smiling and thinking of Sam, she turned to her laptop screen, then glanced at Andie who was looking at her.

"That was my son," she said.

"That's right. You have a son, and he has a dog," said Andie, remembering their conversation from the night before.

"Yes, his name is Sam. He's almost ten."

"Cool," Andie said, smiling and seeming to enjoy knowing something about Falco.

"He's a good kid, and he does well in school," Falco said. "Wanna see a picture?" She pulled up her purse from the floor onto her lap. She leaned forward and handed Andie a wallet-size photo of Sam.

"Wow! He's cute," Andie said. "He's got your smile and your hair."

"I think his smile is actually his father's, but he definitely has my hair." She smiled and shook her head. "Poor child."

"Does he like to read? I have to ask that. It's the librarian in me," Andie said, handing back the photo.

"Oh, yeah, he's always at the library. He even goes in the summer. I started reading to him when he was an infant."

"Great," Andie said, smiling and leaning against the dining room table. She thought for a moment. "There are a lot of really good teen and pre-teen authors out there—Mile Lupica, Gary Paulsen, Rick Riordan, Christopher Paolini..."

"Oh, the book *Eragon*. Yes, Sam really liked that one."

"The second one is even better. I can't think of the title at the moment."

She pinched her forehead again, then turned and headed toward the kitchen. She picked up the phone and dialed Michael's cell phone and left a message. She looked at her watch and spoke in scattered sentences. "He should have been back by now. I hope Roxie is okay. She could have eaten something or gotten tangled up in something. Or maybe he's at the vet with her now, the emergency vet. I wonder what happened to Josh? I hope nothing happened to him, especially since I said he was a leach." She paused, looking around the room. Falco watched her.

Andie stopped talking for a moment then started again. "You know, Josh is nothing like Adam. Michael and Adam were really good together." She looked at Falco as if she knew who Adam was. "They really loved each other. They were really happy. But then Michael decided to pursue a doctorate in psych, and Adam didn't like the idea at all. They broke up once and then got back together. Michael had a really tough time with it all, plus he was in the midst of applying to grad school. And that takes so much energy— the letters of recommendation, the interviews, the loans." She sighed, looking stressed out. "Then Adam got really strange and moved out. Soon after that, Michael found out Adam had virtually drained his checking account. He became a tweaker and had used most of Michael's cash on crystal meth."

"Not good, not good at all," said Falco, shaking her head empathetically.

"Yeah, it was bad. Adam got hooked and really spun out." She caught herself rambling again and stopped short. "I probably shouldn't be telling you this—you know, airing Michael's dirty laundry." She bit her lip and looked away. She thought for a moment then shook her head, then began to pace again.

Andie was making Falco nervous; she wondered whether she was still taking her medication. "Why don't you sit down here and try to calm down?" suggested Falco. She pulled the chair out next to her. "There's nothing you can do right now about Michael or Josh, so try to relax, okay? I'm sure Michael's all right." She turned around in her chair and looked toward the foyer. "You know, I really like that painting over there," Falco said, pointing, trying to get Andie to focus on something else.

Andie looked briefly at the painting and gave Falco a blank expression, as if her words didn't register. She turned and walked quickly to the kitchen and filled a rocks glass with ice. She squatted down and pulled out a bottle of Grey Goose from a lower cabinet and poured some over the ice. She sat on the kitchen floor, hidden between the island and the wall of cabinets. She took a good swallow and let the cold liquid flow down her throat. It felt good. "I'm okay. I'm okay," she whispered to herself, closing her eyes. She looked at her hands; they were shaking. The string quartets continued to crank and jump.

Ten minutes passed. Falco waited, lightly tapping her fingertips on the table. She couldn't see Andie, who was sitting on the floor crossed legged and leaning against one of the cabinets.

"Hey, what are you doing on the floor?" asked Falco as she got up from her chair and walked cautiously around the island. Andie had finished the glass of vodka and was staring at the marble floor as she swayed to the music. Falco came over and sat on the floor across from her. She arranged her shoulder holster around herself to make it more comfortable. "You're not supposed to be drinking that stuff, are you?" she said, leaning closer to Andie.

"No," she said, swirling the ice. "But I have to calm myself somehow during these…episodes. Vodka and Beethoven are so nice together." She stopped swaying to the music and gave Falco a serious look. "I did everything right today, Detective Falco. I took my meds, I blew off some steam on my bike, I beat the crap out of McCaffery."

Falco straightened, stunned at what Andie had just said. She glared at her and placed her hands on her knees to stop her banter. "What did you say?" she asked slowly. "You beat the crap out of whom?" She hoped Andie wasn't hallucinating—or worse, delusional.

"Oh!" Andie said with a smile, tilting her head back and realizing what her statement sounded like. "My punching bag! Sorry!" she said, laughing and putting her hand over her mouth. "It's my punching bag. I have a picture of *him* on it—his mug shot." She bit her lip mischievously and looked at Falco. "It's good for me."

CHAPTER 23

Andie swirled the melting ice in the glass and looked at the clock on the wall. She moved around, desperate for another drink.

"Do you think that vodka is going to help?" asked Falco.

"It usually does. And it works faster than Xanax, and the headache is *much* more bearable."

Andie scooted over to the liquor cabinet and splashed more vodka into her glass. Falco sighed. "Andie, it's not my place to tell you what to do…"

Andie ignored Falco and took a good swallow from the glass; the ice clinked. Falco was feeling a thick sense of dread and sensing that the situation was rapidly getting out of control.

"Okay," she said. "I'm going to take this from you," she said firmly.

"It's okay. Michael doesn't know this is down here," Andie said, missing the point. Her words were beginning to run together. Falco gently took the glass from Andie, got up, poured the rest down the sink, and put the glass in the dishwasher. She turned to Andie, who was still sitting on the floor and said, "Why do you do this to yourself? You work out. You're in great shape."

"I'm a self-absorbed narcissist." Andie laughed, putting her head in her hands.

"Let's go sit over there and try to relax a bit, okay?" Falco said, gently pulling Andie up from the floor.

"I think I'm feeling better already," she said, now on her feet. "See? I'm not shaking anymore." She looked at her hands. "Michael doesn't understand this."

Falco steered Andie to the dining room table, where she sat at a right angle to Falco's laptop. Andie put her head in her hands. "Why can't this all be over with?" she moaned.

"I know this is hard, but the FBI has some new leads, and I really think we'll get him soon," Falco said in earnest.

Andie didn't seem to hear as she drifted off into her thoughts. Finally, after a few moments, she looked at Falco. "It's really hard knowing he's out there. I used to… I used to wake up almost every night in a panic, seeing him, seeing him look at me with those eyes, so angry, so piercing." Falco saw fear in her face. "Sometimes in my dreams he'd be chasing me, then he would grab me. I'd wake up swinging, and Michael would have to hold me down, calm me down. Then I wouldn't be able to sleep." She looked down and said quietly, "He hurt me. I don't think I'll ever…" She stopped and put her hand over her mouth.

"It's okay. Maybe you shouldn't think about all that right now. Let's talk about something else," said Falco.

Andie shook her head as if to rid herself of the image of McCaffery. She stared at the wall in front of her as she rocked in her chair. She was processing something, remembering something. Falco was quiet, tentative, watching.

"My whole life changed on that day, that *one* day," she said slowly. "I can remember it like it just happened, like it's right before my eyes. It was summer, sunny and warm, my favorite time of year. I was feeling good about my job at the library and really liked my co-workers. Most of the staff was in, and we were getting ready to open the library for the day. Our page wasn't in yet, so I decided to empty the outside book drop myself. As I was unloading the books, piling them on a cart, this guy pulled up in a ratty pickup truck. It was green and noisy, and it smelled of exhaust. He left the motor running as he went to the book drop to return his books. I saw that they were ILL books."

Falco interrupted her. "ILL books?"

"Interlibrary loan—books from other libraries outside our system, sometimes from other states," Andie said. She stared off for a moment, losing track of her story.

Falco coaxed, "ILL books."

"Oh, right." She rubbed her forehead and sighed. "The guy came over, and I told him I'd take his books from him because they needed to be discharged differently because they were ILL books. They go in different crates and get sent back to the lending library in these mailing bags."

Falco nodded. "It was McCaffery, wasn't it?"

"Yes," said Andie, looking scared all of a sudden, remembering his face.

"What did he look like when he came to return the books?"

"He was a big guy, dressed in a green shirt, a uniform shirt. He was kind of dirty, and his hair was cut short in a military cut. He had deep green eyes." Andie shuddered. "Deep green eyes." She clenched her arms around herself as she remembered him. She shuddered again and looked down.

Falco gently squeezed Andie's forearm. "It's okay. You're safe here. What do you mean by a uniform shirt, Andie?" she asked cautiously.

"Oh, the kind you wear when you work for a company. It had an emblem on it."

"What was the emblem. Do you remember?"

Andie thought for a moment then shook her head. "I… You know, it was…four years ago."

"Try to remember," Falco whispered.

"I think I told the Evanston police all of this. I can't remember." She continued to shake her head and started to rock a little, forward and back.

"It's okay, really. I was just wondering," Falco said. "Sometimes bits of information you remember from the past can make a difference in solving cases in the present. Still, I know it must be very upsetting."

Andie didn't respond. She stared ahead and slowly moved her index finger over the glass of the dining room table as if writing something. She looked at Falco and said in a tiny voice, "It was strange, and I guess that's why I remembered him. I smiled at him and he just stared back at me. You know, librarians are nice people, and they like people who use the library," she said, nodding at Falco. "He was different, though. He didn't smile. He just stared at me. But libraries attract some strange folks too, so I didn't think too much of it after that."

"He drove away then?" asked Falco.

"Yes."

"Do you remember if anyone else was in the car with him?"

"No, no. I don't remember anyone."

Andie stared at the wall for a moment then looked at Falco. Her eyes glazed over as if she were going somewhere deep inside her head.

She sighed deeply and looked as if she wanted to get something off her chest. Falco watched her, then opened the file on McCaffery and discreetly grabbed a pen and legal pad.

"I remember I took all the books to the work room and pushed the cart of our circulating books next to one of the computers," Andie said. "I took the ILL books. There were a few more beside the books he returned, and I put them on my desk in my office. We opened the library and were pretty busy for about an hour. When I finally got a chance to go back to my office, I saw the books on my desk and went over to discharge them. I tried to carry all of them, but there were too many and I dropped half of them on the floor. Three pieces of paper stapled together fell from one of the books. I was going to throw them away, but I thought they might be mine from my desk. I'm always throwing away stuff accidentally. I glanced through the papers and realized they weren't mine. I saw a map and some diagrams that I couldn't figure out and a copy of some kind of blueprint—a floor plan. First I thought maybe it was someone's homework or research. Sometimes I'd find a name on a report or something, and I'd contact the person if it looked important. People were always leaving stuff in library books: money, Social Security checks, bills, holy cards, letters, all kinds of stuff."

Andie paused a moment to collect her thoughts. She had gotten off track again. Her expression went blank. "The papers," Falco prompted, "You were saying what you saw when you looked through the papers that were left in the book."

"Oh, oh, yeah. I saw the address for the First Bank of Evanston on Church Street, a map of the area, and a time and date. I flipped through the other pages—the floor plan and the diagrams—and I realized what I was looking at. I couldn't believe what I was seeing. It was a plan to rob the First Bank of Evanston." Andie had a look of surprise on her face, as if she were experiencing what had happened for the first time. She looked at Falco fearfully. "I didn't know what to do." Falco nodded. "Then I looked at the stack of ILL books. One was on building and cracking safes and vaults, and the other was on becoming a locksmith. You didn't have to be a rocket scientist—or a detective—to figure that one out." Andie shifted in her seat, her expression suddenly distant as she sorted through the memory.

"I thought about it," she said vaguely, her voice floating upward. "I thought about just throwing all of it away, but then I thought, *What if this bank robbery happens and someone gets hurt or even killed?* I knew then I had to tell someone. Instead of eating lunch, I drove to the Evanston Police Department. I was so scared."

Andie paused and thought a moment, processing her memories. She shook her head and looked off. "I…I think about how they treated me. I was a rational citizen doing what I thought was right," she stammered. "They treated me like I was some…some flake, some crazy person, and I wasn't even crazy back then." She looked at Falco with wide eyes and continued to relive the painful memory. "They took the papers and put them in a file right in front of me. When I was leaving the office, I heard them laughing." She looked down, ashamed.

Falco put her hand on Andie's shoulder and leaned in close. "You did the right thing."

Andie nodded quickly. "When I returned to the library, one of the other librarians told me a man had come in looking for some papers he'd left in some books he had returned. The librarian told him the books had gone back in crates going to the central branch downtown. She said the man was furious and stormed out. Then he came back asking for me, but I hadn't come back from lunch yet. I didn't tell anyone what I'd found in the books. Looking back, I should have done what any self-respecting librarian would have done. I should have thrown the papers away or better yet returned them to their owner—if they showed up for them. I should never have gone to the police," she said quietly. "I bet my life would be different today." She put her head in her hands. She was shaking.

Falco kept her hand on Andie's arm. "Why don't we talk about something else? Okay, Andie? You don't need to tell me about this right now. Why don't we…"

Andie didn't respond. She rested her elbows on the table. Her voice was wavering. She swallowed and continued.

"Maybe two weeks later, I was at a meeting and not in the library. When I came home, I was shocked to hear on the news that the First Bank of Evanston had been robbed and that one of the robbers had been killed. The Evanston police had averted the robbery, but one of the suspects was still at large. The chief of police was being interviewed, and the FBI was posting a bulletin with a picture of the suspect. I saw the picture of the robber from the sur-veillance tape on the news. It was the man who had come into the library. I was so upset I almost got sick. I remember watching the TV anchorman talk, but I couldn't understand him. I couldn't hear him. The room was spinning. I called the Evanston police. I'm not even sure what I said. They picked me up in a squad car. It turns out they were trying to track me down." She shook her head and smiled ironically at the thought. "They questioned me for almost five hours in a tiny room. They asked me all these questions about my job, my finances, my personal life!" She looked desperately at Falco. "I think they thought I was involved with the robbery. I pleaded with them to give me some kind of protection. He knew where I worked. He was out there, and nobody was doing anything to protect me." Andie began to cry.

Falco moved close, put her pen down, and curled her arm around her, saying the police were wrong to not provide her with protection. It was clear why Andie hated cops. Falco took a deep breath and said, "Let's talk about something else. All this stuff about McCaffery is too upsetting, okay?" She had a burning feeling the conversation was getting out of hand, and she knew if she didn't stop it soon she might not be able to stop it at all.

Andie paid no attention; her mind was reeling with the memories. "The next day at the library, it was three staff members and myself. We weren't very busy after eight p.m., so I let two people go because a librarian from another branch was leaving and they wanted to go to the party. So it was just me and Marion, the page. We started shutting down the computers, getting ready to close for the night. I went in the back to get my keys and recalled the sound of the front door opening. We checked around, but it seemed everyone had left. I started turning off the lights. I called for Marion, who was somewhere in the stacks. It got quiet all of a sudden, and I remember feeling something wasn't right. I was very paranoid during that time, as you can imagine, but I kept telling myself not to let my imagination get the best of me." Andie started to get up from her seat but the room begain to stir; she wavered then sat back down. She felt a rush of sadness but took a deep breath and continued.

"I looked around and called Marion again. Then I got really scared. I thought something was wrong with her, that maybe something happened to her. She was eighty years old."

Falco acknowledged with a jerky nod. Andie sighed deeply and put her head in her hands again. She shuddered and shook her head back and forth. Falco was silent, hanging on to every word.

With her head in her hands and her voice muffled, Andie said, "I heard something, like someone was trying to say something or cry out and then stopped short. Then I heard a sort of swish, a crunch. Oh, god," she moaned, recalling the sounds. Her eyes floated upward as if she were having a vision. "It's like it's all in front of me now, like it's happening all over again," she said softly, her eyes glazed over.

Falco looked at her with growing alarm. "Andie, I don't know what you mean. I don't know what you're saying." She gave Andie a little shake, trying to disengage her from her thoughts. "Come on, Andie. Stop this right now."

She got up and wet a dishtowel with cold water from the kitchen faucet. She carefully blotted the back of Andie's neck. "Take it easy, Andie. Come back to me here…now. I don't like what this is doing to you." Andie didn't respond. "Andie! Are you all right?" She shook her gently, trying to jar her back to reality.

Andie's eyes grew wide as she stared ahead. She started to talk softly. "Then I went to find her…and…and then I saw her. She…she…her neck… the…b-b-blood. It was… She was…lying there…in all that blood. I…I couldn't believe my… Oh, Marion. She was…" She shook her hands in front of her as if she were shaking blood from them, then she moaned from deep inside her chest. Her eyes jumped about as if she were looking for something in the room.

"Then he came at me," she said in a flat, disconnected voice. "I could only see his eyes and the knife, the jagged edge coming at me. It was like a flash of light. It was bloody. He was sp-spattered with Marion's blood." Andie's speech grew faster. "Then, then…he tried to grab me. He swung the knife at me!" She gestured with her hands as if to fend him off. "I remember backing away, screaming. I…I remember pushing a book cart in front of him, and he fell over it. I ran around the circulation desk." She was talking between breaths. "I found the panic button under the…the desk… Y-y-you know, you have to press both at once, the buttons, at the same time," Andie reminded herself. "He was so fast and he looked so angry. He called me all kinds of things, names. I knew he was going to kill me. Oh, god."

Andie looked off, consumed in the memory, her hands gripping the table. Falco, pulled into the memory, gripped Andie's arm.

"He chased me into the back and dragged me to the floor facedown. I tried to crawl out from under him, but he was so heavy. I could smell his sweat and feel his hot breath on my neck. His shirt was wet, and I felt his body heat against me. He was so heavy on top of me… I couldn't breathe. I couldn't breathe! I screamed, but I didn't have enough air. I had no strength," Andie whispered breathlessly. "He tried to hold my arms down. Then he dropped the knife, and it fell next to my face." She put her right hand up as if to shield herself from the knife. "He was going to rape me… and kill me…rape and kill me. I managed to my right arm free and swing my elbow into his face. He fell back just enough for me to kick him and break free. Jesus, I don't know how I did it. I managed to make it to the back exit. I remember looking at the door, concentrating, telling myself to get to the door."

Andie drifted off in her memory. Her eyes were pierced and looking ahead; her mouth was open as she gasped for air. She rubbed her palms on her blue jeans and trembled.

"He came at me again and tackled me. I could feel the knife. We…we both fell out the back door and onto the concrete steps outside. Then he dragged me out to the parking lot and threw me down. I was pinned under him. My head hit the pavement. He twisted my arm back, and I felt the knife in my shoulder—so cool at first then hot like fire. My shoulder gave way. I thought he had cut it off. He tried to stab me again. There was blood everywhere. I remember looking at the ground, its texture, its blackness. My head felt so warm. And then I heard sirens."

CHAPTER 24

Michael stood outside his thirty-floor high-rise building, Roxie in tow on a leash. He was angry and distracted, going over in his head what he would do and say to Josh. His apartment was a disaster. Roxie hadn't been walked or fed in two days. He ran Roxie around the block a few times then took the elevator up to his floor. The keys clinked in the lock.

His neighbors, Cindy and Brad, opened their door and saw Michael. "Hey, Michael," Brad said. "How's Roxie? We heard her crying and scratching on the door all night."

"It's a long story. My soon-to-be ex-boyfriend was supposed to stay over to take care of her…only he didn't. I'm sorry if Roxie made a lot of noise."

"We saw Josh. He came on Friday. We saw him take Roxie out 'cause we rode in the elevator with him," said Cindy. "He said you were taking care of your friend Andie. We saw the news about that guy. I can't believe he got out. How's she taking it?"

"Not great. Day by day, sort of."

"We got an invitation to her show. I guess that's not going to happen," Brad said.

"Well, no. The show's still going to happen, as far as we know," Michael said tentatively. He opened the door to his place, and Roxie ran in. "Hey, nice seeing you two." He waved them off, saying, "I've got a big job in here, if you know what I mean."

Cindy and Brad waved goodbye and Michael slammed the door shut.

"I guess I'm gonna have to call a sitter for you, girl!" Michael said to Roxie, giving her fur a rustle with his hand. She spun around in tiny circles of black and grey then waited for Michael's approval. Michael patted her head and said, "Come on baby, you're gonna get the best dinner!"

Roxie jumped up with a woof, her tail waging. After Roxie was fed, Michael sighed and looked around. He was sad and sickened with the state of his place but was more upset that Roxie had been alone without food or water for so long. He admonished himself for having trusted Josh and getting involved with a party boy. "God, I hate him!" he yelled.

Michael cleaned up the vomit, chewed clothing, and dog shit and called his pet sitter. It was nearly four p.m., and he had to track down Josh to get his keys. He said bye to Roxie with a kiss and hug and promised to be back soon. He got in his car and drove down Halsted Street, looking for Josh or some of his party-boy friends. He zoomed around, cutting east on Waveland to Broadway and then circling back north on Halsted. He found a parking spot and put two quarters in the meter. He wandered into the Sidetrack bar and asked the bartender if he had seen Josh. No luck. He walked south to Roscoe's and then to one of Josh's other hangouts, Spin. No one had seen Josh yet that day.

Michael felt pangs of worry. Crystal meth was rampant in the community; it wouldn't take long for Josh to become a tweaker and end up dead on someone's bathroom floor. "He's so fucking self-absorbed," Michael mumbled. He thought about Adam, his lover from years back, as anger rose inside him. "I was so stupid. I *am* so stupid!"

He scanned every person on the sidewalk. He walked farther up Halsted and crossed the street. Suddenly out of the doorway of another hangout called Bobby Love's came a heavily entwined couple hanging on to each other, kissing and giggling. It looked like the two had just rolled out of bed. One boy, with dyed black hair and numerous piercings, wore short cutoffs and was barefoot. The other was blond with wispy long hair, a tank top, and baggy cargo shorts. The two were teasing each other and were half drunk.

"Josh?" Michael said, struck by the blond. "Josh!" he yelled as they brushed past him. "Josh!"

The couple pivoted around, not letting go of each other. Josh looked at Michael with surprise and fear. "Oh, hi…h-h-honey," he said weakly. He glanced at Michael and then his friend. "Uh…" was all Josh could muster.

Michael pushed the dark-haired guy out of the way and punched Josh in the face. The dark-haired guy flew back and fell into the street. Josh lay flat on the sidewalk. He held his head to protect himself as Michael continued to punch and scream at him. He planted a nasty kick square in Josh's crotch, found his keys in Josh's pocket, and stomped off toward his car. "I never want to see you again, you fucking twerp. Go screw up someone else's life!" he yelled. He got in his car and sat there with the door closed. He was so angry and hurt that his whole body shook. He bit his lip and looked out at the street in disgust. *Summer in Boystown. Nothing like being part of the drama,* he thought before he drove away.

CHAPTER 25

The El rumbled outside, filling the dead stillness in the living room. Andie was silent, breathing fast and staring into her memories. Falco had her arm around her tightly. She sat close to her and whispered in her ear, "Try to calm down. It's okay now. You don't have to think about this. It happened a long time ago. It's over now."

Falco had taken nearly a dozen pages of notes. Andie rubbed the perspiration from her forehead and seemed to be emerging from the haze of memories. Blurry eyed, she scanned Falco's face then the table, her eyes fixed on an image half hidden in the open file near Falco's notes. She looked closely at it as Falco followed her gaze.

"That's…that's…" Andie touched the open file with her trembling hand and moved it closer to see the picture. It was a newspaper article about the murder. Falco put her hand on the open file in an attempt to stop Andie from pulling it any closer, but the article slid out easily. Andie angled it to see it better. The image was a cropped picture of a family photo of the murdered library staff member, Marion Kearns.

"Uh, Andie, that's a police file. Give that to me. That's nothing you want to see." Falco got up to move the folder out of her reach, but it was too late.

Andie's breath caught in her throat as she looked at the picture then scanned the photos of the murder scene. "Oh, my… Oh, my god. Marion,"

Andie said quietly to the picture. She touched the photo with her fingertips. "Why, why, Marion? I'm so sorry." The photo shook in her hands.

Falco put her hand on Andie's shoulder and moved to take the picture away from her. "That's nothing you want to see. Come on. Give me that."

"You always brought the birthday cakes," Andie said to the picture in a small voice. She cradled herself with one arm, her body hunched over the picture. She stroked it with her thumb and breathed shallowly, whimpering.

"Okay, enough. Give me that, Andie," Falco said, reaching to pull the picture away.

Andie put the photo down and suddenly stood up, staring forward and wavering slightly. "Marion, I should have… I should have…" Her breathing grew faster and faster, and she leaned into the table. "I…should…have…" She turned almost robotically, and with her hand on her chest, she gasped, "I have to get some air." She spun around, knocking the chair over with her hand, and ran for the back door.

Falco went to grab her but was too late. "Andie! Don't go out there. Wait!"

Andie pushed open the back door, setting off the security alarm. She frantically ran down the wooden stairs as Falco dashed after her.

"Andie! Wait! Don't!"

Her hand on her heart Andie dashed out, saying, "I'm so sorry! I'm so sorry! Why? Why?"

Just as she got to the second landing, two uniformed cops swung around with their weapons drawn. One of them yelled, "Stop right there! Don't go any further!"

Andie slid to a stop as her knees buckled and her body hit the bottom stair. She screamed in terror at the barrels of the guns in her face. Realizing it was Andie, the cops quickly put down their weapons as Falco yelled down to them. Panicked, Andie flung her clenched fists and lurched backward up the stairs. Concerned that Andie would hurt herself, Langer and Riley held her down as Falco steadied her from behind.

Suddenly a voice came from the stairs above. "What's going on? Let me get through here!" yelled Michael, who seemed to appear out of nowhere with a small black pouch in hand. He knew something was wrong the moment he had entered the apartment and heard the loud voices outside.

Falco held fast to Andie, using Andie's arms as a sort of straitjacket. Officer Langer held her legs as Riley looked on. Michael knelt next to Andie. She was gasping for air and trying to break free from the officers. He spoke calmly, trying to ease Andie through her panic attack. Sweat dripped down her face; she was hyperventilating and pale. She took some desperate gasps, then her body went limp.

"I'm so glad to see you," Falco said breathlessly.

Michael gave her an angry look. "What happened?" he demanded. Falco tried to answer but was at a loss for words. Michael handed the black pouch to Falco and said, "Let me get her inside." He put his arm under Andie's shoulders and under her bent knees, pulling her up. He carried her into the living room and gently laid her on the sofa. Her shirt was wet with perspiration; her hair was tangled and stuck to her face. He sat next to her on the sofa and took a syringe and a vial out of his bag. Falco stood back, watching helplessly.

"Are you gonna tell me what the hell happened here, Detective?" Michael asked, pulling the plastic cap from the needle. Falco's files and notes were strewn on the floor. She knew she wasn't going to be able to explain all of this to Michael.

Andie mumbled something and wiped the hair from her face with a clumsy brush of her hand. She looked up and gazed at Michael. "M-M-Michael. Hi…uh…" She absently grabbed the front of his shirt. "I was…I was at the funeral. It was… It was…"

Michael turned his head to look at her. "Andie, lie still." He filled the syringe and then held it between his teeth.

Andie continued to mumble as she looked up at Michael with glazed eyes. "The music. It was 'Ave Verum Corpus.' It was…" She sighed.

"Andie, I don't know what you're talking about right now, but I would venture to guess Detective Falco does."

"Is she going to be all right?" Falco asked, leaning against the arm of the sofa and visibly shaken.

Michael glared at her, his arms crossed in front of him. He scanned the room, and seeing the upended file and papers on the table and floor, he swung past her and jammed them into the manila file. "Gee, I wonder what all this stuff is," he said sarcastically. He picked up Falco's legal pad with the pages of notes, glanced at the words, and slammed it down on the table.

"It's not what you think," Falco said quickly.

He gathered the file and legal pad into one stack and thrust it into Falco's arms. "Get out," he said firmly.

Shocked, Falco said, "Look, it's not what you—"

"I said get out. I warned you this would happen, and you defied me!"

"Listen, Michael," Falco said, trying to gain control of the situation. "Andie just started talking. She… I tried to—"

"Get out, Detective!"

One of the uniformed cops peered through the glass of the doorway upon hearing the shouting.

"Michael, please try to calm down. I can't leave. Give me a chance to explain. Just—"

"I don't give a fuck! Get your stuff and get out!" Michael shouted. He rushed closer to Falco, getting in her face.

Falco backed up. "Don't touch me. Michael!" she warned. "Don't touch me!" She put her hand out. She was furious, her face flushed.

Michael stepped back and collected himself. He looked down, took a deep breath, and then glared at Falco. "I want you to leave...now."

She glared at him, paused, and snatched up her briefcase and files. She gave Michael an angry look and left the apartment. Trudging down the stairs, she informed the officers on duty that she was leaving and that Ballard would cover the rest of her shift. She then called Ballard at home and told him he'd have to come in early, not giving him any information as to why. He grumbled but said he was on his way. It was six thirty p.m.

CHAPTER 26

Falco walked down the block toward her car. She paced back and forth before getting in. She clutched the papers that Michael had thrown at her and gripped her keys in her hand. She got into her car and slammed the door shut. Her car was sweltering hot, having been in the sun all day. Sweat dripped down her face and chest as she tried to calm herself. Realizing she could barely breathe, she started the car, cranked up the air conditioning, and headed south toward headquarters.

The confrontation between Michael and Falco bumped endlessly around in Falco's head. She gripped the steering wheel, trying hard to concentrate on her driving. Her hands rattled; her heart pounded in her chest; and her head throbbed. Had she pushed Andie over the edge? Was Andie all right? Falco admonished herself for letting Andie continue to talk. "I couldn't stop it. I couldn't stop her stream of consciousness. She just drifted off somewhere," Falco whispered to herself.

She drove down Halsted, passing the police station, and pulled into the 7-Eleven parking lot just before Roscoe. She bought a pack of Newport cigarettes, stopped at her car, opened the pack, and lit one up. She took a long drag and shook her head in disgust.

I shouldn't have let Andie go on like that, she thought. "Jesus Christ," she hissed.

A veil of cigarette smoke swirled around her.

* * *

"Hey stranger!" said Lynette Collins, the front desk clerk, as Falco breezed past.

Lynette had been with the police department for thirty-five years and made it her business to know what was happening in the entire station. Falco ran up the stairs to the second floor and careened around a corner of cubicles to her desk. It was piled with paperwork. Ballard's desk, which sat kitty-corner from hers, looked the same. She sighed and moved the stack, pulled out her chair, and sat down. Her eyes met Sam's picture. She studied it as if she hadn't seen him for a while. He had the build of his father and her crazy corkscrew curls. She touched the photo and sighed. She rubbed her forehead and sunk her head in her hands.

"Hey, Falco. I heard you were here." Chief Lassiter stood next to her desk. Falco looked up. "You look like you could use some sleep, Detective."

Falco ignored the comment. "Ballard's covering the rest of my shift. I had a bit of a…problem, sir." Falco lowered her eyes. She pulled the McCaffery file and the legal pad from her briefcase. The papers were a mess, shoved angrily into the folder by Michael.

"What kind of problem?" Lassiter asked.

"I'm in a bit of a jam with Ms. Fulbright's caretaker. He threw me out, and I'm not sure if I can go back there."

Lassiter smiled, amused. "What did you do, Detective?"

Falco didn't return the smile. "Well, I got the interview with Ms. Fulbright. She spilled her guts about the whole thing. I got it all here." She picked up the legal pad and then plopped it back on the desk.

"Good for you, Falco. This'll look good on your app." Lassiter smiled and turned his head to see the notes. "Let's take a look at what you've got. We need a few new leads, and I'd sure like us to get the arrest."

Falco sighed. "Chief, I need to talk about what happened with Ms. Fulbright."

Lassiter looked concerned and took a seat on the edge of Falco's desk. "Okay…" he prompted.

Falco pushed off in her desk chair to get a better look at Lassiter. She began to tell him the details of her conversation with Andie. She glanced at her notes and related the events and emotions of Andie's story. "Ms. Fulbright was agitated all afternoon. Michael Hansen, her caretaker, had left to deal with a personal matter. So we were alone. Ms. Fulbright was pacing and talking nonstop about all kinds of things. I suggested she sit down and at the dining room table where I would try to calm her down. That worked for a short time, then she poured herself a drink, then another. I managed to stop her before she had a third, but she got a bit drunk anyway." Falco shook her head. "She said she was going stir crazy, that she was scared that McCaffery was out there somewhere. She was convinced that he'd find her and that we couldn't stop him from getting to her. Then she started talking about *him*—McCaffery—and her ordeal, everything that had happened from day one. I listened and started taking notes. It was like she was in a dream state, sir. It was weird, bizarre," Falco said, eyeing Lassiter. "She stared ahead as if I wasn't even there. At times I thought she was going to completely lose it. She'd start crying and breathing fast, shaking all over, talking fast."

Falco paused and sighed. "To tell you the truth, Chief, I think she would have told her story to anyone." She brushed her hand through her hair. Lassiter took a deep breath and let it slowly out as he processed the interchange.

"A number of times I knew she was getting way too upset, but I needed to get the information, sir, the interview. At the same time, I was really concerned. She was in such an agitated state, and Michael was nowhere to be found. I didn't want her to lose it, to go over the edge."

"Tough call," Lassiter said.

"She must have talked for over an hour…detailed stuff," Falco recalled. "She told me how Marion Kearns was murdered and about McCaffery's assault on her. It was like she was watching a film and telling me all about it right there," Falco said, shaking her head. "Then I screwed up. Andie noticed one of the photos of the murder in the file that you sent. She pulled it out before I realized what she was doing. She saw the picture of Marion Kearns and the murder scene. It was too much. She started talking to the picture of Kearns—something about birthday cakes—and then she panicked. She ran out the back door, which set off the security alarm. I tried to grab her. Strickland and Langer heard the alarm from outside and stopped her as she ran down the stairs. They had their weapons drawn. She ran right into them and freaked out."

"Oh, Lord," Lassiter said.

"Michael arrived while all this was happening on the stairs."

"Is Ms. Fulbright okay?"

"She passed out—hyperventilated. Michael carried her up to her place and gave her something to calm her down."

"Then he tore into you," Lassiter said.

"Yes." Falco nodded. "It was easy to put two and two together. The papers from the file were on the floor, and my notes on Andie were on the table. It was easy to see what we'd talked about," Falco admitted. "I feel like I put someone I was supposed to protect at risk."

Lassiter paused then stood up and looked squarely at Falco. "Look, you were doing your job. I asked for the interview. You were passive through the whole thing. It was the alcohol doing the talking. You said she was drunk," Lassiter said firmly. "I'll call Hansen and get you back in there. You're the lead on this case. You need to be there tomorrow morning."

He took Falco's legal pad. "I'll take this home with me. You mind?" Falco shook her head. "Go home and get some rest, kiddo. You did good." Lassiter put a heavy hand on Falco's shoulder and left.

Falco sighed and put her head in her hands. She couldn't get Andie off her mind.

CHAPTER 27

Ballard softly knocked on the door of the apartment. He had gotten a gist of what had happened from Officers Riley and Langer. Michael, looking annoyed, opened the door and let him inside.

"Hey, there, Mike," said Ballard, sitting down. "How's the girl?"

Michael snapped, "Andie's fine, no thanks to you guys."

Ballard logged on to the laptop and checked his e-mail. His radio was silent. Michael buzzed past, taking a cold drink out of the refrigerator. "H-two-oh, Detective?" he asked.

"No, thanks. I got coffee. It's gonna be a long night." Ballard sighed.

Michael twisted the cap off his bottle of water and leaned against the kitchen counter.

Ballard looked stridently at him. "You know, Mike, in defense of my partner, she's gonna crack this case. She'll beat the feds. I know it. She never stops thinking…never, ya know?" Michael walked toward Ballard with a curious look. "I'll let you in on a little secret," Ballard said with a wink. The city's adding a profiler division, and Falco's a shoe-in for one of the positions. The chief approached her about applying. It's a big deal and the training's intense." Ballard gave him a knowing nod.

"Hmm…" Michael rubbed his goatee, jutting out his chin. "She got a lot of practice doing interrogation today. I'm sure the stuff she pulled from Andie will be a real feather in her cap," he snarled.

"Every little bit helps," Ballard said.

"Bitch," whispered Michael. He spun around and walked out of the room.

Ballard followed him with his eyes. *Did I say something wrong?* He wondered. "Fags," he hissed.

* * *

Falco took Lassiter's advice and headed home. It was strange to be heading home during the daylight. Once she arrived, she took off her shoulder holster and put it in the locking drawer then collected the mail. Her plants were drooping, and the house was stuffy. She went into the bathroom and took her clothes off, piling them with the other clothes to be washed. She caught a glimpse of herself in the mirror. "Oh, god," she said. "You look like fucking shit."

She washed her face with cold water, but the face in the mirror didn't change much. She sighed and looked at the clock on the vanity. It was seven thirty. *What day is it?* She wondered. *Tuesday.* It occurred to her that Sam had soccer practice on Tuesdays. Surely it was still going on. *Maybe he has a game*, she thought. Her mood lightened.

Falco was tired but couldn't stand the idea of spending the evening alone, and she desperately wanted to see Sam. She checked Sam's soccer schedule that was stuck to the refrigerator door. Sure enough, practice wasn't over until eight. She put on a pair of jeans and a fresh blouse. She freshened her makeup and pulled her hair back into a ponytail. She snatched up her purse and headed out the door. Fifteen minutes later she pulled into the parking lot of the soccer field. Practice was winding down, and the coach was yelling to the players. Falco made her way through the crowd of parents. Kids were running around and climbing on the playground equipment. She looked for

Jeffery and Sam as she walked. Someone recognized her and said hi. Falco returned the greeting but didn't recognize the face.

She found an empty seat on the bleachers halfway up. She spotted Jeffery; he was chewing on a plastic straw and cheering on Sam. Falco followed Jeffery's line of vision and spotted Sam on the field. She smiled seeing him. "Is he really that tall?" she whispered to herself. Guilt filled her. *When did I see him last? Has it been more than a week? Two weeks? No, it couldn't be.*

Practice ended as the players ran off the field. There was a clatter of parents running off the bleachers. They all made their way to the parking lot to find their children among the herd of kids. Falco came up from behind Jeffery and put her hand on his back, rubbing gently. "Hey, you," she said.

Jeffery looked at her with surprise. "Hey, M, what brings you to this neighborhood?" He kissed her on the cheek.

"Our son," she said, scanning the field for Sam. She stood on her tiptoes as she glanced about. "How's he doing?"

Jeffery was staring at her. She ignored him and spotted Sam coming their way. He caught sight of Falco and ran toward her. "Mom!" he yelled, smiling broadly. "You came!" He ran into her with outstretched arms, almost knocking her down. She hugged him long and hard, taking in his scent and holding his head close to her.

"How's my kid?" she whispered to him.

"Great! Soccer is great! I scored two goals!" Sam said, beaming.

"Fantastic!" Falco said with a smile. "I missed you so much!"

"Did you catch that man, Mom? Is that why you came?"

Falco looked at Sam, puzzled. She shook her head. "No, we haven't caught him yet." She hadn't considered that the case was all over the news and that was how Sam knew about it. Jeffery rarely talked about Falco's work with him.

The three made their way to Jeffery's truck. Falco had her arm around Sam. "You look tired," Jeffery, said eyeing her. "You're working those crazy hours, aren't you?"

Falco looked down. "I always work those crazy hours, according to you. Is that a new truck?" she asked, seeing the vehicle with a newly painted logo on the door. "Schuler Construction, Inc. Very nice."

"Yeah, it's new," Jeffery said. "Hey, you want to get a pizza or something?"

"Yeah, yeah! Let's get a pizza!" Sam said as he jumped up and down.

Falco smiled at Sam. "That sounds good and I'm buying."

She followed Jeffery's truck to the local pizza place. Sam was wired from practice and the surprise of seeing his mom. He talked about soccer, his summer math class, and the two-week summer camp Jeffery had signed him up for.

"What kind of summer camp? Falco asked Sam.

"It's a nature camp run by the Boy Scouts. It's got canoeing and fishing, and I'll be staying in a cabin," Sam said, his eyes glistening. "I leave in two weeks; it's way cool!"

"It's way expensive," Jeffery mumbled.

Falco looked at Jeffery and leaned in close. "Since when do you send Sam off to camp without discussing it with me? I thought I'd get some time with him, and now he's going away. Couldn't you have let me know you were going to do this?"

"Look, M, you're not the easiest person to get a hold of. Sam was on the waiting list and someone cancelled. He got the spot. It was as simple as that, and I needed to say yes or no."

"I don't believe that," Falco snapped.

Sam looked up from eating and glanced at them.

"Sorry, but that's what happened, and I don't appreciate being called a liar," Jeffery snapped back, making sure his voice didn't get too loud.

They glared at each other for a moment. Falco looked down at her pizza; she was losing her appetite. She glanced at the TV that was mounted in the far corner of the restaurant. A car was on fire on the Eisenhower Expressway, and firemen were putting out the flames.

Sam leaned close to Falco and gave her a smile as he chewed his food. Falco looked at him and gave him a playful hug. Jeffery clenched his jaw, took the straw out of his drink, and jammed it in his shirt pocket. Sam glanced at his parents, who avoided each other's eyes.

Finally Jeffery leaned back in the booth and said, "I know you made plans to do something with Sam for his birthday, but you're gonna have to change your plans because of camp."

Falco shut her eyes for a moment to think. *Sam's birthday is in two weeks. I completely forgot*, she thought. She felt a stab of pain in her chest. "Well, he's going to camp in two weeks. I guess that's that, isn't it?"

"I didn't plan for it to work out that way," Jeffery said flatly. He looked away then shook his head. "Come on, M. Give me a break already. Sam's really excited about going. There's no way to cancel anyhow. I already paid for it, and they don't give refunds."

Sam looked at both of them and said with his mouth full, "Cancel? You mean I'm not going to get to go?" He looked disappointed. His eyes darted between the two of them.

"No, no. That's not it, baby," Falco said softly, putting her arm around him. "It's just that we made plans for your birthday, remember? Now we have to do them some other time. We'll celebrate when you get back from camp, okay?" She nodded, looking for Sam's approval.

"Okay," Sam said, relieved. He stirred his drink with the straw, making a rattling sound with the ice.

Falco's cell phone vibrated. Startled, she jumped then looked at the caller ID. Annoyed, she answered, "Falco here."

Jeffery looked down and sighed. She motioned to Sam to scoot out of the booth to let her out so she could talk outside.

It was Lassiter. "Hi, Chief. Yes, it's me," she said, making her way to the door.

Jeffery followed her with his eyes. Sam smiled. "Mom's so cool."

Jeffery gave him an angry look. "Cool? How cool is cool when she never sees you?" Sam slumped and played with his pizza. "Sorry, kiddo," I didn't mean that," Jeffery said softly.

"Falco," chirped the voice of Chief Lassiter; it was a bad connection. "Got word of a wreck on the Ike, minivan burnt to a crisp. The feds think it's suspicious."

"Suspicious, Chief? How?"

"Fire crews are down there putting out the blaze. The feds think it might be the van McCaffery stole, and there appears to be at least one body inside."

"Holy shit!" Falco said, spinning around.

"I'll meet you at the station, Falco. I'm on my way there now."

She ran back into the restaurant, looked at Jeffery and Sam, and said, "I'm sorry, but I've gotta go. They may have McCaffery. I mean, he may be dead." She looked at the two, conflicted with relief and regret. "Sam, I'm so sorry."

She turned to Jeffery, who shook his head and said flatly, "Go. Just go."

She put two twenties down. "I'll write you a check for Sam's camp. Just let me—"

"Just go. Be careful."

Falco kneeled down by Sam and looked at him sadly. "I'm sorry, sweetie."

Sam smiled and said, "It's okay, Mom."

"Look," she said, "if all this blows over, maybe we can spend the weekend together. How does that sound? We can even celebrate your birthday; maybe go to Navy Pier or something,"

"Yeah okay, Mom." Sam's eyes drifted to his father as Jeffery nodded yes.

"I'll call you as soon as I know something," Falco said.

"I'm sure we'll see it on the news," Jeffery groaned.

She kissed Sam on the head, glanced at Jeffery, and quickly walked out.

CHAPTER 28

Falco stopped off at home to pick up her weapon then headed toward the twenty-third district headquarters. She pulled into the back lot. Trucks from the local news networks were parked everywhere with their satellites high in the air. She entered through the back to avoid the reporters who waited like vultures. Ballard was still at Andie's place but was getting updates as more information from the feds came in.

Chief Lassiter intercepted Falco as she ran up the stairs. "Falco, this way." He grabbed her elbow and steered her into a room where four FBI agents, including her friend Brenda and two detectives from the department, Steve Grasky and Bob Leighton, waited. Lassiter closed the door of the small conference room and made introductions. Falco knew almost everyone there from the briefing the other day. She smiled at Brenda, who was stirring a cup of coffee from the vending machine.

Special Agent Fred Tedeschi, the FBI agent assigned to lead the case, stood up. He took off his bifocals and rubbed his forehead. He spoke slowly and methodically. "It appears the vehicle that hit a guard rail on the Eisenhower tonight was the one stolen by escaped inmate Brian McCaffery." The room was still. "The van and plate were traced to the man McCaffery killed on the West Side, a Ricardo Gutierrez. Unfortunately there seems to be very little left of the vehicle. It hit the guardrail at a very high rate of speed and flipped over before smashing into a concrete viaduct. Investigators are in the process of towing the vehicle as we speak."

"Was there only one person in the van?" asked Steve Grasky, chewing a wad of gum.

"As far as we can tell, yes," Tedeschi answered. "It appears that the vehicle was carrying some kind of explosives or flammable materials. That would explain the condition of the van when the fire crews arrived."

"But apart from the fact that the van was stolen by McCaffery, what else do we have to go on?" asked Falco.

"Nothing substantial yet. Like I said, we've got a forensic team going over the wreckage."

"I think Ballard should stay put," Falco whispered to Lassiter, who nodded.

"Until we ID the body and process any items found in the vehicle, we're not planning to pull any more agents from this case." There was a collective sigh of relief from the room.

"Any idea when we might know something?" asked Salerno.

"A few hours at least. Let's see. It's nearly ten thirty. Well, I hope before midnight," Tedeschi said. "Based on what we find from what's left of the body and any other evidence, we'll make a determination and go from there."

"What about DNA?" asked one of the agents.

Tedeschi sighed. "Well, you know DNA takes a week. I'm hoping we can determine if it's McCaffery from the body and what we find in the van."

The meeting broke up. Falco and Lassiter left the room together and headed toward Lassiter's office. "I reviewed your interview notes with Ms. Fulbright," Lassiter said, eyeing Falco. "They were pretty good." He smiled. "I've got some ideas to share with you. One thing— do we know where

McCaffery worked? You asked Ms. Fulbright about the emblem on his shirt. She couldn't remember what it was, right?"

"No, she said she may have told the Evanston police about the emblem, but she couldn't remember. Is the EPD cooperating at all with us on this case?"

"Not much. They seem to have their hands full with the child abductions in the north suburbs."

"You know, if we knew where he worked, maybe he made friends there," Falco said.

"That's what I'm thinking. Let's hold that thought, and if this thing doesn't pan out, we can chase that lead in the morning." said Lassiter. "Just in case."

"This would all be a lot easier if we just had the complete file on the guy—work records…all that."

Lassiter gave her a weary smile. "Go home, Falco. Wait 'til the morning with all this. Get some sleep. I'll call you if anything breaks with forensics."

Falco nodded and waved goodnight.

She headed back home; it was nearly eleven. She rubbed her neck and thought about Sam. *I bet Jeffery planned that camp thing from the start*, she thought. "Asshole," she said angrily. She bit her lip and gripped the steering wheel. Her thoughts turned to Andie. *I hope she's okay. God, what a long day.* She took out her pack of cigarettes from a compartment between the two front seats. She pulled a cigarette out with her lips, lit it, and took a long drag.

CHAPTER 29

Chicago was in for another sweltering day with no rain or break from the heat in sight. News stations and city officials were warning residents to check on the elderly and avoid excessive activity. They posted cooling center locations around the city and on TV. Power brownouts were expected if the heat continued.

Andie woke up in a heavy daze. She felt as if she could barely lift her head. Her neck and back hurt as if bruised. "God, did I drink too much last night?" She sighed and grunted as she got up and rubbed her forehead. She was wearing the clothes she had on the day before. Curry and Leo stared at her from the bed. "What day is it?" she whispered. "What happened to yesterday?" The sun was bright in the room as she fumbled her way around the bed to close the blinds. "God, I'm fucking dizzy. Jesus, what happened?" She made her way to the bathroom, brushed her teeth, and combed her hair. She gazed at herself in the mirror; her eyes were bloodshot. "Lovely," she mumbled, holding her head. She changed her clothes and made her way down the hallway looking for Michael.

"Hey, girl," said, Michael hearing her shuffle. "How do you feel?"

"What do you mean, how do I feel?" asked Andie, rubbing her arms. "I'm cold. Did someone crank up the AC or something?" Her hand dragged against a band-aid that held a cotton swab in place at the crook of her left arm. She stopped and looked at it, wavering slightly, trying to focus her eyes.

"Let me get you a sweater," Michael said, walking past her.

Andie studied the band-aid for a moment and then peeled it off her arm. She turned around and followed Michael into her closet. "What is this?" she asked, dangling the band-aid from her finger and thumb.

He avoided her gaze as he helped her put on the sweater. "Let's go talk in the living room." He steered her in front of him and guided her down the hall. "How are you feeling?" he asked again, turning Andie around and setting her in one of the dining room chairs.

"I…I don't know. I'm dizzy and foggy, and my back hurts." She put her head in her hands. "Did I get really drunk last night or something? I don't remember anything. Did I have a blackout?" She gave Michael a sick look.

"Alan's going to be here soon. It seems you had a dissociating episode yesterday. He's coming over to make sure you're okay," Michael said, taking a seat in one of the chairs.

Andie shook her head and looked disorientated and confused. "Alan's coming? Was I drinking?"

"I wasn't around most of the day. I had to deal with my own problems— those being Roxie and another person, who shall remain nameless.".

Andie looked at Michael as if he were speaking another language. She rubbed her neck and put her head in her hands.

"How about some juice and some coffee? I'll make you some raisin toast. How about that?" He got up and moved toward the kitchen. "Is your tummy upset?"

"No, I'm just fucking dizzy, and I have a headache," she groaned. "What day is it?"

"Wednesday, my dear, and Kat has already called twice."

"Who?"

"Kat—you know, Katherine Cohen, otherwise known as the thorn in your side?" Michael said in a cheery tone.

"Oh, god. Just tell her I died, okay? I fell off the back deck onto my head in a big bloody mess."

"Now, now, enough of that wishful thinking," Michael quipped. He was busy making coffee and pouring juice.

Andie's apartment was deathly quiet except for the occasional rumble of the El train. Michael made the toast and kept a close eye on her. Dr. Forrest was running late as usual; it was nearly noon.

Andie peered across the dining room table as a thoughtful look came to her face. "Michael, where is everybody?" she said, turning to him. She got up quickly from the chair, steadied herself, then made her way to the large bay windows of the living room. No cops, no cop cars, no Falco, no Ballard. "Where is everybody?" she asked again.

Michael steered her back to the dining room table and made her sit. He put a glass of orange juice in her hand. "Drink some juice, and I guess I'll be the one to tell you."

Andie looked concerned and very much out of sorts. She put the glass to her lips and swallowed. Michael pulled a chair in front of Andie and sat down. He looked at his watch again, trying to give Dr. Forrest some more time.

"Well, a couple of things happened yesterday," he started. "To refresh your memory, I had to leave to deal with Roxie, who hadn't been walked or fed in almost three days. Needless to say, my place was a mess and Roxie discovered new and interesting food sources in my kitchen and hamper. That's a joke," he said, smiling. Andie's expression was blank. "So I left you here with Detective Ballard. It was about one thirty. Detective Falco most likely arrived soon after that." Michael paused and looked pensive. "I don't know exactly what transpired here while I was gone, and I hope you get around to remembering, but I returned around five thirty, and as I entered your place, I heard all this commotion downstairs. I heard you screaming and Detective Falco was yelling something. I could tell from the kitchen you were hysterical, so I grabbed my little black pouch."

Andie shook her head, not remembering, as Michael continued.

"You were having a panic attack and had fallen on the stairs. By the time I got down there, you were past the point of needing a paper bag. Falco was holding you down from behind, and one of the other cops was holding your legs. You were flinging your fists and kicking up a storm down there. Well, you passed out and I carried you upstairs and put you on the sofa. When you came to, you were talking about all kinds of weird stuff. Somebody's funeral…the music…birthday cakes…Mozart."

Andie's eyes got wide, and she lifted and tilted her head as if remembering something from long ago. "Marion…Marion's…funeral," she said slowly.

"Yes, I gathered that. It seems that Detective Falco managed to get you talking about McCaffery. She took tons of notes. I saw them. Then it appears you started dissociating and ended up having a big panic attack on the stairs."

"But…but I don't remember *anything*," Andie said, finding it difficult to process the story.

"Yeah, well, the thing is, Detective Falco asked me the other night if you'd be able to talk about what happened. She needed more information because the Evanston police weren't as forthcoming with stuff on Brian McCaffery as the CPD would have liked. They sent over an incomplete file, and Falco thought you might be able to fill in the blanks."

"I…I don't remember talking. I'm not getting all this." Andie shook her head.

Michael scooted closer to her with his chair. "She asked if I thought you'd be willing to be interviewed about the case, and I flatly said no. I said you never talk about it, and you were in no state to relive the ordeal for the sake of a skimpy, incomplete police case file," Michael said, exasperated.

"But we must have talked anyway."

"Yes, and you went over the edge. You were in some trance-like state, and then you… You freaked out on the back stairs." He held his gaze, making sure Andie was processing what had happened. "Do you get what I'm saying?"

"Yes, but I don't remember." She shook her head, frustrated. "I was dissociating? I've *never* done that." She put her head in her hands again.

"I'm afraid you have, in the past," Michael said. "Many, many times."

Andie sat up. "Okay, already. I don't know what you're getting at. Is Alan coming here to put me in a hospital…in the crazy house?" she asked as tears welled up in her eyes.

"Oh, no! Dear god, no!" Michael gushed. "I'm sorry. I didn't mean to take you down that road." He paused and collected his thoughts then knelt in front of her. "I just wanted you to know that I believe Detective Falco took you over the edge last night. I brought you back here and gave you something to calm you down. That's why you had the band-aid on your arm, and that's why you feel like shit today. It was the medication. I had no choice." He looked at her intently.

Andie looked hurt. She processed what Michael had said. "You promised me. You know you promised me…no more needles."

"I know, I know, but I had to." Michael said, pleading with his hands. "I'm sorry, but I'm still your nurse, and you were really out there. You were freaking *me* out. So, in short, when Andie goes over the edge, all bets are off."

There was a pause of silence. "I miss her," Andie said quietly. She looked at the floor and then at Michael.

"Well, I threw her out." he said, pacing the room. He spun around. "She betrayed me *and* you. She defied me."

"You threw her out?" asked Andie, biting her lip.

Michael sighed. "Yes, I told her to get out. I picked up all her damn papers and her fucking pad of scribbled notes that she took while putting *your* mental health at risk, and I told her to get out!" Michael said, getting angry all over again.

"Please don't yell," Andie said quietly, closing her eyes and rubbing her head.

Michael put the chair he had been sitting on back in its place and sighed as he looked at Andie. He glanced at his watch. It was nearly one thirty. "Okay, there's one more thing," he said. He paused and knelt and looked deep into her eyes. "Brian McCaffery is dead," he said, gently taking hold of Andie's arms.

Andie looked at Michael in disbelief and gasped. Her eyes were fixed on Michael's; her head moved slightly askew. "W-what?"

"Last night," Michael said, "he either lost control of the stolen van he was driving or he purposely ran it into a guard rail on the Eisenhower. The van burst into flames, and he was basically incinerated."

"How… When did it… Are you sure?" Andie got up from her chair and looked across the room.

Michael followed her. "The FBI closed the case early this morning. Ballard got the call about three thirty. They positively identified the body—prison clothes, personal stuff, tattoos. It was McCaffery."

Andie was silent, looking out the window. She was breathing fast. She turned and looked at Michael. "Are you sure?" she said softly, her eyes full of tears.

"Yes. It's over with. It's really over with," he said with a tearful smile.

Andie fell to her knees, and Michael rushed to her. She was dazed and filled with a mixture of relief and disbelief. She stared at him, pulling him close to her, grabbing his shirt with both hands. She gasped and tried to speak. "I…I can't… It can't be… Just like that? How? How could it?" she said breathlessly. Her eyes searched Michael's face.

"Take it easy," he said, looking at her. "Take it easy."

Her body quaked with sobs. "Tell me. Tell me it's really, really true."

Michael stroked her back and held her head close to his chest, embracing her.

Dr. Forrest let himself in and sat at the dining room table. Michael and Andie were locked in an embrace, gently rocking back and forth. The doctor made eye contact and nodded to Michael. He nodded back; Andie was okay.

The phone rang, bursting through the newly found calm in the room. Michael put his face close to Andie's. "I bet I know who that is. Do you want to talk to her?"

"Okay, okay. I might as well get it over with," Andie said weakly.

Michael answered the phone. It was Kat. Andie got up from the floor, and Dr. Forrest embraced her and whispered something in her ear. He looked closely in her eyes and smiled. "When you're ready…when you're ready," he said, nodding. Andie smiled and took the phone from Michael.

Dr. Forrest nodded to Michael and softly said, "You know, it was four years ago yesterday that this all happened." Michael looked at him with surprise. He leaned close to Michael and said in a low voice, "I think she's okay. Keep an eye on her for tonight." As he made his way to the door he said, "It'll be nice having you back at the hospital, Michael." He gripped Michael's shoulder and added, "This was good clinical experience for you."

"I'm exhausted," Michael said with a weary smile.

Andie was quietly talking with Kat. She was crying again but smiling too. Her show at the gallery was on course thanks to Mario, who had finished mounting and framing Andie's work.

"That'll come off the top of the total sales revenue," Kat told Andie.

"Okay, that's fine." Andie sniffed. She was relieved everything was falling into place.

"We'll start hanging it tomorrow and then finish on Friday. The invitations went out. We've gotten a lot of calls—I mean a *lot*—and it's going to be covered in the *Trib* with photos, I hope," Kat said. "Why don't you come by early tomorrow and we'll celebrate? Okay, girl? There's so much we need to catch up on."

Andie smiled. "I'll be there before noon."

Andie gave Michael a hug and thanked him for his comfort and support over the last few days. Michael said flippantly, "I guess you won't be needing me anymore."

"I'll always need you, Michael," Andie said sweetly.

She turned and bumped her way down the hallway. She entered her bedroom, flopped onto her bed, and quickly fell asleep.

Michael straightened up the apartment and wiped the dining room table with glass cleaner. He arranged the dining room chairs and picked up a navy blue cardigan from underneath one of them. He looked at it, folded it neatly, and placed it on Andie's dresser.

CHAPTER 30

Falco impatiently tapped her pencil on her desk. She was anxious and having a difficult time focusing. She had a pile of paperwork to finish and reports from the past two weeks to complete. She was out of sorts. Ballard took the day off. He probably didn't want to face the paperwork on his desk, she thought. She couldn't believe the McCaffery case had ended with such a whimper. All the drama of yesterday—god, was it just yesterday? She shook her head.

Her side of the office was quiet except for the buzz of the air conditioner. "Okay, let's do this. Nobody else is going to get through this stuff. It's just me and you, kid," she said to her computer screen.

Falco worked for a while then got up and stretched and made her way to the water cooler. She filled a plastic cup and took some aspirin. She leaned against the wall and looked at the ceiling tile. Something didn't feel right. Her thoughts turned to Andie as she smiled. She hoped she was all right.

"McCaffery's dead, but it just doesn't feel right," she whispered into her plastic cup. The feds seemed to be in an awful big hurry to put the case to rest and had wasted no time shifting more agents to the child abduction cases in the north suburbs. Falco wandered back to her cubicle and sat down. *I should go home early*, she thought, feeling an acute sense of fatigue. She rolled her head back, loosening the stiffness in her neck. *Well, at least*

Sam and I can do something this weekend, she thought as she looked at his photo on her desk.

Chief Lassiter breezed past her desk and plopped down the legal pad with the notes from the interview with Andie. "Falco, here are your interview notes. They're useless now, but they were very good." He smiled, and she returned it with a shrug. "That's police work," he said.

She leaned back in her chair and looked up at Lassiter. "How long for the DNA results on McCaffery?"

"At least a week."

She thought for a moment then said, "Sir, don't you think the FBI was a little premature about closing this case? I mean, I don't—"

"Falco, the chance of this not being McCaffery is remote. They found prison clothes in the back of the vehicle, and the dental records matched."

"You know that for sure, sir?" asked Falco. "Because I've gotta tell you, I don't feel right about all this."

"Understandably," Lassiter said. "You've been cooped up in someone's house for almost a week, you're working a crazy schedule, you haven't had a decent night's sleep, and now you're here at your desk looking at a pile of paperwork. Of course you're gonna feel unsettled." Falco processed what Lassiter had said. He eyed her and added, "Why don't you get out of here? Take some time for yourself."

Falco looked at her watch and sighed.

Lassiter smiled back wearily. "I might as well tell you while we're talking, Falco. I'm putting you and Grasky on the child abductions case. It appears the feds have a lead that points to a suspect in our jurisdiction. Go home and get some sleep. Tomorrow's another day."

CHAPTER 31

Michael was working on his laptop at Andie's dining room table, catching up on his e-mails and research notes. He was anxious to get back to his dissertation and his work at the hospital with Dr. Forrest.

Andie knocked quietly on the wood molding at the entrance of the dining room. "Hey, you feeling any better?" Michael asked with a smile.

"I thought you'd left for your place," Andie said.

"I'll stay the night to be sure you're okay, and then I'll get back to my life and all its scholarly excitement tomorrow. Is that okay with you?" He glanced up at Andie from his computer.

Andie had showered and put on makeup and a pair of jeans. She wore a low-cut shirt underneath a printed linen jacket. She was leaning in the doorway and holding something in her hand.

"Hey, you look great!" Michael said getting up from his chair.

Andie smiled. "I'm still not a hundred percent, but I need to go downtown…to buy a tie."

Michael laughed. "You mean you're not going to Sears?"

Andie smiled. "I'm going to take the train."

"Good idea. It'll do you good to get out."

"I'm meeting Aisha for dinner too," she said with a mischievous look.

"I didn't hear a thing!" Michael said, holding up his hands and spinning around.

Andie leaned on the table. "Do you know who this sweater belongs to?" she said, holding the sweater up.

"I thought it was yours. That's why I put it on your dresser. It was under here on the floor," Michael said, pointing.

"It's not mine, but I think I know whose it is. I'll just have to return it in person." She smiled. "Tomorrow."

Michael gave her a serious look. "Please come home tonight. No monkey business, okay? 'Cause you know I'm going to worry."

"Yes, Mother. Don't worry. Plus we're hanging the show tomorrow." She kissed him on the cheek

Andie walked out of her building with a new sense of freedom. The world seemed to look different somehow, a bit brighter, a bit greener. Life had begun again.

CHAPTER 32

Thursday morning was bright and breezy. The heat had taken a little break, and a nice wind came off the lake. Lassiter gave word that Falco and Steve Grasky would be joining the feds and suburban law enforcement on the child abduction cases. Two suspects from the northwest side were under surveillance. One was a registered sex offender, and the other had served time for possession of child pornography. Falco sat at her desk sifting through prison records on her computer.

Steve Grasky was a thirty-five-year veteran with the Chicago Police Department. He was fit but stocky; his hair was mostly gray and cut short; and he had a rubbery face and a wry smile. His friends and colleagues often said he looked like a thinner version of the former Chicago Bears coach Mike Ditka, without the mustache or cigar. He had a penchant for chewing gum after having quit tobacco years ago. Folks around the department gauged Grasky's stress level by the pace of his jaw on the gum.

* * *

The next morning Andie drove her blue Volvo south on Halsted to Addison and found parking a block west. She snatched the small shopping bag from the passenger side of her car, walked east, and entered the twenty-third police district. Her shopping bag contained Ballard's new Burberry tie, nicely wrapped, and Falco's navy sweater. Andie wore a pair of snug-fitting jeans, with the right knee torn, and hitched up with a thick suede belt. She also had on her favorite broken-in cowboy boots and a clingy deep-red shirt with a teal jean jacket. A thin silver chain and bobble dangled from her neck.

"Hi. Can you tell me where I can find Detectives Ballard and Falco?" she asked the woman at the desk.

The woman stared at her for a moment. "Uh…let me see." She looked at a clipboard on her desk, picked up the phone, and dialed Falco's extension. "No answer, and I know Detective Ballard isn't in yet," she said. A uniformed cop swished behind the woman. "Hey, Simon. Simon, honey!" The cop stopped. "Is Falco in yet?" she asked, leaning back in her chair.

He thought for a moment and said, "Yeah, I think I seen her. Yeah, she's at her desk."

The woman looked annoyed. "This lady here needs an escort. You wanna take her up to see Falco?"

"Sure," he said, looking down at Andie. Officer Simon motioned to Andie to follow him. They trudged up two flights of stairs. When they reached the second floor, he smiled and said, "Just down this way. Follow me."

The second floor of the twenty-third district was brightly lit; gray and maroons were the dominant colors. Police and plain-clothes cops and administrator types were buzzing about and phones were ringing. Officer Simon scanned the maze of cubicles and saw Falco sitting at her desk. Detective Steve Grasky was leaning over her, gazing intently at her computer screen. Stacks of files were piled on Falco's desk and on the chair next her desk.

"Detective Falco? You got a visitor," Officer Simon said when they reached Falco's desk.

"Hey, Detective," Andie said smoothly.

Falco looked up from her computer and squinted for a moment, her train of thought broken. She hardly recognized the person in front of her. "Uh…Andie! Hi. I would have never expected…" She smiled broadly, clearly surprised. She looked around for a place to move the stack of files piled on the chair next to her desk. Grasky loomed and smiled at Andie. "Oh, Andie, this is Detective Grasky. We're working on a case together."

Detective Grasky shook Andie's hand then told Falco he was going to make some phone calls at his desk.

Andie clutched the small shopping bag she'd brought. "It's okay. I don't need to sit. I'm going downtown, and I can only stay for a few minutes."

"No, please. It's not a problem. Here, have a seat." Falco moved the stack of papers to the floor. Andie sat down, still clutching the bag. She glanced around the office and at Falco's desk.

Falco was surprised at Andie's appearance; her look was edgy but soft. She wore a touch of makeup and deep red lipstick. Her hair was a tussle of layers and looked gently windblown.

Falco sat down. "It's nice to see you. How are you feeling?" She looked at Andie intently.

"Better than the last time you saw me, I'm sure," Andie said, suddenly self-conscious.

"Yes, I was worried, and I should have called…after all that happened."

"No, no that's okay. Michael was there, and well, I guess you two kind of…"

"Yes, we did, but that's over with," Falco said with a deep sigh. "I was concerned that maybe I pushed you too far. If I did, Andie, I'm really sorry."

Andie shook her head. "No, no, I'm just… I'm a bit foggy about the whole thing, and really, that's not why I came. I just wanted to…" She pressed two fingers to her forehead, closed her eyes, and paused. "Listen, I really don't remember what happened that night. Alan, my shrink, said I was dissociating. I really don't know. But I came here to give Detective Ballard this gift." Andie pulled the gift-wrapped present out from the shopping bag.

"The tie? Did you really?" Falco said, as if she knew the punch line of the joke.

"Well, yeah. I had to replace it, since I ruined the other one, you know." She smiled and scrunched up her nose. "Is Detective Ballard around?"

"He's out for a few days. He took some time off," said Falco as she glanced at Ballard's desk.

"Well, maybe you can give this to him for me?" Andie asked, handing the gift to Falco.

She took it and looked at the wrapping paper. "You didn't go to Sears, did you?" she said with a laugh.

Andie laughed too. "It's very close to the one I ruined. At least I think it is."

"Burberry. *Very* nice," Falco said, smiling. "I'm sure he'll be quite surprised, and I'm sure he'll like it a lot."

Falco felt pangs of loss remembering Andie's laugh, her expressions and mannerisms, her contradictions. Their eyes locked as they shared smiles. She put the gift in the bottom drawer of her desk and assured Andie she would give it to Ballard when he got back.

Andie felt a sudden swell of emotions as her voice caught in her throat. "Oh, one more thing, I think this might be your sweater." She took the neatly folded sweater out of her shopping bag and handed it to Falco.

Falco looked at it and said, "You know, this is mine, but I don't remember leaving it or even missing it. Maybe I forgot it the other night when I left in a bit of a hurry."

"Michael found it," said Andie. There was a moment of cool silence. "Well, my show is on at the gallery. I can't believe it," she said, changing the subject. "We're hanging it today and tomorrow, and the opening is Saturday night."

"Wonderful. I got the invitation, but I'm not sure I'll be able to make the opening. I have Sam this weekend, and I haven't been very…available lately," Falco said, glancing at the invitation that was stuck to her bulletin board. "We're going to celebrate his birthday a few weeks early 'cause my ex made plans for Sam to… Anyway, it's a long story," she said, shaking her head.

"Well, you can always bring him to the opening if you're in the area. I'm not currently doing any…erotica." She gave Falco a sly look then laughed. "Anyway, it'll be up for a month, so if not the opening…whenever." She shrugged.

"I'm glad it all came together. It sounds like there was a lot of preparation involved. Are you excited?"

"Petrified," Andie said flatly. She glanced at her watch and grimaced. "Oh, no, I'm late." She got up from the chair and backed up to leave. "I was supposed to be there by now." Suddenly Andie's cell phone rang. "Kat!" they both said together. Andie eyed Falco then fished the phone out of the pocket of her jeans. "My new cell phone. Now Kat can reach me anytime and any place—unless I smash this one too!" She laughed as she looked at the flashing display.

"Well, don't let her push you around," Falco said with a knowing smile. She got up from her chair and smiled; there was a hint of sadness in her face. "It was nice seeing you, and thanks for returning the sweater."

"Same here." Andie looked at Falco then at the floor. "And thanks for everything…you know…just being…well, putting up with me."

Falco lightly brushed Andie's shoulder. "I'm just glad you're okay, and this is over with."

Andie's phone rang again. "Well, I gotta run," she said, squinting at the incoming number. She backed up, making her exit. "See you…sometime, Detective."

"Take care of yourself." Falco watched Andie make her way through the rows of cubicles and to the stairwell as she talked on her cell phone.

Steve Grasky returned with more paperwork. "That's the Fulbright woman, isn't it?"

"Yeah," Falco said, distracted, watching Andie dash away.

"She's kinda cute," Grasky said, eyeing her as she walked out.

"Yes, she is…" Falco said softly. She quickly turned toward her computer, sat down, and put the sweater on her lap.

CHAPTER 33

Andie dashed out of the police station, frantically making her way to her car and running the conversation she'd had with Falco through her head. She scooted in, slammed the door, and moved her rearview mirror lower, eyeing herself. She took a deep breath and let it out slowly, started her car, and pulled onto the street. She got on Lake Shore Drive at Belmont and headed south. Her head buzzed as she gripped the steering wheel. "She's straight, Andie," she said to herself. "Jesus...and beautiful."

Andie sped down the drive, passing illegally and watching for cops in her rearview mirror. She exited on Grand Avenue and headed west toward Franklin, where she eventually found a parking spot. She was seriously late. She put two quarters in the meter and ran down Franklin to Huron. She knew Kat would be pissed.

A fifteen-foot truck was parked in the loading dock of the Cohen Sloan Gallery. Kat was giving orders to Mario as he unloaded large paintings. Kat caught a glimpse of Andie turning the corner. "You're late, baby," she said with a smile. "Ooooh, don't you look nice?"

Mario smiled and waved at Andie. "I couldn't move them all at once, so I'll have to come back with the rest tomorrow," he said in a slight Spanish accent.

"That's fine with me. I think we've got our work cut out for us right now," Andie said as she ran her hand through her hair.

Kat walked closer to Andie, smiling. "How ya doin'?" she said, snuggling up to her.

Andie smiled and kissed her lightly on her lips. "Don't want to ruin that lipstick," she said, quietly holding Kat's gaze. Kat returned the kiss, sliding her tongue between Andie's lips, touching her jaw with her fingertips. They kissed long and deep.

"Uh, ladies, I could use some help here," said Mario. "You wanna save that for the back office?"

Kat and Andie peeled themselves away from each other. "Sorry," Andie said. "We gotta hang this thing." She gave Kat a serious look and stashed her backpack and jacket in the supply room just inside the loading dock.

Kat and Andie put on cotton work gloves and started to move the large paintings into the warehouse area of the gallery. Kat had Aisha and Mario clear a large wall area of the warehouse as a temporary location for the work. After thirty minutes the van was empty, and the two women began to determine the layout and location of the pieces. Mario stood ready to help with the hanging once Kat and Andie decided where everything should go. It was a huge space, and Andie was feeling overwhelmed.

"We'll do this systematically," Kat said, sensing Andie's looming frustration.

"Systematically? It's artwork!" Andie said, throwing her hands in the air.

Kat gave Andie a crazy look. "There's a method to my madness."

Andie tapped her forehead and scowled. "Well, there's a madness to my methods!"

Kat smiled and started to move paintings. She gave Mario orders to shift and switch works as Andie brought them into the gallery. After an hour the space was taking shape. Andie was impressed.

"I just don't have it in me to do this anymore," she said with a sigh as she rubbed the back of her neck.

"Don't worry, baby. I'll hang your show anytime. Just keep doing the work."

The three surveyed the area and were pleased. "I need a drink," Andie said, looking tired.

"I need a break," Mario said.

"Well, I've got just the thing!" Kat held her index finger up. She turned and scurried across the gallery floor. Her platform sandals made clopping noises on the hardwood. She returned with two cold bottles of Laurent-Perrier Grand Siècle and glasses.

"Oooh, man!" Mario said with a smile and a clap of his hands.

"Kat, what's all this?" Andie said, looking weary.

"We're celebrating life, death, and art! Not necessarily in that order," Kat said and plopped herself down on the bare floor. "Mario, will you do the divine honor of opening these?" She arranged the three champagne glasses on the floor where Andie and Mario sat.

Mario opened the bottles and poured the sparkling liquid into the Champagne glasses. Andie smiled, looking through her glass at the bubbles. Kat got to her feet and raised her glass for a toast. She cleared her throat and smiled, then shook her butt in a little dance and giggled.

Andie and Mario stood up and raised their glasses. Andie stomped her feet on the floor to imitate a drum roll.

"To the visual arts—the highest form of all the arts—and the extraordinary work of my lover, Andrea Fulbright." Kat gave Andie a loving look and a half-bow. "And to Mario for getting my lover out of her proverbial jam." Mario laughed and raised his glass higher. "And to my stepfather, that rich old bastard, for forcing me to study art history and—"

"Can we just drink this now?" asked Mario, as he leaned against Andie and grinned.

"Okay, already. Cheers!" Kat said.

The three clinked their glasses and took long sips of the Champagne. Andie was relieved no one mentioned death or Brian McCaffery. The three sat on the gallery floor until the two bottles were finished. They were buzzed, talking loudly and laughing.

After a while the party broke up. Kat went into her office to make final arrangements for the opening. Mario grabbed his keys and told Kat he'd be back tomorrow before noon with the rest of the paintings. The gallery was quiet. Andie studied the paintings objectively. She was feeling her familiar anxiety about showing her work. She made some mental notes as to where the other pieces should go when Mario delivered them the next day. She listened to her footsteps and the echoes they made as she roamed the space. She walked faster, enjoying the sound. Then she skipped across the room and spun around in a dance with her arms extended. Smiling, she thought of Detective Falco.

Kat's voice came from her office in the back. Andie wandered in and found her giggling on the phone with her wine distributor. "Just deliver a case of white and two cases of red. No, we're not having a bunch of food. Nobody's coming here to eat, and if they are, they're gonna leave hungry and drunk! Yes, and those nice plastic wineglasses… No, not the tall ones. They tip over too easily."

Andie sat on the sofa, sighed, and looked at the ceiling. She was feeling the Champagne. Kat got up from her desk, still on the phone, and closed her office door. She leaned against the front of the large wooden desk, legs extended, smiling and immersed in the conversation.

Andie got up from the sofa and made her way toward Kat. She gave her a wicked look, leaned into her, and started to unbutton her knit shirt. Kat laughed and slapped Andie's hands away. Andie gave her a playful hurt look. She put her hands on Kat's thighs as she leaned on them and traced her tongue between her breasts where her shirt was unbuttoned. Kat tried not to gasp and leaned backward on the desk, giving Andie a piercing look to stop, but Andie continued. She ran her hands up Kat's ribs and caressed the swell of her, then returned to work on the rest of the buttons. She squeezed Kat's right breast, tracing her tongue down and finding her nipple. She took it in her mouth and softly sucked. Kat gasped and grabbed Andie's hair from the back and pulled her head away. Andie gave her a mischievous grin. Kat was blushing and having trouble talking. Finally she got what she wanted from her wine rep and slapped her cell phone off.

"I can't believe you! That was Randy. He knows my father!" Kat shook an angry finger at her. "Jesus, I am so fucking hot. You…" She smiled and pushed Andie backward on the sofa. They kissed and dragged each other's clothes off, making love on the soft leather. Afterward they dozed entangled together, their clothes in a heap on the floor.

Andie rubbed her head and looked at her watch. It was nearly ten p.m. "Oh, baby, I should go. Michael went home today, and I've gotta feed the boys."

Kat looked at her watch then rolled over and kissed Andie. "I missed you."

Andie smiled. "Yeah, I missed you too. God, last week was…surreal." She rubbed her eyes.

She put on her clothes and walked slowly toward her car, dragging her feet. Her head was heavy from the Champagne, and she needed to eat something. Kat offered to buy her dinner, but she said she needed to get home. Her shoulder muscles ached from moving the paintings. She made her way across Franklin and found her car with a parking ticket stuck to the windshield. "Shit!" she said, ripping it from the window. She moved toward the streetlight to get a better look at it. Angry at herself for forgetting to feed the meter, she moved to the driver's side and unlocked the door. An engine started with a roar from a rusty minivan parked behind her. It startled her.

"Get your fucking muffler fixed, jerk face," she mumbled as she looked in the direction of the van. It jutted out of its parking place and onto the street, passing Andie as she got into her car. She drove north on Lake Shore Drive feeling sleepy and drained. Thoughts of the opening and the people who were invited blossomed in her mind. She smiled as she thought of friends she hadn't seen in a while who would be attending—people from the gay and lesbian community, people from the arts scene, art critics.

"Oh, god. I don't want to do this," she said, suddenly dreading the whole scene. *Maybe I'll just hide in back*, she thought. *I'll hang out with Aisha. No, that's a bad idea.* She sighed deeply and smiled, thinking of Aisha, then Falco. "Oh, Detective Falco, why do you have to be so hot?" Andie whispered.

CHAPTER 34

It was three twenty a.m. Andie awoke suddenly from a deep sleep. McCaffery's image exploded in her mind as she'd seen him the day he had returned the books. On his shirt Andie saw a "W" with a dog or wolf baring its teeth. Wide awake, she got up from her bed and paced the floor. Her heart was racing, and she was dripping with sweat. She looked out the window of her bedroom, and a flood of memories from the other night came back. Like a movie in front of her, she saw the picture of Marion Kerns, the blur of wooden stairs, and the flash of Officers Strickland and Torres shoving their guns in her face. In her one ear she heard Falco's voice, "Andie, let's talk about something else. Andie, stop this. You're getting upset!" She turned around to where the voice was coming from; she gasped and stared into the night, remembering.

It was nine a.m. when she called Michael. She told him about her dream, the voices, and the pictures in her head. She told him about Strickland and Torres and how she had heard Falco telling her to stop. "Detective Falco did try to stop me from going over the edge that night, Michael. I know it."

"Yeah, okay, Andie," Michael yawned. "Like the fact that you have the total hots for her isn't clouding your thinking. I still think she's a shifty bitch."

The morning was rainy with violent thunderstorms and predictions of more for the next few days. It was a welcome relief from the last two weeks of heat. The dream and recollection of the other night left Andie feeling unsettled and shaky. She drank some coffee, took her meds, and climbed on to her stationary bike trainer. She plugged in her iPod and took off for a mental ride. Before long she was working up a dripping sweat and breathing hard. After her ride she did some free weights and cooled off with a shower. She was feeling better as the endorphins kicked in. She wrapped a towel around her, walked into her closet, and scanned the racks of clothes, wondering what she would wear to the opening. She sighed and looked down at Leo, who sat at her feet. "Maybe I'll just wear you to the opening," she said lovingly. He purred in response. "I'll deal with this tonight when I get home," she said.

CHAPTER 35

Rain spattered Falco's unmarked police car as she drove west on Division. Steve Grasky was eyeing a map and looking out the window for an address. After poring over stacks and stacks of files and shifting through police and FBI databases, Falco and Grasky had a handful of suspects and acquaintances of suspects to track down. The child abductions had continued and moved south into the city. Four children were now missing. Families all over the north suburbs and the Chicago metropolitan area anxiously waited for some kind of break in the case. Detectives from other districts were being added, and a coordinated effort by the feds and local law enforcement was in full swing.

The abductors had left virtually no clues, except for one lone Converse sneaker, size two, left at one of the scenes. It seemed the four boys had disappeared without a trace. A list of potential witnesses had resulted in only a vague description of one of the men—a short, stocky Latino with sunglasses.

Falco squinted through the windshield wipers and headed north on Austin Avenue. "What a shitty day," she said, gripping the wheel. Grasky was quieter than Ballard, she thought. He didn't talk incessantly about guy things and make annoying comments about hot girls on the street. Maybe it was because Grasky was happily married with kids. *That'll mellow you out,* Falco thought. Her thoughts turned to Sam and their plans for Saturday. She had let Lassiter know that she wasn't going to work that weekend.

Dark storm clouds were looming. "This rain is really gonna cramp our style if it continues into tomorrow," Falco told Grasky. "Sam and I are supposed to go to Navy Pier."

Grasky looked up at the clouds. "Well, it's gonna rain all day today, that's for sure." He stuck a fresh piece of gum in his mouth and crushed the wrapper into a tight ball.

* * *

Andie got off to an early start but got caught in slow-moving traffic on Lake Shore Drive. "Come on people, what's a little rain?" Lightning flashed and thunder boomed. "I hope we don't have this for the opening. Nobody's gonna come," she said to herself. She thought for a moment then said, "That wouldn't be so bad, really."

Mario was in the loading dock, sitting in his truck and waiting for the rain to stop. Kat was in her office with a double latte. Aisha was adjusting large folding tables in the reception area and unfolding table linens for the wine and glasses. Andie quietly walked in, approached Aisha from behind, and kissed the back of her neck. "I just love your neck. I dream about your neck," she whispered in her ear.

Aisha turned around and smiled broadly then pointed in the direction of Kat's office. "Be careful…the wrath."

Andie gave Aisha a disappointed look and lumbered into Kat's office. Kat eyed her as she tugged on the latte from her mug. "We'll start again once the rain stops. I don't have plastic big enough to cover your work." Kat looked stressed out.

"Whatever," Andie said in a distracted tone.

Kat was all business. Her phone rang; it was one of the newspapers. Andie sat down on one of Kat's chairs and casually pulled at the tear in her jeans. Andie had come to hang the rest of the show in her very best "scruffies," as she called them—battered blue jeans and a chambray shirt over a clingy short-sleeve top. She wore her favorite boots, which were great protection from falling hammers; they also made her feel tall.

Mario opened the loading dock door and trudged through the gallery to Kat's office. "It's not letting up. I think I'll go have an early lunch." It was barely eleven a.m.

"So much for getting an early start," Andie said with a yawn.

Mario grabbed a *Chicago Reader* newspaper from a stack outside the door and put it over his head as he ran across the street. The rain filled the gallery with white noise. Kat was still on the phone when the wine delivery came. Andie jumped to her feet, ran across to the back of the gallery, and shoved open the loading dock door. A man smoking a stinky cigar pushed a dolly that held three cases of wine. Andie directed him to unload the boxes where Aisha was setting up. The man was dripping wet. He handed a soggy delivery voucher for Andie to sign.

"Well, it's not like I can sign this. It's soaking wet!" she said, laughing and looking at the drenched receipt and then at the man.

"It's a mess out there and some idiot in a minivan is blocking the alley. I had to get out and knock on his window to make him move!" the man shouted. "Fucking moron," he said under his breath as he wheeled the dolly toward the door.

Andie helped Aisha open the boxes of wine and stack the extras under the table. "You look nervous, girl," Aisha said gently, glancing at Andie's face.

"Oh, I'm just not into the whole opening thing—center of attention and all."

"You should be used to it by now. Isn't this your third show here?"

"Second one here and others at other galleries. And yes, I should be used to it."

Andie paced the gallery and stopped in front of the windows that over-looked the street. The rain finally was letting up. Mario came back as the rain slowed to a drizzle. The sun appeared through the clearing sky, and Kat came bounding out of her office. "Okay, kids, show time!"

Aisha joined the three, and they quickly unloaded the paintings from the truck. Before long the truck was unloaded, and Kat and Andie began the second phase of hanging the show. Aisha waved goodbye to Kat and Andie, saying she'd be back for the opening. Mario dragged his toolbox from the back of the truck and started to hang the pieces that were in place.

Andie and Kat disagreed on the placement of some final pieces, and Mario was having trouble with the nails. "You're gonna need some longer nails with flat heads," Andie told him. "Those aren't going to hold. They'll bend downward or tear out of the wall."

Mario looked annoyed that he'd have to go back for different nails. Kat assured him she had a variety of nails in the supply room near the loading dock.

"I'll go find them," Andie said. She wandered toward the loading dock, humming to herself, while Kat and Mario rearranged the other pieces.

"Andie's not gonna like this," Mario told Kat.

"It's my gallery," Kat said dismissively as they moved a large piece across the room.

CHAPTER 36

Andie walked over a puddle on the concrete floor on her way to the supply room. Mario had left the big door partially open, allowing rain to blow in. She stared at it for a moment, thinking she should try to heave it closed, but she knew it was too heavy to close by herself. She shuffled through some half-empty boxes of wood screws, wire, and nails that were piled high on rusty metal shelving, but she still didn't find the nails she needed.

"Where did you say those nails were, Kat?" Andie yelled. Kat and Mario didn't answer, so she continued to look. She took a few steps back from the wall of shelving and spotted a dusty box from Clark and Barlow with the words "Three-Inch Wire Fasteners." "That'll do," she said out loud.

As she reached for the box, a thick arm grabbed her from behind. Before she could react, a white cloth soaked with a strong-smelling liquid was clamped over her nose and mouth. Startled, she took a breath to scream, but the cloth muffled her voice. Her lungs filled with the caustic fumes, burning her throat as she panicked and gasped for air. She kicked her legs, catching a box of nails on the shelving and sending it tumbling to the floor. She tried desperately to break free. She grabbed frantically at the arm around her, but it was too strong. Her vision blurred as she felt a dull warmth come over her face, neck, and back.

As she drifted into blackness she heard, "Hey, there cunt. Long time no see."

Brian McCaffery dragged Andie's limp body through the loading dock door. He looked down the alley both ways. Mario's truck had hidden the stolen minivan he was driving. He looped Andie's arm around his neck and put his arm around her waist, making it appear they were a couple walking in a sort of embrace. He quickly slid the side door of the van open and threw Andie inside. Her body tumbled into a heap on the dingy floor.

McCaffery scoped out the alleyway; no one was around. He got into the van and gunned the engine. A mass of blue smoke filled the alleyway and drifted into the gallery's warehouse space. He careened around Mario's truck, clipping part of his left mirror and almost hitting a man riffling through a dumpster. He turned around in his seat to see Andie, who wasn't moving. He smiled broadly, nodding his head, and headed west toward the expressway.

CHAPTER 37

Fifteen minutes later Mario and Kat had rearranged most of the paintings they had hung the day before. Kat looked satisfied with the layout and smiled at him. Suddenly she realized Andie hadn't come back from searching for the nails. "I don't know where the hell she is," Kat said. "I hope she didn't go to C&B, because I know I have a box of nails that'll work."

"Well, we sure got the space wrapped up," Mario said, dusting off his hands. "I'm beat."

There was an eerie quiet in the gallery as a faint smell of car exhaust lingered from the loading dock. Kat and Mario looked at each other.

"Okay, I'm sure there are nails back there. Andie, did you find the goddamned nails?" Kat looked toward the back of the gallery then stomped across the floor toward the supply room. Mario followed. The loading dock area was still. "Mario, did you leave the loading dock door open?" asked Kat.

Mario shrugged. "I dunno."

Kat stomped into the supply room. "Are you still looking for those nails, girl?" she asked impatiently. "Jesus, I could have gone to the store and come back by now." She looked around; the supply room was empty. She turned and looked around the warehouse space. "Andie?" Bewildered, she said, "Where is she?"

Mario shook his head and walked into the alley.

Stomping around, Kat looked in her office, the restroom, and again in the warehouse space. "Andie…Andrea! Where the *hell* are you?" The space was quiet except for the patter of drizzle on the skylight. "Andie? Andie!" she shouted. Suddenly Kat had a sick feeling. She spun around and retraced her steps, looking again in places she'd already searched—still no Andie.

Mario was closing the door of the loading dock. "Mario, is Andie out there, maybe in the alley?" she said weakly.

Mario saw the look on Kat's face and got worried. "She's not here. I looked up and down the alley, even inside my truck."

"Andie…Andie!" yelled Kat. Her voice echoed in the gallery. Her breathing grew faster, and her eyes scanned the room. "Okay, I'm not going to panic," she said to herself. "There's a reasonable explanation for where she is."

Mario joined the search. He found Andie's backpack where she'd left it, stuffed in a locker in the supply room. He turned to leave the room and kicked the overturned box of nails that had fallen to the floor. He studied them for a moment then looked up. The box of three-inch nails Andie was looking for was still on the shelf. Dust and dirt from the loading dock had settled with the rain and humidity. He followed the spilled nails and spotted large footprints made by heavy work boots in the dust. Through the pattern of dusty footprints, he saw two long groove marks that resembled those made by skis in snow. Mario was wearing running shoes. *Those aren't my footprints*, he thought, *but the smaller ones are Andie's boots.* Something wasn't right, he thought. A surge of fear shot through him. He turned and ran into the gallery space and collided with Kat.

"Something's wrong, Mario. I think something is seriously wrong!" Kat said, her face contorted with panic.

Mario nodded. "Come with me."

He showed Kat the spilled nails and the footprints. She stared at the scuffle of marks and gasped, putting her hand over her mouth. The prints on the floor looked like Andie had been dragged out to the alley.

"Something's happened to her. Something's happened to her!" Kat said as fear flooded her face.

Mario dialed 911.

CHAPTER 38

McCaffery pulled the van into a secluded wooded area just outside of city limits. It was an empty lot with the remnants of old buildings and over-grown trees. Gang activity was rampant, and abandoned vehicles stolen for their parts made McCaffery's van inconspicuous.

He twisted around and squeezed himself between the front seats, crouching toward Andie. She was barely conscious. He reached into a large box and pulled out some half-inch nylon rope. He pulled Andie up toward the back of the van and tied each hand to an interior corner of the van. He stared at her and cursed her. She was the reason he'd spent nearly four years in a small cement cell. He unscrewed a fifth of whiskey and smiled. He knew he finally had the bitch who had fucked up his life, and he would give her what she deserved. He took a good slug from the bottle and smiled at Andie. His breathing grew faster as he reached down and unbuckled her belt and took her jeans down to her knees. He spread her legs, unzipped his fly, and penetrated her violently, rocking her up and down on the rough floor. He grunted and cursed her until he came, his body falling on top of hers. He was wet and sticky with sweat.

Andie slowly gained consciousness, feeling a deep burning pain inside her. She could barely breathe with the weight on top of her. She opened her eyes and groaned; she felt dizzy and sick. Her vision cleared, and slowly she saw a pair of eyes looking at her—the deep green eyes of some demon; eyes that echoed from her past, a past she had thought was gone forever. She took in the rest of the face: the nose; the freckles; the crooked, evil smile. She felt the jolt of recognition. It was him…Brian McCaffery. Her eyes grew wide as her mouth hung open in fear.

"Oh, god," she gasped. "No, noooo…" She tried to move, but her hands were tied. She twisted her body, looking left and right, looking to escape, to free herself.

Her voice caught in her throat as panic filled her lungs. She tried to scream but didn't have the air. She gasped; tears streamed down her face and into her ears.

"Oh, no. Oh, no…please," she said in short breaths. She desperately tugged at the ropes, her eyes wide as she searched his face, still not believing. "No…no…no!" she cried. She twisted her body, trying to break free, but McCaffery was straddled on top of her, laughing. His penis was erect and hovered just above her abdomen. Finally Andie gathered enough air and screamed loudly, but McCaffery clamped his dirty hand over her mouth to mute her cry.

"Shut up, fucking bitch!" He found a dirty rag that smelled of motor oil, twisted it, and gagged her. He leaned down and whispered in her ear, "Guess who's gonna die?" His breath was hot and smelled of whiskey. He laughed, not taking his eyes off her, then violently raped her again.

Andie was going into shock. Her breathing was fast and shallow and her eyes dazed. No longer seeing her terror, McCaffery grabbed the side of her face, trying to stir a response. "Fucking bitch! Wake up!" He struck her across the face with a heavy blow. "You're gonna die nice and slow, and only when I say so," he said between gritted teeth. Her head had swung to the side; her cheekbone and lip were cut and bleeding.

CHAPTER 39

Falco and Grasky were halfway down their list of interviews. They were striking out: most of the suspects' current addresses were phony or non-existent. The two detectives were feeling drained, and the weather wasn't helping. Falco rubbed her neck as Grasky flipped to his last batch of questions. They were sitting in a dingy Mexican restaurant on the West Side, talking with one of the owners. The man's cousin, an illegal from Mexico, had been spotted in the vicinity of one of the child abductions. Falco could tell the man was lying, professing to know little English. Neither she nor Grasky knew Spanish.

She sighed and looked at her watch. It was three thirty. She was trying to stay focused, but her mind drifted to thoughts of the weekend and Sam. Her radio chirped. It was the dispatcher telling her to contact Lassiter immediately. She unclipped her cell and dialed the chief. No answer. She tried his office phone but got no answer there either. Her radio squawked again. She got up from the table where she, Grasky, and the Mexican man were talking and tried her radio again. "Damn it!" she said. "Everything's screwed up." She looked out the window at the storm clouds above. Her cell rang. This time it was Ballard, back she presumed, from his vacation. He was calling from his car, on his way downtown.

"Falco!" he said. There was a splash of static from his phone. Falco's radio cracked with more static. She turned it off with an angry twist. "Falco!" Ballard yelled again. A bunch of muffled words followed, but she couldn't make out what he was saying. A swishing noise cut in and out. He was yelling about something.

She went outside and ducked under the awning of the restaurant. Finally the signal came in clear. "Falco, it's Ballard. Listen up! Andrea Fulbright went missing about ninety minutes ago. We've got an APB out for her and a description of someone matching Brian McCaffery. You got that, Falco? Andrea Fulbright is missing!"

Falco nearly dropped the phone. Her blood seemed to thicken in her veins. She turned to run to the car then stopped at the entrance of the restaurant.

Ballard was still on the line and didn't know if Falco had heard him. "Falco, are you there?"

"Yes, yes, JB! Where was she… What…?" Her eyes flashed as she tried to grasp the situation.

Ballard gave her the address of the gallery. He said the cops were already there and he was on his way. Falco rushed back into the restaurant; Grasky looked at her with alarm. She grabbed her purse from the booth where Grasky and the Mexican man were sitting and yelled, "I gotta go!" She bolted out to the car and sped away. Grasky was bewildered as he watched the car peel off and careen down the wet street.

"No, no, no," she whispered, rocking back and forth as she drove. "This can't be happening. This *cannot* be happening!" She gasped and bit her lip and tried to focus on the road. With her blue lights flashing and her siren barking, she sped south on Homan and hooked up with Grand Avenue. The traffic slowed. "Shit!" she hissed. She cut over left to Augusta and floored it, heading east. Traffic slowed down again. Just ahead, a school bus inched out of the parking lot of Lafayette Elementary School.

"Damn it!" she said, pounding on the steering wheel. She slowed down and let the bus back up and pull away. A stocky Latino with a mustache waved her on as he pushed the wrought iron gate of the parking lot closed. He glared at her strangely as he recognized her vehicle as an unmarked police car. Falco gunned the car past him and made a quick right onto Washtenaw, then left onto Chicago Avenue. She drove east, racing toward the gallery district.

When she found the alleyway of the Cohen Sloan Gallery, she saw a crowd of gallery owners, artist types, and news media vans. The two uniformed cops who had responded to the 911 call were trying to get a coherent statement from Kat, but she was crying in Mario's arms. The area was cordoned off with police tape.

Falco pulled her car to the left and dashed out. Lassiter was working through the crowd, looking for witnesses. He eyed Falco and pointed in the direction of Kat. Falco was trembling and desperately hoping that maybe this was all some stupid mistake, that Andie had gone for a walk or was trashed at some bar down the street.

Mario located Andie's car parked off Chicago Avenue with another parking ticket stuck to the windshield. It hadn't gone anywhere since she'd parked it that morning. Mario gave Ballard a description of the van he'd seen in the alley, and Aisha returned to give her statement, telling the police about the deliveryman and the van blocking the alleyway earlier in the day. Clutching herself and mindlessly pulling at her dreads, Aisha looked drawn and worried.

Falco made her way toward Kat, who was huddled next to Mario talking to one of the cops, crying and saying, "No, no, she was just here! She was just *here!*"

Falco eyed the uniformed cop. He backed up, letting her take over. "Hi, Ms. Cohen. I'm Detective Falco. Can we talk somewhere?" she asked.

Kat looked up, recognizing Falco. "Let's go in my office," she said, wiping her eyes.

Falco followed Kat to her office, where she motioned for Falco to take a seat on the leather sofa. Kat sat next to Falco and put her hand on the cushion. "God, we were just here together," she said as she cried softly. "Do you think it's him?" Her voice cracked as a flash of anger rose in her face. "Do you think it's that monster, McCaffery?"

Falco shook her head. "We don't know for sure, Ms. Cohen."

"Please. Kat. It's Kat."

"There were two people who saw the same van in the alley. They both saw the driver and gave descriptions that sound like someone who looks like McCaffery, his build, his hair color," Falco said slowly. "But we don't know for sure. We don't even know if Andie was abducted."

"But he's supposed to be *dead*!" Kat said, bolting up from the sofa. "The news said McCaffery was dead!"

Falco looked around the office. On Kat's wall behind her desk, she saw a beautifully photographed image of two women kissing. They were nude and lying in layers of sheets. She stared at it curiously as Kat paced.

"Kat, I'm going to need to get a statement from you. I know you have a lot of questions, but until we know for sure what we're dealing with, we've got to go with what we know and what we can find out. Please, sit down and tell me everything that happened, starting with this morning."

Kat tried to calm down and sat next to Falco. She relayed the morning's events, the delay of phase two of the installation, and Andie's search for the box of nails. Just then Aisha knocked on the office door and gave Kat the pink delivery voucher from the man who had delivered the wine. Kat handed the slip to Falco, who called Ballard to contact the company who employed the man.

Falco looked up from her notepad. "Is there anything else you can remember about this morning? Was Andie okay? Did she give you any indication that she was upset about anything?" Kat shook her head.

Aisha hung by the door and moved toward Falco on the sofa. "Andie told me this morning she didn't want to be at the opening, that she hated the attention."

"That's bullshit! She's never, ever said that to me!" Kat shouted, jumping up from the sofa and glaring at Aisha.

Aisha looked annoyed. "Well she said that to *me*."

Falco waited impatiently as the two exchanged looks and asked again, "Anything else?" Aisha and Kat shook their heads. Falco got up from the sofa. She was anxious to leave. She thanked them for their time and assured them they would do everything possible to find Andie.

Kat turned and leaned forward at her desk, looking up at the photo of Andie and herself. She hung her head in disbelief. "If Andie got cold feet, that's fine. I just want her safe."

Falco left the office and ducked beneath the yellow line of police tape, slowly making her way through the scene. Ballard was questioning potential witnesses and nodded to Falco as she passed. She scanned the area of footprints and the spilled box of nails. She was feeling a little lightheaded from anxiety and dread. She hoped the uniformed cops scouring the area would find Andie hiding out in one of the bars or maybe back at home. But that wouldn't explain the fact that her car hadn't moved all day. She wondered whether anyone had contacted Michael. Maybe he knew where she was.

As Falco walked past the back door of the loading dock, her eyes caught a white object, some kind of cloth jammed under the half-opened door. She pushed the heavy metal door out slightly with her body, freeing the cloth from underneath. She stared at it for a moment then pulled a pen from her front pocket and scooped it up. She held it firmly with the edge of her thumb and examined it through the light. A faint, sweet odor wafted past her nose. She jerked back; the cloth smelled of chloroform.

Falco placed the white cloth in an evidence bag. She made her way through the busy crowd of police and witnesses and found Lassiter. She handed him the evidence bag. He opened it and caught a whiff of the chemical. "Is chloroform used for any purpose other than rendering someone unconscious?" he asked.

"I don't think so," said Falco, feeling very unsettled.

"I don't want to get all worked up over some piece of cloth and find out artists use the stuff to clean their brushes," he said. He took the evidence bag and handed it to a technician. "Find out if this is what I think it is and if it's ever used in the production of artwork." The technician gave Lassiter a curious look and put the evidence bag with his other samples. "ASAP!" Lassiter barked.

Falco walked quickly out to the loading dock and found Ballard. He had finished his interviews and was waiting for her. The two climbed into the car, Falco at the wheel. She turned the ignition key just as the radio squawked. More information about the van was coming in. It had been spotted heading northwest on Milwaukee. Lassiter ran the make and model, and sure enough the van had been stolen in Harwood Heights.

"Damn it!" she yelled, slamming her hands on the steering wheel. She should have followed her instincts about McCaffery's death.

Ballard looked at her and said, "Maybe I should drive."

It was five forty-five p.m., and the sky was red and stormy. Ballard steered the car northwest and handed Falco a bundle of notes he had taken from people in and around the gallery. Falco looked ahead and said in a worried tone, "If this is McCaffery, we may be too late." She felt a dreadful surge of fear. Tears began to fill in her eyes; she gritted her teeth and shook them off.

CHAPTER 40

Friday traffic was heavy and slower than usual because of the rain. Puddles splashed the cars and soaked McCaffery's windshield. The wiper blades were worn out, and he cursed each time a car drenched his windshield. Andie was quiet in the back; he feared she might die before he was finished with her. "You stay alive, you fucking dyke whore. You're gonna pay for my time—*my* time behind bars!" he said, beating his hands on the steering wheel.

He pulled a map out of the glove box and stared at it for a moment. He rushed ahead of the person in the next lane, cutting off the other car. "Yeah, fuck you too!" he said, gritting his teeth. He swerved and headed northwest toward an abandoned industrial complex near the Chicago River. He once saw a man shot dead there, execution style. It was a good place, he thought.

He found the dirt road from the map. It was littered with old cars, tires, trash, and other remnants of the city's inhabitants. It was more overgrown than he'd remembered. He peered at his automatic weapon on the floor of the passenger seat and fingered the eight-inch hunting knife that lay between his legs.

Andie moaned, her voice a muddle of incoherent words and sound. Her body shook involuntarily. McCaffery watched her from the rearview mirror, his eyes beady like a rodent. He drove slowly and found the smooth concrete viaduct that sloped underneath the expressway.

A rotting wooden fence at the top of the viaduct surrounded the area, which led to a steep overhang that led to the murky Chicago River. The rain had made the area muddy, and the van seemed destined to get stuck in the soggy earth.

He stopped and pulled the vehicle between some overgrown trees, hiding it well. He looked at Andie through the mirror again, smiled, and took another deep slug from the whiskey bottle. He got out of the van, slogged around in the mud, and slid open the door. Andie was semiconscious. Seeing McCaffery, she tried to free her hands from the ropes as she screamed through the gag in her mouth.

"Ain't gonna happen, bitch. I got you. I got you!" McCaffery leaned in close to Andie. "But I do have good news. Your time is up!" He jerked her jeans up and haphazardly cinched her belt. "We're gonna take a little walk in the rain." He crawled on top of her so she couldn't move and untied the ropes. "Seems like old times, doesn't it, Andrea Fulbright?" he said, smiling and breathing his whiskey breath in her face.

He retied Andie's hands in front, dragging her by the ropes and pulling her spastic body out of the van. She fell forward onto the muddy ground as her legs followed. She lay motionless for a moment then floundered to stand. "Get up!" he commanded. Andie tried, but her hands were wedged underneath her body; she couldn't use them to push herself up. McCaffery kicked her in her ribs with his heavy boot, lifting her momentarily out of the mud and spinning her backward. She tumbled partially down the incline, sliding in the mud. He careened down the steep concrete slope and said again, "Get the fuck up, bitch!"

Andie shifted her weight to get herself up. She pulled the gag from her mouth and tried to catch her breath. Slowly she got to her feet and staggered backward. She caught a glimpse of McCaffery as he stood before her, knife in hand and the high-powered rifle slung over his shoulder. She raised her tied hands to her face to wipe the blood and muddy hair from her eyes. She was dazed; she stumbled back and stared at him. He seemed smaller and much shorter than she'd remembered. She stood wavering and staring at him. "Just kill me, please. Just kill me," she said in a breathless whisper. Her body felt heavy, her legs weak.

McCaffery's nostrils flared as he took the butt of his rifle and swung it into, her hitting her left arm and shoulder. She spun around and landed on her right side in a muddy heap. She cried out in pain as her arm snapped. The pain radiated from her forearm to her shoulder blade and up her neck. She screamed in anguish, her body curling into a fetal position. Andie tasted blood; her teeth were gritty with mud.

"I'll decide when you die, bitch!"

McCaffery stomped toward her and landed a swift kick into her left rib-cage, sending her body upward and knocking the wind out of her. She cried out, gasping for air as her body slid down through the mud, splattering her face. Andie tried to breathe, but the air turned into mud. She coughed and vomited into the murky ground. A slosh of footsteps came closer. She clawed desperately at the concrete of the abandoned viaduct, trying to stand, to stop her descent down the slippery embankment.

A sour taste seeped into her mouth then a pain rattled through her like shattered glass. Blood appeared through her shirt then flowed down her elbows. Her body curled over, she moaned heavily; her forehead rested on the wet concrete.

"Get up!" McCaffery said once more.

Andie didn't hear him. Her head was throbbing as a pool of blood formed on the ground and churned with the mud. Pain shot through her arm and shoulder in long intense waves. Her ribcage rattled with every labored breath. Her body shook and her teeth chattered. Her arms were drenched with sweat and blood as she tried to hold herself up.

McCaffery looked at her huddled body on the broken pavement and kicked her again in the abdomen. This time she fell backward, spattering blood as she tumbled down the incline. He laughed and slipped down the hill as he took another pull on his whiskey bottle. He looked down at Andie and smiled; it was time. He grabbed the rope that bound her hands and dragged her up the incline to the broken-down wooden fence. Her blood smeared a bloody, muddy path. Overgrown trees and shrubs hid the decaying structure, which sagged against its own weight.

McCaffery ran back to the van and brought the box he had in the back. Andie was turning pale from the loss of blood and moaning weakly with each breath. McCaffery returned, looked at her, and laughed. "This is how it feels to be somebody's bitch! It's payback time, you fucking whore—payback for all you did to me, for all the butt fuckers I had to fight off, for shitting in a bucket, for sitting in solitary, for eating rat shit."

Andie's shirt had taken on a deep crimson where McCaffery had kicked her. Her breathing was labored and made a gurgling sound in her throat. He untied her hands and pulled her up to the horizontal cross post of the fence. Her head fell forward on her chest; her hair was a bloody tussle of ringlets that stuck to her face and neck. He reached into the box and pulled out a tangled coil of rusty barbed wire. He put on heavy work gloves and wrapped each of Andie's arms around the crossbeam of the fence and used the barbed wire to secure them. He wrapped the wires tightly, each barb piercing the fabric of Andie's shirt. When he finished he took out a pair of pliers and twisted the wires once more, sending the barbs deep into her skin. She screamed in pain as she lifted her head. Blood appeared out of the side of her mouth. She counted her breaths to stay conscious, but her vision was blurred and her body was growing weak.

Six, seven, eight were the breaths she took. Something was rattling in her head. She tasted blood, and the barbs hurt with every movement she made. She was growing faint, her breathing difficult; the air felt raw. Then, like a dream, Michael appeared in front of her. He was laughing and dancing in her kitchen. "Michael, I'm so…cold," she whispered. Tears streamed down her face.

Then Kat appeared. She was raising her glass in a toast and laughing. *Oh, your beautiful smile,* Andie thought. Aisha was playing the piano and singing, and Leo and Curry were asleep on her bed. "My kids," she whispered softly.

Andie found herself holding a paintbrush, gripping it with her right hand. She was painting a large canvas with long red and blue strokes, just like the clouds in the sky. Her vision was so blurry, her head heavy and thick. "Think, think," she said with a whisper. "Eleven, seventeen, twenty…" she whispered as she breathed. Falco appeared before her, smiling. "I love you," Andie breathed. Red and blue and purple and white and blue and red, she was painting; she was staring up at the sky.

CHAPTER 41

Ballard and Falco were heading north in pursuit of the rusty minivan. Falco was feeling sick with dread, hoping they were on the right track. Ballard's radio broke in as the dispatcher reported that police had lost sight of the minivan, but a helicopter had been deployed and was scouring the vicinity from Milwaukee Avenue, east to Cicero, and north to Dempster. "There's a lot of trails back there, wooded areas and murky water," Ballard said, staring at the road ahead.

Falco's cell phone rang; it was Lassiter. "Falco, bad news on the cloth. It's chloroform, and there are traces of lipstick on it. No question, we're dealing with a kidnapping—or something worse."

Falco put her hand on mouth and closed her eyes. "Fuck."

Special Agent Fred Tedeschi reigned agents in from the child abduction case and joined the pursuit of Andie's kidnapper. The DNA evidence on the dead body in the minivan hadn't come in yet, but as far as he was concerned, they were screwed. In addition to the prison clothing found in the burned-out van, a shirt from Wolfe Security, a business based in Oak Park, was also found. The feds were considering whether McCaffery had planted a double in the van, filled it with flammable liquids, and crashed it to fake his own death. McCaffery had worked for Wolfe Security during the time he had planned the bank heist. His accomplice was the brother of the owner, Sean Wolfe.

Falco asked Ballard to pull off the road. He parked the car in a Chicago Transit Authority parking lot. She burst out of the car and started to pace, then went back into the car and pulled out a pack of cigarettes. She frantically looked for her lighter and spilled the contents of her purse on the floor of the car. She found her lighter, lit the cigarette, and stepped out of the car. Ballard got out of the car and leaned on the roof, looking concerned. "Take it easy, Falco."

"I just need to *think*," she said in a weak voice and taking a long drag from her cigarette. She looked at her watch and then threw the cigarette down, stomped it out, and got back into the car. She collected the contents of her purse and fished underneath the seat for her cell phone. The image of Andie with her new tiny cell phone flashed before her. "Kat can reach me any time and any place," she heard her say. "Jesus Christ, of course!" Falco said. Hearing Falco's cry, Ballard swung back into the car. "GPS," Falco said. "Fucking GPS! Don't all new cell phone have GPS?" Falco got out her cell and called headquarters.

Grasky and two other detectives from the twenty-third district obtained Andie's cell phone provider information and began to track the GPS signal in her phone. "What if she's got it turned off? Will the GPS still work?" Ballard wondered out loud.

"I don't know." Falco stared ahead, waiting. This was the most promising turn of events so far. She waited with bated breath, crossing her fingers under her raincoat. "Come on. Come on," she whispered.

CHAPTER 42

McCaffery sat on the pavement drinking the last of his whiskey. His head felt heavy as he played with the jagged hunting knife. He watched the pool of blood beneath Andie grow larger and drip slowly down the concrete embankment. It was beginning to rain again, but the late-summer sun was burning a red hole in the storm clouds. Suddenly it was quiet. He walked over and straddled Andie, standing over her. Her head rested on the wooden cross post; blood dripped from her nose and mouth. Her eyes were fixed on the sky, staring at something far away.

McCaffery stared at Andie with clenched teeth. He knelt over her and jerked off the silver necklace that hung around her neck. Then he pulled the silver rings off her right hand and the thick platinum band off the third finger of her left hand. He dropped the jewelry in the pocket of his shirt then started to unbuckle his belt. In the distance he heard the subtle rumble of a helicopter. Was it the cops? He looked toward the minivan. Should he make a run for the van? The rumble grew louder, and he heard sirens in the distance. He was trapped. He could either make a run for the vehicle or take his chances along the river. *There are plenty of places to hide*, he thought, *and I've got plenty of ammo*. He looked down at Andie and kicked her hard in the knee. "See you in hell," he said as he fled down the embankment.

It was six thirty p.m., and the rain came in sudden downpours. Three police vehicles and Falco's unmarked car followed the helicopter. The GPS on Andie's phone indicated her location near the Illinois 58 overpass. "Isn't that where the river splits?" asked Ballard. Falco didn't answer.

Lassiter was in the lead car following the helicopter. They careened down Waukegan Road and found a long-abandoned frontage road that ran parallel to Beckwith Road. Lassiter tried to zoom in on the squad car's computer to get a closer location of Andie's whereabouts. "That assumes she still has the cell phone on her person," Lassiter mumbled.

The helicopter hovered over what appeared to be McCaffery's minivan, hidden under some overgrown shrubbery and trees. The three squad cars came to grinding halts, and six uniformed cops jumped out with their guns drawn and approached the minivan. Lassiter followed.

They shouted for McCaffery as they surrounded the vehicle, but no movement or sounds came from inside. They stormed the van. Ballard and Falco arrived with their weapons drawn. They were too late; no one was in the van. They searched the vehicle. The dingy, rusty floor was smeared with blood. The rope used to tie Andie's hands was stained bloody red and lay among a spilled box of ammunition for a high-powered rifle.

Lassiter ordered a search of the area and called for additional manpower. "If McCaffery has enough ammunition, he could put up a pretty good fight, especially with a Ruger assault rifle," he said.

Just then his radio squawked. It was Ken Masuda from the chopper above saying they had spotted something near the concrete embankment, heading due north. The squad cars and the Crown Victoria edged closer to the concrete viaduct. Weapons drawn, the uniformed cops split up and slowly slipped their way down the embankment, hiding behind vegetation and heaps of trash and other debris. Ballard and Falco picked their way through the wet grass and mud. Falco led the way, squinting against the onset of dusk. She surveyed the area looking for evidence of McCaffery or Andie. Then her eyes fixed on a dark-colored area near the top of the concrete embankment. It was a large irregular shape that looked like a big oil spot. She squatted and touched it; it was blood. "Oh, god," Falco whispered.

She looked upward and saw more blood on the concrete farther up the embankment. She followed it, sprinting. Shots came from below, and the two detectives instinctively ducked. Ballard was searching higher up the concrete incline; Falco heard the rustle of brush against his legs.

Falco looked around but saw nothing. She grew worried that McCaffery had killed Andie and buried her body or thrown it in the river. She shook that thought away. She climbed higher and spotted a decrepit wooden fence and followed it with her eyes. She squinted and saw a dark form and moved closer. She pushed past a large area of brush and saw a large pool of blood on the pavement and next to it Andie's body. Falco ran to her.

"Ballard, over here!" she called out. "Oh, my god. My god," she whispered, looking at the bloody body. She crouched down and checked for a pulse in her neck. She held Andie's jaw and gently moved her head so she could see her face. "Andie?" Falco cried. She looked down at her chest and abdomen; her shirt was soaked in blood, and her sleeves were blotchy with dark crimson stains.

"Jesus… Jesus," she said. "What did he do to you?" She called her name again, this time gently shaking her. Andie's head bobbed lifelessly. "Andie! Come on! Please!" She lifted her head and listened for breathing. Falco wasn't sure what she heard. She listened for a heartbeat as she put her ear to her chest. Maybe…maybe something; she again checked for a pulse as she put her fingers to the side of Andie's neck. She felt a tiny rhythm; it was faint and fast. She couldn't believe Andie was still alive. "Okay…please… stay with me."

Ballard came tromping down the concrete incline. He stopped upon seeing Falco crouched over Andie's body. "Oh, my good god. Is she alive?"

"Ballard, help me!" Falco cried as she tried to free Andie from the barbed wire. She immediately cut the fleshy part of her right thumb with one of the rusty barbs. "Fuck!" she yelled, gripping her hand. Blood filled the wound.

"We need some pliers or wire cutters," said Ballard. He ran back to their vehicle. It was beginning to rain again. Falco checked Andie's pulse once more. She felt cold; her body temperature was dropping. "Come on, girl. You gotta stay with me." She looked up at the sky; it was almost dusk. Falco pulled off her raincoat and covered Andie's body. She couldn't keep Andie safe, but she could keep her warm, she thought.

Ballard returned with a pair of wire cutters. The weight of Andie's body had pulled the barbed wire tighter around her arms and deep into her skin. Ballard's wire cutters were dull and rusty. "Better than nothing," he said as he tried to cut through the metal.

Shots rang from the river—first the sounds of police fire and then the sputter of automatic weapon fire. The helicopter continued to circle, keeping sight of McCaffery.

CHAPTER 43

Falco gritted her teeth while trying to unravel the twisted wire around Andie's right arm. With her help Ballard freed Andie's arm. The weight of her body followed as her right arm dropped to the ground, pulling apart the broken bones in her entangled left arm. Andie's head rose from her chest, and she breathed a soft cry of pain.

"It's okay. It's okay," Falco said. She gently lifted Andie straight up, taking her weight off her left arm. Ballard work feverously to untangle and cut the remaining wires. Andie's arm was badly broken; Falco could barely look at it. "Hurry, Ballard," she said. Gunfire continued, and the detectives heard yelling and the splash of water below.

Andie was suddenly conscious, delirious, and agitated. "He's…he's… I have to get up. I… Help me." She tried to look at Falco but could barely lift her head. Her right arm was flailing as she clumsily pointed down in the direction of the river.

"It's okay, Andie. We're getting help. The ambulance is on its way. Just hang on. Hang on, please!" Falco urged.

Andie mumbled something. "Please… I have to…" Her breath rattled as bloody spittle shot from her mouth.

Suddenly the gunfire stopped, shouts came from near the water, "Freeze, McCaffery! Drop your weapon and get down on the ground now! Now Now!"

"I think we got him, Andie! Did you hear me? I think we got McCaffery!" Falco said, bending down. "Just hang on. Keep breathing!" She heard the whine of an ambulance in the distance.

Ballard was uncoiling the long expanse of barbed wire from Andie's left arm when more voices came from below. Someone was yelling to McCaffery, again telling him to get on the ground. Falco tried to help Ballard pull the unraveled wire away, but with her hand badly cut, she was of little help. Andie stirred, moving her left leg and trying to push herself up from the concrete. She grunted from the effort and mumbled something barely audible.

"Stay still. Stay still, Andie. It's okay," Falco coaxed.

She glanced at Ballard, who was prying the last of the wire from around Andie's broken arm. "Almost done. Almost free. Hang in there," said Ballard.

Bang! Bang! Two gunshots whizzed past the left side of Falco's head. She clapped her left hand over hear ear and instinctively ducked to her right, away from the noise.

"She's got your gun. Falco, look out! She's got…" In an instant, Ballard leapt over Falco and onto Andie, knocking the gun out of Andie's hand.

Shots from the gun scattered the cops below. McCaffery was being cuffed and had just been brought to his feet when one bullet stuck him in the chest, sending him jerking back. A second bullet pierced through his neck, severing his carotid artery and splattering blood everywhere. Andie caught a glimpse of McCaffery for only a second. The gun wobbled in her hand and hit the pavement as Ballard grabbed at her wrist. Andie let out a faint cry then a deep moan; Ballard's weight was cutting off her air.

He quickly rolled off Andie's body and scrambled to his feet. "Son of a bitch!" he said. "Falco! You okay?"

"Jesus!" she cried. "How? What the… What the fuck?" Falco's face was pale; her eyes zipped back and forth in panic and disbelief. She looked down at where her gun had tumbled then at Andie, shocked at what she had just done. Andie let out a long breath and grew strangely still; her eyes were fixed in a distant stare. "Oh, no. Oh, no, no," said Falco in a low voice. "Andie. Andie!" she yelled, shaking her. No response. Andie's eyes were glassy and unresponsive. "No!" Falco shook her; her head fell back against the wood fence. Falco opened Andie's mouth and checked her airway; she had no idea whether it was clear of blood. She started to blow into her mouth and checked for the rise in her chest. She listened desperately for a heartbeat—nothing. "No! Come on, Andie! Fight it. Fight it!"

Falco began chest compressions as Andie's body jerked lifelessly. Ballard slid down the muddy embankment to fetch Falco's gun. He picked it up and slid it into a plastic evidence bag he pulled from his jacket pocket. He returned to the top of the embankment and looked down at Falco, who was frantically performing CPR. He saw the ambulance and waved his arms.

McCaffery lay dead, killed instantly from the two bullets. Lassiter crouched by the body then looked up at Ballard and Falco. The uniformed cops, looking shell-shocked, glanced up the embankment and at the two detectives, wondering who had delivered the fatal shots to McCaffery.

The ambulance arrived. Two EMTs ran to Ballard. "Please make room!" they called out, carrying a gurney and other equipment. Falco didn't move as she desperately tried to revive Andie. "You're not gonna die on me! Come on. Come on, Andie!"

"Detective, please clear the area. We'll take it from here," said one of the EMTs.

The other EMT, a tall lanky African-American male, gently pulled Falco up from the ground. He crouched and saw Andie's massive blood loss as he checked her vital signs and yelled, "Let's get her out of here! Now!"

Falco backed away, feeling weak and shaky. Her eyes followed Andie as they lifted her body onto the stretcher and loaded her into the ambulance. Moments passed as Andie was rushed into the ambulance. It peeled down the muddy dirt road, its lights flashing and sirens blaring into the waning daylight.

Falco bent over and put her hands on her knees. She felt like she was going to get sick or pass out. Lassiter stomped up the incline, struggling to catch his breath. "What the fuck happened up here, Falco?" he wheezed. "McCaffery's dead. What the fuck happened?" Falco was trembling and scattered. She didn't answer. He bent down to look at her and said evenly, "Take some deep breaths."

Ballard scooped up Falco's raincoat in a heap; he shook it out and put it over Falco's shoulders, mumbling, "Looks like the rain's back." He handed the evidence bag containing Falco's gun to Lassiter.

After a minute, Falco managed to regain her composure; she took a deep breath, straightened up and looked at Lassiter. "I'm sorry, sir. She took my gun. I didn't know…and she just…*shot* him." She put a shaky hand to her forehead.

Lassiter thought for a moment; he looked at the pool of blood left from Andie's body and the bundle of bloody barbed wire on the ground. He glanced down the concrete viaduct where McCaffery was lying dead and said, "Come on… I'm gonna fix this…"

He motioned to Ballard and Falco to follow him down to the base of the embankment where the others were waiting for the coroner. He eyed Falco's cut hand as they headed down the concrete incline. "You'd better get that taken care of, Falco."

CHAPTER 44

Lassiter gathered the group of eight cops together as he gripped Falco's Glock 22 in his hand. Falco looked down, eyeing McCaffery's bloody body and wondering how she could have let this happen. The group was quiet. They avoided looking at Falco and waited to hear what Lassiter was about to say.

"Okay, everyone. We all know what happened here," Lassiter began. "And we all know how we got here." He paused and looked down, collecting his thoughts.

"I'm gonna tell you right now, this whole McCaffery case is gonna blow up in everybody's faces—mostly the FBI's for closing the case before the DNA results came in, but you can bet we'll be dragged into it too." He glared at the group. "The feds handled this case badly from the start. We can't help that, especially now, but unfortunately it gives our department a black eye." He looked up at the darkening sky. "What happened here was a fluke, an accident. A civilian used an officer's gun to kill a man. So what I'm about to say may confuse you all. It may even shock you. What I'm going to do is... I'm gonna cut our losses."

He studied the group long and hard. "We all know Internal Affairs could have a field day with what happened here, and heads would most likely roll. But the reality is McCaffery was scum—the lowest kind of scum. And if you saw what he did to that little gal up there, you'd get a real good idea of the kind of monster this guy is…*was*. Better off dead? You betcha."

Lassiter looked at his watch; the feds would be arriving soon along with crime scene technicians and most likely the press.

"So I'm going to change the ending of this story just a little. Let's just say that instead of the story reading 'McCaffery was shot dead by the victim using an officer's firearm,' it'll read, 'Brian McCaffery was fatally shot by police as he went for his weapon.'"

Falco's shoulders sunk, and she shook her head. *This isn't right*, she thought.

Lassiter looked at the group. "This is now the official statement for what happened here, gentlemen and lady, a small little twist that'll keep us all in the clear. This will be the official statement given to the press and reflected in your reports, all of which I will sign off on. As per department policy, Amy Hollander, our spokesperson, will be the *only* person talking to the press."

Lassiter turned as if to walk toward the embankment as the group broke up, speaking quietly among themselves. "Uh, one more thing officers and detectives," he said, turning back toward the group and raising his hand. "Let me add one warning. Anyone—*anyone*—who strays from the official statement or says anything that deviates from what I have just told you *will* be suspended without pay—or worse."

There was a general consensus that Lassiter's twist was best for the department and for Detective Falco, for whom many felt a strong sense of loyalty and respect.

"We've got to protect our own," said one officer to Falco as he walked past her. She ignored him, scowled, and looked down. She didn't buy it.

Lassiter came by and took Falco's gun out of the plastic bag and handed it to her saying, "Clean that when you get home tonight, okay?"

She looked at Lassiter. "Sir, I appreciate what you're doing here but I—"

"Not another word, Falco. I know you like to play by the rules, but in this case, your reputation and my unwillingness to have it tarnished are much more important. The feds screwed this from the start. You know that." He paused and glanced up the embankment where headlights from approaching vehicles appeared.

"Falco, you and Ballard head back to the station," Lassiter said. "Then get to the hospital and handle any press that may be lurking around Ms. Fulbright. Keep them away even if you have to pull a couple of uniforms from the street. Ballard, I want you to coordinate the officers' reports as they come in. Put them in an envelope in a safe place until tomorrow morning when I can look over them. Also, I'll expect drafts of your reports from both of you tomorrow before noon." Lassiter walked away and met up with Special Agent Tedeschi, who was getting out of his vehicle.

Ballard and Falco made their way to their car. They got in just as the rain started again. Falco looked ahead in silence, clutching herself.

Ballard started the car and sighed, "Jesus! That is one fucking craaazy bitch."

Falco glared at him with disbelief then burst out of the car, slamming the door and walking into the rain.

Ballard quickly put the car in park and yelled after her. "Falco! Get back in the car! Falco? What are you *doing*?" He jumped out of the car and started after her.

Falco stormed back, came around the car, and pushed Ballard hard. Her eyes were fiery as she said through her teeth, "What did you say? What did you say, you insensitive bastard?"

Robby Torres, one of the uniformed cops who had worked the McCaffery case the week before, saw the altercation and grabbed Falco from behind just as Falco was about to take a swing. "Hey! Hey! Cool it, Falco. Cool it!" he said.

She struggled to break free and tried to take another shot at Ballard. Her face was flushed with anger, and she was crying. "You fucking bastard!" she yelled. Suddenly she realized what she was doing and stopped cold. Torres loosened his grip on Falco. "It's okay," she whispered. She put her hand out to signal him to let go.

"You okay?" Torres asked, craning his neck to look at her.

She put her hand over her eyes and turned toward the car. She rested her hand on the edge of the roof and said, "God, I'm sorry. Ballard, I'm sorry. I didn't know what I was doing. Jesus Christ."

Ballard collected himself. "No, I shouldn't have said that. I'm sorry, Falco. You have a right to be pissed. It was…um… I was thinking with my ass."

The ride back to the station was quiet. Falco went to her locker and changed out of her bloodstained pants. She stashed them into a plastic bag and searched for a fresh blouse. Not finding one, she decided to keep her raincoat buttoned. She looked for the first-aid kit and cleaned and bandaged the cut on her hand. She saw Ballard on her way out and said, "See you tomorrow, JB."

"Yeah, take care of yourself, and send my best to the family," Ballard said. He shook his head, angry with himself.

CHAPTER 45

Falco got into her car and fished around in her purse for her lighter and cigarettes. She glanced at herself in the mirror; she looked like shit. She looked again in her purse and noticed her hands were shaking. She stopped and put her head on the steering wheel and took some deep breaths. "Keep it together," she told herself. She lit a cigarette, started the car, and headed toward the hospital.

News crews combed the area. Falco avoided them by parking in a restricted zone. She found the emergency room, showed her badge, and inquired about Andie's whereabouts. "Fifth floor, surgery." She felt a stab of pain. The elevator doors opened to a hoard of media types with cameras, microphones, and video equipment. Falco ordered them out with a stern word and a flash of her badge. They left with disappointed faces.

She made her way through the corridors to the family waiting room. The large room was virtually empty. It was eight fifteen p.m., and most surgeries were performed in the morning, leaving the area all but vacant. An elderly woman at the volunteer desk saw Falco and said with a jittery voice, "Miss, can I help you?" Falco came forward, startled by the voice. She showed her ID and badge and asked if Andie was still in surgery. The woman checked her clipboard and said, "Yes, she is." She looked at Falco and added, "Did you chase away all those TV people?" Falco said yes and the woman grinned.

She scanned the waiting area, looking for familiar faces. She was initially disappointed, wondering whether Michael, Kat, or Aisha hadn't yet been notified that Andie was found and taken to the hospital. Then her eyes caught a lone figure leaning on the marble sill of a large window. His forehead rested on the pane of glass. Falco smiled at the elderly woman and thanked her then walked across the waiting room toward Michael. He was wearing stone-colored khakis and a stiff white hospital-issued coat over a tan button-down shirt. He had his cell phone in one hand and a handful of tissues in the other. He stared blankly down onto the street and breathed heavily on the glass.

Falco approached him from the side, tilting her head to see his face. He didn't notice her. "Michael," she said gently. He didn't hear her. She reached up and put her hand on his shoulder. "Michael."

He turned to her with red eyes and looked surprised at first, then angry. "Hi, Detective," he said in a cold voice. He turned around and leaned on the windowsill, his back to the window. He looked at the floor, trying to hold in his emotions, clenching and unclenching his jaw. There was a long pause.

"Michael, I don't know what I can say," Falco said softly.

"There's nothing to say, Detective," he said in an angry tone.

"How is she? Have you heard anything?"

"She's been in surgery for over an hour now. Alan's in there."

His eyes welled up with tears. Falco wanted to reach out to him but stopped. It was obvious he was still angry with her.

"Did you find her?" asked Michael, his voice cracking.

"Yes," Falco said softly.

"What did he do to her?"

"I can't really say. I mean, I can't talk about that right now. It's still considered a crime scene," she said, hoping Michael would understand.

"Crime scene," he sniffed. He wiped his eyes and blew his nose.

Falco turned, leaned against the wall, and looked at the ceiling. She rubbed her forehead and shook her head, thinking of Andie.

"What happened to your hand?" asked Michael, seeing the bandage.

"Oh, I cut it on some… I cut it," Falco said, putting her hand in her coat pocket.

"Pretty lousy bandaging. I hope you didn't pay for that," he said, coming around and gently taking her hand.

"No, I did the bandaging…in haste."

"Mind if I look at it?" Without a response, he unwrapped the bandage and looked at the wound. He eyed her and said, "Pretty nasty. Looks like you might need a stitch or two. Why didn't you get this taken care of?"

Falco shook her head, not having an answer and not wanting to divulge how she had been injured. "It wasn't important at the time," she said, brushing him off and pulling her hand away.

"No, wait. Come on. Let me take care of this," he said, taking her hand and pulling her down a hallway. He found an empty physician's office and steered her into it. Falco resisted at first and then went along. Her hand was smarting with pain, but she was getting used to it. She deserved every bit of the pain.

"Take your coat off so we can clean it," Michael said, very focused. He slipped her coat off. The deep stain from Andie's blood had dried to a dull crimson brown on the lower half of Falco's blouse. It caught Michael's eye, and he gasped, thinking Falco had more injuries. She looked down at her shirt, realizing she shouldn't have let him remove her coat.

"I'm sorry. I shouldn't have let you," she said.

Michael took her hand and gently cleaned and bandaged it without saying another word. After a few minutes, he broke the silence. "That's Andie's blood, isn't it?" he said calmly, not looking at her.

"Yes, it is."

CHAPTER 46

The two went back to the waiting room and sat down. Michael was silent. Falco felt dizzy and exhausted. The rhythmic sound of footsteps grew louder from down the hall. It was Kat.

"Michael! Oh, Michael!" Tears streamed down her face as she grabbed Michael and buried her face in his chest. She was bordering on hysterical.

"Take it easy, Kat. Take it easy," he cooed.

She suddenly pulled away from him, seeing Falco nearby. "What are *you* doing here?" she said angrily, bolting toward Falco. "This is all your fault!" Kat yelled, pointing her finger at Falco. "I heard the news. He was alive, and you let him find her. You let him!"

The elderly lady got up from her seat and looked in the direction of the yelling. She gave Kat and Michael an alarmed look. Michael put his arm around Kat and steered her away from Falco, pulling her into an adjoining hallway. Her sobs echoed into the waiting room and grew progressively louder.

Michael returned looking shaken. "She's going to get some coffee. I gave her a Valium."

Falco barely nodded. She closed her eyes and cradled her face in her hands.

Michael peered at Falco. "Are you okay?" She didn't answer. She put her hand over her mouth, trying not to cry. She shook her head. Michael moved close and sat next to her. He put his arm around her and gave her a hug. "She's strong, you know." Falco nodded, not looking up.

The waiting room was deathly quiet except for the soft voice of the elderly lady, who was talking with another volunteer. Michael absently kicked at his briefcase on the floor. "Hey," he said. "I've got something for you." He bent down and dragged the briefcase closer, fumbled around in it, and pulled out a colorful plastic bag with something square in it. He smiled and handed it to Falco.

She gave him a blank look. "What's this?"

"Well, look *inside!*" he said with a childlike sense of urgency.

She scowled and looked inside the bag. It was the Xbox game her son had wanted. "Oh, my!" she said softly. "I completely forgot about this."

Michael smiled, seeing she was pleased. "Nothing like having connections," he said, satisfied with himself.

"How much do I owe you?" Falco looked relieved. "You know…my son will be…"

"Twenty-five even." Michael said.

She took out her wallet and gave him a twenty and a ten. "Keep the change, for your trouble."

"Okay, I'm not proud." He shrugged, putting the money in his wallet and jamming the wallet in his back pocket.

Falco looked at him; her shoulders drooped. "I appreciate it very much, especially since I didn't have time to get Sam anything yet. This all came down, and well, you probably think I'm a pretty lousy cop right now…and maybe not a very good mother," she said quietly.

Michael thought for a moment. "Well, I don't know what kind of mom you are, but you can't be all that bad of a cop if you're worried about what *I* think." He looked at Falco intently as a little smile appeared on his face. "Peace?" he said, holding out his hand.

Falco took his hand and nodded. "Yes, peace."

They sat quietly for a long while, turning their heads in the direction of anyone coming down the hallway. Andie had been in surgery for more than three hours with no news. Kat returned with a Styrofoam cup of hot coffee. She was calmer and sat on the other side of the waiting room but looked restless. Michael went over to check on her, telling her there was no news.

Falco's head fell forward to her chest as she drifted off to sleep. Michael's eyes drooped as he leaned his head on his hand. "I guess we're both pretty beat," he said, looking over at her. "Want some coffee? I could go get us some."

Falco jerked awake and rubbed her eyes. "Sounds good," she mumbled.

She looked over at Kat, who was asleep on the loveseat across the room. The elderly volunteer was gone, leaving the volunteer desk empty. It was eleven fifteen p.m.

Falco recalled the crime scene. She would never forget what McCaffery had done to Andie: the barbed wire, the brutal beating, her blood-soaked shirt, and her twisted, broken arm. The two gunshots rang in her head. She jerked forward in her seat and chased off the sound and the thoughts that came with it. Images of her father surfaced in her head. She remembered him awakening suddenly after a couple of bourbons, mumbling about gunshots, arrest warrants, and a full cast of bad guys. She wondered whether she would end up like him, her mother's voice telling her, "I told you so."

Michael returned with two steaming cups of coffee. "I don't know how you take yours," he said apologetically. "I forgot to ask."

Falco smiled wearily. "Black is fine."

Michael winced as he took a sip. "This is awful…blah! It's worse than McDonald's!" He stuck his tongue out.

Falco shrugged. "Just put some sugar or that powdery stuff in it if it's that bad."

He took another sip and made a face. "Andie is such a coffee snob. It has to be the best beans and freshly ground," he said, looking off. "I guess I've been spoiled." He looked at his watch and grimaced. "I'm going to see if I can find out something." He got up from the sofa, wandered down the hall, and cut into a nurse's station. After ten minutes he returned looking wearier. "She's still in surgery. Why can't they tell us *something?*"

He picked up a magazine and leafed through it, ignoring the coffee. Then he looked at Falco and said, "You're actually drinking that swill?"

She shrugged and took another sip. "I need the boost."

Michael continued to leaf through the magazine, trying to keep his mind off Andie. He got up and started pacing, rolling up the magazine and thumping it against the palm of his hand.

"I'm going to get some air," Falco, said getting up.

Michael nodded as she walked down the hall toward the elevators. Kat woke up and came over to Michael, who was still pacing. "No news yet, I guess," she said, her voice cracking. "Where's lady cop?"

"Getting some fresh air," Michael said. "I hope when she returns you won't verbally assault her like you did before."

Kat looked pissed. "It's her fault. She interviewed me at the gallery when Andie disappeared. I could tell she knew something. I could tell, Michael."

"Leave it be. This is not the time. Please," he said.

Kat put her finger into Michael's chest. "Well, I'll tell you one thing. You can bet I'll sue for negligence. You can bet on that! I'm calling my father's lawyer tomorrow. They're not getting away with this," she sneered.

"Whatever. Let's just hope Andie's get through this."

Kat spun around once and then turned again to Michael. "I cancelled the opening. I may cancel the whole show. I don't know." She wandered off toward the windows.

Falco returned smelling of cigarette smoke. Michael was back on the loveseat with another magazine. He sniffed and took out a tissue and blew his nose. He looked at the pictures from an article in the magazine and turned it so Falco could see. "This reminds me of a party Andie had about a year ago," he said, smiling. "She had some great parties…lots of people, lots of fun and great food." He sighed and shook his head. "I remember this one party. It was in the dead of winter and Kat came really late. She and Andie got into this huge fight. Oh, god the drama." He smiled, looking down. "It was still a great party, though," he laughed. "I could tell you some stories."

Falco smiled sadly.

Another hour passed. It was nearly one a.m. Falco dozed off. Michael looked at his watch, shot up from the sofa, and said, "I can't stand this." Falco woke suddenly. He got up and began to pace again. "I'm really worried," he said, tears coming to his eyes. "She's been in there almost five hours. There must be something I can…" He stopped then sat down again, feeling help-less. "Tell me, Detective. I know you're not supposed to talk about the crime scene and all, but how bad… How bad was it?" He looked desperate. "Just *tell* me. I need to know *something*."

Quiet footsteps came down the hallway. It was Dr. Forrest, his surgical mask dragged down to his chest. His face was drawn and didn't hide his worry. Kat ran across the room and joined Michael and Falco.

"Come on. Let's sit down," the doctor said, quietly looking intently into their faces. He took a seat in front of them and rubbed the stubble on his chin. "It's not good," he said with a sigh. "She's lost a lot of blood. Every time we tried to stop the bleeding, her pressure would drop." He looked at the floor and sighed. "She's critical…very critical."

"What happened?" Kat asked, her voice hoarse. "Tell me what he did to her." She began to cry.

Dr. Forrest turned his head away. His body sunk into itself, and his head hung low and heavy. He looked off for a moment, carefully searching for the right words. "She's got massive contusions and internal bleeding. Her ribcage on her left side was…*is*…virtually shattered, most likely from being kicked. Her left lung is punctured and collapsed. She's got deep puncture wounds in both her arms, apparently from some kind of sharp prongs. I heard he used barbed wire. I hesitate to go on," he said as he looked at the three, "but her arms were bound almost like a crucifixion. Her weight from being bound cut off the oxygen to her body and to her brain."

Kat walked away in tears, having heard enough. Michael closed his eyes and said flatly, "What else?"

"We had to remove her spleen, and her left arm is broken in three places. She was sexually assaulted." Dr. Forrest stopped and dragged his hand over his face. "I've never seen this kind of brutality. I'm not a surgeon but I remember my ER rotation; this was as bad as it gets. God…after all this."

Falco whispered something faintly into her chest and put her face in her hands.

"We almost lost her, but Andie is tough. Still, she's not out of the woods yet by any means." He turned to Falco. "If it hadn't been for the CPR she got out there, we probably wouldn't be having this conversation." He gave Falco's shoulder a gentle squeeze.

He stopped talking. Each of the three had withdrawn from the situation in their own way. Kat stared out across the room in a daze, looking out the tall window. Michael sat forward, his arms crossed on his chest, as he bit at this thumbnail. Falco's face was in her hands; her heart was filled with sadness and regret knowing she could have prevented all of this.

"She'll be in ICU," Dr. Forrest told them. "There's not much we can do for now except wait." He quietly left, walking heavily down the hallway.

After a few minutes, Michael went over to Kat and told her he was staying the night. Kat got up and decided to leave for home, saying she had to make phone calls in the morning to cancel the opening.

Michael sat by Falco and said, "You should go home already. Did you drive here yourself?" Falco nodded. "Maybe you should take a taxi home. You look exhausted."

"No, no. I'm okay. Are you staying?"

"Yeah, I'll stay here, but if I need to I can get some sleep in Alan's office. He's got a nice sofa." Michael smiled.

Falco sank into herself. She shook her head, fighting off tears. "I don't know what I can *do*," she confessed in a tiny voice.

"Just go home. I'll call you if anything changes," Michael said, looking for more tissue.

Falco got up and pulled her coat closed. She turned, looking for her purse on the sofa and the floor. Michael eyed her sadly and took her in his arms. He held her tightly; he felt the emotion well up inside her. She wrapped her arms around him and buried her face in his jacket and wept.

CHAPTER 47

The rain had finally stopped, but the streets were still wet. It was nearly two thirty a.m. as Falco drove home with a throbbing headache. Her jaw and face ached from the crying and stress. She was drained but thought about cleaning her gun. It haunted her, tucked away in the holster under her arm and touching her ribs. She didn't want to think about it just now, if there was blood on it—Andie's blood.

She got home and changed clothes, taking her soiled pants out of the plastic bag and pulling off her shirt. She looked at the washing machine and decided to put the clothes in the utility sink with some presoak detergent and water to leave for the morning. She wrapped her robe around her naked body and poured a glass of red wine. She took a sip and thought of Andie. "Nothing like a nice Cab for a sleepless night," she sighed, remembering Andie's words. "Why didn't I trust my instincts?" she whispered into the glass. That was a futile conversation that she wasn't going to start with herself.

She rubbed her neck, still in disbelief. She felt strange and different somehow; she had changed in some dark way. She thought about what she could do if she ever left the force—maybe teach high school English or something. She shook the thought away. *Who are you kidding?*

She walked wearily into her bedroom. She couldn't bear the thought of sleeping alone in that bed. The bed had been hers and Jeffery's; she hadn't gotten around to buying a new one. The thought of them sleeping together made her anxious. She turned and walked into Sam's room, looking at pictures of him on the wall, his soccer trophies and ribbons from Boy Scouts. She took another swallow of wine and sat on his bed. His baseball glove was on the floor next to her feet. She picked it up and clutched it. "He's safe. He's safe," she said softly. She lied down on the bed, still clutching the glove, and fell asleep.

* * *

The next morning, Falco's neighborhood was brimming with Saturday morning activity. Lawn mowers buzzed, kids road their bikes, cars were getting washed, and people headed out to do errands. Rain was forecast for the afternoon, so Sam was already planning to ask Falco to take him to the Field Museum where the Pompeii exhibit was in its final days.

Sam ran out of Jeffery's car and waved goodbye. He put the key in the lock of the front door of Falco's house and gave the door a shove. It didn't open. Jeffery watched him, waiting for him to open the door and get safely inside before he drove off. Sam tried the door again, turning the doorknob. The key worked, but the door was stuck. Seeing Sam having trouble, Jeffery parked the car in the driveway behind Falco's gold Camry.

"The door's stuck…or something," Sam shouted to his dad. He gave it another push and then leaned on the doorbell. No one came to the door.

"Is the lock stuck?" Jeffery asked as he got out of the car.

"No, the door's stuck!" Sam said, growing frustrated. He pressed his finger to the doorbell again and then knocked at the door.

"Where's your mother?" Jeffery said, wondering why she hadn't heard the doorbell and Sam's knocking.

Jeffery took Sam's key and put it in the lock. He turned the knob and gave the door a good shove. The door opened partially. "Humidity," Jeffery said to Sam. "The door's swollen shut." He grunted and gave the door one more push. It opened with a whoosh.

The house was strangely quiet as Sam ran in calling for his mom. "Her car's out front," Jeffery said, following Sam inside. He looked at his watch; it was nearly nine thirty a.m. Sam raced through the house calling for his mother, dragging his duffle bag and dropping a laundry bag full of dirty clothes on the floor. Jeffery grabbed the laundry and placed it next to the sofa. Sam ran past his bedroom and into his mother's room. Not finding her there, he careened past Jeffery and ran into his room. Jeffery was growing concerned. Sam peered out the doorway of his room and quickly motioned to Jeffery.

"Dad, Mom's sleeping in *my bed*," Sam said in a whisper, looking a bit confused.

Jeffery entered the room and saw Falco asleep on the bed, her arms wrapped around Sam's baseball glove. He spotted the half-full wineglass and sat next to her on the bed.

"M? Hey, M!" He shook her gently. "Wake up. Are you okay?"

Falco stirred and slowly opened her eyes. Sam jumped on the bed and shook her too. "Mom? Hey, Mom! You're sleeping in my bed!"

Falco closed her eyes and opened them again, trying to focus on the faces before her. "Oh, Sam, honey," she said, seeing her son.

He jumped on top of her and gave her a big hug. "We kept ringing the doorbell, Mom, but you were asleep!" he said, smiling.

Falco looked at her watch; it was nine forty. Her eyes focused on Jeffery. "Jeffery…what are you doing here?"

"It's not really my house anymore, but I can still come in once in a while, can't I?" he asked, getting up and taking the wineglass from Sam's dresser.

"Mom, why are you sleeping with my baseball glove?" Sam asked with a laugh.

"Oh…" She looked down at the glove. "I got home really late, and I guess I wasn't thinking too clearly. I'm sleeping with your glove *and* in your bed!" she said, making a joke. She rubbed her eyes and moved to get up.

Jeffery looked at her intently as she got to her feet. "Are you okay?"

"Of course I'm okay. I'm just a little tired," she said, growing impatient. She immediately thought of Andie and searched for her purse and cell phone. Finding it, she flipped it open. No calls from Michael—hopefully a good sign. She sighed.

"How 'bout I make you some coffee? You look like you could use some," Jeffery said.

Falco gathered her robe around her. "Sure…yeah, great. I'm gonna take a quick shower." She walked past him and took the wineglass out of his hand.

"That woman, the one you were protecting… They said on TV that she's critical," Jeffery said.

Falco nodded. "Yes, I know." She placed her cell phone on the kitchen counter.

"Is that where you were so late?" he asked, measuring the coffee.

"Yeah, I was at the hospital past two."

Sam glanced at his parents then ran outside into the backyard and into the neighbor kid's yard. The two kids connected as they usually did each time Sam came to his mother's house, not missing a beat in their friendship.

Falco took a warm shower, letting the water beat her tired muscles. She wrapped herself in a towel and wiped the steam from the mirror. "Oh, god," she said, looking at herself, "and I still have to go to the station." She dried off and pulled her hair back. Little ringlets fell out around her forehead. She pushed them away and then changed into jeans and a striped knit shirt.

Jeffery met her at her bedroom door, his face grim. "What's this?" he said, motioning with his finger for her to follow him.

"What's what?"

Jeffery turned and headed toward the laundry room as she followed. "This is Sam's laundry. I brought it for you to do."

"Okay…" Falco said.

"So I come in here with the laundry bag and find *this* in the utility sink! Jesus Christ! Is this blood, Monica? What the fuck? Is all this blood?" Jeffery was alarmed and angry.

Falco looked at the utility sink where she had put her soiled clothes to soak. The water had turned to a bright crimson.

Jeffery glared at her. "Are you hurt?"

"No, no. I'm fine."

"Well, what the fuck is this then? All this blood, Jesus Christ! What if Sam had come in here and seen this?"

Falco shook her head and quickly drained the blood-tinged water out of the sink and ran fresh water over the clothes.

"I…know…um… Yes, you're right," she stammered.

"This isn't your blood?" he said looking down at the bandage on her hand.

"No…no. I'm okay." She took a deep breath and collected herself. "Listen, I put this stuff in here because I was tired and needed to go to bed. I just didn't *think*," she said in a pleading tone. "They needed to soak before I—"

"Didn't think? You knew Sam was coming over today. Do you have any idea what kind of reaction he might have had to seeing this? Thinking it's *your* blood, that *you* were hurt?" He pulled the dripping, stained white blouse from the sink then looked squarely at Falco. "This…this is why I have a problem with all this…your work…and how it spills over into our personal life," he said loudly.

"Look, I made a mistake, but you're blowing this out of proportion. And you're beginning to really piss me off."

"Don't you get it?" Jeffery said, getting in her face. "This isn't about your career, Ms. Detective. This is about our son…and the fact that every day he worries about you."

Falco looked down and said in a small voice, "I know, I know. But…"

"But *what*? You're no different than your dad. Look at you. You're bringing it home with you just like he did—and you wonder why he drank himself to death."

"That is so unfair, Jeffery. So unfair!" Falco said, putting her hand on his chest and pushing him away. "You don't know anything about my father except what my mother has told you, most of which isn't true. But it's easier for you to believe *her* instead of me." She turned her back to him and walked away.

"Your mother has nothing to do with this," he said. He walked after her and put his hands on her shoulders. She jerked away out of his grasp.

"Fuck you, Jeff!" Falco said, lurching toward him. "I'm sure you and my mother are still so fucking cozy. She probably calls you all the time!"

Jeffery took a different tone. "Well, when was the last time you called her? She thinks you're too damn busy—too damn important—to call her," he said loudly.

"Hey, I don't have to report to you when I call my own mother," Falco said, feeling threatened. The reality was she hadn't spoken to her mother in more than a week-and-a-half. "She fucking drains me. Every time I talk to her I feel like I'm talking to you," she yelled. She glared at Jeffery angrily then put her hand to her forehead. "Look, I can't do this right now."

The back door slammed, and Sam ran in saying something about playing with this friend's Xbox. He stopped short and got quiet seeing his parents, realizing they were arguing again. Falco suddenly remembered the game in her purse. She bent down, took a breath, and managed to smile at Sam. "Hey, you. I got you something for your birthday."

Sam perked up. "Give me my purse over there, okay?" Sam ran and got it.

Falco gave Jeffery a dirty look. She rummaged through her bag and pulled out the brightly colored bag containing the new Xbox game. Jeffery looked on suspiciously.

Sam grabbed the package and pulled the game out of the bag. His face lit up.

"Oh! Oh, Mom! Thunder Crash Car III!" He held it to his chest and jumped up and down. "Wow! I can't believe you got it! I can't believe it. I can't believe it." Sam continued to jump up and down and yell with delight.

Falco smiled broadly, feeling she had at least done something right today. She glanced at Jeffery, who was trying not to look jealous. "Where'd you find that?" he asked quietly.

"Oh, some pusher on the street. You know the kind of people I hang out with."

Sam hugged his mother and dashed next door, yelling to Riley about his new game.

Falco looked at her watch; she needed to get to the station and to the hospital. She'd stop by the Fergusons' to see if Sam could stay over and play with Riley until she got back.

Jeffery was still angry. He made his way across the living room and stopped at the front door. "This door is swollen, M. You might want to do something about it." He gave the door a strong pull and opened it. He turned and scowled at Falco and left.

"Fuck you," she said under her breath and took a swallow of the coffee.

Jeffery had made the coffee way too strong; she downed the rest, making a face. She sat on her sofa and turned on the TV, looking for the weather forecast. It was ten and the local news was on. The McCaffery story was the top news item. The TV station ran footage of Amy Hollander, the police spokesperson who handled the department's statement to the press. The report included a brief interview with Chief Lassiter, followed by a live feed outside Northwestern University Hospital. Andie's condition was still critical.

Falco put her head in her hands and looked at the coffee table. Her eyes fixed on the postcard announcing Andie's exhibition; it would have been tonight. She picked it up and stared at it, remembering the look on Andie's face the morning she had come by the station. She thought about the tie Andie had bought Ballard and what he had said in the car. "I've gotta get going," she said out loud, shaking her thoughts away. Rain was in the forecast. She thought about what Sam would want to do instead of spending the day at Navy Pier.

She closed and locked the front door with a thud. It was sticking, but she wasn't going to deal with it right now. She made her way across the front yard to the Fergusons' and knocked on the door.

Riley answered. "Hi, Mrs. Schuler. Wow, Thunder Crash Car III rocks!" he said, opening the door for Falco. His mother, Megan, smiled seeing Falco. "Hey, lady. I never see you anymore. How's life?" Megan asked.

"Busy, just busy," Falco sighed. "Megan, I've got to run to work for an hour or so, and then I need to stop off—"

"You need me to watch Sam?" she said, knowing what she was going to ask.

"If it's okay, if you don't have plans for the next two hours…two hours max."

"We don't have anything planned. Danny's working on the car in the garage, so we're not going anywhere," Megan said with a smile.

"Great," Falco said. She followed the noise of the video game into Riley's room. She bent down and told Sam she'd be back in two hours. He nodded, not taking his eyes off the TV. Falco smiled at Megan, thanked her, and made her way toward her car.

CHAPTER 48

The first floor of the twenty-third district was noisy for a Saturday. The front desk phone was ringing faster than the receptionist could pick it up. A ragged group of homeless teenagers argued loudly with two uniformed cops. Falco entered, swept past the teens, and climbed the stairs to the second floor. She was tired. As she reached her department, a hush preceded her as she made her way to her desk. She felt the stares with every step.

Ballard was at his desk looking sheepish, still stung from their confrontation the day before. He glanced at Falco as she sat at her desk. "You all right?" he asked, getting up and leaning over his cubicle to Falco's.

She looked at him as if she didn't notice he was there. "Yeah, I'm okay."

"Fulbright is still critical, didja hear?" he said quietly.

"I know."

Two uniformed cops strolled by and stared at Falco. She gave them a pierced look. She rubbed her forehead and scanned her desk. Ballard had finished their report; it was waiting on Falco's desk.

"Is this the report?" she asked.

"I was here early so I took a stab at it," Ballard said, making it sound like he had done her a favor.

She looked at it, thumbed through the pages, and eyed Ballard's signature at the bottom. "I'm supposed to sign this?" she asked, looking up at him.

"Yeah. Lassiter wants us both—"

"No, JB. This is a draft, not a final copy," she said, sounding bitchy.

Ballard looked uncomfortable. "Well, I thought…"

"I'm *not* gonna sign this," she said, her eyes darting around the pages. She started marking up the report with a pen, circling text and correcting grammar. Ballard looked at his watch, sat down at his desk, and sighed.

Falco was in a dark mood. She didn't want to be at work and hated the attention she was getting. Lassiter came by and stood at her desk. She was still going over the report, pen in hand. She spotted Lassiter's khaki pants and looked up.

"Hey, Falco, how's that hand?" he said, smiling. Falco didn't return the smile. She looked down at the report and said firmly, "It's fine, sir."

"Are you almost done with that?" he asked, referring to the now scribbled-up report.

"I'm working on it," she said flatly.

Lassiter peered over at Ballard, who gave him an annoyed look and shrugged.

"What do you say, Falco? Ten minutes?" Lassiter asked.

She gave him a weary look. "Um…fifteen," she said, wiggling her mouse and looking at her computer screen.

"Great," Lassiter said and walked down the hall.

Falco put her head in her hands and sighed. She found Ballard's report on a shared document file and made corrections and changes. Ten minutes later the printer whirled and she eyed the revised copy. She drummed her pen on her desk and made more changes to the printed copy. Ballard waited and ran his fingers through his hair. His stomach growled.

The printer whirled again, and the final draft of the report was complete. Falco read through it once more and handed it to Ballard to read.

"Oh, that's okay. I'll just sign it. I'm sure it's perfect," Ballard said, reaching for his pen.

"Read it. If you're going to sign the damn thing, you'd better read it!" Falco snapped.

Ballard's face flushed. He sat down quickly and read through the report. Falco gazed at Sam's picture and felt a pang of anxiety. She looked at her watch. It was almost eleven, and she had promised Megan she would only be two hours.

Lassiter returned and saw Ballard sign the document. He handed it to the chief, who scanned it and said to Falco, "Were you an English major in college?"

"It was my minor," she said quietly.

"This is good, Falco. Detailed yet to the point," he said, signing it and turning the paper toward Falco for her signature.

Falco looked at the page and the blank line that awaited her signature. She stared at it, hesitating, thinking. Lassiter waited patiently.

"You're not going to make more changes are you?" Ballard whined, standing up to leave.

She didn't respond. Chief Lassiter pulled out a pen from the left pocket of his shirt and held it for Falco. She continued to stare at the document. Lassiter was growing impatient and leaned on her desk. "You okay, Falco?" he asked, growing concerned. He had never seen her behave this way.

Falco quickly got up from her chair and said loudly, "Why is everybody so fucking worried about me?" She shot a dirty look around the room and then at Lassiter. She snatched the pen from him and quickly signed her name to the report, then pushed it at Lassiter and placed the pen on top. He stepped back at her brisk response, surprised and dismayed. She shut down her computer, snatched up the navy sweater from her desk, and stormed out, whispering to herself.

She got in her car and lit up her last cigarette. She cursed the empty pack.

CHAPTER 49

The hospital parking lot was busier than during the workweek. Falco had to park on the roof of the parking structure. The sun was blistering; she looked up at the sky and put on her sunglasses. It felt like rain was coming on. She walked quickly to the elevator and made a mental note where she had parked. She made her way through the busy corridors and took an elevator to the eighth floor, intensive care. Stopping at the desk, she felt a surge of dread as she recalled her father's illness and his subsequent stroke and death. "I hate hospitals. God, the sanitized smell," she whispered.

"Can I help you?" asked a middle-aged woman with red hair.

"I'm here to see Andrea Fulbright."

"Is she here in ICU?" asked the woman as she scrolled through names on her computer screen.

"Yes," Falco said quietly.

"She's in surgery. You'll have to wait on the fifth floor."

"Surgery?" Falco asked weakly.

"Fifth floor," said the woman.

Falco felt pangs of panic; she turned and walked back to the elevators. She pressed the button for the fifth floor. The doors opened to the fifth floor surgery family waiting area, as they had the night before. The bright corridors were now familiar as was the artwork that hung on the walls. She entered the large waiting area. Michael saw her immediately and waved. Falco walked quickly to him.

"I tried to call you, but I got your voicemail," he said, looking concerned.

"Is Andie okay? What's going on?"

"More bleeding."

Falco shook her head. She sat on the loveseat and unbuttoned her light-green cotton jacket, revealing the brightly colored shirt underneath.

Michael took her hand. "Sometimes this happens…more bleeding. The good thing is her blood pressure has stabilized."

Falco nodded, looking down at the carpet. "I can't stay long. Sam and I have plans for the afternoon."

Michael smiled. "Did he like the game?"

Falco smiled back and gave him a nod. She looked sad for a moment and then looked away. She thought about how sweet Michael was—sincere, caring, funny. She was glad to know him. Her thoughts turned to Jeffery, and pangs of anger returned.

Michael studied her, tilting his head to make eye contact. She looked back at him and then avoided his eyes. "I've never seen you in street clothes—I mean, normal street clothes," he said with a smile. "You look really nice." Falco smiled and managed a laugh, embarrassed. "No, really! A little color does wonders for you," he said, looking at her intently.

Her eyes filled up with tears. "Michael, you're so sweet," she said in almost a whisper.

"Hey, I didn't mean to make you cry!" He put his arm around her.

She wiped her eyes with a tissue and looked down. "I just had a bad morning…with my ex. Then I got to the station and everyone was worried, staring at me…like if…well…I just…" She cut herself off and rubbed the back of her neck then looked at the floor and sighed. "And then with Andie… I guess I let myself get too close, and I shouldn't have."

"You should take some time off, girl. Get some sleep, get a massage," Michael said, hugging her again and giving her a playful shake.

CHAPTER 50

Navy Pier and her time with Sam took Falco's mind off Andie and her guilt about the abduction and memories of the dreadful crime scene. On Sunday night she drove Sam back to Jeffery's and bought another pack of cigarettes on her way home. She thought again about quitting the force. She wondered what it would be like to be a full-time mother like Megan.

Monday morning came too soon, and Falco thought about taking the day off. Her head was heavy with the events of the past three days, but she decided to go to work anyway. Traffic was unusually light for a Monday morning. The day was set to be another hot one, steamy with a chance of afternoon thunderstorms, possibly heavy.

She made her way to her desk, seeing Steve Grasky and Ballard. They both waved good morning, but she barely noticed. Ballard came by with a cinnamon roll in hand saying, "Morning, Falco. Somebody brought these in. Want me to get you one?"

She looked at him as if he were an alien being. "No, no, thanks, Ballard."

She riffled through her desk looking for aspirin and came across the gift Andie had bought for Ballard. Ballard was busy munching on the roll when Falco leaned over with the box. "Hey, I forgot about this," she said, handing him the gift. He eyed it and looked at Falco, thinking she was giving him a peace offering. He wiped his sticky fingers on a napkin and stood up to take the present. People in nearby cubicles looked over and made jokes.

"It's not your birthday, is it, Ballard?"

"Hey! I want a present too!"

"Hey, Falco! What'd you bring for me?"

Falco sighed. "Ballard, it's not from me," she said plainly, giving him a pierced look.

Everyone looked at the two detectives, waiting for Ballard to open the gift. It appeared that most of the department had heard about Falco's run-in with Ballard Friday night and assumed she was giving him the gift to make amends. Falco glanced at the others, who were gawking around Ballard. She shook her head and sat at her desk. "It's not from me, folks," she said to the room.

Ballard unwrapped the gift, ignoring the attached note. He opened the box, and his eyes narrowed as he saw the tie. He pulled it out of the box, draped it over his hand, and whistled. "This is a beauty!" He held it up for the others to see. Guys from the adjoining desks admired the tie, telling Ballard he'd have to get a whole new wardrobe to measure up.

Grasky came by Falco's desk and quipped, "Ballard sure is lucky to have you as his partner."

Falco said firmly, "It's *not* from me."

She stood up from her desk and looked at Ballard. "Isn't there a card attached somewhere, JB?" He gently placed the tie in its box, eyeing it once more, and looked for a card. It had fallen to the floor. He picked it up and read it. His face went pale.

Detective Ballard,

Sorry I ruined your tie. Hope this one is a worthy replacement.

Best,

Andrea Fulbright

CHAPTER 51

Grasky and Falco convened to review Grasky's progress on the child abduction case and the suspects on the West Side. "Dead ends, Falco," admitted Grasky, chewing a wad of gum.

Later that day, the two detectives were to meet up with other law enforcement departments in the area that were working on the case. Local politicians continued to apply pressure to the police to break the case and locate the missing children.

Falco was finding it hard to focus, haunted by the images of Andie and the sounds of gunfire in her head. She shook the thoughts away.

Lassiter stopped her as she and Grasky were leaving for the meeting. "Just to let you two know, Katherine Cohen, the owner of the Cohen Sloan Gallery, has filed a civil suit against our department and the feds," he said quietly. "Our legal department is looking at it. They think we'll be cleared, but who knows."

Falco suppressed a flash of anger in her face. "God, I hate that woman," she said under her breath.

* * *

Grasky drove the police vehicle west on Irving Park Road and headed north to the Kennedy Expressway. Falco was quiet, processing the news of the lawsuit and whether Internal Affairs would be snooping around the case. Her stomach was in knots, and she was getting a headache.

"Hey, Falco, you okay?" asked Grasky. "You don't look very happy."

"I'm okay. You're about the tenth person to ask me that in the last day or so." She rubbed her neck and avoided his eyes.

"Did you ever think about talking to someone? You know like somebody from EAP or peer support?"

Falco sighed and didn't respond right away. "Maybe…maybe I should check into that," she said in a noncommittal tone. "I might be able to help," shrugged Grasky.

The meeting was at the Glencoe police station. The familiar faces from the FBI were there; Special Agent Fred Tedeschi was there as was Brenda Salerno. She smiled seeing Falco and grabbed a seat next to her. "Hey, Monica baby," she said, smiling broadly. Falco gave her a little smile and fumbled through her briefcase then pulled out a pen and a legal pad. "Any news on the profiler gig?" she whispered.

Falco shook her head. She scanned her notes and flicked her ballpoint pen.

Grasky sidled up next to Falco, scooting in his chair with a loud groan. The meeting began with lots of questions.

"Do we have descriptions of any of the suspects?" asked a rookie agent.

"Have we checked recent parolees who are sex offenders?" asked a burly detective from the south suburbs.

Special Agent Tedeschi moved to the back of the room and held up his hands. "I know we all have a lot of questions, all of which will be answered in one form or another with everyone's reports. Let's hear from CPD first. Detective Grasky?

Grasky reviewed their meager progress on their suspects while Falco stared at her legal pad. Her mind wandered to Andie and then to Kat, then to the bloody crime scene. Gunshots echoed in her head, then she recalled the clickity-clack of her gun as it tumbled down the embankment. Suddenly the room darkened and she looked up. Agent Tedeschi turned on the laptop and overhead projector and began to review mug shots of suspects near the locations of where the four children had disappeared. Falco chewed the end of her pen, trying to concentrate.

Tedeschi droned on and on. Brenda Salerno leaned into Falco. "God, this guy is so boring."

Falco nodded. She barely noticed. Mentally she was somewhere else.

* * *

Grasky and Falco returned to the station with no fresh leads. Wiretaps were in process for the suspects they had interviewed that rainy Friday, and the two detectives planned to question them again. The good news was that no more children were missing; the bad news was they had nothing to go on. Falco glanced at the clock as she returned to her desk. It was nearly four thirty. She grabbed her raincoat and briefcase and waved goodnight to Ballard, who was on the phone.

Ballard held up his hand for her to wait. He hung up the phone, leaned over his cubicle, and said, "You know, I feel really bad about what I said the other day…you know, about Andrea Fulbright."

Falco gave him a blank stare and said flatly, "I can't help you with that, JB" and walked away.

Ballard hung his head. That wasn't the response he'd wanted. He thought he knew her. They'd been partners for almost two years, he thought. He sat down at his desk, shook his head, and thought, *Falco is tough, but what's this all about?*

CHAPTER 52

Kat was riding the elevator to the eighth floor. It stopped on three and Michael got on. "Hey, Kat," he said quietly, avoiding her eyes.

"Have you been up to see her yet?" she asked Michael.

"No, but Alan said she's the same."

Kat nodded. They got off the elevator and walked toward the reception desk. Michael stopped and stood motionless, looking at the floor. Kat, seeing he was no longer walking with her, turned around to see where he was. He was still looking at the floor; something was on his mind.

"Michael?" she said, walking back toward him. "Aren't you coming?"

Michael shook his head and looked at Kat suspiciously. "How's the show going?"

Her eyes avoided his. "Uh, it's going well...*very* well."

"I thought you were going to cancel it," he said, anger rising in his voice.

"I thought about it, but I have a lot of expenses, Michael."

He looked up at the ceiling trying to hold his tongue.

"I had to pay Mario…and…and…I did cancel the opening."

He gave her an angry look. "Well, I guess you'll sell a few of Andie's paintings, and you won't go in the hole. And with Andie clinging to life, I guess it'll be a good investment opportunity for you. So why *would* you cancel the show?"

Kat gasped. Her mouth hung open in surprise. "Michael! How could you even…?" She walked toward him.

"I know how it works," he said bitterly. "Artist dies and the work doubles in price!"

Kat stomped closer to him. "You fucking asshole! How could you insinuate…how *could* you?" She glared at him.

A couple of people at the reception desk stood up and gave the two startled looks. Michael glared back, then turned and walked away.

"Michael!" Kat yelled after him as he hurried down the hall at a good clip.

* * *

Falco stopped by the hospital and took the elevator to the eighth floor. She had been depressed all day and knew coming here wouldn't help matters. She checked in at the reception desk; the red-haired woman remembered her. "You're the police officer," she said, smiling. She checked her visitor's list and said, "There's someone up there now. She just arrived. You'll have to wait a few minutes—maybe twenty if she stays the entire time. Only one visitor is allowed at a time in the ICU."

Falco nodded. It was probably either Aisha or Kat, neither of whom she wanted to see. She backed away from the desk and said she'd try tomorrow. As much as she didn't want to be there, she wanted to see Andie, to make sure in her own mind that she was still alive.

She waited for the elevator to take her to the first floor. She fingered the pack of cigarettes in her coat pocket. She thought about the child abduction case, Kat's lawsuit, and Ballard's tie.

"Detective Falco? Detective Falco?" came the voice, almost in singsong. It was soft at first, and then the voice grew louder and someone was touching her shoulder. Falco jerked out of her thoughts and looked up toward the voice. Smiling at her was Dr. Forrest.

"I wasn't sure I had the right person. You sure look like the Detective Falco I know, but you weren't answering," he said with a laugh.

Falco tried to hide her distraction. "Oh, hi, Dr. Forrest. I guess I was… thinking or something."

"You sure were," he said kindly. "Off somewhere?"

"I was here to see Andie, but it appears she has a visitor. I'll try again tomorrow. Is there any change?"

Dr. Forrest shook his head grimly. "Not really. She's still not breathing on her own, but at least we've controlled the bleeding." Falco looked sad and shook her head. "Michael's been keeping you posted, like I'd asked, hasn't he?" Dr. Forrest asked, turning his head and bending down a bit to get a better look at Falco.

"Yes," she said.

He paused and gave her a long look. She glanced at him then looked away. "Well, it was nice seeing you Dr. Forrest. I've got to get home." She backed away and punching the button for the elevator.

He nodded, brushed her shoulder with his hand, and gave her a serious look. "Take care of yourself, Detective."

She glanced back and got into the elevator before the doors closed.

CHAPTER 53

Two days later Michael's phone calls had become less frequent. *I guess nothing's changed*, Falco thought. Over the last few days she couldn't shake her sadness. She couldn't sleep but resisted drinking, not wanting to get in the habit of needing alcohol to relax, and sleeping pills weren't her style. She was restless and had developed a cough from the cigarettes. Every day seemed to require more and more effort to get things accomplished at work and at home. The front door was still stuck, and the laundry was piling up.

"Get a grip," she said to her reflection while getting ready for work. It had been one week since McCaffery had kidnapped and brutally beaten Andie, leaving her for dead. It seemed like a month to Falco.

Sam was leaving for camp on Saturday afternoon, and Falco planned to go to Jeffery's house to see him off. She had called Jeffery two days earlier, asking whether Sam needed anything for his trip, but Jeffery didn't return her call.

At the station her desk was a mess, files were piled high, and a stack of messages awaited her attention. Grasky waved as he passed her and said he'd be back to talk as soon as he'd made copies. Falco looked at her watch; she'd come in late. It was almost ten a.m.

Her phone rang, startling her. It was Lassiter asking to see her in his office. She sighed and got up from her chair and headed down the hall.

Lassiter was taking another phone call as she appeared in the doorway. He motioned for her to come in. She hovered around his desk then looked out the glass window that enclosed his office.

Lassiter got off the phone. "Please, have a seat, Detective." He moved around his desk and quietly closed the door. He sat down at his desk and peered at Falco. He took a deep breath and said, "Falco, I'm gonna be real honest with you. I'm a little worried about you. I know it's only been a week since that whole McCaffery business went down, but I've gotta tell you, you're carrying something real heavy here, and it's not good for you."

Falco gave him a serious look then avoided his eyes. "Well, sir, I've been a bit stressed out lately. My ex has been…difficult." She rubbed the back of her neck. She sighed and paused to collect her thoughts.

"Look, Falco. It isn't just me who's noticed. A lot of folks around here have come to me with concerns about you."

"Who came to you?" Falco, said sitting forward in her chair and feeling threatened.

"I'm not going to get into that, Detective." He paused and said, "The reason we're having this conversation is that I want to make you aware of our Employee Assistance Program, and I want to encourage you to take advantage of it. There are some very good people on staff there, and they're useful for situations like this."

Sulking, Falco looked down and said softly, "I know about the program, Chief." She shifted uncomfortably in her seat, her face pinched.

Lassiter got up from his desk and leaned against the front of it, arms folded. "Let's face it, Monica. You've been distracted lately. You haven't spoken to anyone except Grasky and maybe Ballard. You've come in looking depressed and worn out, and someone said you've taken up cigarettes again. I know it was hard for you to quit a couple of years ago." He stopped himself and added, "Of course your cigarette smoking is none of my business."

Falco rubbed her eyes and cupped her mouth in her hand. She shook her head and said softly, "You're right. I know you're right." She fought back a wave of regret and sadness.

Lassiter looked concerned and finally said, "Why don't you take the rest of the day off? Go do something fun. Go to the beach. Get some sun. I don't know."

Falco nodded, not looking up. She bit her fingernail and looked at the floor. Another moment passed, and she was still silent.

"Falco?" Lassiter said.

"Okay, sir." She got up from the chair. "Anything else, sir?" she said, glancing at him and looking pissed.

"No."

She turned and walked back to her desk. She shut her computer down and walked past Grasky's desk, where he was waiting to have their meeting. She came by, avoiding his eyes, and said, "I need to get out of here, Steve. Can we do this on Monday?"

Without a reply she walked away and headed downstairs and out of the building. Grasky watched as she walked through the rows of cubicles and desks and toward the stairwell. Others watched her too, thinking, *she never leaves early.*

* * *

Falco drove south on Lake Shore Drive toward the hospital. She was smoking a cigarette and feeling sick to her stomach. Lassiter's conversation had come out of nowhere, she thought. "I'm really okay. I am," she said out loud. She looked at the cigarette in her hand, made a face, and tossed it out the window. "That's it," she said.

At the hospital she took the elevator to the eighth floor. There was a different person at the reception desk; a young Latina named Claudia with large hoop earrings. Claudia checked the list for Falco's name and gave her a visitor's pass. Falco slowly walked down the hall to the glass-enclosed ICU. She opened the door and showed her pass to an African-American volunteer who smiled and directed her to Andie's room.

She entered the room and immediately felt pangs of sadness. Andie had a large tube in her mouth that was attached to a machine that helped her breathe. Another tube ran through her nose, and another was attached to an IV that connected to other tubes that carried more liquids from IV bags. Yet another tube collected urine that drained near the foot of the bed. A machine tracked her heartbeat, and another monitored her blood pressure.

Falco's eyes drifted over Andie as she took a seat in the lone plastic chair next to the bed. It was the first time she had seen her since that rainy Friday. Andie was pale; bandages were fixed to her forehead and on the side of her bruised face. Her left arm was immobilized at a right angle with splints and bandages covering the puncture wounds from the barbed wire. Her face appeared expressionless, and her eyelids hung half open. The ventilator rhythmically pushed air into her lungs, making a wet squishing sound.

Falco leaned closer and gently put her hand on Andie's shoulder. "Hey, Andie, it's me, Detective Falco – uh…Monica. I've…I've missed you." A deep sadness swelled inside her. She covered her mouth with her hand to stifle the emotions and fumbled for a tissue in her pocket. Her breath caught in her throat, "Andie, listen to me. I wish I could fix this. I should have tried… Jesus…to stop him. I feel so horrible. You didn't deserve this. I hope you'll forgive me."

She began to cry again and put her face in her hands. After a few moments, the waves of sadness softened, and her thoughts drifted to the first time she had seen Andie, almost two weeks before, scruffy and sweaty, her hair full of sawdust. Then she pictured her on her boat, head bleeding and out of sorts, and later that morning after her workout.

Falco leaned in close. "I remember when you came into the living room after you worked out. You looked so strong, *so strong*. I know you can get through this. I know you can, Andie," she said desperately. She looked at Andie's body; it was so still, so seemingly thin and fragile. Falco sat up straight and then slumped in the chair. She stared at the floor and said, "It's all my fault. Kat was right to say that. I screwed up the interview. I pushed you too hard. I was the one who caused you to panic out there."

She rested her head on her hands and tried to process the past week. "What's happened to me?" she whispered. "Why I am so wound up about this? What the hell is going on?" She shook her head and stared at the floor.

A tiny knock came at the glass door. Falco was lost in thought and barely heard it. The door opened slowly with a swish of air. It was Dr. Forrest. Falco quickly lifted her head from her hands; her hair dangled in her face.

"We meet again," Dr. Forrest said with a smile.

"Hi, Doc," she said as she fished through her pockets, found the pass, and got up to leave.

"Oh, you don't have to leave yet," he said. "I'm just going to be a minute, checking vitals."

"No, I really need to go. My son is leaving for camp tomorrow, and I'm going to see him off...and I..." She was starting to ramble and stopped herself.

Watching Falco, Dr. Forrest smiled, flipped open Andie's chart, and made notes from the machines.

"Any change?" she asked quietly.

"Not really. Her progress is slow, but there's a lot going on..." His words drifted off as he made notes in Andie's chart.

"I'd better go," she said, grabbing her purse from the floor next to the chair. She scanned Andie's body as if to say goodbye for now.

Dr. Forrest closed the chart and tucked it under his arm. He took a step toward Falco as she approached the door. "Just a minute, Detective," he said. She stopped, growing uneasy and waited. "I don't mean to pry, but I can't help notice a change in you after all that's happened. You seem troubled, sullen."

Falco's body tightened, and she looked down. "I know what you're going to say, Doctor. I've already had this conversation—today, as a matter of fact. I know all about it," she said tersely. She turned, opened the glass door, and hurried out.

CHAPTER 54

Falco gave her front door a good push; it opened reluctantly. It was one thirty, and the rest of the day was wide open. She looked around her living room. Mail was piled on the coffee table next to a week's worth of the *Chicago Tribune*. She sorted through her bills and junk mail and gathered the newspapers, unbundling them from their rubber bands and flattening them out for the recycling bag. Saturday's paper caught her eye. The headline read, "Woman Kidnapped and Brutally Assaulted." She scanned the article. Her name and Ballard's were mentioned as well as Katherine Cohen and the Cohen Sloan Gallery.

Falco sighed as she glanced through the article and read the official police statement on McCaffery's death. She shook her head and put the paper in the stack and dumped it into a blue bag. She sat on her sofa, took off her holster, and switched on the TV. CNN was airing a news conference with the president. She zoned out looking at the screen, then turned off the TV. She got up and looked out the front window. The front porch swing gently drifted back and forth in the summer breeze.

It was almost two when Falco walked into the kitchen, opened the refrigerator, and pulled out a bottle of Chardonnay. She uncorked the bottle and poured some wine into a glass. She walked across the living room, grabbed the doorknob of the front door, and gave it a good pull. The sun had warmed the smooth wood of the swing. She sat down and took a long sip. The wind softly blew through her hair; it felt nice. In the distance she heard the groan of a lawn mower.

* * *

Falco woke up on the sofa. The sun was beaming into the living room. She looked at her watch; it was eight a.m. The TV was blaring some cheesy sci-fi movie. She glared at the screen, fumbled for the remote, and turned it off. Her half-eaten dinner was still on the coffee table as was a copy of the *Chicago Tribune*. "When did I turn on the TV? God, I don't remember what I did last night…eating this food," she whispered, rubbing her stiff neck.

She got up and stumbled forward, feeling dizzy, then she remembered Sam was leaving for camp at noon. "I'd better get a move on, maybe call Michael to see how Andie is," she said quietly. She went to the kitchen to make some coffee and picked up the warm bottle of Chardonnay. She held it up and looked through the green glass. "Most of the bottle…not good," she muttered. "That would explain the headache, stupid," she scolded herself. Her stomach didn't feel that great either.

* * *

The gold Camry was steaming hot when Falco got in. She opened the doors on both sides and waited for the hot air to drift out. Megan Ferguson waved hello, saying something about having seen her name in the *Trib* last week. Falco smiled and started the engine. She made her way west on Devon Avenue toward Park Ridge.

Jeffery's truck was parked in the driveway. The front door of the house was open, and Sam was dragging a duffle bag down the stairs. He waved as he saw Falco's car. She got out and saw Jeffery, who was walking down the front stairs with Sam's backpack and sleeping bag. Sam ran to his mother and gave her a big hug. She bent down and kissed him on the cheek.

"All set?" she asked as she ran her fingers through his hair and studied his face.

"Yep! Dad took me shopping yesterday for a flashlight and a canteen," he said, his face beaming.

Jeffery came over and plopped the sleeping bag on the ground and handed the backpack to Sam.

"Are you taking him to the bus?"

"No, the Desais are picking him up."

"Who are they?" Falco asked, squinting at him, her hand shading her eyes from the sun.

"We know them from Boy Scouts," Jeffery said, barely looking at her.

She sat on the front steps and waited with Sam. Jeffery left them alone and went to talk with his neighbor.

"Are you excited, sweetie?" Falco asked, smiling.

She loved to look at him; she could see her father in his face and in his mannerisms. Even when her father was ill, suffering from liver failure, a child-like spark appeared in his eyes. He would lean in close to Falco and whisper some secret to her. She chased the memory away and watched Sam as he talked.

"It's gonna be so great, Mom. There's a lake, and we can go fishing and canoeing, and there's a tree house and…"

Falco's eye caught sight of a black Saab that was slowing down in front of the house. Jeffery waved and turned to Sam. "Let's go buddy. Your friend is here!"

Falco felt surge of panic. It was too soon; she wasn't ready to say good-bye yet. Sam got up and snatched up his backpack. He ran over to the black car as it pulled behind Falco's. She got up from the steps and made her way toward the car. Jeffery introduced Falco to the Desais as he helped Sam put his things in their trunk.

Sam ran to Falco to say goodbye. "Have a good time, okay?" she said, trying not to let her voice crack.

Sam hugged Jeffery then piled into the car with his friend. Mr. Desai waved, saying, "It was nice meeting you, Monica!" He pulled the car out from the driveway and headed out to the street. Falco watched the car as it disappeared into traffic.

"Come on inside out of the heat," Jeffery said. Falco followed him as he opened the door. "Coffee?" he asked.

"No, thanks," Falco said.

"Want something to eat? I can make you an omelet," he said, sitting down at the dining room table.

"*You're* gonna cook for *me*?" she asked, smiling.

"Sure! I've gotten more…domestic in my old age. It comes from taking care of a growing boy," he said, ending his sentence with a scowl.

"I'm sorry. Cooking isn't my thing either. I'm the last person who should say that to you." She looked down with a frown.

Jeffery got up and looked down at Falco. "I'm not gonna tell you that you look tired, but you look tired." He moved behind her and put his hands on her shoulders and began to massage them.

Falco gasped; she closed her eyes and put her head down. "Oh, god. My neck is so stiff," she said.

"Yeah, well, you've got a nice knot in your shoulder." He continued to massage her shoulders and moved down her back.

"Jesus," she moaned. He leaned close and pulled her hair to one side and kissed her neck. He kissed her again and breathed softly into her ear. Falco sighed. Her mouth opened slightly as she quietly moaned.

Jeffery came around in front of her and kneeled. He ran his hands up her shoulders and cupped the back of her neck with one hand, bringing her close. He kissed her softly. Falco opened her eyes and looked at him. He caressed the side of her face with his hand, lightly touching her jaw. He looked at her intently and kissed her again, this time deeper. She breathed softly and pulled him close, responding, parting her lips and opening her mouth as her tongue found his. Their breathing grew faster, as did their kisses, their tongues touching and intertwining. Falco ran her hands up the side of Jeffery's ribs and under his shirt, feeling his strong back. He lifted her from the chair and guided her into the bedroom.

The bedroom was dark and cool. Jeffery pulled her close again and unbuttoned her shirt then unfastened her bra. It fell to the floor along with her top. He clutched greedily at her breasts, sucking on her nipples until she gasped, breathing faster and faster. He took her in his arms and laid her on the bed. She unbuckled her belt and peeled off her jeans and panties. Jeffery dragged off his clothes and climbed on top of her. He was warm and smelled of sweat and soap. He kissed her deeply and moaned as he explored her body with his mouth. He caressed her inner thighs and touched her; she was wet. She winced at the touch. He maneuvered up and gently penetrated her.

Their bodies became one, as they had so often in the past. Their love-making was rhythmic and explosive. Falco's body arched into Jeffery's in an electric jolt of ecstasy. He rocked her faster and deeper as she quickly came once more. She cried out, clenching his pulsing back, as tears ran down her face. Jeffery held her close, surprised at her tears. She let go and relaxed in his arms, her heart rattling in her chest. He looked deep into her face and brushed her tears away. "You're crying, babe," he whispered softly, looking concerned.

"No…no, I'm not crying," she said breathlessly.

He held her as their bodies calmed. Jeffery lay back on the bed, and Falco moved closer, putting her arm around his sweaty chest and feeling safe.

* * *

"Hey," Jeffery said softly. "M?" He shook her gently and moved out from under her arm. She slowly opened her eyes. "I'm gonna get some water. Do you want anything?" he asked with a gentle smile.

"No…no," she mumbled.

Jeffery left for the kitchen. Falco pulled his pillow over and let her head sink into it. When he returned, she was breathing deeply, sound asleep. He looked at her for a moment and smiled, then gently pulled the blankets that had fallen to the floor over her. He sat at the side of the bed and studied her, then softly kissed her hair.

It was almost six p.m. and Falco was still asleep. Jeffery climbed in next to her and shook her gently. "M? Wake up, M. Hey," he said softly. She barely stirred.

"Come on, sleepy. It's almost six," he gently coaxed. Falco lifted her head and opened her eyes slightly. She rolled onto her back and rubbed her forehead. "Hey, it's almost six," he said again. "Boy, you really passed out."

"Six o'clock?" she groaned. "I'd better get going." She pulled the blankets away.

"You hungry? I've got two beautiful steaks. How 'bout I make them with a couple of baked potatoes?"

Falco thought a minute, still sleepy, and said, "Okay, that would be nice, really nice. I'm starved."

Jeffery smiled. "I was going to run out to the store while you were asleep, but I was afraid you'd wake up and cut out on me."

Falco smiled and absentmindedly searched for her clothes. Jeffery had folded them neatly and put them on his dresser. She washed her face and brushed her hair, not spending too much time in front of the mirror. She was feeling chilly and fished around in Jeffery's closet for a sweater or shirt. She found a plaid flannel shirt and put it on and rolled up the sleeves.

Jeffery was busy salting and peppering the steaks. She came around him from behind and put her arms around him and buried her face in his back. Jeffery smiled and said, "Careful, careful. I've got a weapon!" Falco smiled and drifted to the kitchen counter, where she watched him prepare the food.

They ate and talked mostly about Sam. Jeffery brought out some pictures from Sam's last two soccer games. Falco smiled as she looked at them. "He's getting so big."

Jeffery smiled. "Yeah, pretty soon he'll want a cell phone and won't want to talk to either of us."

Falco frowned, not relishing the thought.

CHAPTER 55

The next morning, Falco arrived at the station early. The station was practically empty—no Ballard or Grasky. She looked up the number for the Employee Assistance Program and made an appointment for Tuesday at four p.m. She craved a cigarette. Thoughts of the weekend entered her mind: Sam swinging his backpack over his shoulder and heading for the car; making love with Jeffery; Andie's frail body; her conversation with Lassiter.

By the time she and Grasky gathered for their meeting, she was feeling a little better. Even Ballard noticed. "She actually said more than two words to me," he whispered to himself as he took a sip from his coffee mug.

The phone taps on the suspects on the West Side were in place, and Grasky was encouraged by the results. Falco and Grasky were planning to visit the two later that day.

Officer Tim Strickland searched the second-floor cubicles looking for Falco. He found her sitting with Grasky at his desk. "Hey, Detective Falco," he said, hesitating as he approached. "Uh, I don't know if you heard about it, but there's going to be a thing for Ms. Fulbright at the Cohen Sloan Gallery on Wednesday night."

Falco looked up at him from her chair and shook her head. "What kind of *thing*?"

Strickland shrugged. "I don't know. Some kind of service or something. I guess Ms. Cohen is having it. Michael told me about it. It's at seven."

Falco felt a surge of fear. Had something happened to Andie that she didn't know about? She hadn't heard a word from Michael. She got up from the desk and looked Strickland square in the eye. "What are you talking about? Is Andie all right?" A look of panic crossed her face.

Strickland backed up. "No, no. I mean, yes, as far as I know. I ran into Michael over the weekend, and he told me about it. I guess Ms. Cohen closed the gallery last week. She's going to open it Wednesday night with some kind of service—or something—for Ms. Fulbright. I don't know what he called it." Strickland was getting nervous, not knowing how to explain himself or how to react to the look on Falco's face.

"Michael told you?" she asked.

"Yes. It's at seven on Wednesday," he said, backing up.

Falco thought for a moment. "Thanks for letting me know, Strickland." She wondered why Michael hadn't told her about the service. Maybe she wasn't invited.

* * *

On Tuesday, Falco found the address of the EAP office on West Irving. It was next to the Lincoln Diner, a local dive with a huge portrait of Abraham Lincoln painted on the side of the building. She entered and was directed by the receptionist to take the elevator to the fourth floor. The offices were run-down, with gray carpet and sticky-looking vinyl chairs. The elevator wasn't much better. Its doors slid open with a clatter and closed behind Falco as she got in. She pressed the yellowish button for the fourth floor. All was quiet. She looked up at the numbers above wondering if the elevator was actually moving or just sitting at ground level. She pressed the button again. The elevator rumbled as it ascended.

The doors bumped open to a brighter, less-dingy waiting area. Another receptionist gave Falco a clipboard with a short form attached to it and a pen. "Maggie will be with you in a moment. Just have a seat."

Falco sat down impatiently, picked up a magazine from the coffee table, then tossed it back on the table. She was trying not to be nervous and fidgeted with her cell phone.

A door opened across the room. "Monica?" asked the woman. She appeared to be in her late thirties and wore funky linen pants, sandals, a boxy shirt, and big earrings.

Falco got up and said in a weak voice, "Hi."

"Come on in." The woman motioned with her hand. "I'm Maggie Simonds."

CHAPTER 56

It was Wednesday night, and the Cohen Sloan Gallery was set to open at six thirty. Kat wasn't sure what to call the event since Andie didn't have any official religious affiliation. She did have lots of friends, many of whom were members of the gay-friendly Ebenezer Lutheran Church on Foster Avenue in Andersonville, a neighborhood often called Girls' Town.

Andie attended their services occasionally, so choosing Reverend Phillips to speak seemed like a good choice. Kat's rabbi offered to speak too, but Kat didn't want the event to be overly religious. Candles, a word from Reverend Phillips and some friends, some music and wine were fitting.

The show was as Kat and Mario had left it upon finding Andie missing that Friday. Kat had Mario and Aisha set up the main gallery space with two sections of folding chairs facing a podium. Behind the podium was a blank white wall where pictures of Andie, her work, and her life would be projected. Greg Roth, a longtime friend of Kat and Andie, originally had produced the endless loop of photos and pictures for the exhibition. He arrived with an LCD projector and quietly set it up toward the back of the room.

Aisha, dressed in a flowing deep-blue dress, sat at the piano. She shuffled through the sheet music, stacking it and stashing it inside the seat of the piano bench. She played through the opening music, making sure Kat had the piano tuned. She saw her strained reflection in the black finish of the Steinway. She looked away and stared at the ceiling, feeling a deep wave of pain and loss.

Kat arranged the last of more than fifty candles that were positioned around the space. "Jesus, if these catch fire, I am done with," she whispered to herself. She adjusted the dimmers, leaving just enough light for people to safely enter the space. It was six o'clock. She told Mario and Aisha to start lighting the candles at six twenty-five; she'd open the doors at six thirty.

Reverend Phillips arrived, as did the cellist and oboist, who joined Aisha at the piano. Kat opened the box of printed programs for the service and placed a stack at each entrance. She gave a copy to the reverend, Aisha, and Greg, making sure each of them knew what they needed to do and when.

"Mario will bring up the dimmers just before we start. Aisha, that'll be your cue to start the music. Greg, give the music about twenty seconds and then start the images. After the music ends, I'll say a few words." Kat's voice caught in her throat. "Then Reverend Phillips, you'll go on and the rest will follow the program. Aisha, you'll end with the Nancy Rumble piece. Everyone got that?" They all nodded.

Kat was stressed out but managed to conceal it. She was wearing all black—a Vera Wang tie-front jacket with a matching flowing skirt accented by chunky white gold jewelry. Her dark lipstick added to her dramatic look, which offset the seeping sadness in her face.

She had hired wait staff to serve the wine, leaving Aisha free to play the piano. Aisha huddled with the handsome cellist and repeated a middle C as he tuned his instrument. The portly oboist looked on and fidgeted with his reed.

A tiny knock came at the glass door of the gallery. Mario ran to the door. It was Seiko, the bike messenger and a longtime friend of Andie. He was talking loudly through the glass.

Mario unlocked the door saying, "My man!" They shook hands and smiled.

"Can I stash my bike in back?" Seiko asked.

Mario looked at the bike; it was filthy. "Bring it around back. I'll open the loading dock door, and you can put it in the warehouse."

"Cool," said the young man.

Seiko's real name was Sean Harris. "Seiko was the nickname his fellow bike messengers had given him for his speedy, on-time delivery. "Like the watch," he would say, introducing himself. He was a stringy tall kid in his late twenties, with red hair spun into dreadlocks. He was an artist and a set designer but made his living on his battered blue Cannondale delivering documents and packages all over the city. Seiko guided his bike into the back and stashed his dingy backpack underneath. He made his way into the gallery space and spied Aisha, who gave him a little smile.

Seiko wore a thin cotton short-sleeved checkered shirt over a faded gray T-shirt. His tan cargo pants were cut at mid calf and frayed. He wore thick black socks with a scruffy pair of sky-blue Converse high tops. His nose and lips were host to numerous piercings, and his arms were a colorful map of cartoonlike tattoos. He grabbed a copy of the program and nodded nervously, then gave Mario an uneasy look. "I don't know what I'm going to say…yet."

Mario shrugged and pulled a lighter from his pocket and started to light the candles. It was almost six twenty-five. Seiko fished through the breast pocket of his shirt, found his lighter, and helped Mario. Kat whisked by, eyeing Seiko up and down and giving him an annoyed look.

"Hey, Kat, you are some piece of work in that dress!" Seiko said, eyes sparkling.

Kat kept walking. "Hurry up with those candles you two."

"She's got a nice ass," Seiko whispered to Mario.

It was six thirty-five, and people milled about the gallery door. Mario and Seiko finished lighting the candles. Kat appeared looking out of sorts, a tissue in her hand.

"Okay, everybody. Mario's going to dim the lights and then open the doors. Let's get this started." She spun around and made herself scarce. Aisha and the other two musicians took seats in the back.

CHAPTER 57

Falco found a parking spot a block away from the gallery. "Two quarter's enough?" asked Jeffery as he got out of the car and looked at the change in his hand.

"I think so," Falco said, slamming her door and hitting the alarm button.

Jeffery made his way around the car and put his arm around Falco. They crossed the street together. Jeffery's blue blazer and burgundy tie waved in the breeze. "Feels like it's going to storm," he said, leaning close. She was distracted and paid no attention to what he was saying. She looked at the sidewalk as they headed toward the gallery.

The wind off the lake was cool for July. Falco wore her black suit; the jacket was a welcome shelter against the chilly breeze. "You look nice, M," Jeffery, said smiling. He couldn't help notice her darkening mood. "Is Jim Ballard coming?"

"I don't know. Everyone from my department knows about it, but whether he makes it…" Falco's words drifted off. She looked at the street and then to her left, down the alley of the Cohen Sloan Gallery, remembering the crime scene. She closed her eyes briefly and sighed. Jeffery looked down at her and squeezed her tightly as they walked. She wrapped her arm around him.

The gallery door was open, allowing a steady stream of friends, acquaintances and well-wishers to enter. The space was dim except for the candles. Their reflections danced off the jet-black Steinway positioned to the left of the podium. To the right and left were two of Andie's largest pieces, barely visible in the darkness. They formed a sort of diptych and were flanked by four smaller paintings also hidden in the dark. The rest of the gallery spaces were closed off and darkened, preventing anyone from viewing the balance of Andie's work

People quietly drifted in, programs in hand. Gallery owners from the River North area nodded to one another as they took their seats. Officers Tim Strickland and Robby Torres entered together. Ed Lassiter followed them, slipping quietly into a back seat. A group of young women dressed as men made a noisy entrance, attracting stares. An assortment of queens and coupled men followed, as well as a motley group of artists dressed in an assortment of vintage black clothing, bike messenger types, and musicians. The mood was grim.

Falco and Jeffery entered the foyer and followed the stream of people through the dimly lit space. It felt like a starkly lit church. Emotions gripped Falco as she took in the mass of glistening candles. Jeffery steered her to a row of seats near the middle. She was feeling a wave of sadness and kept her eyes down, hoping it would pass. They sat down.

Falco saw Tim and Robby sitting to her left. They were wearing dark suits and looking solemn. Jeffery put his arm around Falco and whispered, "Interesting group." He handed her one of the programs. She took it and clutched it tightly in her hand. The room was almost at capacity with people standing in the back. Seven o'clock neared, and the room took on a cool hush.

Aisha appeared from the darkness and made her way to the piano. She was followed by the cellist, who took a seat to her right and in front of the piano. She looked down and waited as the room stilled. She gave a tiny nod to the cellist and began to play the rolling notes of "Summer Fields" by Wayne Gratz. As she played, the cello quietly joined her. Slowly the lights of the gallery space came up from above, gently lighting the diptych and then the other paintings in the room. Falco gasped as the light slowly illuminated Andie's work. Her eyes dashed around the space as the paintings slowly appeared. Something was undeniably familiar—the colors, the brushstrokes. It struck her like a memory long forgotten.

It was Andie's work, she thought. It was her work that she had seen on vacation with Jeffery at that little gallery in South Beach. The painting she had obsessed about for weeks and the piece hanging in Andie's foyer—that was Andie's, too. She swallowed hard and shook her head, trying to comprehend the irony. "Oh, my god," she whispered.

Slowly, just above the podium, projected on the wall, appeared images of Andie's artwork—paintings and sculptural pieces. Other images emerged in random sequence: photos of Andie painting a large canvas; Andie as a young woman smiling, topless, fists clenched and marching with friends at the annual Dyke March in Andersonville; misty black-and-white photos of Andie and Kat embracing; Andie smoking a joint, a cloud encircling her profile; Andie finger-painting with a group of children.

Falco's heart swelled with sadness at the images, as did most in the room. She pressed a tissue to her eyes as her body shook. Jeffery glanced at her and frowned.

The slideshow had taken on new meaning tonight for its producer, Greg Roth. He originally had done the slide presentation as a favor for Andie as a substitute for a written bio and retrospective catalogue for the exhibition. Now it was a telling portrait of the life of a beloved artist and friend.

As the music ended, the images of Andie faded and the room was silent. Aisha put her head down and wiped tears from her eyes. She and the cellist took seats off to the side of the gallery space. Finally Kat appeared from the right side, looking down, as she approached the podium. She tried to maintain her composure. Her eyes were red as she looked out at the crowd. She looked away and put her fingers to her forehead, then to her lips. She again looked out at the crowd.

"This…this is the hardest thing…for me, you know. You just never know how fragile all this is—life, I mean." She paused and shook her head. "I'm sorry. Let me start again. I'm Katherine Cohen. I own the Cohen Sloan Gallery, and I've known Andrea Fulbright for many years. She's been my lover, my confidant, my friend, my inspiration. Through that time we've shared a great deal, and well, it hasn't always been…an easy ride," she smiled wistfully then looked down. "But the things we shared—the work, the process, our love…"

Kat's eyes drifted off then she roused herself.

"I recall a time once when Andie called me in the middle of the night. It was one of her sleepless nights…fleeing off to her studio at three a.m. She was talking nonstop about her work, what it meant to her. I had just told her I wanted to show her paintings at my gallery, and that was way before we were lovers."

Kat paused again and scanned the paintings in the room.

"I loved her *work* before I knew I loved *her*," she said. "The confidence of her colors and how she worked the paint, the way she made your eyes dance around the canvas."

Kat paused and put a fist to her mouth; she closed her eyes and looked away. "Please give me a moment." She turned away and wiped her eyes with a tissue then took a deep breath.

"Well, Andie didn't want the show. She didn't want to exhibit her work at all," Kat said with a sad smile. "I didn't understand initially. Most artists would kill for that kind of chance, that kind of opportunity. But I realized she wasn't about showing her work to the world."

She paused again then gripped the podium, her voice suddenly strong. "Andie once said this to me, and I hope I get this right. She quoted the painter Francis Bacon. She said, 'I should have been a conman, a robber or a prostitute, but it was vanity that made me choose painting—vanity and chance.'"

Kat smiled to herself.

"That, to me, really sums up Andrea Fulbright as an artist, and for those who know her as a *person*. She would never *ever* admit that she was doing something important, something that really mattered. That…self-deprecation, that humility was…*is*…a big part of who Andie is."

Kat paused briefly, closing her eyes. "Now, as I look at this room full of her work, at the paintings that continue to thrill me, all I want—*all* I want—is her back here with me. With all of us…right now."

She hesitated, looked down, then turned and walked into the darkness.

The service continued. Reverend Phillips talked about Andie's creative spirit, sacrifice, and the path toward healing; Seiko told the story of how Andie had paid to repair his bike after a taxi had cut him off and bent his frame; Aisha played Liz Story's "Worth Winning"; a member of the Chicago Kings—a large woman dressed in a man's suit, with slicked-back hair and a mustache—talked about Andie's activism in the lesbian community; a board member of the Gerber/Hart Library talked about her generosity and her passion for gay and lesbian literature.

Afterward, the crowd dwindled. Falco nodded to Lassiter as she and Jeffery slipped out. She wondered if she had missed Michael somehow. Surely he would have come—and Dr. Forrest. Falco felt empty as she and Jeffery walked slowly down Huron. The noisy group of Kings passed them, their hands in their pockets, their gaits full of swagger. Jeffery eyed them curiously and shook his head.

"You want me to drive?" he asked. Falco nodded.

They drove off in silence. Falco's face betrayed her feelings. She stared out the window and clutched the program. Jeffery glanced at her as he drove north on the Kennedy. Before long they were in front of Falco's house.

"Hey, we're home," Jeffery said gently.

Falco looked at Jeffery then got out of the car. She backed up as he came around the car toward her. "Thanks for coming with me, Jeffery."

She put her hand out for the keys. He placed them in her hand then watched as she walked into the house and closed the door behind her.

CHAPTER 58

It was Thursday morning, and Michael awoke on Dr. Forrest's sofa. His neck was stiff, and his jaw ached. He sat up and rubbed the stubble on his cheeks. He had spent the night with Andie, who was having fits of violence as she emerged from the sedation. Michael had taken an unexpected fist to the jaw last night. The pain was the first thing to greet him when he woke this morning. Andie's physical condition had improved. She was breathing on her own now after almost two weeks. Dr. Forrest attributed her violent behavior to the pain medication, which was still being administered in large doses.

Michael's cell phone rang as he put on a fresh shirt. It was Falco. "Hey, did I miss you last night?" she asked.

"No, I wasn't there," he said, clearing his throat.

Falco sensed there was something wrong. "Are you okay?"

"Yeah. A lot of things came down last night, and Andie was one of them. She's been having violent fits, swinging and kicking. Alan thinks it's the pain medication, but we don't know yet. She's a bit more than the nurses can handle right now."

"Oh, no," said Falco quickly.

"We're probably going to move her to psych."

There was a long pause.

"Oh," said Falco faintly.

"It doesn't mean she'll stay there," Michael assured her, "but for now it's probably the best thing."

"Can I still see her?"

"Not right now, unless you want a fist in the jaw too. She'll be evaluated, and then we'll go from there."

"Okay," Falco said weakly.

"How was the service?" Michael asked. "I haven't spoken to Kat in a week."

"It was very nice. Actually, it was quite beautiful. Kat did a nice job." She paused. "I had never seen Andie's work."

"It's pretty amazing, isn't it?" Michael said. "I planned on being at the service, but… Tim said the service was nice too. He also said you brought someone with…" Michael said in a leading tone.

"With?" Falco asked.

"Yes, like a man."

"Oh, that was Jeffery, my ex. I didn't want to go alone," she said quietly.

"Well, too bad I missed meeting him."

* * *

Falco pulled her car into a parking spot and swung open the back door of the police station. There was a ruckus in the hallway and noise coming from the second floor. She walked up the stairs, where the noise grew louder. There was mass of staff members. Uniformed officers and detectives gathered around a large table in one of the conference rooms.

Steve Grasky stood around with the others, chewing gum and holding a Styrofoam cup. Falco walked by, peering in, when one of the uniformed cops motioned for her to join them.

"Hey, Falco! You're missing the party!" Ballard said.

She looked around the room at the smiling faces. "What's going on? Someone getting married or pregnant?" she asked, half smiling.

Grasky came around the table and put his arm around her. "I'm retiring."

She looked surprised and smiled broadly at Grasky. "When? When did you decide…?" She shook her head in disbelief.

"My wife and I have been talking about it. My son is starting a security company, and I thought I'd help him out with that, and you know my daughter just had a baby," Grasky said, almost apologetically.

"When's the big day?" asked Falco, trying to remain upbeat.

"October 15th, that'll give us some time to wrap things up and all."

Falco got a little teary eyed. She had grown to like Steve. He was a lot like her—patient, thorough, played by the rules. In the back of her mind, she had hoped they might end up as partners, but that wouldn't happen now. She glanced at Ballard, who was chomping on a cinnamon roll and laughing, crumbs on his shirt. She wished the profiler gig would happen, but it was the City of Chicago and things took forever. She felt sad, empty, and with her back against the wall.

"Hey, Falco. Want some coffee? I made a fresh pot," Ballard said with food in his mouth.

"No, thanks." She made her way to her desk and checked her voicemail. "You have seven messages," said the automated voice.

"Hi, honey. It's Mom, please call me."

"Shit," Falco hissed as she heard her mother's voice. She erased the message and pressed the number three button on her phone repeatedly until the phone disconnected. "Shit!" she whispered. "Can this day get any worse?"

Elaine Falco was a petite woman with an affinity for nice clothes and jewelry. She wore her hair in a smart pageboy cut that complemented her classic wardrobe. Falco always resented her mother for not being more like her two grandmothers—roll-up-your-sleeves, salt-of-the-earth types. As a young wife, Elaine had wanted nothing to do with housework, cooking, or managing a family. She had played along anyway, raising two children and living the life of a policeman's wife. Falco's father, Piero "Pete" Falco, was a family man who had struggled with the priorities of a wife and kids and his career as a cop.

Falco was close to her father and had been by his side when he died during her junior year in college. She always blamed her mother for her father's drinking and for driving her brother Peter away. Falco had no idea where her brother was now. He had left college during his sophomore year and never returned. She got a note from him postmarked somewhere in Mexico sometime later and never heard from him again.

She dialed her mother's phone number, hoping she would still be in bed. It was nine twenty a.m.

"Hello?" came her mother's singsong voice.

"Hi, Mom," said Falco, trying not to sound guilty. It had been almost three weeks since she had spoken to her, and she knew she was going to hear about it.

"Monica? Is that you?"

"Yes, of course it's me. Do you have another daughter you haven't told me about?" Falco said sarcastically. She wasn't going to play that game.

"No, it's just that I forgot what your voice sounded like. It's been so long since we've spoken."

"Yes, yes…I know that. I'm sorry, Mom. I've been swamped here," Falco stammered.

"At work you mean? Oh, yes. I saw your name in the paper, the article about that woman."

"Yes, that and a bunch of other things."

"I told Howard all about you and your job and showed him the article with your name in it," Elaine said in a gushing tone.

Falco sighed and closed her eyes—Howard Larson, the retired car salesman with the pinky ring.

Her mother went on at length about Howard, the gifts, the dinners out, the theater tickets. Falco was hardly listening, fixating on what her mother had said. It seemed the only time her mother was proud of her was when she was bragging about her to her friends. Any other time she was a lousy mother, a lousy daughter, and worst of all, she was a cop like her father.

The phone was suddenly silent. Her mother had stopped talking and had asked Falco a question, catching her off guard. "Are you still there, dear?" she asked.

"Yes, Mom. Sorry. Someone just…" She shook her head and looked up at the ceiling in annoyance.

"So is Saturday okay?" her mother asked.

"Saturday?"

"Yes, for dinner with Howard and me. We'll make reservations for seven and you can meet us here."

"This Saturday?" She flipped open her calendar, knowing she had nothing going on. "Sure, sure. That would be great." She hung up the phone and rubbed her forehead. "Fuck," she said with a sigh.

CHAPTER 59

Grasky was hovering near Falco's desk waiting for her to hang up the phone. He was still buzzing about the announcement of his retirement. He had his briefcase in his hand and his sport coat over his arm. Falco looked up with surprise.

"Falco, we're late," he said with a smile. "It'll take us twenty minutes at least, so come on!"

Falco drew a blank. She had just turned her computer on and had seven files to review. She glanced at her calendar for Monday. It said, "Morton Grove PD @ 10."

"Sorry, Steve, I had to call my mother," she said, getting up and pulling on her blazer and gathering the files.

The two detectives made their way out of the building, climbed into their vehicle, and headed northwest.

"How's your mom?" Grasky said, making conversation.

"Okay…same old thing," Falco mumbled. "Center of the universe."

Grasky laughed and glanced at Falco. "Yep, they get that way."

When Falco and Jeffery had bought the house from Falco's mother after they were married, Elaine had moved into a luxury senior citizen community and made fast friends. The facility had a variety of social activities, and her mother had adjusted quickly. Before long she was chairman of the social committee and had set up her second bedroom as an office.

Falco was pleased her mother had friends and activities to keep her busy and out of her hair. Jeffery seemed to miss his mother-in-law and volunteered to remodel her second bedroom into a functioning office space.

"She's not getting paid to do this. I don't know why she needs an office," Falco had complained.

"Well, we can still make it a more useful space for her," Jeffery had said.

Sucker, Falco thought.

"Hey, have you heard anything more about the Fulbright woman?" Grasky asked, putting on his sunglasses and getting on the expressway.

Falco was staring out the window processing her conversation with her mother. Grasky's voice brought her back to reality. "Uh…yeah. She's doing better physically, but her doctor's aren't sure about her…mentally," she said dryly. "She's being evaluated."

Her eyes caught the back window of a car just ahead of them in the right lane. A small boy with white-blond hair looked out the back window then disappeared as if pulled down by the person sitting next to him. It seemed strange to Falco. The boy had a scared look on his face. He caught Falco's eye just as he disappeared.

She sat up and watched the car as Grasky talked, not really listening to what he was saying. The car with the boy slowed down and was changing lanes. This time she got a better look. It was a green Ford Escort with rusty wheel wells. The back driver's side door was dented and probably didn't open. Falco looked over at the driver as he sped up to change lanes again.

He was male, probably in his early forties, Hispanic, with a mustache and sunglasses. The passenger visible in the back was a younger male, Latino and wearing a Cubs baseball cap. The driver glanced over and caught Falco's eye then quickly veered right and took the Foster exit off the expressway.

Falco squinted at the plate number. She took out her pen and wrote VK86 on the palm of her hand. She twisted her neck back, following the car as they passed. "Damn it!" she hissed. "Grasky, take the next exit, if you can. Quick!" She craned her neck, keeping her eye on the green car.

"Peterson Avenue?" Grasky asked, nervously chewing the gum in his mouth.

"Yeah, yeah!"

Grasky checked his rearview mirror and veered over two lanes toward the next exit. "What'd you see, Falco?

"Something's weird with that car we just passed. Damn it! They got off at Foster. Maybe we can backtrack."

Falco looked around as Grasky made the exit then headed east. "Turn right. Turn right! Take Cicero. We might be able to intercept them," she said, looking frantically. "It's a green Escort, a beater with lots of rust. Two guys were in it…"

Her words drifted off as she scanned the street. Grasky slowed down, watching the road. Falco looked over to the left side of the street, hoping the green car would be heading north just as they were going south.

"They could be anywhere at this point," Grasky said.

"Shit!" she said, scanning the street. She gripped her radio and called in a description of the vehicle and the passengers.

"Blond kid with two Hispanics?" Grasky asked. "Are you sure?"

"That's what I saw. The kid looked right at me, and he looked scared."

Grasky eyed the street then made a U-turn and headed north again. He pulled over and parked the car off the street. "You sure it was green?"

"Yes, I'm sure, goddamn it!" She got out of the car and looked out in the distance. "I'm assuming they'd be heading up this way, but who fucking knows?" Her heart sank as she scanned the street. "They probably pulled off somewhere."

"At least we got a description of the vehicle," Grasky said. He looked at his watch. "Come on, Falco. We gotta go."

They headed back to the Edens Expressway toward Morton Grove.

* * *

Grasky parked the car near the back of the Morton Grove police station. The building was a boxy modern structure of red brick and teal awnings. They entered through the tinted front doors and found their way to the spacious meeting room near the back of the building. The room was packed. Falco and Grasky found seats along the wall. A large white screen awaited another slide presentation by the FBI. Brenda Salerno stood near Special Agent Fred Tedeschi, who was at the podium. The meeting had just gotten underway. Tedeschi held up his hands for quiet as Brenda backed up to lower the lights.

"Looks like we've got more people on the task force," Falco said.

Grasky nodded. "We need it."

As Tedeschi started to talk, Falco couldn't get the image of the blond boy out of her head. *He looked like he was in some kind of trouble. What else could it be?* she thought. *Well, it's up to the Lincolnwood police now. Those two guys really looked suspicious.* She shook her head, admonishing herself for not getting Grasky to tail the vehicle.

Grasky looked over at her. "Let it go, Falco. We did what we could, and you called in the description of the vehicle and the partial plate. For all we know, they're getting picked up right now."

Falco nodded then pulled out pictures of the missing children from her files. She stared at their faces then glanced at the mug shots of the potential suspects. None of them looked like the men in the car, and she wasn't sure about the blond boy. She sighed and chewed the cap of her pen.

The meeting lasted longer than last month's, with new leads and dead ends. Wiretaps had revealed little information, and the handful of promising suspects had dried up. Three had disappeared, and the other two were arrested for unrelated crimes.

Falco knew that even though sexual predators and offenders must register with local police when they move into a neighborhood, most rarely comply with the law and often disappear from the system altogether. Many who do comply with the law often give false addresses such as those of abandoned buildings or empty lots. If a child gets molested or turns up missing in a neighborhood where a sexual predator is registered, the cops often face dead ends when trying to track down the suspect, thus allowing the predator to hurt more and more innocent children.

The meeting finally wound down after almost ninety minutes. Brenda Salerno turned the lights back on, and the crowd filtered into the hallway. Falco gathered her files and the paperwork the feds had passed out as Brenda made her way through the crowd looking for her. "Hey! Falco! Don't leave yet!" she waved, catching her eye.

Falco smiled. "Hi, Brenda. How's it going? The feds keeping you busy?"

"Oh, yeah. Same old, same old... Hey, I'm gonna be in the city this week. You want to have lunch or something?" Brenda asked, smiling.

"Sure, let me get my calendar out." Falco rustled through her briefcase and found her calendar.

"You like Thai food? There's this good place on Clark not far from the station."

"Sure." Falco shrugged. She didn't really care what kind of food she ate; she hadn't had much of an appetite in a while. The two made a date for lunch on Thursday at Thai on Clark in Uptown.

"Don't forget!" Brenda yelled, looking back as Falco and Grasky left the room.

CHAPTER 60

The Edens Expressway was a parking lot as Grasky muscled the car into the slow-moving traffic. "Construction…what else?" he moaned. "It's nearly three p.m. We won't be back for another hour with traffic moving like this. Boy, oh, boy. I won't miss this."

Falco was silent. Was she going crazy, or did the driver in the green car look like someone she had arrested a few years back? Where had she seen that face? He almost seemed to have recognized her—or maybe her mind was playing tricks. She gazed out into traffic, deep in thought.

Grasky pulled the car into the right lane and exited at Kimball. They made their way east on Irving Park Road, where traffic came to a dead stop once again at Western Avenue. "Now what?" Falco moaned, sitting up in her seat and looking around.

Grasky pulled the car into the right lane and floored it, heading south on Western. Falco put her fingertips to her head and closed her eyes. She was getting a banger of a headache; it started at her forehead and slowly moved down the back of her neck.

"Oh, it's a fucking Cubs game. I should have known!" groaned Grasky. "I'm gonna flash the lights and part the seas once we make Addison," he said, losing his patience. "Fucking suburbanites…in *my* city!"

"Pissing on the lawns," Falco added.

"That's why I'm a Sox fan. Those are the real people who live and work in the city—not a bunch of suburbanites from Mount Prospect or Naper-fucking-ville!"

Falco burst out laughing. "Naper-fucking-ville? That is sooo funny, Steve."

Grasky looked over at her and smiled. "I haven't seen you laugh like that in a while. You used to be a bit of a cut-up yourself, you know?"

"Yeah, well, it's just a bunch of stuff. Maybe I'm just getting old," she said flatly, her hand still on her forehead.

* * *

Falco left the station soon after they arrived. Traffic would be a picnic on the way home too, she thought. She downed some Motrin with some cold water, snatched up the files she had planned to review earlier that morning, and headed down the stairs and out the door.

Ballard was making his way in passing Falco; his shirt and tie were dark with sweat. "Hey, Falco, you leaving for the day?" he asked breathlessly.

Falco eyed him with concern. "Are you okay? Your face is really flushed."

"Yeah, yeah, it's fucking hot out there, dincha notice?" he snarled.

"Yeah, I know. We just got back too. Did ya ever hear of air conditioning?" Falco joked.

Ballard gave her a dirty look and waddled down the first-floor hallway toward the elevator.

* * *

Jeffery had left a message for Falco on her voicemail at home. She thought about their making love and let out a deep sigh. She felt herself pulling away from him. Her mind went back to a time when they were married, and a surge of anxiety swept through her. She poured herself a glass of Chianti and some put some frozen French fries in the oven. She remembered she had an appointment with Maggie on Wednesday. Maybe she should mention her lousy appetite. *I've lost weight*, she thought. *Mom will notice right away.*

It was nearly nine thirty p.m. Falco had gotten through five of the seven files. She finished her second glass of wine when the phone rang. It was Jeffery.

"Hey, Jeff," she said, seeing the caller ID.

"Hey. Did you get my message?"

"Yes, I did. I guess I lost track of time here. I needed to review some files. What's up?"

"Well, for one thing, Sam called and he's having a blast."

"Great!"

"Yeah, he caught a couple of fish and went kayaking, and I guess he found some arrowheads and stuff. What's new with you?"

"Nothing, just work, you know," Falco said, distracted.

Jeffery was silent. It seemed he had something on his mind. Falco took off her reading glasses and waited for him to say something. She heard him breathing on the other end.

"So what's new with you?" she asked, wondering why he was so quiet.

"Not much…just work stuff," Jeffery stammered then was quiet again. Falco heard him take a deep breath. "Listen, M. I need to ask you something."

"Sure, what?" Falco asked, glancing at her empty glass.

"I'm getting some mixed signals from you, which is nothing new. I mean, last week when we made love, I guess I thought that maybe we might start something—you know, maybe try again."

Falco sighed and made a pained face. "Well…"

"And then you asked me to go to that service, and I thought, *Hey, this is good*," Jeffery said then paused again. "Well, that was almost a week ago, and I thought maybe I'd call you over the weekend, but then I reconsidered." He paused again. "Look, M. I'm just gonna come out and say it, okay? I'm putting two and two together here—the crowd at the service, those gay people, whatever. I mean, you were pretty upset, and then you got so quiet afterward. It made me wonder. Do you…do you have a thing for that Fulbright woman? I mean she is a dyke."

Falco put her hand over her eyes and let out a deep breath. She shook her head, not saying a word. Several moments passed. "I don't know how to respond to that, Jeff," she said quietly.

"Just answer me…as your husband."

The trouble was that Falco didn't have an answer for Jeffery. She didn't know what she was feeling for Andie. Clearly she felt responsible for what had happened; that was part of the flood of emotions she felt when she thought of her. But she knew she was struggling with something more, something deeper, something very new.

Finally she said, "Jeffery, come on."

"That's not an answer, M," he persisted.

"If you're asking me if I have somehow become a lesbian, I'm going to flat out say no," she said, relieved she was able to verbalize it.

Jeffery paused but wanted more from her. "You just seemed so…at ease with them, like it was no big deal—and those women, dressed in suits with sideburns and mustaches."

"It's no big deal!" Falco said getting frustrated. "Look, I live in the city. It has a diverse population. I work at the twenty-third district, which happens to be smack dab in the middle of Boystown. You know what that is. And just north of us is Andersonville. Some call it Girlstown. You get my drift, Jeffery."

"Yeah…well, it's just that," he stammered.

"Look, when I transferred to the twenty-third district, it was a whole lot different than the sixteenth. I went through a bit of culture shock too. Attitudes are different at the twenty-third. They're more accepting."

Jeffery was silent for a moment then said, "I guess that stuff isn't in my realm of experience."

"Well, it's obvious that *you* have the problem. You're homophobic," Falco said with a laugh.

Jeffery considered that for a moment then said, "Let's have dinner on Saturday."

She paused and welcomed the change of subject. "I can't. I'm having dinner with Mom and Howard, the car salesman," she said in an annoyed tone.

"Oh, oh, yeah. That's right. I forgot."

"Forgot?" Falco asked. "How did *you* know about it?"

"Uh, I talked to Elaine the other day. I recommended a plumber for her kitchen."

"Jesus!" Falco snapped. "I can't believe you. I just can't!"

"Hey, wait a second. Don't get mad. I just—"

"Listen, Jeff. I need to go to bed. I've got an early meeting tomorrow, okay?"

Jeffery heard the tension rising in Falco's voice. "Yeah, okay. I'll talk to you soon then."

Falco slammed down the phone. She a poured another glass of wine and drank it in one gulp.

CHAPTER 61

Tuesday morning was just as hot as the morning before. Falco got into her Camry and headed toward Devon Avenue. She pulled out her cell phone and dialed Michael but got his voicemail. She hung up without leaving a message.

Traffic on Devon was unusually slow. Falco sighed, wondering how much of her life was spent sitting in traffic. She quickly made a right turn onto Pulaski and headed toward the Edens Expressway. She careened around some slow-moving cars to Peterson, gunning the car from the merge lane into the rush of oncoming traffic. The Edens also was moving slow, but she wouldn't be on it for long.

She turned on her radio, looking for traffic and weather. It felt like rain. She peered into her rearview mirror and pulled at her hair. "I don't need a weather report. I just have to look at my hair," she said.

Falco fished around for her sunglasses as the morning sun blasted off her windshield. Far up ahead she saw the steady stream of brake lights and realized she was in for another slow commute. "Great," she muttered. She reached for her mug in its holder and took a sip. She tasted the bitter brew and curdled milk from the previous day's coffee. She swallowed the cool milky liquid, making a sour face and putting her hand on her mouth, "Yuuucck!" She'd left her other mug filled with fresh coffee on the kitchen counter. *It's Jeffery's fault*, she thought. Their conversation stirred in her head again as she studied the road ahead.

Her AC was cranked, but her shirt was beginning to stick to her sweaty back. She smelled the sour odor of exhaust from the car ahead. Dust off the road from too many dry days swirled around like sandpaper over her windshield. She squinted to assess the traffic ahead. Was it moving? She couldn't tell. She glanced at the car in the next lane just ahead of her; its tailpipe was belching out dirty exhaust for all to share. Not paying attention, she found herself too close to the car in front of her. Its brake lights flashed.

"Jesus!" she hissed as she slammed her brakes. She rubbed her eyes and told herself to pay attention. The car belching out fumes drifted into her lane, almost cutting her off. She braked again. "Nice job," she said sarcastically.

Just then the letters "VK" appeared before her on the license plate, then the numbers 8 and 6. She focused on the characters for a moment then slowly took in the rest of the vehicle.

It was the green Ford Escort.

Falco took a deep breath and let the car get a bit more ahead of her. She followed it, trying not to get herself noticed. She grabbed a pen and wrote down the rest of the vehicle's plate numbers, making sure she got them all this time. She studied the car and its driver. The person at the wheel was smaller, possibly a woman driving alone—no blond kid in the back this time.

The car made its way past Kimball and moved to the right lane to exit at Belmont. Falco waited then looked in her mirror to change lanes. With her directional blinking, she checked her blind spot and made her move to the right lane. Just then, out of nowhere, came a buzzing motorcyclist screeching his brakes to avoid the Camry and sending the car next to Falco into the far-right lane. The motorcyclist cut her off and gave her the finger as he raced ahead at almost eighty miles an hour.

Her heart beating in her throat, Falco missed the Belmont exit. "Fuck you!" she yelled to the motorcyclist, who had already disappeared. She looked for the next exit, which was Fullerton. She knew there was no way she would find that car.

* * *

Falco got to the station late and ran the plate. She printed the vehicle information and headed out again. She asked Ballard if Grasky was in. He told her he was downtown at personnel putting in his papers. Falco looked annoyed and let Ballard know she was leaving to check out a lead on the West Side. He nodded as she left.

Falco got in the Crown Victoria and headed west on Addison. The green Ford Escort was registered to Alicia Quinones of West Wabansia in Humboldt Park. If this person and the other two males were involved with some kind of child porn ring, they lived close to the suspects she and Grasky and had interviewed that rainy Friday. *Maybe they're all connected*, she thought. She drove west and cut south on California.

Traffic rumbled down the street. Delivery vehicles were double parked, and rusted-out cars with huge stereos jockeyed around with deafening bass notes. Little girls with babies in strollers peered around the stream of cars as they tried to make their way across the street. Vendors on the sidewalk with food carts sold ice cream, hot sweet corn with mayonnaise, and other Latin standbys.

Falco zigzagged with traffic, turning right onto North Avenue, then past historic Humboldt Park. The grass and pond had taken a beating from the hot weather, and it appeared no one was hanging out there. "Too hot for anyone today," Falco said, looking to her left.

She continued to head west toward Kedzie, scanning addresses as she drove. She found Ayers and turned right then veered left onto Wabansia. "Let's see. Springfield, Harding," she said out loud as she squinted at the street signs. She crossed Pulaski and continued to look for the cross street.

"Karlov...okay," she said slowly. She circled the block, looking for the address. Spotting the house, she slowed down. It was a gray brick bungalow with a large wooden front porch. A rundown chain-link fence with a BEWARE OF DOG sign surrounded the house.

The green Escort was nowhere in sight. She cruised around the street then circled back through the alley. The garage was dilapidated; she couldn't imagine parking a car in there. The backyard was dismal with abandoned furniture and rusty car parts littering the area. Some street-gang types noticed her and stared at her car suspiciously as she drove by. She circled back once more and parked down the street, the dingy bunga-low still in view.

Falco ducked low in her seat and locked her doors as she scanned the street and the house. An hour passed with no movement. She wondered whether the address of the plate was old or phony. She hoped she hadn't reached another dead end.

A noisy minivan rumbled down the street, drifting through the four-way stop. It slowed down and parked in front of the house. Falco perked up, squinting to see the license plate. The stocky older man who was driving the Escort the other day got out carrying a box and walked quickly into the gray house. Falco waited.

A younger man, possibly the person she had seen sitting in the back of the Escort, got out of the passenger side and unlocked the back cargo doors. He started to unload what appeared to be two Dell computers and monitors. The older man helped the younger one carry the boxes into the house. They both were working fast and looking around.

Falco waited as another hour passed. Two young men wearing white T-shirts appeared at the corner just ahead of where she was parked. She squinted, studying them. Another man soon appeared. The three were talk-ing and gesturing. She figured they were either Latin Eagles or Spanish Cobras. She was getting a bad feeling.

She unsnapped the strap holding her Glock 22 and rubbed her sweaty hands on the car seat. Then she waited watching the windows of the bungalow and the guys on the street. She cranked the car to a start and slowly pulled out, watching the house as she passed. She turned down the alley and drove past the back of the house. She took note of a half-filled black garbage bag and two crumbling cardboard shoeboxes stacked on top of each other. She quickly backed the car up behind the dilapidated garage and grabbed the bag and threw it into the backseat. She squatted and lifted the two boxes; she felt them both give way as she put them in the car. The boxes smelled of mildew and mold. Gravel gave way to dust as she gunned the car toward the street. She glanced in her mirrors and circled around to the front of the house. Looking straight ahead and avoiding eye contact with the three as she passed, she squinted at the license plate of the minivan and memorized it. As she reached North Avenue, she peeked in her rearview mirror. The three men had disappeared.

"Outta here," she said to herself. Her heart was racing. Her vehicle looked like an unmarked police car, and clearly she was a white chick in a largely Latino neighborhood. Even so, the block was quiet and virtually deserted, except for those three men. *I can pass as Latina*, she reasoned. She couldn't wait to run the mini van's plate number.

Something was eating at Falco. That man, the driver of the Escort and the minivan—she knew him from somewhere, but where? She headed past Western Avenue to Milwaukee and Damen. She waited for the light as a scattering of pedestrians crossed the street.

A slim African-American woman pulling a large suitcase on wheels crossed her line of vision. The woman struggled to get the bulky suitcase up the curb and looked frazzled. Falco did a double take and realized it was Aisha Lockwood, Andie's friend. She slowly pulled over to the curb and put her flashers on, pissing off the driver of the car behind her.

Falco hit the button for her passenger side window and yelled, "Aisha? Aisha!" She beeped the horn. Aisha looked around for where the voice was coming from, then bent down to look in the car. She gave Falco a blank look. "Aisha?" Falco said again. "It's Detective Falco. Do you remember me?"

Aisha looked confused for a moment then recognized Falco. She smiled and waved. "Do you need a ride?" Falco called out. Her voice collided with the rumble of a CTA bus.

"What?" Aisha asked, making a face and gesturing to her ear.

"Do you need a ride? I'm heading east!" Falco said, pointing ahead. Aisha dragged her suitcase closer and bent down next to the car. "Hi! You look like you need a lift. I'm going east. Can I drop you off somewhere?" Falco asked.

"I'm going downtown to pick up the Orange Line to Midway Airport," Aisha said.

"Come on. Get in. I'll give you a lift."

Aisha thought for a moment as she glanced at her suitcase. "All right, why not?" she said, giving her suitcase a pull. She opened the back door of the car and pushed the suitcase onto the seat with a grunt, then got in the front seat and shut the door. She looked at Falco and smiled. "What are you doing in Bucktown?"

"I had something to do in Humboldt Park," Falco said, checking her left mirror and making her way into the intersection. "That's a big suitcase. Are you going to be gone long?" she asked, glancing at Aisha.

Aisha paused and looked down. "I'm going to graduate school," she said quietly.

"Really? That's great! Where are you off to?"

"NYU. It's an MFA program in theater and set design."

"That's *very exciting*...and New York City. Wow!" Falco said.

"Yes, well, the semester starts in a few weeks, but I need to find a place to live and maybe a part time job," she said, looking a bit sad. "I wrapped things up with Kat at the gallery last week. There wasn't much to do. I had hoped to see Andie…before I…" Aisha looked out the window, and her words stopped short.

Falco glanced at her then looked ahead. "Yes, I know."

Aisha put her head down and crossed her arms in front of her. Tears streamed down her face. Falco glanced at her and then did a double take. "Hey…hey, are you okay?"

"Yes, I'm okay. I've been crying for the last few days, saying goodbye to everyone. They've all been so great. I just wish…well…" Aisha paused and brushed the stream of tears away. "Kat had a little party for me at the gallery, but I know she hates me for leaving."

"Why would she hate you?" Falco asked, surprised. "Graduate school in New York is an amazing opportunity."

Aisha laughed and looked over at Falco. "She's a bitch, that's why—self-centered, egotistical, manipulative…and a lot of other things. That's why, we…Andie and I were…well." She shook her head. "Kat walked all over her, you know. I don't know why Andie took it for so long," she said, looking angry then sad. "I just wish I could have said goodbye."

"So…you two…" Falco began but decided her question was too personal.

"For about a year-and-a-half," Aisha volunteered. She stared out the window. "I love her."

Falco nodded. They both were silent the rest of the way.

CHAPTER 62

Falco pulled into a shady spot in the twenty-third district's parking lot. She pulled open the back door of the car and heaved out the garbage bag. Sitting sideways on the backseat, she pulled open the bag. It was full of shredded paper. "Fuck," she muttered. "I should have known."

Rooting further into the bag and sifting the shreds through her fingers, she came across half of a torn envelope. She looked at it then searched deeper for the other half. She dragged the bag flat on the pavement and shuffled the contents around. Larger pieces of paper, spared by the shredder, clung to the bottom of the plastic bag. Falco grabbed a handful and scanned the half-torn sheets. Half of a crumpled yellow credit card receipt jutted out from the mass of white bits of paper. Barely visible from the printing were the words "Canon Hi-Def Cam $3,999" then below them "Sony Hi-Def Mini-Cam $3,699." Falco squinted at the merchandise total with tax and tried to make out a signature for the charge slip. She dropped the paper into the breast pocket of her blouse.

She searched again through the bag and found the other half of the receipt; the purchase was made at Best Buy on Elston Avenue. She called Grasky from her cell phone. "I'm in the parking lot," she said. "I got a bag of stuff from the bungalow. I think we got a lead."

Within minutes Grasky appeared, walking quickly through the parking lot. He smiled and shook his head as he spotted Falco leaning over one of the tattered shoeboxes.

"Whatcha got there, Falco?"

"I found a receipt in this bag of shredded paper," she said, squinting up at Grasky. "You wanna go through this other box? There's nothing worthwhile in this one, weird stuff, worthless shit—old *TV Guides*, Spanish comic books, playing cards, pens, markers."

Grasky pulled the other shoebox from the backseat. "You staked out the bungalow on your own, didn't you?"

Falco nodded. She took the receipt from her shirt pocket. "Look at this. It's a receipt from Best Buy for two hi-def camcorders."

Grasky took the receipt. "What else you got?"

"Another plate number," she said with a smile.

Grasky smiled and chewed a wad of gum. "Falco, Falco, Falco."

The two shoeboxes netted nothing for the two detectives except an assortment of empty paper video boxes, sheets of yellowed sticky labels, expired coupons, dried-up permanent markers, yellowed playing cards, and moldy comic books. They threw the two boxes and the garbage bag of paper in the trash then made their way toward the building's back entrance.

"Let's run that plate number," Falco said as they climbed the stairs to the second-floor offices.

Her heart grew heavy as the excitement of finding the receipts wore off. Her thoughts turned to Aisha; she had looked so lost. So many things were left undone.

***

Best Buy was chilly. Ear-shattering bass notes rumbled from the electronics department in the back. Grasky pointed in the direction of a display of camcorders. A young Latina with heavy red lipstick caught the detectives' eyes.

"Can I help you with something?" She put her hands in the back pockets of her jeans and smiled shyly.

Falco and Grasky flashed their badges.

"Two camcorders were purchased here," Grasky said, holding out the torn receipt. "We don't have a date from the receipt, just the address of this store. Can you check your inventory or your computers to find out when they were purchased and by whom?"

The girl looked around for a moment then bit her lip. "I'll have to find the department manager. He can help you. Okay?"She disappeared for a moment. Then a young man with a goatee and tattooed arms came around the camcorder display. "Officers, how can I help you?"

The three gathered at the customer service counter with Kurt, the manager of the electronics department. He ran the inventory numbers of the two camcorders.

"They were purchased August eighteenth," he said. He stared at the computer screen then shook his head. "I don't have access to customer names, you know. All I can tell you is when they were purchased. Sorry."

"Can you tell us who sold the stuff to them? Which employee? Maybe that person might remember," Falco offered as she glanced at the computer screen then back at the young man.

Kurt made a few keystrokes then scrunched his face. "Hmm…" Grasky and Falco waited. "Hector Salazar was the employee. He's not with the store anymore." He leaned into the detectives and whispered, "Had to let him go…for stealing."

"Do you have an address for Hector Salazar?" Falco asked.

Kurt shook his head and flattened his lips. "I'm not privy to that information, plus I think the company's gonna press charges."

"Is there someone else we can talk to? Someone who would have access to that information?" Grasky asked, tapping his fingers on the counter.

"The store manager will be in tomorrow. I'll have him call you," said the young man.

"The girl that helped us, the one with the lipstick…did she work with Salazar?" Falco asked.

"Naw. She started two weeks ago."

She slid her business card across the counter to the young man. "Thanks for your help."

The two turned and headed toward the exit. "Salazar should have an arrest record," Grasky said as he opened the door for Falco.

Falco and Grasky headed back to the station buzzing with leads. Falco checked her voice mail at her desk, note pad and pen ready. Elaine Falco left a message on her voicemail to remind her about their dinner date on Saturday. Falco scowled as her stomach churned. She checked the rest of her messages; the store manager from Best Buy had an address for Hector Salazar. He asked her to return his call. Falco's heart skipped. *Great*, she thought.

She dialed the number and was connected to Alberto Dominguez, the store manager. He gave her Hector Salazar's last known address. He paused then said, "You know, Detective Falco, I never forget a face."

"What do you mean?" she asked.

"Hector was the person who took handled the purchase of the two camcorders. I'd bet the entire inventory of this store that he knew the two guys."

"Guys? Were you there when the purchase was made?"

"Well, the purchase had to be signed by a manager cuz it was over $5,000. Lot of good that did, huh?"

"Did you sign off on the purchase?"

"No, it was the large-appliance manager, but I was nearby at the time. It was weird when I look back on it. Hector was acting nervous, and so were the two guys. After the credit card cleared and they left, I forgot about it. But here's the kicker. I think those two guys were back here buying computers a few days ago. In fact I helped them load two computers into their van out front."

"Two computers? They purchased them at your store?"

"I'm almost sure of it. Two guys, one skinny and one stocky with a mustache."

"Do you think you could ID one of them from a photo?"

"Yeah. Like I said, it was just a few days ago."

"Let me fax it to you," Falco said.

After he received the fax, Alberto Dominguez told Falco he was sure the man in the photo, Ernesto Oporto, was one of the men who had purchased the computers two days ago.

Now all we need is to find Hector Salazar, Falco thought as she hung up the phone.

She ran Salazar's name and address through the CPD databases and came up with two names. One suspect was doing time for armed robbery; the second man was in his twenties with a large build and muscular. He'd been arrested for possession of stolen property and burglary. Falco printed the description, arrest record, and mug shot then looked at her watch; it was nearly noon.

CHAPTER 63

Falco made her way to Grasky's desk as he ran the plate of the mini-van on his computer. The owner of the vehicle had a criminal record that included child pornography and rape.

"Bingo!" he said, eyeing the results.

Falco leaned closer and peered at the computer screen. "Ernesto Santos. I know that name. Don't you know that name, Grasky?"

"Hm…maybe," he said.

She peered at the mug shot of Santos. "Where have I seen this guy?" she whispered to herself.

"Maybe we should make another visit." He looked at his watch; it was nearly four. "You up for it?" he asked, chomping on a fresh piece of gum.

"Sure. Let's go."

They took Grasky's car this time to avoid getting noticed. Grasky drove a beat-up Ford Taurus with tinted windows. They got into the car and headed west. "Aren't tinted windows illegal in Illinois?" asked Falco with a little smile.

"Not if you buy the car in a state where they're legal and transfer the title," Grasky said with a grin.

Falco adjusted her brown leather shoulder holster; it hadn't felt the same since she'd spent two hours slouched in the Crown Vic earlier this afternoon. She rubbed the back of her head. "I hope this pans out," she said.

For once traffic was moving on North Avenue. Before long Falco saw Ayers and directed Grasky to turn right. They cruised to Wabansia going the same way Falco had driven earlier that day. She glanced around for gang activity, knowing this area was a hot spot for rivalries and drivebys, especially after dark. "You know, you shouldn't have staked out this place by yourself, Falco," said Grasky. "This isn't a place for a white woman to be hanging out alone, even if she is an excellent marksman."

"I thought about that when I saw those three gang members staring at me, but I needed to get that plate number, especially after seeing the same two men out front."

"You shouldn't take chances like that," Grasky said.

They came upon the gray bungalow. This time the green Ford Escort was parked in front, but the minivan wasn't. They circled the block and found parking just north of the house. The sun was getting low, but no lights came on inside the bungalow. A car cruised up next to Grasky's then slowed down, passing them. A large Latino put the car in park, opened the door, and stood on the street looking around. He looked anxious and was talking into a cell phone clipped to his ear. Soon two young men wearing baggy white T-shirts appeared and exchanged cash for two small, neatly folded paper bags. They had no idea the cops were watching the whole scene just fifteen feet away.

"Pack runners," whispered Falco.

"Keep it light," said Grasky. He unwrapped a fresh piece of gum and shoved it into his mouth.

The deal was made, and the car drove away, leaving the two gang members sprinting for North Avenue. "Service with a smile," said Grasky.

They waited, watching the house closely. Falco was beginning to feel antsy. "I wish I knew where I've seen that guy before."

"It could be nothing. Sometimes people look like other people, you know? When I first met my future son-in-law, he looked like someone I knew too. It bugged the shit outta me for a week. Then it dawned on me. You know who I thought he looked like?" Falco looked at Grasky and shook her head. "Fucking Jeffery Dahmer!" Grasky laughed.

"The serial killer?" Falco asked, not believing him.

"Yep, and you know what? I never told my daughter that!" Grasky said with a chuckle.

"Good move."

The two detectives staked out the house for three hours. It was nearly eight thirty when the minivan drove up and parked behind the green Escort. The older stocky man got out of the driver side and opened the sliding side doors to let out two children who appeared to be no more than eight years old. Falco and Grasky watched closely, trying to see what the kids looked like.

"I can't see a thing, Steve," Falco whispered. "We should have brought the binoculars."

"Wouldn't do much good in the dark."

The porch light went on; someone had been inside the house all along. The three ran up the steps and entered the house. A small woman—possibly the one who had driven the Escort—looked out the door and up and down the street. She then disappeared inside.

"Couldn't get a good look at those kids," Grasky said.

The lights went on in the basement of the house. "You wanna take a closer look?" Falco said, her hand on her gun.

Grasky eyed the house as he chewed his gum nervously. "Yeah, let's go."

He switched off the automatic dome light and quietly opened the car door. Falco followed. They glanced up and down the street; it was empty and quiet. They made their way down the sidewalk and stopped outside the cyclone fence.

"There's a BEWARE OF DOG sign out front, but I haven't seen any dogs," Falco whispered.

"Hey, as long as we stay on this side of the fence, we're just two neighbors going for a walk."

"Yeah, right."

They approached the side of the house with the view of the basement. A bright overhead bulb lit the room. Falco and Grasky peered closer as they leaned against the fence. "You want to chance it?" Falco asked, meaning jump the fence.

Grasky scanned the yard. His vision had adjusted to the darkness. He didn't see or hear any dogs. "I'll go first."

He put the toe of his shoe into one of the rhombus-shaped links of the fence, swung his other leg around, and quietly landed on the ground inside the yard. Falco did the same. They waited for the sound of dogs. All was quiet. "Let's go," said Falco.

Just fifteen feet ahead was the window, hidden only by a half-dead lilac bush. They approached slowly, half crouching, Falco on the left and Grasky on the right. Reaching the basement window, they squatted and craned their necks to see inside. The young man Falco had seen earlier was hooking up the computers. They saw a large-screen TV and what looked to be video equipment. The woman who had appeared at the front door brought food on a plate for the young man. Grasky glanced to the left and saw some kids' games, a playhouse, and toy trucks.

They continued to watch as the stocky man with the mustache entered the room and checked the computer equipment. He spoke to the young man, who was now hunched over his plate of food, eating. The two seemed to be having a disagreement and were gesturing and pointing. The scene went on for a few minutes. The young man got up suddenly and walked out of the room and up the basement stairs.

The slam of the front door startled the two detectives. They ducked and hid against the side of the house. The young man got into the Escort, started the noisy engine, and drove off.

"Shit, that was close," Falco whispered.

They continued to observe the two in the basement. A door opened in a back room, revealing a vertical bar of light that grew wider. Falco squinted to see what was going on. It appeared to be a bathroom. She saw the Latina doing something with a white towel. It looked like she was drying off a child; she made out skinny legs and arms amid the swirl of terrycloth. "Look over there," she whispered to Grasky.

He fixed his eyes on the half-open doorway. "Nothing unusual," he said.

"If it's her kid," said Falco.

The boy ran out of the bathroom naked as the woman finished with the towel. The light of the bathroom illuminated a full-size bed and a number of overstuffed pillows strewn about the floor. The woman followed the boy and turned off the lights, leaving that part of the basement dark. The stocky man hovered around the computer equipment then followed the woman and the child up the basement stairs and turned off the lights. "Damn it," Grasky hissed. "Did you get a look at the kid?"

Just then they heard voices from the alley. It sounded like a group of teenagers. A car crackled over the gravel of the alleyway, moving slowly past the gray bungalow. Grasky and Falco held their positions. They heard Spanish being spoken and threats being made. "Fuck you" was interspersed with other profanity in English and Spanish. "Great," Falco whispered, looking back near the alley.

They heard the shuffle of feet and the sounds of someone being beat up. Grunts and groans came from the alley then the sound of running feet and the burn of tires. Dust rose from the alley and cast a gray cloud over the streetlights nearby. Then all was quiet. They waited. A young man got up from the ground, holding his stomach, and limped north up the alley. He fell to his knees once, then got up and slowly walked into the darkness.

"Pumpkin head," Falco whispered.

"Let's get out of here," Grasky said.

They quickly made their way over the fence and to the car. Grasky started the engine and headed for North Avenue.

CHAPTER 64

Falco didn't get home until nearly eleven. She was exhausted but wired thinking about the events of the day. *Something's going on in that house*, she thought. She and Steve planned to stake out the place again the following night. In the meantime they were going to check school records for kids living at that address. If nothing came up, they might have a nibble.

Falco took off her holster and locked it in its drawer. She peeled off her clothes and shoved them into the hamper. It was overflowing again, and the mail was a six-inch stack on the coffee table. She poured some red wine in a glass, reminding herself about her appointment tomorrow with Maggie Simonds. She went to bed and dozed off quickly.

Bang! Bang!

Falco woke up with a start. Her heart was racing. She thought she had heard gunshots outside. She looked out the window of her bedroom then walked through the hallway into the living room. She peered out the picture window to the street. *Was I dreaming?* She looked out the other windows of her house, out into the street and in the backyard. It was two-thirty and all was quiet.

She sat on the sofa and stared into the darkness, confused at what had awakened her.

"Did I hear gunshots or was I dreaming about gunshots?" she whispered. She remembered the sounds of her gun going off in her left ear like it was yesterday and the clickety-clack of her gun hitting the pavement and sliding down the embankment. She still couldn't believe Andie had shot Brian McCaffery. The images and events haunted her: the blood, McCaffery's body, the sound of Andie's breathing, her deathly stare. Falco got up from the sofa and started to pace. Her knee caught the corner of the coffee table, sending her nearly to the floor. "Shit!" she said, holding the side of her leg. "Goddamn it!"

She limped back to the window and looked out again. Convinced she was dreaming, she went back to bed. The room was dark except for the occasional reflection of headlights from the street. She stared at the ceiling then rolled over facedown into her pillow. She thought about Aisha and her suitcase rolling through the streets of New York City. She thought about Michael. She hadn't seen him in almost two weeks. *People go on with their lives*, she thought. She rolled on to her back and stared again at the ceiling. She could taste the loneliness.

At least I have Sam, she thought. She wondered how he would do if he lived back in the city with her. *Babysitters*, she thought. She cursed her life and her job. "That wouldn't work," she whispered.

Sam has Jeffery. He's a good father. He's probably dating someone. He's handsome, responsible, a good catch, she thought. *Michael has lots of friends—Alan and Andie and Aisha and Kat and maybe Strickland…who knows? Grasky is married and so is Ballard. Lassiter has a girlfriend from way back. Mom has Howard.*

She continued to stare at the ceiling and considered her life—work, work, work…and whenever she could see Sam.

She thought about her day then remembered the scenario with the gang bangers. They had noticed her. "What if I'd gotten shot and never made it back to the station? I'd be rotting in that hot car and no one would even know," she whispered to the ceiling. A wave of sadness filled her. "Jesus," she said as she got up from the bed and wandered into the laundry room. The bright fluorescent light hurt her eyes as she sorted through the dirty clothes—the whites, the colors. She opened the lid of the washer and turned the knob. A rush of water filled the machine.

CHAPTER 65

Wednesday morning was muggy and rainy. The moisture seemed to perk up the grass and trees, giving everything a fresh green look, but Falco was anything but fresh. She had hardly slept all night, and her head felt swollen. She was also aching to see Sam and looked forward to his return from camp on the weekend.

She dreaded dinner with her mother and that phony, pinky-ringed man she called her boyfriend. She wondered what her dad would think of him as she drove to work. She got to her desk just after nine and already had messages on her voicemail. Grasky had signed in for the day but wasn't at his desk. She started to check her messages, writing down names and numbers. She was surprised when she heard Michael's voice asking her to call. She finished checking her messages and immediately called him.

"Hey, Monica," he said. "How's it going?"

"Okay. I tried you a few days ago and got your voicemail, but I didn't leave a message. How's Andie?"

"Not great. She won't let anyone near her or touch her."

"What's going on?"

"Well, she doesn't know who she is or where she is. She just goes around slamming her hands on things, the walls, the floors, people. She broke her finger the other day slamming her hands against a wall. It's not good. But we're going to try some other things, some different meds, and see what happens."

"Is that a typical reaction to a traumatic event like what she's been through?" asked Falco quietly.

"Nothing is typical about behavior like that—the anger, the aggression, the withdrawal. We're trying some new drugs. Some are effective, but others exacerbate the symptoms.

The subject of Kat came up and then Aisha. Falco told Michael about her chance meeting with Aisha on her way to the airport. Michael trashed Kat for treating Aisha badly and keeping the gallery open the week Andie was in the ICU. "I guess some of the larger pieces sold," he said. "I hope none of them were pieces Andie listed as not for sale, but knowing Kat she'd sell them anyway."

Michael told Falco he'd been spending some time at Andie's place, making sure he gave Curry and Leo some quality time.

"You're a really good person," she said.

"I promised her. That first night when you and Ballard came, I promised her I'd take care of her boys if something happened to her. I never thought I'd be doing it, though," he said sadly.

Falco hung up the phone feeling sad and hallow. She wished there was something she could do to help Andie.

Grasky came by and stopped at her desk. "Hey, you get some bad news or something?" he asked.

Falco looked up at Grasky's smiling face and fought back a wave of emotions. She put her face in her hands and said, "No, I'm just tired or something." She didn't want him to see she was about to cry.

Grasky took the hint. "I'll come back in a few."

* * *

The afternoon flew by. Falco swung by Grasky's desk to confirm their stakeout at five thirty. She arranged to use another unmarked car, a dark blue Impala, for the night.

She drove to the EAP office on Irving and parked on the street. She took the pokey elevator up to the fourth floor and signed in at the reception desk. Four o'clock loomed, and Falco was antsy. She glanced out the window and looked at her watch. The office door opened. It was Maggie Simonds smiling. "Hi, Monica. Come on in."

She was fighting off another headache and rolling through her dark mood. Maggie couldn't help notice she had things on her mind. She waited as Falco sat silently and stared at the carpeting. After a few moments Maggie said, "I can see you're struggling with something today. Where would you like to start? Anything happen recently that has been upsetting or troubling to you?"

Falco sighed and put her fingertips to her eyes. Tears streamed down her face, slowly and then almost uncontrollably. She covered her face and cried softly. Maggie quickly gave her a handful of tissues and looked at her intently. After a few moments, Falco managed to quell her tears. She wiped her eyes and blew her nose and said quietly, "I'm sorry. I didn't mean for that to happen."

Maggie gently put her hand on Falco's. "It's okay. It's okay. Let's talk about it."

Falco took a few deep breaths and put her hand to her forehead. "I've been really stressed out. There's so many things going on inside my head. I can't seem to stop thinking about them, and I haven't been able to sleep much. And I have to have dinner with my mother this weekend, and I just don't want to see her."

Falco rambled on, talking about the child abduction case, the gang bangers, Andie's admission to the psych ward, Ballard, Grasky's retirement, and missing Sam. "I'm juggling so much, it seems, but I'm just going through the motions." She sighed. "It's like I'm on a fast-moving train that won't stop, like I'm watching my life streak by but everything is so…superficial. I don't have any control over any of it."

The session blew by, leaving Falco feeling dizzy and drained. Her headache loomed as she drove east on Irving and back to the station.

CHAPTER 66

Grasky waited patiently at his desk. Falco gathered her things, swallowed two Motrin, and joined him on his way out to the parking lot. They located the blue Impala and headed west to Humboldt Park. Grasky drove, leaving Falco to her thoughts. He knew she was dealing with some personal issues, so he let her be. North Avenue was moving slowly; he turned north and then west on Wabansia then found a parking spot with the bungalow in view.

The house looked empty with neither the Escort nor the minivan in sight. Grasky settled in and glanced at Falco. "You okay?" he asked, fidgeting with a pack of gum.

"Yeah…yeah, I'm okay. Just dealing with some stuff, you know?" Falco said weakly. She focused her eyes on the bungalow. "I sure hope we get something tonight."

It was nearly seven forty-five with no movement anywhere, no cars, no lights. Falco was tired and thirsty, and Grasky tried to fend off sleep. He turned on the engine to rev up the AC as Falco rubbed her eyes and yawned. Dusk loomed red and purple.

Falco's neck was stiff. Her appointment with Maggie ran around in her mind. She felt some sense of relief when she thought about dinner with her mom. Was it really normal for her to dislike her mother so much? She wondered as she stared into the darkness. Grasky was nodding off. Falco glanced at him. She wished she could sleep like that. She smiled and wondered what it would be like to be married to a man like Steve. She imagined sleeping next to him. *He's so solid*, she thought.

She looked at her watch; it was nearly nine. She wondered whether the gang bangers she had seen yesterday afternoon had alerted the people in the bungalow. They could be staking out an empty house for all they knew. She was getting restless; she crossed her legs and felt the bruise on her knee. She looked at Grasky and softly shook his arm.

He grunted, realizing he had dozed off. "Sorry. I didn't realize…"

"It's okay. Nothing's going on. No cars, no lights on in the house." She stared at the street, straining her eyes.

Grasky looked at his watch. "It's been a long day. Want to give it until nine thirty?"

"Sure," Falco said.

Grasky rubbed his eyes and stretched. "Ballard's hot on the trail of those car thefts in Uptown," he said, making conversation.

"Well, I'm glad he's got some leads. He really knows the neighborhood. I guess he grew up around Lawrence and Clark. I've learned some handy back alley shortcuts from him," Falco said with a smile.

"I didn't think you two got along so well."

"Just between you and me, he can be an insensitive clod. And he's pretty lazy, but other than that…" Falco chuckled.

Grasky smiled and nodded. "He's a character. That's for sure."

Nine-thirty came and went. Grasky and Falco decided to call it a night. Grasky started the Impala and headed east toward Lakeview. Thunderstorms were booming out over the lake. Falco didn't relish the drive home. *I won't make it home until ten thirty at best*, she thought.

* * *

Thursday morning was dark and stormy. Falco's alarm woke her from a dead sleep at six fifteen. She felt groggy as she bumped her way to the kitchen to make a pot of coffee. It gurgled and sputtered until the four cups were done. She took a warm shower and put on a crisp white blouse and dark khaki pants. She brushed her hair, letting it air-dry in the humidity. Dark circles hung below her bloodshot eyes. She glanced in the mirror with a look of disappointment then returned to the kitchen for some coffee. She sat at the dining room table and put her head in her hands. "Thursday," she sighed.

The summer was hitting its dog days. Falco always dreaded August and the onset of the school year. Even though her school days were long past, she still felt the burden of their approach as if she were a kid. The rituals of shopping for new clothes and school supplies never had excited her, even though she was a good student who enjoyed most subjects, especially English and history. She sighed as she drove east thinking about Sam coming home and her dinner date with Howard and Elaine. Her stomach felt mildly upset and she knew why.

The station was buzzing with the news of a hate crime in the vicinity of Roscoe and Halsted. Two guys in a pickup truck had gone after two gay men leaving the 7-Eleven. The Cubs game had gone into extra innings, and the two attackers were probably drunk and looking for trouble. Both of the men who were jumped had cuts and bruises but neither could identify their attackers.

Falco waved to Ballard as she glanced at his desk. He was on the phone. *He must be really on to something if he beat me to work*, she thought. She peered at her calendar. "Shit!" she whispered. "I'm supposed to meet Brenda for lunch." She sat down with a sigh, not feeling very social or interested in food. She walked over to the water cooler and filled a cup.

REACTION TO THE VICTIM

Tim Strickland brushed past. He was all smiles. "Hey, Detective. How's life?"

"Fine, I guess," Falco said blandly. She had the distinct feeling he and Michael were an item, but she'd wait for Michael to tell her. "Do you know anything more on that hate crime on Roscoe?"

"Not really. That kind of thing really gets the community up in arms."

"Yeah," Falco said, turning back toward her desk. She figured Bobby Leighton would be put on the case along with the police GLBT liaison.

Grasky came by Falco's desk with a chocolate-frosted doughnut. She glared at the sticky mess in his hand and said, "You're not gonna make it to retirement eating that stuff." She smiled, scrunching her face.

"Hey, ya gotta live a little," Grasky said, pulling over a chair and sitting down.

Falco was hoping he'd go away with that doughnut; the sweet smell was making her sick to her stomach. She swallowed some cold water and moved her chair out of the doughnut's range.

"Got an update on the bungalow. No school records of kids living at that address," Grasky said.

"Get the fuck outta here!" Falco sat forward and smiled at him.

"I say we do the same as yesterday and take the Impala. How does five o'clock look for you?"

"Plan on it," she said breathlessly. She suddenly felt focused. *Now we're on to something*, she thought.

CHAPTER 67

Falco's mother left a message on her work voicemail to remind her about their dinner date on Saturday. She scowled as her stomach churned. She checked the rest of her messages then made arrangements to use the Impala for the evening's stakeout. She ran down the stairs and out of the building. It was steamy outside. The August heat felt different than the heat of July or June. August heat was morbid, as if the spirit of summer knew her impending fate and was taking her wrath on Earth's lowly inhabitants one last time.

Falco climbed into her hot car. The stale coffee from her commuter mug, still in its holder from the other day, smelled sour. She opened her door and dumped the coffee onto the street. She started the car and headed north on Halsted, then west to Clark. Finding a parking space just off Wilson, she crossed the street to the Thai restaurant. She was five minutes late.

"Hey, girl!" came Brenda's voice.

"Hey, yourself," Falco said with a smile, finding her friend in a booth near the middle of the restaurant. She sat down. "Sorry I'm late."

"No biggie," said Brenda with a wave of her hand. "You been working hard?"

"Weird hours mostly," Falco said, not wanting to give Brenda any information about their hot lead on the gray bungalow. "Anything new on your end on the child abductions?"

"Fucking no. It's so frustrating. I bet these guys skipped town weeks ago," she said, leaning in and not wanting anyone to hear. She took a sip from her water and scanned the menu. "This is my favorite place for Thai food. They make it real hot, so I'm warning you now."

Falco gave her a pierced look. "Hm…"

"Hey, are you all right? You look a little beat."

"Weird hours, you know? And I've had some trouble sleeping," Falco said, avoiding Brenda's gaze.

They ordered their food. Brenda asked for chopsticks; Falco stuck with the fork. Brenda talked nonstop about work, her family, and her condo. Falco mostly listened and picked at her food. She was enjoying hearing about someone else's life for a change. *I need to get out more*, she thought.

Brenda stopped talking and smiled. "I'm sorry to be blabbing on and on. We just don't get together much anymore." Falco nodded in agreement. "So, how's single life treating you?"

"Okay, I guess. I see my son as much as I can."

"That's not what I'm asking and you know it. Are you seeing anyone?"

She was taken aback by Brenda's question. "No, I'm not seeing anyone." She laughed, as if the idea were preposterous.

Brenda gave her a puzzled look then smiled and looked at her plate. She paused for a moment then grinned. Noticing Brenda's wry smile, Falco looked at her askance. "What's up Brenda? You're gonna tell me something, aren't you?"

Brenda continued to smile and then blushed. "Well, I do have some interesting news."

Falco put her hands out as if to say, *Let's hear it.*

"You know, I had a reputation when I was at the twenty-third district," Brenda said, holding Falco's gaze. "I'm sure you knew about it. It was no big secret."

Falco shook her head. "I try not to get involved with that kind of thing—rumors, gossip."

"Well, you know what the guys used to call me—Butter Salerno. And it wasn't because I'm related to the bakery folks…Salerno Butter Cookies, you know," she said with a laugh.

Falco nodded. "Yes, I know."

"Well, I got around, and it wasn't because I had this need, this insatiable need for men…for sex, you know. Looking back on all that, I realize I was trying to find myself. When I got to the FBI, I had to change my ways. I didn't need a rep there. That's for sure."

Falco nodded.

Brenda looked around then sighed. "The thing is, I met someone," she said, smiling.

Falco perked up. "That's great."

"Yeah, it is great, really great," Brenda said, beaming. "The trouble is…" She looked away. "The trouble is…her name is Beth."

Falco sat back and stared at her, her eyes wide. Brenda paused, gauging Falco's reaction. Falco continued to stare until Brenda finally said, "Uh…hello in there."

"Oh…sorry, Brenda," Falco stammered, putting her hand to her forehead. "That is a bit of news."

"Well, I hope you're okay with it," she said pointedly.

"Oh…sure…it's not a big deal…at all."

"Good, 'cause I figured you'd be cool with it. Beth and I have been seeing each other for about two months. She's a paralegal. I met her at the court-house of all places. It's so weird, girl. I can't begin to tell you how alive I feel, how in touch I feel with myself now that I figured all this out."

Falco nodded. "That's really wonderful."

"I mean, before I came out to myself as a lesbian, I couldn't figure out why I wasn't happy with guys. I guess that's why I fucked so many of them. I'd think, *Oh, he's the one* or *This guy is perfect.* Then I'd wake up with them and think, *Yuck! What is this hairy thing in my bed?*" Brenda laughed then looked around, hoping she wasn't getting too loud.

Falco smiled but was stuck on Brenda's initial admission. She wanted to be accepting and supportive, but her head was spinning and her heart was beating fast. She took a swallow of water and tried to focus on what her friend was saying.

"Beth is so wonderful. We connect on so many levels, and when I wake up and see her, feel her next to me, I know it's perfect and so right. No hairy men in my bed…ever again!"

Falco smiled, trying to relate while resisting the image of two women together in bed. She thought about that misty black-and-white photo of

Andie and Kat in the gallery office and wondered what a woman's soft skin next to hers would feel like. She shook the thought away.

Brenda paid for lunch, apologizing for going on and on. They walked across Clark and found Falco's Camry. She leaned against it as Brenda moved toward her.

"I need to tell you one more thing," Brenda said, "and then I'm gonna shut up and let you go."

"There's more?" Falco said, half joking then looking at Brenda intently.

"I've always…been attracted to you, Monica, right from the start. In fact," she said, getting close, "I've often thought about what it would be like to kiss you."

Falco held her gaze as Brenda leaned closer. She felt Brenda's breath faintly on her lips as she put her hands on Brenda's shoulders and whispered, "I don't… I don't think that's a good idea."

Brenda pulled back and gasped. "Sorry, girl. I'm sorry." She looked down, embarrassed. "I guess I got caught up in the moment," she laughed. She stepped back and smiled. "I'd better go."

Falco turned to her car and said, "I'll see you sometime, Brenda."

"Take care, girl." Brenda spun around, looked back at Falco and smiled, then disappeared around the block.

Falco got into her car and started the engine. She took a deep breath and stared at the car parked in front of hers. Sweat was beading on her forehead, dripping down her chest, and pooling underneath her breasts. She switched on the AC full blast and pulled onto Clark Street. She gunned her car right and onto Lawrence and headed east. Traffic was stopped at the stoplight on Broadway. The homeless were drifting into shady alleyways. She made a quick right and headed south to Addison. Distracted and driving a bit too fast, she pulled into the station's parking lot and cranked the engine off.

She sat in her car and stared at the red brick wall in front of her. Her heart was racing and her palms were sweaty.

How close did she come to kissing me?

Why did I let her get so close? she thought, feeling Brenda's breath on her lips.

Did I want her to kiss me?

How would it make me feel?

Would it change me forever?

The car suddenly felt overwhelmingly hot. Her blouse was sticking to her back and chest. She was finding it hard to breathe. She pushed open her car door and almost fell onto the pavement. Her chest felt tight and she felt dizzy. "Oh, god," she whispered, standing up and leaning into her car. She put her fingers to her forehead and took a deep breath, then her keys dropped to the pavement.

Her legs felt heavy as she made her way to the back entrance of the twenty-third district. The cool of the air conditioning was a welcome relief as Falco huffed her way up the two flights of stairs. She ducked into the rest-room and splashed water on her face. She looked in the mirror but didn't recognize the image. The long hours were catching up to her, and so were the sleepless nights. She thought again about Brenda's near kiss as a smile surfaced on her face.

"She made a pass. I guess you could say she made a pass…a big pass," Falco whispered. "Jesus Christ."

She returned to her desk with a cup of water. Grasky swung by and pointed to his watch. She eyed him and nodded. "We're all set."

She had messages to return but felt distracted and strangely exhilarated. Her hands shook as she put the Styrofoam cup to her lips. She pushed her chair back with her legs; it moved easily on the tile floor then stopped abruptly as if stuck on something. She twisted around and found her navy sweater on the floor; one of the wheels had run over it. She moved the chair forward and picked it up, shaking off the dust from the floor and wheel. She folded the sweater, set it on her desk, and stared at it. Thoughts of Andie came to her mind—her smile, her presence that day she had come by the station. She placed the folded sweater on her lap and whispered, "I *miss* you."

CHAPTER 68

It was nearing five, and Grasky knew they would hit the peak of rush hour traffic to Humboldt Park. "Let's get a move on and beat the rush," he said, briefcase in hand.

Falco gathered her things and adjusted her holster. She put her sunglasses on and followed Steve down the stairs and out the building.

Despite the traffic, Grasky and Falco arrived at Karlov and Wabansia in twenty minutes. Grasky had absconded with a pair of night vision binoculars from one of his SWAT buddies. Falco fumbled with them as Grasky found an appropriate parking space. "We're in luck," she said, eyeing the green Escort; it was parked in front. The gate of the cyclone fence was ajar.

"Maybe we'll have some movement. When it gets dark, we'll bend the block then park again," Grasky said. Falco nodded.

The car was hot but Grasky managed to find a thick maple tree to park under out of direct exposure of the scorching sun. They waited as dusk settled and the sun cooled to shades of orange, ochre, and purple.

Falco had plenty to occupy her thoughts.

It was nearly nine when the minivan drove up in a rumble. Three adults tumbled out of the front seats and moved toward the van's back cargo doors.

Out came four children: one blond, the other three with dark hair. None of the four kids was over three feet tall, making them all within the height of the missing children.

Grasky and Falco perked up in their seats, eyeing the six as they made their way into the house. The four kids appeared to be boys; they were dressed in skimpy shorts and thin tank tops. One boy ran ahead but was reined in by one of the adults. The smaller adult turned out to be the woman they had seen two days before in the basement.

Minutes after the front door closed the basement lights went on. Falco and Grasky made their move across the street, quietly over the fence and into the yard. They peered into the basement. The four children weren't Latino. The woman unpacked bags of carryout food while the kids waited. They looked thin and despondent but well behaved. The older man with the mustache watched the four children as the younger man sat at the table of computer equipment and started up the machines. Someone turned on overhead lights as the four boys huddled over the bags of food.

Falco peered into the basement window and squinted at the four boys. She had memorized the faces of the missing boys from the suburbs, but it was hard to tell if any of them matched the descriptions in her mind.

"They look so thin," she whispered.

Grasky nodded. "I can't tell if they look like any of the missing kids. Can you?"

Falco shook her head.

The boys ate while the three adults moved equipment around the basement. Near the back, where Falco remembered seeing the child in the bathroom, was the full-size bed with oversize pillows. The younger man dragged out a large box with wheels; it looked like a suitcase. He laid it on the floor and opened it. Inside was a video camera with lights. He took out the lights and pulled apart the telescoping stands. He then unpacked the camera.

There was a flurry of activity near the bed as the three adults arranged the lights and pillows. The young man positioned the camera and focused the lens on the bed. Next he unloaded a handheld camera and placed it on a small table.

"This doesn't look good," Falco whispered, getting nervous. Grasky grimaced as he eyed her. He was chewing a wad of gum with his front teeth.

Before long the lights in the front of the basement dimmed, and the four boys were herded into the bathroom. The door closed. The younger man took off his shirt and handed the video camera to the older man. Just then Falco and Grasky heard the gate of the cyclone fence open and clang shut. Someone from the street had entered the yard and had climbed up the front wooden steps. He knocked at the front door. The woman in the basement ran up the stairs to let the person in.

The two detectives watched as the woman led the young man to the basement. He was a big kid, no more than fifteen years old, white with tattoos up and down his muscular arms. The older man held a bottle of clear liquid, possibly tequila, and downed a mouthful. He handed the bottle to the young man, who took a swig then gave it to the teenager, who tipped the bottle upside down and let the liquid flow down his throat.

The woman stood behind the large video camera on the stand and focused the lens on the middle of the bed. She dimmed the lights and walked toward the bathroom and opened the door. The four boys were naked and filed timidly out of the bathroom. Falco's heart was beating fast. "We can't let this go too far," she said. "These boys are going to get hurt. I know it!"

"Take it easy," Grasky said. "We need evidence."

The lights dimmed in the back room. They saw the teenager take off his shirt and pants. A light came on from above as one of the young boys, the blond, was directed to get onto the bed. The teenager joined the boy, glaring at him, talking and gesturing. The boy appeared frightened of the muscular teenager, who seemed to take pleasure in intimidating the child with his size and presence.

"Jesus, Grasky. We have enough right now!" Falco whispered.

"Let them get something on film. Hold on."

They both watched in silence. The blond boy was crying. Falco couldn't stand it and looked away.

"I'm calling for a squad, Steve. I've seen enough!" she whispered with a cry in her voice. Her hands shook as she radioed for backup. Quietly she reached for her weapon and took it in both hands.

"Take it easy," Grasky warned, touching her forearm. "Wait…wait."

CHAPTER 69

Within minutes two squad cars appeared in front of the house; another crept in the back. Four uniformed cops slid out of their vehicles and quietly pushed their car doors closed. Grasky motioned for them to take positions on each side of the front door. The other two were to stay in the yard. Two officers from the alley were positioned to break down the back door and charge the basement from the rear.

Falco scanned the yard and street, looking left and right, her weapon ready. She and Grasky would enter the front door and storm the basement with the two uniformed officers following. It wasn't clear whether any of the suspects downstairs had weapons; with four squad cars outside, they would be heavily outmanned if they did.

Grasky and Falco climbed the wooden stairs. The two officers followed. Falco tried the front screen door; it was locked but still ajar. She pulled the metal door open then quietly tried the wooden storm door. "It's locked," she whispered.

Grasky motioned to the two uniformed cops. The two detectives backed out of the way as the officers stepped back to force the door open. They kicked the wooden door in with a loud thud, sending the adults in the basement scrambling. Guns drawn, Falco and Grasky blew into the house and trounced down the basement stairs. The cops from the alley broke down the back door and entered the basement with guns drawn.

"Police! Don't move!" they yelled as they descended the stairs and saw the stunned suspects.

"On the floor! Everybody! On the floor!" Falco shouted, her gun pointed toward the four adults.

Grasky circled behind her. "Don't move! Everybody on the floor! Now!"

The suspects held their hands in the air and dropped to their knees, then went facedown on the basement floor. They'd been caught completely by surprise. Grasky and the other officers searched and cuffed the three men and read them their rights. Falco did the same to the woman.

After the suspects were secured, Falco walked to the back of the basement looking for the four boys. She found them huddled together in the bathroom. She put her gun in her holster and approached them cautiously. "Everything's okay now," she said. The boys were trembling in terror and whimpering. "It's okay. I'm a police officer. I'm not going to hurt you. We're gonna find your clothes and get you back to your families right away, okay?" she said gently.

More squad cars surrounded the house. Lassiter arrived, as did the FBI. The four suspects were seated on chairs near the computer equipment. Evidence technicians filed in, taking photos and bagging and boxing evidence.

Falco looked around the basement for clothes for the boys. She wasn't finding anything except what they were wearing before and a bunch of dingy bath towels. She approached the Latina. "Where are the boys' clothes?" The woman gave her a blank stare and spat something at her in Spanish. One of the Latino officers saw the exchange and asked the woman the same question in her native tongue. She blurted something at the officer then was silent. "She's not cooperating," he said with a frown.

Falco gave each boy a towel to wrap himself in and went in search of their clothes. Lassiter intercepted her as he made his way through the crowd of feds, technicians, and cops. "Great work, Falco. *Great* work," he said, beaming and putting put his hand on her shoulder.

She gave him a distracted look. "Uh, thanks, sir. Excuse me. I've got to find some clothes for those boys." She walked past him and climbed the stairs.

A uniformed officer accompanied a young woman into the house. It was one of the department's social workers assigned to talk with the boys.

Upstairs, the house was dark and musty. Trash, newspapers, and clothes were piled on the floor and on the sparse furniture. Falco bumped into a floor lamp, almost knocking it over. She felt the walls for a light switch, but when she found one it didn't work. She wondered whether anyone actually lived in the house or just used it for filming and other illicit activities.

She felt her way farther into the darkness and tried more light switches along the wall with no luck. She grabbed her flashlight from her belt and punched it on. Cockroaches scurried from the light. "Ewww," she gasped, clenching her teeth.

Falco made her way into a room then decided to turn back and get a strobe light from one of the technicians downstairs. Just then she heard something in the darkness. It was a squeak, then a little cry. Alarmed, she followed the sound down a short hallway. The beam from her flashlight led her into a tiny room. She tried the light switch—nothing. She pointed the flashlight around the room, scanning the walls and floor. Cardboard file boxes were piled up six high along an eight-foot wall. Each box was cryptically labeled with dates. She walked closer to the wall of boxes with her flashlight and squinted at the labels.

Suddenly out of nowhere came a yelp and a bark. A black pit bull barreled through the room and pounced on Falco. The dog was chained to a metal cage and dragged it along as Falco and the dog fell to the floor. The dog let out a ferocious series of growls, barks, and snarls as it chomped down on Falco's right arm. Her flashlight had fallen to the floor; its beam caught the glow of the dog's eyes and the flash of its teeth. "Get the fuck off me!" she yelled as she punched the dog with her left hand and pummeled its belly with her knees. She tried to pry the muscular jaws from her arm with her free hand, but the dog held fast.

Gunshots rang out from the left side of the room, sending bursts of yellow fire. The dog yelped once, then again, and fell silent. Its body rolled lifelessly off Falco and onto the floor with a sickening thud. Blood from the dog sprayed on Falco's face and formed a warm puddle on her chest and stomach. Lassiter and a uniformed cop rushed to her and pulled her up from the floor.

"Jesus Christ. Are you all right?" Lassiter said, kneeling at her side.

Falco was gasping and holding her bleeding arm. They pulled her out of the room and set her on one of the dingy chairs. The room was lit with two huge floodlights. Falco was shook up but not badly injured. "Let's hope that fucking dog doesn't have rabies," she cursed.

Grasky dashed up the basement stairs after hearing the gunshots. "Falco!" he yelled. He saw the blood on her and then glanced at the dead dog. "Holy shit!"

"That explains the BEWARE OF DOG sign," she said, pulling at her bloody sleeve.

"Are you hurt?" Grasky asked, bending down to look at her and all the blood.

Lassiter put his hand on Grasky's shoulder. "It's the dog's blood. We sort of …blew it away."

"I can see that," Grasky said with a grimace.

"We'd better get that arm looked at, Falco," said Lassiter. He grabbed one of the uniformed cops. "Take Detective Falco to the nearest emergency room ASAP."

The officer eyed all the blood and glared at Falco. "Don't you think we should call an ambulance?"

"It's the fucking *dog's* blood. I'm worried about her *arm*!" Lassiter snarled.

The puncture wounds weren't serious. The ER physician on duty theorized the dog was old and losing its teeth. "You'll have some nice bruises, though," he told her.

"Lucky me. I get bit by an old dog," Falco joked as he bandaged her arm and gave her a tetanus shot.

CHAPTER 70

The scene was still alive when Falco and Sergeant Moran returned from the ER. The media was all over the gray bungalow. Camera crews and reporters rushed to Falco as she got out of the squad car. Amy Hollander, the police spokesperson, intercepted her and pulled her into a police van. "We aren't giving an official statement yet," Amy said. "But the press is going to want to talk to you and Detective Grasky," she said, smiling. "You guys cracked the case!" Falco let out a deep sigh and nodded, then smiled.

The four boys had given their names to the social worker, who also had managed to find their clothes. They were positively identified as the missing kids from the north suburbs. The boys were scared but largely unhurt and asking for their parents. An ambulance took them to the hospital, where a pediatrician and a mental health professional would examine them.

Lassiter banged on the door of the police van. "Amy, let's get this show on the road." He briefed her and Falco and gave Amy permission to round up the press. Amy Hollander exited the police van and informed the media that Chief Lassiter was ready to release an official statement, just in time for the tail end of the ten o'clock news. The horde of media positioned themselves around the van as Lassiter stood next to Amy and was flanked by Detectives Grasky and Falco.

Amy Hollander introduced Chief Lassiter, who summarized the case as it had originated in the north suburbs and eventually had involved his law enforcement team at the twenty-third district. He said the four suspects were being booked on numerous charges, including child endangerment, kidnapping, possession of child pornography, possession of stolen goods, and possession of property with the intent to produce and distribute child pornography. The teenager was wanted on two outstanding police warrants, one as an accessory to murder.

Lassiter praised the outstanding police work and professionalism of Detective Monica Falco and Detective Steve Grasky. "Their tireless work and dedication to bringing these children home safe and putting an end to the dangerous and sick activities of these four suspects is deserving of our department's highest commendation."

"I hope my wife is watching," Grasky whispered to Falco. She smiled and crossed her arms over her bloody shirt.

Lassiter turned the microphone over to Amy, who would field questions for the two detectives.

Marjorie Green from the NBC affiliate broke in with her microphone. "Detective Falco, were you injured in the arrest of the four suspects?"

Falco leaned into the microphone. "I was attacked by a pit bull in one of the rooms. Most of the blood was from the dog. Two officers shot it to get it off me."

A rush of questions and shouts rose from the crowd.

"What was the turning point in the case for you, Detective Falco?" asked another reporter.

"I spotted one of the missing children in a car on the Edens last week. The vehicle looked suspicious, and the child looked scared. We got the plate number and went from there," Falco said.

Grasky stepped in and interrupted, "That's an oversimplification of what happened. It was good police work with a lot of female intuition, by my partner, Monica Falco. She noticed the child and followed her instincts. We wouldn't be here answering questions with four suspects in custody if it hadn't been for her superb police work and tenacious follow-up." Falco looked down, embarrassed.

Grasky and Falco took questions for another twenty minutes until Amy Hollander broke up the press conference. The crime scene was winding down and being secured by evidence technicians. Lassiter made his way through the crowd and found Grasky. "You two get outta here and go home. It's been a long day, okay?"

Grasky found Falco, who was looking through the file boxes in the small back room. The pit bull's body had been bagged. "Hey, Falco. Let's get out of here."

She looked up from one of boxes. "These are full of videotapes, and those over there, the brown boxes, are full of photos. Really sick stuff."

"Leave it," Grasky said.

The two detectives headed out of the bungalow and through the yard. The crowd of reporters was still holding out for more. "Shit. Let's make it fast," Falco said.

The hungry journalists with their mass of cameras and microphones spotted the detectives and rushed toward them, asking more questions and seeking more comments regarding the suspects, the boys, and what was in the house. Grasky moved in front of Falco and put his hands up. "Look, everybody. It's been a long day, and I think we've answered all your questions. Can ya give us and break and let us go home?"

The crowd persisted, but the two ignored them, walking fast to the blue Impala down the street.

"We're outta here," said Grasky as he started the engine and made his way through the reporters, TV cameras, and vans.

* * *

It was nearly midnight by the time Grasky and Falco reached the station. They trudged up the stairs to the second floor, where they were met by the night shift, who applauded and cheered as they made their way to their desks.

"Oh, come on, guys," Falco said as they passed through the cubicles.

"Thanks a lot, everybody, but we just want to go home," Grasky said, smiling.

They gathered their things and headed out the building. Grasky stopped at Falco's car on his way to his.

"Thanks for the nice plug with the press, Steve," she said, looking up at him.

"This was really your arrest, lady. I'm proud to have been a part of this case and to have had the opportunity to work with you. It's been a privilege, Falco."

"Thanks, but the privilege is mine." She pulled him closed and kissed him on the cheek.

He smiled and laughed, then gave her a hug and backed away from her. "Get some sleep, Detective."

"I'll try," she said as she unlocked her car. "See you tomorrow."

Falco started the engine then pulled out of the parking lot and onto Addison. She headed west to Damen. She was exhausted and her arm ached. She drove in silence, listening to the hiss of the AC. She turned right on Damen then left onto Foster. The streets were deserted for midnight on a Friday. She felt herself calm down and processed the events of the day. The faces of the four boys surfaced in her head, then the surprised faces of the four suspects. *Sick bastards*, she thought. She stared ahead, watching the road. Slowly but surely a smile appeared on her face. She felt it widen and allowed it happen. She nodded slowly, gripped the steering wheel, and quietly whispered, "Yes!"

CHAPTER 71

It was eight fifteen a.m. when the phone rang. Falco woke from a dead sleep. Her body ached as if she hadn't moved a muscle since she had lain down. She sat up and immediately felt pain from her bruised arm and the bite wounds. She then felt the dull ache of her weapon deep in her left side. She leaned forward and let the phone ring then looked down at her bloody shirt and realized she'd slept in her clothes with her holster on.

"Great," she sighed, getting up from the bed. She took off her holster and wrapped the straps around the pistol. Then she took off her shoes and peeled off the bloody shirt, which had adhered to her abdomen. "Fuck," she whispered. "This stain is never coming out."

The phone rang again. She made her way around the bed and grabbed the receiver clumsily, knocking it to the floor. She snatched it up and put it to her ear. "Yes. Hello?" she said, her voice hoarse.

"Hey, M. Congratulations," Jeffery said. "Did I wake you up?"

"Oh, hi. Well…I guess I overslept," she said, rubbing her eyes.

"I saw you and Detective Grasky all over the news last night and this morning too. Congrats."

"Thanks. It's all a bit much right now," she said, looking at her watch.

"I hope you and Grasky get a nice bonus for all your hard work on the case."

"Oh, I'm sure that's not going to happen. It doesn't really work that way. Listen, Jeffery. I'm running late. Can I call you later, like tomorrow or something?"

"Well, I'm going to be picking up Sam tomorrow from camp sometime in the afternoon," Jeffery said.

"Oh, I forgot! Sam's coming home tomorrow!" She put her fist to her forehead, admonishing herself for forgetting.

"Why don't we get together on Sunday? Maybe get a pizza somewhere?"

"Great," Falco said, feeling let off the hook. "I'll call you Sunday morning."

She grabbed the heap of dirty clothes and put them in her hamper. She turned on the shower and carefully pulled back the bandages from her wounds. Her arm had started to bruise, but the puncture wounds were looking a little better. She got into the warm shower and let the water run over her aching body. Her neck and upper back were stiff from having hit the floor with the dog on top of her.

Jeffery's phone call popped into her mind. *How typical of him not to ask me about the dog bite*, she thought. *He's so afraid of me getting hurt that he won't even talk about it. It's a reality of the job…and sometimes it's only a dog bite.* "Stupid, nasty dog," she muttered.

Falco grabbed the *Chicago Tribune* from her porch and tossed it into the living room as she pushed her front door closed. She scanned the street, looking for TV vans—nobody. Relieved, she got into her car and pulled onto the street. Her right arm ached as she gripped the steering wheel. Her cell phone rang as she drove east on Devon. She fumbled for it in her purse.

"Falco here."

"Hey, girl. You know, I should be really, really pissed at you!" It was Brenda Salerno.

Falco grimaced. "I never thought you'd hold out on an old CPD buddy! Academy chum and all!"

Falco paused, wondering whether Brenda was really mad or pulling her chain. "Well, Brenda, it was like…"

"Hey. I'm just kidding, girl. Nice work! Congrats! We're pretty pissed off over here, though," she said, laughing. "I bet Lassiter is walking on air."

"Thanks, Brenda, but it was mostly about being in the right place at the right time. We just got lucky."

"Oh, you're so fucking modest. Jesus Christ! Ride it out, girl. Take it all in and enjoy. That's what I say. Great arrest, baby!" Falco smiled but didn't say anything. "Hey, are you okay from that pit bull attack? Was it bad?"

Falco was distracted and tired of talking about the dog bite. "It's no big deal. My arm is just bruised. Luckily the dog was old, or it could have been much worse."

Thankfully Brenda got a phone call and had to cut the conversation short. Falco thought about what Brenda had said about enjoying the accolades and glory then shrugged it off.

* * *

The twenty-third district headquarters was mobbed by TV station vans parked along the street and in the parking lot. Falco's heart sank as she pulled into the back lot. She looked in her rearview mirror for approaching reporters. "Maybe I can sneak out and make a run for the door," she said out loud. She peered around the parking lot and quickly slipped into the station and closed the door behind her.

Jim Ballard was waiting for the elevator with a cup of coffee and a cinnamon roll. Falco eyed him as she turned the corner for the stairs.

"Hey, JB. What's going on?" She flashed him a smile.

"Oh, you're all smiles today," he said, chewing.

She leaned against the wall next to the elevator and gazed at him. She could see a hint of jealousy in his face.

"Congratulations are in order. Nice work!" he said, lifting his cup in a toast. "I guess you're the new rising star in the department!"

Falco laughed. "I hardly think so."

Ballard stuffed the rest of the cinnamon roll into his mouth and punched the elevator button again. "Too bad Grasky's retiring. I'm sure you two would make a great team."

She didn't want to comment and turned toward the stairs. She grabbed the handrail of the stairwell and started to head up.

"Hey, Falco!" yelled Ballard. "Lassiter brought pastries in for everybody to celebrate. There's more upstairs."

"Hm…none for me. Thanks. You're looking a little pudgy there, JB. You might want to cut back on those. Didn't you tell me you were borderline diabetic?" she said flatly.

"Ooooh, Detective Falco, the finely oiled machine!" Ballard shot back as the elevator doors opened.

"Jerk," she hissed as she climbed the stairs.

Falco surfaced on the second floor. As she made her way to her desk, people rose from their seats and clapped and cheered. Some came out and patted her shoulders. Grasky had made it in before her and had received the same welcome. Falco blushed with embarrassment and looked down smiling as Grasky stood at his desk applauding. "Okay, okay. That's enough. Thank you, everyone," she said, taking her seat. She looked at her watch; it was only ten. *It's going to be a long day*, she thought.

Chief Lassiter announced there would be an eleven a.m. briefing in the conference room for everyone. He then called Falco into his office. She went down the rows of cubicles and slipped into his office.

Lassiter smiled broadly at her. "I hope you got some sleep last night."

"Yes, I did," she replied quickly.

"How's the arm?"

"A bit sore. I'm going to have some nice bruises, but other than that it's okay. Thanks for saving me from that thing. I guess I forgot to tell you that last night."

"Hey, all in the line of duty. What a night, though, huh? I'll tell you, I didn't sleep much!" he said, beaming.

Falco nodded, wondering why he had called her into his office.

Lassiter came around to the front of the desk and leaned on it, gazing at her. "Listen, clear you calendar for this Tuesday, okay? I don't care what you have going on. Even if you plan to fly to Hawaii, clear your calendar. I've already spoken to Grasky and told him to do the same."

"Okay, but what's going on? We going to Disney World?" she joked.

Lassiter let out a big laugh then smiled broadly. "You know, I've missed that in you this last month or so—that kooky sense of humor of yours. I've really missed it."

Falco smiled and shrugged.

"The deal for Tuesday is you and Grasky will be getting a special commendation from the big guys downtown," Lassiter said. "Superintendent Kline and the mayor will be there to present the commendations. Also, from what I'm hearing, folks from the suburbs will be there with some kind of special recognition too. It's going to be a big thing—big for you and big for the department. I've invited some special folks from our district, the alderman and some council members—political types. A lot of people from the department will be there too. I'll get some more invitations by the end of the day, so make sure you come by and get a handful from me if you want to bring your husband and family. Oh, and I should also mention that you'll probably be asked to say a few words."

"How many people?" Falco asked, biting her lip.

"It's taking place in the winter garden of the Harold Washington Library on State and Congress."

Falco scrunched her face. "The winter garden – that's huge. I'm glad you warned me."

CHAPTER 72

Falco and Grasky sat at the large conference table waiting for the eleven o'clock briefing to start. Lassiter was held up with a phone call. The room was buzzing about the child abductions and the four suspects. Grasky described the arrests for everyone—especially the looks on the suspects' faces. Falco looked on and smiled.

Lassiter entered the room beaming and formally congratulated Grasky and Falco on their outstanding police work. Everyone at the table and in the room applauded again. He then looked serious and unfolded a computer printout. "A couple of updates on the four suspects, Ernesto Santos, Alicia Quinones, Corey Van Fleet, and Ricardo Mendez. They've been formally charged with the following: kidnapping, child endangerment, download-ing child pornography from the Internet with the intent to distribute, pos-session of stolen goods, possession of controlled substances, sexual assault on a minor…"

Falco looked at Grasky and shook her head. "Those poor boys. If only we could have gotten to them sooner."

Lassiter read further from the list of charges. "Bail has been set at two million each," he said, looking up. Applause came from around the room as Lassiter held up his hands for quiet. "In addition, Detective Falco's run-in with a pit bull netted some interesting evidence and charges. "You want to tell us all about what you found in that back room, Falco?" he asked, turning to her.

"Well, besides the pit bull…" Laughter rumbled through the room. "We found at least sixty cardboard file boxes full of photos of kids, really young kids, involved in pornographic activities and video recordings dating back almost three years."

Eyeing the room, Lassiter added, "So our suspects—these monsters—were involved in the child porn industry, operating virtually undetected, for three years…collecting the stuff, distributing the stuff, hurting little kids. I'm hoping one of the four will cop a plea and help us turn over more rocks where more of these creeps are hiding and put a real monkey wrench in their sick business," he said with a fist to the table.

As the meeting wound down, Ballard got up and made an announcement. "Hey, everyone, I want to invite all of you to a party some of us are pulling together for our two infamous detectives! It starts right after work. Three-ish." Everyone laughed. "Oh, I mean five-ish at Murphy's Pub on Sheffield and Waveland."

Someone from the back yelled, "Hey, we know where Murphy's Pub is! Most of us can crawl home from there!" Everyone laughed.

"Detectives Grasky and Falco will be our honored guests, and we'll be picking up the entire tab until we close the place," Ballard said. Cheers erupted in the room. "And I expect Detective Falco to be there with her drinking shoes on!"

Falco smiled, not wanting to disappoint her colleagues.

Grasky leaned in to her and whispered, "I gotta call my wife and tell her. We were supposed to go to dinner tonight. I don't want to be a party pooper."

"No, you don't want to be a party pooper and leave me with Ballard, Riley, and Bobby Leighton," she said, giving him the evil eye.

* * *

Falco returned to her desk and checked her voicemail. Thirteen messages awaited her attention. "Shit," she sighed. Ballard came by and slid a copy of the *Chicago Tribune* under her line of vision. He had circled an article just under the lead front-page article about the child abduction case. She scanned the page as she wrote down messages from her voicemail. Her eyes dropped to the bottom of page one, where Ballard had circled a block of text and drawn an arrow. The headline read, "Rising Star Follows in Dad's Footsteps."

Falco glared at the headline then quickly began to read the article. There was an old police photo of Detective Pete Falco, and to the right was Falco's photo. She hung up the phone, stood up, and stared at the article, then picked up the paper in both hands, peering at it closer. Her heart was racing.

The article traced the career of Falco's father as a Chicago cop, highlighting key cases, including the arrest and conviction of a notorious rapist and murderer. They paralleled Falco's career, starting from college where she had majored in forensics; to her career as a young street cop; to her promotion to detective and transfer to the twenty-third district. Comments on both father and daughter were taken from numerous sources, including retired cops still living in the city and Falco's colleagues and those who had served as her mentors. The article went on to mention her father's early retirement from the force and his untimely death at age fifty-two. "Jesus Christ," she whispered. She felt both exposed and betrayed.

"Hey, looks like you've seen a ghost," Grasky said, eyeing Falco.

She looked up at him, startled. "This article…about me and my father. I can't believe they'd print this without asking me." Grasky leaned in and peered at the headline. Falco continued to scan it, her eyes darting around the text and the photos.

"Well, it's a nice article. That's for sure," Grasky said, reading over her shoulder. "I didn't know your dad had died so young."

"That's exactly the point! Nobody needs to know this… about me or especially my father." She stared at him, visibly upset. "I can't believe this.

They found people he worked with and people who knew me at the academy and when… I'm surprised they didn't print what brand of fucking tampons I use!" she hissed.

"Hey, take it easy. Take it *easy*, Falco. I can understand how you feel, but the article is hardly malicious. In fact it's very complimentary. I think you should calm down and read it again." Falco stared at him and Grasky saw the anger leave her face. He put the article in front of her and said, "Read it like you're just interested in the detective who cracked a very important case."

Falco closed her eyes for a second and breathed deeply. She sat down and reread the article. Grasky walked back to his desk and left her alone. He sat down and smiled, eyeing her from across the room. *What a firecracker*, he thought. *High strung, passionate, and smart*. He shook his head and smiled then unwrapped a fresh stick of gum.

* * *

The rest of the day passed quickly. Falco was busy returning messages and compiling her report on the abduction case. Ballard walked past her desk and said, "Thirty-five minutes until Murphy's Pub."

Falco glanced up. "Do you want this back, JB?" she asked, handing him the newspaper.

"Only if you autograph it," he said with a smirk.

"Yeah, whatever," she said, tossing it in the trash. She thought for a moment then fished the paper out of the wastebasket. She grabbed a pair of scissors and cut out the picture of her father, then stuck it on her bulletin board and smiled sadly.

Ballard left early and headed to Murphy's with fellow detective Bobby Leighton and a handful of others. Falco was immersed in her report and didn't notice it was past five p.m.

Grasky drifted past her desk and peered at her computer screen. "Come on," he said. "It's after five, and our presence at Murphy's is required."

She smiled and closed the window she was working on and shut down her computer. Grasky waited patiently. She got up and turned to Grasky. "Ready to party," she said.

He smiled. "After you, Detective."

They left their cars in the police station parking lot and walked to the pub. It was an old neighborhood bar built of red Chicago brick. Inside it smelled of stale beer and cigarettes; its décor was vintage oak and deep green. Murphy's was dark for an early summer night, but this was Wrigleyville, home of the Cubs, where the partying starts early, especially during base-ball season.

Falco and Grasky entered the bar and were met with cheers from their fellow officers, the bar owners, and patrons. Most of the folks at the twenty-third district were regulars at Murphy's, although Grasky and Falco rarely frequented the place. The two detectives sidled up to the bar as the bartender told them their drinks were covered all night.

"All right!" said Grasky, elbowing Falco. He was ready to celebrate.

Two shot glasses appeared in front of the detectives. Grasky downed his without asking what the liquid was; Falco peered at the tiny glass and ordered a Chardonnay.

Jim Ballard and Bob Leighton made their way through the thickening crowd of cops and staff. Chief Lassiter came by without his ever-present jacket and tie and sat next to Grasky. "Sure you want to retire, old man?" he said, slapping him on the back.

Grasky downed Falco's shot. "Paperwork's in, Chief. I can't turn back now!"

Lassiter looked at Falco and said, "Well, you're a youngster. I can count on you being around for a while."

"I'm not that young, Chief," she said, eyeing him.

Ballard burst in, overhearing their conversation. "Well, you're old enough to be drinking something stronger than that, Detective. Come on, Pauley. Set us up with some more shots!"

Lassiter got up and sat next to Falco. "Hey, nice article about you and your dad in the *Trib*. You saw it, didn't you?"

She nodded. "Ballard gave me a copy."

"Did you know I knew your dad just before he retired?" Lassiter asked.

She looked at him with surprise. "No, I didn't know that."

"Yeah, I was more than a couple of years younger than him and still pretty green. He was real decent to me, taught me some stuff, and gave me some good advice. It's too bad he retired so young." Falco looked down and nodded.

Ballard pushed the shot in front of her and leaned in. "Come on, Falco. Don't be such a fucking lightweight!"

She smiled at Ballard and downed the shot without flinching, as the crowd around the bar cheered her on. Bobby Torres and Tim Strickland came by with beers in their hands and sidled up to the bar next to the two detectives. It was only six thirty, and they were already loaded.

"You guys here together?" Falco asked, half joking.

"Together? Like *together,* together?" Torres asked, looking at Strickland. "No way! My girl's working the night shift at the hospital."

Falco laughed. "And I'm spoken for, at least currently," Strickland said. "In fact, Detective, I think you may know him."

Falco looked at Tim sideways then smiled. "I thought something was up between you two! Good for you."

The bar grew more crowded, and the two detectives were the center of attention. Falco saw old acquaintances from early in her career and retired cops who had known her father. Grasky came by with two more shot glasses and slid one over to Falco. "Come on, girl. The night is young."

"That's what I'm afraid of," she said, downing the shot. She was feeling the first one and had no rational idea why she would do another.

Chief Lassiter stood on a chair and attempted to quiet the crowd. He wavered for a moment, almost losing his balance. "People! People! Let me say a few words to benefit those who no longer regularly frequent the twenty-third district! I see a lot of old familiar faces, and I'd like to make sure *they* know why we are celebrating tonight. I'd like to introduce our two illustrious detectives, Monica Falco and Steve Grasky." Applause and cheers broke out in the bar. "Their…" Lassiter continued trying to quiet the crowd, "their tireless work on this difficult case and their amazing police work make us all really, really proud!"

He jumped down from the chair and grabbed Falco and Grasky by the shoulders, giving them both manly pats on the back and half hugs. A uniformed cop brought another round of shots to the two detectives. The crowd got thicker and noisier.

"Do these look bigger?" Falco asked Grasky, looking down at the double shot glass. He didn't hear her as he downed the drink, laughing. "Jesus Christ, Grasky. Somebody's gonna have to drive you home," she said. He was looking very happy, and his face was flushed. She downed her shot, then said, "Somebody's gonna have to drive *me* home."

By eleven o'clock, the crowd at the pool tables had diminished, but the dart games were going strong. The bar was still loud and rowdy, typical when cops blow off steam. Bobby Leighton and Ballard were loaded and smoking cigars. Ballard had his arm around a plump waitress as he made his way through the noisy room. They found Grasky and Falco yucking it up with one of the bartenders near the back. The shots had taken their toll on Falco. She was weaving and hanging on to the edge of the bar.

"Hey, Falco, I didn't think you could get wasted on white wine!" Ballard said, laughing.

"Fuck you, Jim," she laughed. Her head was spinning, but she didn't care.

Ballard wrapped his arm around the waitress and ordered another drink. "She ain't half bad when she's drunk!" he said to the woman.

It was nearly eleven thirty when two more shots appeared before Grasky and Falco. Grasky downed his automatically then looked over at Falco. She had her head on the bar and wasn't moving. He slid off his barstool and waddled close to her. "Falco, you still alive?" She didn't respond. He gave her a little shake then whispered in her hair, "Falcoooo…are you okay?"

She raised her head and smiled weakly, "I'm okay, just a bit…" She put her head back down.

Grasky looked around and snagged Lassiter, who was playing darts with a noisy bunch of old-timers. "Falco's gonna need a ride home," he said, motioning with his thumb.

Lassiter looked over at Falco with her head on the bar. "Oh, boy. Let me call the station and get a squad car over here."

Within minutes a car pulled up. Officer Jeremy Foley got out and entered the bar, looking for Lassiter. Foley was a rookie in his mid-twenties, tall and muscular with short brown hair. A group of cops from the station razzed him as he walked past. He eyed them comically and said, "You guys are wasted!"

Grasky grabbed Officer Foley and steered him to the back of the bar. He nudged Falco, who had virtually passed out. "We're gonna need to get Detective Falco home," Grasky said, slurring his words.

Foley looked over at Falco and said, "Detective Falco? Are you there?" He nudged her gently. Falco picked up her head but didn't open her eyes. The room was spinning.

"Yeah. What, Steve?"

"I'm not Detective Grasky. I'm Foley, Officer Jeremy Foley. I'm going to give you a ride home, okay?" he said, eyeing her.

"Okay, but let me get my car," she said, her words running together.

"No, Detective. I'm going to give *you* a ride home."

Falco raised her head and tried to focus on Officer Foley's face. "Do I know you?" She scrunched her face and looked confused.

"I'm Officer Foley. I'm going to give you a ride home. Can I help you off the stool here?" he asked, gently taking her arm.

Falco drifted off the stool and steadied herself as she got to the floor. She closed her eyes and leaned against the bar. "Oh…this is sooo not gooood," she said quietly.

Officer Foley took her arm and started to help her to the door. Falco stopped and said, "I need my keys." She turned back to the bar and bent down for her raincoat and keys. Foley intercepted her and grabbed her coat then held her steady. She leaned back into him, and the two turned toward the back door of the bar. "You really know your way around this place," Falco said, looking up at him. "What was your name again?"

Officer Foley told her his name and steered her out of the bar and to his squad car. She stepped around to the passenger side and nearly got hit by a passing car. Foley grabbed her around the waist and pulled her from out of the street. "Jesus!" he yelled.

"Oops," laughed Falco as she dropped her keys.

Foley held her arm, opened the passenger door, and steered her into the seat. He closed the door, came around the car, picked up Falco's keys, and slid in behind the wheel. He started the vehicle and waited for Grasky to return with Falco's address.

Lassiter came out with a slip of paper. "Someone will drive her car back tonight or tomorrow morning," he said, eyeing Falco, who was passed out, her head leaning against the window. Lassiter handed the piece of paper to the rookie. "She's just south of Devon, and put on her seatbelt, okay?"

Foley glanced at Falco. "Yeah. You bet, Chief."

CHAPTER 73

Officer Foley drove west on Addison. He found Cicero Avenue and headed north to Devon. Before long he was straining his eyes at the piece of paper and looking out at house numbers for Falco's address. He found the blond brick house and pulled into the driveway.

"Hey, Detective." He gently shook her. She didn't respond. "Detective Falco," he tried again. She woke up slowly, her eyes drooping. "Detective Falco, you're home. We're gonna need to get you out of the car, okay?" Foley said, gently shaking her again.

She rubbed her eyes, glanced out the window, then looked at Officer Foley. "I guess I need to go to bed."

"Yeah, but we need to get you out of the car and into the house first."

Falco looked at him. His face was serious. She stared at him, smiled, then burst out laughing. "You are so adorable!" she said. "And soooo serious! You've got to be new…a rookie, right?" She shook her head. Officer Foley smiled and tried not to be embarrassed. "I can spot you new guys a mile awaaaay," she said, laughing.

Officer Foley unlocked the car doors from his side and helped Falco unfasten her seat belt. She leaned into the door and dragged herself out of the car, dropping her wallet and keys onto the pavement. "Shit!" she hissed as she bent down to pick them up. Officer Foley came around with her rain-coat and gently took her arm. "Jesus, you're tall," she said, looking up at him. She laughed and almost lost her balance. "I…I don't usually drink like this, Officer," she said comically. "I've never had a DUI before. Can you let me off with a warning?" she asked, laughing.

Officer Foley smiled. "You know, Detective, I haven't been on the force long, but a lot of us rookies think you're one of the best cops in the depart-ment."

"Really? That's you and maybe one or two others?" she asked sarcasti-cally.

"No, Detective, you have a great rep all over the north side. I'm just glad to be in the same district as you. Maybe I'll learn something."

"Yeah…okay," Falco shook her head and stared at the front steps as she tried to maneuver them. When they reached the top of the stairs, Officer Foley looked at her handful of keys as she tried to figure out which one opened the front door. She looked at him and smiled. "The big rectangular one."

He found the key and turned it in the lock. The mail dragged along the carpeting as he shoved open the heavy wooden door. The house was dark. "Let me try to put some lights on," he said as the two entered the living room.

Falco leaned against the door as it closed and put her hand to her head. She leaned forward to walk across the room but decided to wait until Officer Foley returned. A light went on in the living room, and he returned to the front door where she stood holding the doorknob to steady herself. He picked up the mail from the floor and the copy of the *Tribune* she had tossed in from the porch that morning and set the pile on the coffee table.

"Nice house," he said, quietly looking at her. She seemed to be getting her bearings a little better. She fumbled with her holster then took it off and put it on a table next to the door.

"How are you doing? Looks like the fresh air did some good," he said with a little smile.

Falco smiled back weakly. "God, I shouldn't have drunk so much. I don't even know what was in those shots."

Foley laughed then came closer. He looked at her and said, "I was serious about what I said about your rep. I hope someday we might work a case together."

Falco smiled at Foley, then said, "Soooo serious…all the time." Their eyes met. She held his gaze and leaned her head against the front door. Officer Foley looked down at her and leaned in closer. He had a look of tender longing on his face.

Falco put her hand on his black leather belt and gently pulled him close. He bent down closer and searched her face. Their lips met lightly, barely touching. They kissed softly, then again. Falco sighed and pulled him closer, kissing him deeper, her lips parting and wanting more. Foley moved in and put his hand softly around the back of her neck, caressing her ear then her jaw.

Falco slipped her arms up and around Foley's back. She felt the ripples of his muscles in his broad shoulders. She moaned as he pulled her collar aside and kissed her neck then unbuttoned her blouse. He pulled her closer and wrapped his arms around her. She fell back, almost losing her balance. He caught her and clutched her body as he scanned and explored her neck then her breasts with his hand. She laid her hand on Foley's chest, pushing him away for a moment. He stopped and looked at her. He was breathing fast, probing her face, hoping she wouldn't want him to stop.

"Come with me," she said softly.

CHAPTER 74

Jeremy Foley looked at his watch; it was almost one thirty a.m. He had fallen asleep after making love to Falco. He quietly eased out of her arms and slipped out of her bed. She was sleeping soundly. He gazed at her as he hopped into his pants and pulled on his shirt. He was sweaty and smelled of sex. He cinched up his holster and adjusted it on his waist. He sat on the bed and looked over at Falco, caressed her hair, and smiled.

He got up and milled around the room, finding a tiny pad of paper and pen near the phone. He pulled off a sheet and wrote a note. He folded it twice lengthwise, slipped it into her hand, then gently squeezed her fingers around it. He made his way through the dark house and into his squad car then drove off to finish his shift.

* * *

Falco's phone rang. The sun was beaming happily into her bedroom. Her eyes opened slowly as she stared at the digital clock on her nightstand. The blurry amber numbers read ten a.m. She lifted her heavy head and immediately felt the pain. It was a bad one. She wondered how she would feel once she got herself vertical. She dreaded the thought. She slid her hand to the other side of the bed and sleepily stared at the sheets. They were rumpled and twisted. She moved her hand to her face as a small folded piece of paper fell to her chest. She unfolded it and read:

Detective Falco,

You are a beautiful woman!

—Jeremy

She stared at it for a moment, rubbed her eyes, and stared at the note a bit more. Her hand fell heavily on the bed as she crushed the paper in her hand. "Oh, god," she moaned, turning on to her stomach and putting her face in her pillow. She smelled the scent of a man in her bed and felt the tingle of sex from last night.

"Oh, god," she moaned into her pillow. She lay there until sleep came upon her once again. She dreamed of Jeremy, recalling the blur of their lovemaking. She moaned into her pillow as she made love to him again in her mind. Then the phone rang; it startled her awake. "Fuck," she whispered breathlessly. She pulled herself up from the bed and fumbled for the phone. "Hello?" she croaked.

"Hi, dear. It's Mom how *are* you?"

She fell back onto her pillow and put her hand over her eyes. "Hi, Mom."

"Honey? Are you there? You sound sick. Are you sick?"

She had the phone upside down and was talking into the earpiece. She looked at it and then turned it around. "Hi. No, I'm not sick," was all she could think of saying. Her head was pounding and her stomach was rocky. She wanted to moan in agony but figured it wasn't the time. She felt around for the crumpled note in her bed and smoothed it flat on her chest as her mother discussed at length where they were going to have dinner. She stared again at the note and shook her head. "Fuck," she whispered.

"What, dear?" her mother asked.

"Uh, nothing, Mom. I was just saying…how nice it will be to see you." Falco grimaced.

She made a fist and pounded her forehead. They made plans to meet at seven at her mother's apartment. They would "visit for a while," then Howard would take them in his Cadillac to the restaurant, a nice Italian place, as her mother put it. Falco dreaded the thought but felt it was fitting penance for her having fucked Officer Foley. *Oh, my God. I am heartily sorry for having offended thee, and I detest all my sins…*

Her mother went on to briefly mention seeing her on TV with that handsome other detective. Falco shook her head. *Please stop talking, Mother,* she thought. *We can talk later. I need to take some aspirin…or morphine…or rat poison.*

Falco heard a car in her driveway. She then heard a door slam, then another door. A tiny knock came at her front door. She heard the scratch of keys going through the mail slot then quiet. She hung up the phone and slowly got up from the bed. "Jesus, it's worse than I thought," she whispered, willing herself to stand. Her head was banging, and her neck and back were stiff. She was dizzy and her stomach felt like a bowl of acid. She bent over her bed and leaned on her hands. "Oh, shit."

She made her way out of the bedroom and into the bathroom, where she avoided the mirror altogether. She washed her face and attempted to comb her hair. She took two aspirin and put on her robe. She bumped her way into the kitchen and made some weak coffee.

"I need to eat something, some carbs to sop up the acid in my stomach." She opened the refrigerator and peered inside; it was empty. She pulled open the freezer and found some ice-encrusted Eggo waffles she had bought for Sam. She unwrapped them from the plastic and put them in the toaster. The coffee gurgled as she lowered herself to the sofa and waited for the aspirin to kick in.

"I'm a mess," she whispered. "I hope I didn't do anything stupid at the bar. I sure did something stupid afterward." She put her head in her hands and cursed herself.

The sofa was as far as she got for the rest of the morning and early afternoon. The waffles had made her feel a little better, as did the coffee and aspirin. At about one thirty she felt well enough to peer out the picture window at the bright sunshine and see her car parked safely in the driveway. Someone from the station had driven it back and slid the keys through the mail slot.

Falco made her way back to the sofa and closed her eyes. She wondered how she was going to deal with Jeremy. She hoped he wasn't going to get all droopy eyed when she told him their encounter was just a one-night thing, a very stupid one-night thing.

CHAPTER 75

The sun was sliding behind some storm clouds as Falco squinted to see the highway ahead. She wore her navy suit and low-heeled pumps with the pearls her father had given her when she graduated from high school. The last remnant of her hangover was still hanging on, as was a small red mark on the side of her neck. "Jesus Christ, a fucking hicky. I'm forty-seven years old," she steamed.

She had made the forty-five-minute trip to see her mother many times, but the terrain looked different today. The hot weather had made the rolling lawns and trees brown and stiff.

The Connerton Senior Living Community was a sprawling facility with three hundred acres of golf, tennis, bike trails, and other amenities. Meals were included with the yearly fees, which was great for Elaine, who couldn't cook her way out of the box her microwave came in.

Falco searched for her mother's apartment building. Happy gray- and white-haired people dressed in the plaids and florals of summer floated toward one of six dining areas. Falco smiled as she passed a group of them. "God, I hope I never get old," she said through her teeth. She was right on time as she pulled into a parking spot. She touched up her lipstick and glanced at the mark on her neck then scowled.

The staircase up to her mother's apartment was gray stone. It winded up a circular path that led to an elegant entrance. She buzzed her mother's apartment number. The closed-circuit camera light blinked, and the door buzzed open. She took the elevator to the fourth floor and heard her mother's voice as soon as the doors slid open.

"Hi, sweetie!" her mother said as Falco made her way down the hall toward the apartment. Her mother smiled and kissed her on the cheek and gave her a tiny hug.

"Hi, Mom. You look good."

Howard, the car salesman, who was standing behind Elaine, scurried over and gave Falco a hug. "How's the famous detective?" he said, smiling.

Howard Larson was a round man pushing seventy-five years old. He dyed his hair a cheap Grecian Formula brown and never seemed to have a decent haircut. He wore suits that were tight fitting in the wrong places and ties that never seemed to match. He had bulging eyes and big teeth, and his fingernails were long and yellow.

Falco shivered at the thought of those fingernails as he hugged her. She had to admit she did like his car, though. It was a big white Caddy with lots of bells and whistles. She couldn't imagine Howard had enough money to afford a car like that, especially the way he dressed. She figured he lived in some cheap, dingy apartment somewhere near the expressway—or maybe he lived in his car.

Don't be so evil, she told herself.

She sat on her mother's huge sectional sofa and smoothed out her skirt. Her mother eyed her. "Monica, you look so thin. Haven't you been eating?"

"Of course I've been eating," she said, already irritated. "I'd be dead by now if I weren't."

"My daughter, the comedian," Elaine said, shaking her head.

Howard leaned in. "The news said you got attacked by a pit bull. I figured you'd have a big bandage on yer arm or somethin.'"

Oh, god, the pit bull story again, she thought. She smiled and sat up straight. "It was really nothing. The dog was old. I just had a few bruises on my arm." She held up her right arm and clenched and unclenched her hand. "See? All better!"

"My daughter, the detective," Elaine said, dragging her words out. "I worry about you so much, dear, every time I hear about a shooting or a robbery in the city where someone gets hurt. I just pray it's not you!"

"We've been through this before…a number of times. It's my job," Falco said flatly. She didn't want to have this conversation again, especially with Howard around.

"Well, I made a decent living selling cars, as you know. I think the sales professions are wonderful careers, especially for a young lady as attractive as you," Howard said.

Falco looked at him with a blank face then burst into laughter, covering her face.

"I wasn't trying to be funny, Monica…really," he said.

Elaine looked at the two of them then changed the subject. "How's Jeffery? Have you seen him lately?"

"He's fine. I saw him a few weeks ago," Falco said, still laughing.

"And Sammy?"

"He's fine too. He was at a Boy Scout camp for two weeks. He's coming back today."

"Yes, yes. I know. Jeffery told me. He gave me the number for a wonderful plumber for my kitchen faucet. It needed to be replaced. What a nice young man he was, so friendly and helpful."

The room fell silent, and Howard took the opportunity to remind them that their dinner reservations were for eight and that they needed to get going. They piled into Howard's Cadillac and headed for the restaurant.

Falco felt her headache returning and started to get a sick feeling sitting in the backseat of the car. It smelled like stale cigars and "old people," as Sam would say. She smiled at the thought of him coming home from camp. *I bet he grew another inch*, she thought. *What a long two weeks.*

They arrived at the restaurant, the nice Italian place, as her mother referred to it. It was crowded and noisy. Fortunately they were seated at a table near the back where it was quieter. Howard immediately ordered a bottle of Chianti with dinner and a gin and tonic. He spotted the waiter and asked for two glasses of water, no ice. Falco needed a drink but decided to wait and have the Chianti with dinner.

She eyed Howard and Elaine. They both studied the menu, their heads bobbing as they peered through their bifocals. *Our worlds are so different*, she thought, staring blankly at the menu. Louis Prima was playing in the background; it made her think of her father. He loved music and dancing and food, especially Italian food. He loved life, she decided. Her mother was so different, sort of a solitary soul, reserved and very proper. She thought of the guys in the department gathering together last night at Murphy's Pub. *I guess all my friends faded with the divorce*, she thought. *They all seemed to quietly side with Jeffery and his ideas on what a wife and mom should be. I guess I'm not that. Should I be?*

Elaine put her hand on her daughter's arm and said something to her, but she was deep in thought. "Monica, honey?" her mother said, looking at her intently. She and Howard were staring at her.

"What? I'm sorry. I was…somewhere else," she said, rubbing her forehead.

"Are you ready to order?" asked Howard, his eyes bulging.

"Uh, sure, sure," said Falco. She hadn't really decided but it didn't matter. She wasn't very hungry anyway, and her stomach was still iffy.

The table jerked as Howard kicked the leg of the table with his foot. The water glasses rattled back and forth, as did everything else on the table. "Sorry, ladies. Sometimes I get a little crampy in my right leg," laughed Howard. He immediately kicked the table again, sending Elaine's glass to the table in a loud clink and then to the floor. Falco grabbed her napkin and placed it on the puddle of water.

"Oh, dear," said Elaine, looking at the glass on the floor.

"Good thing they've got carpeting," Howard said, embarrassed.

The waiter brought Falco another napkin and picked up the water glass from the floor.

"Sorry," she whispered. Her head was beginning to pound again. She grabbed her purse from the seat next to her and fumbled for some aspirin or Motrin. Finding nothing, she thought of her penance and then the Chianti.

Elaine and Howard let the conversation wane between them as the table grew silent. Falco was having a hard time concentrating, so the quiet was welcome. Howard looked around for the waiter to take their order. Seeing him, he rudely snapped his fingers and motioned with his finger. He kicked the table again. This time everyone immediately put their hands over their water glasses to keep them from falling over. *Jesus*, Falco thought as she tried not to show her disgust for the man.

The waiter appeared. Howard ordered for himself and Elaine then asked for the bottle of Chianti.

After Falco ordered her food, Elaine gave her a stern look. "Did you read that article in the *Tribune* about your father?"

"Yes, I did," she said stiffly.

"Did someone tell you they were writing the article?" Elaine, said sounding annoyed.

"No, I knew nothing about it."

"Well, it was a little unnerving to look at the paper and see your father's picture there. I relived that part of my life all over again when I saw it," she said. "And that photo of you was not flattering at all."

"Those were both department-issue photos, Mom," Falco said through her teeth.

"Well, I didn't think it was appropriate that they wrote the article without talking with the widow."

"Mom, it wasn't like Dad died in the line of duty."

Howard kicked the table again, and again everyone put their hands over their glasses to keep them from toppling. Falco smiled then started to laugh. She covered her face with her hands then excused herself to go to the ladies' room. Her heels were noisy as she entered the restroom. She slipped into one of the stalls and leaned against the closed door. The steel door felt cool on her back. She stared at the mustard and red-colored tiles and clutched herself as tears came to her eyes. "Why today?" she whispered. She brushed the tears away, washed her hands, and headed back to the table. *And I detest all my sins because of thy just punishments.*

* * *

The food came in enormous quantities. "That's why we like this place!" said Howard, winking at Falco. She glanced at her plate of steaming chicken parmigiana and looked around for the waiter and the bottle of Chianti.

"Something wrong, honey?" Elaine asked.

"No, no, nothing," she said. She seemed to have lost her appetite. *Maybe I can get an order of Eggo waffles*, she thought and smiled. Her mother caught her eye and looked at her suspiciously.

Howard was eating happily when the Chianti came. The waiter poured the wine, spinning around as he filled each glass. Falco took a long sip, glanced at her mother, then took another. She waited for Howard to kick the table again and send the wine onto everybody's lap.

I need a cigarette, she thought. She took another long sip of wine. Before long her glass was empty. *I have no business drinking*, she thought. She sighed and took a stab at her chicken parmigiana.

The table grew quiet. Howard eyed Elaine; she caught his eye and nodded. He poured more wine for Falco and for himself then lifted his glass for a toast.

"I'd like to make a little announcement, if I may," Howard said. He looked at Falco, who stopped eating, put her fork and knife down, and looked at him intently. "Monica, we had initially asked Jeffery and little Sammy to be here, but Sammy was coming home from camp and, well, it didn't really work out," he said with his glass still in the air.

Falco nodded slowly, waiting for the boom to fall. "Well, I guess this will be a one-person announcement unless it's something Mom doesn't know about yet," she said, looking at her mother for a clue.

"No, no, I know all about this," Elaine said, laughing and looking sweetly at Howard.

"Well, Monica, honey, you know I've known your mother for almost three years, and we've talked a little about the future," he said slowly.

Falco looked at the two of them then took another swallow of the Chianti. She felt a scowl coming to her face. She was feeling the wine.

"Our announcement, sweetheart, is that I've asked your mom to marry me!" Howard said endearingly, raising his glass higher.

"And you said *yes*?" Falco blurted as she glared at her mother.

Elaine turned to her. "We're planning a fall wedding."

"Fall?" Falco said, her voice cracking.

Howard kicked the table again. The bottle of Chianti wobbled just as Falco snatched it and grabbed her own glass. Elaine's glass teetered then tipped over; it rolled along the table and onto her lap. Howard tried in vain to catch his glass, but his clumsy fingers pushed it over. It toppled to the floor and bounced, spilling wine everywhere.

"Shit!" Falco spat as she grabbed her napkin from her lap and helped her mother soak up the wine on her skirt. "Oh, dear, looks like this will need dry cleaning," her mother said, half joking.

Falco shook her head and tried not to laugh again. *My mother is marrying an idiot*, she thought. *I hope he'll buy a decent suit for the goddamn wedding.*

CHAPTER 76

A dark mood settled over Falco as she drove home from dinner. Her life seemed to be a series of dead ends with no viable options. She felt stuck and terribly alone, and she felt the burden of the night before with Jeremy. "God, I'm so stupid!" she said out loud. "He was awfully sweet, though," she reconsidered.

I hope no one caught on that he spent part of his shift fucking me, she thought. The whole idea was absurd. She laughed as she focused on the road ahead. She was a little buzzed from the wine and craved a cigarette. She opened the window and thought long and hard as she drove. "I work too much…and my social life is a joke…and I'm a complete idiot for sleeping with a rookie cop, or anyone else from the department."

She focused on the road and gripped the steering wheel. "Okay, okay. Wait a sec. Let's take a big step back," she said. "You come in midway through the child abductions case and crack the fucking case! We outdid the North Shore cops *and* the feds," she said. Her mood lightened as she glanced at the speedometer. She was doing eighty-seven on the freeway.

Falco arrived home feeling drained. She turned on the TV to some cheesy cable movie and lay down on the sofa. *We're planning a fall wedding*, she heard her mother say. "Jesus Christ," she whispered. She thought about Howard kicking the table then started laughing. She rolled onto her stomach as her body shook. The ridiculousness of the evening waned as her laughter turned to tears. She sat up on the sofa and tried to think of something to fend off the sadness and loneliness, but the tears rolled down her face.

* * *

Sleep overcame her as early morning loomed. Falco heard herself gasp and felt her arm jerk suddenly. Her body bolted awake. It was three in the morning. She heard a dog in the next yard barking fiercely. Her head was heavy from sleep as she found herself gripping her arm. *The pit bull*, she thought. Her heart was racing.

She got up from the sofa and looked out her picture window. The neighborhood was deathly quiet. She couldn't remember whether the neighbors on her left had a dog. *They don't have a dog*, she remembered. *They have a ferret*. She sighed and rubbed her eyes. The house was stuffy. She walked across the living room and turned the air conditioning down a notch then went into Sam's room and fell asleep.

The phone rang, waking Falco from a sound sleep. It was eight thirty.

"Hey, M, did I wake you?"

"No, no. I was up," she lied.

"Are you planning to come over today?" Jeffery asked.

"I thought around noon. How does that sound?" She got up from Sam's bed.

"That's fine. Sam came home with a little cold."

"Oh, no. Do you need me to pick something up for him, like some Tylenol or something?" she asked, suddenly worried.

"No, we're covered. I gave him some last night and he's still asleep."

"Does he have a temperature?"

"I haven't checked this morning yet."

"Well, why don't you *check*, Jeffery. Feel his forehead," Falco said, getting irritated.

Jeffery put the phone down with a clunk. Falco drifted into the kitchen and started some coffee. She was troubled that Sam had come home sick. Jeffery came back on the line and said, "No fever. He's just got some congestion and a runny nose."

"I'll be there before ten," Falco said.

* * *

She got to Jeffery's house just after ten. She was feeling the Chianti from the night before and swearing to lay off alcohol starting today. Church bells rang in the distance as she got out of her car and headed toward Jeffery's front door. He met her with a concerned look. She eyed him and slipped past toward Sam's room.

Sam was flushed and looking sleepy. "Hey, buddy," Falco said quietly, looking worried.

Sam's eyes were droopy as he saw her. "Hi, Mom." His voice was hoarse, his body shivering.

She pulled him close and kissed him on his head. "I missed you so much. You don't feel so great, huh?" She felt his forehead; he was burning up. She took a short breath and looked at Jeffery, who was leaning in the doorway. "Did you take his temperature?"

"No, I just felt his head," he said, looking at the two of them.

She shot up from the bed and walked quickly past Jeffery. "Do you have a thermometer?"

She went into the bathroom and opened his medicine cabinet. A small box of condoms fell out. Jeffery followed her.

"Let me look for it," he said, getting angry and pushing her aside with his forearm.

"He's burning up," Falco hissed. "What's the matter with you?"

Jeffery glared at her then searched for the thermometer. Finding it, he walked past her toward the bedroom. Falco found a bottle of rubbing alcohol and a cotton ball and followed him into Sam's room.

"Wait," she said as Jeffery pulled the thermometer out of its container and pointed it toward Sam's mouth. She put her hand out for the instrument and wiped it with the alcohol-soaked cotton ball then went over to Sam. "Okay, you know how we do this, right?"

Sam let his mother put the thermometer under his tongue. They waited. After a few moments, she gently removed the thermometer from Sam's mouth and squinted at it through the sunlight. Her hand dropped. "We've got to get him to a hospital right now, Jeffery. His temp is a hundred and four."

They bundled Sam up in a light blanket, climbed into Jeffery's pickup, and headed to Lutheran General Hospital. Sam was visibly weak as he lay between Falco's legs, wrapped in her arms. She quietly told Sam about the pit bull attack, trying to keep his mind off going to the hospital.

They registered at the desk in ER and waited. Sam shivered as his parents got progressively worried. Impatient, Falco walked up to the registration desk looking for an attendant or nurse. A man dressed in scrubs came around the desk and eyed her.

"Has someone helped you?" he asked with a smile.

She stammered, "I just…my son has a high temperature…and he's…"

The physician squinted at her and said, "Let's take a look."

He put down his clipboard and quickly followed her to where Jeffery and Sam were huddled. He looked at Sam and felt his forehead. "Okay, let's get him admitted," he said.

Falco sighed with relief. The physician disappeared for a moment then came back with a wheelchair and an ER nurse. He quickly sat Sam in the chair and told Falco and Jeffery to follow them.

Falco bent down in front of Sam and said, "It's okay, Sammy. You're gonna be okay now."

Sam shivered and gripped the blanket they'd brought him in. The nurse backed the wheelchair up and turned it toward the hallway as Falco stood and eyed the physician. He held her gaze and smiled. "You're that detective who solved the child abductions in the north suburbs, aren't you? I recognize you from TV."

She was caught off guard. "Yes, I'm…I'm the one, along with my partner."

The physician stuck out his hand. "Nice job, Detective."

Falco shook his hand but couldn't find the words to respond. Jeffery put his arm around her and followed Sam and the nurse down the hall.

Sam spent the night at the hospital, as did Falco and Jeffery. He was released the next morning.

CHAPTER 77

Summer sizzled as Falco pulled her car into the station parking lot. It was after lunch, and she felt frazzled and distracted. She made her way to the second floor and was met by Bob Leighton. "Hey, Falco. How's your head?" She stared at him for a moment as she slipped by him. He looked at her and chuckled.

Chief Lassiter saw her as she made her way through the cubicles to her desk. He followed her as she pulled out her chair and turned on her computer. "There she is," he said with a little smile. "I was worried when I heard you were coming in late."

Falco looked up at him. "My son spent the night in the hospital. He came home from camp with a cold, and he was running a high fever."

"Sorry to hear that. Is he okay?"

"Yes, he was released this morning. He's with Jeffery at home now," she said quietly.

"You get home okay on Friday?" Lassiter asked, leaning on her desk.

She closed her eyes and said, "Yes, I got home okay."

"Good – that was some party." He smiled and walked toward his office.

Falco checked her voicemail messages. Her mother had called and asked her to call when she got home from work. Michael called requesting the same.

Steve Grasky made his way to Falco's desk and pulled up a chair. "Hey, Falco. How ya doin'?" he said with a gentle smile.

She sighed as she wrote down the last of her messages. "Hey, Steve. How's it going?"

"Fine, fine. Working on our reports. You get home all right on Friday?"

"Yes, I got home all right," she said mimicking his tone.

"You were pretty wasted," he said with a chuckle.

"Yeah. You were too, Detective."

"My wife was pissed 'cause I was hung-over on Saturday. Didn't even make it to four o'clock mass."

Falco glanced at him and smiled. "I know what you mean, but I had to have dinner with my mother and her boyfriend—who is now her fiancé!" She shook her head and laughed.

"I think you beat me there," Grasky said. He put a heavy hand on her shoulder and walked away.

CHAPTER 78

The Winter Garden of the Harold Washington Library Center is an expansive space with a huge skylight and towering roman columns. The room was set up for one hundred people with round tables and chairs arranged in neat rows that faced a stage and podium.

Falco and Steve rode with Chief Lassiter and his guest and longtime companion, Iris. Steve Grasky had invited his wife, daughter, and son-in-law. Falco had completely forgotten to invite Jeffery and had avoided mentioning the event to her mother and Howard. The room was noisy as wait staff poured water into glasses from stainless steel pitchers and set platters of pastries, bagels, and fruit on each table.

Falco wore a powder-gray matte jersey suit and a silk blouse with matching leather slingbacks. Lassiter smiled as she got out of the car. "Falco, you look great!" he said.

Iris playfully slugged Lassiter as if she were jealous. Falco smiled. They followed Lassiter as he made his way through the rows of tables. They were early, but the space was filling up quickly with dignitaries from city government and the suburbs. News media milled about, setting up cameras and microphones. Falco recognized some of the reporters from TV and others from public events.

Lassiter led them to a reserved table and politely pulled out chairs for Falco and Iris. Grasky waved to his family, who took seats near the back. Falco smiled at Grasky's wife, Dinora, who gave her a little wave from across the room.

Lassiter leaned into the two detectives. "Don't forget our suspects are being arraigned tomorrow at the courthouse. I expect you both to be there." Falco and Grasky nodded.

Someone came up from behind Falco and whispered in her ear, "Hey, girl. You look hot!"

It was Brenda Salerno, along with Special Agent Tedeschi. They stopped at the table and congratulated Lassiter, Grasky, and Falco. "Great work, Detectives," Tedeschi said. "Anytime either of you wants to join us downtown, we'd love to have you."

"I'm retiring in a month," Grasky said, staring ahead and taking a sip of coffee.

Tedeschi looked at Falco. "No, thanks, sir. I'm pretty happy where I am," she said, smiling.

"It's because she loves her boss. That's why," Lassiter said, eyeing Falco and then Iris.

Brenda turned and gave Falco a thumbs-up, then followed Tedeschi to a table near the back.

The ceremony was a blur. Mayor Richard M. Daley gave an impassioned speech about the dedicated people of the Chicago Police Department and praised the superb police work of the two detectives. He introduced the two detectives and asked them to stand and be recognized. Grasky was feeling overwhelmed; Falco was feeling uncomfortable.

The mayor and Police Superintendent Kline presented the detectives with official police commendations, which consisted of large heavy plaques ornately engraved with their names and titles and emblazoned with the seal of the City of Chicago and the seal of the Chicago Police Department. Falco and Grasky had their photos taken with Superintendent Kline and Mayor Daley. Representatives from the northern suburbs gave their own commendations as the crowd showed their appreciation with a standing ovation.

"Can we go home now?" Falco whispered to herself.

Grasky and Falco both said some words. Grasky talked about his time on the force and his impending retirement; Falco spoke about law enforcement's duty to protect children from sex offenders and pedophiles.

After the formal ceremony ended, the two detectives stayed around, shaking hands and taking more pictures with community leaders and politicians from the city and the suburbs.

It was nearly two-thirty when they finally piled into Lassiter's car and headed to the station. Grasky and Falco were both drained. Lassiter was wired, talking nonstop about the mayor and the politicians with whom he had chewed the fat. When they returned to the station, the two detectives went back to their desks amid cracks and jabs on their snazzy appearances. Falco checked her voicemail then waved goodbye to Ballard, Grasky, and anyone else within her line of vision.

Ballard gave her the eye as she walked past him. "Like the suit, Ballard?" she asked, seeing him look at her up and down. He looked away and picked up his phone.

CHAPTER 79

Falco dashed down the stairs and through the parking lot to her car. She could hear the Cubs game a few blocks away. She pulled her keys from her purse and turned off the car alarm.

"Hi, Detective," said a voice behind her.

At first she wasn't sure of the voice, but then it was unmistakable. She spun around and looked up. It was Jeremy Foley. The blood seemed to drain from her face. She peered up at him, squinting in the sun. He had on mirrored sunglasses and smiled at her knowingly.

"Hi, Officer Foley," said Falco. "How are you?" She felt a cold chill down her spine.

"Can I talk to you for a moment?" he asked, glancing around the parking lot.

"Sure." She shielded her eyes from the sun with her hand and felt at a distinct disadvantage.

"Uh, the other night…" Foley started to say.

"Yeah…the other night," she repeated. "Listen, Jeremy, I thought the note was really sweet, and you were really sweet too, but I don't think we can continue anything beyond…"

"Yeah, I know, Detective. I hope you didn't think I took advantage of you the other night."

"No, I don't think you did. I...I was pretty wasted and...obviously not thinking very clearly," Falco stammered, her voice rising. She looked at him again in the bright sunlight. He was still as tall and handsome as he was that night in her living room. She felt her heart skip a beat. She took a deep breath and said, "You know that I can't see you again, and I hope you understand that the other night was a crazy thing to do...a bad idea...and a mistake."

Jeremy looked away then looked at Falco and said breathlessly, "Yeah, Detective. I guess I just got... Well, I guess I acted on a crazy impulse. I mean, I've always thought you were really—"

She held up her hand to stop him then looked around the parking lot. "Let's just leave it at that then," she said evenly.

"Our secret then?"

"Yes...our secret."

"Great," he said, breathing a sigh of relief, "cuz I just got engaged last month."

Falco gasped. "Well...congratulations." She gave him a look of dismay.

"I'll see you around then, Detective," he said, backing away.

"Yeah, see you around, Officer Foley." She held his gaze for a moment then opened her car door and got inside. "Jesus Christ," she whispered as she started the car. "He just got engaged?"

* * *

Falco called Jeffery's cell phone on her way home. Sam was doing fine and had spent the day with him riding in his truck to various job sites.

She delicately mentioned the commendation ceremony and apologized to Jeffery for not inviting him. He seemed annoyed but said he probably wouldn't have been able to attend anyway. Falco hoped to take the rest of the week off starting on Thursday and asked if Sam could stay with her during that time. Jeffery agreed and said he'd bring him over Wednesday night.

She called Michael on his cell phone when she got home. He didn't answer, so she left a message. She then called her mother, but she wasn't home either. She changed her clothes and pulled out the half bottle of Chardonnay in the refrigerator and poured the rest into a glass. She took a long sip then drifted outside to her car and retrieved the two commendation plaques from the backseat. They were heavy as she cradled them in her arms and brought them into the house and set them on her bed.

She looked at the plaques and thought of those four boys. Their frightened faces and skinny bodies sent surges of pain through her heart. All the self-congratulations suddenly felt superficial. It wasn't about cracking the case; it was about getting those boys back to their families and far away from those sick people. It was a big case for sure, she thought, but would it really stop the hundreds or possibly thousands of other predators and sex offenders out there, or put a dent in the multimillion-dollar child porn industry? Probably not, she thought.

She sat at the edge of the bed. It was just a week ago when things were heating up at the gray bungalow. A week later she and Grasky were stars of the department and all over the news. She got up from the bed, stacked the two plaques on top of each other, and shoved them under her bed.

CHAPTER 80

It was sunny and warm as Steve Grasky leaned on a banister halfway up the cement steps of the Cook County Criminal Courts Building on South California Avenue. He was looking for Falco, who was running late. She jogged up the stairs waving as she saw him. "Hi. Sorry I'm late. Traffic was unbelievable," she said. They made their way into the building and through the metal detectors and long halls of courtrooms and offices.

"Over here," Grasky said, motioning to Falco.

They opened the huge wooden doors of the courtroom where a tall wooden desk towered over rows of wooden chairs. Men and women dressed in suits mingled and watched the door that led to the judge's chambers.

"I want to finish our report today, if at all possible," Falco whispered to Grasky. "I requested the rest of the week off to spend some time with Sam."

"Good for you," he said with a smile. "You need to take the time. You've been burning the candle at both ends for a while. You can't keep up that kind of pace forever, lady. It'll catch up to you."

Falco shrugged. Just then a voice came from the front of the room announcing all to stand as the judge entered the courtroom then sat down at the tall desk. A series of court formalities ensued, then the judge read the names of the people to be arraigned. They entered wearing handcuffs and orange jumpsuits with "Cook County" printed on the back. Falco and Grasky glanced at the four suspects as they appeared at the front of the courtroom.

Falco squinted at the older man with the mustache, the one who had driven the Ford Escort that fateful morning. She cleared her mind, and finally it came to her. The mustached man was the person she had seen closing the gate at Lafayette Elementary School the Friday Andie was abducted. He was the one who had stared at her suspiciously as she frantically drove to the Cohen Sloan Gallery. At that point all she could think of was his daily contact with the students at the school. Was Lafayette Elementary a recruiting ground for him? She felt sick and put her hand to her forehead.

"What's wrong?" Grasky whispered.

"I'll tell you outside."

After the arraignment, the courtroom let out; as they made their way through the echoing corridors, she told him about the mustached man. "I *knew* I recognized him from somewhere, Steve—that chance encounter, that rainy Friday." She shook her head as her face darkened. "Lotta good it did us."

"Point is, Falco, we got 'em. That's all that matters." He looked around and turned. "Hey, I'm parked south. I'll meet you at the station."

Falco waved then looked at her watch. It was nearly noon. Her heart was heavy that her memory had failed her with the mustached man. "Shit," she whispered. Suddenly turned around, she looked for the exit signs over the doorways that would lead her to where she had parked her car. She turned down a hallway, but it ended with a stairwell. Thinking for a moment and trying to get her bearings, she stopped midway then turned around to head back in the opposite direction.

"Jesus Christ, where the fuck am I going?" she said quietly. She wanted to get back to the station to finish her report before she left for the week. "Damn it!" she said, frustrated as she scanned the room numbers and looked for exit signs. She found a map of the first floor mounted in Plexiglas on a wall. Her eyes followed the direction of where she had parked her car; it appeared she had been going in circles. She quickly turned and immediately ran into someone. His dark suit and green-and-blue tie assaulted her field of vision.

"Oh, I'm so sorry," she said, backing up and putting up her hands.

"I'm not!" said the man, smiling down at Falco. It was Dr. Forrest dressed for a court appearance.

"Dr. Forrest! I…I hardly recognized you!" Falco said with a gasp. "I'm sorry. I was trying to figure out where I parked my car," she said, smiling and looking frazzled.

"Funny, I always seem to catch you at some moment when you're running off somewhere or distracted, deep in thought. You must live a very interesting life," he said with a gentle smile.

"Oh, not really. Believe me."

The two exchanged reasons why they were at the courthouse, and Dr. Forrest congratulated her on her work on the child abduction case. The conversation turned to Andie, and he grew serious. "Well, I guess you hadn't heard," he said, looking concerned. Falco shook her head, searching his face. "Andie tried to take her life a few days ago."

Falco put her hand to her head, and her eyes fell to the floor. "Oh, no," she huffed. "How? What happened?"

"She's going to be okay, but we placed in another wing of the hospital."

Falco looked confused and upset as she stared at Dr. Forrest.

"She's isolated herself and still can't carry on a conversation. We're trying a new round of meds. Hopefully they'll make a difference."

Falco hung her head. This was the last thing she needed to hear.

Dr. Forrest studied her for a moment. "I can see I've upset you, Detective. I'm sorry. I wish I had better news." She nodded, avoiding his eyes. He eyed her thoughtfully then said, "Look, Detective, if you ever need to talk—about this or anything else—feel free to call me." He pulled out one of his cards and placed it in her hand. He looked at her closely and added, "We're not giving up yet. I don't want you to, okay?" He smiled as Falco met his eyes. "Nice seeing you, Detective." He waved then turned and walked away.

CHAPTER 81

Grasky and Falco finished and signed off on their reports. Falco gathered her things and turned off her computer. It was four thirty, and she was cutting out. She still felt something hanging over her. She mentally checked off in her mind any loose ends she needed to tie up with Grasky and the child abduction case. *All finished*, she thought.

Andie weighed heavily on her mind as she drove home. She thought back to the last time she had seen her at the station that Thursday morning. She processed the chain of events that followed and the death of Brian McCaffery. She wondered whether the truth would ever come out about who actually had killed him. She wondered whether Andie had any recollection of what she had done.

A cold shudder came over her. *We'd all be fired if the truth came out. Heads would roll. We'd all be out on the street, pensions gone*, she thought. She shook the thought out of her mind. "I've got to quit worrying so much," she whispered. She thought of Maggie Simonds and wished she hadn't canceled her appointment with her yesterday.

* * *

Sam rang the doorbell as Jeffery made his way up the stairs of Falco's house. "She probably hasn't gotten the door fixed yet," Jeffery mumbled.

Falco pulled the door open and smiled at the two. "Hey, honey, you look so much better!" she said to Sam. He hugged her then ran into the house toward his room. "You wanna come in?" she asked Jeffery.

"For a bit," he said.

The kitchen was a mess with bags of groceries yet to be unpacked. "I needed to go shopping," she said apologetically. Jeffery helped her as Sam jumped on the sofa and turned on the TV.

"So did you bring them home?" Jeffery asked, looking askance at Falco.

"Bring what home?" she asked, folding up the paper shopping bags and shoving them under the sink.

"Your commendations, I saw the news."

Sam jumped off the sofa upon hearing their conversation. "Yeah, Mom, did you bring them home for us to see?"

She scowled and looked away. "Since when are you so interested in my job, Jeffery?"

"Since you became so famous," he said with a teasing smile.

"Are you kidding me? You've got to be kidding me because that's exactly what my mother does! She complains about what a burden my job is to her and then brags about me when something good happens or when I'm mentioned in the news."

"Whoa! Wait a minute, M," Jeffery said, putting his hands up. "I was just kidding around. Come on, already. I didn't mean to get you all riled up. We're *proud* of you." Jeffery and Sam both glowed with pride.

Falco looked at them then looked away. "You're right. I'm sorry. Come into the bedroom. I have them there."

In the bedroom, Jeffery looked at the plaques and gave Falco a tiny hug. He offered to hang them on the wall, but she said they were fine under her bed. Sam beamed with pride as he ran his finger across the engravings and seals. Jeffery backed out of the room, eyeing his watch. "I gotta go," he said. He hugged Sam, waved goodbye to Falco, and walked through the living room.

"I'll bring him back Sunday night," Falco yelled as Jeffery yanked the swollen door open.

"Think about getting this door fixed," he said, glancing back.

Sam followed his mother into the kitchen. "Dad's got a date," he said, squinting up to look at her.

"A date?" she said, almost laughing.

"Yeah…with a lady he met at work, on some job."

Falco thought for a moment, avoiding Sam's gaze. He was measuring her reaction. "Well, that's your dad's business," she said lightly. "So what would you like for dinner?"

Falco and Sam spent the next few days catching up and doing a variety of "really cool things." They saw two movies, ate lots of pizza, and visited the Shedd Aquarium, the Field Museum, and Navy Pier. By the time Sunday rolled around, Falco was exhausted but happy that she was able to spend some quality time with her son.

Sam had gotten the news from Jeffery about his grandmother's engagement to Howard. He seemed confused and a little unhappy about the whole thing. Falco confessed to Sam she felt the same way and left it at that. She didn't want to put any of her negative ideas in his head.

"Maybe we'll all come around to liking Howard," she told him. She wished her father had lived long enough to see the birth of her son and see him grow up. *They'd be two peas in a pod*, she thought.

CHAPTER 82

Michael had his head in his hands as he sat at a conference table with Dr. Forrest, another psychology intern, three psychiatric nurses, and Dr. Forrest's colleague, Dr. David Levinkind. It was their weekly Monday meeting where they discussed patients' progress, therapies, and medications.

Michael was disturbed by Andie's suicide attempt and wanted to discuss treatment options. Unfortunately her name was at the bottom of the patient list, and he felt they would run out of time before they would be able to discuss her case. Most of the participants in the meeting had good news and wanted to report positive progress and pat themselves on the back. Michael frowned as he took notes. Dr. Forrest glanced at him, sensing his frustration.

The meeting broke up without any discussion of Andie. Michael was concerned and pulled Dr. Forrest aside. "What's our strategy with Andie? We didn't even get to discuss her case," he said as he gripped his legal pad.

"We're going to meet with David at four. This isn't anything we can cover in a short meeting," Dr. Forrest said.

Andie's suicide attempt wasn't unusual for someone with a history of post-traumatic stress disorder. While she had managed to attain a somewhat normal and functioning life after McCaffery's first attack four years before, this ordeal was far more severe.

It had been nearly two months since that terrible Friday in July. Andie's arm was healing slowly with three pins holding it together. Her ribs and internal injuries would take longer to heal. While pain medications helped ease the physical pain, they also contributed to her uncontrollable behavior and fits of violence. Her memory was all but gone, and she barely responded to her name. She had no recognition of Dr. Forrest, Michael, or Kat and spent days huddled in the corner of her tiny room clutching herself. Her behavior seemed to stem from a barrage of recurrent memories and sounds.

Traditional talk therapy is a valuable tool for many who suffer from PTSD; however, it seemed absurd for Dr. Forrest or Michael to use it on Andie at this point in her treatment. Her team of psychiatrists and nurses had to first establish the correct combination of psychotropic medications to help bring her out of her current emotional state.

Andie had been moved to the area of the hospital designated as the D ward, a place for patients who needed constant monitoring for their own safety and the safety of the staff. There were no visitors to the D ward. After a little more than two weeks of taking a new series of drugs, she had attempted suicide again by repeatedly striking her forehead on the tile floor of her room. By the time hospital staff had discovered her, she was unconscious in a pool of blood from her bruised and bleeding forehead. The little fingers on both her hands were broken from her having slammed her fists on the floor. She was treated for a slight concussion, lacerations to the head, and two broken fingers.

Michael and Dr. Forrest were aware of the high suicide risk for patients suffering from PTSD resulting from unusually high levels of intrusive memories and what psychiatrists call arousal symptoms: irritability, angry outbursts, and exaggerated startle responses. Andie also showed typical symptoms of depression, which in a vast majority of cases were more predictive of suicide attempts. Her incoherent state was likely the result of feeling overwhelmed and trapped by recurring memories of the attack. For Andie, suicide was the only means of escape.

That afternoon, Dr. Forrest, Dr. Levinkind, and Michael discussed new treatment strategies for Andie. They decided to treat the depression as the primary disorder, theorizing that Andie's inability to speak more than a few words was the result of high levels of anxiety. "She suffered from a mild anxiety disorder before all this happened," Michael noted. "We treated it with Zoloft, but every so often something would trigger a full blown panic attack."

Michael returned to his office and checked his messages. He wrote himself a note to call Falco. He knew he was avoiding talking to her since the news wasn't good. Kat called, saying she was going to Barcelona and would return in two weeks. She left a number where she could be reached then hung up. "Must be nice," he said as he slammed down the phone.

* * *

Falco woke up on Monday morning feeling tired but happy. Her couple of days off with Sam had rejuvenated her. She had a feeling that her perspective on life had changed just a bit. She had a full refrigerator of food, had plans with Sam to go shopping for school supplies, and hadn't drunk a sip of wine since Wednesday. Even her eyes looked brighter as she glanced at herself in the bathroom mirror.

She got off to an early start and headed to work. Michael popped into her mind. She wondered why he hadn't returned her call on Wednesday. She glanced at her cell phone and saw no new messages and frowned. *Stop worrying*, she told herself. *Just have a normal day.*

"A normal day?" she said out loud. "Where did you get that from? You're a cop. There are no normal days."

* * *

Andie woke up in the darkness of her tiny room. It appeared different, more gray or green. She couldn't really tell. Her hand moved up to touch something on her forehead; it was a bandage. Pain surfaced in her head and hands. She got up slowly, feeling more pain in her neck and upper back. She sat at the edge of the bed and stared into the blackness.

Across the room appeared a pair of green eyes. She watched them as they moved closer. She heard a familiar voice from behind the bed, then a laugh. She quickly turned as the eyes moved in front of her. Startled, she waved them away with her bandaged hands. "No…no…no," She heard someone say. Was it her voice, so faint?

"No…no!" She swung her hands around, trying again to chase away the eyes. The room was suddenly hot as her breathing grew faster and faster. She felt sweat drip down the front of her thin cotton shirt. She got up from the bed, rushed to the window, and looked through the obscured view of a protective metal grid. She squinted, wondering where the voice had come from and where the eyes had suddenly disappeared to.

"No!" She slammed her hands into the window as pain jolted through her broken fingers and through her wrists. She bent over from the throbbing, panting through it. She dashed to the other side of the room. Lights from the parking garage illuminated the wall. She saw an image and ducked out of its way. It was her shadow. The voice came again. "No…no…no…no!"

She leaned against the wall and slid to the floor. "Andie, Andie, guess who's gonna die?" came the whisper. Laughter rattled in her head as she covered her ears and shut her eyes tightly. "No…no…no," came the voice again. She heard a loud noise. It came from her left. She turned in its direction. *Bang! Bang!* She scrambled to her feet and quickly moved to the other side of the room. *Bang! Bang!*

She ran to the door and hit it with both hands. Pain raced through her hands and up through her elbows. She fell to her knees. The room began to spin. She tried to get to her feet.

"Guess who's gonna die?" came the voice. It hovered like a whisper close to her left ear then rose over her head. "Guess who's gonna die?"

She buried her head in her hands, not knowing where to hide.

CHAPTER 83

For once it was a slow day at the twenty-third district. Bob Leighton had tracked down the two suburban twenty-somethings who had beaten up the gay couple a few weeks before. The gay press was all over the story and the arrests. Falco took advantage of the lull to catch up on some reports and statistics. She hadn't seen or spoken with Ballard for more than a few minutes in the last few weeks, and when they had spoken, the conversation was strained at best.

She vowed to start mending her relationship with Ballard starting that day. She looked over at his desk; it was piled with paperwork. The clock read eleven forty-five. Maybe he was out on a call or coming in late for some reason. She cleared her desk of odds and ends and cleaned her computer screen with Windex from the janitor's closet.

"Fall cleaning?" came a familiar voice.

Falco looked up. It was Dr. Forrest. "Hi! What are you doing here?" She couldn't hide her surprise.

He smiled. "I was in the area. Actually I was supposed to meet Michael around here for lunch, but he canceled...something about Josh. Anyway, I thought I'd take a chance and track you down and ask if you'd like to have lunch."

Grasky peered at Dr. Forrest from his desk, wondering who the guy with the suit was.

Falco thought for a moment then said, "Sure, I guess. I'm not real busy today. Why not?"

Dr. Forrest smiled and looked at his watch. "If we leave now, we can beat the rush. What do you think?"

"That's fine with me. I rarely eat breakfast, so early lunches are good."

"You know, you really should…" he said, snatching Falco's sweater from the back of her chair.

"Should what?" she asked, taking her sweater and pulling it over her shoulders.

"Eat breakfast." He rattled off some information from a recent article from the *Journal of the American Medical Association* then stopped short and smiled. "You know, Detective, you look well rested today, more so than I've seen you in weeks."

Falco smiled. "Well, I can't say I'm well rested, but I did take some time off to spend with my son. We ran around everywhere, and I'm a bit tired today, but it was definitely worth it. We had a really nice time."

"Good!" he said. "By the way, may I call you Monica?"

She laughed. "Of course."

"Well, then it's Alan for me."

Alan pulled up to an Italian place in Andersonville called LaDonna. Falco had driven past it many times, and lots of people in the department raved about the food, but this was the first time she had set foot in the place.

"Michael loves this restaurant," Alan said as he opened the door for Falco.

"Speaking of Michael, I haven't heard a word from him since the middle of last week. Is he okay?" she asked as a waiter seated them.

"He's got some problem with his boyfriend or ex-boyfriend...uh...Josh, and he's been pretty swamped at the hospital and dealing with Andie."

Falco nodded. "Do you think Andie will pull out of this?"

"I hope so, but it's too early to tell. I've known her for a number of years. She's a strong person, but her current psychological state, her inability to speak—to verbalize all but just a few words—and her failure to recognize key people in her life isn't good. Some of what she's dealing with is classic PTSD, and some of it's classic depression. The two often occur simultaneously along with symptoms manifested in anxiety disorders. All those things combined, and we're pretty much talking about Andie's condition with ambient voices and hallucinations thrown in."

"She's hearing voices and hallucinating?" Falco asked, looking surprised.

"It's not unusual with PTSD. Many of the recurring memories come in the form of voices and hallucinations," Alan explained.

"That last night when I was with Andie, when she had that huge panic attack, it seemed like she was hallucinating." She shook her head, remembering that day.

"I think in that instance she was dissociating." He put his hand on Falco's. "I know Michael tore into you that night and accused you of pushing Andie over the edge."

"He definitely threw me out...and said some unpleasant things. Looking back, I wonder if I *had* pushed her too far, or maybe I should say I didn't try to stop her from talking, at least not as hard as I should have. I still feel really bad about it."

Alan smiled. "You know, you're kind of a softy for a cop."

Falco laughed. "I have been called many things, Doctor, but never, ever a softy."

Their food arrived, and Falco found her appetite had returned. Alan talked about medical school and how Michael reminded him of himself as a young, idealist student, bent on healing the world. Falco could see that in Michael.

The conversation drifted again to Andie and how Alan first had become involved with her. "I was dating her lawyer at the time, believe it or not, a Holly Greene. She was a spunky little thing but smart and ambitious and really, really cute," Alan said. "She was the prosecutor for the McCaffery trial. We started dating around the same time.

"So you were there through the whole thing, since the beginning?"

"Not exactly, I treated Andie as a favor to Holly. She was growing concerned for her as the trial date grew closer. Andie was having a lot of anxiety and mood swings and even some full-blown panic attacks."

Falco listened closely.

"Holly had the McCaffery case all but sewn up. The guy didn't have a chance, but she put Andie on the stand anyway and made her recall all the events that took place, even the murder of the eighty-year-old woman. She didn't have to put her through that," Alan said, looking off. Well, some other things happened and I found out who the real Holly Greene was, and I changed my opinion. But to make a long story short," he said with a quick smile, "I knew Michael from the hospital, and when the caretaker opportunity came up as part of the civil case settlement, I recommended him. Before long he was working with—or for—Andie, and we all sort of got to know each other and became friends. Of course I'll always be Andie's psychiatrist first and her friend second. She's a hell of a woman and a brilliant artist."

Falco recalled the gathering at the Cohen Sloan Gallery. Seeing Andie's paintings in her mind's eye, a heaviness came to her. Suddenly the future felt bleak and her mood darkened. Alan kept talking but his words turned into dark blobs that floated around her head.

CHAPTER 84

After lunch Falco slipped back to her desk and checked her voicemail. The cubicles around hers were strangely quiet, and Ballard still wasn't at his desk. She wiggled the computer mouse and continued working on her spreadsheet. She felt better now that she was sitting at her desk with work to do. Grasky appeared next to her and said, "You holdin' out on me, Falco?" He jammed a piece of gum in his mouth.

She looked up, taken off guard. "What?"

"You holding out on me?" he repeated.

Falco looked confused then shook her head.

"The suit…the guy…*lunch*?"

She smiled and touched her forehead. "Oh! That guy!" she said with a laugh.

"Yeah…*that* guy!" Grasky said sarcastically.

"That was Andrea Fulbright's doctor. His lunch date cancelled on him, so he asked me to lunch. It was more like he was in the area than actually…asking me to lunch, like on a, you know, *date*." Falco found herself stammering.

"Okay…hm…a doctor, eh?" Grasky smiled. Falco scoffed and waved him off.

She immersed herself in the spreadsheet but wondered where Ballard was. She glanced at his desk as she saw Chief Lassiter walk out of his office and head toward her. She smiled as he approached. He looked serious. "I got some information just now about some mini meth labs operating on west Belmont and way north on Broadway and Bryn Mawr. We got a guy this morning dealing the stuff, and he's talking. I want you and Ballard to follow up on any leads this guy gives us, okay?"

"Yes, sir. We'll get right on it, but where's Ballard?"

"Toothache," Lassiter said.

* * *

It was nearly five forty-five when Falco glanced at her watch. Her eyes were beginning to ache from the spreadsheet. *Time to go home,* she thought, pressing her fingertips to her eyes. She turned off her computer and snatched up her sweater and purse. She looked around the office and realized she was virtually alone. She shook her head, marveling at her ability to tune out the rest of the world. She trotted down the stairs and dropped some paperwork off with the front desk receptionist then headed out the front doors to the street. The wind whipped around the building, catching her hair and blowing it in her face. She brushed it back and pulled her sweater close. "I should have worn a jacket," she said, bracing against the wind. She noticed a strangely familiar figure twenty feet ahead on the sidewalk. He was pointing and gesturing to another man. Falco walked closer as she headed to the parking lot.

As she approached the two men, she recognized one of them as Michael and slowed down. "Hey!" she said with a smile.

Michael's face dropped. "Monica," he sighed.

The man he was talking to stared at Falco, looking her up and down and eyeing her badge. She hesitated, not wanting to intrude. It looked like Michael was pissed off at the young man. He was blond, with numerous piercings in his nose and eyebrows. She smiled politely and headed toward her car.

After a moment Michael ran after her. "Hey, wait up!"

She stopped and turned around. "I didn't want to interrupt anything," she said, brushing the hair from her face.

Michael looked down. He seemed to be upset about something. He glanced back down the sidewalk where the young man had disappeared. "That was Josh," he said. "He got arrested this morning for dealing crystal. He just got out now." He looked back again and sighed. "I guess the cops—the police—questioned him most of the day."

Falco nodded, trying not to look unsympathetic. "Are you okay?"

He sighed. "Yeah, I'm just completely drained and fed up with him. It was over between us a month ago, but then he got into some trouble—started doing crystal—and now he's dealing. Fuck!" he yelled, jamming his fist into the palm of his hand.

She figured Josh was the person Lassiter was referring to who had spilled his guts about the mini meth labs. She listened as Michael vented about Josh, his screwed-up friends, and his eminent road to ruin. She could tell he still cared about Josh but hoped he had enough sense to know when to cut him loose.

Michael realized he was ranting and stopped short. He smiled and shook his head, embarrassed. "I'm sorry. You want to go home, and I'm going on and on."

"It's okay, but I have to admit I was worried about you." She thought for a moment and added, "You know, it's none of my business, but I hope you'll be careful with Josh. This whole meth business—the labs and the devastating things the stuff does to people—I'd hate for any of that to touch you or your life in any way. I'd hate to see you get hurt."

Michael looked down. "I know what I'm doing." He smiled and gave her a hug. "I've missed you, Detective."

Falco looked a bit sad. "I've missed you too, Michael."

CHAPTER 85

Andie's head was aching as she woke. Her body felt as stiff and cold as the floor she found herself lying on. The sun was rising and cast a glow in her room. She pushed herself into a corner and gathered her legs up. The sun grew brighter, creating shadows on the opposite wall. It seemed to mock her in its freedom, making her eyes hurt, making her angry.

The door of her room slowly opened. Her eyes grew wide as she prepared herself for the intruder. A tall woman dressed in a pastel nurse's uniform entered the room cautiously. She carried a tray of food and two tiny cups. She looked around for Andie then spotted her on the floor. "I brought you some breakfast and your medication, Andie." She put the tray down. "Do you think you can swallow these for me?" she asked, taking the tiny cup of pills and the paper cup filled with water. She approached Andie slowly then bent down.

Andie shook her head and pressed her body deeper into the corner. The nurse sighed as if they had gone through this before. "I'm going to come a little closer, okay? I need for you to take these. I need to make *sure* you take these."

Andie jumped to her feet and pushed the nurse aside, sending her into the opposite wall and the water and pills into the air. She rushed to the door, pulled it open, and ran down the corridor and through a dimly lit stairwell. The nurse rushed after her and called for help. They caught up with Andie as she made her way down to the next floor. As Andie swung and kicked, two male nurses and one orderly managed to overpower her and get her back in her room. She was breathless and sweating as they forced her to swallow the pills. They left her alone, staring at her breakfast.

Andie looked at the tray of food then let her body drop to the floor. The floor felt good; it was cold and unforgiving. She squinted at the rising sun as it sent strange rainbows around the walls. They were engaging for a while then turned into orange fire. *Bang! Bang!*

She jerked away from the noises as they echoed through her head and around the room. She clapped her hands over her ears as her body tightened. What was that noise? The residual clatter rattled in her head, and she closed her eyes. *Maybe that nurse is still here hiding somewhere making noise to scare me*, she thought. She bit her fingernail and cowered in the corner. Her eyes followed her fingers to her palms then fixed on the bandages and metal splints on her little fingers. *Where did these come from?* She wondered, eyeing the bandages. *Whose hands are these?*

Andie got to her feet and held her hands in front of her, studying the splints on each hand. She walked in a circle, looking, staring. She spun around as if someone else were in the room playing a trick. Suddenly she realized these were not her hands. She was sure of it. She had to get the bandages off. Surely her real hands were underneath these bandages. She tore into the white tape and pulled off the metal splints and gauze on both fingers. She stared at her palms then at the broken fingers. They were bluish purple and swollen. "No, no," she whispered.

CHAPTER 86

Kat cruised east on Chicago Avenue, heading toward Northwestern Memorial Hospital. Fresh from two weeks abroad, she was on her way to pay Michael a visit. Her black Lexus SC sped across Michigan Avenue as she glanced at herself in the rearview mirror. She had gotten some sun in Barcelona. She saw it in her hair and on the bridge of her nose. She sighed, thinking of Andie.

At the hospital, Kat took the elevator to the third floor. As the doors opened, she ran smack into Alan. "Kat!" he said with surprise.

Kat returned the smile, surprised herself. "I'm looking for Michael. He hasn't returned my calls since I got back from Spain. I want to know about Andie. How's she doing?"

Alan gave her an update. She looked sad and frustrated, turning away as she put her hand on her forehead. "I feel so damn helpless," she said. "Why can't I see her?"

Alan shook his head, saying her behavior was much too erratic for visitors. Kat looked at the floor with disappointment then pulled her tapestry bag open and gave him a paper bag containing a square-shaped box. "Please give these to Andie," she said and walked away. Alan took the bag and peered in. It was a box of crayons in sixty-four colors.

* * *

Andie's fingers were bandaged and re-splinted. The attending physician warned her not to take them off again. The noises in her head muffled most of his words. To Andie, he was merely moving his lips.

The medication had significantly calmed her violent fits, but the voices and the flashes of memories still tormented her and cut her off from the real world. She resisted entering her room, stopping short of the door. Two nurses gently picked her up off her feet and set her inside, shutting the door before she could try to slip out.

The walls had turned their familiar green-gray as the sun began to set outside. She felt a deep unsettling ache inside her. Then a whisper came from behind as she quickly turned to see who was in the room. "Guess who's gonna die?" came the voice. She let out a gasp. Her stomach knotted. The voice came again. "Guess who's gonna die?" She spun around. Losing her balance, she fell to her knees. Her eyes blurred as she looked around the room. A laugh came from under her bed. She dropped to the floor, searching for the noise. She got to her feet again and grabbed the edge of the bed, lifting it and pushing it on its side. The pillow and bed linens fell in a heap, followed by the flimsy mattress. She climbed on top of the toppled bed and frame and grabbed at the wire springs. Three nurses ran in upon hearing the racket and tried to pull Andie from the overturned bed. Her fingers were bleeding as she gripped the metal netting. "Nooo! Nooo!" Andie yelled.

She jerked away from their clawing hands as they tried to pull her off the overturned bed. She freed her right arm and swung it into the face of the male nurse, sending his glasses across the room. He jumped on top of Andie, and the two fell off the bed to the floor. Andie tried to break free, kicking and swinging. Finally the three managed to subdue her.

Alan arrived after being paged. He was mystified at Andie's outburst. He had thought she was making some progress with the new medications. He peered into her room; it was back in order. Andie was curled up on the floor.

The next morning Alan entered Andie's room and found her huddled in the same corner, rocking and moving her lips. She had her right hand on her right ear and was shaking her head. He approached cautiously. "Andie, do you know who I am?" he asked, trying to make eye contact. Andie hid her face. "Come on, Andie. Look at me. You know me," he pleaded. Andie didn't respond. She clutched herself and held her hand over her ear. "Is something wrong with your ear?"

He came closer, watching her reaction. She looked up and glared at him suspiciously then pulled herself in tighter. Alan moved toward Andie's right side and peered at her right hand. A stream of blood ran down her forearm and dripped off her elbow. It formed a small puddle on the floor. Alan gasped then attempted to kneel down to get a closer look. Andie got to her knees and quickly moved away. He got a better look at the blood and saw she was bleeding from her right ear. A thin three-inch rectangular piece of metal lay on the floor in the blood. He squinted at it and identified it as one of the metal finger splints. It appeared that Andie had used the splint as a knife and had cut away at her right ear. Had the piece been thinner or pointier she most likely would have punctured her eardrum.

He took a chance and reached for the splint. Andie's eyes followed him and caught his wrist just as his fingers touched the bloody piece of metal. Her grip was strong as rage surfaced in her face.

"No!" she yelled, glaring at him. Startled at her strength and the anger in her face, he dropped the metal splint and quickly moved back. Blood streamed from Andie's ear. Alan rushed off to get help.

* * *

"How did this splint get left in Andrea Fulbright's room?" Alan demanded.

The two nurses who had been on duty the day before sat sheepishly in his office. "We know she unwrapped her bandages and pulled off her splints. How could you throw one splint out and not the other?" he asked, looking at the two in disbelief.

Andie had managed to sharpen the splint by methodically scraping it against the mortar between the tiles on the wall. Michael felt sure Andie's attempt at hurting herself wasn't a suicide attempt but some action to rid herself of something she was experiencing. Alan agreed. "I still think we're on target treating the depression first and the PTSD as a secondary disorder," Alan said, and Michael nodded.

CHAPTER 87

"I can understand why you couldn't make our last appointment, Monica," said Maggie Simonds. "You were everywhere on the local news. Congratulations."

Falco looked down. "Thanks. I'm just glad we found those four boys. All that media attention was a little silly, if you ask me."

Maggie sat forward in her chair. "The last time we spoke, you were working through some things with your ex-husband and your mother. How's all that going?"

Falco told Maggie about her dinner with Elaine and Howard and the news of their wedding in a month.

"A month?" Maggie asked.

Falco nodded. She went on to talk about her mother's reaction to the newspaper article and her own reaction to Jeffery and Sam wanting to see her commendations. She discussed her feelings toward her mother and Jeffery and the risks that came with her job. She talked about the support she had received from her colleagues after the capture of the four suspects in Humboldt Park but steered clear of her night of partying with the boys and her encounter with Officer Foley.

"It's been a crazy, mixed-up week," she said, looking away. She was quiet for a few moments.

Maggie looked at her sideways, seeing something was on her mind. "Anything else you want to talk about today?"

Falco put her hand to her mouth and looked out the window. "I'm having a hard time letting go of someone I was protecting, the woman who was kidnapped and brutalized."

"Andrea Fulbright?"

"Yes." Falco looked away then looked at her watch.

Maggie smiled. "We still have some time. Let's talk about that, okay?"

Falco's forehead tightened. She wished she hadn't brought up Andie. She wanted to take it back and talk about something else—something safe—but it was too late. "I'm worried about her, and I think about her all the time. I think I've gotten too close," she blurted.

"It's perfectly normal for you to feel a connection with someone you were protecting. You felt a strong sense of responsibility toward her. You may still be feeling that now."

"I don't know what it is, really." Falco paused, feeling uncomfortable. "Look," she finally said, "I failed her. I was supposed to protect her, and that monster came after her anyway. I couldn't stop him, and she got hurt."

"I can tell you're pretty angry with yourself," Maggie said quietly.

"Angry…disappointed…sad…guilty." She looked at the floor, trying to quell her emotions.

"How is she? Is she still in the hospital?"

"Yes, of course she is!" Falco said, getting up from the chair and walking toward the window across the room. "She's in the psych ward. I found out last week she tried to kill herself." She spun around and looked at Maggie. "It's my fault. It's all my fault!"

"Monica, that's not true. You know that's not true."

Falco looked down as tears streamed down her face. She brushed them away and shook her head. Maggie waited.

"It's just… I don't know. I had this strong connection. Something about her affected me. I guess it was the things she loved—music, art. Andie had come so far from the first time McCaffery had hurt her. She was dealing with PTSD issues, but somehow she managed to work through them. She was able to live like a normal person for the most part." She looked down. "She managed to find beauty and get excited about life all over again. Maybe it was her inner strength that affected me. "

Maggie was silent, letting Falco collect her thoughts.

"I guess…" Her words drifted off. "After my divorce I lost a lot of friends— our coupled friends. They still see Jeffery at soccer games and all, but they certainly aren't interested in being friends with me anymore, the lady cop," she said with a little laugh. "What did we really have in common anyway? I have more in common with the guys at the twenty-third, for god's sake. But what I realized is that for a good two years or so I was just bumping around, hoping my marriage would get better. I was working a lot, trying to keep up with my son, taking care of the house and my husband, trying to be a good a mom and a good cop."

"Is that all?" Maggie asked ironically.

Falco countered, "Well, then you take away the marriage and the kid and the only thing you've got is work, work, work. And you know police work can take up your whole life if you let it."

"Go on."

"Well, my partner and I were assigned to protect Andie until McCaffery was apprehended. A job like that is usually a real drag, long boring hours, babysitting. But I got to know her. She was engaging, challenging, passionate, eccentric, funny…beautiful." Again her words drifted off. "Toward the end I looked forward to seeing her, to talking with her." She looked down, as if almost ashamed. "Then everything changed. We got the word McCaffery was dead in a burned-out van on the Eisenhower. The next morning we were informed that the FBI had closed the case, that they had found prison clothing in the van and that the dental records matched McCaffery's."

She got up from her chair, crossed her arms in front of her, and looked down. "But something didn't feel right. I kept thinking it was all too neat and tidy. The feds seemed way too eager to close the case. I kept thinking they should have waited for the DNA results. We should've kept someone on to protect Andie until we knew for sure McCaffery was dead. Then, that Thursday, after everything appeared to be back to normal, Andie came by the station. She looked so calm, so beautiful…almost radiant. The monster was dead. It was all over. After four years she was free, really free."

"How did you feel seeing Andie?" Maggie asked.

"I was happy to see her. It was a wonderful surprise. She returned my sweater, which I had left at her place. She couldn't stay long. She was going downtown to hang her show." Falco's voice caught in her throat. "It was the last time I saw her…happy, not like I saw her later the next day and again in the hospital with tubes going everywhere." She got up and walked across the room, her fists clenched. "I just…can't handle it sometimes—everything that happened, the fact that I could have prevented it all if I had listened to my gut." She put her hand over her eyes and leaned into the wall. "Oh, Andie. I just want you to be okay."

CHAPTER 88

Falco was sound asleep when her phone rang. It was three thirty a.m.

"Falco? It's Lassiter. We got a floater off Belmont. I want you and Ballard out there ASAP."

"What, sir? A…a…*where,* sir?" she stammered, sitting up in bed.

"Belmont, by the yacht club…you know. You and Ballard get out there right away."

She cursed as she looked at the time then rolled out of bed. The floor was cold on her bare feet as she made her way to her closet. She pulled a wool sweater over the T-shirt she was sleeping in then put on a pair of jeans and black boots. She looked outside; it was cold and raining. "Fuck," she whispered, rubbing her eyes. She called Ballard and told him to meet her at the rocks. He knew what she meant.

Before the city was granted federal funds to rebuild its crumbling lake-front with the smooth, concrete step-like structures that exist today, the huge broken concrete boulders off Belmont Harbor were called "the rocks" by locals. They were a place to get high or drunk or fuck, and the debris from years and years of activity was strewn about and wedged deeply within the crevasses of the decaying structure. Now, after years of renovation, the lake-front was coddled from erosion by protective concrete steps that supported bikers, sunbathers walkers, runners and even a fisherman or two. In the summer the cement remained fairly dry, but in the winter it braced against a fierce gray-green lake, lashing it with waves topping fifteen feet—waves that sometimes spilled over onto portions of Lake Shore Drive.

Falco's body tightened against the late-September wind as she dashed toward her car. It started without a whimper. She cranked up the heat and the windshield wipers and headed toward the expressway. It was still pitch black outside, but folks were on the road, either drunk or going to work. Before long she was exiting on Belmont and heading east toward the lake. Ballard was on his way and promised to bring coffee.

When she drove up, two squad cars and an ambulance were parked precariously close to the edge of the concrete embankment. She waved to two uniformed cops she knew from the twenty-third district. They stood around with their hands in their pockets waiting for the medical examiner. The fire department was in the process of pulling out the victim. Falco walked closer, squinting at what appeared to be a white male. "He hasn't been in there long," one of the officers said as Falco approached.

She rubbed her hands together. "Fucking freezing out here," she said to herself.

She made her way around the area, looking for clues about the victim. She scanned the asphalt path for people who might have seen the victim jump in or get pushed. At four thirty a.m., no one was around. She switched on her flashlight and searched the ground for a wallet, some kind of ID or something. Twenty minutes later Ballard came trotting over with two cups of coffee. The two uniformed cops looked at the detectives longingly, coveting the hot brew.

"What'd you find out, Falco?" Ballard asked.

"Nothing yet. They can't get the fucking body out," she said, letting the steam from the coffee warm her face. "They had it out and then it slipped back in. Now they can't find it."

"Fucking cold and murky down there," Ballard said, peering out over the lake.

"Yeah, I looked around but didn't find shit," she said, pulling the hair out of her eyes.

Voices came from where the firemen were diving. It appeared they had located the body and were bringing it up. The medical examiner waited with a gurney and was flanked by two shivering EMTs. After they loaded the body into the ambulance, the vehicle headed onto Belmont then south toward downtown. Falco and Ballard followed in their cars.

At the morgue the two detectives waited for the medical examiner to give them preliminary details about the victim. After twenty minutes the white-jacketed man met the two outside a set of swinging doors. He told them the body was that of a white male between the ages of nineteen and thirty. He had no wallet or ID in his pockets. Ballard theorized it was a robbery gone bad. He eyed his watch and buttoned his coat, itching to get home.

"I'd like to see the body," Falco said.

Ballard glared at her. "Why do you want to see the body?" he snarled.

"I just want to make sure of something."

The coroner motioned for them to follow him. They made their way past the swinging doors and down a cold, dingy-yellow corridor. He pushed open a steel door that led to another long corridor. Their footsteps echoed off the walls.

"Like a fucking morgue," Ballard hissed.

"You got that right," Falco mumbled.

They entered a large elongated room lined with long rectangular drawers. Everything was hard-edged stainless steel. The room reeked of death and acrid chemicals.

"Over here, Detectives," said the coroner. He gripped the steel handle of one of the lower drawers and used his body weight to pull it open. It wheezed and hissed as it came to a halt, revealing the young victim inside a frosty transparent bag. He looked at the two detectives and pinched the zipper pull.

"Ready?" he asked, eyeing them.

Ballard stepped back, not wanting any part of this. Falco nodded as she looked down at the body. A cool rush of air exuded from the bag as the coroner quickly unzipped it. The body was naked and blue.

"No bruises that I can see," she said to no one in particular. She studied the young man's face. He had blond hair and numerous piercings in his nose and eyebrows. She peered at his arms, then at his hands, spotting a thick silver ring on his left little finger. Ballard approached, not wanting to get a whiff of the body.

"What ya thinking, Falco?"

She eyed the body again, then the face. "I think I know this young man," she said sadly.

CHAPTER 89

Michael mindlessly watched Roxie run after a dirty yellow tennis ball as he sat on a bench at Doggy Beach just south of Addison. The beach was empty; the weather was cool even for dogs. He glanced at his cell phone and frowned. He hadn't heard from Josh in five days. He called after Roxie and bent down to attach her leash to her collar. "Yeah, we gotta go, Rox. Your daddy has to do something."

He dropped Roxie off at home and headed out again. He climbed into his red Honda Civic and drove north on Broadway. He stopped by the book-store across the street from the Riviera Theatre and asked if Josh Michlin had shown up for work. A chunky young girl with bluish-green hair and purple lipstick said, "We haven't seen him in a week. He never called in either, so his ass is grass."

"When was the last time he worked?" he asked, leaning into the check-out counter.

"Who knows? He came in maybe a week-and-a-half ago and was fucking wasted. Keith, the manager, made him go home. I don't think we saw him after that."

Michael called Josh's home phone again then his cell but got no answer on either. He got back in his car and turned left onto Lawrence, heading west. He was getting a bad feeling.

Meanwhile, Falco sat at her desk and stared at her phone. *I can't do anything until the autopsy results come in. We've got no ID and no missing person's report. What if I'm wrong about this kid and call Michael? No way. I can't do that,* she thought.

* * *

Lawrence Avenue was backed up before Damen. A truck delivering a mattress was double-parked, causing cars in the right lane to merge into the left lane to pass. Michael glanced at the cross streets and looked for Kimball.

New construction was going up everywhere, but this part of Lawrence was still a bit grungy. He found the street and made a quick left. A few blocks south was Josh's apartment building, a dingy nondescript brick structure with heavy brick balconies. Michael spotted Josh's rusted-out Chevy Nova. It had two faded parking tickets stuck to the window and a flat rear tire. Michael parked behind it and peered inside. It was a mess. He tried the door, but it was locked. The front seat was littered with half-eaten food in paper and Styrofoam containers. Cans of diet Coke, Mountain Dew, and Old Style were wedged under the seats and intermingled with what appeared to be a sweatshirt and a pair of jeans.

He ran up the front stairs and rang the buzzer for Josh's apartment. A raspy voice with a thick accent answered.

"I'm looking for Josh," Michael said. "Is this Ricky, his roommate?" Static followed, and he waited.

"Who you look for?" came the voice.

"Josh Michlin. I'm looking for Josh," he said, almost yelling into the intercom.

"Josh? He's not here. I have not seen him three days, and if I did I wouldn't let him in!" cracked the angry voice.

"Can I come up?" asked Michael. "I'm his boyfriend." *Ex-boyfriend*, Michael said to himself.

The door buzzed as Michael pushed it open. He ran up the three flights of stairs to Josh's apartment. The door was open, so he walked in. A man, presumably the landlord, was loading a large trash bag with what looked like rotting and dripping food containers from the refrigerator and cupboards. The place reeked of spoiled food, stale beer bottles, and vomit. The landlord had the window open, but the fresh air didn't help the stench. The man peered at Michael as he entered. He was of eastern European descent, possibly Bosnian.

"You know this Josh?" he asked, looking angry.

"He's my boyfriend. I think he's in trouble. When did you see him last, sir?" Michael asked, a little afraid of the man.

"I see him three days ago with friend…a big guy. They make too much noise. I get complaints, so I go up and they don't answer door. I pound loud and get nothing. Then it is quiet, so I leave and go back to my place. The next day I smell something bad—real bad—and I knock on door. Nothing, so I knock again. I don't like this, so I get master key and open door. They leave place in big mess. Like what you see. I change lock and throw out his stuff."

"You evicted him?" Michael asked.

"Yeah, I throw out all his stuff on sidewalk," the man said.

"When was this?" Michael asked.

"Two days ago. He not pay last month rent, so I keep deposit."

Michael nodded. All of Josh's possessions were most likely on their way to the landfill. He thanked the man and left. As he came down the stairs, he considered breaking into Josh's car in hopes of finding a phone number, a name, or an address where he might be staying. But none of his tweaker friends had names that could be found in a phone book. Mickey Fine, Suede, and Rudy Tuesday were names of people making short appearances in life, Michael thought. His last option was to cruise the bars and start asking around. He didn't want to do that but headed east toward Halsted Street.

CHAPTER 90

"Party boy," said Ballard as he scanned the autopsy report. "Still no leads on who he is, though." He looked at Falco and handed her the report. "You think you know this kid?"

She scowled as she flipped through the file. "He died of blunt force trauma to the back of the head and drowning. The body contained large amounts of crystal meth and a variety of other drugs and alcohol," she said, reading from the report.

"That'll do it," Ballard said flatly as he popped open a can of diet Coke.

Falco looked through the plastic bag that contained the silver ring the victim had worn as well as an assortment of metal studs and earrings. She opened the bag and took out the silver ring, feeling it with her thumb and forefinger. She searched her desk for her reading glasses. Finding them, she looked closely at the ring for marks. "Ballard, do you have a magnifying glass?" she asked. He handed her the glass over his cubicle. She took it vaguely, not taking her eyes off the ring.

"You got something there?" he asked, craning his neck to see what she was looking at so intently.

Inside the ring she saw a tiny engraving that read, "10-30-06.""It's a date," she whispered.

Just then Falco's phone rang. It was Lynette Collins, the receptionist from the front desk, telling Falco she had a visitor, a Michael Hansen. Falco moved the autopsy report to the opposite side of her desk and put the ring in her top drawer. Before she had a chance to consider the reason for Michael's visit, he appeared looking around for her. She smiled as she caught his eye. He looked worried as he made his way through the maze of cubicles.

"Hey, what's up, Michael?" Falco asked as concern quickly clouded her face. She pulled her coat off the chair next to her desk and motioned for him to sit. He was upset and breathing fast.

"I…I just took a chance to see you. I'm beside myself," he said quickly. He was wringing his hands.

"How can I help?"

"It's Josh. Something's happened to him. I just know it. I spent the afternoon looking for him. I went to his job. He got fired. He hadn't been to work in a week. I went to his apartment and found out he was evicted two days ago." He looked at the floor; his eyes were red from crying. "I just came back from his place. I spoke with his landlord. God, it was a wreck. It smelled of beer and vomit. Ugh." He put his head in his hands. "Jeeesus," he whispered.

Falco scooted her chair in front of him. "When did anyone see him last?"

"Two days ago, I guess. He was with some friend, some big guy, as his landlord put it."

"Then his landlord was the last person to see him?"

"Yeah, two days ago."

Falco took a deep breath. "Do you want to file a missing person's report?"

"Yes, yes, I do," he said, biting his lip. "I never thought I'd be doing this. I knew he was a party boy when I met him, but he was young and beautiful, and I thought... Well, I thought..." His eyes filled with tears, and he put his hand over his face.

Falco grabbed a handful of tissues and handed them to him. She came close, hesitated, then put her arm around him. Ballard eyed the two as he scooted out of his cubicle.

After a moment, Michael slowly pulled away from her, blew his nose, and took a couple of deep breaths.

"You okay?" Falco asked gently.

"Yes, I think so," he sniffed.

"How long were you and Josh together?" she asked softly, taking her seat.

"Almost a year-and-a-half. We met at a Halloween party, I was Cap'n Crunch, and he was...Harry Potter or somebody. I can't remember what Josh was for sure," Michael said, looking off.

Falco put her hands over her eyes and traced her fingertips down her face. Michael read her expression and stared. He took a deep breath and said, "You know something, don't you? You do. I can see it."

Falco pulled her top desk drawer open and picked up the silver ring. "There's a date on the inside of this ring. Does it look familiar to you?" she asked, handing the ring to him.

Michael looked at it and said, "It's Josh's ring. I gave this to him. It has the day we..." He stopped short. "How did *you* get it?" Falco's face flashed with sadness as she avoided his stare. He held the ring in his fist and shook his head, "Oh, no. Oh, god, no."

Falco put her hand on his and said, "Michael, I'm really sorry. It's bad news."

CHAPTER 91

The North End was quiet for a Wednesday night. The pool tables were empty and the bartender looked bored. Michael was on his fourth rum and Coke. Falco sat quietly, opposite of Michael, staring at her glass of white wine.

"I've got so many calls to make. I don't know why I'm sitting here getting drunk," he mumbled. "I have to call Josh's parents in St. Louis—that'll be a real trip—then figure out how to, you know, get him back home." Michael's face was full of pain, and his eyes were red and puffy. "Who could have done this to Josh?"

Falco shook her head. "We'll find him, whoever he is. Somebody had to have seen something. We'll talk to the landlord tomorrow and follow up on any other leads or ideas you might have. I'll need a list of his friends, his roommate's name, and the bars he…" She stopped short and rubbed her forehead then looked at him. "I'm sorry. I'm sounding more like a cop than a friend."

Michael gave her a little smile. The image of Josh's dead body flashed in his head. "He was so beautiful…like a statue," he said, remembering the body, cold and blue-gray.

Falco put her hand on his. "Enough of that right now, okay? Don't torture yourself."

He looked down as tears came to his eyes. He downed the rest of his drink and looked at his watch. "I'd better go home," he said.

Falco's eyes followed him as he got up from his chair. "Can I drive you?" she asked, seeing him waver just a bit.

"No, I'm okay, sweetie."

Falco wasn't so sure. She grabbed her jacket and followed Michael out of the bar. He headed up Halsted and found his car.

Falco looked down the street. Her car was still parked in the lot at the station. "Stay here and let me get my car. I'll follow you home." Just then a tall figure ran across Halsted Street. "Michael, hey!" It was Tim Strickland. The two men said nothing as they embraced. "I'm so sorry," Tim said. He looked at Falco, who waved goodbye and headed down the block to her car.

* * *

The next day, Falco and Ballard followed up on the information Michael had given them the day before. They headed to Josh's apartment on Kimball to speak with the landlord. Falco was worried about Michael and called him on his cell phone but got his voicemail.

"Too bad about Mike," Ballard said quietly. "Small fucking world."

CHAPTER 92

"Answer the fucking phone, Michael!" Kat snapped as she heard his recorded voice kick in. She slammed the phone down and fidgeted with an envelope. *What's going on with him?* she thought. She dialed his work number and got a lengthy message that he would be out of the office until Monday. She cursed and spun around in her desk chair, got up, and went into the back office. She crouched and opened the safe and placed the envelope inside. She slammed it shut and gave the dial a spin.

Michael spent the day making phone calls to Josh's family and friends and fielding calls from the *Chicago Tribune* and the gay press. He made arrangements with a local funeral home to transfer Josh's body to St. Louis. He booked a flight for eight p.m. and called his pet sitter.

* * *

"Sometimes I really hate this job," Falco told Ballard as they drove west on Lawrence.

"What? You? Really?" Ballard said, surprised.

Falco stared out the window. The two detectives pulled up in front of Josh's apartment building just shy of a fire hydrant. The police had towed Josh's car the day before after Michael had identified his body.

Ballard punched the button for the landlord on the rusty wrought iron gate. He identified himself, and the inside door buzzed. The landlord appeared outside his apartment just as Ballard and Falco reached the top of the stairs. He was a large, middle-aged man with light brown hair cut short. He had a rubbery face with a large forehead and a deep scar just over his left eyebrow. His plaid cotton shirt was unbuttoned, revealing a grubby white T-shirt. His pants were baggy and paint splattered, and he wore a pair of beat-up huarache sandals.

"Police, eh?" the man said as Falco and Ballard approached.

The two introduced themselves and showed their badges. "We're here to talk to you about Josh Michlin. He was your tenant as of just a few days ago," said Falco, flipping open a notepad.

"He was no good. Lots of trouble. I throw him out, put all his stuff on sidewalk." He glanced at the two detectives. "Someone came yesterday looking for him, a boyfriend," the man said with a laugh.

"Yes, we know about him," said Falco quickly. "Josh had a roommate named Ricky Grimes. Have you seen him?"

"No, no. Ricky move out long time ago."

"Did you see anyone else with Josh after the roommate moved out?" asked Falco.

The man looked at her and smiled. He stared at her chest for a moment then looked at her askance. "You know, you are a very pretty lady," he said with a little smile, his eyebrows raised.

Ballard stepped closer. "You wanna to answer the lady's question?"

The landlord gave him an angry look. "No, I see no one else except for big man three…four nights ago, I think."

"What did this big man look like? Can you describe him?" Ballard said, taking over the questioning.

"He was a big guy. That is all!" laughed the man.

"Look, was he blond? Dark? Young? Old? He wasn't just a *big man*!" Falco said, getting impatient.

"Okay, okay, little lady. He was maybe six two, bigger than me. Maybe Hispanic or Italian like you," he said, smiling again at her. She sighed and looked away.

"That's all you can think of?" Ballard asked firmly.

"He had tattoos…big tattoos on hands and neck."

"What did the tattoos look like?" Ballard asked.

"They look like *tattoos*!" said the man, getting annoyed. "He had on jacket, so I only see hands and neck."

"Why did you evict Mr. Michlin? Did he not pay his rent, or was it something else?" Ballard asked.

"He had too much noise and the place stink! I open door and apartment a big mess. Beer bottles, clothes, food on floor, stuff on stove. It stink!" said the man. "I throw trash out and put stuff in bags and throw out window on sidewalk. Then I change locks!"

The two detectives sighed and looked at each other. "We're gonna need to see the apartment," Falco said. "Has there been a trash pickup since Monday?"

"Trash collector come tomorrow."

"We're gonna need to look in the dumpster," she said, putting away her notepad. "Let's start there."

Ballard called for a forensics team. The dumpster was wedged between two tall brick buildings. The alley was damp and dark, and the black asphalt showed remnants of a cobblestone street. The landlord led the detectives down a narrow corridor between the apartment building and the one next door. The sidewalk was slick with moisture, and dryer lint hung like Spanish moss from rusty vents from the neighboring building.

Ballard felt claustrophobic and walked faster. He eyed the sides of the two buildings and heard the scuttle of some kind of animal, a cat or maybe a rat.

"Here is dumpster," said the landlord. The grungy metal box on wheels was overflowing with garbage bags. "Sometimes animals open trash," he said, eyeing a torn and leaking trash bag. "You finish, come back, and I have apartment open for you." He turned and walked away. Falco and Ballard gave each other pained looks and put on rubber gloves.

An evidence team arrived within an hour. Ballard and Falco had gone through the dumpster and collected a large bag of evidence. It contained two empty metal cans of acetone, an empty antifreeze container, duct tape, and a paper bag full of what appeared to be coffee filters stained reddish brown.

"I think we're done here," said Ballard. He swung the heavy dumpster lid closed, and the two detectives made their way up to Josh's apartment, bringing the bag of evidence with them.

Rita Bragg, one of the evidence technicians, looked over from the kitchen area and spotted Ballard and Falco. "Stop right there, Detectives," she said through her facemask. "The place has been aired out, but I wouldn't come any farther. They were cooking it up in here. It's in the stove and on the walls." She looked up at the ceiling then down to the bag Ballard was holding. "You got more stuff there?" she asked.

"Yeah, a bunch of stuff from the dumpster," said Ballard.

"Leave it," she said, pointing to the floor.

Rita conferred with another tech and said, "I think we're good here. We'll check the dumpster again, but I think we've got enough evidence right now. We'll go through it and send over any names, phone numbers, or whatever else we find. Sound good?"

"Works for me," Falco said, turning away from the open door.

They made their way down the grimy pink carpeted stairs and out to the front steps. Falco felt like she needed to change clothes and take a shower. She couldn't wait to get rid of the rubber gloves and wash her hands.

"You wanna get lunch somewhere?" Ballard asked.

"Do I want to get *lunch* somewhere? We fucking smell like a dumpster and you're thinking about *lunch somewhere?*"

"I guess that's not such a good plan," he said, scrunching his face. They left in silence.

* * *

By the time the detectives returned to the station, they had stacks of messages, and the tiny red voice message lights were blinking on their phones. Falco rooted through her locker and found a clean blouse to change into. Ballard went home for lunch and returned in fresh clothes. Lassiter snagged Ballard as he walked past his office, asking for an update on the Michlin murder and the meth labs on west Belmont. He told the chief they were waiting for the evidence techs to finish at the victim's apartment but that he and Falco had pulled a substantial amount of evidence from the dumpster.

Falco looked through her messages hoping Michael had returned her call. She was worried about him but also wanted the names of Josh's roommate and friends he had promised to get her last night. Grasky came by Falco's desk and loomed cautiously, waiting for her to finish on the phone. She looked up and smiled, putting her index finger up, meaning she'd be done in a minute. He nodded and milled around her desk. She hung up the phone and motioned for Grasky to sit.

"I was in the chief's office and heard you and Ballard went dumpster diving this morning," he said with a laugh.

"You came all the way over here to tell me that, Steve? You didn't get a whiff of us from back at your desk?" she said, giving him a sour look.

"I don't smell anything," he said, lifting his nose in the air.

"Well, I changed my shirt, but the pants... Well, don't get too close," she said with a laugh.

"I wanted to tell you I just got put on the case with you two," Grasky said.

"That's great. We could use the help. I hope that doesn't mean the chief thinks we're dragging our feet," she said, suddenly concerned.

"No, I don't think so. Lassiter said I should help you guys out since he doesn't want me into something too deep just before my retirement date," Grasky said with a smug look.

"Well, good for you."

She leafed through her stack of messages, sorted the ones pertaining to the meth case, and handed them to Grasky with a smile. "Let me track down Ballard and give you a briefing."

CHAPTER 93

Andie stared at the door of her room. A dark shadow had formed around its edge. She was afraid to go near it. The darkness of the night had descended on her room, but the glow of the parking lot lights below illuminated the door. It taunted her; it called her name. She shook her head and pulled at the bandage on her ear to silence the voices. Then she stared at the door.

The heat kicked in. She heard the warm rush of hot air from the vent way above her head. Something rattled slightly then stopped. She swallowed hard then slowly got to her feet. She crept across the room; the floor felt cold. She found herself staring at the door. A hand reached out and touched the silver doorknob; it was cold too. She held her breath and pulled gently, almost timidly. The door floated open with a tiny click. Andie peered out the door of her room and down the dark, empty corridor. The floors were shiny, reflecting the long rows of dimly lit overhead lights. She stepped out as the door closed behind her. She felt a little smile come to her lips. She gasped in anticipation.

"Go, Andie," said the voice.

She turned slightly, looking to her left then to her right. She then moved cautiously into the corridor. She heard the voices of a man and woman ahead. She turned back and headed in the opposite direction then found a tiny stairwell. She shoved the door open. A fire extinguisher startled her as she ran down the first flight of stairs.

"Go, Andie. They're going to find you. Hurry!" said the voice almost playful.

She was out of breath as she made it down another flight. Then she heard more voices. It was the sound of two women talking. She smelled cigarette smoke. They were smoking in the stairwell. She pushed open a door and found herself on the fifth floor. The clock read 1:34; the hallway was empty.

Suddenly Andie felt confused. She stopped and looked around then headed to her right toward a hallway of offices. A light had gone off in one of the rooms as a small, thin man with glasses exited and walked quickly down the opposite hallway. Andie watched as he turned the corner and disappeared. She approached the door and peered through the window and into the dark room. She squinted then pulled the door open. The room was dimly lit by the lights from the parking lot, but the smell was unmistakable. Andie gasped as she looked at the wall of shelves that teemed with books of all shapes and sizes. "Ooooh," was all she could whisper.

She strained her eyes to read the handwritten sign: LIBRARY USERS, PLEASE SIGN OUT BOOKS HERE. Then she looked over at a tiny desk. Above it a sign read, WELCOME TO THE PATIENT/STAFF LIBRARY. PLEASE BE RESPECTFUL OF THE MATERIALS.

Andie looked up at the two towering shelves. Her mouth hung open as she scanned the hardcover books and paperbacks. She ran a finger over the spines as she scanned the titles and authors, then stepped back and gave the shelves a scowl. Her eyes scanned the collection, top to bottom, left to right. She was suddenly filled with anxiety and a strange exhilaration.

"Nooo," she said quietly, annoyed. She pulled books off the shelves and piled them on the floor and tables. She didn't dare turn on the lights. She worked quickly and deliberately in the darkness.

Abbot, Abrams, Albom, Allison…Cervantes, Childs, Chopin, Clark, Crichton, Coombs. Gibson, Gide, Grisham, Hesse, Jackson, Jakes, Kafka, Kellerman…Lawrence, Macomber, Mann, Maupin…O'Connor, Patchet, Patterson, Porter, Preston, Robb, Roberts, Sanford, Steel, Trollop, Turow, Updike, Vachess…Wilde, Woolf…

* * *

It was eight a.m. when the nurse found Andie's door ajar and her room empty. She alerted the morning shift and grabbed those from the previous shift to help in the search. The head nurse paged Alan, who was parking his car in the garage across the street.

"We have no idea when or how she got out," said a red-haired nurse from the evening shift.

Alan walked quickly down the hall with a look of anger and worry. "How did this happen?" he demanded.

"I don't know, Dr. Forrest. I just started my shift and went into Ms. Fulbright's room, and she wasn't there," said a heavyset nurse with dark eyeliner.

Donald Hopkins, one of the orderlies on duty, drifted by, buttoning his coat.

"Ask Donald," said the heavyset nurse, pointing. "*He* worked the night shift."

Alan turned to Donald, who looked at Dr. Forrest with wide eyes. "Did you check Ms. Fulbright's room any time last night?"

"Uh…yeah. I checked around midnight. She was sleeping on the floor like she usually does," Donald said.

"Did you check on her any other time during the night, Mr. Hopkins?" asked Alan, getting angry.

"No, I didn't, but I think Anita did," he said slowly.

"Anita Jaworski?"

"Yeah," mumbled Donald.

"Nobody's leaving until we find Ms. Fulbright. Understand? There is no excuse for this kind of thing to happen. I don't care how long it takes. Nobody's leaving! Now all of you take off your coats and start looking," Alan said loudly.

Alan left and went into Andie's room looking for bandages or blood. The rest of the night shift stashed their coats and purses and combed the corridors, empty offices, restrooms, closets, and stairwells. He wondered how far Andie had gotten. Was she even in the hospital anymore? The temperature was forty degrees outside, and he knew she had only the clothes she had on. He decided to call the police just in case. He went to his office and pulled out Falco's business card and dialed her number.

"Hi, Dr. Forrest—uh, Alan—how are you?" Falco said.

"Hi, Monica. I need your help. I wasn't sure who to call, but Andie is missing. She left her room sometime last night. I've got our staff searching the wing of the hospital, but if, god forbid, she left the hospital, I need to get the word out," he said. "I've never had this happen before." He spoke quickly, panic in his voice.

"When did you say she went missing?" Falco pulled a pen and paper out of her desk drawer.

"Sometime last night. I was told by the nursing staff it was after midnight."

"That's a long time to lose track of someone," Falco said, feeling pangs of worry. "What are the chances of her getting out—you know, walking out of the hospital?"

"I think pretty slim, and maybe I'm jumping the gun here, but…" He looked toward the door of his office. His secretary, Margaret, was waving, trying to get his attention. "Uh, just a minute, Monica."

"They found Andie, Dr. Forrest, on the fifth floor," Margaret said.

Alan's head dropped to his chest in relief. He got back on the phone and said, "We found her. I've gotta run down to the fifth floor. She's down there. Sorry to bother you," he said with a sigh of relief. He quickly hung up the phone and took the stairs to the fifth floor.

Falco sighed and put her head on her desk.

Grasky looked up from his computer screen. "Never a dull moment, eh, Falco?"

* * *

A small crowd had gathered at the entrance of the makeshift library. Alan pushed his way through the nurses, staff, and patients. "Let's clear the area," he said, focusing ahead. He grabbed one of the night-shift nurses and Donald Hopkins and told the others the library was temporarily closed. He found Andie on the floor near the back of the room holding four books in her arms and staring at them.

The library was in pristine shape. The fiction was alphabetized by author, and the small collection of nonfiction was also neatly organized and shelved. The small man with glasses Andie had seen in the wee hours of the morning looked at Alan as he approached and said, "She redid the entire collection. It's wonderful!" Alan ignored him and slowly approached Andie.

"Nice to see you in your element, Andie," Alan said, bending down on one knee. Andie tensed up and held her books close to her chest. She glared at him then mouthed some words. Alan took a chance, sensing she was worn out, and sat cross-legged on the floor across from her. "Someone told me you did a wonderful job organizing the collection here," Alan said with a gentle smile. "It must have taken you most of the night."

Andie looked up at him, and her expression relaxed a bit. She looked at the books in her arms and quietly said, "Can I have these?"

Alan and the two staff members got her back to her room. She wouldn't let go of the books until the three left her. She sat on the floor and stacked the books in front of her, *Don Quixote*, *The Metamorphosis*, *a book on Renaissance Art*, and a collection of poems by Virginia Woolf. She touched the covers of each book with her fingers as if they were long lost treasures.

CHAPTER 94

It was nearly seven by the time Falco got home. She called Jeffery so she could talk to Sam, but no one was home. She wondered how Michael was doing and whether he had made the trip to St. Louis. She hoped Andie was okay and hadn't tried to hurt herself again.

She started a load of laundry and poured herself a glass of wine as her cell phone rang. It was Alan. "Hi, Monica. I just wanted to call and let you know Andie's okay," he said in an upbeat tone.

"Oh, that's a relief," she said, taking a sip of wine. "Where did you find her?"

Alan sighed. "She was in her element. We found her in the patient/staff library. She alphabetized the entire fiction collection!" Falco smiled. "I hope I didn't alarm you with my call. You were the first person I thought of who could help. There was no telling where Andie had gone, so I was just being careful."

"That was perfectly appropriate, Alan. If she were trying to head home, she would be in my jurisdiction anyway. If she were out somewhere near the hospital, it would have been the eighteenth district."

"Uh…just a minute," Alan said. There was a pause in the conversation, and she heard someone talking to Alan in the background. "Listen, Monica, I have to run, but I wanted to ask if I could take you to lunch sometime next week— for two reasons. One is strictly a social one. It'd be nice to see you again, but I'd also like to talk about a few things in connection with Andie." She tried to say something, but he cut her off. "I'll call you first part of next week, okay?"

"Sure," she said as the phone clicked off on the other end. She put her cell phone on the counter and eyed her glass of wine. Cool droplets of condensation had formed around the edge of the glass. She swirled the wine and took a long sip. "Interesting," she said.

* * *

Friday was busy at the twenty-third district. Grasky had tracked down the leads Falco had given him; Ballard was pulling files and mug shots of suspects with prior meth arrests; and Falco called the landlord in for further questioning. The evidence team had packaged the remainder of the items from Josh's apartment as well as the bag full of evidence that Ballard and Falco had pulled from the dumpster.

"No names, no nothing," said Ballard, referring to the evidence.

Grasky grabbed his keys from his desk and quickly walked past the two detectives. "I got a lead on another lab off Western and Division. I'll be back."

"You need company?" Falco asked, wanting to get out of the office.

"Sure. Get your coat."

Ballard grunted as the two walked quickly toward the stairwell. "Guess I'm chopped liver or somethin'," he said into his coffee.

When they got into the car, Grasky looked over at Falco. "Why do I feel so comfortable with you sitting there?"

"Not for long, buddy."

"You gonna miss me, Falco?"

"Yeah, I'm gonna miss you, Steve," she said, nodding sadly.

CHAPTER 95

After spending the night reading *Don Quixote*, Andie finally fell asleep after two a.m. Alan was encouraged by her interest in the books and her uncanny focus on her impromptu library project. The library volunteer snagged Alan later that day to tell him Andie had organized the tiny non-fiction collection using Library of Congress classification. "A major feat," he said, "especially since they had no spine labels."

Alan smiled graciously. "Maybe I'll send her back in a couple of weeks."

The next morning Alan appeared in the doorway of Andie's room. He watched her closely and entered slowly then knelt on the floor where she sat with one of her books. "I got a deal for you," he said with a little smile. "You take these without a problem, and I give you what I have in my hand." He was holding a small green case behind his back.

Andie looked at him suspiciously. "I just took some of those," she said, her words stubborn in her mouth.

"That was last night," he countered. Andie flinched and rubbed her ear. She was quiet. "Something going on in that ear, Andie?"

"No, no," she said, shaking her head.

"Do we have a deal?" Alan put the tiny container of pills on the floor and slid the cup of water closer. Andie placed the book down and rubbed her eyes. She looked at Alan and processed the offer. "Come on, Andie. You know me. I'm a man of my word. I wouldn't play a trick on you."

She glanced him and then at the pills. "Okay," she whispered. She tipped the container of pills into her mouth and swallowed the cup of water. She set the two containers down and looked back at Alan.

"Great," Alan said as he brought his left hand around and set the small green case on the book Andie was reading. She stared at the green object, not knowing what it was. She touched it cautiously then fingered the snap that held the case closed. Recognition came to her face as she unsnapped the case and pulled out her tortoiseshell reading glasses. She took a deep breath and opened her book. A tiny smile appeared on her face.

CHAPTER 96

Falco went to bed early, bringing some case files with her to bed. She settled in and opened the first file; a mug shot slid out. She glanced at it then put it back in the file, closing it and setting it next to her on the bed. Her eyes were tired. She dragged her glasses from her face and rubbed her forehead. *I wonder how Michael is doing? He looked so beside himself the other night.* She thought about Andie alone in the hospital. *She must be doing better physically if she can disappear to another floor of the hospital.* She smiled at the thought of her and recalled her image that day in the kitchen. A deep sigh filled her chest. She closed her eyes and sunk into her pillow, reached between her legs, and squeezed.

"Hey, Detective…"

"Andie, what a nice surprise! Come and have a seat."

"I brought your sweater. You left it at my place."

"Oh, yeah. That is my sweater."

Falco ran the conversation in her head. In her mind she saw Andie looking at her. Andie moved closer and softly touched the front of Falco's blouse. She eyed her longingly then drew her closer, gently playing and pulling at the buttons. Andie brought her lips close to Falco's, brushing them lightly with her breath. Falco gasped then moved in toward Andie, parting her lips.

Their mouths met, wet and soft, as their breathing grew faster. Andie ripped open Falco's blouse, sending buttons flying.

"Oh Jesus!" Falco woke with a start. She was breathing fast as she grabbed her chest then touched her collarbone, where a pool of sweat had formed in the hollow. She squinted from the light then sat up, wondering where the noise had come from. She looked at the floor and saw the files had slipped off the bed. "Son of a—," she whispered. Her heart pounded as she fell back onto her pillow. "Oh, my…god," she said. She stared at the ceiling, remembering her dream, desperately wishing it hadn't ended. "Fuck," she whispered breathlessly. "I am so wet." She put her hand over her eyes and whispered, "Oh…lord of heaven."

CHAPTER 97

Sam and Falco spent Sunday together shopping for a new winter coat and soccer shoes. It was nearly eight thirty when she dropped him off at Jeffery's house. Jeffery motioned for her to come in as she watched Sam enter the house from the car. Falco sighed and turned off the car. She slid out and headed up the sidewalk.

"What's up, Jeffery?" she asked as she walked up the steps and into the living room.

"Your mother called me about the wedding. She wants me to give her away," he said fighting back a frown.

"What?" Falco blurted. Her face cracked as she burst into laughter. "You have got to be kidding me!" She put her face in her hands and flopped on the sofa. "Oh, god!" she said between fits of laughter. Her body shook as she fell face first into the sofa cushion and pounded it with her fist. "She wants you to give her away! Now that…" She sat up, trying to collect herself. Jeffery grimaced and folded his arms across his chest. "Jesus Christ, is she gonna get the Pope to do the ceremony?" she asked, wiping tears from her face. She looked at Jeffery's expression, which only made her laugh harder.

Jeffery looked at her annoyed and gnawed on his thumb nail.

* * *

Seventeen voicemail messages greeted Falco on Monday morning. It was eight fifteen and Indian summer in Chicago. Sunny and pleasantly cool, it was a welcome reprieve from the last few weeks of frigid, damp weather. Ballard drifted in and heaved himself down at his desk. Falco smelled coffee and the sweet fragrance of a French doughnut. He was wheezing as he scooted in his chair. Falco could hear the creak of the springs as it held Ballard's weight.

Michael had left a message early saying he was back from St. Louis and would drop by the names and phone numbers he had promised last Wednesday. Her mother called with an update on the wedding. More messages came in with leads on suspected meth labs in the area. Falco was beginning to figure some landlords were calling in as a way to harass their tenants. She was getting pretty good at weeding out the bogus calls.

Alan Forrest left a message about lunch. Falco wasn't sure how she'd be able to fit a lunch date into what was already looking like a hectic week. She scrunched her face at her calendar as she tried to jostle suspect interviews, meetings, and the open-ended days of chasing down leads. She sighed. *Maybe dinner*, she thought.

She looked at her watch. It was ten o'clock and time to meet Sadik Ostoja, the landlord from Josh's building. He graciously had volunteered to come to the station to meet with Grasky, Ballard, and Falco. Ballard gulped down the rest of his coffee and got up slowly from his chair.

Falco stared at him. "You okay, JB? You look a little stiff."

"Oh, the body's seen better days and so has my tooth," he said, rubbing his jaw.

"Toothache again? I thought you took care of that."

"Yeah, so did I." He nodded at Grasky, who was chewing gum and looking anxious.

"Let's go, kids," Grasky said. "Mr. Ostoja is waiting, and he came all this way to visit with us and look at these mugs."

"No, he came all this way to look at Falco's mug," teased Ballard.

"Okay, don't start." She shot Ballard a dirty look.

"Children," said Grasky, almost in song.

The three jogged down the stairs toward one of the interrogation rooms. Mr. Ostoja sat patiently at the bottom of the stairs with a bottle of diet Coke in his hand. He smiled as he saw the three, recognizing Falco first. Ballard introduced Mr. Ostoja to Grasky, and the four made their way to one of the empty interrogation rooms. Three dingy chairs surrounded a wobbly laminated table. Ballard went out to find another chair as Falco pulled out a stack of mug shots. Mr. Ostoja was wearing a blue short-sleeved shirt and a pair of shiny pleated trousers. He reeked of Old Spice and deodorant soap.

He smiled broadly at Falco as she stacked the photos in front of him. Ballard noisily hauled another chair into the room. He was out of breath and flushed. Falco glanced at him with concern then focused her attention on Mr. Ostoja.

"Just take your time with these, sir," she said, avoiding his gaze.

The man put on a crooked pair of plastic reading glasses and carefully looked at each mug shot, not commenting on any of them. His aftershave was giving Falco a headache. Grasky glanced at her as she got up to get some fresh air. "Excuse me," she muttered. Mr. Ostoja looked up as she moved to leave the room.

"She'll be right back," Ballard offered.

Falco walked outside and took a few deep breaths. The closeness of the room and the guy's aftershave had made her dizzy. She leaned on the brick wall just outside the heavy door leading inside, enjoying the resurgence of summery weather. *It won't last*, she thought.

Grasky appeared at the open door. "We think we have a positive ID." Falco turned and followed him back into the room.

"This is man…boyfriend," said the landlord. "I am sure this is boyfriend."

Cornell Raphael Cordero, otherwise known as Cachao Cordero, was a member of the Latin Kings street gang and a notorious drug runner. He had served time at the federal penitentiary for trafficking cocaine and attempted murder and was just recently paroled.

"He's probably using his connections in Mexico to smuggle ephedrine and pseudoephedrine," said Grasky.

"Or distributing recycled solvents," said Falco.

Mr. Ostoja looked pleased with himself. He pointed to Cordero's mug shot. "See, tattoos," he said, looking up at Falco.

"Great, Mr. Ostoja. We really appreciate your coming in," said Falco. She quickly gathered up the files, handed the Cordero file to Grasky, then left the room.

Mr. Ostoja scowled.

Grasky and Ballard were smiling as they returned to their desks. "Boy, you really know how to duck out of a room, Falco," Grasky teased.

"The guy was making me nervous," she said, not looking up from her computer. "I've got three known addresses for Cordero. I put out an APB too."

Her phone rang. It was the bank manager from the Chase Bank on Sheffield and Belmont. He had pulled up Josh Michlin's checking account statement and found that a withdrawal of $600 was made the night of Josh's death.

"Do you have the transaction stills for the cash machine from that night?" she asked.

"We have them on disk. I can pull them up for you if you want to come by the bank," the manager said.

"Great, I'll be there in half an hour."

Just then her phone rang again. It was Michael wanting to drop off the names and phone numbers of Josh's friends.

"I'll be there before five," he said.

"Great. I'll wait for you," Falco told him.

Ballard peered over her cubicle. "Me and Grasky are gonna head to west Belmont. You checking out the bank?"

"Yeah. I'll catch up with you guys later," she said, grabbing her jacket and purse.

CHAPTER 98

Halsted was slow moving all the way to Belmont. Falco made a right and parked in a tow zone in front of Berlin, one of the oldest gay bars in Boystown. The bank manager came into the lobby and greeted Falco, gesturing for her to follow him into his office. He was a tall man with thinning blond hair and tiny black glasses. He pulled a chair close to the computer at his desk and motioned for her to sit.

"We don't usually get this kind of excitement at our branch," he said with a laugh. "Usually it's the West Side or the South Side where they get the trouble." He pulled up Josh's account and scrolled down, showing the time and date of the $600 withdrawal. "You see, it was just as I said on the phone, early morning when the withdrawal was made." His eyes moved to the top of the screen. He tilted his head slightly and focused on another line of the account. "Well, I'll be damned," he said slowly. He looked closely at the numbers. "Detective, it appears the account has been completely drained… zero balance."

"Zero balance? You just said over the phone…" She squinted at the screen.

"It appears someone just blew the balance as of about an hour ago," the manager said.

Falco's heart jumped. "Where was the transaction made? I'll need that and a photo—a still from the cash machine—if you can get it. How soon can you get it?" Her hands were sweating as she rubbed them on her jeans.

"I can get the transaction location right here online," the manager said. "It's at our Bucktown Branch, North Avenue and Western."

"I've got to call this in," she said, pulling out her cell phone.

She got Ballard on the phone and gave him the location of the Chase bank where the suspect had made the last transaction. Ballard and Grasky weren't far. "If it's Cordero we'll call for backup," Ballard said.

The manager picked up his phone and dialed a number to the downtown branch. He explained the situation to the person on the other end, then nodded and hung up. "We should get a fax in five minutes or so," he said almost breathlessly.

"Great," Falco said with a firm nod.

He pulled a disc from a plastic box and inserted it into the CD drive of his computer. "Let's see if we can find the guy who made the transaction that Monday at one twenty-two a.m." He scrolled up the screen of Josh's account. Falco waited as the disc whirled in the drive. "These discs contain enormous amounts of information. I hope this doesn't take forever," he said apologetically.

Falco peered at the screen. The manager typed in some information, a date and time, and hit "enter." The disc whirled again. They waited. Across the room, the fax machine hummed and hissed then jutted out a piece of paper. It floated to the floor. Falco let the manager pick it up; he scanned it and looked a little disappointed. "It's not a very clear image unless you know what the guy looks like," he said, handing it to Falco.

She studied it and nodded. "This is the guy," she whispered. The image was blurry, but she could see the man's substantial size. He was a black man, medium complexion, with dark glasses and a strong jaw. Part of what looked like a leaf pattern appeared from under his shirt, most likely tattoos sprawling across his chest and neck.

She called Ballard again. "We got the photo from the cash machine on Western. It's Cordero. I'm sure of it." Just then the disc stopped spinning, and a file matching the time and date the manager had typed in appeared. He moved his mouse and clicked on an icon that opened up a series of photo stills on the screen. He clicked on one of three images. A large black male with a Cubs baseball cap appeared on the screen. This time he wasn't wearing dark glasses. Falco squinted at the picture. It was Cordero. The manager printed the photos for her. Falco thanked him and dashed out.

"We've got him," she yelled to Ballard from her cell.

Ballard and Grasky were hot on his tail.

Falco couldn't do anything but return to the station. The suspense was killing her. Lassiter looked pleased as she walked through the cubicles to her desk. He smiled and gave her the thumbs-up sign. She nodded in response.

CHAPTER 99

It was just after five when Michael appeared at the station looking tired and thin. He smiled as he made his way to Falco's desk. She gave him a hug and looked at him affectionately. He sat down with a sigh and unfolded a piece of paper.

"How did everything go?" she asked.

"It was one of the most difficult things I've ever had to do. I'm just glad it's over with. I met Josh's parents, and I can understand why he was so screwed up."

"Well, we have a positive ID on the guy the landlord saw Josh with just before he died and bank records showing the same person withdrawing cash from Josh's checking account early that morning," Falco said. "We also had an evidence team go through Josh's apartment, and Ballard and I went through the dumpster. We found clear evidence he was manufacturing meth in his apartment. He probably had help getting some of the chemicals. That may be how the killer got involved."

"Oh, god. That's dangerous," Michael said, looking alarmed.

"It just goes to show you how desperate Josh got," Falco theorized. "It's so tragic. People who get involved with that stuff get so screwed up. Josh messed with the wrong person or persons and got himself killed."

Michael nodded and stared off. "Funny thing is, I miss him now more than ever. I wish I could have done something before he got so far gone." He looked at the sheet of paper and slid it over to Falco. "I guess giving you this is all I can do now."

"Thanks. I'm sure it will help."

He got up from the chair. "Listen, I can't stay. I have to be at the hospital. I've got a shit load of work to do, and it'll help me keep my mind off the weekend, if you know what I mean." He got up to leave then smiled. "Oh, by the way, I heard you may be having lunch with Alan this week. Do tell!"

Falco blushed. "I need to call him back. I'm not sure I can do it. This meth case is really heating up so…"

"Okay, then, but you know I'll be interested," he said as he spun around to leave. "See ya, girl."

"Yeah, see ya, Michael. Thanks for the names," she said with a wave.

CHAPTER 100

Alan briefed Michael on Andie's progress. Her new round of meds clearly made a difference. She was still dealing with some auditory disturbances, especially in her right ear, but the four books she had borrowed from the library had given her new focus. Alan was encouraged.

"How are you doing, Michael?" he asked with a hint of sadness.

Michael shrugged. "It was hard to see someone so beautiful die so young." He looked off, avoiding Alan's eyes. "But Monica said they may have a positive ID on the guy who killed Josh."

"Monica Falco? Did you see her recently?"

"I was just at the police station. I dropped off the names and phone numbers of Josh's roommate and some of his friends," Michael said. He looked at Alan, who seemed to zone out for a moment. He smiled. "She said she'd call, by the way."

Alan smiled back. "Thanks for letting me know."

They both got up to leave as Alan stopped short. "Oh, I meant to tell you. Kat has been looking for you since early last week. You should call her."

"I know. She called this morning. I'm stopping by the gallery on my way home tonight," Michael said.

Alan glanced at the brown paper bag on his desk. "I wonder," he said as his eyes fixed on the package. "I wonder if you might stop at Pearl Paint over on Chicago Avenue on your way."

"Pearl Paint? The art store? That's where Andie gets her supplies."

Alan reached into his wallet and gave Michael a $20 bill. "Buy some large newsprint," he said.

A warm breeze drifted off the lake as Michael made his way to his car. It was still light out, but the sun was setting earlier each day. He put on his sunglasses and headed north on Michigan Avenue then cut west on Ontario. He found parking just off Chicago and jogged into Pearl Paint. He looked around and found the newsprint and riffled for the $20 bill. He dragged the oversize bag with the large pad of paper to his car and stashed it in the trunk. The wind had shifted. He zipped up his jacket against the quickening breeze and dropping temperature and walked briskly toward Huron.

The Cohen Sloan Gallery looked dark as Michael tried the door. He gave it a gentle pull, but the door was locked. He found the button for the buzzer and pressed it with his thumb. A tall red-haired woman pushed the door ajar. "Hi. Can I help you?" she asked with a smile.

"I'm here to meet Kat. Is she around?" Michael asked.

"Um, yeah. Just a minute." She let the door close, leaving Michael standing on the sidewalk, then turned back and opened the door again. "What's your name?" she asked.

"Michael Hansen," he said, growing irritated.

The red-haired girl turned and walked back into the gallery, presumably to look for Kat. After a few minutes she returned and opened the door. "She's in her office."

"Thanks," he said, sliding past her and heading across the large gallery space toward the back.

Kat was on the phone. She saw Michael and motioned for him to come in. Michael noticed she had gotten some sun and lost some weight. Kat hung up the phone and gave him an annoyed look. "I called you all last week, and you just got around to returning my call this morning. What gives?" she said, as if to start a fight.

"I'm sorry, Kat, but I had some bad stuff happen last week. Josh was murdered."

Kat's eyes grew wide, and her mouth hung open. "Murdered? Josh? Dead? What happened? Oh, my god."

Michael filled her in on what had happened along with the new information he had received from Falco regarding Josh and the suspect.

Kat came around from her desk and gave him a hug. "Jesus Christ, so much tragedy," she said. She paused and studied his face. "How's Andie?"

Michael gave her an update, saying her new round of meds seemed to be working well and that she had taken an interest in reading.

Kat nodded then looked away, distracted. "Michael, I have to give you something." She walked around her desk and into a back room. Michael followed her with his eyes, not knowing if he should venture back there. He saw Kat bend down and then disappear from view. After a moment she returned to the office with an envelope.

"Here. This is for Andie. I know you'll know how to handle it," she said briskly.

Michael looked at the envelope.

"Open it."

Michael opened the envelope and peered inside. He gasped then looked at Kat.

"It was a good show," she said, turning around and sitting down at her desk. She stared off then put her hand to her forehead. "I wish… I just wish…" she said quietly, as her words trailed off.

Michael nodded, knowing exactly what she wished for.

He stashed the envelope in his breast pocket and headed toward his car. He started the engine and locked the doors. He sat quietly for a moment then pulled out the envelope from his jacket pocket. He opened the flap and peeked inside again. It was a check made out to Andie for $86,700. "Wow," he said with a sigh.

CHAPTER 101

It was a warm night for late September. Falco opened the window in her bedroom then got into bed and pulled a light blanket over her. The TV buzzed at the other end of the bedroom. Cordero was out there somewhere, she thought. Surveillance teams were in place, and cops were trolling the streets of Humboldt Park, Little Village, and Wicker Park. *It's just a matter of time before we bring him in*, she mused.

Her mother had left a message on her home phone asking her to call. It was about the wedding; she was sure of it. She couldn't deal with her mother or the wedding right now. She'd have to wait until this case blew over.

Falco switched off the TV news and the bedside table lamp. The room was dark and quiet. She drifted off to sleep. She dreamed of Michael and Josh, remembering his reaction to seeing Josh's body. "Michael!" she shouted, waking up with a start. Her heart was beating fast as she sat up then climbed out of bed. She went into the kitchen and drank some water, then laid her head on the cold marble countertop. "Jesus," she sighed.

She made her way back to her bedroom and sat on the edge of the bed. Her thoughts turned to Andie. Thinking of her calmed her. She didn't know why. She got up again and paced the room, replaying the events leading up to that fateful Friday, her botched interrogation, and the debacle at the river. "I can't believe I still show up for work," she said. Suddenly she realized she had totally spaced out her Tuesday appointment with Maggie Simonds.

"Shit!" she whispered, punching the mattress. She felt terrible and paced the floor some more. Finally she calmed down enough to climb back into bed. She pulled the blanket over her and stared at the ceiling. Thoughts circled in her mind. She rolled over with a jerk onto her side and clutched the extra pillow on her bed. She thought of Brenda Salerno and then of Andie.

The next morning she drove to work feeling achy. She had hoped to hear that Cachao Cordero had been apprehended overnight. He had managed to elude Ballard and Grasky and the other patrol cops on that beat the day before. Most likely he was in hiding. Raids were planned overnight at the three suspicious apartment buildings on West Belmont and West Division. No one had called her with an update, and the morning news said nothing about Cordero or the raids. She headed to work feeling less than optimistic. Her cell phone rang as she waited for the light at Lincoln and Foster.

It was Jeffery. "Hey, M. I'm not sure the coat you bought for Sam was a good choice."

"Why not?" she asked, scrunching her face.

"I don't think it's warm enough, and the zipper keeps getting stuck."

"It's a down coat, and I think it was rated for thirty below. How much warmer of a coat does Sam need?" Falco said. She heard the rustling sound of the coat on the other end. Obviously Jeffery hadn't taken the tags off yet or bothered to read them.

"Hello…Jeffery? And what's wrong with the zipper? Did Sam try it on again?"

She was getting frustrated. It seemed Jeffery was in a bad mood and wanted to take it out on her. "Are you still there?" she persisted.

"Yeah. Okay, I see the label. I guess if it's warm at thirty degrees below zero, it'll be fine."

"Sam really liked the coat. Now tell me about the zipper," she said, finding patience deep inside her.

"Oh, we'll just deal with it. Maybe it was stiff 'cause it's new or something," he mumbled. He grew quiet then said, "Have you spoken to your mother lately?"

She clenched her teeth as she jutted into the intersection to make a left turn. "No, she called me yesterday and left a message, but I couldn't deal with her just then. I'll call her today. I'm sure it's about the wedding."

"Yeah, she wants Sam to be part of the ceremony, the ring bearer, I guess," he said with a little groan.

"Well, I guess it would be a good experience for him."

Traffic on Foster had come to a halt. Falco saw flashing blue lights ahead. She craned her neck but couldn't see past the huge Range Rover in front of her. "Shit," she whispered. "Listen, traffic's a bit of a mess right now. Can we talk about this later? How about I call you tonight?"

"We've got a soccer game tonight. I told you that last week. Sam's team is playing a tournament game at five thirty. It'd be nice if you showed up," he said, not hiding the accusation in his voice.

Falco paused for a moment, thinking of her schedule for the week. "I'll try to make it. I'll *really* try," she said in a pleading tone.

"Sure, whatever."

* * *

Falco was late getting to the station. Ballard was hunched over his desk talking on the phone and writing something. She saw Grasky down the row of cubicles working on his computer.

"Hey, Grasky, what happened yesterday?" she said, walking toward his desk.

"He's still at large. We thought we spotted him, but it wasn't Cordero. We're still hot on his tail, though. It's just a matter of time," he said, chewing a ball of gum.

"We've got the task force in that area. Aren't they involved?"

Grasky nodded. "I think they'll be the ones who bring his ass in. Like I said, it's just a matter of time."

Falco returned to her desk and read her e-mails. The three raids on the meth labs on the West Side had netted empty apartments and no suspects. She shook her head in frustration. *Cordero's behind it*, she thought.

Ballard got up to get a refill of coffee and waved at her. He didn't look so good. When he returned, she looked piercingly at him. "You feeling okay, Ballard?"

He sat down with a huff. "Yeah, yeah, just the usual shit."

CHAPTER 102

Michael arrived early at the hospital with the large pad of newsprint. He snagged Alan, who was on the elevator heading to another floor for a meeting.

"Hey, that looks like newsprint," Alan said, seeing Michael's bag from Pearl Paint.

"You want me to put it in your office?"

"No, I want you to give it to Andie along with the box of crayons on my desk."

"Crayons?" Michael looked confused.

"Kat brought them for Andie last week. I initially thought she was joking, but actually I think it was a brilliant idea. Give Andie the crayons and the newsprint. We'll see what happens," he said with a smile.

"Okay," Michael said, intrigued. "Right away."

Michael hadn't seen Andie in almost a week. She looked pale and thin but seemed engaged in one of her books. He entered her room cautiously. Andie eyed him suspiciously over her reading glasses then put the book down on her lap, saving her place with her finger. She had her right hand on her ear and mindlessly pulled at her earlobe. She was mouthing something Michael couldn't make out. He put the crayons and newsprint on the bed and watched.

"I brought these for you, Andie. How are you doing?" Andie said nothing but mouthed some words. "What's going on?" he asked, wondering what she was saying. Andie shook her head and pulled at her ear. "Are you hearing something in that right ear?" he asked, craning his neck to see her. Andie shook her head and glared at him. She glanced at the box of crayons and newsprint then shrunk down and pulled her arms around her knees, drawing herself close. Michael sighed. "Come on, Andie. You know me. It's Michael," he said, almost pleading. Andie shook her head and mouthed some more words, then Michael got up to leave. He moved toward the door. "You should check the crayons out, girl, and the newsprint."

After Michael left, Andie put her face in her hands. Her head was rattling with the noises in her ear. "Please make it stop," she whispered.

CHAPTER 103

The day breezed by. Falco called Maggie Simonds and apologized for having missed her appointment and confirmed next week's session for Tuesday at four. She left a message for her mother and Alan; everyone seemed to be out today.

Indian summer was still in the air. The sun took on a delicate glow through the south windows of the second floor of the police station. Falco's phone rang. It was Lassiter; Cordero had been apprehended by a special task force from the Police Narcotic and Gang Intelligence Section (NAGIS) in the Little Village neighborhood. They were bringing him in.

"Yes!" Falco said, loudly jumping up from her seat and clenching her fists in righteous delight. She spun around and looked at Grasky, who had gotten up from his desk upon hearing her shout. "We got him!" she said over the cubicles. "They're bringing him in right now."

Ballard got up from his seat and smiled broadly. "All right!"

* * *

It was four thirty by the time Cornell Raphael Cordero arrived at the twenty-third district station. The place was abuzz with activity and positive energy. The gang task force had acted on an anonymous tip and found Cordero hiding out in the back room of a grungy grocery store. When they raided the place, they also found chemicals and equipment for the production of crystal meth, a half-kilo of cocaine, and a cache of firearms that included semiautomatic weapons.

The three detectives waited impatiently for Cordero's arrival. They had a slew of questions to ask him after he was booked. Falco looked at her watch; she wasn't going to make Sam's soccer match.

She heard loud voices and footsteps near the back entrance of the first floor. The familiar clanging sounds of handcuffs and the rustle of close contact grew louder as two heavily armed officers from NAGIS led Cordero down a corridor for booking. Falco stood on her toes to see above the tall men and get a glimpse of Cordero. He was easy to spot; he towered over everyone. *Josh didn't have a chance*, she thought.

Formal charges were pending. The two task force officers nodded to Grasky as they left, their job done. "Nice work, Steve," said one of them.

Cornell Cordero was part Cuban, part Jamaican. He had grown up in Cuba and had entered the US illegally with his parents at the age of fifteen. As a teenager he had found easy money dealing marijuana and coke on the streets of South Florida. His father was killed by cops in Ocala after a routine traffic stop; his mother took her own life soon after.

Once on his own, he made his way to Chicago's West Side and stayed with relatives. Later he found both a home and family with members of the Latin Kings street gang. By the time Cordero was twenty, he had a long rap sheet. He had eluded law enforcement for two years before he was arrested for accessory to murder and drug trafficking. He served three years at Statesville Prison in Joliet and recently had been released on parole.

Cordero was a towering six foot three and weighed 220 pounds. He had a large square head and a prominent jaw that complemented a smile made crooked by a scar that ran down the left side of his mouth. His was black, as were his eyes, and his hair was a mass of dirty dread locks. His arms, chest, and back were covered with tattoos of crowns and crosses and on his back was a large lion of Judah tattoo. The three detectives waited for Cordero to be fingerprinted and booked. Down the hall they heard him denying the charges. "I didn't whack that fucking gump!"

Ballard was getting impatient and glancing at his watch. He ran his tongue over his sore tooth and grimaced.

"Still having trouble with that tooth, JB?" Falco asked.

"Yeah. I gotta get this taken care of," he said with a groan.

"I thought you did already."

"Yeah, so did I. Guess I gotta go back. Jeez, I hate dentists." He glanced down the hall. "I'm gonna go take some aspirin. Be right back." He turned and walked down the hallway toward the elevators.

Just then Cordero appeared outside booking, cuffed from behind and flanked by two officers. He looked angry, and his eyes darted about. Falco and Grasky perked up as the officers led him down the hallway to an interrogation room. Grasky led the way as the uniformed cops held Cordero by the arms. He walked past Falco and gave her an evil smile; she backed out of the way. The clinking of handcuffs and keys echoed down the strangely quiet hallway. Grasky opened one of the large interrogation rooms and motioned for the cops to head his way.

Falco, clutching her notepad, followed the three from behind. *This is going to be good*, she thought. Her eyes traced the figure of Cordero, his broad shoulders and huge arms baring the intricacies of his tattoos. His handcuffs were tight around his wrists, but something appeared to be wrong. Falco's eyes suddenly fixed on his wrists, the cuffs. She noticed one of the links was broken and the chain connecting the bracelets was hanging loose. Between Cordero's two fists was a jet-black handle. Falco's heart jumped. She rushed forward toward the two uniformed cops. "Hold on a second, officers!" she yelled.

Cordero quickly twisted free and swung the black object in one hand.

"Look out! He's got a weapon," she yelled. "Grasky, look out!"

She rushed toward the two cops, who were now in pursuit of Cordero. She caught a flash of Cordero's weapon as he ran toward Grasky. It looked like an eight-inch knife with a short blade.

"Grasky, he's got a knife! Grasky! He's got a fucking knife! Stop him!" Falco reached for her weapon.

Cordero immediately turned, seeing the hallway was blocked. He swung the knife, slashing Grasky in the forearm, and spun toward the exit, pushing past the two uniformed cops. One cop jumped him from behind, but Cordero threw him off.

Falco blocked Cordero's path. She gripped her Glock in both hands and pointed it in his approaching face. "Hold it right there! Get down, Cordero, or I'll shoot!" she yelled.

Cordero weaved sideways as the two uniformed officers attempted to grab him. Falco kept her weapon on the man as he kept coming. Then, with the grace of a dancer, Cordero lunged at Falco with the knife and pushed her weapon away with his other hand. The Glock went off, two rounds shattering ceiling tiles above. The knife sliced into the left side of her abdomen just under her rib cage. The blade felt cool at first. Falco felt no initial pain, just a strange jolt of surprise.

Her mouth fell open as she caught the steely eyes of Cordero. She looked down and saw the blade again, this time covered in blood. The man disappeared in a blur. She heard shouting everywhere as her gun fell to the floor in a clatter. She looked at her hands as they gripped her stomach. A strange warmth seeped through her fingers. Time slowed. She focused her eyes down the hallway her thoughts running rampant, dizzy. Chaos mounted as officers chased Cordero and others rushed to Falco, yelling and holding out their hands.

"Officer down! Officer down!" came the loud voices. Gun shots fired and took Cordero down. He scrambled to get up as a flurry of officers swarmed him.

Falco was icy cold and confused, everything was happening so fast. She felt the strangest urge to kneel down, her body heavy. The floor seemed to pull her down. She felt the jolt through her body as she dropped to her knees. Her head and arms felt thick and clumsy as she swayed backward, looking up at the walls then at the ceiling and the rows of fluorescent lights. Her head fell back as her body followed. She landed heavily on the cool tile floor.

"Falco!" Grasky yelled as he rushed to her.

She was lying in a growing pool of blood, her knees up and her body twisting in pain. Tears and sweat streamed down her face as she clutched the gushing wound and gasped for air. "He cut me, goddamnit!"

Grasky's face appeared in front of her. "Hang on, Falco. We got a bus on the way. Hang on!" She gripped his hand like a vice; it was sticky with blood. She glanced toward her left. Someone had ripped her blouse open and was applying pressure to the wound. It was Lassiter.

Falco winced in pain. "Oh…god," she whispered, her words tumbling from her mouth. Her eyes followed the faces around her. Everything was happening so fast she couldn't keep track.

"Just breathe, Monica. Just breathe," someone was saying. She glanced at Grasky. He looked scared, but his eyes didn't leave hers.

She took a short breath and said, "Is it bad?" She was shivering.

"No, no. Just hang in there. It's not bad. You're gonna be fine." He put his left hand on her shoulder then gently brushed her hair from her eyes. She glanced to her left at the doorway. "Where is he?"

"Don't worry. We got Cordero," Grasky said. "Just be still." Falco felt a swell of pain as she clenched her teeth and arched her back. "Easy, Falco. Easy!" Grasky said, feeling her grip tighten. "I hear the sirens now. It won't be long. Stay with me!" He looked at Lassiter, who was on his third package of sterile gauze pads; the other two were on the floor soaked in blood.

Falco felt another swell of pain, this one worse than before. "Oh, oh… Jesus," she said through her teeth. She felt the room suddenly shift as she gasped for breath. A strange lightness came to her head as the burning pain in her side began to tingle and fade. She took a few shallow breaths and felt her eyelids close and her jaw heavy.

"Falco! Falco!" yelled someone.

She was dizzy and wanted to say something but her mind was blank. On her left she heard Ballard talking, saying something to her. Lassiter was talking too. Grasky's face began to blur. She squinted, trying to focus. She took a shallow breath, her voiced cracked, "Call my kid." A heavy blanket of blackness overtook her as her body sank to the floor.

CHAPTER 104

Sam tied his new soccer shoes and looked at them with a smile. Two of his teammates pushed past him as he turned to meet up with the rest of the team outside the locker room. "They're too new," Sam said as he looked down at his shoes. Still, they felt good on his feet.

Jeffery hung out with the other parents, waiting for the game to start. He looked at his watch and glanced at the parking lot, wondering whether Falco was going to show up. "Miracles," he muttered as he chewed on a plastic drinking straw. His cell phone vibrated in his pocket. He glanced at the number and ignored it. *Nobody I need to talk to right now*, he thought. He settled into one of the bleacher seats and took off his sunglasses. The sun would be setting soon, and the lights of the soccer field were already glowing.

The team came running out to the field as the crowd cheered. Jeffery clapped and searched for Sam. He smiled as he saw him take his position on the field. A tiny voice came over the public address system welcoming both teams and their parents. Everyone rose from their seats as they patiently waited for the playing of the National Anthem. The crowd joined in, singing along with the tinny recording. As the applause faded, a whistle pierced through the noise and the game began.

Footsteps to Jeffery's left came loudly on the wooden bleachers as someone called his name.

"Jeff?" It was Ron Pettibone, the father of one of Sam's friends. Jeffery turned and smiled, giving Ron a manly handshake. Ron looked at Jeffery and said, "I guess everything is okay if you're here for the game."

"Huh?" Jeffery said, looking sideways at Ron.

"Didn't you hear on the news? A detective was hurt at the police station in Wrigleyville. I think it was a woman."

Jeffery felt like a bolt of lightning hit him. He glared at Ron. "What? What happened?" He didn't wait for an answer as he immediately pulled out his cell phone and checked his messages. He cursed the phone as his hands shook and his fingers fumbled with the buttons. He gave Ron a desperate look as his messages began to play. The voice was that of Chief Lassiter telling Jeffery that Falco had been hurt and that he needed to call the police station as soon as possible. Jeffery bolted down the bleachers as the second message played. It was Steve Grasky saying that a suspect at the station had wounded Falco and she was being transported to Illinois Masonic Hospital.

Jeffery ran out onto the sidelines and grabbed the coach. "Pull my kid. Pull Sam out of the game now!" The coach gave Jeffery a blank stare then looked out at the field. "It's an emergency. I need him out now. We have to leave now!" Jeffery turned to run out to the field to get Sam when the coach blew his whistle to stop the game. Everyone looked over at the sidelines. Jeffery grabbed Sam and pulled him off the field. "Mom's been hurt, Sam. Come on. We gotta go!"

The two dashed down the field toward the parking lot and piled into Jeffery's pickup. Sam was crying as Jeffery dialed Steve Grasky.

"Grasky here," came the voice on the other end.

"It's Jeff Schuler. My wife, Monica, is she okay?"

"Thank god we got you," Grasky said.

"Is she all right? Damn it! Is Monica all right?" Jeffery yelled. Sam was crying and looking at Jeffery. He'd never seen his father look so scared. It made him scared too.

"She's in surgery right now. We don't know anything else. There's nothing you can do but get here right away. Be calm, pay attention to the road, and get here," Grasky said deliberately.

"I want to know what happened! Was she shot? What the hell happened?" Jeffery cried. He gunned the engine of the truck and peeled onto the street.

"She was stabbed in the abdomen on her left side. She lost some blood, and like I said, she's in surgery now," Grasky said, trying to calm him down. "That's all we—"

Jeffery clicked off his phone and looked over at Sam. He was pale and sobbing. They stopped at a red light, and he reached over to fasten Sam's seatbelt. "It's gonna be okay, Sam. We're gonna get through this," he said, running his hand through Sam's hair.

"I'm scared for Mom. I don't want her to die!" Sam said, crying and rubbing his eyes.

"We're on our way to the hospital right now. Mom's friend said she's in surgery, so that's good. Let's just be calm and get there safely. That's what Mom would want, right?"

Sam nodded.

The drive to the hospital seemed to take forever. Jeffery parked the truck in the parking garage and raced to the ER with Sam. News crews milled about as they rushed past. A young woman behind a Plexiglas-enclosed reception area directed them to the seventh floor.

Sam clung to Jeffery. Both were breathing fast from running through the parking lot. They found an elevator close by; Sam punched the "up" button.

Jeffery swallowed hard as he watched the numbers light up for each floor: four, five six, seven. The doors opened quietly as the two stepped out and looked for a sign directing them to the waiting room.

"This way…I think," Jeffery said weakly.

Sam followed. Jeffery's heart beat fiercely as he gripped Sam's chilly hand and jogged down the long corridor to what looked like a waiting room. The two stopped and peered inside the glass-enclosed room, where three men sat staring at the floor. Jeffery recognized Jim Ballard and grabbed the steel handle of the door and swung it open. All three men rose to their feet when they saw Jeffery and Sam. Their faces couldn't hide their concern.

"Hey, Jeff," Ballard said, quietly putting out his hand.

"How is she?" Jeffery said breathlessly as Sam stayed close.

"She's still in surgery," said Ballard.

Jeffery looked down and hugged Sam close. Lassiter came over and shook Jeffery's hand. "We met a year or so ago at…some event. I'm Ed Lassiter, commander of the twenty-third." He looked down for a moment then eyed the two. "She's a tough lady, you know." He bent down in front of the boy and put his hand out. "You must be Sam, the soccer player." Sam nodded and shook his hand shyly.

"We just came from a game in Park Ridge," Jeffery said, placing his hand on Sam's head.

Grasky loomed close. "I'm Detective Steve Grasky," he said, shaking Jeffery's hand. His eyes got teary as he looked away for a moment. "We've worked a few cases together, Monica and I. We were working on this one too." He put his hand on Jeffery's shoulder. "She was the first one to see the knife. He was going after me. He would've got me in the back, but instead I just got cut," he said, showing Jeffery the bandage on this forearm. "Monica saved my life." His voice wavered. "She saved my life."

For the next couple of hours, they all stayed close by the waiting area hoping Falco would soon be out of surgery. A tall uniformed cop timidly pushed open the door and entered the room. His face looked strained.

"Officer Foley," said Lassiter, getting up and walking over to the young man.

"Hi, sir." He nodded to everyone else in the room. "How's Detective Falco? Have you heard anything?"

"Nothing yet, kid," said Lassiter. "You still on your shift?"

Foley looked down as if caught doing something wrong. "Yes sir, but I just needed to stop in, you know, for a minute or two."

Lassiter put his hand heavily on the rookie's shoulder. "I'll let Detective Falco know you stopped by, okay?" Foley nodded. He eyed the others then slipped out, walking steadily down the dimly lit corridor.

"Nice kid," Grasky said, remembering that night partying at Murphy's Pub. He sat down and rubbed the back of his neck.

CHAPTER 105

The stabbing of Detective Falco was all over the news. Reporters were asking how a weapon had made it into the police station undetected. Lassiter was going to face a barrage of questions not only from the public but also from his superiors. He didn't plan to return to the station and didn't dare venture into the rabble of reporters that awaited him outside the hospital. He sat back on the loveseat in the waiting room and stared at the ceiling.

Jeffery and Sam sat quietly as Lassiter wandered over and sat next to them. He glanced at Sam's soccer shoes and said, "Nice shoes, Sam. Bet you can run real fast in them and kick that ball hard too."

Sam smiled shyly. "Mom got them for me last week," he said, kicking his feet.

"Did your mom tell you about her encounter with the pit bull?"

Sam nodded with a little smile.

"Knocked her down to the floor," he said, giving Sam a wry look. "She's a tough lady." Sam smiled sadly and looked at his shoes.

It was nearly seven fifteen when Grasky glanced at his watch. He got up and stretched his legs then caught sight of a man dressed in surgical garb walking quickly toward the waiting room. The man was in his early fifties, short, and a bit portly, with curly salt-and-pepper hair that stuck out from his green surgical cap. He caught Grasky's eye and nodded, letting him know he was coming to speak to them. Grasky opened the door for the man as Ballard, Lassiter, Jeffery, and Sam got up from their seats.

Dr. Otto Hagler introduced himself and took off his wire-rimmed glasses. "Who is the husband of Mrs. Falco?"

"I am. I'm Jeff Schuler, and this is Sam, our son," he said, suddenly out of breath. "I'm, uh… She's…my ex-wife," Jeffery stammered.

Dr. Hagler eyed the others then smiled at Sam. "Your wife is a very lucky lady, Mr. Schuler. The knife was maybe four or five inches long—the blade, I mean. It could have done a lot of damage. It cut through mostly muscle and connective tissue and just grazed the large intestine."

Jeffery shook his head, trying to understand what the doctor was saying.

"She lost some blood, but the damage could have been much worse. We stopped some internal bleeding, sutured inside the wound, then closed it up with a few more."

"Is she going to be all right?" Jeffery wanted to know.

"Yes, she'll be all right. We'll keep her here for a couple of days, put her on some antibiotics, and give her something for the pain. She'll mostly likely have considerable pain."

Jeffery's head dropped to his chest in relief. He put his hands over his face and let out a deep sigh.

Dr. Hagler looked down at Sam and smiled. "You look very much like your mother," he said, putting his hand on his shoulder. He glanced at the worried faces in the group and dragged his surgical cap off his head. "That's all I have for you now. I'll be in to check on Ms. Falco later tonight. She'll be in recovery for maybe forty-five minutes. Someone will come and get you when she's in a room. In the meantime you can wait here." The doctor nodded to everyone and left.

Grasky came over and gave Jeffery and Sam a hug. "I'm so relieved," he said quietly.

Sam leaned into Jeffery. "Mom's okay. She's gonna be okay."

* * *

Every local news outlet covered Lassiter's press conference about the stabbing. The knife Cordero had smuggled into the twenty-third district was an eight-inch long nylon composite knife with a four-inch blade. Its nylon composition made the knife undetectable by a metal detector; its compact design enabled Cordero to hide it in the small of his back. How he had managed to break the chain links of his cuffs was still under investigation.

Jeffery bit his little fingernail as he and Sam waited to see Falco. It was nearly ninety twenty, almost ninety minutes after the surgeon had come in. Sam was sleepy and leaning on Jeffery. Lassiter had left for the press conference, and Ballard had gone home after hearing Falco was all right. Grasky amused himself watching a rerun of *CSI: Miami* on the waiting room's TV.

Jeffery looked at Grasky. "I thought cops didn't watch cop shows."

"Oh, well, lots of us do," Grasky said with a smile. "They're pretty realistic, but my beef is sometimes people watch them and think they can do the same thing in real life. You know?"

Jeffery nodded. "I used to watch cop shows, but when Monica and I got married she wouldn't watch them with me. She'd say she didn't need to work overtime, so I stopped watching them altogether," he said with a little smile.

"You know, she's a hell of a cop, Jeff. I'm retiring in about two weeks, but I'll tell you, if she were *my* partner and not paired up with Ballard, I'd have given the department another couple of years."

"How does your wife handle it? Your being out there day after day?"

"Well, she's glad I'm retiring. That's for sure," he said with a chuckle. "I've been lucky, though, real lucky. I could have been the one in that ambulance today. I could have got it in the back. Cordero was right behind me when he broke free." Grasky looked at the floor and shook his head. "Falco was there, watching. She's always watching, observing, like a hawk. She had my back, she saved my life."

CHAPTER 106

Elaine Falco eased herself into her overstuffed sectional sofa. The brief spell of Indian summer weather was waning. She pulled a crocheted throw over her and sipped a gin and tonic. On her lap was a stack of catering menus from various companies. She glanced through them as she grabbed the remote and turned on the TV. The volume was low as she looked up at the screen. Another Chicago police officer was hurt in the line of duty, the reporter said. Elaine shook her head, tuning the news out. Then her phone rang. It was Howard.

"Honey, Elaine…Do you have the news on?" came his voice in a panic.

"Yes, I have it on, but I'm not really—"

"Turn on Channel Seven right now," Howard said.

Elaine jumped to her feet, sending the menus to the floor. The Channel Seven news was already on; its top story was the stabbing of a police officer at the twenty-third district. Falco's picture flashed on the screen as Elaine tried to make sense of what happened. "My…lord," she whispered.

Chief Lassiter appeared in a news conference talking about a knife and Cornell Raphael Cordero. Elaine's face went pale and trancelike as she drifted across the room and straight into the glass coffee table. She ignored her clumsiness and the pain in her kneecaps as she glared at the TV screen.

"Oh, my. Oh, my dear god," she whispered.

She hung up the phone and called Jeffery. There was no answer. She fumbled for the phone book on the top shelf of her pantry. It was an old Chicago phone book, torn and tattered. Her heart was racing. She looked up hospitals; her hands shook as she found a number for Illinois Masonic Hospital. She dialed the number; it had been changed.

"Oh, my little girl. Oh, god, let her be all right," she cried. She ran back to the living room to look at the TV. The reporter was in front of the hospital saying Detective Falco was out of surgery.

Elaine fell back, clutching the page from the phone book. She dialed Jeffery's cell phone but got his voicemail. "Jeffery, please call me, honey. I saw the news. Please let me know where you are, if you're at the hospital. Please call me." She put her hands over her face then got up from the sofa. She turned and stared up at a large family portrait taken when her daughter and Peter were in middle school. She gazed up at her late husband as a fiery look came to her face. "Damn you!" she yelled at the photo. "Damn you!" she said pointing at the photograph. "You did this to my little girl!"

* * *

Jeffery scooped up Falco's hand and kissed her forehead. Scared and uneasy from the ordeal, Sam held back tears as he hid behind his father. Falco was pale and very still, but her heart was strong and steady. The room was quiet except for the hissing of the ventilation system and the steady beep of the heart monitor.

The door opened with a tinny creak, then a voice cut the silence. "Oh, hi, I didn't think there'd be anyone here so late."

It was Alan Forrest with a bouquet of flowers and a pink envelope. Jeffery looked up and stared at him suspiciously. Alan walked in and set the flowers on a table and slid the card underneath the vase. He came over to the opposite side of the bed and looked pointedly at Falco as he scanned the jumping line and flashing numbers of the heart monitor. He touched her wrist gently then checked her pulse.

Alan wore a brown leather car coat over a cream-colored shirt and a silk tie. He had taken a detour on his way home after hearing the news on the radio. Professional courtesy at the hospital allowed him to visit after eight p.m. when visiting hours were over. Alan felt Jeffery's stare and eyed the two over his spectacles. "Sorry. I'm Alan Forrest. You must be Monica's ex-husband…and Sam?"

Jeffery nodded protectively then eyed the flowers.

"I'm…just a friend," Alan said, feeling uneasy. He paused a moment then gave Falco's hand a little squeeze. "She's gonna be okay." He nodded to Sam and Jeffery then said goodnight.

"Who was that, Dad?" Sam asked.

Jeffery frowned and shrugged. "Don't know."

Grasky peered in with a cup of coffee. He looked at his watch and said, "Hey, I can stay if you guys need to get home."

Jeffery looked at Falco then at Sam. "I'd like to be here when she wakes up," he said, "but I also need to get Sam home. He has school tomorrow."

Grasky shrugged. "I can stay if you want. You'll see her tomorrow."

Falco stirred, having heard the voices. Her eyes slowly opened.

"M? Hey, are you awake?" Jeffery said quietly as he leaned on the bed. She brought her hand to her head and sighed. She tried to focus on the voices and Jeffery's face. "Hey, how are you feeling?" Jeffery said, gently putting his hand on her arm.

Falco looked confused as Sam came closer. "Mom?" he said in a whisper. She tried again to open her eyes, then saw Sam and smiled. "Mom, *wake up*," he said a little louder.

"Hey," she whispered.

Sam came close and put his arms gently around her. Her right arm came around him and held him close. Jeffery looked on, his face serious. "How are you feeling, honey?"

"Okay."

"You're at Illinois Masonic. I didn't want to leave until you woke up," he said. "Do you remember what happened to you?"

Falco thought for a moment as she held Sam.

"You got *stabbed* Mom," Sam blurted out.

She smiled then scrunched her face, feeling a flash of pain. Jeffery looked around and said, "Are you in pain, baby? Let me get a nurse."

She put her hand on his. "No, it's not bad…really. Just stay here with me." She closed her eyes and tried to remember what had happened. She found herself in the hallway looking at the broad back of Cordero. Her heart quickened, and she shook off the memory. "God, it happened so fast," she whispered.

Jeffery filled her in on what the doctor had said. She dreaded looking at the bandage.

Steve Grasky waved. "How ya feelin', girl?" he asked, moving to the opposite side of the bed. She smiled back and shook her head. He knew what that meant.

A nurse appeared and asked Falco about her pain. She showed her the morphine pump attached to the IV. "Don't hesitate to use it, especially tonight. Don't let the pain get to be too much for you," she warned.

After the nurse left, Grasky stayed while Sam and Jeffery went home. He settled into the chair by the bed, putting his coffee cup on the floor, then leaned into Falco and took her hand; it felt cool. He put his other hand over it as she smiled then drifted off to sleep.

CHAPTER 107

Andie held her head against the cold floor. She was breathing fast. The noises in her head came in loud waves as the narrative from Kafka's *Metamorphosis* echoed around the room. "Why did I let them come inside my head?" she asked, looking at the books on the floor across the room. "Mistake, mistake," she admonished herself. "They tricked me. They tricked me and now they want to stay." She winced as the noises rang in her head again. "Please stop," she whispered, wrapping her arms around her head, and pulling her knees up. She closed her eyes and felt the warm presence of someone close. Alarm rose in her as a familiar voice said, "Andie, Andie, guess who's gonna die?"

Andie bolted to her feet and took a swing at the voice. She spun around and landed on her knees. Her body fell forward as her arms and chest dropped to the floor. Her heart pounded and her body ached. She pressed her forehead to the cold floor. "Please stop. Please leave me alone," she groaned. She heard the voice again, this time from deep in the floor somewhere. She rolled onto her back and felt the sick warmth again. "No, no," she whispered. She could smell him and feel his breath on her face. Her chest tightened as she gasped for air. He was on top of her.

CHAPTER 108

Tim Strickland brought Michael a steaming cup of coffee to the tiny table at the Starbucks on Roscoe and Broadway. It was eight fifteen in the morning, and they were both on their way to work. Tim warmed his hands on the paper mug as he dragged over a discarded copy of the *Sun-Times* from another table.

Michael yawned and thought about his day then smiled at Tim. "You look tired," he said quietly.

"Gee, I wonder why," Tim said, smiling and looking up from the paper. "You always keep me up way past my bedtime, sweetie."

Michael looked out the window at people with jackets and coats heading to work. "Indian summer sure didn't last long."

* * *

Lassiter was up to his ears with questions and inquiries about the stabbing. He was dressed in a dark suit and looking stressed out. Phones rang incessantly on the first floor of the twenty-third district. The shuffle of feet and the banter of voices consumed every inch of every office and corridor. The second floor, however, was strangely quiet. Falco's absence was a haunting reminder of the dangers cops face every day on the streets and even in the perceived safety of the police station.

Internal Affairs interviewed Grasky and Ballard as well as the two members of the gang task force who had brought Cordero in and the two uniformed cops who had escorted him to the interrogation room. The knife sat on top of an evidence bag. Traces of blood were visible on the blade and inside the plastic bag.

Grasky eyed it wearily. "Where do ya get something like this? It's got to be illegal in Illinois."

"They're pretty easy to get on the Internet, and we have no laws against them right now," said the representative from IA. Grasky shook his head, "Shoulda shot the guy dead."

Ballard came by and sat at the conference table. "How late did you stay last night?"

"Oh, until about one. Falco woke up just as Jeff and Sam were about to go home, so they got to see her and make sure she was okay. She was having some pain when I left, so I got the nurse. She's also got a little pump thing attached to the IV that she can squeeze and get pain medication. It's the neatest thing," Grasky said with a look of amazement.

Ballard nodded. "That was pretty close, I tell you." He glanced at the knife. "Pretty close for sure."

* * *

Alan stopped by the hospital just before visiting hours. Falco was sitting up but seemed to be in a good deal of pain. "Hey, how are you?" he asked. She was slumping over to her left, her breathing labored.

She looked up and barely smiled. "Hi, Alan. Thank you for the lovely flowers." Her voice was weak, her face strained.

Alan looked concerned and sat on the side of the bed. He glanced at the tray of food by Falco's bed; she hadn't touched it. "Not hungry?" he asked.

"You should try to eat something. You'll feel a lot better, and the meds will be easier on your stomach."

Just then Jeffery appeared, looking a bit frazzled and flushed. He was wearing a red flannel button-down collar shirt and brown khakis. He was surprised to see Alan back and irritated that he was sitting on the bed.

Falco smiled and said with a sigh, "There you are."

Alan got up from the bed and greeted Jeffery, who had brought the newspaper and some books. She looked at the two men and said, "Jeffery this is Alan Forrest. Alan, this is Jeffery, my ex-husband."

"Yes, yes. We met yesterday, although briefly, and I met Sam also," Alan said.

The rest of the day was a blur as a steady stream of well-wishers came to visit. Chief Lassiter brought ice cream and Michael brought a tiny stuffed bear with a package of French roast coffee.

* * *

The D Ward of Northwestern University Hospital was eerily quiet. Michael peered into Andie's room but didn't see her anywhere. His heart jumped as he quietly entered. He looked behind the door then walked around to the bed. Andie lay flat on her back, sweating and breathing hard. She was having a full-blown flashback. She had been screaming, but she was very quiet now. Her eyes were wide and glassy as she stared at the ceiling.

Michael appeared at her side. "Andie," he whispered, "it's only a dream. Come on, Andie. Come out of this. This isn't really happening."

Andie didn't respond. She just stared straight up and gasped. She shook her head and mouthed some words, but Michael had no luck making them out. He sat on the floor next to her, holding her hand and waiting for the memory to dissipate. He studied her, listening to her breathing and any words that came from her lips.

"Andie, come on. You've got to trust us. You're safe. There's no danger here."

For a few moments Michael was transported back in time. He was at Andie's place. He saw her listening to music, hanging out with Kat, laughing and smiling. Then he thought of Falco sitting at Andie's dining room table with the laptop. He remembered blowing up at her that night after Andie had gone over the edge. Then he thought of Falco this morning at the hospital; she seemed to be in so much pain. He thought of Josh and his violent death. He missed Josh. He missed Falco. He missed Andie.

CHAPTER 109

It was Friday, and Falco got word from her doctor that she'd be released from the hospital later that day. Jeffery arrived just after one to take her home. Dr. Hagler wrote prescriptions for antibiotics and painkillers and said under no circumstances should she return to work or drive for two weeks. Falco was annoyed at the news but figured she could work at home.

By the time she and Jeffery got to her place, she was exhausted and in a great deal of pain. Jeffery helped her get out of the car, up the stairs, and into the house. She was breathing fast and sweating. *Maybe the two weeks off isn't such a bad thing*, she thought.

"This is far enough, Jeffery," she said breathlessly.

Jeffery looked worried as he helped her to the sofa. "I'm gonna bring Sam over after school, and we'll stay the weekend," he said as he brought a light blanket from Sam's room and covered her with it.

Falco was immersed in waves of pain and nodded. "Fine…fine."

The phone rang; Jeffery quickly answered it. There was a hesitation on the other end. It was Elaine fumbling with Howard's cell phone. "Hello? Hello? Is someone there?" came her voice at the other end.

"Hi, Elaine. It's Jeff," he said, recognizing the voice.

"Jeffery? Is that you?" Elaine continued to struggle with the cell phone. A muffle of voices and static ensued, then the line went dead.

"That was your mom. I'm guessing they're coming over."

Falco put her hand over her face. "Oh, please... Shit."

Thirty minutes later the doorbell rang. Falco was dozing off, her hand over her face as she had left it. Loud voices came from outside and grew louder as Jeffery opened the front door. He hushed them as they entered. Howard held a plastic container of cookies. Elaine peered woefully at her daughter, who was lying on the sofa. "Oh, dear, my sweetheart." Elaine had been crying.

Falco stirred, suddenly feeling her mother's eyes on her. "Hi, Mom," she said with a sigh, her hand still on her forehead. Her mother sat next to her on the sofa. Falco heard the delicate clink of jewelry and smelled the hint of hairspray.

Her mother spoke quickly and lightly. "I knew it was just a matter of time before something happened to you. I just knew it. Are you in pain, honey? Did they catch the man who did this to you? Oh, I wish... I wish you didn't..."

Falco took her hand from her forehead and, without looking, put her hand on her mother's forearm. "Please, Mom, just stop. Please," she said flatly. She felt the fabric of Elaine's wool coat.

"You're *so thin*, dear," Elaine persisted.

Falco put her hand back on her forehead and ignored her with a sigh. Howard sat silently on a chair opposite the sofa. He pulled the zipper of his coat open then fiddled with the gold ring on his little finger. "Nice flowers," he said, eyeing the roses.

"Oh, yes. They are lovely! Were they from your friends at the police station?" Elaine asked, trying to make conversation.

Falco didn't answer.

"They're from a friend of Monica's," Jeffery answered flatly.

"Oooh," Howard and Elaine said in unison.

Howard shifted in his chair. "Wow, first the dog bite then this." He looked around, waiting for Falco to respond. "They say things happen in threes." Elaine shot him a worried look. "I'm...I'm just pointing that out," he stuttered.

Howard and Elaine didn't plan to stay long; neither of them had taken off their coats. Silence loomed as the two shifted in their chairs. Finally Elaine said, "Well, we've got to get going. Howard has an appointment in Skokie."

She looked at Jeffery. Howard zipped his jacket closed and got up from the chair. Elaine glanced back at her daughter as the two made their way toward the door. Falco had her hand over her eyes and was breathing slowly.

Jeffery set his jaw as he eyed the two. "Thanks for stopping by."

Elaine gave him a fearful look. "She's going to be okay, isn't she?"

Jeffery nodded. "I'll take good care of her. Don't worry."

Elaine gave him a kiss on the cheek then she and Howard walked out-side.

A tiny trail of tears streamed down Falco's face from under her hand. She wiped the tears from her face and sniffled. Jeffery sat on the sofa and gazed down at her. It was painfully obvious that the mother-daughter estrange-ment wasn't going to ease anytime soon.

"Things happen in threes," Falco said. "Of all the things to say."

The rest of the afternoon was a blur to her. Jeffery left to pick up Sam from school. It was five thirty before the two returned with two pizzas. Sam sat next to his mother, talking nonstop about soccer and school. She listened quietly, taking comfort in Sam's closeness.

"Mom, you're not eating," Sam said, eyeing her closely, a wad of pizza crust in his cheek.

Falco blinked and tried to focus on him. "I'm a little spacey, Sam." She took a bite of her pizza and chewed it, not taking her eyes off him.

"I'm starved," he said. He glanced at his plate then looked at his mother closely. A glint of sadness appeared on his face. Sam wanted to say something. His face was pinched as he looked at Falco and chewed.

Falco stopped eating and looked at him. "What's wrong, sweetie?" she asked gently. "I don't want you to worry about me. I'm going to be fine in no time." Sam scrunched his face and looked away, but she persisted. "Hey, Sam. What's the matter?"

He stopped eating and sat on the floor and put his head on the sofa cushion. She put her arms around him and ran her fingers through his hair. "You okay?" She looked down at him. He nodded and sniffled. "It's all right, my little man," she cooed.

Sam quickly wiped a tear away, embarrassed that he was crying. "You're gonna be okay, aren't you, Mom?"

Falco smiled. "Yes, of course I'm going to be okay. It'll take a few days or so, but I'll be as good as new before you know it." She looked at him sadly, seeing the worry in his face. She sighed and swallowed hard.

A gentle knock came at the front door. Jeffery was out back taking out the trash. Hearing the knock, Sam perked up. "You want me to answer the door?"

Falco nodded. "I don't know who that could be," she said, glancing at her watch. It was nearly seven and most everyone from the department had made their obligatory visits at the hospital.

Falco gritted her teeth through another wave of pain, then looked at the two vials on the coffee table and wondered when she had taken her medication last. She heard voices on the other side of the door—Sam's voice and someone else's, vaguely familiar. Sam cautiously opened the door for a tall man wearing dark jeans and a black leather jacket.

"Hey there, Detective," said Michael with a big smile. He was carrying a gift bag with a ribbon around the handles.

Falco smiled weakly and shook her head. "What are you doing in my neck of the woods? Isn't it a bit boring for you?" she asked with a little laugh then winced with pain.

Michael came around the coffee table and put the bag down next to Falco. "How ya doin'?" He gave her a careful hug then looked at her closely.

"Not too bad. I'm having some pain."

He picked up the medicine bottles from the coffee table and squinted at them. "Good stuff," he said.

Sam slowly came up to them and looked at Michael.

"Have you met Sam?"

"At the door. Yes, I did," Michael said, smiling. "You look like your mom."

Falco pulled Sam closer and rubbed his back. "Sam, Michael was the person who got you that crash collision game, or whatever it's called."

Sam perked up. "Wow. How did you manage to find it? Nobody at school has it except me and another kid. It's way cool!"

Michael smiled. "A friend got it for me. She can get all kinds of stuff, so let me know if you can't find any other games, and I'll see if she can track them down for you."

Falco shook her head. "Michael…"

"It's okay, really," he said, smiling at the two.

Sam smiled broadly. "Cool!"

The back door slammed loudly as Jeffery came in from the backyard. He took off his coat, tossed it onto the kitchen counter, and wandered into the living room. He lifted his head curiously and looked suspiciously at Michael. Sam was talking nonstop about the Thunder Crash Car game, comparing the newest version with the others. Michael was paying close attention, having played the game himself. Falco shook her head at the two, not bothering to comprehend the inner workings of the game. Jeffery eyed Michael and the gift then looked over at Falco.

"Hi. You must be Jeffery," said Michael, getting up from the sofa and extending his hand.

Jeffery shook Michael's hand as Falco craned her neck to see him. "Jeff, this is Michael Hansen, a friend of mine. Michael, that's Jeffery, my ex-husband." She pointed back and forth then let her hand drop to her chest.

Sam interrupted to tell Jeffery that Michael was the one who had found the Xbox game he'd wanted for his birthday. Jeffery smiled curtly, not taking his eyes off the angular man. Michael broke from Jeffery's glare and sat down again next to Falco. "Listen, I'm not going to stay long, sweetie, but I wanted to bring you these fabulous chocolates and some various sundry items from the hospital, namely extra gauze, sterile pads, and bandages… and some magazines. You're gonna need to change that dressing sometime soon, you know."

Falco looked at him. "Gauze? Bandages?"

"You know, M, you don't have any of that stuff," Jeffery interrupted. "You only have a box of band-aids and some tape and an old bottle of Bactine."

Michael looked up at Jeffery and then at Falco. "There ya go. We have tons of gauze and sterile pads at the hospital. I figured it would save someone a trip to the drugstore. Plus this stuff is the *good stuff*," he said, pointing to the bag on the coffee table.

"Oh, well, that was very thoughtful of you..." Her voice trailed off as she winced from another wave of pain.

Michael glanced at her, then looked at the medicine bottles. "Is it time for your pain meds yet?"

She looked up at Jeffery, who looked at his watch. "Uh, yeah. It's time." He headed toward the kitchen and got a glass of water, feeling a little threatened.

Falco looked frustrated. "The pain is *relentless*, but the meds kind of zone me out."

Michael smiled then looked at her tentatively. "You mind if I take a peek at your bandage, for my own peace of mind?"

She smiled. "No, if you really want to see it."

She pulled the blanket down and pulled up her shirt. "I am a nurse, you know. I just don't play one on TV." He looked at the bandage as Jeffery returned with the water.

Jeffery winced and stepped back upon seeing the size of the bandage. He grimaced and said, "M, take this." He guided the glass of water into her hand. She set it on the coffee table next to the vials of pills.

Michael carefully pulled her shirt back down and pulled the blanket over her. "I'll swing by on Sunday and change the dressing, okay?"

Jeffery furrowed his brow. "Uh, that won't be necessary, uh, Mike. I can do that."

"It's no big deal really. Plus I'd like to take a look at the wound…you know, for inflammation, infection, that sort of thing," he said, looking at Falco then at Jeffery.

"It's okay. Michael is a nurse, Jeffery," she said.

Sam got up from watching TV and looked at Michael sideways. "I thought only *girls* were nurses."

Jeffery let out a hearty laugh. Michael smiled and said, "There are both male and female nurses. Usually it's the male nurses who get to do the really cool stuff, especially when their natural strength is needed." Sam looked at him skeptically. "Listen, I could tell you some stories from when I worked in the ER—crazy homeless people going berserk, big burly guys wielding—"

Falco put her hand on Michael's thigh to stop him. "Okay, okay. That's enough. I'm sure Sam would love to hear about all the blood and guts, but I think we've had our share of blood and guts lately."

Michael chuckled. "Sorry Sam, maybe some other time."

He left, giving Falco a kiss on the forehead and waving goodbye to Sam and Jeffery.

Jeffery pouted as he shut the front door. "Another one of your…your…"

Sam turned to Falco wide-eyed. "Is Michael a homo?"

She looked at Sam and gave both him and Jeffery a dirty look. "Michael is gay, okay? Not a homo, not a sissy. It's *gay*, okay? And he's *very* sweet *and* a good friend."

Jeffery seemed out of sorts the rest of the evening, not saying much to Sam or Falco. That was fine with her. She appreciated the quiet as she mulled over her mother's visit and Jeffery's darkening mood.

CHAPTER 110

It had been only a few days since she was injured, but Falco missed her old life: Grasky, the guys at work, even Ballard. She missed Andie, realizing she had neglected to ask Michael how she was doing. She wondered how long Andie would have to stay in the hospital. She couldn't imagine staying any longer than a day or two. She hated hospitals.

After the ten o'clock news, Jeffery helped her into bed and pulled the blankets up around her. He sat at the end of the bed, watching her, his jaw clenched.

"You feeling all right?" Falco nodded, closing her eyes. Jeffery sat there without saying a word then finally said, "Sam's pretty upset, you know."

She looked at Jeffery then looked away. "I know," she said in a tiny voice.

"It's gonna be hard on him when you go back."

"Go back? You mean back to work?"

"Yeah," said Jeffery.

"Well, I don't have much choice. It's my job."

"You don't have much choice? You have a choice, M, and you know it."

"What are you saying?" Falco asked, slowly sitting up in bed.

Jeffery paused, looking at her as she stared at him. "You could quit. That's what I mean."

"Quit? You're suggesting I *quit*?" she asked, feeling anger rise inside her.

Jeffery didn't respond.

"We've had these conversations before, but I can't believe you'd actually come out and suggest that I quit!" She sat up further but winced, stifled by the pain. She squeezed the bridge of her nose with her thumb and index finger and shook her head. "This isn't easy for me. You know I don't do 'sick' very well. But for you to suggest that I give up my career because of this…"

"I'm not suggesting that. I'm asking that you consider pursuing something *else*…in your department…something less—"

"Less dangerous? Like a fucking desk job?" she jeered.

"I don't know… You know what the options are," he said, looking uncomfortable.

"Fuck you, Jeffery. Fuck you. I've worked very hard just to get where I am. You have no idea. Fuck you," she said with tears in her eyes.

"Oh, yeah, your career…*your* career," Jeffery said dryly.

"What's that supposed to mean—my career? Why do I feel like I'm talking to my mother? Why do I feel like my career is disposable, that somehow it's not a part of who I am?"

"Look, babe, things have changed. You've been lucky, but now that you got hurt I see what it's already done to us, what it's done to *Sam*."

"Sam's a big boy," Falco said tersely.

"What if this happens again? What if you get hurt again? Can you imagine what that'll do to him? Don't you even care about that—about *him*, about *us*?" he said, trying not to raise his voice.

"Of course I care about Sam, and I know he worries and I know everyone worries, but this is part of the job. You know it and Sam knows it. My mother knows it. There's a lot of bad stuff out there. All of us take risks every day. You could fall off a roof, get electrocuted, cut your fingers off. How is that any different?"

Jeffery frowned. "You can't compare the two. There's no fucking way."

"But if you got hurt, I wouldn't ask you to quit your job and work at Home Depot. This is the fucking real world here, and it's my world. It's not the suburbs. It's the city, and sometimes it's a mean, mean place."

"And it's your job to fix it, right?" Jeffery said angrily.

"That's not fair!" She winced in pain then leaned back on the propped-up pillows. Her head was spinning and her forehead was shiny with sweat.

Jeffery sighed, knowing the conversation wasn't getting anywhere. He sat on the bed next to her and said, "Look, I'm sorry I brought the whole thing up."

Falco shook her head and avoided his eyes. "This is why we split up. This is why we'll never get back together. My job will always be the wall that divides us."

Looking hurt, Jeffery turned and left the room.

* * *

The tension between the two continued the next morning. Falco was feeling dizzy and out of sorts and thought a shower would make her feel better. The water was warm and a sharp contrast to the cold marble floor of her bathroom. She shivered and wrapped a towel around herself, eyeing the bandage that she'd managed to keep dry. She thought of Michael coming over later that day and felt a smooth sense of calm. Thoughts of Jeffery swelled inside her like acid.

After her shower, she bumped over to the bed and made a feeble attempt to arrange the covers over the pillows. Jeffery approached her from behind and put his arms around her shoulders. "I'm sorry, honey," he whispered in her ear.

Falco hardened, "Nothing's gonna change" she said, not looking at him. Jeffery clenched his jaws and helped her make the bed, then left the room.

Sam joined his mother on the sofa with a bowl of cereal. "Dad said we've got to go home soon, Mom," he said quietly.

She gave him a hug. "Well, you've got school tomorrow and homework to do, I'm sure."

"Yeah. I've got a spelling test tomorrow."

Falco nodded, suddenly feeling empty and acutely out of touch.

The two left before noon, leaving her alone and in a dark mood. She lay on the sofa and stared off, her head feeling heavy and hot. The emptiness of the house buzzed in her ears.

CHAPTER 111

It was six p.m. when the phone rang. It was Michael. "Hey, Monica. I'm about three minutes away."

Falco got up slowly from the sofa and made her way toward the front door and unlocked it. It was cold and rainy outside; the weather fit her frame of mind.

Michael ran from his car to the door and twisted the knob. He entered the living room as a gust of rainy wind blew past him. He smiled at Falco, who was sitting on the sofa, and said, "Nasty out there!" He took off his wet coat and hung it on the doorknob and walked across the room to where she was sitting leaning her head on her hand. She waved and glanced briefly at him. She looked tired. He sat next to her. "Hey. How's it goin'?" he said.

She didn't look at Michael, but the tears in her eyes spoke volumes. She looked away and put her hand over her eyes.

"What's going on?"

She shook her head, not wanting to talk.

Michael waited then finally said, "Okay, so if the patient doesn't want to talk, we deal with the physical symptoms." She brushed away a stream of tears as a tiny smile came to her. He took her pulse as he glanced from his watch to her face. "You feel a little warm, sweetie." He placed his hand on her forehead then nodded. "I think you're running a fever. How do you feel?"

Falco sighed. "Not so good. I'm tired and a bit dizzy, out of sorts."

Michael nodded and fished a small plastic beige case from his compact briefcase. He slid out a thermometer, sterilized it, and prompted her to open her mouth.

He glanced at the two vials of pills then looked closely at the antibiotics. "You've been taking these as prescribed?" Falco nodded. He took the thermometer from her mouth and held it up to the light. "One-o-two," he said. "You've got aspirin or Tylenol in your medicine cabinet?"

She pointed toward the hallway. "Over there."

Michael got up, found the bathroom, and located the Tylenol in the medicine cabinet. He returned with a glass of water. "Take these. Did you eat anything today?"

"Not really. I wasn't feeling that great."

"Everybody leave?" Michael asked, looking around.

"Yeah, Jeffery and Sam left around noon," she said into her chest.

"You should eat something. Those meds will tear up your tummy if you don't." The two were silent. Finally he sat next to her and said, "Let's change that bandage okay?"

Twenty minutes later, with the fresh bandage, Michael helped Falco back to the sofa. She was shivering; he wrapped her in an extra blanket. She winced with pain as perspiration glistened from her brow. "I'm cold, but I'm sweating," she said shaking her head, exasperated.

"It's okay," Michael said. "The Tylenol will help bring your fever down. We'll keep an eye on it. I'm not going anywhere."

Falco glanced at him as she settled in. "God, this is such a fucking pain in the ass. I really hate this." Her voice cracked.

Michael looked at her sadly. "I know, but it's going to take a little time. The pain, your mobility—it's hard. You're gonna have to be patient."

"Jeffery wants me to quit," she said quietly. Her eyes, full of hurt, drifted up to him.

"Quit? Quit what?"

"My fucking job. Quit my fucking job…as a cop!"

"That's absurd," Michael said dryly. "You can't quit."

"I know, but then I think of Sam, the look on his face the other night. He looked so worried about me, so sad. I just don't know."

Tears flooded her eyes as Michael came around next to her, sat close, and placed his arm gently around her. She let her head fall back against the sofa and sighed.

"Other kids have parents with normal jobs—accountants, teachers, social workers," she sniffed. "They don't worry about their parents, whether they'll finish their day on a gurney headed for the hospital or worse. Then I thinkGrasky's got kids. He's been on the force for close to forty years. Ballard has a son and a stepdaughter. Torres has a little girl. I can think of a lot of people…"

Her voice drifted off as if she were alone in the room. She looked down and studied the pattern on the blanket.

"It's just been so crazy these last couple of months. So many things have happened. It's almost like everything is coming to a head, staring at me in the face, forcing me to take a good look at my life...as a mother, as a cop."

Michael gave her a reassuring hug. "I know, Monica. You've been through a lot—the McCaffery case, those boys and the porn ring, Josh's murder, and now this."

"Andie," Falco added weakly.

"Yeah, and Andie," he said quietly, nodding his head.

"Grasky's retiring, and I won't be able to be there for his last week. Then my mother is getting married. It's just too much." The phone rang. Falco glanced at it with dread. "That's probably my mother now. Shit."

Michael handed her the phone. She squinted at the caller ID then put the phone on the sofa cushion. "Oh, no," she said, smiling. "Officer Foley," she whispered.

"Officer who?" Michael asked, intrigued.

"Oh...that's...he's...well," she said, scowling. "Fuck me..."

Michael looked at her teasingly. "You *seeing* someone?"

"No, no, no." She shook her head.

"No?" Michael teased.

Falco gave him a pierced look then fell silent. She closed her eyes and shook her head, processing the last few months. "Jesus, what a bunch of shit. Maybe things'll settle after all this, at least for a while."

"Then the holidays," Michael prompted.

"Oh, thanks for reminding me. You're a real pal."

"You gonna buy Officer Foley a present, like for Christmas?" Michael teased.

"No, Michael!" She shot him an angry look as he laughed. "Shithead," she said, smiling. She fell silent again, putting her hand to her head. "You know, my father was a cop."

Michael nodded. "Tim told me. He said he had a great reputation when he retired."

"Yeah, he was a good cop—straight, smart, intuitive, thorough. My mother hated him for it, for all of it. I loved everything about him, flaws and all, but especially that he was a cop."

"You were close?"

"Yeah, then he got sick. I took care of him. I was in college then, so I did what I could, but, yeah, we were close. He started drinking when my brother and I were in middle school. He'd come home late. Dinner would be cold. He'd either be happy or ugly...angry. My mother would yell at him, and he'd have another drink then fall asleep on the sofa. He never missed work, though, because of his drinking. He'd always get up and be back at work before anyone else got there. How he managed to keep his head on straight is still a mystery to me."

Michael nodded. "Sometimes I wonder the same thing about you."

She gave him a curious look. "Me? Why would you think that about me?"

"Well, you were pretty wound up about the McCaffery case even after it all blew over, and you were pretty upset about Andie," Michael said. "You're still carrying that around, I'm sure."

"I hope he thinks I'm a good cop," she said with a sigh.

"Who?"

"My father. Sometimes I wonder if he's looking down on me…somewhere…smiling, I hope. That sounds kind of crazy, I know."

Michael smiled. "Not really."

"My dad died from complications of liver failure," she said. "He started getting sick then had a stroke on top of everything. It all happened so quickly. He got so thin. He deteriorated to next to nothing. He died late one night. I was with him. I held his hand. My mother had gone home. It wasn't until Jeffery and I bought my mom's house and moved my mother into the senior living center that I discovered what really happened to my dad."

She paused for a few moments then continued, "I always assumed he had died from drinking, from alcoholism. There were times I remember him polishing off a case of beer on a Sunday afternoon watching football or baseball on TV. Other times, like when he'd come home from work, it was scotch—mostly scotch. He'd pass out on the sofa mumbling to himself about work. Sometimes I'd help him to bed." Michael nodded.

"Jeffery and I had been in the house for about three months. We finally got to the point where it felt like it was ours and not my mother's. We painted and bought new furniture—this sofa, actually," Falco said, putting her hand on one of the cushions. "One Saturday I was going through some boxes in the attic, stuff my mother professed she couldn't bring herself to go through. I found a box of files containing my father's retirement papers, pension stuff, insurance. Then I found some computer printouts—you know, the old kind with the holes on the side that ran through a track with a daisy wheel?"

Michael chuckled. "Yeah, I remember those. They were noisy."

"Well, I glanced through them, not really paying any attention. I was going to throw them out. Then I realized what they were. The printouts said 'Lutheran General Hospital' at the top. It turned out they were test results from blood work done on my dad when he was first admitted to the hospital.

I found more test results dated after those. I couldn't believe my eyes. I read through them twice then I looked further and found his death certificate. My mother had hidden it from me, and I never knew why. She said I didn't need to see it, that I was too young to handle seeing my father's name, the cause of death…the reality of it all."

"Well, she was protecting you," Michael said.

Falco looked at him. "Jesus, I was a senior in college. I had watched my father wither away in that hospital, and somehow my mother felt like she needed to protect me." She shook her head. "But I left it at that. I guess I sort of forgot about it. I just never thought he died of something other than liver failure and the stroke."

She looked away then continued her story. "Just about three years before my dad was to retire, he and another detective were tracking down a suspect on the West Side, a crack dealer. They followed the suspect into a dilapidated building. It was a flophouse—you know, a shooting gallery, heroin mostly. They called for backup then raided the place. Everything was cool. They found the guy they were looking for, and my dad went to cuff him. The perp went nuts. He stabbed my dad with a used hypodermic needle, right through the fleshy part of his thumb. A few months later, he tested positive for HIV, or whatever they called it back then."

"Oooh Shit," Michael said.

"Once my mother found out about the HIV, she would have nothing to do with my dad. They slept in separate bedrooms, used separate bathrooms. He washed his own dishes and clothes. She completely turned away from him."

"You were away at college?"

"Yeah, so I had no idea this was going on. Then he called me one night just before finals in my junior year. He said he was retiring early. I could tell something was wrong, but he wouldn't let on. It wasn't long after that his liver began to fail. Then he had the stroke. I spent the summer of my senior year at home. I worked a part-time job and spent my free time at the hospital, then at the hospice. Looking back at how the hospital staff treated him, how they protected me, I know they had strict instructions not to tell me that my dad was dying of AIDS. Whenever they drew blood or there was any kind of bodily fluid around, they'd scuttle me out of the room while they cleaned it up. Of course they wore gloves and masks. It made sense to me later after I found out."

"Did your mother care for your dad at all?"

"Oh, yeah, she came to the hospital, but I'm convinced she was there for the sympathy from the guys in the department, from the family. She loved the attention, the 'poor me' shit, the long suffering wife."

She looked down for a moment then said, "I remember coming home one day from work. I got off early because Dad wasn't doing well. My mother was busy out back in the yard. I went to look for her and saw her throw two trash bags out in the alley. I guess I startled her because she dropped one and it fell open. The bag was full of my father's clothes—some of his uniforms from when he was a street cop and other clothes, ties, pants, a few suits. I just glared at her." She took a deep breath and brushed a tear away. "Later I went through the bags and pulled out his uniform. I still have it. It's hanging in my closet."

Michael nodded slowly, processing the story.

"I really didn't put the whole thing together until after that day in the attic. I ran into one of my dad's buddies at a retirement party. He was there when Dad had gotten stuck with the needle. He was the one my dad had confided to about the HIV. He never said a word to anyone until he told me at the party." Falco paused, staring off. "Looking back, I feel like there were so many times my father seemed to want to tell me something. I wonder if that was it. We shared so much those last few weeks…but not that."

"Are you okay with that?" Michael asked.

She shrugged. "I wish my mother would have told me. I guess I'm more angry about that."

"Does she know you know?"

"We've never spoken about it. I know she left those papers there for me to find. She wanted me to know what really happened to my father. Maybe she thought I'd read them and magically decide to quit the force and become an English teacher or something. Or maybe I'd think my father was up to something illicit and then I'd write him off like my mother did. Fucking bitch."

She paused then smiled. "But I guess I got my little bit of revenge…in retrospect. All through college I told my mother I was majoring in English, that I was going to be an English teacher. In reality I had switched my major to forensics and criminal justice after my sophomore year. I minored in English. My mom didn't find out that my degree was to prepare me for a career in law enforcement until I walked onto the stage to get my diploma."

Michael laughed. "Touché!"

"My dad knew, though. It was one of the last things I told him before he died. I'm not sure how lucid he was, but we seemed to connect for a moment. He smiled and winked at me and said something like, 'You'll do good, kiddo.' After my graduation, my mother didn't speak to me for almost two months. I applied to the police academy not long after that. That was the beginning of a period of estrangement between my mother and me that still exists today."

The two sat in silence as the wind howled outside.

"I'm sorry about your dad," Michael finally said. "I lost a lot of friends to AIDS. It's a devastating disease, especially in the early days when we didn't know what we were dealing with." He looked at the floor, lost in his thoughts, then roused himself. "You need to get something into that tummy of yours, plus you're about due for a pain pill and the antibiotic."

Falco groaned. "Check the fridge."

Michael peered into the refrigerator then the freezer. "Uh…not much here. Eggos? You *eat* these things?"

"They're for Sam, but they come in handy sometimes. Hangovers…" Her voice trailed off.

"You've got three eggs. How about an omelet?"

"Sure."

Michael whipped up the omelet in no time and set it before Falco. She realized she was hungry after all. Michael felt her forehead and sighed. "You're still a little warm. You want me to stay the night?"

"No, no. I'm feeling a little better, really."

He smiled. "You just needed to eat something. That's probably why you were feeling so lousy. You need to stay hydrated too. Now, what's with the frozen waffles?" he asked, giving her a funny look.

Falco laughed. "Ohhh, you don't want to know."

"Yeah, I do 'cause I used to eat those as a kid then maybe a year or so ago I had one for breakfast at someone's house, and they were really, *really* horrible. Rubbery and tasteless. I just couldn't imagine ever eating another one again!" he said, making a face.

"You're a food snob," she said as she scrunched her nose. She was silent for a moment as she looked off to the other side of the room. Then she smiled.

Michael looked at her, knowing she was about to tell him something. "Sooo, are you gonna tell me?"

"Okay, I'll tell you. Yet another tale from the fascinating pages of the life of Monica Falco." She glanced at him and smiled.

He sat down and got comfortable. "Okay…"

"Ballard and another detective from the twenty-third district had a party for Steve Grasky and me after we cracked the child abductions case. It was at Murphy's over on Waveland and Sheffield. Well, I'm not a big partier. I never have been. Even in college I was usually in bed by midnight. Everyone from the department came to the party. There were people I hadn't seen in years—folks from the academy, guys who knew my dad. The tab was on Ballard and Bob Leighton and probably Chief Lassiter. Well, Steve—Steve Grasky—was bent on getting shit faced and I wasn't. I planned to stick to one, maybe two glasses of wine and that was it. Well, Ballard was putting shots in front of Steve and me, and Steve was downing them left and right. He was even drinking mine. Then Lassiter got up to say something, and before you know it the guys are egging me on to do a shot. Ballard called me a lightweight and all. He's such a fucking idiot."

"So you did the shot," Michael said.

"Yeah, and before you know it I did another, then another." She shook her head. "After a while I was feeling *no pain.*" She sighed and smiled. "I don't remember a whole lot after that. I do remember sitting in a squad car and someone putting my seat belt on for me. I must have passed out. God, I was so stupid!"

"Somebody drove you home, I assume."

"Yeah, there was no way…" Falco mused. "Well, next thing I knew I was getting helped out of a squad car by this tall kid I had never seen before. Even though I was wasted, I figured out he was a rookie 'cause he was so serious. He was also really, *really* cute."

Michael's eyes were wide. He nodded enthusiastically. "Then what?"

"Well, I remember taking off my weapon as Officer Foley turned on some lights in my house. The next thing I knew, he was looking down at me with these beautiful eyes. I pulled him close. Then we started kissing."

"And then what?"

"We ended up in bed. *Christ*," she murmured.

"Was it good?" he asked teasingly.

"I honestly couldn't tell you. I don't remember much except the fact that I fucked Jeremy Foley, rookie cop, during his eleven to seven shift!" Falco gushed. "It was a stupid, reckless thing to do." She put her fist to her head and closed her eyes. "Stupid, stupid, stupid."

"Sounds like you're still punishing yourself for it."

"That morning I was a wreck. I was feeling really bad. It was the worst hangover I could remember."

"Did you throw up?"

"No, but my head was throbbing, and my stomach felt like it had a hole burnt through it. I had nothing in my refrigerator except some-ice encrusted Eggos in the freezer. So I put them in the toaster and ate them."

Michael cringed. "Bleck!

"I felt a lot better. I really did. I took some aspirin and just lay on the sofa for about three hours. Those Eggos saved me," she said with a rueful smile.

"So are you and Officer Foley an item?"

"Oh, god, no! That morning, when I realized what I had done, I planned my escape. It seemed Officer Foley had a sort of schoolboy crush on me. I ran into him about a week later, and we agreed that our encounter was a one-time thing and a mistake." She smiled. "Then he told me he had gotten engaged the month before!"

Michael's jaw dropped. He fell back in his chair and laughed. "Nice!"

She shook her head. "No, not nice. Stupid, stupid, stupid."

Michael smiled then looked pensive. He got up and peered at a row of photographs on the wall behind the sofa. "That must be your brother," he said pointing to faded photo of a dark-haired teenager.

"Yes, that's my brother Peter. We've lost touch," Falco said.

"You never see your brother?"

"I haven't seen him in over twenty years. He left college after spring break his sophomore year, and he didn't go back. I figured he got some girl pregnant or something. But he never came home even after our dad died. He didn't show up for the funeral…nothing. A year or so after I graduated, I got a postcard from Mexico. That was it, though. I'll probably never see him again. Sometimes I search his name in the police databases, but nothing comes up. At least he's not in trouble or in jail, as far as I know. Looking back, it was my mother who drove him away. Actually she favored him over me. She thought he walked on water. That changed when he cut out. Then Dad got sick and died, and my mother realized she only had me."

"Was she nicer to you, then? More accepting?"

"She kind of treated me like her spouse for a while. I was good for giving her a ride here and there. She hated to drive. She'd ask me to do things around the house, stuff she could pay someone to do, but when she didn't need me she'd cast me off. Then I met Jeffery and we got married, and Jeffery became her surrogate spouse. He fell for it head on. He still bends over backwards for her," Falco sniffed. "Of course now she has Howard, but he's pretty worthless."

"When's the wedding?"

"You know, I don't remember, really. I think it's coming up, though."

When Michael left it was almost ten p.m. He drove home through the rain, deep in thought. Images of the last few months flashed through his mind, as did Andie, Josh, and Falco. He recalled his first impression of Detective Falco; she was tough, no nonsense, impatient. He smiled at the memory.

After Michael left, Falco slowly made her way into her bedroom. She was tired and felt weak. She pulled the covers down on the bed and stared across the room at the closet door. She walked around the bed and pulled the door open. She shuffled through her suits, pants, and dresses until she got to the very back of the closet. There it hung, stored in a plastic ward-robe—the deep-blue jacket adorned with metals gold and red, the starched blue pants, and the crisp white shirt. She unzipped the plastic and touched the fabric, the metals. She ran her finger over the nameplate. It read "Peter Falco."

CHAPTER 112

Andie stared at the pad of newsprint and crayons from across the room. She had managed to chase the voices away for a time but was feeling sluggish and sleepy. Someone had taken the books away. She wasn't sure if she wanted more. Each came with its own set of voices.

The splints had disappeared from her fingers, but noises in her right ear still startled her. Alan was visiting more frequently, as was Michael. She wondered where they went when they weren't in her room. Over the last week, she had developed a strange tick; her head twitched sideways to the right as her right shoulder jerked up in a sort shrug in one quick motion. Alan attributed the tick to the meds and Andie's reaction to whatever she was hearing in her right ear.

"I wish I knew what she was experiencing. If only she could verbalize it…" Alan said to Michael as he looked up from her file. "We know she's been flashing back from the sexual assault. Luckily that's diminished somewhat, but whatever happened during the abduction or afterward occurred somewhere off to the right of Andie's body. Surely it was something frightening or painful," he theorized. "But when the ambulance brought her in, there was no evidence of an injury to her ear. Both eardrums were fine." He sighed and scanned the file. "It's been three months, and although she's made progress—she's talking more and eating—I don't get the impression she really knows what happened to her or that she has a firm grasp of who she is."

Michael agreed. "Do you think she could handle visitors? Maybe Kat could come, or Aisha next time she's in town?"

Alan thought for a moment. "You know, Michael, as much as I think that's a bad idea, it might be worth a try. Andie has only seen you and me over the last three months, and the nursing staff. We're significant people in her life, but we're males. Maybe having Kat come is something to consider. Why don't you call her and run it past her for starters?"

"Okay. I'll do that," Michael said.

Kat's voicemail clicked in, saying she'd be out of the office for one week and that the gallery also would be closed. Michael wondered where she was off to. She virtually lived at the gallery during the fall months; it was gallery season. He left a message then tried her home phone. A woman answered then went to find Kat.

Kat picked up the phone sounding happy as she said hello.

"Hey girl, it's Michael."

"Michael. It's…nice to hear from you," she said, her voice suddenly tense.

"Hey, I got a question for you."

"Yeah…what?"

"Alan and I are thinking Andie could use a visitor. She's at the point where she needs to connect with someone important in her life. We're thinking it might help reassert her identity, so to speak," Michael said. "Can you come by in the next day or so? Or even next week?"

Kat paused. Michael heard her breathing. She flipped through her calendar on her desk. Her blue eyes reflected the cold waters of the lake from her high-rise window. "Just a minute," she said tersely. Michael heard muffled voices on the other end. Kat was speaking to a woman. He closed his eyes and shook his head. He knew what was going on. Kat had moved on.

Kat said she couldn't commit to anything, her calendar was booked. She'd get back to Michael if something opened up. He hung up the phone feeling profoundly empty. It all made sense now: the check for the paintings, Kat's persistence in contacting him, her trip to Barcelona, the suntan, and the new, slimmer figure. "She didn't even ask about Andie," Michael said to himself. "Four, almost five years, and she says she'll get back to me." He put his head in his hands and whispered, "Fucking bitch."

* * *

Steve Grasky called Falco at home, asking if she needed anything.

"I could use a ride to the doctor on Friday, if you're up for it," she said.

"Be glad to lady," Grasky said, sounding genuinely happy.

"I don't want to ask Jeffery. He's a little angry with me. Well, I should say I'm angry with him. So if you could drive me and wait while I get my stitches out, then get me back home, I'd be very, very grateful."

"Just let me know when and I'll be there."

Falco smiled and hung up the phone. *Kiss my ass, Jeffery.*

* * *

Michael felt betrayed after talking with Kat. He wondered if she was going to bother to call him back. He wondered how Andie would respond when she found out Kat had someone new. "I hate her," he whispered to himself.

He dialed Falco's number as he stared at the stack of files on his desk.

"Hi, Michael," she said, her voice somewhat upbeat.

"Hey. How's that fever, girl?"

"It's gone. I took my temperature this morning, and it was normal, right on the button. Thanks for staying with me last night. It was very nice of you. I hope I didn't talk too much or bore you with—"

"No, no, it was fine. *You* were fine, really. I learned a lot about you, and that was good," he said with a hint of sadness in his voice. He paused, not saying anything.

Falco waited and listened. "Hey, are you still there?"

"Yeah, I'm still… Sorry. I was just processing something. I just had a disturbing conversation, but it's not important," he said briskly.

"Disturbing? Like how? Is everything all right?"

"It's about Andie…and Kat."

"What about them? How is Andie?"

"She's doing okay," Michael said. "A little better. In fact I just got off the phone with Kat. Alan and I were discussing Andie's case. We thought maybe she needed to connect with someone other than the nurses and Alan and me. She's still a long way from going home. She has no firm recollection of her own identity. Remnants of herself are floating around in her mind, but memories of the attack have clouded her sense of self in space and time. Alan and I are thinking that having a person significant from her past, like Kat, visit may bring Andie back to the present. It could bring about a turning point in her therapy and recovery."

Falco listened, not sure what specifics she was privy to or what about Andie's state of mind was actually her business.

Michael continued, "Kat and Andie were together almost five years, so bringing her in was key. I called her to ask her to visit, explaining what we hoped to accomplish. I figured she'd jump at the chance to see Andie after almost three months."

"And did you talk with her?" Falco asked tentatively.

"Yes. I called her at home. Kat closed the gallery for the week, which is something I've never known her to do, especially this time of year. Well, some woman answered, and it was quite obvious that she wasn't some secretary or cleaning lady or personal assistant. When I asked Kat to come to the hospital, she wouldn't commit. She said she had a busy week and would get back to me. I was so shocked, so surprised. I couldn't believe it. I still can't believe it," Michael said, exasperated.

"What do you think is going on?" Falco asked, feeling a little intrusive.

"Kat has moved on. She's found someone new. That's it. *Finis!*"

"But you don't know that. Maybe she *was* busy." *Or maybe she can't handle it*, Falco thought.

"I know Kat," Michael said flatly. "Andie isn't of use to her anymore. In fact a few weeks ago she *summoned* me to the gallery, saying she wanted to give me something. She was distant—*very* distant—to me. I think she was cleaning house, getting rid of people, stuff associated with Andie. She handed me an envelope and said I needed to take care of it for Andie."

He paused for a moment, realizing he was talking too fast. "Let me back up. Kat and I had a big argument about her closing the gallery after Andie got hurt. I sort of accused her of reaping the potential returns of Andie's paintings if she, you know, didn't survive."

"*Ooooh.*" Falco winced.

"I know that was a low blow, but I needed to say it. Well, that day at the gallery she demanded I look in the envelope. I opened it and found a huge check made out to Andie for her share of the work that was sold. I guess Kat wanted me to know she hadn't taken advantage of Andie's condition and that she was keeping her end of the contract even though Andie was incapacitated. It wasn't obvious at the time, but now I know she was clearing out the old and bringing in the new, settling her accounts…and attachments."

"I'm sorry to hear that."

"Well, Kat may still come and visit, but I doubt her heart will be in it. I just hope it makes a difference for Andie."

Falco hung up with Michael and stared across the room. She wished she could find out more about Andie's state of mind. Alan had mentioned she was hallucinating and having auditory disturbances when they'd had lunch together. She was troubled as to why Alan thought she might be helpful in Andie's recovery. Could Andie have made a reference to the shooting? She eased herself back in the sofa, pondering her conversation. She had a strange feeling in her chest. She put her hand over her heart and realized it was racing.

CHAPTER 113

Steve Grasky unwrapped a piece of gum and zigzagged it into his mouth. He was on his way to the courthouse on California Avenue for Cornell Raphael Cordero's arraignment. He felt a sense of freedom and excitement as his retirement date approached. This was probably the last time he would have to drive to this part of town, he thought. He was meeting Jim Ballard in the foyer of the first floor.

"I'd rather be meeting Falco," he muttered, "but JB's okay."

Grasky's wife, Dinora, had made a large dish of carne guisada for Falco and was on her way to deliver it as he pulled into the parking lot of the courthouse. *She's gonna like that*, he thought with a laugh. *Dinora's carne guisada is world famous, and Falco could use some meat on those bones.*

He parked his pale blue Ford Taurus and walked quickly down the pass-through toward the courthouse steps. He looked around for Ballard, who was nowhere to be found. He pulled the heavy brown metal doors open and looked around again. *Okay, I'm a little early and Ballard is always a little late. Traffic was bad. I'll give him a few,* he thought as he glanced at the clock on the wall.

Grasky watched the parade of families make their way through the foyer. They were mostly poor folks witnessing the decline of some family member to gang activity, drug dealing, domestic violence, or prostitution. Their faces showed desperation, fear, and helplessness. They were caught up in a cycle that had started long before they were born. Grasky wondered how any of them could break free. Would education make a difference? Maybe. Would living in a better neighborhood change things? Probably not. Would religion keep the evil at bay? Not likely.

He could spot the addicts as though they were wearing nametags, their drawn and lifeless expressions hanging from skeletons of faces. Even their walks, their gaits, spoke of their plights—tiny steps like those on heavy psychotropic drugs, a sort of tentative shuffle that seemed to take them nowhere.

"Hey, Grasky. Sorry I'm late," said Ballard. He was pale and out of breath. His jacket was unzipped, revealing the sweat-stained front of his shirt.

"Did you run from the parking lot?" asked Grasky.

"Yeah, yeah. I'm really out of shape these days," he said with a little smile. He turned quickly when he saw a drinking fountain and ducked over to get some water. "You hear from Falco at all?" he asked, panting and wiping the water from his mouth.

"Talked to her this morning. She's not going stir crazy yet. I'm giving her a ride to the doc on Friday. She's getting her stitches out."

Ballard nodded, still looking pale. They walked quickly up the stairs to the third floor, Courtroom 9B.

Cornell Raphael Cordero was being arraigned on charges that included the murder of Joshua Michlin and the attempted murders of Detectives Monica Falco and Steven Grasky. Additional charges included possession of a concealed weapon, drug trafficking, and distributing illegal substances with the intent to manufacture crystal methamphetamine.

* * *

Falco was feeling better but was troubled by her conversation with Michael. She was pretty well versed in the language of the psych community but was confused by Michael's report that Andie had lost a sense of her identity. She couldn't imagine how that could possibly happen, then she recalled the brutal crime scene: the blood, the barbed wire, the massive contusions, the rape. Add all that to the mix that was already churning in Andie's head, and she might lose herself just to protect herself - but would the memories ever allow Andie to reemerge?

* * *

Grasky returned to the station after leaving the courthouse. He slowly gathered his personal items from his locker and desk. He felt pangs of sadness, recalling mostly the good times, the camaraderie, the personal triumphs. It was a strange, sweet sadness. He looked around the large room, his vision bumping along the cubicles and desks. His eyes stopped at Falco's desk. It was empty and very much as she had left it before the stabbing. He sighed and remembered the incident, the blood, her gripping his hand. Then his eyes scanned Ballard's desk. He hadn't made it back yet from the courthouse. *He must've stopped for lunch*, Grasky thought. Ballard loved lunch. Ballard loved breakfast too.

Lassiter meandered by and stopped at Grasky's desk. "Looking pretty empty on that desk of yours," he said with a hint of sadness.

"Yeah, I didn't realize I had so much stuff here, but after thirty-five years I guess it accumulates," Grasky said with a laugh.

"I called Falco this morning but got her voicemail. How's she doing?"

"Okay. She seemed pretty chipper. I'm taking her to her doctor's appointment on Friday. She's getting her stitches out. I'll wait and then take her home."

"She can't drive for a few weeks, eh?" Lassiter said.

"No, she's stuck at home. I don't know how mobile she is either. Her voice sounded a little strained when she first got to the phone."

"She's tough," Lassiter said with a smile. "Well, now that we've wrapped up the meth case and Cordero is off the streets, it looks like you're good to go." He put a heavy hand on Grasky's shoulder then walked slowly away and back to his office.

* * *

Grasky was immersed in the spreadsheet of statistics Falco hadn't finished. He rubbed his eyes as he glanced at his watch. It was nearly two p.m. Tension had risen in his neck; he rolled his head back and around, closing his eyes and taking slow, deep breaths. Ballard had come in sometime while Grasky was busy with the spreadsheet. He could see his sandy gray hair peeking out from over his cubicle. Grasky got up and stretched, rolling his neck some more. He wandered over to Falco's desk then around to Ballard's. His computer was off, and Ballard was still, his head leaning on his hands. Grasky peered at him, wondering if he had fallen asleep at his desk.

"Ballard? Hey, JB! You asleep?" he asked, bending over. Ballard didn't move. "Hey! Jim, Jim…you okay?" Grasky gave him a sturdy shake. His head fell to his desk with a thump; he was a frosty blue.

The ambulance arrived quickly and took Ballard away on a stretcher, with an IV and oxygen to keep him stable. Grasky had managed to get Ballard's heart going again by frantically pumping his chest and blowing into his lungs. The entire department was tense and shaken. Another officer was gone—first Falco and now her partner, Jim Ballard.

Lassiter's office door was closed. He had his face in his hands. *Jesus Christ,* he thought. *Three good cops out. Falco's out for at least a week or more. Grasky's retiring. And now Ballard's out. Must've been a heart attack or something. Fuck. If Grasky hadn't found him he would have been DOA.*

CHAPTER 114

Falco visited with Dinora Grasky on the front porch. They both enjoyed the spell of temperate weather and the wooden swing. Dinora shared their plans for Steve's retirement and his new job working at his son-in-law's new security business. Falco listened, happy for Dinora and Steve. "Thirty-five years as a cop is a long, long time. I hope I make it," Falco said with a chuckle.

Dinora looked down as a flash of sadness came to her face. "Monica, I know Steve mentioned this already, but I just want to thank you for...stopping that man."

Falco put her hand on Dinora's and smiled. "It's okay. I was just doing my job. That's all." Tears came to Falco's eyes, and she looked away. "Steve's a good man, a really good man and a good cop. It was a real pleasure to work with him over the years. I just wish we could have been partners. We could have accomplished a lot, made a real difference."

She thanked Dinora for the food and waved goodbye as she drove off. She slid the covered dish into the refrigerator, lowered herself onto the sofa, and clicked on the TV. She stared at the screen then put her head back and closed her eyes. The phone rang and jerked her from sleep. She leaned over and found the phone, seeing the call was from work.

"Falco here," she said.

"Hey, Falco. It's Ed Lassiter. How are you doing?"

"Hey, Chief. The pain's been better, so I'm able to move around a bit more. I just get tired easily. I'm getting the stitches out on Friday."

"Great news," Lassiter said. His voice sounded weary.

There was a pause in the conversation. Falco thought someone had come into Lassiter's office then she heard a deep sigh on the other end of the phone.

"Listen, Falco. I know you're home and, you know, dealing with your own thing over there, but I've got some bad news," he said slowly.

"Bad news? What's wrong?" She felt a cold chill.

"Jim Ballard was taken to the hospital this afternoon. It appears he had a heart attack…here…at his desk."

Falco's head fell back in shock. Her mouth gaped open as she said in a tiny voice, "Oh, no. Oh, my god." She put her hand over her eyes and shook her head in disbelief.

"We don't know anything yet, but I wanted to let you know before you heard it on the news." Lassiter sighed. "Everyone here was just getting over what happened to you—and now this. We're all sort of shell-shocked. Then Grasky's out the door in a few days."

"What hospital was he taken to?"

"Illinois Masonic. Grasky found him at his desk. They were just at the courthouse this morning. Cordero was arraigned. Grasky came over to talk with Ballard, and he was already blue."

Falco swallowed hard, trying not to let her emotions overwhelm her. She thanked Lassiter for the call and hung up, then sat motionless on the sofa. The room was quiet except for her breathing. Images of Ballard drifted through her mind: Ballard driving through Uptown; cuffing a suspect; standing over Falco with a cinnamon roll and coffee; going through the dumpster with her at Josh's building; doing shots at Murphy's. A wave of sadness came over her like a heavy blanket. She put her face in her hands and cried.

CHAPTER 115

Michael's voicemail had six messages; one was from Kat. He heard her distinctive voice and grimaced. *Here it comes,* he thought. To his surprise, she agreed to come to the hospital on Saturday, saying that was the best she could do. Michael felt encouraged and dialed her number. He wanted to confirm her visit before she reconsidered and backed out. He rubbed the stubble on his cheek as Kat's home phone rang. A female answered the phone, the woman he had spoken to before. Kat wasn't in, so he left a message with her confirming Kat's visit on Saturday at two.

He sighed and made his way to Alan's office. The door was closed, so he headed down the hall toward the elevators to visit Andie on the ninth floor. He peered into the small square window of the door to her room. He craned his neck to see her then turned the handle and pulled the door open. He was shocked at what he found. He didn't see Andie anywhere in the room, but the floor was covered with the sheets of drawing paper—layers and layers of paper, each page covered obsessively with images both recognizable and abstract. The crayon box was empty and torn apart. Tiny broken nubs of crayons and the colored paper they were wrapped in lay littered around the room and intermingled with the drawings. The cardboard that backed the pad of paper was also drawn and scribbled upon.

"Andie?" Michael called cautiously. He scanned the room. Slowly he entered the bathroom and found her lying on her left side in the tile shower. Her hand gripped the last of a black crayon; her fingertips and nails were a murky greenish brown. She looked dazed; her right hand rested just under her earlobe.

Michael quickly knelt down. "Andie, you okay? What's going on?" he asked urgently. She didn't respond. He bent down to look at her face. Her eyes were blank. He got up and quickly left the room, searching for Alan and the nurse on duty.

A few moments later, he returned with Alan. He scanned the room of paper and debris. "They're all gone? The crayons?" Alan asked, looking around the room.

"As far as I know," Michael said, "and the paper is used up too."

Alan looked around with confusion and concern. He walked into the bathroom and saw Andie on the shower floor. He bent down and put his hand on her arm. She was cold but seemed to be okay physically. He tried to make eye contact then crouched and tried to get her to sit up. She awoke from her daze and grabbed Alan by the shoulders, startling him. Her eyes were wide and fearful. "Bang, Bang!" Alan winced, struck by Andie's words. He held her arms and looked closely at her. She gripped his shoulders, almost rocking him backwards. "Bang! Bang!" she barked again.

Alan tried to make sense of her outburst and tried to calm her with words to coax her out of the shower. She held fast, not moving, anxiety mounting inside her. The nurse on duty appeared at the bathroom doorway. Alan glanced at her and waved her away. Andie held fast to Alan, her eyes darting from the room to the ceiling and back to his face. Her tick surfaced as she repeated the words, softly then louder, "Bang! Bang!" Her right hand let go of Alan as she pulled at her ear. "Bang! Bang!"

Michael gathered the armful of newsprint and eyed the images. He saw violent abstractions of red and murky pink colors alongside brutal streaks of black and orange. He saw images of guns and hands holding guns and knives dripping with blood. He saw fire and stormy skies and bulging, bloodshot eyeballs hanging from red and blue veins. He saw images of cockroaches and crucifixes with large penises, nails, guns, hammers, and piercing circles and triangles and other shapes. Some of the other drawings were calmer and reminiscent of Andie's abstract paintings. The more Michael looked at the images the more uneasy he became. Nausea bubbled in his stomach and throat. He put the armful down on the bed and took a deep breath. He walked into the bathroom where Andie was gripping Alan.

After what seemed like hours, Andie's strength faded. Her cries quieted as she loosened her grip on Alan and her breathing slowed. Alan managed to get her off the floor and led her toward the bed. She glared at the stack of newsprint that Michael had set down and stopped suddenly. Alan looked at her. The fear returned to her face. She stepped back and tried to break free of him. "No, no, no," she said quietly. She pushed him away as she grabbed at his coat.

"It's all right, Andie," Alan said gently as she glared at the stack of papers.

She twisted her arm and broke free of him, rushing toward the drawings. "No, no, no!"

Michael grabbed her just as she reached for the papers and pulled her onto the bed. She took a swing at him with her left fist. The drawings slid off the bed and scattered to the floor. Andie wrestled with Michael then grew still as she caught sight of the images on the floor. Fear and alarm washed over her as her head twitched to the right. "No...no, not that," she whispered. Andie tensed. She put her hands to her face, collapsed into herself, and withdrew completely.

CHAPTER 116

Falco was antsy as she paced the floor of her living room. She was tired and felt surges of pain, but her thoughts and worries drove her to move. She entered her kitchen and looked in the refrigerator for a bottle of wine—nothing. "God, I need a drink," she whispered. Then she remembered the pain medication label, "Do Not Mix with Alcohol."

She suddenly felt lonely. She picked up her cell phone and stared at it. She didn't want to bother Michael and didn't want to talk to Jeffery. Sam was still in school. She hadn't heard from anyone at the station about Ballard's condition. She shut off her cell phone and threw it onto the sofa. The walls seemed to suddenly close in. They took on a drabness she had never noticed before. The carpet too, looked dismal and gray, and the furniture seemed so tired. "I'm tired of you too," she shouted pointing to the furniture and carpet. She closed her eyes and put her hand to her forehead. "What the fuck is wrong with me? I'm talking to the furniture!" She sighed and turned away. "Get a grip, Monica." She ran her hands through her hair and dragged her fingers down her neck and to shoulders.

* * *

Michael and Alan gently gathered the drawings and quietly left Andie's room. Her face sunk in her hands.

"I'm not sure about this," Michael said as they walked down the hallway. Alan said nothing but had a strange look on his face. Michael wasn't sure whether it was fear or exhilaration.

They walked quickly toward Alan's office. Alan held open the door and motioned for Michael to enter. "Put the drawings on my desk," he said, pulling up a chair. He picked up his phone and buzzed Margaret, his secretary. "Hold all my calls."

Michael waited and watched Alan, who went through the drawings one by one. Michael said nothing as he watched. Alan spoke quietly to himself as he studied each piece, putting on his reading glasses and nodding at the pictures. After almost thirty minutes, Alan dragged his glasses off his face and looked at Michael. "I want you to look through these in the order I sorted them and tell me what you see. I want you to tell me what assumptions I've made about them and which ones are significant to Andie's recovery."

Michael looked at the three piles of papers and glanced at Alan. After carefully listening to Alan's instructions, he got up from his chair and started with the first stack while Alan quietly left the room.

* * *

"I've got to get out of this house," Falco said as she snatched her keys and put on her coat. She walked out the front door and pulled it closed as she winced in pain. She made her way down the front steps and looked at her car. "Sorry, baby. I gotta walk." Her car seemed to look at her longingly. It had been parked in the same place for a week.

The neighborhood was strangely noisy—cars rushing by blowing their horns; kids yelling and screaming from the park nearby, their basketballs thumping loudly. Even her own footsteps seemed to radiate up through her body and rattle inside her head. She walked for almost five blocks and entered the neighborhood White Hen Pantry. She wandered to the back, toward the packaged liquor section. She bent down slowly, found the white wine, and selected a Turning Leaf Chardonnay. "Overpriced," she mumbled, "but it'll do." She paid for it and scanned the cigarettes but passed on those. "Let's not go totally down the tubes." She smiled as she pushed open the aluminum door. A gust of damp fall wind blew through her, swinging her jacket wide open and tousling her hair in her face. "Jesus, that's all I need—to catch a chill and end up with pneumonia," she said to herself.

The phone was ringing as she pushed open the front door. She picked up the receiver, but whoever called left no message. Falco put her pain pills away in the medicine cabinet and uncorked the bottle of wine. She poured a generous glass and put the bottle in the refrigerator. She studied the glass, taking in its golden color, then took a long sip and swallowed it slowly. "Okay, this is good," she whispered.

The phone rang again. This time it was Jeffery. "One swallow of the evil brew and he knows it," she said to the phone. Defiantly she answered, "Hi, Jeffery."

"Hey, M. How are you doing?"

"I'm okay. Going a little stir crazy, though."

"Did your mom call you?"

"Haven't heard from her. Someone called before but didn't leave a message."

"You know the wedding is this weekend."

"Huh? Did I get an invitation? I don't remember getting an invitation," Falco said, looking around for her stack of mail. She was already feeling the wine.

"Well, it's this weekend. Saturday at three at Our Lady of the Hills Church."

"Fucking great," she hissed, not caring that Jeffery heard her. "I'm assuming I don't have to do anything except make sure Sam is there to carry the rings. And I'm assuming I don't have to get up and read anything, 'cause if I do…and she's going to spring that on me…"

"Are you drunk?" Jeffery blurted.

"No, I am not *drunk*. Why the hell would you ask me *that*?"

"You seem to be more hostile toward your mother, and that doesn't usually happen unless you're drinking," he said in an accusatory tone.

"My drinking is none of your business. I'm still on the pain meds. You can't drink when you're taking *those*." She shook her head at the blatant lie.

"Okay, whatever. Sam needs to be at the church at one o'clock for the rehearsal. I got him fitted with the tux. I'm picking it up Friday night."

"Anything else I need to do? Besides show up and pretend I'm happy for them?"

Jeffery paused, taking in her growing obnoxious tone. "No. You just need to be there for the service and the reception, which is at Carlucci's downtown."

"You mean the place I had dinner with them a while back?"

"Yeah, that place."

She laughed, remembering Howard kicking the table and sending her mother's glass of wine onto her lap.

"What's so funny?" Jeffery asked.

"Nothing. Really. Nothing is funny about that place."

"What time should I pick you up?"

"Pick me up?" She suddenly realized she had to get a ride to the church since she wasn't supposed to drive for two weeks.

"Shit," she whispered. "I'll let you know. I'll call you, okay?"

Jeffery hesitated. "You sound out of sorts. Are you okay?"

"Yeah, yeah, I'm okay. I just got some bad news about somebody in my department," she said, not wanting to tell him it was Ballard.

"Do you want some company? Sam and I could be there in twenty minutes if you want."

"Oh, no, no," Falco said, looking at the ceiling. "What day is it anyway?" she said lightly.

"Tuesday. You sure you're okay?"

"Yes, Jeffery, please. I'll call you Friday, okay?"

"Sure. Whatever. But you'd better plan to be there."

"Of course I'm going to be there," she said tersely.

She hung up the phone and cursed him then cursed her mother too. She was feeling the wine as she drifted toward the refrigerator for a refill.

She hadn't finished her third glass when the phone rang. She was drifting off on the sofa and mindlessly watching a police series on TV.

"Hey, Falco. It's Grasky. How are you?"

"Uh, I'm okay, I guess. What's up with Ballard?"

"That's why I'm calling. He's in surgery for a quadruple bypass."

"Holy fucking shit!" Falco said, getting up from the sofa.

"Yeah. It's gonna be a while before we know anything, so hang in there, okay? I'll call you as soon as we know something."

"You staying the night?"

"His wife is here and pretty upset. Yeah, I'll probably stay the night."

"You're a good man, Grasky," Falco said, her tongue thick.

"Aww, get outta here, Falco," Grasky muttered.

"It's *true*," she said quietly.

CHAPTER 117

Michael frowned at the challenge Alan had proposed. "I'm not an art therapist," he said with a sigh. He glanced at each stack, grabbed the one closest to him, and sat down. Systematically he looked at each drawing—clinically at first, then once again subjectively—and made mental notes about the literal images, then the colors and the manner in which the colors were executed. He had been immersed in the drawings for nearly two hours when Alan returned.

"Okay, talk to me," Alan said, giving him a wry look.

Michael looked up wearily and cocked his head to the side as he collected his thoughts. He concluded that most of the drawings were Andie's subconscious working through both the physical and sexual assault. The cockroaches and crucifixes with penises and the nails and hammers were images that related to the rape. The cockroaches most likely symbolized McCaffery and reflected Andie's feelings of being violated and polluted by the rape. He thought the images of clouds, fire, lightning, and stormy skies were Andie's recollection of having lost consciousness.

One drawing Michael completely set aside. It was a sketchy image of a woman floating above a field of what looked liked barbed wire. He glanced at it again. "Angel of death maybe, it has no face," he noted then moved to the final stack of drawings. The images of guns, knives, hands, and decapitated heads baffled him somewhat. Everyone assumed Andie had been unconscious by the time the police arrived. He surmised that she experienced the rescue subconsciously, hearing the gunfire and subsequent killing of Brian McCaffery.

Michael rubbed the whiskers on his chin. "Andie's always had an aversion to guns, so I'm a bit confused about these series of drawings: the hands, the guns, the fire coming from the gun barrel. The knife with the blood I can understand. McCaffery had a fishing knife with him. But the guns, the heads…"

Alan nodded. "Very good." He agreed with most of it but added his own theories about the circles and triangles. He looked over at the faceless angel and separated it from the rest of the stack. "I'm puzzled about this one, it doesn't seem to fit," he said thinking. "I'm also bit fuzzy on the gun drawings. They made me realize that we really don't know a lot about Andie's rescue. We know what happened to her, her injuries, but nothing more."

Alan phoned Falco. She fumbled for her phone, finding it embedded in the cushions of the sofa. She realized she was in no shape to be talking on the phone, so she let it ring.

* * *

Wednesday morning was dull and gloomy. Falco woke on the sofa with a headache. Her wound ached. She had fallen asleep on her left side, somewhat twisted around. "Shit," she sighed as she got up slowly. She was dizzy and dehydrated. "Oh, god, what did I do?" she moaned. She remembered only parts of her conversation with Jeffery as she bumped her way to the kitchen. She glared at the empty bottle of wine on the countertop. "What did I do?" she said to herself.

Her cell phone was beeping with several messages, and her home phone also had numerous messages. "God, I hope Ballard is okay. Jesus, I must have passed out," she mumbled. "You'd better get a grip. You'd better get a fucking grip." Her mother had left messages on her cell and home phones. Alan and Grasky had also called. She leaned back on the sofa and wondered whom she should phone first. Just then her cell phone rang, startling her. It was Alan.

"Monica?" Alan said through a burst of static. "It's Alan Forrest."

"Hi, Alan," she said, looking at her watch, her voice a bit hoarse.

"How are you feeling?

"I'm okay. Sorry I didn't call you last week."

"Oh, I understand." Alan's phone crackled. The noise on the other end was making Falco's headache worse. After a few moments the static faded, and his voice became clear. "Hey, I thought you might have a good case of cabin fever by now, so I thought maybe you'd like to have lunch…or dinner."

"That sounds nice," she said, rubbing her eyes. She really didn't feel like being sociable but thought Alan might be a beacon to save her from what might be her steady decline over the next few days.

"How's Saturday look for you?"

"I can't do Saturday. My mother's getting married on Saturday." She chuckled at the absurdness of her words.

"Oh, well, that's wonderful. Good for your mom."

Falco quickly squashed the idea of inviting Alan to be her date, envisioning the cold stares of her mother, aunts, uncles, and cousins, then imagining the fistfight that would ensue between Alan and Jeffery. She was sure Jeffery would provoke it; she wondered who would win.

"Hey, Monica? Did I lose you?" Alan broke in.

"Uh, no. I'm sorry. My brain's a little muddy today," she said, sitting up straight on the sofa.

"How about Sunday. Maybe dinner?"

"Dinner sounds great." They agreed on a time. Alan would pick her up at seven.

She drifted toward the kitchen and made some coffee. She looked for something to eat but found only the leftover carne guisada from Dinora Grasky. She opened the freezer door and pulled out the box of Eggos and smiled at the thought of Michael.

CHAPTER 118

Elaine was furious. She had just spoken with Jeffery, who delicately told her that her daughter was not planning to participate in the ceremony. She hung up the phone in a huff then dialed her daughter.

Falco cursed the phone as she tried to walk quickly back to the sofa. "Great," she said, seeing the caller ID. "Hi, Mom."

Without a greeting, Elaine hit her with a barrage of accusations and insults, starting with her not having returned her two calls days ago to things she had done years before. Falco sat on the sofa and listened, her hand on her throbbing forehead. It was only toward the end of Elaine's verbal assault that she found out Jeffery was the one who had told Elaine about her refusal to take part in the ceremony. She felt rage build inside her; she clenched her jaw and shook her head in disgust.

Elaine went on, "And you always make me feel like I'm not important, that I'm dead in the ground like your father. You never liked Howard. He's a decent man, not like your father, who drank himself to death and left me alone with you and your brother to fend for ourselves. I've always been there for you, for Sammy and Jeffery, and your father couldn't have cared less about—"

"Mother, please stop! That is enough!" She got to her feet, suddenly feeling a sharp pull in her side. She put her left hand to the bandage as she gripped the phone with the other. She winced. "I'm sure you've kept a running list of everything I've done to hurt or disappoint you since my birth, but I won't stand here and listen to you bad-mouth Dad. You never forgot all the times he disappointed you or made you angry either. But he was a good man and a wonderful father. He provided for you and Peter and me and you know that," Falco said, almost pleading. "You drove him away because you couldn't handle him being a cop! You treated him like he was nothing, like what he did wasn't good enough for you, like he didn't make enough money for you."

Falco heard her mother sigh but continued, "When the neighbors bought a new car, you wanted one too. When another family got a new TV, you wanted a new TV too. When the Brolins' remodeled their basement, you wouldn't even go with Dad to see it. You were jealous of them all, and Dad knew it. But he tried. He worked overtime so we could have more, and he *loved* you! He even loved you through all those times you turned your back on him when he just needed someone to talk to, when something was bothering him from work." Her voice cracked. "Sometimes he'd confide in me...a kid...maybe Sam's age. You shut him out and you've shut me out."

Elaine broke in, "Shut you out? That is such a lie. How could you say that to me? I'm the one who had to call you just now. I'm getting married and I wanted you to share in the celebration of our happiness by asking you to take part in our ceremony and—"

"You need a prop, Mom. That's all. You need me to be there to let the rest of the family know that your daughter is still devoted to you. And Sam's the other prop. He'll be there to let everyone know your daughter the cop managed to do *something* right."

"How dare you," Elaine hissed. "I have so much to do for the wedding, and you're making crass...outrageous...insulting and hurtful accusations."

"Mom," Falco said, her voice tired, "if you never loved Dad...if you hated him for being a cop...if you didn't think he provided for us, why didn't you divorce him? We might have ended up happier. Maybe he would still be alive, and Peter…Peter might—"

"I was not the problem!" Elaine shrieked. "No one got divorced back then, especially Catholics."

"Fuck the Catholics!" Falco shouted. She looked at the ceiling in exasperation. "Look, Mom, this conversation is going nowhere. Just tell me what you want me to do, and I'll do it, as long as it doesn't involved jumping up and down or running or dancing or lifting over ten pounds," she said sarcastically.

Elaine was silent on the other end. Falco detected the sound of sniffling. "No, I don't want you to do anything that you don't want to do," Elaine said. "I've already given the reading to your cousin Emily, Anita and Ken's daughter. She's a theater major in college."

"Great. We can always use some more theatrics."

Elaine sighed, letting her daughter's comment drop. "You're coming with Jeffery then?"

"Yes, he's picking me up. We'll be there with Sam for the rehearsal."

"Fine," Elaine said and hung up the phone.

Falco sat down slowly on the sofa. Her left side was stinging. She pulled her shirt up and saw a quarter-size spot of blood on the surface of her bandage. Alarmed, she called Michael.

* * *

"You popped four stitches," Michael said quietly. He pulled two strips of tape from the roll and gently stuck them to the area, pulling the opening closed. "How the heck did you do this?" he asked, looking up at Falco, who was holding her shirt up.

She scowled. "I was having an argument with my mother when I got up too fast from the sofa. I'm sorry. I feel so stupid."

"Don't worry about it. I'm glad you called me, though. How are you getting to the doctor on Friday?" he asked, straightening up.

"Steve Grasky, the detective I worked with on the child abduction case, is taking me. He's retiring soon, so it'll be a good time for us to say goodbye." Tears came to her eyes; she looked away and brushed them from her cheeks. Suddenly a wave of sadness overcame her. She slunk down, leaning against the bathroom vanity, and started to cry. Her hair hung over her face.

Michael gently rubbed her back. Falco blew her nose and wiped her eyes. "I'm sorry," she whispered. "I'm a mess. I'm going a little stir crazy here. Too much stuff is floating around in my head, you know?" She avoided his eyes then said into the marble sink, "Did you hear about Jim Ballard?"

"Yeah, Tim told me. Too bad, I hope he's going to make it."

"I know..." Falco's words drifted off. She let out a deep sigh and turned to Michael. "Thanks for being a friend, for being a bright spot for me through this, and for today."

He hugged her. She felt safe in his arms. "Keep an eye on that bandage, and take it *easy*—no calisthenics!" Michael smiled and made his way toward the front door. "Call me. You know you can always call me."

After Michael left, the only thing she could think of was to call Jeffery and tell him off. "Fucking...whining...goody two shoes...manipulative..." She stopped short and took a deep breath. She wandered into Sam's bedroom then gently lowered herself to the bed and closed her eyes. Her mind was flooded with images: Steve Grasky, Chief Lassiter, Maggie Simonds, Ballard, Kat, Aisha, Andie. She let the image of Andie float through her mind. "Andie, if only I could see you, talk to you somehow," she said with a sigh.

CHAPTER 119

Saturday morning was bright and sunny, almost summery if the temperature weren't forty degrees. Falco felt freer and somehow lighter with the stitches out. The huge bandage had been replaced with a much smaller one. Her doctor warned that she still needed to be careful. She figured it was a good reason not to get up and mingle with her relatives at the wedding. *I'll just be part of the furniture, the folding chairs,* she thought.

She showered and pulled her best suit out of the closet, along with her favorite pair of shoes. She carelessly pulled at her hair. "I need a haircut," she said, eyeing herself in the bathroom mirror. She leaned forward and looked up at her crooked part. "When did I get all these gray hairs?" she said to the mirror. She gave herself a disappointed look. "I feel old."

Jeffery arrived on time with Sam. Sam's tux hung in the back of his truck. "How about we drive your car, baby?" he asked with a smile. Falco couldn't shake her anger at him. She avoided his eyes as Sam ran to her.

"Hi, Mom. Does your cut still hurt?" he asked, blinking at the sunshine.

"Not too much. I'm doing a lot better, sweetie, a whole lot better." She felt a pang of sadness that Sam had remembered her pain first and foremost. She hugged him, but her heart felt heavy.

"You look great," Jeffery said. He could tell she was still pissed at him.

On the way to the church, Sam talked nonstop. Jeffery looked at Falco as she tried to keep up with everything Sam was saying. He put his hand on her knee and said, "You okay over there?"

"Yes. I'm okay," she answered tersely, not looking at him.

"You didn't call me about giving you a ride to the doctor to get your stitches out," he said in a leading tone.

"Steve Grasky took me. He's retiring next week. He took me," she said flatly.

"You were gone most of the day. I tried you on your cell and at home."

"Yeah, well, I forgot my cell phone on the kitchen counter, and after the doc's we went to the shooting range."

Jeffery scowled. "The *shooting* range?"

"I needed to blow off some steam," she said, almost to herself. She stared out the window and thought of life without Grasky. She thought of Ballard recovering in ICU. *He'll be out for a while*, she thought. *You'd better get well and change your ways, JB.*

* * *

On time as usual when Jeffery was driving, they arrived at the church at one p.m. Falco had a strange feeling—something between uneasiness and dread. Jeffery appeared diligently at her side as she opened the car door. He smiled and gently grabbed her arm and helped her out of the car. She expected a jolt of pain but was pleasantly surprised at its absence. *Maybe I'll sneak back to work early*, she thought. They made their way up the church steps as Sam dashed ahead. One of the doors swung open for them as a pudgy man with thinning hair greeted them with a broad smile.

"There she is! Monica! Do you remember me?" the man said, stepping back to see her better. She had no idea who the man was. "It's Tom Brolin from the neighborhood," he said. "We used to live right next door to youse."

"Oh, my god, Mr. Brolin! I would've walked right past you," she said, smiling and giving him a hug.

He glanced at Jeffery and said, "We lived next door. Monica used to babysit for my little Sara and Sherry."

"I remember spending a lot of time with your girls." She smiled. "I still live in that house."

"You do?" Mr. Brolin asked with surprise.

"Yes. It's a long story," she said, smiling.

Howard came and steered Jeffery, Sam, and Falco to the rectory. The ceremony was starting in just under two hours, and Sam needed to change into his tux.

Sam stuck close to his mother and eyed the tux, which was wrapped in dry cleaner's plastic. "You okay with this, Sam?" she asked.

Sam's face twisted. "Yeah, I guess so."

Falco knelt next to him. "I know you're not thrilled about this, but consider it a good experience. And it's a nice thing to do for Gram, okay?"

Sam scrunched his face and nodded.

Howard seemed to be coordinating things. He walked over to them and smiled. "How are you, Monica, honey?" he asked. He seemed to know she'd had words with Elaine.

"Where's my mom?" she asked.

"Oh, she's getting dressed. She won't let me in the room, says it's bad luck," Howard said with a chuckle.

Falco wondered if her mother was wearing white or red.

* * *

"I don't like this tie, Mom. It's stupid," Sam said.

"Well, it's part of the tux, sweetheart," Falco said, adjusting the clasp around his neck. After all the buttons were buttoned and the hooks and eyes fastened, she stepped back to look at him. "Wow! You look fantastic!" She held back a gasp of both sadness and joy at the sight of her growing son. "I can just imagine you at your first prom," she gushed, trying not to cry.

"Prom? No way. I'm not going to any prom. That's stupid," Sam said firmly.

Falco smiled and steered him out of the room and down the hallway where other members of the wedding party had gathered. Jeffery had changed into his tux and seemed relieved upon seeing them.

"You look smashing," Falco said with a smile.

"So does our son," Jeffery added. "In fact I can just imagine what you'd look like at your first prom, Sam."

Falco gave him a dirty look. "We've already discussed that, and he's not going to any prom…ever!" she whispered.

Jeffery chuckled and put his hand on Sam's shoulder. "Do you know any of these people?" Jeffery whispered to Falco.

"No, I haven't seen anyone I know yet except for Mr. Brolin."

Elaine wore an ivory silk two-piece dress with a handkerchief hemline decorated with hand-sewn pearls and tiny beads. Falco knew her mother would be dressed to the nines. She looked good for an older woman, she thought, but Elaine was well kept and never had worked a day in her life.

Elaine walked past her daughter as she took Jeffery's arm. Falco sighed and smiled. *I guess we won't be speaking to each other*, she thought.

The conversation she'd had with her mother the other day echoed in her head. As she sat in the back of the church where it was dark, her heart was heavy with guilt as thoughts of her father floated in her mind. She saw her dad smiling at her with the familiar twinkle in his eyes. She shook the image away and fumbled for a tissue from her purse. *Don't start crying*, she told herself.

CHAPTER 120

"She's fucking late. I don't believe it," Michael hissed. He looked at his watch; it was nearly two fifteen. He hoped Kat hadn't forgotten about their appointment or decided to blow it off. He paced Alan's office then headed toward the elevators. As the doors slid open with a rush of air, Kat appeared wearing a fitted black coat, a turtleneck, blue jeans, and black boots.

"Hi, Michael, sorry I'm late," she said breathlessly. "I couldn't get a cab."

He looked relieved. "Come on. Let's put your stuff in Alan's office."

"Is he coming with us? Is he going to be there when I…?"

"It'll be just you and me. We don't want to overwhelm Andie."

Kat looked nervous. She took off her coat and slid her bag off her shoulder and placed them on the leather sofa in Alan's office.

Michael led her into the hallway. The ninth floor was chilly and deathly quiet. Kat looked around, feeling a sense of dread and fear. "This is so dismal," she said.

Michael said nothing as he gently guided her down the ice-blue corridor toward Andie's room. He stopped and peered into the little window in the door. "I'll go in and check on her. Wait here." Kat's face flashed with fear. "It's okay, Kat. If she's too agitated we'll do it another time."

"I came today, and we'll do it today," she snapped.

Michael sighed and quietly entered the room. Kat turned around, leaned against the wall, and looked at the ceiling. Her face tensed as she held back a flood of sadness. "Be strong," she whispered.

Michael found Andie on the floor next to her bed. She was drawing on the tile floor with the nub of a black crayon. "We forgot to get you more crayons and paper. Sorry, Andie."

Andie didn't look up but scooted herself into a ball and moved back against the wall. Michael frowned. It bothered him that she reacted to him this way.

"Hey, I brought someone to see you today, Andie, a visitor," he said slowly, kneeling down. "You remember Kat, don't you?" he asked, gauging her reaction. Andie mindlessly pulled at her ear. "I brought Kat to visit. Do you remember Kat?" He tried again but got no visible response.

He sighed and got to his feet then made his way to the door. "Okay. Come on in, Kat. I don't know how much of this she's getting," he said, frustrated. "Don't get too close and don't try to touch her. She's too unpredictable."

Kat steadied herself and entered the room. Slowly she came around the bed to where Andie sat with her arms around her knees. In front of her on the floor was an amorphic shape of intricate swirls made with one noninter-secting black line. Kat eyed it, not wanting to step on it. She looked at Andie, who had covered her face with her left hand. Kat bent down slightly and gently said, "Andie, it's Kat."

She studied Andie. Her hair had grown a few inches; it was full of loose curls and wild around her face. She looked painfully thin and fragile. Her hands shook as her head jerked to the right. Kat scowled and looked at Michael. "Try again," he coaxed.

Kat sat on the bed and bent forward, close to Andie. "Tell me about this design here on the floor." Andie looked down at the shape then turned away and covered her face, gripping the crayon in her right hand. "Come on Andie, you've always talked to me about your work. This is very different. Why don't you tell me about it?" she said gently. Andie squirmed a bit then shook her head.

Kat heard a tiny voice say, "No…no."

She waited, watching Andie, then took a chance and slid off the bed and sat cross-legged on the floor in front of her. Andie winced and shirked away. "Kat!" Michael whispered.

Kat waved him off. She put her hand gently on Andie's arm and looked for a reaction. "Come on, Andie. It's me, *Kat*," she whispered. "You know *me*. You know who I am. It's been so long since I've seen you. *Talk* to me, babe."

Andie relaxed a bit. Kat moved closer and took Andie's hands in hers. Andie stared at her through her straggly hair as her shoulder twitched. "See, that's right. It's me," Kat cooed. Andie looked closer at Kat, studying her face, looking into her blue eyes. Andie's eyes appeared hallow and full of hurt and fear. Kat held her hands gently and massaged them with her thumbs. "It's okay," Kat said.

Andie followed their intertwined hands then looked curiously at the rings on Kat's fingers. Slowly, almost methodically, she studied each one then stopped at the intricately shaped ring on Kat's left third finger. She pivoted the ring and peered at it closely. Kat stirred with emotion and whispered, "You know this ring, Andie. You have one just like it, remember?" Andie looked up at her, her expression blank.

Michael came closer and whispered urgently, "I think that's enough for now, Kat."

She glanced at Michael then took a deep breath and leaned close to Andie. "I'll always love you, baby, always, no matter what." She gently swept the hair from Andie's face and touched her cheek. Andie pulled away slightly but didn't take her eyes off her. Kat ran her fingers under her jaw, guided her lips to hers, and kissed Andie softly. Andie looked at her strangely. Kat met her eyes and kissed her again, this time feeling a soft response as Andie leaned closer.

Michael held his breath as he watched the two, his fingertips to his mouth.

"It's time for me to go, baby," Kat whispered as she ran her hands down Andie's shoulders. "I'll come back soon, okay?" She brushed a stream of tears from her face as she got up slowly from the floor. Andie watched her. "You take care of yourself, okay?" She turned to Michael, avoiding his eyes, and quickly walked out of the room. Michael came around the bed to check on Andie. She was staring at the door, her hands flat on the floor.

Down the hallway, Michael looked for Kat, who was already at the elevators. She was turned, facing the wall, shaken and blowing her nose. Michael put his hand on her shoulder. "You okay?" She quickly nodded yes.

* * *

Alan returned to his office and looked at Michael and Kat anxiously as they entered. "How did it go?" he asked.

Kat's sadness turned to rage. "Andie looks horrible! She's skin and bones, and her hair is dirty…and why isn't she wearing some decent clothes instead of those hospital rags? She's so drugged up she can't even speak!"

Alan and Michael listened patiently until finally Kat stopped herself. She looked at the two then sunk into the sofa. She pressed a tissue to her eyes and shook her head in frustration.

"She's…just so thin, so…" Kat whispered, almost to herself. Feeling suddenly vulnerable, she got up from the sofa. Her eyes scanned the faces of

Alan and Michael then caught sight of Andie's newsprint drawings on the desk. Her eyes narrowed as she walked closer to Alan's desk and stared closely at the bundle of drawings. Her head angled to one side as she studied the images on the top of the stack. "Is this… Are these Andie's?" she asked, her voice weak.

"Yes, they're all Andie's," Alan said.

Kat glanced at Alan then rustled through the drawings as she eyed them wildly. Her expressions shifted with each drawing, ranging from confusion to disgust. "Jesus, Andie *did* these?" They both nodded, and she gasped. "Jesus, the images—the penises and cockroaches, the bloody eyes and heads, the guns… Some are so primitive, so brutal, so unlike her work," Kat said, staring at each piece.

"We're sorting through them ourselves," Alan said, taking the stack gently from her and straightening them. She glared at the drawings as Alan took them protectively in his arms.

"This is *Andie's* work?" Kat asked again, shaking her head. She swallowed hard, trying to make sense of the images. "Jesus," she whispered again, putting her hand to her forehead.

Alan leaned forward on the desk and placed his hand on the stack of papers. "They're a release for Andie and useful to the therapeutic process."

Kat ran her fingers through her hair. "Therapeutic process." Her eyes dashed across the room. "What will you do with them when you're done with them? When they're done being *therapeutic?*" she asked carefully.

"We'll destroy them," Alan said flatly.

"*Destroy* them?"

Michael came closer. "Yes, we'll destroy them."

Kat got the message and looked at the floor. She nodded to herself as if surrendering to a verdict. "Are we through here, gentlemen?" she asked as she grabbed her coat and slung her bag over her shoulder. "

"Yes, we are," said Alan.

She turned and headed toward the door.

CHAPTER 121

The wedding ceremony was uneventful, as it was short. Sam walked tentatively up the aisle with the rings, conscious everyone was looking at him. Jeffery looked gallant walking Elaine up the aisle, and Howard actually looked handsome in a garish sort of way as he beamed at Elaine from the front of the church. Falco wondered what the rings looked like. *Maybe Howard got her a matching pinky ring*, she thought, amusing herself.

After the ceremony, a stream of well-wishers and relatives made their way to the back of the church. The bride and groom stood in the foyer greeting the guests as the organ boomed a joyous wedding hymn.

Jeffery found Falco in the back and flashed a disapproving look. "Why'd you sit way back here?" he said, taking her arm.

"It felt right to me. Where's Sam?"

"He's riding with Elaine and Howard. Come on. Let's get out of here. This tux is hotter than hell."

Jeffery held her arm and steered her toward the exit doors, where the bride and groom stood hugging and kissing relatives and guests as they filtered out of the church. Falco eyed her mother as they approached. "You look great, Mom. I'm happy for you," she said as she gave Elaine a hug and kissed her on the cheek. Elaine's eyes filled with tears as her daughter smiled then looked away.

"Hey, Monica, sweetheart," said Howard, taking her in his arms. "I hope you'll call me Dad," he whispered in her ear as he hugged her.

She winced at the thought and at the pain she suddenly felt in her side as he embraced her. She pulled away slightly as Howard moved his hands to her shoulders. "I hope I didn't hurt you, sweetie. I forgot about…"

She nodded as she pulled farther away. "It's okay. I'm fine." She avoided his eyes and looked for Jeffery to rescue her. He stood faithfully behind her.

"She's still not one hundred percent," Jeffery said to Howard.

"I'll be the judge of that," Falco snapped.

The two men nodded to each other. She was as stubborn as her mother.

* * *

The restaurant was noisy and playing the same Louis Prima music as the last time Falco was there. *At least I'm not hung-over,* she thought. Jeffery helped her take off her coat then followed the stream of guests to the banquet area. He placed his arms around her and Sam as the threesome drifted through the crowd. Familiar faces appeared. Cousins, aunts, and uncles Falco hadn't seen in years greeted them and marveled at Sam. Falco felt distinctly out of touch, like she had been living the life of a hermit. She had nothing to say to these people and wondered how they had remembered her after all this time. *Italians never forget,* she thought with a cynical smile.

The three sat at their designated table. Sam was antsy, fingering his silverware and gulping his water. "Cool it, Sam," Falco whispered to him. He stuck his tongue out at her. Jeffery sat close and put his arm around her. She glanced at him as he looked around the room. *Why is he so clingy?* she thought, feeling annoyed.

Louis Prima blared from the other room, singing a duet with a woman, *My dreams are getting better all the time…* The song reminded her of Officer Foley. She smiled at the thought of him kissing her. She wished she could remember the rest of their encounter.

"Something funny?" Jeffery said curiously.

"No, not really." She smiled. "I just like this song."

Sam squirmed and looked up at her. "Mom, can I take off this stupid tie? It hurts my neck."

"I think you should leave the tie on," said Jeffery.

"Well, maybe it's too tight," Falco said, gently pulling on it. She ran her fingers around to the back of Sam's collar and unhooked the clasp in back.

"That's better," Sam muttered, looking at the salad that suddenly appeared before him.

Falco folded up the tie and slipped it into the pocket of Sam's jacket. Sam dug into his salad. "I'm starved," he said with a tomato in his mouth.

She leaned over and said, "Don't talk with your mouth full, *please*, and use your other fork…for the *salad*." Sam rolled his eyes as his mother gave Jeffery a pierced look. "You might continue with the manners, Jeffery," she whispered.

Jeffery casually put his arm around her as he scanned the room, ignoring his salad. He rotated the ring on his third finger as he looked about.

"You're not going to eat that?" Falco asked looking at Jeffery's salad.

"No, I hate salad. Don't you remember?" He pushed the plate over to her then got up and went to the bar. He returned with a bottle of Miller and a glass of white wine. Falco studied the glass in front of her then took a long sip.

After dinner, speeches and toasts were made to the new couple. Jeffery left for the bar, and Sam found a boy his age to play with. Falco let him play; she wasn't about to try to keep up with him. Before long, Jeffery returned with another bottle of beer and another glass of wine. He sat close to Falco and put his arm around her. "Sorry I left you here by yourself," he said softly.

"It's okay. No one's come by to talk to me anyway, and that's fine with me. Sam's running around with some kid."

She watched Elaine and Howard dance to a schmaltzy tune. Feeling a bit drained, she pushed the glass of wine away. Jeffery continued to cling to her; she wondered what he was up to. She glanced at his left hand and spotted his old wedding ring. She felt a distinct stab of pain. *Why the hell is he wearing his wedding ring?* she thought. *He hasn't worn it in over a year, since the divorce was final. He rarely wore it when we were married! Why the hell would he have it on now?* She gave him a scornful stare.

"What's up, babe?"

"Nothing." She reached for the glass of wine, which was now warm, and took a long sip.

Just then her Aunt Dorothy came over to their table. "Hi, Monica," she said, smiling with her bad set of false teeth and her beehive hairdo.

"Hi, Aunt Dorothy. It's been a while," she said, not wanting to talk to her.

"How's your handsome son? I can see your husband is still as handsome as ever." She grinned, eyeing Jeffery. Her sweet perfume mixed with the scent of her peppermint gum.

"Sam's fine. He's running around somewhere."

"I miss seeing you during the holidays and the summer months. You know I have a picnic every Fourth of July," Aunt Dorothy said.

"We're always so busy during the summer and holidays."

"Sam is really into soccer. We're always taking him to practice and tournaments, you know, that kind of thing." Jeffery added, rescuing her.

"Are you still working as a police officer?"

"Detective…I'm a detective."

"Oooh, such dangerous work, just like your father…sweet man. Are you still living in Chicago? In that big old house on… What was the name of that street?"

"Yes," Jeffery said, quickly cutting into the conversation.

Falco glared at him. She was beginning to see what Jeffery was up to. Aunt Dorothy left, giving Falco and Jeffery hugs and kisses. Falco took the opportunity to excuse herself and find the restroom. A growing sense of anger rose deep inside her.

It wasn't long before one of her cousins yelled over the music, "Hey, Monica!" Falco waved and kept walking.

Sam ran into her sweaty and out of breath. "Hey, Sam. Why don't you cool it a while? Jesus, you're all sweaty."

"Can't, Mom. Ricky is after me!"

She shook her head as he ran off. She was feeling acutely tired and figured her injury was rearing its ugly head. *Maybe we should be getting home,* she thought. *That would be a relief.* She remembered her date with Alan on Sunday and felt a sense of comfort at the thought of returning to her real life. She wondered how Ballard was doing.

She caught sight of Jeffery as she left the ladies' room. He was sitting up straight, looking for her across the room. He appeared concerned until he spotted her. She came around the table and sat down gingerly. She glanced at Jeffery and finished off the rest of her wine. It was nearly ten p.m.

"Jeffery, I need to go home soon. I'm feeling really tired."

"So soon? I thought maybe I could talk you into a slow dance," he said with a little smile. She gave him an absurd look that squashed the idea. "How about we wait until ten thirty?" he said, looking at his watch.

"I really need to go home now. Is there any reason we should stay longer?"

"No, not really, I guess," he whined.

Falco scowled and started to get up from her seat. "I'm going to find Sam."

"No, I'll go," Jeffery said, looking annoyed. He looked around the room then made his way toward Elaine and Howard, who sat at the head table talking with relatives. He leaned over to Elaine and said something in her ear. She glanced over at her daughter, who felt her gaze upon her.

The tension was thick in the car as Jeffery drove home. Sam was asleep in the backseat. Deep in thought, Falco found herself frowning. Both her mother and Howard were stiff as boards when she had said goodbye to them at the banquet hall. Before long the car came to a stop. "We're home," Jeffery said, looking back at Sam from the front seat.

Falco whispered back at Sam. He awoke and yawned then fumbled his way out of the car and into Jeffery's truck. "No kiss?" Falco asked, following him out.

"He's tired," Jeffery said.

Sam settled into the front seat of Jeffery's truck and promptly went back to sleep. Falco stared at Jeffery and squared herself for what she was about to say to him. His body hardened as he saw anger rise in her face.

"I know what you were doing back there, at the wedding. You had me a little confused at first, but I figured it out," she said, glaring at him.

"What are you talking about?"

"You know damn well what I'm talking about. The sitting close, the touching, the hanging on to me. Did my mother put you up to this?"

"M, come on. Give me a clue here," Jeffery said, putting his hands out.

"Jesus Christ! Do you really think I'm that stupid?" She spun around and started to walk away.

Jeffery ran his hand through his hair. "Wait, M, wait!"

She turned around as if to give him one more chance. He scowled and looked as if he wanted to say something but didn't know what.

"Come clean, Jeff. Come on. Did she put you up to this…this charade?"

"Monica, you got it all wrong."

"All wrong? All wrong?" She grabbed Jeffery's left hand. "What's this on your finger, sweetheart? You never wore your wedding ring when we were married! Why the hell would you wear it tonight?"

Jeffery looked down and said nothing.

"I can't believe she put you up to this! She played you and you played me," Falco said bitterly. "You're a fool, Jeffery, a goddamn fool."

She walked up her front stairs, unlocked the door, and closed it behind her.

Jeffery sheepishly walked toward his truck, got in quietly, and started the engine.

CHAPTER 122

Falco dragged her suit off and craved a cigarette. She piled her clothes into the overflowing hamper, brushed her teeth, and slipped into bed. Her body ached as she slowly lay back. She moved her left hand down her side and felt the bandage on her abdomen. She closed her eyes and saw a flood of faces from the wedding: relatives, people from the neighborhood, and Elaine's friends from the senior center. "They all think they know me," she whispered. She draped her arm over her eyes, feeling alone and empty. *They don't know me.*

* * *

The next morning was chilly and wet. Falco was in a dark mood, thinking about Jeffery and her mother. "Manipulative bitch," she muttered. She missed work and being at her desk. She wondered about Ballard and considered going to the hospital to see him. *He must be doing okay,* she thought. No one had called her. *Poor JB.*

She spent the first part of the day cleaning the house and doing laundry. The activity lightened her mood, as did the look of her place. The furniture looked a bit tired, and she needed to do some painting and redecorating. *I bet Andie would have some ideas*, she thought. She wondered how Kat's visit had gone.

It was nearly six when the doorbell rang. It was Alan dressed in a dark suit with a stunning blue tie. His black Volvo S80 idled in the driveway. He smiled broadly, seemingly surprised upon seeing Falco. "You look amazing! I never figured a lady cop could be so beautiful," he gushed.

She smiled. "Well, I never knew a shrink could look so dashing."

"Quick…very quick," said Alan, stepping inside.

She grabbed her coat as Alan scanned the living room. "Early American, middle-of-the road, ranch," she said, a little embarrassed.

Alan laughed. "I still have a leather chair from my college years."

"Well, some of it's mine and some of it's from…my marriage, you know…" Her words drifted off as she slipped on her coat.

"We've got reservations for seven. Do you do foie gras?"

"I thought it was banned in the city."

"In the city, yes, a few years back, but not where we're going." He smiled as they made their way to his Volvo and opened the door for her.

Forty minutes later, Alan pulled into the parking lot of the restaurant. "Carlo's is one of my favorite places to eat," he said as they were seated. He was in a jovial mood and talked at length about his years in medical school, his first and second marriage, and his daughter, Alona.

"She's in law school at U of C. She'll be making six figures before long, and then I can retire," Alan said jokingly. He smoothed his napkin on his lap. "I was there for a benefit for the law school a month or so ago and ran into Holly Greene. It was rather unpleasant," he said with a laugh.

"Holly Greene was Andie's lawyer for—"

"The McCaffery case. Thankfully she lives in Cleveland now, and she's married. Still, it was awkward. How long were *you* married?"

"Almost ten years."

"What happened?"

"A lot of things happened, but it was mostly about my career, my being a cop," Falco said flatly.

"Your career?"

"Jeffery felt I should do something that wasn't so dangerous. He and my mother think alike. My mom couldn't handle my dad being a cop either. It's a long, complicated story," she said, looking away.

Alan asked about Falco's injury and the wedding. Falco talked about Sam and Grasky's retirement and Ballard's bypass surgery. "As much as I want to go back to work, I kind of don't want to go back," she said with a sigh.

"It must be a stressful life," Alan surmised. "Being a cop."

She gave him a pierced look. "Okay, now don't *you* start."

He looked at her askance then realized how his words sounded. "Oh, yeah, uh… I'm sorry. I didn't mean…"

She put her hand on his and smiled. "I'm just joking."

"Well, I have to tell you, I was a bit concerned about you a few months back, after the McCaffery case." Alan said. "You were looking pretty stressed out, like you were carrying something pretty heavy."

Falco nodded. "It was hard for me. I felt—I *feel*—I have a certain responsibility for Andie. I knew something wasn't right when the FBI closed the case. I should have listened to my gut, insisted we continue protecting her until the DNA results came in, but they shifted me to the child abductions case and moved Ballard too. It left Andie out there, vulnerable, and now…"

"You shouldn't feel responsible, Monica."

"It's hard not to."

Alan thought for a moment then looked off. "It's hard for me too and for Michael. We feel the void…and seeing her the way she is now, well…" He looked pensive. "I've known Andie for a while. I think I told you before how I met her through Holly. I was her doctor through her first hospitalization and subsequent shorter periods of hospitalizations. She had issues with agoraphobia when she was transitioning to the outside. Michael helped her through much of that until things came to a head one day at the house. Andie had an episode there, and three weeks later the place was sold."

"She sold her house?"

"She had a small house in Edgewater. It had a lot of ghosts in it—for her that is," Alan said, leaning back in his chair. "Before the trial, Andie took a leave from her job. She felt she was being harassed by some of the Evanston police, but she couldn't prove it. Holly confided in me she that thought Andie was losing it back then. Then one night Andie met someone at a bar in Evanston and was picked up on her way home by the Evanston police for DWI."

"Was she drunk?"

"The cops claimed she was, but no breathalyzer test was ever given, according to the police report. She spent the night in jail. Andie said no one let her make a phone call until hours later. She called Holly to bail her out. When she got home early that morning, she found her house had been broken into and her paintings vandalized."

"Oh, no," Falco said, leaning closer to Alan.

"Andie said it was a setup and that her house had been vandalized by the cops."

"No, that couldn't happen…no, no." Falco scowled and shook her head. She pondered Alan's story. *That explains why Andie hates cops*, she thought. *Maybe it also explains why the Evanston police wouldn't release more information about the McCaffery case.*

"She got pretty paranoid after that," Alan continued. "After the trials, after she was released from the hospital, she sold her house and moved to Uptown. It was still a transition for her, but then she hooked up with Kat. She was stable and good for Andie."

"How did they meet?"

"Kat was doing research for a class she was teaching in pre-Columbian art. She came to the library where Andie worked and requested some journal articles and books. Kat found out Andie was a painter and showed up at a group show Andie was in. Kat loved Andie's work and immediately wanted to show it at Cohen Sloan. It took a lot of convincing on her part to get Andie to do it. Andie's kind of…tentative when it comes to showing her work. Sensitive—maybe that's the better word."

They ordered dinner, and Alan ordered a bottle of wine. The food was exquisite. Falco had Chilean sea bass and Alan New Zealand venison.

Just as Alan signed for the check, his beeper went off. "Damn it," he whispered, putting his pen down and looking at the little square device on his belt. He glanced at his watch; it was nearly ten. "I'll deal with this later. I'm not the MD on call tonight. They probably paged me by mistake," he said, looking annoyed.

"Dinner was amazing, Alan. Thank you," Falco said, giving his hand a squeeze.

"Well, I hope we can do this again sometime. I've enjoyed our conversation and our time together."

Falco nodded with a smile.

Rain had started to come down in steady sheets as Alan drove toward Falco's house. He talked about his car, pointing out its special features and how the newer models were even more advanced. Falco listened, pretending to be interested. She was feeling tired. It had been a busy couple of days. She was glad to be out with Alan; Jeffery was such a schmuck.

Alan's beeper went off again. Scrunching his face, he pulled the beeper from his belt and glanced at it. "Hm…don't know what this is about." He took a deep breath and placed the beeper on the dashboard; it was flashing a phone number.

He pulled into Falco's driveway. They scurried out of the rain and under the awning of the front porch. Alan's cell phone rang. He sighed and looked at the number. "I'm gonna have to take this call," he said.

Falco nodded. "It's okay."

Alan slipped the phone into his jacket pocket and put his hands on her upper arms, pulling her close. He kissed her lightly. She slid her arms around him as they kissed again. They gazed at each other momentarily. Falco put her hand on Alan's chest and ran her hand down his silk tie. "I had a nice time."

"Me too," he said with a smile. He moved to kiss her again as his phone rang. He stopped, eyebrows furrowed. "I'm gonna have to say goodnight."

Falco nodded. "Sure."

Alan ran to his car and ducked in as she watched him drive away.

CHAPTER 123

A groaning noise came from the other side of the wall, waking Andie from a deep sleep. "Kat," she whispered. She sat up straight, hearing the noise again. "Kat," she whispered, not recognizing her own voice. She searched the room as shadows loomed on the walls. She felt her lips move. "Kat."

She dragged her hand through her hair and over her right ear. She got up slowly and walked to the door. She leaned close to the window and looked out. Something rattled strangely; she stepped back, startled, eyeing the door. It was ajar. A flood of memories came suddenly: the staircase, the library, the books.

"Kat," Andie whispered. She realized the voice she heard was her own, soft but clear. She put her hand on the metal handle of the door. It was icy cold. She turned it carefully and pulled. The corridor was dark and desperately quiet. Time seemed to stand still as something became very clear to her. She needed to find Kat.

Andie walked quickly down the hallway and pulled the stairwell door open. It was strangely familiar. She glanced at the faded face of a clock above a bright-red fire extinguisher; it was eight ten p.m. In her bare feet, she ran down the stairs, past a door with a large "6" painted on it. She continued down more stairs, past a number 5, a 4, then a 3. Before long she reached a dreary gray door unlike the others. On it a sign read, AUTHORIZED PERSONNEL ONLY.

Andie looked curiously at the door then turned the knob. The door popped open with a gust of wind. Cautiously she entered the space. It was long and rectangular, with pipes of various sizes running along the ceiling and walls covered in what looked like papier-mâché. The door closed behind her with a thud, shutting off the remaining light in the basement. Large air compressors and giant fans created a steady rumble.

Disoriented from the sudden darkness, Andie turned back and searched for the doorknob. Not finding it, she turned around again and headed toward a tiny source of light that came from the floor some two hundred feet away. She walked quickly toward it and ran hard into a steel pillar, striking her left shoulder and sending her bouncing in the opposite direction. She steadied herself and looked for the light again. Carefully, with arms extended, she walked toward it.

"Kat," she called out breathlessly.

The line of light appeared at her feet, revealing a doorway that led to another room, a well-lit room. Andie gave the door a pull as she twisted the doorknob. The door didn't budge. She tried again, this time giving the door a hard push. It caught a gust of cold wind and swung open, taking Andie with it. She fell to her knees onto a cold, wet gravel surface. She was outside.

A bitter, wet fall wind swept past what appeared to be large air conditioning units surrounded by a ten-foot-tall cyclone fence. Large incandescent lights flooded the area with light. Andie got to her feet, chilled by the wind and disoriented from the surroundings. The door closed behind her with a heavy thud.

The gravel on her bare feet was cold and sharp, and the rumble of the street, car horns, and the El train swelled in her head. She slapped her hands over her ears and gritted her teeth. "Stop!" she cried. The rattle around her swallowed her voice. She rushed back toward the door and grabbed and turned the icy doorknob. The knob didn't turn; a key was needed to open it from the outside, keeping intruders who might scale the fence from entering the bowels of the hospital. Andie stared at the door as if willing it to open. She gripped the doorknob with both hands and pulled it frantically. "No, no!" she cried. She stepped back, unable to comprehend what was happening. She pounded at the door then pulled at the knob again. She was trapped.

Gasping for air, Andie found herself on her knees gripping handfuls of muddy gravel. She was wet and cold. As she pulled herself up from the ground, she peered at the door. She looked up and around and saw the outline of a giant construction crane standing idle. Looking for a way out, she followed the perimeter of the fence. She spotted a gate at the far end of the enclosure that was partially hidden by overgrown bushes. She got to her feet and ran to the gate; a large chain was looped around the opening, secured by a sturdy metal lock. Andie studied it, grabbed the chain, and pulled at it frantically. Tears and rain streamed down her face as fatigue and frustration began to drain her.

She pulled again at the chain. The gate rattled and clanged against the fence post. Just then she noticed a small opening between the gate and the post, an opening not more than a foot wide. She pulled the gate open as far as the chain allowed, crouched down, and squeezed through the narrow gap. Her flimsy cotton shirt caught the sharp end of one of the chain links, stopping her midway between captivity and freedom. She frantically pulled at the fabric as the wind rattled the gate against her ribs and spine. "Let me go. Let me go!" she cried. Finally the fabric tore free as Andie squeezed her lower body through.

The hospital grounds were undergoing an expansion project. Oversize industrial equipment littered the darkness and loomed from above a large cordoned-off area. Andie ran into the street as lights from above cast a peppered glow on the darkness. The pavement was cold but welcome over the sharp gravel of the fenced-in area. Anxiety and desperation rose inside her as she looked about, wondering what to do next. Her breath was white in front of her, and her body shook from the cold. She found a dark doorway, a shelter from the wind and rain. She pulled at the steel door, but it was locked. She gasped with frustration and fear, pulled herself close, and huddled there. Kat's face flooded her vision; her smile, her scent comforted her.

She dragged her dirty hands over her face, brushing away strands of hair and tears. Then she heard voices in the distance and the gritty approach of a car on wet pavement. Frightened, Andie waited, pulling herself into a ball against the cold metal door.

The squad car slowly moved through the alleyway. Andie heard the banter of its radio as it passed. It stopped at the corner, just past the doorway, and idled there, filling the enclosure and alley with choking exhaust. Desperate for air, Andie got to her feet and ran wildly in the opposite direction looking for another doorway in which to hide. Her feet were numb from the cold; she could barely feel them as they hit the pavement. Her throat and lungs were on fire.

Billowy puffs of steam filled the alleyway; it smelled of clean laundry. After running nearly six blocks, Andie collapsed onto the wet pavement. She dragged herself to her feet and followed the sweet scent. It was dry and warm between two large metal dumpsters just under a large dryer vent. She sat down and pulled her knees to her chest. The warmth of the steam calmed her shivering somewhat, but her flimsy cotton shirt and baggy cotton pants were no protection against the rain and cold wind. Exhaustion overwhelmed her as she tried to stay alert. She wondered about Kat.

Sleep overcame her as her head drifted back to the cold brick wall she leaned against. Her sleep was fitful, her breathing difficult.

"Miss? Miss? Are you all right?" came a voice from the darkness. A hand gently shook Andie's shoulder startling her. She instinctively thrust out her hand, made a fist with the other, and swung blindly at the voice.

"Hey there, little lady. We're not gonna hurt you. We've come in Jesus' name." The words were syrupy and rung low and deep in Andie's head.

Another voice was a woman's. "Yes, yes, in the blood of Christ we come!"

"Amen!" said the two voices.

The two figures peered down at Andie as she quickly got to her feet and looked to run down the alley, but the two large dumpsters between her blocked her path. She glared at them with her fists clenched. "No…no…no!"

"It's all right. We ain't gonna hurt you! We've come to give you aid, child," said the man in a ringing Southern accent.

"Nooo. No. Go away!" Andie said through her trembling.

"But you're cold and wet! Let us take you to a shelter. You're gonna freeze by the morning out here," said the woman. Andie held her fists up like a boxer ready to fight.

The woman was thin with long brown hair pulled back in a ponytail. The man was black and wore a long, dark leather coat and a fedora-type hat. They each carried shopping bags and huddled under one umbrella.

The man got closer to Andie. "Sister, let us take you to a shelter. We're not gonna hurt you. We've come in the name of our Lord and Savior, Jesus Christ. We've come to help those just like you…to find a better path, a path toward righteousness and salvation."

"Kat," Andie whispered. "Kat!"

The two retreated for a moment as the woman riffled through her shopping bag. She pulled out an oversize sweatshirt with a zipper, stuffed a sandwich wrapped in plastic wrap into the jacket pocket, and cautiously guided it toward Andie.

"Here's a jacket for you, sister, and food."

Andie didn't take the jacket. She eyed them threateningly and flattened herself against the brick wall, her fists clenched. The woman hung the jacket by its hood on a metal bar that came out from one of the dumpsters.

"Blessed are you in the blood of Christ Jesus," said the two. "May the Lord protect you and save your soul." They backed away cautiously, giving Andie looks of foreboding. She heard chants of prayer come from them as they disappeared into the rain.

Andie eyed the sweatshirt; it was already getting wet. She put out her hand to touch it. Carefully she pinched the fabric. It fell to the ground along with a brightly colored piece of paper. Bending down, she snatched up the jacket then the piece of paper and looked both ways down the alley. She pulled the jacket on and wrapped it around her tightly. The sleeves were thankfully long; she pulled them over her hands and huddled back under the vent. Andie unfolded the paper and looked at it carefully. "Jesus saves," she said.

CHAPTER 124

Alan started the car and flipped on his phone, autodialing Michael.

"Hi, Alan," said Michael. "Andie's missing again."

Alan sped toward the expressway, pounding on the steering wheel as he drove. He was livid. Michael had called from the hospital and had already joined the search. Crews of available volunteers and nursing staff scoured the area, looking in closets, empty hospital rooms, offices, the library, stairwells, and restrooms. Andie was nowhere to be found.

Alan ordered that no one leave the hospital and told Michael to lead a second search. "She's there somewhere, goddamn it!" He clicked the phone off and rubbed his forehead. He looked up at the rain and hoped Andie hadn't found her way outside.

* * *

The next morning was rainy and cold, and Michael's head throbbed. He and Alan had spent the night searching the hospital for Andie and now were considering the very real possibility that she had left the hospital and was wandering somewhere outside.

Alan looked at his watch and rubbed the stubble on his chin. He eyed the phone then looked out his office window. "It's bloody cold out there," he said, looking over at Michael.

Michael nodded and closed his eyes. "She doesn't have a coat or shoes. She could be anywhere," he said quietly. "Where would we even begin to look?"

Alan nodded, then picked up the phone. He thought about calling Falco but dialed the eighteen police district instead.

* * *

Daylight beaconed in the alley where Andie had spent the night. A delicate layer of frost had formed on her sweatshirt. The dryer vent was no longer billowing steam. The loud noise of an engine woke her with a start. It was a garbage truck slowly making its way down the alley, lifting up dumpsters and tilting their contents into the slimy pit of its huge compactor. A man was yelling as the dumpsters banged loudly just north of where Andie took shelter.

Andie grabbed her ear. She looked around madly, hearing the noise again. "Bang! Bang," she said as she bolted down the alleyway, her jacket filled with cold air as her sleeves flapped wildly. She ran west down a long series of dark corridors between towering buildings, parking garages, and loading docks.

Her bare feet pounded the pavement. She stopped in the middle of a street and bent over breathlessly. Suddenly something caught the sleeve of her sweatshirt, spinning her around and sending her down hard to the pavement. A tinny screech of rubber circled around her as she felt a stinging pain in her right elbow and left knee.

"Hey! Hey, lady. I'm real sorry. Are you okay?" The clatter of a bicycle hitting concrete and the clomp of cycling shoes came somewhere from Andie's left. Stunned and disoriented, she slowly pulled herself up, eyeing the shoes in front of her.

"I'm really sorry. Are you okay?" the man said, crouching down and picking up the folded piece of paper that had flown from Andie's hand. She didn't look up but attempted to crawl away on her hands and knees. The shoes followed her. "Hey, are you hurt?" the cyclist asked as he set the folded Jesus tract on the pavement.

"Go away!" Andie managed to say. She got to her feet and glanced at the young man through a tangle of wet hair. She stumbled back, staring, then picked up the paper and ran down the street into another alley. The cyclist rubbed the stubble on his reddish goatee and watched the woman disappear. He adjusted his helmet, picked up his bike, and sped off as his radio squawked, "Seiko…Seiko! Do you read? Got a quickie at Burnett."

CHAPTER 125

Falco was feeling chipper and hopeful that her doctor would authorize her to go back to work by the end of the week. "Next Monday, for sure," she said as she took a sip from her coffee mug. She thought about her date with Alan and wondered if she should invite him to Grasky's retirement party. *That would create quite a stir*, she thought. She looked at her watch; it was nearly nine thirty a.m. She had nothing planned for the day except changing her bandage, maybe for the last time. She thought about getting a haircut, but her hairstylist was across town; she'd have to drive.

The phone rang, and she got up to answer it. "Hello?" she answered, clearing her throat.

"Hey, Falco. Did I get you up?" It was Steve Grasky.

"No, I'm up," she said. "How ya doin'?"

"I'm great. I miss you, though. It's so lonely here—no Falco, no Ballard. I may as well just retire," he said with a chuckle. "How are you doing, Detective?"

"Pretty good. I'm hoping to be back next Monday at the very latest," she said.

"Great! You'll be here for my last week and then for my retirement party. Did you get the invitation?"

"Yeah, I'm planning on it, Steve, even though I hate that you're leaving."

"Terrific!" Falco heard him chewing gum on the other end. "Hey, one other thing. Did you see the news this morning?"

"No, I don't usually watch the morning news," Falco said, taking a sip of her coffee.

"Oh, then you haven't heard."

"Heard what?" She immediately thought of Ballard. "Your friend, uh, Fulbright. She went missing last night from the hospital. There's an APB out from the eighteenth district."

Falco put her coffee down, almost spilling it on the carpeting.

"What? Andie? Missing?"

"Yeah...uh...since—"

"Jesus Christ, Steve!" Her eyes darted around the room. "What do you know about it? How long? How long has she been missing?" She fumbled for the TV remote, hoping to catch some local news. Suddenly she thought of Alan's pager going off last night around ten, then again as he had said goodnight and sped off. Did he know last night that Andie was missing? Fear and anger rose in her. Her head spun as her thoughts blocked out what Grasky was saying.

"Steve, I gotta go. I gotta make some calls." She clicked the phone off then found her cell phone and dialed Alan. She got his voicemail. She called Michael only to get his voicemail too.

"Shit!" she said, throwing the phone onto the sofa. She stared at her cup of coffee and wondered what to do. "Alan knew. He *knew*. Why he didn't tell me?" she yelled. "But what could I do? Tag along with him looking for her? Yeah, why not?" She felt angry and frustrated. She began to pace, thinking... thinking.

* * *

Andie's knee was bleeding from the encounter with the cyclist. A relentless wind blew through the alleys, carving its way between the cavernous buildings just east of the River North area. Trendy shops were still dark as trains squealed and buses blew past delivering workers to their destinations. Those on foot walked briskly with steaming cups of coffee, their winter coats blowing in the wind.

Andie's face was red with windburn, and her fingers and feet were swollen and pale. Her teeth chattered as the twitching grew worse, and a hoarse cough rattled inside her. She looked up at a street sign as it shook against the wind, Superior and Wells. Something was strangely familiar; a memory came to her as a surge of pain shot through her head. She gripped her forehead with her sleeve-covered hand and headed west toward Huron.

"Kat."

* * *

Falco waited by the phone for a call from Alan or Michael. She picked up her purse, fished through her wallet, and found Alan's office number. She dialed it and got Margaret, his secretary, who wasn't helpful. She said she couldn't give out patient information over the phone and said she'd have Dr. Forrest return her call as soon as he got in. "Fuck," she whispered. She suddenly felt chilled and achy. It was nearly two p.m., and the rain had returned, pounding the sidewalks and forming dirty puddles everywhere. She took a warm shower but didn't feel much better. She picked up her cell phone again then set it back down on the coffee table. "Jesus Christ," she whispered, putting her face in her hands. Finally she got up. "That's it," she said. She changed her clothes, clipped on her badge, and grabbed her coat and car keys.

* * *

Andie was exhausted. Her vision was blurry, and her feet grew clumsier with each step. Her body shook with tremors and a heaviness grew deep in her chest. Somehow she knew she had to press on to find Kat. Rain returned as the wind shifted off the lake. She drifted down another alley just east of Franklin Street. She stumbled upon a small loading dock hidden by a dumpster that was filled with construction debris. It looked warm and inviting. She dropped to the ground and pulled her legs up close; her body was stiff from the cold. She pulled the large sweatshirt around her legs and curled her feet underneath. She was dirty, wet, and freezing. Sleep came to her quickly as her face fell to her knees. She drifted slowly to her left side as her arms relaxed around her and her head came to rest on the pavement.

* * *

Falco sped south. Her only thoughts were on Andie and whether she should have brought her weapon. It was better left at home, she reasoned. The rain pelted her windshield as the wind whisked around her car, driving it into the right lane in unexpected gusts. Her stomach was upset as anxiety swirled inside her. She gripped the steering wheel as she headed downtown.

Falco didn't have a plan; she had no idea where Andie might be. Maybe she'd drive past her place first then stop by the eighteenth district. She popped open her glove compartment and fished around for her radio and turned it on. The APB for Andie was still active.

Traffic slowed as she approached Uptown. The neighborhood looked cold and dreary. Everyone on the street seemed to be bracing for another dismal winter. Falco found the alley behind Andie's place and drove south. She pulled into the parking lot behind Andie's blue Volvo. A thick layer of leaves and debris reflected the car's lack of use. Falco got out and walked around the vehicle. She then stepped back to look up to the third floor at Andie's place for a light or something that would indicate someone was up there. A stream of memories came to her. She remembered that night when Andie had run out onto the stairs. So much had happened since then. It seemed so long ago, yet it also seemed like only yesterday. She recalled the warmth of that day then felt the sting of the cold rain. She stared at the blue Volvo; it looked almost abandoned and made her feel sad.

She got back into her car and stared at her rain-drenched windshield as her mind wandered. She missed Uptown. She missed Ballard. She missed work. She missed Andie.

Just then she saw one of Andie's neighbors walking down the wooden steps. Her shoes made a loud clomping sound. Immediately Falco thought of Kat the day she and Andie had argued about the paintings. Then it hit her. Did Kat visit Andie on Saturday? Alan didn't mention it, but what if she had? How did Andie react to seeing Kat? Falco could hardly guess. They'd been together a long time; maybe Andie had left the hospital in search of Kat. She didn't know where Kat lived, but she did know where her gallery was located and it wasn't far from the hospital. She started her car and headed toward Lake Shore Drive. Her heart raced as she merged into traffic from Montrose Avenue. The lake looked green and threatening as she thought of the *Nigel T* adrift. She wondered who was taking care of Andie's affairs. She wondered who was taking care of Andie.

Traffic slowed to a dead halt just before North Avenue. It was a parking lot all the way to Randolph. "Shit," Falco whispered. She slowly made it to Grand Avenue, where she got off the drive and headed west. It was nearly four p.m. and darkness loomed.

Unless she's in some homeless shelter, she can't possibly be outside in this weather. No way, Falco thought. Suddenly she got a sick feeling. She wondered whether anyone had checked the morgues. "No!" she said out loud, hitting the steering wheel with both hands. "Please, no," she said as a prayer.

Traffic was bumper to bumper on Grand as tempers flared and horns blared. Falco was getting impatient herself and reached for her cell phone. No calls, no messages. She was growing angry with both Michael and Alan. "Stop it. This isn't about you," she scolded herself.

She made a left on LaSalle and headed south to Huron then made a right, heading west again. She drove slowly, eyeing anyone who looked lost or homeless. She spotted the Cohen Sloan Gallery and pulled over. It was dark. Many of the River North area galleries were closed on Mondays, she thought. Falco spotted the alley that led to the gallery's loading dock. She stopped the car and got out. The concrete dock area had been painted a bright white and the heavy door looked new. The image of Brian McCaffery dragging Andie into the stolen van came to her. She shook her head as she felt a renewed sense of guilt and dread. "Oh, god, Andie," she said with a sigh.

The alley and the concrete area surrounding the dock looked clean, and the dumpsters appeared to be empty. She saw no trace of anyone having stayed there recently. She looked up and down the alley then got into her car and drove north. She got back on Huron and continued west then turned into another alley. Two homeless men were under a tarp drinking from a bottle in a paper bag. Falco pulled over and got out of her car. She had two $5 bills in her hand.

"Gentlemen?" she asked as she crouched to see them under the tarp. They looked at her bleary eyed. "Have you seen a small white woman with brown hair anywhere near here?"

The two looked at each other and shook their heads.

"Are you sure? She may have been wearing hospital clothing…any idea?" Again they shook their heads. She straightened up and sighed. "Shit."

She looked back as the two men hovered over the bottle of alcohol. She thought of Andie lost somewhere in the city. A sick feeling swelled inside her. The rain persisted as she walked back to her car. Then a blue flashing light off her windshield caught her eye. She spun around and looked north across the street into the other alley. A squad car was parked off to the side, its Mars lights flashing. She spotted two patrolmen behind a dumpster.

Falco jumped into her car and sped north across the street, parking just behind the squad car. Hearing her approach, the two uniformed officers stood up and peered over the dumpster. Falco got out and flashed her badge and ID.

"Detective Falco, up and around I see?" It was Sean Donleavy, a smart-ass cop Falco knew from her days at the sixteenth district. The other cop was a rookie and gave Falco an abrupt nod as she made her way toward the dumpsters.

"Got a woman…homeless. We don't know if she's the one we're supposed to be looking for," said the rookie.

Donleavy smiled and shook his head. "Who fucking cares? Homeless is homeless."

Falco came around past the two dumpsters as the two cops parted the way. Seeing the figure, she quickly bent down and pulled the hair from the woman's face. She was pale, her lips and nose blue. "We called an ambulance," the rookie said quietly.

"Is she the nutcase that got loose?" Donleavy asked, looking over at Falco.

She scanned the body. She wasn't sure if was Andie. The woman was painfully thin; her feet were bare, frostbitten, and blotchy; her face was drawn and bony; and she had dark circles under her eyes. Her mouth moved involuntarily as her body shook with tremors.

Falco gently shook the woman's shoulder but got no response. She then pulled back the hood of her sweatshirt and checked her pulse at the base of her jaw. The woman's skin was cold, but Falco detected a faint pulse. She partially unzipped the sweatshirt and saw that the woman wore what looked like a thin cotton shirt. Gently Falco took the woman's left arm and pulled the long sleeve up over her wrist. It revealed a white plastic wristband. She gasped and squinted at the text printed on it.

NORTHWESTERN MEMORIAL HOSPITAL

FULBRIGHT ANDREA 7-22-07

PSY 9 — 24D

115638477-000000032

Falco's head dropped. "Jesus. It's her. It's Andie...Andrea Fulbright." Falco yelled to the two patrolmen, "Where's that ambulance!" She sat back on her ankles and looked up at the sky. "Thanks, God."

The rookie cop radioed the information to the dispatcher; an ambulance was on its way. Falco looked over at Donleavy and tossed him her car keys. "I've got a blanket in my trunk," she said.

Falco leaned close into Andie and draped the blanket around her. Andie seemed to be saying something; it was hardly a whisper. She gently put her hand on Andie's head and brushed the hair from her face. She felt clammy and feverish. "You're gonna be okay, Andie," she said softly. "I'm so glad to see you."

A car rattled up the alleyway and parked behind the squad car and the Camry. Falco looked over and saw Alan walking quickly toward them, his jaw clenched. He nodded, seeing Falco, then crouched and checked Andie's pulse then felt her forehead. "She's been outside all this time," he said bitterly.

Falco didn't look at him but muttered, "The ambulance is on the way."

Andie's left fist clenched as her right hand gripped the Jesus tract. Her eyes floated open, and her lips slowly formed the word "Kat." She stared off blankly for a moment then tried to push herself up. "Kat," she said hoarsely.

"Stay still. We're gonna get you out of here," Alan said softly.

The ambulance appeared and made its way down the alley. Two EMTs dragged a stretcher out as the two uniformed cops stayed close.

"You think we're gonna need to cuff her?" asked Officer Donleavy.

Falco got to her feet as Alan gently took Andie's arm to help her up. Andie flinched and tried to push Alan away. He held her firmly as he gently pulled her to her feet.

"No…*nooo*," Andie moaned, trying feebly to break free. She was weak and barely able to stand.

The EMT guided the stretcher close. Andie was confused and shivering as she gripped the paper in her hand and weakly fought to free herself from Alan's grasp. Officer Donleavy came over to help, taking Andie's right arm. She shot a piercing glance at him then spotted his holster and weapon. She wrenched her arm free, taking Donleavy by surprise. Her head twitched to the right as her shoulder shrugged involuntarily. "Bang! Bang!" she said with a cough. "Bang! Bang!" She put her hand with the Jesus tract to her ear.

Alan grabbed her right arm and quickly twisted her around sitting her down heavily on the stretcher. "It's okay. Everything is all right. We're taking you home now, where it's nice and warm," Alan said. Andie fell back weakly on the stretcher as the EMT attached restraints to her ankles and hands. "Bang, bang," she breathed. "Jesus…saves."

Falco stepped back from the ambulance, her face drained of color upon hearing Andie's words. She realized Andie's memory of McCaffery's death was as vivid as the day it had happened. She stared blankly ahead, processing the last few moments.

Alan came toward her looking troubled. "How did you know… How did you figure out where to find her?"

Falco glanced at the ambulance as it pulled away, then looked at Alan and said flatly, "Alan, it's what I do."

She followed the ambulance to the hospital, reeling from the revelation that Andie remembered shooting Brian McCaffery. "But she was barely conscious," Falco reasoned as she drove. "She was going in and out of shock when she got my gun. *Jesus.*" She put her hand to her head and drove toward the hospital.

CHAPTER 126

At the hospital Falco caught sight of Michael and Alan. Alan hadn't changed clothes since their date the previous night. He looked exhausted, and so did Michael. She waited, hoping she could see Andie once they got her in a room. She worried about her fever and cough and hoped she would be okay.

Alan came by and sat heavily next to Falco. "I owe you an apology, Monica," he said quietly.

"Yes, I think you do," she said, not hiding the anger in her voice.

"I should have let you know what was going on. I'm sorry I didn't return your calls today, but I didn't want you to worry. I figured you had enough to handle dealing with your own recovery."

She shook her head. "Listen, Alan, I know it's part of your job to make decisions for people, but you hardly have to make decisions for me."

His head dropped to his chest. "You're right. I shouldn't have…"

Falco sighed and looked at the ceiling. "Forget it, okay? I'm pretty angry with both of you right now, but this isn't about me. My biggest concern is that maybe we could have found her sooner. That's all."

Alan nodded with resolve. "They're checking her over now. She dehydrated and hypothermic, and she's got a fever and congestion in her lungs. I just wish I knew how she managed to get out."

"She was looking for Kat, wasn't she?"

"Yeah, Kat visited on Saturday, and I guess it affected Andie enough to go looking for her."

"So is that good or bad?" she asked, looking at Alan askance.

Alan sighed and pulled off his tie. "I don't know."

* * *

Falco drove home in the rain light headed and distracted. Andie looked bad, barely recognizable. Her face was bruised and sunken, blotchy and red from the windburn and frostbite; her arms were thin, and her hands were red and scraped up. Alan said she had bruises on her legs and a large laceration on her knee. She could only imagine what Andie had gone through all night.

Her mind went back to that rainy Friday in July. She saw the blood and heard Andie's labored breathing. She felt the panic and recalled the frantic attempt to free her from the barbed wire. She recalled Ballard's face grimacing as he held the pair of wire cutters. She heard the shots in her ear, the clatter of her gun, and Ballard's voice as he knocked the gun from Andie's hand. "Damn it all!" Falco said, slamming her hands on the steering wheel.

She pulled into her driveway and scurried to the front door. It was raining hard, and the wind only made it worse. Once inside she took off her raincoat and tossed the blanket from her trunk on the floor. It was damp and dirty. She was beat. "I've got to sort through this," she said out loud. "I can't let this go on." She sat down heavily on the sofa and put her face in her hands, then got up and started to pace.

* * *

At the hospital, Michael sat slouched in a plastic chair, zoning out and listening to Andie's breathing and sporadic mumbling. He wondered how she had survived the night in the rain and cold. He wondered who had given her the sweatshirt with the sandwich. He wondered how she had gotten so bruised and scraped up. Did someone try to hurt her? Did she get hit by a car? He rubbed the stubble on his chin and stared at the floor. *We may never know*, he thought.

* * *

"Hey, it's me," Jeffery said cautiously. It was nine p.m.

"Hi, Jeff," Falco said, gripping the phone. *What the fuck does he want?* she thought.

"Just wanted to call and see how you are," he said in a leading tone.

"I'm fine. How's Sam? Did you return the tux?"

"Yes, of course I returned the tux," he said tersely.

Tension rose as neither said a word. "I saw the news…about your friend, Andrea," Jeffery finally said.

"Yeah, she was in pretty bad shape. She was hardly wearing anything when we found her," Falco said, suddenly realizing she shouldn't have said what she said.

"You were out there?"

Falco sighed. "Yes."

Jeffery was silent for a moment. "Are you back at work?"

"No, I'm not back at work."

"Then… Why…?"

"I went looking for her, okay, Jeffery? I had a feeling, a hunch, and I went looking downtown near the gallery." She knocked her forehead with her fist, admonishing herself for saying too much.

"Oh…" Jeffery said in a judgmental tone.

She cut him off. "Listen, I'm really tired and chilled. I need to get to bed. I'll call you later this week, okay?"

She hung up the phone without getting a response. "Fucking asshole," she muttered.

CHAPTER 127

Falco woke with a start; it was early morning, three a.m. She was sweating and breathing fast, having dreamt about the damp blanket from her trunk, Andie's sunken face, and gunshots. Her head was throbbing. "I've got to see Maggie," she whispered.

The next morning, she was feeling tired. She hardly had slept and she felt a distinct pull near her wound. Still, she picked up the phone and called Maggie Simonds as soon as her watch said nine a.m. The receptionist found an opening at eleven. Falco downed a cup of coffee and headed for the shower.

The weather had cleared overnight, but the sun seemed cold and the air damp. Winter was threatening. Falco drove south, taking the Kennedy and exiting at Kimball. She headed west on Irving Park and found a parking spot near the alley. Her heart felt heavy. She wasn't sure what she was about to reveal to Maggie, but she knew somehow, someway she had to get this McCaffery thing off her chest. She hoped she wasn't putting her career in jeopardy; if she were, more heads would fall in her wake. She sighed and turned off the car. She was right on time but hesitated going in. Finally she willed herself to open the car door and headed toward the drab gray doors of the EAP office.

She rode the slow elevator up and entered the drab reception area, where she made eye contact with the receptionist before sitting down. Piped-in music was playing smooth jazz as Falco closed her eyes to calm herself. An old Anita Baker tune filtered into the room. *What have you done to me? I can't eat, I cannot sleep, and I'm not the same anymore. I don't know what to do, 'cause all of me wants all of you…* Falco knew the song; she smiled ironically as the lyrics seemed oddly fitting.

Tapping her foot and feeling anxious, she glanced at the clock. After a few minutes, Maggie appeared at the doorway, smiling, and motioned for Falco to come back to her office. Falco's heart skipped a beat; she suddenly felt anxious and a little scared. Maggie closed her office door and sat down, eyeing Falco.

"How are you feeling, Monica?" she asked, leaning toward her in her chair.

"I'm better. Thanks."

"That was a pretty scary thing to happen to you."

"Yes, it was scary, but I'm okay now. I hope to be back at work next Monday."

Maggie waited while Falco geared up to talk. She could tell she was sorting through some things and having trouble getting started. "I heard about Andrea Fulbright. Is she all right?"

"Yes, I guess," said Falco weakly.

"Is that why you're here?"

She remained quiet then said, "Part of the reason, yes."

"Still feeling responsible, or is it something more?"

"I don't know where to start, really."

"Try," Maggie said.

Falco paused and shifted in her seat. "I saw her yesterday, Andie. I hadn't seen her since that day I came to ICU, back in July. It was hard. She's gotten so terribly thin, and yesterday, well…"

Falco went on to tell Maggie about the chain of events that had led to Andie's disappearance and her hunch about where Andie might have been. She described Andie's condition, the windburn and frostbite, the scraped hands and sunken features.

"I didn't recognize her until I found the hospital ID bracelet on her wrist. I was relieved we had found her but disturbed by her appearance. Jesus," she said, looking away as emotion rose in her face. She paused, trying not to get overwhelmed, but her hands shook and tears had welled up in her eyes. She brushed a tear away and after a few moments said, "I just can't seem to shake this…*her.* I don't know what I'm feeling. Is it just guilt that makes me hurt *so much*, or…"

"Or what? What are you thinking, Monica? What are you feeling?"

Falco twisted in her seat and said nothing. She ran her fingers through her hair and down the back of her neck, then shook her head.

Maggie looked at her squarely. "You know, it's not unusual for people who work in law enforcement, or any of the helping professions, to sometimes have a reaction to someone they're helping."

"I know that. I know that!" Falco snapped. She bolted from her chair and walked across the room. "It's just that this has gone on for so long—months—I mean, I dream about her. I…"

"What are your dreams?" Maggie asked evenly.

She shot Maggie a pierced look from across the room. "Well, I've…I've had a lot of dreams, weird dreams about what happened." She swallowed hard, putting her hand to her throat. "Then I've had others, like when Andie came to the station that day before all this happened."

"I remember you used the word 'radiant' to describe Andie when she came to see you that day. Andie doesn't look that way now, does she?"

"No. Not in the least. She's pretty much a wreck…physically and emotionally," Falco said.

"Maybe you're dealing with those issues: guilt, disappointment, shock."

Falco nodded, processing Maggie's interpretation. "Sure, that could be part of it, and other things that I mentioned before. Her life. My life. The differences. How she made me see that I should want more out of my life. That I shouldn't just settle, That I spent the last years of my marriage in a fog."

"She did all that?" Maggie asked, giving her a look of disbelief.

Falco stared. "Well, maybe she was the means for a lot of self-assessment."

"That's good then?"

"Yes, it's good…for the most part. Oh, I don't know what I'm saying." She started to pace. Somehow she felt she was off track.

"What else, Monica?"

The Anita Baker song was rolling through her head. "I…I…think." She sat down again heavily and put her face in her hands. "I…don't know."

Maggie waited, giving her space.

"Look, I'm just going to go ahead and say it, Maggie. I think for the first time ever, *ever* in my life, I'm attracted to a woman, to Andie. And I'm having a hell of time with it. In fact I can't even believe I've actually said it out loud to you. I haven't even said it to myself!" she said, sliding back in the chair. "Oh, god."

Maggie was silent but had a tiny smile on her face. "I understand. Monica. That's a pretty big revelation. You've never had feelings like this before?"

"No, never. That's why this is so weird, so fucking hard! I wake up thinking about her. I dream about her. She's on my mind all the time, and…the worst part is, I may never know that person again. I mean, what if she never recovers? What if she's in that hospital the rest of her life?"

Maggie sat beside Falco and put her hand on hers giving it a tiny squeeze. Falco wiped her eyes and continued. "When we first got the assignment, it was just that—an assignment, just some stupid protection gig…babysitting. I didn't think much of it except that I had to rearrange my weekend with Sam. My first impression was that Andie was this sort of offbeat creative type. I could tell she didn't care for me or Ballard. She was pretty upset when we told her about McCaffery. Her friend Michael was part of the mix, handsome… gay."

Falco hunched over and scanned the floor. "It was funny too, almost prophetic…Andie's work, her paintings. One in particular was hanging in her foyer. I was almost stunned when I saw it the first time Ballard and I walked in. I'd seen a painting very similar to it in Miami a year before. I remember I was sort of obsessed by it for a couple of days. I couldn't afford it, of course, but I remembered that painting all over again when I saw Andie's piece on the wall that first day."

"Did you find that you were attracted to her then, when you first met her?" Maggie asked.

"No, I don't recall being attracted to her at first, not until that Sunday morning, the day after she slipped out of her apartment and took off on her sailboat." She watched Maggie, measuring her response.

"Sailboat?" Maggie asked.

"It's a long story, but we got her back in one piece." Falco smiled. "She got a bit banged up thanks to my partner, but all in all she was okay. Then the next morning, I was on duty, and Michael was waiting for some groceries to be delivered, and this person appeared in the kitchen. I thought at first it was a teenage boy, muscular—well, more sinewy—and sweaty. I wondered how he had slipped in. Maybe he was a boyfriend of Michael's. I was confused. Then the person turned around and faced me, and I recognized the person as Andie. I was shocked. She was…so…strangely beautiful in a boyish sort of way, strong and sensuous. Something stirred inside me. I couldn't take my eyes off her."

Falco let out a breath, consumed in the memory.

"Jesus, I can still see her in my mind. I resisted the attraction at first, but it haunted me. Then, over the next few days, I got to know Andie through Michael and through conversations with her. She was so different—interesting, passionate, perceptive. I'd never met anyone like her."

Maggie nodded. "Tell me more. What else besides her physical aspects were you attracted to?"

"Her passion for life, for her art, for music—classical music. I think music was the catalyst for her work, a source of release. She seemed to feel it so deeply inside. She'd hear some part of piece of music by Beethoven or someone, and it would almost consume her. I don't know much about classical music, but I've been listening to it more and more, trying to tap into what she was feeling, to figure out how it can move a person as much as it did Andie."

"What else?"

Falco paused and thought a moment. "She reminds me somewhat of my father. It's strange. She drinks too much, and so did he. Well, sometimes I drink too much," she said with a sigh. "But they shared the same passions. My father loved music. He would dance around our living room. Sometimes he'd pull me in, try to teach me to dance. He loved my grandmother. They used to cook together. My mother is so different. She stifled him."

Falco paused for a few moments and stared at the floor.

"It just seemed to me that despite all that had happened to Andie, she still managed to live a full and vibrant life. She had lots of friends who supported and loved her. She was active in the gay community. She did lots of fun things. Like I said, she made me look at my own life. I realized all that I wasn't experiencing, all the things I stopped doing, all the things I shut out of my life. She made me think about the friends I'd lost after my divorce; how I used to cook, go to parties, concerts, and stuff when I was married. I realized I'd been living in a holding pattern, maybe just waiting for something to happen. I lived to see Sam on the weekends, and I lived to work."

"So do you really think it's an attraction issue, or do you just want Andie's life?" Maggie asked.

"Her life?" Falco asked, her face scrunched.

"Yes, her life."

She was silent, processing Maggie's question. "No, no. That doesn't account for the dreams, the dreams of us together. The dreams of her kissing me, of her pulling open my blouse and making love to me on my desk… at work," Falco said shaking her head, embarrassed.

"Would you like that? Would you like Andie to make love to you?"

"You mean if I dream about it, I must want it?" Falco asked, bolting up from her chair and walking over to the window. "Yes! I guess. I mean… I don't know. I want to kiss her. Jesus Christ, I want to touch her. I want her to touch me…to… Oh, lord!" Falco put her face in her hands. "Fuck," she moaned. "I've never wanted this before." She looked helplessly at Maggie.

"I've never kissed a woman before. I don't even know if I'd...*like* it. You know?"

She sat down heavily and slumped in the chair. Thoughts of her brief encounter with Brenda flashed in her head. "I just need to sort this out," she said.

* * *

Falco left Maggie's office feeling acutely exposed. The word was out. The universe now knew she was attracted to a woman, to Andrea Fulbright. *Does that make me a lesbian?* she wondered. The session had gone by so fast; she hadn't even gotten the chance to talk about what had happened that rainy Friday, the day Andie had killed Brian McCaffery.

She sat in her car and watched tiny raindrops appear on the windshield. She felt strangely foolish, exhilarated, and painfully disappointed. "I'm just going to have to tell Alan that Andie shot McCaffery, tell him all of it, for Andie's sake. I hope it'll be worth it," she said quietly. She pulled onto Irving Park Road and headed east toward the lake.

* * *

"Hey, JB," Falco said as she slipped into Jim Ballard's hospital room. The TV was blaring ESPN.

"Falco!" Ballard said with food in his mouth. He pushed away a tray of what looked like lunch.

"How ya doin'?" she said, taking a seat in a molded plastic chair.

"They ripped me open," he said, pulling on his pajama top. "That's what hurts...and the fact that I gotta go on this strict diet now."

"No more cinnamon rolls, I guess," Falco said with a smile.

"No. Well, maybe once in awhile," he said with a wink. "You going back soon? I don't know how they're surviving with us both out." He let out a chuckle.

"Yeah. I hope to be back on Monday."

They were both quiet for a few moments.

"God, that was something else, my heart attack. I'll never forget the pain that hit me. Couldn't move, couldn't do anything but sit there."

"I heard Grasky gave you CPR, got you breathing again. Lucky thing."

"Yeah, Stevie. Too bad he's leaving. You going to the party?"

"Of course."

"Should be fun. Have a few shots for me, will ya?" Ballard said with a hint of sadness.

Falco drove home somewhat distracted. Visiting Ballard took her mind of the stinging realization that someone else knew her secret. She picked up her cell phone and dialed Alan. She left a message for him to call her as she headed home. She had a lot of thinking to do.

CHAPTER 128

Kat walked quickly from her car, through the parking lot, and into the hospital lobby. She impatiently pressed the "up" button of the elevators then muscled her way into an already crowded elevator car. She was angry after having heard Michael's messages about Andie's disappearance on Sunday night then his subsequent message on Monday telling her Andie was okay. She had been in Miami looking at an artist's work and sported a sunny glow on her cheeks and the bridge of her nose.

Kat hugged a paper bag to her chest that contained a box of crayons for Andie. She walked quickly to Alan's office and pulled open the door. Margaret greeted her. "Sorry, Ms. Cohen. Neither Dr. Forrest nor Mr. Hansen is available right now."

Kat clenched her jaw. "I want to know how Andie is. Do you know if she's okay? Can I see her?"

Margaret saw Kat was agitated and tried to calm her, but Kat seemed bent on telling someone off. Just then Alan walked into the office, running straight into Kat as she was about to storm out. "Alan! Just the person I want to see," she said sarcastically. "We need to talk."

Alan placed his coat on one of the leather office chairs. "All right, come into my office. I just have a few minutes."

"This won't take long," Kat said briskly.

Alan led her into his office. She set the bag with the crayons on his desk. "These are for Andie. How is she?"

"She's recovering. She has some congestion in her lungs and some frost-bite, some scrapes and bruises, but she'll be okay, thankfully."

"Yeah, thankfully. Listen, Alan, I'm taking Andie out of here. I'm putting her in a different hospital near my father's house, in the north shore. I'd like you to arrange that. I think she'll do better in a private facility."

Alan was taken aback. "You can't do that," he said flatly.

"Yes, Alan I *can* do that, and I plan to do it. It's for Andie's own good, and at least I'll know she'll be taken care of. She'll be fed some decent food, and she'll be in a place where she won't likely wander off."

"Kat, you're not in a position to make decisions for Andie. You're not her legal guardian."

"Yes, I am." She pulled an envelope from her purse. "I met with my law-yer this morning, and based on her care here, he arranged for me to have temporary guardianship over Andie, long enough for you to arrange for her transfer to another facility…of *my* choice."

Alan laughed. "Let me see that!" Kat handed him the document.

"Michael is Andie's legal guardian. I arranged for that a long time ago, Kat," Alan said, eyeing the official-looking document. He ran his hand through his hair. Kat smirked.

"I also have another document for you, Alan. It gives me legal rights to any artwork that Andie produces. In other words, you won't be able to destroy those drawings once they've outlasted their 'therapeutic' value. You must give them to *me*. All of them. Furthermore, when Andie is no longer a patient of yours, and that will be very, very soon, those drawings will become *my* property."

Alan leaned on the edge of his desk, crossed his arms, and snapped, "I know what you're up to, Kat, and it's despicable. If you think for one minute you're going to get away with this…"

"Andie spent an entire night and most of a day outside in the blistering cold with skimpy hospital clothes on. She could have died out there! She could have been raped or murdered" Kat's nostrils flared as she pointed at Alan with every word she spoke. "When I saw her on Saturday, she was skin and bones. She didn't know who she was, and she sure as hell didn't know who I was!"

"Look, Andie has a number of issues we're dealing with. She's under-gone—"

"She's not getting better. I saw her… She's—"

"Kat, you don't understand. You just can't turn mental illness on and off like a light switch."

"Stop it. I'm sick of hearing all that. You call what I'm doing despicable? Her care here is what's despicable, *Dr.* Forrest."

She spun around and stormed out of Alan's office. He ran after her with the envelope. "Kat! Wait, you… You can't…"

She turned abruptly around to face Alan. "You just try, Alan. I've got enough on you and this place. My lawyer will go after you *and* this hospital for malpractice if you cross me, and I hardly think your lawyers are any match for mine."

Kat stormed out as Margaret gave Alan a blank look. He dashed back into his office and asked Margaret to connect him with someone in the hospital's legal department. "Good god!," he hissed as the phone rang on the other end.

CHAPTER 129

Falco had a bad feeling. She was tired and feeling lost and empty. She checked her voicemail, but there were no messages. She pulled off her coat, went into the kitchen, and poured herself a glass of wine. She felt pangs of doubt, wondering whether what she had told Maggie was really true. *I'm not a lesbian. I'm not*, she thought. *I was married for ten years. Jeffery and I had a perfectly satisfying sex life. There are lesbians all over the department. I was never attracted to any of them.* Then she thought of Brenda Salerno and how had she felt when Brenda leaned in close to kiss her.

"Jesus, I've never kissed a woman."

Her mind took her back to that day at the station. She saw Andie walking away, talking to Kat on her cell phone. Her heart beat faster. "I can't deny what I feel," she whispered. She set the glass of wine down and pulled her coat back on and headed out the door. She searched her wallet for her library card and got into her car. *Maybe some Mozart will help me sort this out.* She started her car and drove west.

* * *

Something seemed very different to Andie. Her room had been rearranged, the door was on a different wall, and the window had moved too. She rose from the bed and walked toward the door. She pulled the handle, but it didn't budge. She tried again, pulling the handle with both hands—nothing. She rubbed her forehead then studied the palms of her hands; they were scraped and bruised. "Jesus Saves," came a voice from nowhere. She sat on the floor, remembering her escape; her run-in with the cyclist; the Jesus people; and the faint memory of the alley near the gallery.

Andie traced her right index finger on the floor, drawing an invisible design. She found herself in the back supply room of the Cohen Sloan gallery. She was staring at a row of steel shelving filled with dusty cardboard boxes with words scribbled on faded labels. "Three-inch nail fasteners," she whispered. Suddenly she was overcome by a caustic odor; it overwhelmed her senses and made it difficult for her to breathe. She gasped and got to her feet, running into the bed and smacking her shins on the steel frame. She fell onto the bed then rolled to the floor. She got to her feet and pulled the bed over. The linens and pillow fell to the floor as the bed frame toppled. She crawled underneath the tumbled mess and for a few moments felt safe.

Bang! Bang! came the sudden noise, startling her from underneath the bed. "Where am I?" she heard herself say. She climbed out from under the bed and stood in the middle of the room as lights from the street cast eerie shadows everywhere.

Bang! Bang!

Andie spun around and clapped her hands to her ears. *Bang! Bang!* came the noises again. The room filled with the sounds of voices yelling something indiscernible. She ran to the nearest wall and huddled in a corner then crawled back under the bed. She pulled at her right ear and whispered, "Jesus save me."

* * *

"I can't sleep," Falco said in disgust. It was two a.m. She got up, turned on a light in her bedroom, and paced. Her mind went in circles as she ran her hands through her tangled hair. "This has got to stop," she moaned into the darkness. She paced some more, went into the kitchen, and looked for a bottle of red wine. Finding nothing, she looked in the refrigerator for some white. No luck. "Fuck," she whispered. She drifted into the living room, her CD player was loaded with *Mozart for Your Mind,* a CD she borrowed from the library. She hit the remote to start the CD and sat down heavily on the sofa. She listened to the music, waiting for her heart to stir like Andie's. She walked into the kitchen searching again for a bottle of wine, but stopped short. *No, I'm not going to start.* She turned the music off and went back into her bedroom.

Wondering what to do next, she fixed her eyes on her closet then her dresser. *Okay,* she thought. Peering into her closet she got an idea. She decided to pack up her summer clothes for the season and bring out her winter clothes. Of all the tasks that came with the changing seasons, she hated this one the most. She loved the transition of winter clothes to summer, but the task of packing away her summer things always made her uneasy and sad.

For a moment she felt overwhelmed at the undertaking. The flood of emotions associated with the winter months swelled inside her along with the uncertainty she felt about the future. She reran her session with Maggie in her head and wondered whether Maggie had given her revelation any thought after she'd left her office. Suddenly Falco was filled with anxiety and doubt. "It's guilt and anger," she said out loud. "It's not *attraction.* I am *not* a lesbian. I don't have a thing for Andie. It's guilt."

She sat on her bed amid a stack of wool sweaters and pants. The clothes suddenly looked strange, almost foreign. Who was the person who wore these sweaters, these pants? She wondered, staring at the heap of browns, blacks, and greens.

What's happened to me? I don't know who I am anymore, she thought.

She picked up a plastic bin from the floor and arranged the blouses and shirts inside. As she shifted the stacks of clothing in the bin, her hand brushed against a folded piece of paper sticking out of the pocket of a pair of linen pants she hadn't worn since the previous summer. She looked curiously at the folded card; her heart raced, jarred by a distant memory. She unfolded the postcard and took a quick breath. It read:

ANDREA FULBRIGHT

PAINTINGS AND MIXED MEDIA

May 9–June 6, 2005

Trace Gallery

810 Lincoln Road

Miami, Florida

A full-color photograph of one of Andie's paintings appeared on the flip side of the postcard. Falco gasped as she stared at the words then at the photo. Suddenly Kat's words came to her, "I loved her work before I knew I loved *her.*"

Stunned, she sunk down on the bed and stared off. She looked at the postcard again then found herself pacing, staring off, then staring again at the postcard. "No, no, no," she whispered, shaking her head. She sat on the bed and gripped the card, then ripped it in two and threw it in the trash.

CHAPTER 130

"Hey! Hold it already! What are you trying to do?" exclaimed Tim Strickland as he guided the barbell to the rack on the bench press. Michael was breathing hard, his muscles bulging and twitching. "What's the matter with you today? You trying to kill yourself?" Tim asked, glaring down at him.

"Come on," Michael said. "Let me finish this set." He gripped the barbell as Tim positioned himself to hoist it off the rack. He finished the set and wiped his forehead as Tim continued to look at him.

"You gonna talk to me or what, Michael?"

"It's not you," Michael mumbled.

"What then?" He gave Michael a worried look.

"It's my stuff—you know, the drama I call Andie…and Kat."

"Oh…" Tim said, suddenly understanding the cause of Michael's mood. Tim followed as Michael wandered to the free weights and took a drink from his water bottle. He watched as Michael took hold of a pair of twenty-five pound weights and sat on a bench.

"Kat's causing big problems at the hospital," Michael muttered, not looking up. "She got her lawyer to grant her temporary guardianship of Andie, and she's trying to move her to another hospital."

"Can she do that? I thought you were Andie's guardian."

"I am, but that might change if Kat's fancy lawyers have anything to say about it. Papers were filed a few days ago, and the hospital's lawyers are going over them now. There may be a malpractice suit too if Kat gets really pissed."

Tim sat next to Michael on the weight bench and put his hand gently on his back. "What can I do?" he asked.

Michael smiled sadly. "Not much."

* * *

The sun was rising, sending early morning sunlight into the back windows of Falco's house. She squinted at the bright light as she stacked two plastic bins on top of each other full of summer clothes. *I'll deal with these later*, she thought, reminding herself she needed to watch how much weight she lifted. *It's been a long two weeks*, she thought.

She had been up all night but barely felt tired. Her mind was still buzzing, so she decided to keep going. She went through Sam's closet, sorting through old clothing and boxes of tattered toys. She rooted in the basement for cardboard boxes and brought them upstairs. *I'll take these to the Brown Elephant Resale Shop when I go back to work on Monday*, she thought. It was Wednesday and Monday seemed a long time away. One task loomed; she needed to talk with Alan about what had happened that rainy Friday. She felt a stab of anxiety.

* * *

The ropes that bound Andie's wrists burned as she tried desperately to free herself. She felt the road under her as the van sped through the driving rain. Her throat felt raw as the caustic odor hovered around her nose and mouth. She drifted off, awakening to a shattering pain in her head and neck. She drifted off again but was startled by the sounds of someone crying, sobbing in the darkness.

* * *

Alan pushed his cup of coffee out of the way as one of the attorneys representing the hospital set down three thick manila file folders on the small conference table. It was seven-thirty a.m. He pulled out his bifocals and studied the papers Kat's lawyers had delivered to the hospital bright and early that morning. Alan was feeling a little queasy but was confident in what the team of attorneys had said: Kat had no rights when it came to Andie and no legal claim to Andie's guardianship.

Bill Kucer, one of the hospital's attorneys, looked up from the documents. "Ms. Cohen and Ms. Fulbright aren't legally married, and as you know, the state doesn't recognize civil unions or same-sex marriage. That works for us here. In addition, Ms. Fulbright and Ms. Cohen haven't lived together for three years. They were never registered as domestic partners, so Katherine Cohen would be hard pressed to use that in court. However, Ms. Cohen's claim to Ms. Fulbright's artistic work may be more difficult to sort through. Unfortunately that's not my area of expertise."

"Are you suggesting that I not destroy Andie's drawings once we're through using them in her treatment?" Alan asked.

"I'd suggest you keep them in a safe place even after you're through with them. I'm sure Ms. Fulbright has legal counsel for her artistic property. You might find out who that is and get advice on what to do with the work before Ms. Cohen's attorneys draw up something new."

Alan nodded. Kat had known what she was doing when she had brought over those crayons, Alan thought. *No, that's not true. No one could be that devious.* His cell phone buzzed in his coat pocket. It was Falco. He scowled as he looked around the conference table; the discussion was thick with no end in sight. *I'll call her later, if this meeting ever ends*, he thought.

The discussion continued for another hour, covering every aspect of the thirty-six-page document Kat's lawyers had drawn up. The team of attorneys representing the hospital determined that Kat's claims of negligence by the hospital were unfounded and concluded her case for guardianship was weak at best. They were confident Michael would remain Andie's legal guardian and that Kat would have no legal say as to where Andie received treatment. The hospital's legal team planned to file a countersuit on the hospital's behalf, knowing full well the legal wrangling was far from over.

* * *

Margaret put down her cup of freshly brewed coffee as the phone rang. "No, detective, Dr. Forrest has been in a meeting since early this morning. Yes, I can check his schedule. One moment, please." Piano music followed as she put Falco on hold.

Falco wondered why Margaret annoyed her. *She's on a power trip*, she thought. Margaret was middle aged or older. *The job was probably all she had, she surmised. I bet she's menopausal too. Was that a sexist comment? Probably*, she thought. *She reminds me of Mom. Their voices, their intonations are strangely similar.*

"Detective Falco, Dr. Forrest has a very, *very* busy schedule today and… Wait one moment, please." She put Falco back on hold again as tinkling new age piano music filled her head. "Christ," Falco groaned, rubbing her forehead. "Uh…yes, Detective. I think I can squeeze you in around twelve thirty, if that will work for—"

"Yes, yes, please. That'll work fine for me. Yes," she said eagerly. She hung up the phone and sighed. "This is it. Today is the day we tell how the story really goes."

CHAPTER 131

The gold-levered handle of the dark wood door felt chilly as Falco nervously pulled it down and jerked the door open. Margaret Bremmer was seated at her large stately desk like the keeper of the gate. She glanced at Falco over her baby-blue bifocals. Her spectacles matched the steel gray of her hair, which was wrapped around her head like a turban. *She looks like a smoker*, Falco thought as she made eye contact with the woman.

"Detective Falco, I presume?" Margaret asked in a low voice.

Falco nodded. She scanned the room and sat in one of the leather chairs, then looked at her watch. Margaret glanced at her suspiciously. Falco avoided her stare. *This woman is making me nervous*, she thought. *Good thing I'm not a psycho or a serial killer coming in for my weekly chat. This woman might put me over the fucking edge.* She tapped her foot on the carpet. *I've got to do this. Alan's got to know what really happened out there.*

Just then Michael breezed in with a steaming cup of Starbucks. He was surprised to see Falco. "I hope this is a social visit," he said, giving her a wry look and shifting his weight to his right leg. Falco's face twisted, she quickly looked down. Michael caught her reaction as worry crossed his face. "Hey, what's up?" Falco looked away for a moment then sighed in resolve.

"I'm here to talk to Alan, and actually, I'd love if you could stay too." Michael looked at his watch. "My appointment is at twelve thirty. Do you think you can stay?" she asked weakly.

Michael continued to give her a worried look. He scratched his forehead then pulled out his phone. He frowned for a moment then looked at his watch again. "I'll be right back, okay?" He quickly left the office.

Falco heard Alan's voice from the hallway. He was talking loudly with a colleague. He pulled the door open and immediately saw Falco. She felt her anxiety kick up a notch.

"Hey, Detective, what a sight for sore eyes," he said with a broad smile.

She didn't return the greeting or the smile. "Alan, we need to talk." Alan's face flashed serious as he brushed her shoulder. "I have an appointment," she added firmly.

Alan looked at her askance as his expression changed to worry. "Come on in," he said.

Michael returned, out of breath and looking confused. He glanced at Alan then at Falco and followed the two into Alan's office. The door shut quietly as she took a deep breath and sat down.

"You want to take your coat off?" Michael asked.

She didn't seem to hear him as she sat up straight near the edge of the leather chair. Alan sat down slowly, watching her; he then clasped his hands together as he did most times when patients were close to revealing something important.

"There's something you both need to know, and I didn't realize the significance of this until the other day when I saw Andie...in that alley." She glanced tentatively at Alan then at Michael as the two waited for her to continue. "That day, that rainy Friday in July, we found Andie in pretty bad shape. She was going in and out of shock, and as you know, she had lost a lot of blood."

Falco swallowed hard.

"There was a lot going on. Ballard and I were trying to free Andie's arms from the barbed wire while the other officers went after McCaffery. It was… *intense.* We were dodging gunfire and, well, trying to keep Andie alert, telling her to keep breathing, that she was going to be all right." She forced her emotions down. "I'm sorry. I didn't…"

"It's okay. Continue," Alan said gently.

She closed her eyes for a moment. "Andie seemed to be loosing blood with every breath. It was everywhere, coming from her nose and mouth, her side, from the punctures in her arms. She kept going in and out of consciousness. Sometimes she would try to say things but…"

Falco paused as if to shake off the memory. She straightened in her chair and embraced herself. "Ballard and I were so close. We managed to free her right arm, but then her body sank to the right from her weight. It was pulling on her left arm, the broken one, which was still bound up by the wire. She was in so much pain. I tried to straighten her up, to take some of her weight off her left arm. Then the shooting stopped. I remember the dead silence… and Andie's breathing and the sound of the rain. Ballard and I were working frantically, trying to free her arm, when Andie started getting agitated. I looked down the embankment and saw that McCaffery had been captured and was being cuffed. I told Andie to stay still, that we got him, that the ambulance was coming. She started to say something. I looked away for an instant, then I heard loud gunshots to my left."

Falco put her head in her hands. "Oh, god." After a few moments, she lifted her head and looked up at the two men. "Andie shot Brian McCaffery. She shot him once in the chest and again in the neck. She used my gun to shoot him…to shoot him dead."

Alan and Michael were stunned. She glanced at them and then looked down. The room suddenly felt large and open then suddenly it shifted and shrunk down around her.

"The official police statement of course never told that part of the story. It said McCaffery had been killed by police fire as he went for his weapon, but, as I said, that was not the case. When I saw Andie the other day, it was obvious that she remembers the event. I never, ever thought she would remember it. She was barely conscious, but then I saw her in the alley, holding her right ear and saying—"

"Bang, bang," Michael said quietly.

"Yes. I only hope that after all this time…that maybe knowing this… what really happened that day…"

"Is significant, Monica, yes," Alan said quietly. He sank into his desk then put his head down as if deeply relieved. After a few moments he looked up, his face red as if from holding back tears. He closed his eyes and nodded. "It explains a lot."

* * *

Falco left Alan's office feeling empty and a bit scared. She hoped she might feel lighter now that the burden of what really happened that day was off her chest. Alan assured the confidentiality of her disclosure then embraced her warmly before she left his office.

"I knew Monica was carrying something around about that day," he told Michael after Falco left the office. "I saw it in her face. It was eating at her."

"Well, she couldn't say anything without putting her career on the line," Michael said. "Wow, tough call."

Alan paced the room. "Jesus Christ. Andie killed Brian McCaffery!" He sat down heavily at his desk then thought for a moment and looked at

Michael. "As far as I'm concerned, we're at square one with Andie." He picked up the stack of crayon drawings and started to resort them. Michael looked on feeling acutely optimistic.

* * *

At the Cohen Sloan Gallery, Kat was livid. She slammed the phone down and grabbed her coat and purse, virtually knocking her assistant down as she dashed out of her office. "I'm leaving, Renee. I may not be back, so take messages. If Simon calls, tell him I'm on my way." She grabbed a cab just outside the gallery. "One eleven South Wacker," she yelled to the driver as she slammed the door. "This is not over, not by any means," she sneered.

CHAPTER 132

Steve Grasky was wearing a dark-blue suit and steel gray tie as he greeted the stream of law enforcement personnel, friends, and family as they made their way into the banquet room of Monastero's Ristorante & Banquets. He chewed his gum nervously as his wife stood at his side smiling broadly at the guests.

Ed Lassiter trudged by with Iris. He winked at Dinora and said, "I hope you two are planning a little vacation before Steve starts his new gig."

Dinora smiled, "No, no. Steve starts at Precision Security on Monday."

"No rest for the weary," Lassiter said, smiling at Grasky.

Bobby Leighton appeared with his latest girlfriend, a hot Latina with dark red lipstick. Tim Strickland came in with Robby Torres and Dan Reilly; Jeremy Foley brought his fiancé.

"Where's Falco?" Grasky asked, looking across the crowd. "She said she was comin'." He glanced at his watch and frowned. Before long the shrill sound of a microphone being turned on came from the packed banquet room.

"Ouch," Falco said, putting her hands to her ears.

"Just in time for the speeches," Alan said as he swung open the door of the restaurant.

Falco and Alan quickly walked in and made their way around the crowded tables. *Nothing like making a grand entrance*, she thought as everyone checked out her date. Steve Grasky made his way over to her; he was smiling.

"I was beginning to think you weren't gonna show, lady!" he said, giving her a big hug, almost lifting her off her feet. He looked at Alan, who appeared rather dashing in a black suit and blue shirt and tie.

"Uh, Steve, this is Alan Forrest."

The two men shook hands as Grasky led them to two saved seats at his table.

"Figured this was the last time we'd have lunch together," he whispered to Falco. She smiled and rubbed his back affectionately.

"How's Ballard?" Grasky asked, sitting down.

"He's okay. I saw him on Monday. He wants me to do a few shots for him," Falco joked.

"Shots? Did you say shots? Bring a few over here!" said Grasky, motioning to one of the waitresses.

"Oh, no, Steve. I was kidding, *really*." Falco laughed. *Oh lord.*

"What? You're not gonna get shit faced with me?" Grasky said, purposely making Falco feel uncomfortable in front of Alan.

She gave him a dirty look. "No, I'm too old for that and so are you!"

Grasky gave her an evil smile then sped off to talk with Bobby Leighton.

Dinora came by and bent over to whisper in Falco's ear. "You're creating quite a little stir, my dear." Falco looked up at Dinora, not knowing what she meant. "Your friend," she said, shifting her eyes to Alan.

Falco smiled and glanced around, catching a few eyes in the process. "Nothing like a little gossip," she said with a smile.

Alan looked at her and leaned in close. "I'm glad you invited me." She smiled and gave his hand a squeeze.

"I wasn't sure, after our conversation on Wednesday," Falco admitted.

"That was work. *This* is personal," Alan said, gently leaning close. "You seem happier somehow. I know it wasn't easy to unload all that."

Falco sighed. "Well, I feel a little better, but I'm still haunted by the fact that we could have stopped the whole thing from happening, if we'd just waited a few days, waited for confirmation that it was actually him in that van."

"That decision wasn't made by you, Monica," Alan said.

"I know, I know."

After dinner Falco's colleagues from the district greeted her, asking when she'd be returning to work. Lassiter smiled at her and Alan as he carried two mixed drinks to his table. "You're back on Monday, right?"

Falco nodded. "I can only imagine the stacks of paperwork on my desk." She suddenly felt sad. *Grasky's gone*, she thought. *Ballard's out for a while.* "Jeez," she whispered, touching her forehead. "It's gonna be a lonely place."

* * *

Alan hit the alarm button on his keychain and walked with Falco to her front door. "Nice night," he said quietly.

"Yeah," she said, looking up at the sky. "Feels like winter, though. Even the stars look cold."

Alan smiled as he looked up. "Interesting…I guess they do look cold up there."

Falco turned to him and leaned against the front door. Alan bent down and moved in close. She smelled the wine on his breath and a faint hint of soap or some kind of cologne. She breathed it in as he touched her face with his hand, guiding her mouth to his. They kissed softly. His lips seemed warmer than hers, as did his breath upon her cheek. He kissed her deeply. She felt his warmth fill her and flow through her body. His mouth moved to her neck then under her ear, his hot breath burning as he moved lower and unbuttoned her coat.

"Let's…let's go inside," Falco said quietly, catching his eye. She fumbled for the doorknob with her right hand, not taking her eyes off Alan.

He held her gaze and dragged himself away from her momentarily as she opened the door. Alan used his body to move them both inside as he guided her into the living room and closed the door with his left hand. He leaned into her once more and dragged her coat off; it fell heavily to the floor. His mouth was on hers, kissing her deeply, passionately.

Falco gasped for air. "Oh, fuck." Alan worked his way down her neck, running his lips over her cool skin, biting softly at her neck. He pulled open her blouse and ran his tongue between her breasts as her breathing grew faster. She pulled Alan's coat off and slid her hand under his suit jacket and ran her hands up and down his back and around to the front of his pants. Hands shaking, she quickly unfastened the buckle then the button of his pants.

She started to slide down to the floor, but Alan stopped her. "Where's the bedroom?" he asked, his eyes darting to hers. Falco smiled and took a handful of his shirt and pulled him toward the hallway.

They quickly peeled off each other's clothing. The sheets were cool against their hot, clammy skin. Alan pulled Falco under him and sucked greedily at her breasts. She cried out in pleasure, reaching down and stroking him. He was smooth and hard. "Jesus Christ," he moaned, sliding his hands under her and thrusting himself deep inside her. She was welcoming and wet. Falco's head fell back into the pillow as she gasped and moaned.

Alan cradled her and took long, deep, rhythmic thrusts inside her. He was much stronger than he looked. Their bodies slid easily over each other as the sheets crumpled and twisted. He pulled her on top then guided her back down to the bed, where their bodies tensed tightly together then released with shudders and gasps. Alan fell onto his back, taking deep satisfied breaths and putting his hand on his sweaty chest. Falco turned on her stomach, finding a spot where the sheets were dry and cool. Tired from their lovemaking, they fell asleep intertwined in the blankets and pillows. The bedroom was quiet except for the sounds of the street outside.

Falco drifted awake to the salty, sweet smell of the bed linens. The early morning light drifted in between the wood shades. She rubbed her eyes and felt the heat of someone next to her. Alan was asleep, breathing deeply, his mouth half open. She smiled as his face came into focus. *God, that was amazing. He was amazing*, she thought. Her body held the memory of the previous night. She was sticky and tender between her legs, and her throat was scratchy.

Quietly she craned her neck to look at the time; it was nearly six a.m. *It's Saturday*, she reminded herself. *Too early to get up*. She slid back comfortably into the bed and moved closer to Alan. She studied his face; a faint cast of whiskers had grown on his chin overnight. He looked rather ordinary, she thought, like a guy who would come to fix her refrigerator or paint her house. Surely this was not the abundantly published Alan Forrest, MD. She leaned on her hand and watched him sleep, then smiled and laid her head on the pillow and closed her eyes.

CHAPTER 133

Falco heard herself groan as another sound made its way into her consciousness. It was a light tapping somewhere near the front of the house. She sat up suddenly and looked at the clock radio; it was nearly nine a.m. The knocking persisted as she quickly untangled her legs from the wrinkled sheets and blankets and pulled on her robe. The house was chilly; it hinted of the onset of winter. Feeling sleepy and only half awake, she followed the sound into the living room, where she caught a glimpse of Jeffery's truck in the driveway. Sam was knocking on the door. "Oh, great," Falco said. "It's Saturday. How could I have forgotten?"

She opened the front door as Sam piled in, carrying a rucksack and a stack of books. "Hi, Mom! Lost my key," he said, running into her and giving her a hug. "I thought you were still asleep!" he said, much too loudly.

Jeffery followed Sam looking a bit annoyed. "Didn't you hear us knocking? I think your doorbell is broken. We tried it, but I didn't hear it from outside."

"Neither did I," Falco said sheepishly.

"Were you asleep? You look like you just got up."

"Yeah, I overslept," she said, pulling the front of her robe closed.

"Mom, Riley's outside. Can I go over there?" Sam asked excitedly.

"Sure, just put your stuff away in your room."

Sam stormed in and threw his books on his dresser then jammed his bag in a corner on the floor. "See ya later!" He waved and ran out the front door.

"So…back to work on Monday?" Jeffery asked, leaning against the living room sofa.

Falco looked around, wishing he would hightail it out of there like he did most Saturdays. "Uh, listen, Jeffery. I, uh, kind of have a…"

Her bedroom door crept open as Alan appeared wearing his pants and no shirt. He pulled his hand through his hair and caught Jeffery's eye.

Embarrassed, Falco shook her head, then looked over at Alan. "Hey," she said easily, smiling at him.

He came over to her and kissed the side of her neck from behind. "Good morning. Things get started early around here, huh?" He smiled, looking at the two of them.

Falco gave Jeffery an annoyed look then quickly took Alan's arm and steered him out of Jeffery's earshot. "I'm sorry. I forgot that my son was coming over today."

"Not a big deal. I'd take you out for breakfast, but it looks like I've got a call I'm going to have to take." Alan squinted at his phone.

Falco gave him a sad look, "I'm sorry."

Alan smiled. "It's okay." He made his way back to the bedroom and searched for his clothes.

"Sorry, M. I guess I didn't think to…" Jeffery stopped short, not knowing what to say. He huffed in frustration then decided to keep quiet. "I'd better go," he said, backing up toward the door.

"Okay," Falco said, not wanting to show her relief.

"I'll come by around seven to pick up Sam. He's got homework to do too."

Falco nodded. She heard Alan in the bedroom talking on his cell phone. After a few moments, he emerged, pulling his arm into the sleeve of his shirt. "So," he said, buttoning the front, "does your ex make frequent unannounced appearances?" He glanced out the living room window and saw Jeffery pull away.

"Not usually. Most of the time he just manages to call me when I don't want to talk to him."

Alan laughed. "Funny. My ex used to do the same thing. Now she doesn't call at all."

He tucked in his shirt and glanced at his watch. "Hey, I'm starving. Do you have any eggs? I've got to stop in at the hospital then head home. I sure could use a bite to eat. Nothing like some hot sex to ratchet up the appetite," he said with a wry smile.

Falco was relieved to find an unexpired carton containing seven eggs in her refrigerator. "You make the coffee, and I'll whip up these guys," Alan said.

"Sounds like a plan," she said playfully. She came close and put her arm around his waist. "Last night was…"

"Amazing," Alan said, finishing her sentence. He leaned over and kissed her, putting his arm under hers and pulling her into his chest. The whisk fell to the floor, sending tiny streams of egg with it. "Oops. My mother would say, 'Cook or get out of the kitchen!'" Alan chuckled. He eyed her affectionately, picked up the whisk, and gave it a rinse under the faucet.

They sat at the dining room table and ate the eggs and drank coffee.

"Have you made any progress with Andie?" Falco asked.

Alan cocked his head to one side. "We tried to get her to talk about the drawings yesterday, but it's going to be slow going." He took a bite of toast and looked off thoughtfully. "She recognizes the work as hers, so that's a good start. She's got other issues too, some of which we've been working on way before all this happened—unresolved stuff."

"Besides McCaffery?" she asked. She heard Sam and Riley outside.

"Her dad committed suicide. He shot himself in the head with a shotgun when Andie was in her twenties."

"What?" she said, putting her fork down.

"Yeah, so Andie has had an aversion to guns from way back." He took a sip of coffee. "Do you know anything about her? Did she ever talk to you about her family?"

Falco thought for a moment. "I don't know much about her really, other than what you and Michael have told me."

Alan put his fork down and wiped his mouth. "Andie was the only child of a wealthy steel mill family. Her grandparents owned the land on which most of the steel mills in the area were built. After the steel industry waned during the late seventies and eighties, the family sold the land and her dad invested the money in oil and the computer industry—Microsoft and Apple, specifically. He was also a successful attorney, civil cases mostly. Her mom was a socialite and a free spirit, liberal and heavily involved in politics and environmental causes."

"So Andie is originally from around here? Falco asked.

"Yes, north side, Rogers Park," Alan said chewing his toast. "Andie went to the best schools, traveled Europe, and adopted the same liberal viewpoints as her mother. She and her mom were close. Then, when Andie was in high school, her mother caught her father in bed with a colleague and promptly threw him out of the house and filed for divorce. Her mom took him to the cleaners. She got the house and made sure she and Andie were set financially. Andie and her dad never really got along. That relationship grew more distant when she came out as a lesbian. After the stock market crash of 1987, Andie's father lost a huge amount of money. Despite efforts to recoup his losses, he became despondent. He tried to reconcile with his wife, but she would have no part of it. About a year later, on Christmas Eve 1988, he put a shotgun to his head. Andie had just arrived at her dad's place from grad school when someone heard the shots from a back bedroom. Andie found him dead."

"My god," Falco said, shaking her head.

"Andie and I have never spoken about her father's death," Alan said. "I found out about it from an acquaintance who knew Andie's father. She knows I know about it, but she's never wanted to talk about it."

"Where's Andie's mother now?"

"Somewhere in California. She's had some health problems and is living in a nursing home."

"Does Andie keep in contact with her?"

"Not much anymore. After her mother started losing her memory, Andie couldn't take seeing her mother so dependent. She didn't recognize Andie, so she stopped going to visit. She told me the last time she visited she ended up in Napa, got drunk, and almost drove her car off a cliff. I guess that was it for Andie and California."

CHAPTER 134

Monday was rainy as winter approached. It was October thirtieth, the day before Halloween. Falco made plans to take Sam trick-or-treating the next day with Jeffery. *This might be a bit uncomfortable*, she thought as she drove east to work. "Fuck him," she said out loud. "Who I fuck is my fucking business." Falco smiled at her poetic profanity.

She found her usual parking spot at the twenty-third district and quickly walked in through the back door. The heat was on in the building; it smelled familiar and comforting. She was greeted by smiling faces and waves. "Hey, Detective," said Tim Strickland as he headed past her down the stairs. Falco smiled. She wondered whether Tim knew what she had discussed with Michael and Alan on Wednesday. She shook the thought off; she was sure Michael would keep her confidence.

She approached her desk and her heart sank. "What the fuck?" she whispered. Stacks of files and paperwork were piled high on her desk, almost covering the entire surface. She dragged her coat off and draped it over her chair, not taking her eyes off the mounds of paper and overstuffed file folders. She couldn't imagine what all this stuff could be. A new case perhaps? Something really pressing? Suddenly she felt everyone stare at her as a scowl came to her face.

She looked up and glanced around as laughter rumbled around the room. Suddenly she got it. Falco straightened up as her scowl turned to an annoyed smile. "Okay, okay. Ha ha. I get it already…not funny!" She cast her eyes around the room as everyone laughed.

Bobby Leighton careened by her desk with a huge blueberry muffin and a card signed by everyone. "Welcome back from all of us!"

She smiled broadly. "Thanks, all of you. It's good to be back. Now does someone want to take this stuff *off* my desk?"

Ed Lassiter walked through the rows of cubicles wondering what the laughter was all about. His eyes focused on Falco. He nodded to her as he approached.

"Detective, welcome back," he said, stopping at her desk. He looked around the room then leaned in close. "Why don't you come into my office?"

Falco tried to read his face then got up and followed him. He shut the door and motioned for her to take a seat. He had a manila file folder in front of him. "Pretty lonely over there with Grasky gone and Ballard out of commission," he muttered.

"Yeah, I hope Ballard will be back soon," she said, eyeing Lassiter closely. He had a strange look on his face, one she had trouble reading.

Lassiter took the manila file folder and smacked it against his hand. He walked over to the window and looked out. "You know timing is everything…in sports, in life." He turned to Falco then gave his hand another smack with the folder. He sat down again at his desk and smiled. "You know, I've had this song in my head all morning. I think Barbra Streisand recorded it. It goes, *What are you doing the rest of your life? North and south and east and west of your life?* Do you know it?"

"No, I'm not a big Streisand fan, sir." She gave him a strange look. "Can you tell me what you're talking about? I'm confused."

Lassiter looked at the file and smiled. "The profiler positions came through, and you're on the list, Detective."

Falco's heart skipped a beat. She had forgotten about her application. It had been months since she had applied, and rumors had swirled about funding and union issues with the program's implementation. She had assumed the whole thing was on the back burner.

"You're kidding," Falco managed to say, rattled by the news.

"I kid you not. Just found out on Friday, wasn't going to mention it at the retirement party."

"When then? What's next?"

"Well, you know how the city works. Things are slow usually. But with this promotion, and I use that word very loosely…"

Falco gave Lassiter a confused look. "It's not a promotion?"

"Let's just put it this way, Detective. There's good news and bad news. The good news is you're going to attend a highly competitive and rigorous training program sponsored by the federal government and Office of Homeland Security. The bad news is the profiler positions will only be part time at best for now and utilized on an as-needed basis. That was a cost-cutting decision made by the powers that be. However, we do expect the positions will eventually become full time. Each team member will be placed in one of four quadrants around the city. Most likely you'll remain here at the twenty-third after training. Now, that could all change quickly if we were to be under threat of a terrorist attack or something like that."

"I see."

"Now for the other bit of bad news, Detective."

"More bad news?" she asked, biting her lip.

"Training begins next Monday, November sixth, in Quantico, Virginia. It'll be a total of eight weeks with two breaks in between, one for the week of

Christmas and New Year's. You'll need to talk with Lynn downstairs about arranging for airfare and the like."

"Wait a minute, sir," Falco, said not believing her ears. "You mean I have to be in Virginia on Monday, one week from today?"

"Quantico, Virginia, yes. That's where the training is. You're familiar with the FBI's training?"

"Yes, sir. I'm familiar with it. I mean, I know all about it." Falco's head was spinning. *This whole thing came out of the blue*, she thought. She had things to arrange. She had to tell Jeffery, Sam…Alan.

"Look, Falco. You were chosen for one of the positions. Three people are waiting in the wings if you decide it's not—"

"No, no, sir. That's not it. I want to do it, absolutely, yes. It's just…well…"

"Falco, this is a good time for you. You're between cases, you don't have a partner, and by the time you're done with the training, Ballard will be back."

She looked down. "Jesus, I can't believe this all came through. This came out of nowhere."

"Yes, I know, and I understand how you're feeling, but that's how the city works. The funding came through just before the calendar year was up and the department got the go ahead. So, Falco, are you in?"

"I'm definitely in," she said, suddenly excited. *This is it*, she thought.

Lassiter handed her the official letter, signed by Superintendent Cline and the mayor. He placed the rest of the documents on a nearby table and pulled out a blue ballpoint pen. "Paperwork," he said, motioning for Falco to take a seat. After twenty minutes she had completed the forms and added her signature to each. Lassiter called the superintendent's office to let them know Falco was on board.

She walked back to her desk feeling lightheaded. Behind her she heard Ed Lassiter's voice. "People, I'd like to make an announcement."

* * *

"Nice going, girl! You're gonna love the training!" Brenda Salerno said from her cell phone. "I don't know if it's anything like the training I had, but you can bet your tits you're gonna be fried. But hey, there are some really great bars south of town. I suggest you check them out before you get in too deep. You're gonna thank me for that one, lady!"

Despite what Brenda had said, Falco was walking on air. She was booked on a flight for Richmond for Sunday morning. She headed home with a long of list of things she needed to accomplish. She needed to pack for four weeks.

* * *

Jeffery left a message on Falco's voicemail. "Hey, I hope we're still on for tomorrow tonight."

"Of course we are," she said to the recording. She went to the closet and pulled out an old hat box and carefully unwrapped her father's police hat and holster. She eyed it lovingly, wondering whether her father would mind Sam wearing it for Halloween. "He'll be careful," she said to the hat, "and I'll be there." She studied the tiny marks and scratches on its brim and the hat-band that was yellowed with age and sweat. "I hope you're proud of me, Dad. I got the profiler gig. It's a big deal. I hope it's a good move. I hope I get through the training." Suddenly she was filled with self-doubt. "I just have to do my best…that's all."

Falco wondered whether she should call Jeffery and tell him the news now or wait until tomorrow to tell him in person. He'd be less likely to look pissed and complain about her being gone for eight weeks with Sam around. She knew Sam would be excited for her; Jeffery was another story. *It's a decent raise*, she thought. *You can't argue with ten percent.*

CHAPTER 135

The ninth floor of the hospital was strangely quiet. The solemn chime of the elevators interrupted the hushed tones of voices. Michael and Alan walked quickly down the dull corridor to Andie's room. Michael carried a carefully selected bundle of Andie's drawings. Their strategy was to gently show them to Andie, one by one, starting with the milder ones then move to the more disturbing drawings.

"Andie's on the brink of something based on the drawings themselves," Alan said earlier that day. "Hopefully she'll want to talk about them."

Andie sat on the tile floor, drawing on a large piece of newsprint. She recoiled upon seeing the two men as they entered. Michael and Alan sat on the bed and placed the drawings on the floor. Andie glared at them from across the room.

* * *

"This hat almost fits your head, Sam. I can't believe it," Falco said with a laugh. "I guess big heads run in the family."

"He just needs a good haircut," Jeffery said.

Falco tightened her father's belt around Sam's waist and adjusted the holster. "Okay, where's your weapon?" she said, giving him a serious look. Jeffery handed the plastic-green squirt gun to Sam.

"That's a mighty big gun, Sam. Who are you, Dirty Harry or someone?" Falco joked as she slid it into the holster and snapped it in.

"It's a three fifty-seven, Mom, and I'm Horatio Caine from *CSI*."

"A three fifty-seven. That gun's got a heck of a kick. I hope you can handle it," she said, playing along.

"Let's hope you never have to use it," Jeffery muttered

"Oh, we're just kidding around, Jeff," Falco said, looking up at him suddenly annoyed.

Sam straightened his hat and pulled his necktie tight around his collar then ran to a mirror to check out the final result. "Cool! I look like a real cop!"

Falco smiled, hearing him from the other room. "Don't forget your flashlight! You can hook it on your belt, but you're probably going to need it to see."

Jeffery seemed annoyed and distracted. "He's got a trick-or-treat bag here somewhere," he said as he shuffled through a stack of newspapers on the kitchen table.

Falco sighed and felt a surge of anxiety. She knew Jeffery was still dealing with Alan's presence at her house the other morning. She also knew he wouldn't take the news of her promotion and the eight weeks of training very well either. She watched him look for the trick-or-treat bag as the doorbell rang.

"It's probably Kareem. Sam, get the door!" Jeffery yelled. A thunder of heavy footsteps followed as Sam ran to let his friend in.

"Jeff, I have something to tell you," Falco said cautiously.

He looked over from the other side of the kitchen and came over to her. "Does it have anything to do with that…doctor?"

"No, nothing to do with Alan," she said flatly. "I, um, well, I just found out I got the promotion I applied for last summer, one of the profiler positions."

"Congratulations," Jeffery said.

"I was one of only four selected out of a hundred and thirty-seven applicants. I'm the only female."

"Well, you must be really excited," he said blandly.

"I am. The trouble is, the training starts Monday. I'm on a flight to Richmond, Virginia, Sunday morning. The FBI Academy is in Quantico. I'll be gone for eight weeks, but they'll be two breaks in between."

"Eight weeks? You're going to be gone eight fucking weeks?" His face suddenly teetered on beet red.

"There's a break after the first four weeks. I'll be home for the weekend of December second. Then we have a weeklong break for the holidays starting on December twenty-second. I'll have to be back on January third."

"Well, it'll be nice for you to grace us with your presence for Christmas, M!" he said sarcastically.

She was surprised at his response. "I know this comes out of the blue. It did for me, but I accepted the promotion, and I have to be there for the training. There's no way around it."

Jeffery slammed his hand on the kitchen table, making Falco jump. "What the fuck do you want *me* to do about it? I guess you won't be around for the holidays, for Sam's Christmas concert, *or* for the entire Christmas season. But

I suppose you didn't think of that when you accepted the promotion, did you?"

"I told you we take a break for Christmas," she said, glaring at him.

"Great! Sam and I will look forward to seeing you then. Maybe you can leave a recent photo of yourself before you leave so Sam doesn't forget what you look like."

"Oh, that is so fucking childish," she snapped.

"Listen, did it ever occur to you to check with me about all this? That maybe *I* have something planned, like maybe a vacation to the fucking Poconos or something?" Jeffery glared at her, not waiting for an answer. "Of course not!"

"*Are* you going on vacation somewhere?" she asked weakly.

"Well, I hoped the three of us might go somewhere, you know, for the holidays. Geneva, Wisconsin, I don't know. I thought maybe Sam would like to try skiing."

"I'm sorry, Jeff, but I have to do this. We can go in January or February. The snow's usually better—"

"Whatever." Jeffery left the kitchen and went to the closet to get his coat. "Are you coming?" he asked, storming back into the kitchen.

Falco tried again. "Listen, you're the one who said not more than two weeks ago that I should quit my job or find something in the department that wasn't so dangerous. Well, here it is and you're still giving me shit."

"It's always the job with you, Monica, always. How come we never argue about my job, huh?" he asked as he walked away and buttoned his coat. "You guys ready to go?" he yelled to Kareem and Sam.

She followed Jeffery and grabbed his arm, pulling him back into the kitchen. "I know this leaves you with Sam for all those weekends. I mean, if you did have something planned, my mother—"

"Your mother? I just spoke to your mother the other day. She hasn't heard from you since the wedding. That was two weeks ago. Now you think I can just bail you out and dump Sam off at Elaine's? Yeah, right."

"Okay, you're right. I just… Look, Jeff…" She was flustered. Jeffery had her exactly where he wanted her, and after the uncomfortable scenario with Alan over the weekend, she was coming across as very irresponsible. She stood squarely and looked at the floor, her arms crossed. Quietly she said, "Jeff, I need to do this…*please.*"

Jeffery walked out of the kitchen and followed the boys out the door.

* * *

Michael left Andie's room, leaving Alan with the drawings. Alan watched Andie as he carefully placed one of the pieces of paper in front of her and slid it close to her on the floor. "Andie, I want you to look closely at this drawing. Do you know who drew this?"

Andie gritted her teeth then cast her eyes upon the images. Violent streaks of green, yellow, and red erupted out of a large, heavily outlined triangle. She shrunk away from it momentarily then looked at it again. "Do you know who drew this?" Alan tried again.

"I did," Andie said quietly, twitching.

"Can you tell me what this drawing is all about? Maybe tell me about the colors?"

She scowled as her breathing grew faster. "No," came a tiny breathless voice.

"Can you tell me about the colors?" he asked, quietly watching her. Andie paused then looked away. Alan saw she was having a hard time looking at the drawing. He asked her again with his eyes as he bent lower to look in her face.

"They are poison," Andie said.

"Poison? The colors are poison? Why are the colors green, red, and yellow poison?"

"They…just are."

"Can you tell me about the triangle?"

Andie recoiled and shrunk back. "No."

Alan took another drawing and placed it before her. "How about this one. Do you know who drew this?"

"It's me. It's *me*!" Andie said, slamming her hands on the floor.

"Okay, okay. Calm down," Alan said, troubled by her impatience. "Can you tell me about this one?"

She turned her head and looked carefully at the images of dark clouds, violent X marks, and bloody hands. A dark fury seemed to rise inside her. She jumped to her feet and ran to the opposite wall. "Let me go! Let me go!" She slid to the floor and covered her head as her neck and shoulder jerked violently. "Please…*please*!" she screamed.

Alan turned the drawing facedown and came over to her. Andie jumped to her feet again and pushed past him, nearly knocking him down. She ran for the door and yanked the handle with all her strength. "Let me go! Don't… Don't hurt me!"

Alan pulled her away from the door, spun her around, and set her on the bed. She gasped as tears ran down her face. She rolled off the bed and took a swing at him, narrowly missing his chin. He jerked back and tried to grab her arms, but she twisted away, snatching up the two drawings and wrapping her arms tightly around them. "No!" she shouted, holding the papers close to her chest.

Alan sank back and watched her. "Andie, Brian McCaffery isn't in this room. He isn't anywhere in this room. You're safe here."

Andie shook her head in disbelief. "He's here. He's here."

Alan cautiously gathered the stack of papers from the floor and left the room.

* * *

Kat looked out the window of her condo, watching the traffic inch south on Lake Shore Drive. She nervously tapped her pen on the windowsill as she waited for her lawyer to call. "This is fucking ridiculous," she snipped, turning away from the window and pacing the room. She headed to her desk and picked up the phone.

"Schulman, Greenberg, and Robbins," came the voice on the other end.

"Simon Schulman, please."

"Mr. Schulman is on another call. May I take a message?"

"This is Katherine Cohen. Please tell Simon to call me. I've been waiting most of the day," she said tersely.

"Ms. Cohen, Mr. Schulman will be leaving shortly after four today, but I'll give him the message that you called."

"Give him the message that I called? Listen, I want to speak to Simon *before* he leaves today. I don't care if he's leaving at fucking four. You tell him to call me." Kat slammed the phone down. "I pay you enough. You damn well better be at my fucking beck and call!"

CHAPTER 136

Falco wiggled the mouse as her computer came to life. *Let's see*, she thought. *Weather for Richmond, Virginia. Oh, great. Cold and rainy, highs in the upper thirties.* Her face contorted. *Good thing I unpacked my winter stuff.* Despite the buzz of her promotion, she was fighting a dark mood. Jeffery had contributed to 90 percent of it; the other 10 percent came from the weather forecast and the dull feeling of being overwhelmed with arrangements and other things she needed to do before she left. She smiled as she thought of Sam the other night dressed as a cop. *That really got under Jeffery's skin*, she mused. *Sam was so happy for me. Maybe I could get him some kind of T-shirt or something and send it to him. He's the only one who understands me.*

* * *

"This is bullshit, Simon. You mean we're just going to roll over and play dead? What the fuck am I paying you for?" Kat yelled. "I want that guardianship challenged, and I want Andie out of that hospital. What? You've exhausted all avenues? Then you try something else. Yes, you know what I mean. I want you to start on the malpractice suit. I want to see preliminary paperwork by Friday. You got that Simon? No! I don't fucking care if you're going away with the wifey-poo. I want progress by the end of the week. And find out about Andie's drawings. Nobody has gotten back to me on those either."

Kat didn't wait for an answer as she hung up the phone.

* * *

The rest of the week was a blur to Falco; she had so much to pull together. She wished she had more time to prepare and make arrangements. Her suitcase was as full as it was going to get. She dreaded heaving it off the bed as she zipped it up. She sat on her bed for a moment and stared at the wall, then she heard a car horn blare out front. *Time to go*, she thought. She dragged the suitcase from the bed; it thumped loudly to the floor. She slid her coat on and wrapped her scarf around her neck then dragged the suitcase behind her and out the door. Just then the phone rang. She waved to the taxi driver to wait a minute as she rushed back inside to answer the phone. The caller ID flashed Jeffery's number. She let it ring and went out the door.

"Fuck him," she muttered. "He's probably offering to give me a ride to the airport. No way. I can get there myself. I don't need his long face or a lecture just as I'm leaving." The taxi driver heaved her suitcase into the trunk as she slid into the backseat. "Should have brought an umbrella," she mumbled, watching her house as the taxi pulled away.

The flight was delayed because of the rain. Falco was feeling nervous. She fidgeted with a paperback book she'd brought along then stashed it in her purse. After an hour the announcement that the United Airlines flight to Richmond, Virginia, with a stop in Indianapolis would soon be boarding. She got up and draped her coat over the handle of her suitcase and focused her eyes on the boarding gate. Her legs felt stiff and achy. *Must be the dampness*, she thought.

The coffee was weak as she watched the surface of the liquid flow to the left as the plane glided toward Indianapolis. She took a sip and thought of Michael that evening at the hospital. "How can you drink that swill?" She didn't get a chance to talk with Michael or Alan over the last few days. She hoped they'd understand she was under a major time crunch. She wished she could have said goodbye to Alan. She wondered about Andie.

Before long, Indianapolis came into view. The plane rumbled onto the runway. Its high-pitched brakes and rattling touchdown gave Falco an instant headache. After what seemed like forever, passengers from Indianapolis boarded as the hint of jet fuel and exhaust floated into the cabin. A stocky man with tiny wire glasses, a white shirt, and a blue jacket jammed the corner of his suitcase into Falco's seat. "Sorry," came the voice now behind her. It sounded hoarse but squeaky and more like a woman's voice.

The snap and shuffle of people and suitcases continued as a baby cried mercilessly near the back of the plane. Falco rubbed her forehead. *I hope that kid doesn't keep it up for the whole flight.* She recalled a flight to Miami with Jeffery almost two years ago. A rude kid had made it his mission to kick the back of her seat for the entire flight. She was ready to kill him by the time they disembarked.

Before long the plane was back in the air, and Falco was sipping a glass of white wine. *It's nearly noon Chicago time*, she thought, and *I'm getting drunk.* She looked out at the clouds; they appeared heavy and gray. The baby screamed again as the mother desperately tried to calm it. Falco heard rustling in the back. The mother with the baby was trying to make her way to the back restroom. Cursing ensued from the back of the plane. The stocky man with the white shirt who had rammed her seat earlier strutted past her toward the front restroom. To Falco's surprise the cursing had come from him; he was pissed that there was a noisy wait for the restroom. The man smelled of a mixture of cigarettes and something spicy and sweet. Falco took a long sip of the wine just as the baby let out a piercing wail. "Oh, Jesus," she said under her breath.

The wine made her sleepy. Her eyes drifted closed as her book tumbled out of her hand. She awoke with a start and looked out the window to what appeared to be a city emerging from the clouds. *Maybe we're going to land,* she thought as her heart jumped. Just then a voice came from the speakers. It was the pilot thanking the passengers for flying United Airlines and telling the flight attendants and crew to prepare for landing. "Welcome to Richmond. The current temperature is thirty-four degrees with fog and rain."

Falco sat up in her seat and stared out the window. "God, I hope I don't have to wait long for my suitcase," she whispered as the plane taxied slowly toward the gate. A mixture of excitement and fear filled her as the passengers unclipped their seatbelts and riffled for their belongings. *It's still pretty green here for November*, she thought as she looked out the window and across the runway.

Crowds drifted around the baggage claim area waiting for the release of luggage and cargo. Falco was feeling impatient and craved a cigarette. The man with the white shirt quickly found his suitcase and lifted it effortlessly from the carousel then strutted off. Falco looked after him enviously. "How does he rate?" she said under her breath.

* * *

Monday morning, day one of her training, came quickly as she found her way to a squat limestone building and up the surrounding steps. A man dressed in some kind of military-looking uniformed read Falco's face and pointed her in the direction of the Investigative Training Unit wing of the building. The large auditorium buzzed with people. "Jeez, I thought I was early," she said to herself as she scanned the room.

Finding a seat near the center, she put her purse down and took in the space and the people milling about. A thick manila folder and pen were set on each chair, numbering more than sixty-five places. For a moment Falco wondered whether she was in the right room. She looked over the day's itinerary and assured herself she was in the right place. Sixty-five people were more than she had expected for the training.

The rest of the day was a blur. More than twice, the participants were congratulated for being chosen for the training program, which was underwritten by the Office of Homeland Security, the Department of Justice, the FBI, and each attendee's local law enforcement department. Falco scanned the crowd, making eye contact with only two other females.

CHAPTER 137

Andie studied the two drawings she had taken from Alan the other day. Something was rising deep inside her. She placed the drawings on the floor and smoothed out the wrinkles. Her hands were shaking, her body sweating. Slowly her vision began to blur, as if she were losing consciousness. She felt someone's hot breath against the back of her neck. She got up suddenly and spun around, looking for the source of the heat, but found no one. A great pain ran through her as she buckled and fell to the floor. She pressed her cheek against the hard tile surface; it felt cool against her skin. The pain returned like a hot steel rod deep inside her. She cried out, holding her stomach, then vomited a stringy yellow liquid.

Swallowing hard and pressing her hand against the floor as if to will away the nausea, she saw the pool of vomit change from yellow to green. She studied it as it turned to red. Was she bleeding from the mouth? Had she vomited blood? The pain persisted, weakening her until she fell over on the floor. Grimacing as the jolts rocked her body, she gathered herself into a ball.

* * *

Falco wandered around the Academy grounds wondering whether after eight weeks she might call it home. She worried about her house, whether her neighbor would watch it as closely as she had said. She hoped the timers would go off as she had set them. She wondered whether Sam would miss her, whether Jeffery would rake the leaves and collect the mail.

A brisk wind came out of nowhere, pulling her coat open. Falco took it as a sign that she should head back to her hotel suite and get something to eat for dinner. Suddenly she felt terribly alone. All the things she took for granted about being home beckoned her: her kitchen, the sound of the El train, traffic on Devon Avenue, her car, her desk at work. *Come on, girl,* she coaxed herself. *It's just the first day. Treat this like an adventure, a really cool adventure!*

She slid the plastic electronic key into the slot of the door and pulled the lever. The handle didn't budge. She looked closely at the plastic key and tried again. "Fuck," she whispered. She slid the key in again and looked for the little row of green lights to blink. Nothing. She held the plastic card up to the light then tried again. "Fuck!" she whispered and stared at the card.

"Hey, need some help there?" came a voice from the other side of the ice machine.

Falco looked around then craned her neck to see who was talking. To her surprise it was the stocky man from the plane, the one who had banged his suitcase into her seat, the one who had cursed the crying baby and the long wait for the restroom. The man came over. He seemed shorter than before. Falco eyed him and suddenly realized the stocky man was actually a stocky woman.

"Let me try that," she said, smiling broadly. "You've got to rub the contacts, the magnetic strips. They're probably dirty. She rubbed the card on her knobby corduroy pants then inserted the card into the slot, immediately setting off the row of green lights. She jiggled the handle, and the door opened with a swish. "Voilà!" she said, making a swishing motion with her hand. Falco gave the woman an amazed look for her practical genius and for the fact that she had mistaken this woman for a man not once but three times!

"Hey, weren't you on the flight with me? The United Airlines flight?" the woman asked.

"With the screaming kid?" Falco said, not wanting the woman to know she had noticed her.

"Yeah. Jesus H. Christ! I'm glad I've got dogs and not kids." She laughed, getting out of the way of the door, then handed Falco her key card. "I'm Christine Sommers, but most folks call me Chris. I take it you're here for the profiler training?"

"Yes. I'm Monica Falco," she said. "Thanks for the help with the door." She slid past the woman and pulled off her coat. The woman stepped back, taking the hint that she wanted to be alone.

"Hey, maybe I'll see you tomorrow, okay?" Chris said in a gruff voice.

"Okay, yeah. See you then."

Falco shut the door quietly and looked for a phone book. "I could use a drink," she said to herself, "and some food." She ordered a pepperoni pizza, then scooted out of her room, down the elevator, and into the bar. It was dark, smoky, and filled with noisy men. She ordered a glass of red wine and tipped the bartender heavily. She left with the glass and headed back to her room. *I've got to find a liquor store somewhere*, she thought as she sipped the wine and watched the elevator's lights.

The elevator doors opened. She walked past the ice machine and past Chris's room. The TV was blaring, and she smelled cigarettes.

* * *

It was nearly six a.m., and Falco woke before her alarm buzzed. She decided to head out early and scope out a grocery and liquor store. She showered and dressed quickly. She gathered her books and folders and shoved them into her canvas briefcase, pulled her coat on, and headed out the door. The morning was crisp as a musty wind blew open her coat. She walked past an Enterprise Rent-A-Car office and pondered renting a car. *No, the walking will be good for me, and this is temporary*, she reminded herself.

She walked into a trendy grocery store and smelled freshly ground coffee; it reminded her of Michael. It reminded her of Andie. She bought two granola bars and ate part of one as she made her way to the Investigative Training Unit building.

Folks milled about in the room as Falco found a seat off to the side and stuck the half-eaten granola bar in her coat pocket. "Mind if I join you?" came a woman's voice, raspy from cigarettes. Falco looked up. It was Chris.

"Uh, hi, Chris. Good morning," Falco said, moving her coat to the other chair.

"You were out the door early!" Chris said, almost getting in Falco's space.

"Well, I needed to check out the area, get a sense of where things are, you know?"

"Stick with me, kid. I know this area like the back of my hand," Chris said with a smile. "I've got family here, folks I've known for years. I used to come here almost every spring. Spring is amazing here, by the way."

"I just need a good grocery store for staples and such, since we've got a microwave, sink, and all that in our rooms."

Chris nodded. "There are a few grocery stores within walking distance," she said as another attendee squeezed between them to take a seat next to Falco, "and there are some good restaurants, cheap and expensive, also nearby. If you're one for having a drink or two, there are some great bars on the south side of town, but you'll need to take the bus or cab it from here." Falco nodded as the crowd in the auditorium quieted.

The group split up into two areas of specialty—one group concentrating on forensic evidence and the other on behavioral science. Falco smiled as Chris gathered her things and joined the forensics group. She flipped through her textbook as the instructor went to the podium and introduced himself.

CHAPTER 138

With two weeks of training under her belt, Falco felt she was getting to know the Quantico/Richmond area. She had developed a routine, which included an evening walk and a healthy dinner. Sam called her most evenings, talking mostly about school. He also let her know that Jeffery had checked on the house. Falco and Alan continued to play phone tag, which was fine with her at this point. She didn't need the distraction of a relationship during the next few weeks.

The behavioral science course was grueling. Falco was reading an average of seventy-five to a hundred pages a night and reviewing her notes after each six-hour class. The information was riveting; she hoped her other classes would be as good.

Friday night was rainy. She was fussing about the test she had taken earlier in the day. *I'm not good at tests*, she thought as she looked inside her mini refrigerator. Her mind went a mile a minute as she reviewed each question and the answer she had chosen. "I knew the stuff," she said with a scowl. Self-doubt filled her. She changed her clothes and drifted downstairs to the bar; it was six forty-five.

The bar was filled with loud voices and oldies music. Falco recognized most of the faces in the crowd as fellow law enforcement taking part in the training. Someone got up from a barstool and mimed what looked like a fistfight. The group of men watching laughed loudly as the person got back on the stool and slammed a fist to the bar. Falco quietly avoided the raucous group when suddenly she heard someone call her name. It was Chris at the bar, asking her to join them. Falco stopped and smiled, catching her eye, then walked over.

"Hey, you missed my best story!" Chris said as she punched the air with her fist.

"Sorry. I'm just here for a glass of wine," Falco said. "I'm a little tired."

"Yeah, we're all fried here."

The men around her chimed in and made room for Falco. A tall man with reddish hair slid off his stool and guided her to sit.

"No, no thanks," she said. "I'm not going to stay."

"What do ya mean, not gonna stay? Get this girl a drink!" Chris said, sliding a ten spot to the bartender. Falco smiled and ordered a red wine as Chris lit up a cigarette. Some of the men meandered to a pool table as the crowd around her thinned.

"You play pool?" Chris asked.

"No."

"Darts?"

"Noooo."

"Softball?"

Falco shook her head.

"How about golf? You must play golf!" Chris said, taking a drag from her cigarette.

"Nope, no golf either."

"Okay, I thought I hit it with golf. You look like the cerebral type!" Chris laughed. "So what do you do to have fun, you know, blow off steam?" she asked, tilting her head.

Falco thought for a moment then looked at her glass of wine. "I guess I drink and maybe go to the shooting range but not at the same time."

"Ha! I like that! But you look kind of sporty. I figured you were into—"

"Sporty?" Falco said with a laugh. She felt a little uncomfortable, and she couldn't figure out why. It was obvious Chris was a lesbian. *Wouldn't you know she'd gravitate to me?* she thought.

"Where are you from, Monica?" Chris asked, blowing a cloud of smoke then swishing it away from Falco's face. "Chicago?"

"As a matter of fact, I'm with the Chicago Police Department. I'm a detective."

"I knew it. The Chicago part, that is. It's your accent."

"Accent?" Falco frowned. "I hardly think I have an accent," she said dryly.

"Sure ya do. I can place almost anyone anywhere in the country just by how they say certain words. I'm from Chicago too, from the South Side. Now that's a whole different accent," she laughed. "I live in Indy now. I'm with the police department there, mostly homicide."

"How'd you end up in Indianapolis?" Falco asked, taking a sip of the wine.

"My dad died, and my mom moved there to live with her sister. I visited her a few times then met my partner, Jenny. She convinced me to apply to the police force there, and the rest is history. Been in Indy five years now."

"And before that?"

"I was in law school for a while at Northwestern. Then a friend of mine convinced me I was wasting my time. She was a cop with the Evanston Police Department and persuaded me to apply. I got hired and spent five years there before moving to Indy." Chris noticed a tiny scowl on Falco's face. "Hey, you got a beef with EPD?"

Startled by Chris's keen observation, Falco gave her a piercing look. "No, not really."

Chris held her gaze. "Okay," she laughed. "Just checkin.'"

CHAPTER 139

When Andie awoke, the room was filled with darkness. The pain had subsided. She ran her hand over the floor in front of her as she looked for the pool of blood; it was gone too. The drawings were where she had placed them, their wrinkles smoothed by her own hands. She sat up on the floor, listening and watching. She pulled the drawings close and studied them. Each had a predominant color: green, yellow, or red. She frowned as she eyed them. Had she hallucinated the vomit on the floor? Was the pain not real either? She rubbed her head and paced the room, then found the box of crayons and dumped them all on the floor.

* * *

Alan sat at his desk and stared a brief e-mail from Falco.

Alan, I'll be out of town for a training, but I'll have a break in a week. I'll tell you more when I see you, or I'll try you on your cell phone.

—Monica

He counted the days to her return but had little to report about Andie. Progress was slow, hampered further by Kat's legal wrangling over Andie's hospitalization and the drawings. Kat was persistent, but so were the hospital's lawyers; they weren't about to get pushed around.

I just wish we were at the point where we could confront Andie with the shooting, Alan thought. *The drawings all point to it as the culmination of the disastrous chain of events, but she's not ready to talk about it.* He looked thoughtful and tapped his pencil impatiently.

A knock came at the door. It was Michael. "Alan, I think you'd better come see this."

Alan gave him a curious look then got up and followed him down the hallway, to the elevators, up three flights, and into Andie's room.

As they entered the room, Alan saw a massive amorphic shape drawn on the floor. Streaks and squiggles and images both discernible and indiscernible of blue, green, black, orange yellow, and red filled every tile, every inch of the floor. Andie didn't pick up her head or stop drawing as the two men entered. They stopped short, wondering whether it was okay to step on the huge work in progress.

Michael called Andie's name but got no response. Alan scanned the markings as he walked slowly toward her. The enormous drawing was extraordinarily intricate, violent yet delicate; none of its lines intersected. At first glance it looked like a meshwork of veins or the ringlets of a huge vine. Interspersed were geometric shapes that contained the same sort of violent images Andie had drawn on the newsprint.

Huddled in the far end of the room, Andie had virtually drawn herself into a corner. Alan heard the faint hum of some melody coming from her. He eyed Michael strangely from across the room as he cautiously approached and squatted near her. He called her name gently, but she didn't respond. Alan touched her arm and called her name again. The crayon froze in her fingers mid stroke. She turned and looked at him, squinting, recognizing Alan and then Michael. Her head ticked to the right.

"I don't like people coming into my studio…unannounced," she whispered. Her eyes flashed at them then back to the floor. Alan said nothing, backing up and giving her space. She whispered as she began to draw again. "You can wait by the door until I'm through," she said quietly.

Andie spoke very little during the hour it took her to finish the drawing on the floor. When she did speak she mumbled about color theory and trompe-l'oeil painting.

Alan and Michael left Andie's room. They walked silently toward the elevators as if under a spell. Finally, in the elevator, Alan broke the silence. "I'm not sure if I should be saying this, but I remember saying to Kat that you just can't turn mental illness on and off like a light switch."

A smile came to Michael's face as he watched the lighted numbers of the elevator. "I was thinking the same thing," he said, "but I didn't want to jinx it."

The two quickly went into Alan's office and reviewed Andie's session. Michael noticed a fine tremor in Alan's hands as he opened the locked credenza and set the stack of drawings on his desk. "This is how I think we should proceed," he said.

CHAPTER 140

The third week of training flew by. Phase I of Falco's coursework in the Behavioral Science Unit had ended, and Phase II was set to begin at the National Center for the Analysis of Violent Crime (NCAVC). Falco studied the handout as she thought about the next three weeks. The unit covered an organized path: assessment and state of mind of the offender, criminality of the offender, geography of the offender, predicted behavior of the offender, and interview strategies and threat assessment. Her textbook was almost three inches thick. She flipped it open, put on her glasses, and started to read. Just then a loud knock came to her door.

"Monica Falco! I know you're in there! Come on. Open up! It's the police!"

Startled by the knocking but recognizing Chris's raspy voice, she smiled, walked across the room, and opened the door.

Chris looked at Falco with her book in hand and rolled her eyes. "What the hell are you doing? Tomorrow's our break. We're both on a flight home in the morning. It's time to *party*, girl! We've got a long weekend ahead of us!"

Falco smiled. Chris was already two sheets to the wind. "Come on. Get yer coat on. We're going to my favorite bar, and I'm buyin'!" Chris said, pushing past her and finding Falco's coat. "Put the book *down*," she said deliberately. "You can read it on the airplane tomorrow."

Smiling and playing along, Falco let Chris put her coat on and tie her scarf neatly around her neck. "Where are we going?" she finally asked as they were suddenly outside in the cold.

Chris smiled and waved for a cab. "We're going to one my favorite bars this side of the Appalachian Trail. I hope you're ready to party!" she hooted.

"I'm not about to get wasted, Chris, but it looks like you're on your way."

The cab sped down the street, heading south. Falco wondered what she had gotten herself into. The bar was off the beaten path of south Richmond. It was a greystone painted a hideous pink color. Chris handed a chunky female bouncer a $10 bill and guided Falco into the bar. On the walls were murals of voluptuous women in various stages of undress. The place was smoky and dark.

"Let's find a booth. What are you drinkin', girl?" Chris yelled over the thumping music.

"White wine!" Falco yelled back. She slid into a booth and took off her coat as she looked around. Women were everywhere, playing pool, dancing, and holding hands. *This is a lesbian bar*, she thought with a sigh. *Jesus Christ. She took me to a fucking lesbian bar.* She laughed and shook her head.

"Hey, all they had was tequila, so I had them put it in a wineglass!" Chris said, putting the drink down.

Falco raised her eyebrows and looked at the glass. She smelled white wine and shot Chris an evil look. "Yeah, right! Listen, I'm getting pretty fed up with your antics here," she said, pretending to be mad. Chris gave her a look of alarm, wondering whether she was pushing Falco too hard. She grinned and gave Chris a wry look. "Gotcha, girl!"

Chris laughed loudly and watched Falco check out the women. She downed her drink then looked around and said, "There used to be a bar like this back home…in Chicago, in Uptown. It was the best."

"Yeah? I work in Lakeview at the twenty-third district. Uptown's part of our jurisdiction," Falco said above the noise.

"You ever been to a girl bar?" Chris yelled.

"Never!"

"Then I guess you never made it to Paris," Chris said.

"Paris?" Falco looked at her, confused.

"It was a lesbian bar in Uptown. It looked a lot like this one, the murals especially," she said, glancing about. "Paris was the place to go if you were a dyke looking for some fun or to meet someone…or get lucky. It had a great dance floor, pool tables, great music. I'd go every weekend; stay out all night…on the prowl. There were some beautiful women there. Hooooot!"

Falco smiled. "Did the bar close?"

"Yeah, a fucking developer bought it, knocked the place down, and put up condos. What a fucking tragedy! The funny thing is, we heard later that the developer had a hard time selling the condos 'cause all the views overlooked a cemetery! Ha!"

"Paris was across from a cemetery?" Falco asked, taking a sip of her wine.

"Yeah, on Montrose and…what…Racine, maybe? Oh hell, I can't remember anymore. Don't get me wrong. There were other good bars too. CK's, Big Chicks, Augie's. There'll never be another Paris, though," Chris said sadly, looking up as she lit a cigarette. "I remember there was a sign on the bathroom door, ONLY ONE PERSON IN THE RESTROOM AT A TIME, PLEASE. See, on many occasions two or more gals would end up in there, you know, doing what girls do," she laughed. "So the sign went on the door."

Falco raised her eyebrows and chuckled quietly.

"The bartender… God, what was her name? She'd come stormin' around the bar and pound on the door, screaming above the music. Sometimes she'd pull the door open and find girls half naked gettin' it on! One other time I was at the pool table with a very nice girl—a tiny thing and *real* cute—then *bam!* outta nowhere somebody whacked me on the back of the head with a pool cue. Son of a bitch, that hurt! I almost fell over on the table. I had blood all over the back of my shirt. Well, this gal I was hitting on ended up taking me to the emergency room in her car. What was it…ten stitches in my head? She drove like crazy to the ER and was pale as a ghost seeing all that blood. I told her I was used to it 'cause I was a cop. When I came back into the waiting room, she was nowhere around. The nurse said the girl cut out on me—left me in the ER with a big ol' bandage on my head and no way home!"

"Maybe she didn't like cops," Falco offered.

Chris eyed her and nodded. "I saw her on the street not long after that. She didn't even acknowledge me or ask how my head was."

It was two a.m. by the time Falco shut the door of her room. She chided herself for staying out so late and set her alarm clock for seven. She laid out her clothes for the flight and haphazardly put the rest of her things in her suitcase. She was feeling the wine as her ears buzzed from the loud music. "I can't wait to tell Michael I hung out in a lesbian bar—with a dyke from Indy." She climbed into bed, put her hand over her eyes, and fell asleep.

* * *

Falco waved goodbye as Chris pulled her carryon from the overhead compartment. "See ya Wednesday, Mo," Chris said, her voice rough. Falco settled in for the rest of the flight. Her head ached as she thought of home.

O'Hare Airport was sunk in a thick fog and traffic was moving like molasses. After 45 minutes in a cab, Falco was home. She dragged her suitcase up the steps of her house, put the key in the lock, and pushed the door open. The mail was piled neatly on the coffee table, as was the stack of *Chicago*

Tribunes. I should have cancelled the paper, she thought. Jeffery had been by at least once; the leaves had been raked in the front, and the grass looked like it had been cut too. She felt her heart soften toward him as she picked up the phone to check for messages. She dragged her suitcase into the laundry room and dumped the clothes on the floor. She pulled off her coat; it still smelled smoky from the bar. Falco smiled, thinking of Chris and their night out. She felt somehow that she was leading a double life. She shook off the thought as she threw a load of whites into the washing machine.

* * *

Michael was about ready to jump out of his skin. A combination of Andie's emergence and Kat's tenaciousness had made him a nervous wreck. He paced his bedroom talking to himself as Tim slept peacefully in Michael's bed. He reran the last few days with Andie in his head. *Next week it's do or die*, he thought. *McCaffery and Andie will meet again.*

CHAPTER 141

Falco eased herself into the sofa, glass of wine in hand. She needed to make some phone calls but needed some time for herself first. Just then the phone rang. She sighed and looked at her watch, then picked up the phone and eyed the caller ID. It was Alan.

"Hey," she said warmly.

"You're home. I *missed* you, Monica. I'm sorry we weren't able to connect except by e-mail, so impersonal."

"I know, and I'm sorry I didn't get to tell you about my promotion, although I did try to call."

"I can't believe it's been only three weeks. It seems like six months," he said with a sigh. "Listen, I'd really like to see you. Can I take you to dinner?"

"Well, I have to be back in Richmond on Wednesday at eight a.m. I've got a four o'clock flight on Tuesday. Today's not good, and I have plans to see Sam on Sunday."

"Sounds complicated."

"How about Monday night?" she offered.

Alan thought for a moment, "Hm. Monday night is no good. How about lunch on Monday, near the hospital? Can I meet you?"

"That would be great."

"I have some good news about Andie," he said.

"*Good* news about Andie? Her heart jumped. "Tell me."

"I think we've had a breakthrough. She's talking more and relating to the images in the drawings. We hope we'll be able to talk about McCaffery sometime next week."

"McCaffery? You think she's ready to talk about the shooting?" Falco sat up straight.

"That's what I'm hoping," Alan said. "I'll see you around one. How about the Corner Bakery Café on Saint Clair?"

* * *

Falco spent Sunday with Jeffery and Sam. They went out to dinner and saw a movie. Jeffery still acted like a hurt puppy; she did her best to ignore him. "Thanks for taking care of the house and doing the outdoor stuff," she said to him over dinner.

He frowned. "You didn't notice. I fixed your door too." She looked away, trying to remember something about the door. "It was sticking all last summer, honey. I took it off the hinges and planed it," Jeffery said as his shoulders hunched.

"Thanks, yeah. It *was* sticking." She glanced at Sam as he snuck a smile at her.

At lunch with Alan the next day, she talked at length about her behavioral science coursework at the FBI Academy. Alan was intrigued at the depth of the material and how she would use it as a profiler for the police department. "Of course a lot of this stuff is geared toward terrorism," Falco said, "but it can also be applied to domestic situations, homicide, motiveless crimes, serial crimes, that sort of thing."

Alan thought for a moment. "You know, I've got an idea."

"What's that?"

"After we're done here, would you mind coming to my office? I'd like to show you some of Andie's drawings. I might be able to use your insights, your objectivity on some of them. Interested?"

Falco shrugged. "Sure, I'm not sure how helpful I can be…or objective."

"Sometimes the difference between failure and success is a new thought," he said as he signed for the check.

"Have I heard that quote somewhere before?"

"Probably. *Casebook of a Crime Psychiatrist* by James Brussel," Alan said with a smile.

"The psychiatric criminologist who profiled the Mad Bomber in New York City during the 1950s…"

"You're a good study, Detective," Alan said as they crossed the street.

He swung open the door of his office and took Falco's coat. Margaret shot Falco a pierced look as Alan told her to hold his calls. He shut the door quietly and walked over to the credenza where Andie's drawings were stored. He unlocked the drawer and pulled out a thin stack of rumpled paper. "Okay, here are the ones I think are most relevant to the events," Alan said, setting the stack of eight drawings on his desk.

Falco looked at the first one and scowled. "Jesus, this is scary stuff. Andie did these?"

"Yep. She was quite prolific, but these are the ones we think are the most relevant."

Falco took a deep breath and studied the first drawing. She clenched her jaw and shook her head as she looked at the images and colors. She systematically went through each drawing and spread half of them on the desk. She scanned them curiously; her face went from wonder to deep concern and disgust. "They seem…" she started to say, as she looked at one then another. She searched through the stack and pulled out another drawing. "They seem connected in some way, like they're part of something else or they lead to something else. I can't explain it," she said, looking up from the drawings.

"There are more here, if you want to look at them," Alan offered.

Falco nodded. She shuffled quickly through the other set, pulled out two, and set them next to the original eight. She glanced at the faceless angel drawing and put it back in the large stack. Alan noted, "I'm not sure about that one, it doesn't fit anywhere." Falco continued to study the drawings, turning them one way, then the other. She stepped back and scanned the set of ten, feeling satisfied with the result.

"Hm…" Alan said as he scanned the ten drawings that covered the surface of his desk. "I didn't notice that before." He stood up straight and thought for a moment. "I think you may be on to something."

She continued to study the drawings. "I'm no art therapist, but somehow I just… These drawings seem to want to take me somewhere. Notice how the streaks go off the pages. They almost look like the outline of tree branches, and they seem to carry the images off the pages." She looked up at Alan, who nodded in agreement.

He sat down at his desk and stared. "Are you in a hurry to get home?"

Falco looked at her watch; it was two thirty. "Not really. I'll probably just pack for my flight and do some reading."

Alan picked up the phone. He hesitated then hung up. "How do you feel about taking this further?"

"Further? Like how?"

"Any interest in seeing more of Andie's drawings?"

"Sure, if you think I can help somehow."

Alan made a phone call from the front office then motioned for Falco to follow him out of the office. "Where are we going?" she said, glancing up at him as they walked.

"There's another drawing I want you to see." He held the ten drawings in his one hand and held her elbow with the other. They walked briskly to the elevators and took one up three flights.

Alan led her down a dimly lit hallway. He swiped his ID and pulled open a set of double doors labeled with a large "D."

"Are we going to see Andie?" she asked cautiously.

"No, we're going to see Andie's *room*. She'll be in another room while we're in there."

"I don't get it," Falco said. "What are we doing here?"

Alan smiled. "You'll see in a minute."

He slowed his pace and approached the door to Andie's room. He peered through a small window in the door. He swiped his ID again and inserted a key in the door handle then pulled the door open. Falco looked around as she followed him into the room. Immediately she caught sight of the marks on the floor. She stared at them, following the lines and images with her eyes across the floor to the room's perimeter and back. "Oh, my god," she said quietly, taking in the images, the lines, and the colors.

"Come on. It's okay to walk on it." Alan took her hand and led her farther into the room. Falco looked stunned; her eyes scanned the floor, back and forth, and all around. "I…I never imagined this, never in my wildest dreams," she finally gasped. "It's beautiful and disturbing, so violent yet almost graceful, lyrical." Emotions rose in her; she swallowed and pushed them aside.

Alan crossed his arms over his chest and let her continue to study the drawing. She walked back and forth and around the room, taking in the energy of the design. After a few moments, she put her hand out and without looking at Alan said, "Can I have those drawings?" Alan promptly put them in her hand.

She stepped to the right of the room and shuffled through the papers. Finding one drawing, she placed it on the floor over a section of the design. She did the same with another drawing, then another. Alan watched but said nothing. She scanned the room again then strategically placed the other seven drawings on various locations on the floor. She stepped back once more then walked over to Alan.

He squinted, trying to figure out what she had done. "What do you think?" Alan asked, glancing at her and then at the floor.

"I think it's a maze, sort of a memory maze, and it ends in that far left corner," she said, pointing. But I'm not sure that last one fits. Maybe there's another one we haven't considered.

Alan walked over to the first drawing. He studied it then picked up each one in the order Falco had laid them down, noticing how the drawings matched the movement of the images and lines on the floor. He stopped, squatted, and scanned the floor. "This is incredible." He rubbed his forehead and looked at the drawings again. "The drawing here on the floor is a system of lines, conduits for the flow of images relating to Andie's memory," he said. "And the individual drawings fit within it. It makes sense, at least from our perspective. This is good, Monica, really good!" He gasped, looking up.

"It wasn't difficult, Alan," she said as they gathered the drawings and left the room. "You just needed a fresh eye looking at them."

"No, no. I've been looking at those images over the last couple of weeks. You shouldn't be so modest, Monica. This is an amazing discovery, very significant, huge!" Alan spouted as they walked toward his office. "I only wish you could be around when we explore this with Andie," he said thoughtfully.

"She probably doesn't even remember me," said Falco quietly.

"Oh, no. That's not true at all," Alan said as he gently opened his office door.

"Well, if she does, it's probably not in a very good way."

"We've got a lot of work to do," he said, helping her with her coat. He gave her a sad look. "You take care of yourself, and I'll keep telling myself that it's only three weeks until you're back. I gotta tell you, it seems like a long time."

He gently pulled her into his office and kissed her.

CHAPTER 142

"Monica!" said Chris as she found an empty seat on the plane to Falco's left. She smelled of cigarette smoke, but Falco didn't mind. She scooted her things farther under the seat in front of her, making room for Chris.

"Cat got yer tongue?" asked Chris, getting in her face.

"No, I'm just tired."

"Too much partyin'?" Chris said, eyeing the flight attendant.

"Oh, yeah," she said dryly. She was preoccupied with thoughts of Andie and the images in the drawings. She was hopeful that Alan and Michael would make some progress, but the images in Andie's work haunted her terribly.

The row of seats jerked as Chris got herself settled and buckled in. "It's raining in Richmond again, but I brought an umbrella this time," she said, glancing at Falco. "Hey, you *are* tired, girl! You feelin' okay?"

Falco smiled. "I'm a little distracted." She opened her textbook and adjusted the reading glasses on her nose.

"Oh, come on, Monica. You're not gonna read *now* are you? I thought we'd get some time for some girl talk, some chitchat," Chris said in a whiney voice.

Falco closed her eyes and took off her glasses. She gave her an annoyed look. "All right, chitchat away. I'll listen."

Chris pouted then looked for the flight attendant. "I need a drink and so do you."

She talked non-stop about her long weekend. She and Jenny, her partner, had spent the break doing yard work and putting up storm windows in their house. "It's a seventy-five-year-old bungalow, real nice. It was a wreck when we first bought it, but Jenny's real handy, and we did most of the repairs and renovations ourselves."

"My ex is a contractor," Falco said. "He fixed my front door while I was away. It was sticking."

Chris smiled and waved the flight attendant over. "Can I get a scotch on the rocks and a white wine please?"

Falco put her hand on Chris's arm. "No, no. I'm *not* going to start drinking. It's only—"

"Six-thirty in Richmond. Lighten up, will ya?" Chris gave her a nudge with her elbow.

"I haven't eaten yet today," Falco mumbled.

"Well, whose fault is *that*? Here, have my peanuts," Chris said, tossing the tiny packet into Falco's lap.

Falco rubbed her head. She was fighting a dark mood as the plastic cup of wine appeared.

"So what's up? What's buggin' you?" Chris said, taking a swallow of her scotch.

"Nothing really. Maybe I'm feeling a bit overwhelmed," she finally admitted.

"What? With the reading? Phase two?"

"Yeah." Falco took a sip of the wine and looked out the window. The sky was clouding up, and the cabin was getting dark. "And I'm worried about a friend."

"What? You have friends?" Chris kidded. "Come on. Tell me about him. Is he a cop too?"

Falco laughed at Chris's conclusion that her friend was a man, a boyfriend. "It's not a man. My friend… Well, she's had some bad stuff happen to her. I'm just hoping she's going to come around," she said, taking another swallow of the wine.

"All right. Well, at least you shared *that* with me," Chris said empathetically.

"It's complicated."

"Okay. 'Nuff said."

For a fleeting moment Falco thought about telling Chris about Andie, how she felt about her, the dreams, the fantasies. *It's just the wine*, she thought. *I'd regret it in the long run.*

Chris grumbled then crossed her arms over her chest and closed her eyes.

CHAPTER 143

"It's been almost three weeks. I thought the paperwork was filed. You're not keeping me informed, and it's really pissing me off!" Kat's nostrils flared as she glared at Simon Schulman, her attorney.

"Look, these things take time," Simon said, leaning forward on the table. "If you think the world is going to open up just because we filed a malpractice suit, you've got another thing coming. These things take time. We know they got the paperwork, but the hospital's lawyers have to go through it in order to prepare a response. We've been through all this before."

"I want them shaking in their boots. I want them wondering what we're going to do next. Do you get that, Simon? Are we doing that, Simon?"

"Look, Kat—"

"Don't *look, Kat* me! Weeks have gone by since the fiasco with Andie walking out of that hospital. Who's going to make sure she doesn't do it again? *You*? Alan? The fucking hospital lawyers? They could give a rat's ass. She's not safe there, and I want her moved somewhere else. That's not so complicated. Secondly, where is the paperwork that says I'm Andie's legal artistic representative? I thought you were going to put something together."

"That whole thing is just not going to wash. I can't conjure up proof that you're Andie's artistic representative as long as Andie's attorney says it isn't so. Can you spell fraud? Can you spell disbarment?" Simon said, getting pissed.

"Fuck you!" Kat got up and spun around, toppling her chair over. "If you can't produce, I'll find someone who can!"

"Kat! Stop! Get a grip already for chrissakes." Simon stopped short of running after her as she grabbed her coat and stormed out of the office.

* * *

"This is amazing," Michael said. "And I haven't even seen these drawings with the drawing on the floor yet. Jesus, how did Monica figure this out?"

Alan nodded and smiled. "I don't know. She said it was just a fresh set of eyes."

Michael chuckled. "I don't believe that. The woman is brilliant!"

Loud voices came suddenly from the outside office. Alan heard Margaret stomping around and talking loudly. Within seconds her voice grew louder as Alan's phone buzzed. Before Alan could answer, Kat burst through the door.

"I've had it with your bullshit, Alan, and you too Michael *and* your goddamn lawyers! You're stalling. I…" Kat stopped mid-sentence upon seeing Andie's drawings on the desk. Alan put his hand strategically on them as she came closer.

"Those drawings are mine, Alan. They're mine and I can prove it!" Kat jeered.

"Okay, go ahead and prove it," Alan countered. "I have paperwork that says that Andie's attorney, Karen Graham-Jennings, is her legal artistic agent. In fact Andie's contract with your gallery is the *only* legal document that holds water between the two of you."

Kat glared at him. "I want those drawings. They're of no use to you. The only reason you're keeping them is to keep them from me." Kat took a breath. "You can't do this, Alan. They're all I have left of her!"

Kat began to cry. Michael calmly walked over to her, put his hands on her shoulders, spun her around, and led her out of the office. "You are so full of it, Kat," he said, "and so are those tears."

The next day, Alan sat opposite a somber-faced attorney with the malpractice suit in hand. "It's a pretty strong case, Dr. Forrest."

"What are you saying, Bill? Should we be concerned?"

"Unless we can cut some kind of deal and settle the whole thing with Katherine Cohen and Schulman, Greenberg, and Robbins."

"What kind of deal?"

"I don't know," Bill Kucer said as he sat heavily at one of the conference table chairs and tapped at the manila file folder. Alan took a deep breath and shook his head.

* * *

Michael looked out the office window and chewed on his thumbnail. Alan was on the phone with one of the attorneys as another line flashed. Michael listened closely as he looked at the traffic below. Alan took the other call without a word in between.

"Can we do that? It sounds like questionable legal wrangling… So if she took the deal, Andie's work would *only* be part of her *private* collection? Well, that sounds good to me as long as Karen Jennings agrees." Alan nodded and looked relieved. He hung up the phone and spun around to speak to Michael.

"Let me guess, the hospital's attorneys are going to use Andie's drawings as a bargaining chip," Michael said.

"In so many words, yes."

"What about Andie and the guardianship, all that business with Kat wanting to move her to another hospital?"

"We're going to dangle the offer of the drawings in front of her and the rest may quietly resolve itself," Alan said with a knowing smile.

"Very nice," Michael said with a nod.

CHAPTER 144

Chris Sommers tapped her pen impatiently on her notebook as she waited in the crowded auditorium for the speaker to start. She was distracted. She walked into the hallway thinking she might see Falco pass by.

God, I hope she doesn't have a bug up her butt about something. I sure hope it isn't me, she thought. *She can't be so immersed in the reading that she won't even answer her door or her goddamn phone.* "Shit," she whispered, banging the pencil hard on her notebook.

It was nearly six thirty; darkness seemed to come earlier each day as winter deepened. Chris ran out for a pack of cigarettes and bumped into Falco as she bristled against the cold.

"Hey, Chris," Falco said as she grabbed her arm.

"Hey, stranger! I haven't seen you since last Wednesday. What's up? You mad at me or somethin'?"

Falco laughed then frowned when she saw Chris's expression. She eyed her for a beat. "Did you think I was *mad* at you?"

"Yeah, I did. I called you a couple of times and knocked on your door, but you didn't answer," Chris said, looking a little hurt.

"I'm sorry. I've been going to the library across the way. You can see it from here," Falco said, pointing. "It's quiet and I can do the outside reading there after the lecture."

"God, you're an overachiever," Chris nagged. "Well, I'm just glad it wasn't something I said or did. Sometimes I can be a bit over the top."

Falco smiled. "Hey, how about we go have dinner tomorrow night? My treat."

"You're on, kiddo. How about six thirty? Meet you at your place?"

"Sounds like a plan."

* * *

"How many drawings are there?" asked Karen Graham-Jennings, Andie's attorney.

"About thirty-five," Alan said. "Uh, well, Andie took two of them from me a week ago, so let's call it thirty-three drawings in all. That number does *not* include the one on the floor of her room."

"The floor of her room?" Karen asked.

"Andie did this huge drawing on the tile floor of her room here at the hospital. It's all in crayon, as are the other drawings."

"I hardly think Katherine Cohen is going to get her sticky paws on that one," she said with a chuckle. "When do you think you'll be finished using them in your sessions with Andie?"

"That's hard to say. We hope to make some progress this week. Actually we're going to have to do some pretty intensive work because the drawing on the floor is slowly wearing away."

Karen frowned as she thought for a moment. "I see. So what's a good timeline for me to float over to Schulman, Greenberg, and Robbins?"

Alan scratched his chin. "Let's say two weeks."

* * *

It was eight thirty a.m. when Alan and Michael entered Andie's room, drawings in hand. Andie's hair was wet and disheveled from sleep and a shower. She pulled her thin cotton shirt over her abdomen and gave the two men a threatening look.

"What's that?" Andie whispered, looking at the armful of drawings Michael held close to his chest. She cowered in the left side of her room where Falco had said the maze ended. "You can't make me," she said. "You can't make me draw those!"

"Andie, no one is asking you draw anything. Calm down. Just calm down," Alan said. Andie looked confused then stared at the drawings Michael had in his arms. He looked for a cue from Alan from across the room. Alan nodded. "Michael, go ahead."

Andie glared at Michael then at Alan as a look of terror crossed her face. "No. No. Don't let him!" she shouted. Michael took the drawings. They were numbered in the order that Falco had placed them on the floor. He reconstructed the arrangement as Falco had indicated.

Andie gasped as Michael worked. "What are you doing?" she asked as she rushed toward Michael.

Alan intercepted her and set her down on the bed. "Take it easy, Andie. I want you to pay attention. Look at what Michael is doing. Look at the drawings. Look at the images in the context of the drawing you made on the floor." Andie stared at Alan then at the drawings now arranged as before on the floor. "Tell me about the work, Andie. Tell me about the sequence of drawings you created."

She looked at the images. "Who *did* this?" she asked, looking up at Michael then at Alan. Her breathing quickened. She got up from the bed and looked at the first drawing. "The box of nails," she said, looking at the two men. "It was the box of nails, and the figure is Aisha…so beautiful. I love…the back of your neck," she said as her eyes glazed over.

She put out her hands as if she were making her way through a dark room.

"Look…look. The nails. I found the nails and the champagne that Kat brought and the knife that…that *he* brought." Andie touched the image of the hunting knife then quickly pulled away as if it were sharp. She cautiously looked at the second and third drawings. She touched them as if they were velvet. Yes, yes, this is mine…and my body…and Kat is so gentle, so…" Andie sighed.

Suddenly Andie looked off as the images spurred a new memory. She gasped and swung her hands in the air. "No, no, not you, not *you*!" She pointed to someone. "Let go of me! She screamed, backing away from the drawings. *Please! Please!* Go away. You're dead. You're supposed to be dead!" She backed up and hit the wall then fell to her knees. "I can't breathe. I…I can't *breathe*!"

Michael moved to help her. "Leave her be," Alan said, grabbing him by the arm.

Andie clasped her hands over her head and rolled to her side. "Please, don't hurt me!" She dragged the drawing to her, smothering it with her body. She gathered the paper under herself as her body pulsed. A stream of vomit dripped from her mouth and to the floor. She dragged her fingers to her lips and stared at the wetness. "It's blood. It's blood. Please, no more. *Please*!"

She gasped then quickly sat up. The front of her shirt was wet with perspiration and the yellow liquid. "Just kill me," she groaned, looking down. "Please. *Just do it*. I can't stand the pain. I can't take seeing you again," she cried as she leaned forward onto her hands. Her eyes drifted up, as if speaking to McCaffery. "Just kill me. *Do it!*"

Andie waited, as if looking for a response, as she held the crumpled drawing to her chest. "Please! Do it!" she yelled as she stared into thin air. "You filled me with you poison. Now just fucking do it!" She pounded the floor with her hands. "Just…" Andie looked at Alan and squinted. She moved toward him and grabbed is arms as if to pull him down to the floor. "Please, please end this…I'm begging you!"

Alan gently released himself from Andie's grasp and guided her to her bed. He was convinced she'd had enough. He watched her closely and wondered what to do next. Andie got up and gathered the other drawing and pulled it close to her chest. "It hurts so much, so much," she moaned, pulling her knees close. She clenched her arms around the drawings and closed her eyes. "Please, please," she said softly.

Alan approached." Andie, it's okay. You're safe. Try to calm down. You're not in any pain now. We're going to take the other drawings away."

Michael picked up the other sheets of paper and discreetly moved away from Andie and headed toward the door.

As he and Alan made their way down the hall, Michael looked at him. "Did we make any progress?"

"I think so. She got through the first five." He let out a long sigh. "That was intense."

"This may sound stupid, but do you think she really wants to die?" Michael asked.

Alan scratched his head. "I guess we'll have to ask Andie that."

CHAPTER 145

"Detective Falco, you look wasted!" Chris said as Falco closed the door of her room.

"I haven't had much sleep," she said, her voice rough.

"Let me guess. You've been staying up studying!" Chris said as they pushed the doors of the hotel lobby open and felt the rush of cold air.

"I've been keeping up with the reading, yes, but I go to sleep and I wake up, then I can't get back to sleep. It's an endless cycle. I think I slept three hours last night. Then I'm wired in the morning and feel like crashing after lunch."

Chris frowned. "The reading puts me to sleep. I'm way behind."

"Well, at least you're able to sleep," Falco said as her phone rang. The caller ID flashed Alan's number. She spun around and said, "Chris, I need to take this call. Can I meet you across the street?"

"Yeah, great. I'll get you a glass of wine."

Falco nodded as she flipped the phone open. "Alan, hi, how are you?"

"Good. I'm so glad I got you. I wanted to tell you Andie managed to work through five of the drawings today. We reconstructed the order of the drawings on the floor."

"How did it go? How did she react?"

"She screamed a lot. She relived the abduction and the assault. It was intense. At one point she got physically sick. I wanted to stop the whole thing then, but we got through it."

"How's she holding up?"

"She was pretty shaky when we left her room. We had to convince her McCaffery wasn't in there with her. She was bouncing off the walls, screaming at him. Depending on how she is tomorrow, we may wait a day or two before proceeding to the next drawings. As you know, they're the most violent and they contain the bloodiest images—the guns and the decapitated heads."

Falco sighed. "I wish there was something I could do. I'm so out of touch out here."

"I think once we get through the rest of the images, and the part about the shooting, a lot of what Andie is experiencing will hopefully be resolved, at least theoretically," Alan said. "The biggest hurdle is the killing. That'll be the most significant and disturbing part for Andie *and* for Michael and me."

Falco wandered into the restaurant and found Chris huddled with a glass of scotch. Her white wine waited for her across the table. She slid into the booth.

Chris scowled. "I may have to run out for a smoke. This is a no-smoking establishment."

"Oh, sorry." Falco half smiled.

"Everything okay with your phone call?"

"Yeah, everything's fine." Falco picked up the menu.

"Then how come you're shaking?" Chris asked, eyeing the menu as it wiggled in Falco's hands.

Falco frowned and put the menu back down on the table. "Well, it's *cold* out there!" she said, giving Chris an evasive look.

"All right, all right. Monica's going to try to pull the wool over my eyes," she said, looking at her sideways. "You forget I'm a cop with a degree in psych. Come on. What's up?"

Falco took a deep breath and looked over to the next table.

"It's your friend, right?" Chris asked, eyeing her as she polished her silverware with the cloth napkin.

"Yeah, but it's complicated, and it's a long story. I don't know if—"

Chris looked at her watch. "The night is young."

Falco unraveled the story of her initial involvement with Andie, whom she called "the victim." She told her about McCaffery faking his death, the abduction, and the subsequent killing with her weapon. She talked about the victim's breakdown, the drawings, and her own guilt about having failed to protect Andie, the victim.

"Jesus Christ," Chris said. "That's a lot of heavy stuff." She thought for a moment then said, "You said this person is a friend of yours?"

Falco nodded. "I consider her a friend."

"Do you usually call your friends 'the victim'?" Chris asked, giving her a piercing look. "Does your *victim* have a *name*?"

Falco sighed. "It's Andrea…Andie."

"I see," Chris said as a look of realization came over her. "Ah ha, that explains a lot. You know I was with the Evanston PD when that stuff went down. I'm sure you figured that out."

"Yeah, I figured it out. Were you involved?"

"I was on my way out during that time. I was going back and forth to Indy, but I knew the guy who set your friend up."

"Set her up?"

"Yeah, the officer who got her nabbed for the DWI and had someone ransack her house."

"*What*?" Falco yelped and slammed her hands on the table. "Who the fuck was it?" she demanded.

"Take it easy, lady! Yeah, they wanted to send your friend a message to back off the civil case. They wanted to make her look like a kook to undermine her credibility. When her hotshot lawyer started asking questions about the arrest, someone in the department made the DWI paperwork disappear and the break-in was never solved. The two cops involved in the hanky panky got early retirements. Go figure. Small world, eh?"

Falco's eyes grew wide with Chris's revelation. She stared at the table, processing what she had just heard.

"Hey, don't think *I* had anything to do with it, girl." Chris balled up her napkin in her fist. Falco stared off. After a minute Chris passed her hand in front of her eyes. "Hey! Back to Earth, Detective. Come on!"

Falco blinked. "I thought the Evanston cops were on the up and up, but they were fucking with Andie just as she'd suspected."

Chris sat back and let go of the napkin. "Well, that whole administration is gone now. I still talk to my friend there. She said I was lucky to get out before all the ethics probes took place. I guess it was sort of a witch-hunt. A lot of folks retired early or were asked to leave."

Falco was quiet. She shook her head and stared off.

"So your friend Andrea is where now?"

"Still in the hospital. Some other things happened. It got so fucking complicated."

"Sounds like you got to know her pretty well, though," Chris said.

"Well, it's funny. We got to know each other when I was protecting her, but I learned more about her afterward, from her friends, people connected to her."

Chris nodded. "So why the interest, Detective? Perhaps you're having some kind of reaction to the...uh...the victim?"

Falco scowled. "Reaction to the victim?"

"I mean, if you haven't seen her in close to five months, why the obsession?"

"Obsession? I'm not *obsessed*," Falco said, glaring.

"All right. I'm just asking, observing."

"It's not obsession. It's concern, a feeling of *responsibility* for Andie. I'm trying to make a right out of a wrong." She glared at Chris as a tense silence fell upon them. "You know, I really don't want to talk about anymore," she said briskly, rubbing her forehead.

Chris tried to change the tone and subject of their conversation, talking about her partner and their bungalow. She feared she might have made a fatal mistake. She may have ruined what could have been a nice friendship.

CHAPTER 146

The next week flew by with no word from Alan or Michael. Falco wondered if she should call one of them for an update, but she immersed herself in the reading and coursework instead. The word "obsession" kept coming to her when she thought of Andie. Her last conversation with Maggie Simonds also echoed in her mind. *I've got to sort this out,* she thought as she drifted across campus.

Alan decided to postpone any further exploration of the drawings with Andie for a week. After working through the first five, she showed symptoms of physical illness and deepening depression. A growing sense of despondency and isolation overcame her. Alan and Michael were both concerned. On top of that, where was no word from Schulman, Greenberg, and Robbins; Alan was worried.

* * *

A light snow was falling to the ground. Falco watched it glisten in the streetlight from her booth at Sharkey's Bar and Grill just east of the sprawling FBI Academy compound. She brought her textbook with the hope of reading, but her mind was on other things. She had been avoiding Chris and had even spotted her in the library looking for her. Chris had called a few times, but the frequency had diminished. Falco stared at her third glass of wine and the pack of Newports she had bought two days ago. "Fuck," she whispered and sunk her head in her hand.

The only bright spot in her day had been her conversation with Sam. He'd made it to the semifinals of the school's spelling bee. He and Jeffery had been studying feverously; their work obviously had paid off. Falco smiled at the thought of him as a tear drifted from her eye. She grabbed the pack of cigarettes and tapped one out, put it in her mouth, and lit it. She took a long drag and blew the cool smoke out, slowly watching it drift to the ceiling. *One more week*, she thought, *then the holidays.*

She moped back to the hotel through a wet lace of snow; it was hardly enough to make footprints but enough to bring a hush to the night. She made her way to her room and fumbled for the keycard. Chris's TV was blaring then suddenly went quiet, as if she had heard Falco in the hallway. Falco quickly entered her room and shut the door. It was almost one a.m. *Brenda was right*, she thought. *I am fried.*

She slept through her alarm and scrambled to make it to her morning lecture. She was feeling the three drinks from the night before and admonished herself for being at what she felt was only 80 percent for the morning's lecture. She sighed with annoyance as she found only the back row of seats available. She found Chris at the far end, moving her coat so she could sit.

"Hey," Falco said breathlessly. "I'm late, I know."

"No problemo. I decided to skip the lab and catch part of this lecture. Good thing I did, 'cause I got you a seat."

"I usually sit up front but not this morning, it seems." She gave Chris a little smile as she sat down and pulled her notebook from her briefcase.

Chris reserved judgment as she pretended to take notes. She wondered what was up with Falco, if she could help in some way. Falco found her heart racing. She took deep breaths and tried to calm herself. Chris turned to her and whispered, "Must be cold outside, huh?"

Falco moved her hands from the desk to under her thighs. "Yeah, it is cold."

Chris kept her distance at the break, watching her secretly. Finally she came over to her in the hallway. "Hey, girl. Friday is our last day. When's your flight?"

Falco thought for a moment. "Saturday at two, I think."

"United Airlines?"

"American," Falco said.

Chris nodded then slipped outside for a cigarette.

CHAPTER 147

Michael wandered into Alan's office and found Margaret there early. "Hi, Margie. Where's Alan?"

"He has an early meeting," she said flatly.

"So early?"

"Attorneys."

Michael felt a surge of anxiety. *Jesus. Kat and her team of hotshot lawyers,* he thought. *Oh, shit.*

He occupied himself in the library with his dissertation, which had been on the back burner for a while. Just before noon, Alan made his way through the stacks looking for Michael. Seeing him with his laptop at a table in the back, he waved. Michael perked up, seeing Alan's face. "Michael, hey. Come on. We need to talk," Alan said. They made their way to Alan's office.

"Our attorney's are ninety-five percent sure that Kat agreed to the deal," Alan said.

Michael frowned and wrung his hands. "I can't believe Kat would settle for the drawings after going through all the accusations and the threats. I knew she was conniving, but I never thought she was unscrupulous."

Alan nodded but was more diplomatic. "Who knows what Kat's motivations are? I'd like to think she still cares about Andie and her best interests. I guess we'll know more if she takes the deal and drops the malpractice suit."

Michael grunted his doubts and thumbed through the stack of Andie's drawings on Alan's desk. "So who decides which ones Kat will get?"

"Karen Jennings. Andie already has ruined a couple of them and will most likely ruin the remaining five. I can't imagine Kat would want those. I'm sure Karen will handle it well. The other twenty or so should be interesting enough for Kat."

"I hope you're right. Kat saw the first ones. I hope she's not going to want those," Michael said.

"Karen will handle it. We've got to concentrate on the other five and how they'll help Andie."

* * *

Falco woke with her textbook drooping on her chest. She threw the blankets off her as her book hit the floor. Her T-shirt was wet with perspiration. It was two forty a.m., and suddenly she was wired. She stared at her book as it lay sprawled on the floor. An overwhelming feeling of finality and absurdness came over her. She crawled to the middle of the bed as tears came to her eyes. She put her face in her pillow as her body shook with sobs.

* * *

Andie looked drained as Alan entered her room with the other five drawings. She stared at them as if they were a death sentence. Alan scanned the floor and saw a shiny clean surface, void of all marks, lines or designs. He looked again at the floor, thinking that the glare from the morning light had made the drawing temporarily disappear. His shoulders sank as he saw the two mounds of newsprint balled up in a far corner of the room. Andie had wiped the floor clean.

"Andie, where's the drawing?" Alan asked with dread. She gave him a blank stare. Suddenly he felt acutely stupid. How could he trust that Andie would leave the drawing on the floor alone after all she had gone through with the first five? He put his hand to his head and turned toward the wall. "Goddamn it," he moaned.

He felt a tug from behind as the drawings under his arm loosened and fell to the floor. He turned and saw Andie looking up at him. She bent down and picked up the five and sat on the floor. "The big one had to go," she said plainly. "It wouldn't stop talking to me, making noise at night. It was a pest."

"What did the drawing say to you?" Alan asked.

"It said it wasn't finished. It said there was a drawing missing, but I don't know what it is," Andie, said looking off.

Alan followed her lead and cautiously sat on the bed near her. He looked at her closely. "Do you think you can talk about these…the next five?"

Andie put a shaky hand out and took the five drawings. Her breath caught in her throat as she relayed her memory of her seemingly last hours as depicted in the images she created. The pictures prompted a stream-of-consciousness narrative: the incessant rain, the pain of the barbed wire twisted tightly around her arms, her own hot blood heavy on her shirt, Falco's words calming her, telling her to breathe. She cried softly as she saw Brian McCaffery's eyes. "Green as vomit," she said. On the seventh drawing, Andie gently touched the image of a woman as her face clouded over. Blues and purples depicted dusk as a tremble came to her hands. She cast the drawing to the floor and looked away. "I'm feeling sick," she whispered, her breathing labored.

Alan gave her a few moments to process her memories then decided to push forward. He gently placed the eighth drawing in front of her. Andie's eyes darted across the page as her breathing grew fast and shallow and her body tensed. Suddenly she jerked away as she erupted into a fit of flying fists and screams. Alan braced against her fury, moving quickly out of her violent path. She threw herself into a corner and cowered against the wall as her body heaved. Her mouth bubbled with vomit. Alan handed her a wad of paper towels. Andie wiped her mouth then blotted her forehead.

"My head. I'm dizzy. My head hurts." Andie covered her face then wiped the liquid from her lips. "I tried…to breathe, to stay with her, to stay with Monica. Am I… Am I *dying*? I feel like I'm slipping up…into the sky, and the light is so soft and the pain is leaving me. Please just let me go, Detective. Just let me…"

Andie gripped her left arm, cradling herself as she dropped to the floor.

"I'm scared. I taste blood. I smell blood…and metal and fireworks. But the sky is so red and purple. I can see the day fading away…so beautiful. They're coming now—Michael and Kat and Aisha…and my boys. I hear music, voices singing. It's a choral piece…Mozart."

She appeared to get dizzy and swayed back, leaning against the far wall where the maze had ended. She grew quiet and still.

Alan looked at his watch, nearly two-and-a-half hours had passed. Andie's shoulders drooped as she rubbed her head and shivered from the emotional release. The drawings were crumpled in her arms, wet with sweat and vomit. The room was silent.

"The worst part is over," he said quietly, coming close. "You did very well today. I know it was difficult Andie, very difficult."

Andie stared off; Alan wasn't sure she was hearing him.

"What you told us last week about the attack, the beating, and the assault—the sexual assault—that was the worst part, don't you think?" he asked in a leading tone.

Andie stared off. "He raped me…like a dog. He put his poison inside me," she said weakly.

Alan nodded sadly. "I know. I know."

He weighed the risk of confronting Andie with McCaffery's death then felt a cold chill of doubt. Should he wait or take a chance on bringing up the shooting now while Andie was somewhat lucid and talking, while her memories were still swirling about the room? Would knowing that McCaffery was dead ease her torment, including the torment Alan himself had just put her through?

Andie put the three drawings on the floor in front of her and eyed the two remaining in Alan's hands. "Please, I'm so tired." She sank to the floor.

Alan left her room and walked down the hallway to the elevators. He wondered whether telling her about the shooting was a good idea at all. Was she even aware she had killed someone? He wondered whether all the work of the last few weeks would rid Andie of the incessant tick, the flashbacks, and her violent, unpredictable behavior. Would it be enough to allow her to leave the hospital and live a normal life again?

He considered the drawing Andie had done on the floor. Why did she say it was incomplete? Was there another drawing that would spawn a new flood of memories? One that would help her put the whole terrible incident behind her? Alan's gait quickened as he headed to his office.

CHAPTER 148

Falco couldn't believe it was finally Friday, December twenty-second. She had a flight back to Chicago the next day at two p.m. She gathered her things, wondering how in the world she'd get her Christmas shopping done. "It's gonna be gift card city," she whispered as she arranged her suitcase. She felt antsy and decided to go down to the bar and have a drink. She ordered a Cabernet and fumbled in her purse for her pack of cigarettes. She lit the cigarette as the waitress brought over the glass of wine.

She pulled out a notepad and a pen and started making out her Christmas list. *Let's see. I was supposed to find a T-shirt for Sam*, she thought. *Jeffery needs some shirts but no socks— we're not married anymore. I'll get Mom and Howard a few bottles of wine and Sam some crazy game for his Xbox.* Before long she was on her second cigarette and third glass of wine. She tipped the waitress as she brought her another drink.

"Always working on something, aren't you?" came a gruff voice to her right. Falco looked up to find Chris standing with a drink in her hand. "I didn't know you smoked. You being a bad girl?" she said with an evil smile.

"I don't smoke actually," Falco said, barely returning the smile.

"You look like you need a diversion," Chris said as she slid into the seat across from her. "What's that you're doing there?" She grabbed the pad of paper and spun it around to look at it. Falco scowled. "You mean you haven't even started your Christmas shopping yet?"

"No, when the fuck did I have *time?*" she hissed, as if it were Chris's fault.

Chris laughed. "I'm just messin' with you! Jenny did all of ours, and I got her stuff online."

Falco put her hand to her forehead and shook her head. *Aren't you special?*

Chris sat back. "So, Monica, what did the bartender say to the horse?"

Falco gave Chris an absurd look. "*What?*"

"What did the bartender say to the horse?"

She thought for a moment then gave Chris an annoyed look. "How the fuck do *I* know?"

"Hey, why the long face?"

Falco tried to hide the smile that surfaced on her face as Chris slapped the table and laughed.

"So let me ask *you* then. Why the long face, Monica?"

She scowled and didn't answer.

"Look, I'm trying to cheer you up, girl. It's the holidays. We must all be happy, happy, happy!" Chris danced in her chair.

Falco continued to scowl.

Chris looked up at the ceiling and ordered another scotch. "All right. You're mad at me. Come on. Admit it. I crossed the line the other night about your friend. I shouldn't have pushed you. I'm *sorry*," Chris said as she gave her a hurt look.

Falco flattened her lips and looked away then nodded as if to say it was okay. She sunk her face in her hands and said nothing. A few minutes passed. Finally Chris said, "Hey, if I'm gonna watch you hide your face there, I might as well go upstairs and watch cable or somethin'. I think the Westminster Dog Show is on."

Falco didn't respond, but Chris heard a faint sniffle. She hunched down to look closer. "You okay?" she asked gently. Falco picked her head up; Chris could see she was upset and her eyes were teary. "Any news? I mean, about your friend?"

"No, nothing." Falco looked away then turned to Chris. "You know, just because you're a lesbian, it doesn't make everyone else a lesbian or a closet case," she said with a hint of pain in her voice.

"Hey, I never called you a closet case! Jesus, I'd never do that! I was just pointing out that… Oh, what the fuck. I don't know." Chris shook her head and frowned.

"It's just that I don't know what's wrong with me. Is Andie an obsession? I mean, I think about her all the *fucking* time. I can't figure it out," Falco said slowly. "Does that make me a lesbian?"

"I don't know," Chris said. "It took me a while to figure it out myself. My family more or less knew before it dawned on stupid me! But look at me. I'm not exactly a femme. Sure, I tried to hide it for a long time. I wore skirts and stuff, even heels sometimes, but then I got tired of trying to pass and I just stopped."

"Trying to pass?"

"Yeah, you know, trying to pass for a straight person."

Falco nodded. "I guess I'm not up on the lingo."

Chris burst out laughing. "It's not like we're the Masons or something—secret handshakes and all. But now that you mention it, there is a terminology, though, like 'bull dyke.' That's me. Then there's femmes and lip-stick lesbians and…sporty types…and…"

Falco shook her head. "I don't need to know all that." She grew quiet all over again.

Chris tried a new approach. "So how do you feel about her? Did you find her attractive at some point?"

Falco avoided Chris's eyes. "Yes, I did and it scared the fucking shit out of me. I remember the exact moment. I couldn't take my eyes off her. It was so weird. I felt…*stung* somehow. I don't know."

She took another swallow of her drink. Chris's eyes were kind as she waited for her to say more. "Have you told anybody else about this?"

"Just my therapist, Maggie."

"How did it feel to say it to someone?"

"Scary, then I regretted it."

"You've never been attracted to any other woman? Not even as a kid? Gym teacher? School nurse?"

"No. Absolutely not!" Falco said, her voice louder.

"There are late bloomers. Some women get married and raise kids and everything then find the right gal and their life changes."

"That's not me," Falco said flatly.

"Then we're back to talking about obsession again. Do you think about her in a sexual way? Dream about her?" Chris took a chance asking her that, seeing they were both a little drunk.

Falco put her head to her forehead. "Yes...yes...yes!"

Chris considered her answer. "You think you'd ever *act* on those...desires?"

"I don't know. She in the fucking psych ward. I don't even know if I'll ever know her as she was before...during the summer." She got sad again and looked away. "Oh, it's so screwed up."

Chris played with her drink then smiled. "I remember the first time *I* kissed a woman. I was in my late twenties. It just sort of happened, but it felt so right. I went home and looked at myself in the mirror, thinking somehow I'd look different." Chris laughed. "After I kissed her, I thought of Sister Mary Louise D'Agostino, my home room teacher in high school. I expected her to smack me with a ruler or something and condemn me to fucking purgatory." Chris put her palms together as if to pray and wined, "'But Sister, she's a *Catholic!,'* I'd tell her!" Falco smiled. Chris put out her cigarette and changed her tone. "Any idea if Andie might feel the same way?"

"I don't know." She has a longtime girlfriend, a partner, but she also was seeing someone else. She was always very sweet and attentive when we interacted, but I never felt she was coming on to me or even making a pass."

"Well, this is what I think, Monica. Take a chance with her. Let's hope when she gets out she'll be the same person. I'd make a move and see how she reacts."

"Make a *move*? Jesus Christ. I wouldn't even know how to do that...not with a *woman*."

"It's not a whole lot different than with a man, and women like to be pursued," Chris said, "even if they might be a top. Jenny came on real strong when we first met, but she's a bottom and I'm a top."

Falco's eyes clouded over. She shook her head and looked confused. "Listen, I gotta go to bed. The room is spinning, and I think I might just pass out."

The next thing Falco knew, Chris was holding her up and trying to open her door with the key card. "Fuck, I thought I fixed this thing!" Finally she guided Falco through the door and sat her on her bed. "You know, dykes hold their liquor a whole lot better than you."

Falco wavered on the bed. "I think I'm okay now, Chris. Thanks," she said as she grabbed Chris's arm.

"Don't worry. I'm not gonna jump yer bones. Just sit there and—"

"No, no. Just let me…" Falco eased herself back onto the bed.

Chris pulled Falco's shoes off, gently swung her legs onto the bed, and carefully put a pillow under her head. She wrote a note on the hotel stationery.

Happy Holidays! I hope you work this out!

See you on the third!

—Chris

CHAPTER 149

Alan got to his office and quickly pulled the remaining drawings out of the credenza. With Kat soon to make a deal, he wanted to make sure she didn't get her hands on the drawing that could be critical to Andie's recovery. *We'd never get it back from her,* he thought. *Then we'd be back to bargaining again.* He was beginning to think Kat didn't care about Andie at all. He riffled through the stack of newsprint then saw it, the drawing Michael had pulled from the stack and set aside almost as an anomaly, the same one both he and Monica thought didn't fit, the faceless angel. It was one of the original drawings Andie had done, one of the original twenty or so from which Falco had selected.

The angel had long flowing hair and floated up to the sky above a strange and sprawling landscape. She held what resembled barbed wire in one hand and a lightning bolt in the other. The woman was goddess-like and wore gold armor and a long flowing skirt. Alan interpreted the image as a symbol of Andie's spiritual self, her soul floating off to the afterlife. Did she draw it as a way to work through her brush with death? Was it based on a near-death experience? Was this the final drawing in the maze? Where did it fit in with the McCaffery shooting? Alan added the angel to the final three. Somehow he felt it was tied to all of the drawings, including the one on the floor. He reviewed the final three once more; they contained the most concrete images of the shooting: hands holding guns and rifles, streaks of orange and red representing gunfire and blood, blue lights perhaps symbolizing police, more barbed wire references, a bloody cross, and images of decapitated heads. Alan knew these final pieces were key to Andie's recovery, but would they lead to catharsis or catastrophe?

* * *

Falco glanced at the note from Chris and crumpled it in her hand. She had forty-five minutes to pull herself together to get to the airport. Her head ached and her stomach felt terrible. "I can't believe I passed out," she whispered as she bumped her way to the bathroom and turned on the shower. It was nearly ten thirty; her alarm had been buzzing for close to an hour. *Get a grip*, she thought as the warm water drenched her aching head. *Christmas is in a few days. The mall will be a madhouse. Then there's Sam's Christmas concert tonight and Christmas dinner at Mom's with Jeffery.* She sighed, dreading it all. "Oh, god," she said. "I feel like shit."

* * *

Michael scanned the images in the three drawings then looked at Alan. "We're so close, just these three," he said.

"No small task, though," Alan said, looking out at the street below. Winter had settled into the city, casting a gray mist over the holiday lights. "I've been thinking," he said as he turned to Michael. "I've been thinking of asking Monica to be there when we show Andie the last three drawings.

Michael nodded. "If she'll do it. When?"

"She's coming back tonight. I'll see when she's available."

"It's Christmastime too," Michael reminded him.

Alan nodded and looked down again at the street below.

* * *

The taxi pulled up to Falco's house. It was nearly six p.m. Traffic was a disaster as people headed to the airport for a long weekend; Christmas day was Monday and most had the next day off. Falco's cell phone rang as she pushed open her front door and wiped the snow off her shoes. The living room was dark. She wondered if her timers were screwed up. She fumbled for the light switch, found it, and flicked it on. "Shit. The bulb's burnt out," she muttered. She managed to turn on another light as she pulled her cell phone out of her purse—missed call, unidentified number. She sat heavily on her sofa and perused the mail that Jeffery had stacked neatly on the table. *All trash*, she thought as she bundled it up for recycling. She did the same with the pile of *Tribunes* then dragged her suitcase into the laundry room. "Hello, house," she said with a sigh, already feeling calm but still hungover. It didn't matter; she was home.

Her phone rang again. She barely heard it over the buzz of the washing machine. It was Alan. "Hey, how are you?" she asked softly.

"Better now," Alan said, flirting with her. "What's that noise?"

"My washing machine. It's kind of loud. It may be on its last leg."

"Well, if it starts to smoke, call the fire department," Alan said with a chuckle. "Any interest in a bite to eat? No frills, just something for the weary traveler?"

Falco leaned against the wall of the laundry room. "That would be really nice, but I have to warn you, I might not be the best of company."

"That's fine. I'd just like to see you."

Falco tensed up, suddenly remembering something. "Wait. Oh, no. I can't, Alan. Shit!" She looked at her watch and froze. "Shit!" she hissed, spinning around. "I've got Sam's Christmas concert at the school tonight. Oh, god. I'm sorry. It starts at seven, or was it seven thirty? Oh, shit!" She put her hand over her eyes.

"It's okay, I understand, Monica. Just calm down." Alan laughed. "Sounds like the holidays suddenly caught up with you. I'll call you. Maybe tomorrow?"

"Yeah, yeah, that's great. I'm sorry."

She rushed into the shower and found the load of laundry had depleted the available hot water. She shivered from the icy shower as she wrapped a towel around her. Suddenly she felt the urge to sit down and cry but fended it off. "God, I'm a mess," she whispered.

She put on makeup, earrings, and a black wool turtleneck dress; grabbed her coat; and ran out the door. The cold shower had chilled and energized her at the same time. Her car started stubbornly as she gunned it out of the driveway and onto the street. *I vaguely remember telling Jeffery I'd meet him somewhere, but fuck if I remember where,* she thought as she bit her lip and headed west on Devon.

Falco arrived at the school and found a parking spot at the far end of the lot. Her heart sank as she heard music coming from the auditorium. "I'm late," she said sadly. "I hope I can find Jeffery." She bought her ticket and found an empty seat in the last row next to two senior citizens in wheelchairs. As the lights went up for a scenery change, she could see Howard's shiny bald spot glistening from a few rows up. Falco got a sick feeling inside. *I'm gonna hear it from all of them, from Mom and Jeffery. Howard will just smile politely, which is far, far worse,* she thought. She forced herself to concentrate on the concert and looked for Sam in the chorus.

After the concert was over, she made her way through the crowd of parents, grandparents, and siblings outside the auditorium. She heard Sam's voice somewhere in the crowd and turned as he ran to her. "You made it back for the concert!" he said beaming.

"I wouldn't miss it for anything, sweetie," she said as she crouched to hug him.

She spotted Jeffery's wingtip shoes just to her left. Her eyes moved up, following his khakis and leather jacket to his face. He tried to hide his anger as he looked at her. "Guess you were late," he said dryly.

"Yeah, I sat in the back," she said, looking at Sam and trying to hear what he was saying. A few uncomfortable moments passed that only got worse when Elaine and Howard appeared.

"Hi, dear, nice to see you. When did you get in?" Elaine asked sweetly. The cold had made her face dry and flaky.

"About six. Traffic was a mess near the airport," Falco said, not wanting to make excuses for herself.

Jeffery continued to show a self-righteous expression as she avoided his gaze. "We're going to dinner. I hope you'll join us."

She thought for a moment and decided to be courageous and take a pass. Her mother and Howard looked at her in shock as she pulled Sam aside and said, "Look, sweetie. I'm *really* tired from the flight. Are you gonna be mad at me if I don't come along?"

Sam looked disappointed but straightened up and took her side. "It's okay, Mom, if you're tired. It's not a big deal. You should go to home and get some sleep," he said, putting his hand gently on her shoulder.

Falco smiled at her son's blossoming maturity. She buttoned her coat and embraced each of them. "I'll see you Christmas Day," she said as she backed away and made her way toward the exit.

CHAPTER 150

Andie spent most of the next few days recalling the images of the drawings and dealing with a rash of disturbing memories. She studied the vacant floor as vague images of her paintings came to her. Colors of her larger pieces drifted through her mind as her heart throbbed.

A flash of a tumbling box of nails startled her as sweat seeped from her skin and drenched her body. She fell back on the floor, suddenly paralyzed as tremors rippled through her. Her body ached as a moan rose from deep inside. Her fingers gripped the floor, grasping for something to hang onto as the room turned upside down. She tried to scream but had no breath, no air to support it. Her arms tingled as the metal spikes probed her skin deeper and deeper, spilling pools of warmth as the wires grew tighter. She gasped as her body rocked from within. Her stomach heaved a slimy liquid that burned her throat and lips. She panted, trying to calm herself, but a flood of sour spit made her cough. Her fingers scratched desperately at the floor as she tried to crawl away, to make her way to the bed, to hide.

She pulled herself under the bed and gripped the web-like mesh that held the mattress above her. *Bang! Bang!* came the tormenting noise. Andie tried to hold on as a scream erupted from inside her.

* * *

"Ms. Fulbright?" The steel examination table felt cool on her forehead as she lifted her head and squinted at the bright fluorescent lights.

"Ms. Fulbright?" came the voice again. Andie's vision cleared as she became aware of the heaviness in her head. "Ms. Fulbright?"

"Uh…" Was all Andie could muster. The rest of her body seemed to come to life again as she felt something tight around her hands and wrists. Thinking she was bound by ropes, she pulled her hands away and cradled them to her chest.

"Take it easy. We're not finished," came the voice again; it was sterile and tight as a wire. Andie looked up and blinked as a man slowly appeared before her. He was dressed in pale blue and wore glasses. She frowned at him, confused.

"You want to tell me what happened, Ms Fulbright?" Andie stared blankly at him and said nothing. "Your hands are covered in cuts. How did you manage to injure yourself like that?"

Andie looked down and saw her shirt had been changed. It no longer smelled of vomit nor was it wet with sweat.

"You're not going to talk to me, are you?" asked the physician. He finished bandaging Andie's left hand and gently moved it to her lap. Andie looked at it curiously then stared at the bandage on her other hand. A wave of dizziness came over her as her head grew heavy again.

* * *

Falco slept twelve hours. Her clothes were a heap on the floor, the blankets on her bed virtually undisturbed as they covered her. Her eyes drifted open as she felt a surge of unfamiliarity.

Where am I? She sat up and looked around as the cold winter sun streamed into her bedroom. Suddenly her bed felt infinitely familiar and comforting. She sunk back into it and promptly fell back asleep. After an hour the cheery notes of her cell phone made their way into her consciousness. She sat up and looked at the clock; it was ten thirty. "Oh, god. It's so late." She rustled through the blankets and swung back the comforter as her feet touched the floor. She searched for her cell phone, following its annoying ringing.

"It's probably Jeffery wanting to tell me off," she muttered as she reached for the phone. She dragged on her robe and turned up the heat, hearing the familiar buzz as the furnace kicked on. The missed call was from Alan. She felt relieved but out of sorts. She knew Jeffery was going to call her. She knew he wouldn't be able to resist making her feel irresponsible and self-centered. "Okay, I've been a little of both lately," she told herself as she dialed Alan's number.

"Let me guess. You're out Christmas shopping!" Alan said, answering the phone.

"No, no. In fact I just woke up."

"Wow, you must have been exhausted," he said kindly.

"Yeah, I was, nothing like sleeping in your own bed."

Alan told her he had hoped to see her today but that his daughter Alona had dropped by with her new boyfriend, and Alan had offered to take them out to dinner. Falco didn't really mind since her shopping list was heavy on her mind.

He paused for a moment, then his voice changed from jovial to serious. "Monica, I need to ask you something important."

"Yes? What?"

"Andie's at a critical junction with the drawings. We've gone through all but two, and then we discovered another one that was important to the set. I'd like to explore the McCaffery shooting with her this week. It's time, and, well, there's another element at play with the drawings. How would you feel about being present when we go through the last three with Andie? I think you'd be a big help, since you were there with her when all this happened." His words were clumsy with anticipation.

Falco considered his request. She hadn't seen Andie since that day in the alley. "I'm not surprised you asked me to come," she said. "But she probably doesn't remember me, Alan."

"Yes, she does," Alan said quickly. "You came up in the drawings. She remembers you," Alan said, hearing the reluctance in her voice. "You'd really be helping us out. There are things Andie remembers but other things she tends to embellish. You'd help her stay on track and fill in the blanks."

Falco thought a minute then said, "All right, yes. I can be there if you think I can help, but you must know that day wasn't easy for me either."

"I realize that, and I'm not going to tell you it'll be pleasant, but this session is critical."

Falco nodded to herself, feeling a combination of fear and relief.

"Okay. I'll be there. When?"

"How does tomorrow look for you?"

"It's Christmas day, Alan. I can't do that."

"Sorry. How about Tuesday? Say, two p.m.?"

"Okay. I'll meet you at your office."

"Thanks. I really appreciate it…and Merry Christmas."

Falco hung up the phone as her heart and mind felt heavy. She shook off the feeling and got dressed for the mall. "I hate this," she said under her breath as she grabbed her keys, her Christmas list, and coat and dashed out the door.

CHAPTER 151

Christmas day was frigid but clear. Dinner at Elaine and Howard's was at five, but the family gathering was at two. Falco woke up early with Andie on her mind. *Christmas day in the psych ward. Fuck. Do they put up a Christmas tree there? Will anyone come to visit?* She felt a wave of sadness and emptiness. She wondered what Andie had done for Christmas last year. She wondered what lovely gifts Kat may have given her. She picked up the phone and dialed Michael.

"Merry Christmas. Hansen residence." The voice didn't sound like Michael.

"Michael? Uh, hi, is Michael around?"

"Yes, may I tell him who's calling?" Falco heard loud music and lots of voices in the background. Michael had company.

"Monica Falco."

"Oh, hey, Detective. It's Tim Strickland, Merry Christmas," came the jovial voice. "Welcome home."

Falco smiled as she heard the phone being handed to Michael.

"Hey, sweetie. You're back and alive and well from Camp FBI!"

"Yeah, I called to wish you a Merry Christmas. I haven't spoken to you in a while."

"Oh, girl, yeah, but I understand. Was the camp cool? Did you meet any hot FBI types?"

Falco could tell Michael already had been hitting the eggnog. "No, nothing like that, but it's been very good—and very draining. I'm glad we have a little break for Christmas."

Michael grew serious. Falco could tell he had stepped into a room away from his guests. "Alan told me you're going to be there when we talk with Andie about the McCaffery shooting."

"Yes, I am. I'm not looking forward to reliving that again, but I know I need to be there."

"I'm really glad, Monica. Did I ever tell you you're a saint, an honest to fucking goodness saint?" Michael's voice cracked.

"No, but I'm hardly a saint, and you know it," Falco said flatly. She wished she had a cup of eggnog to loosen up her holiday too. She hung up the phone saying she'd see Michael at two o'clock tomorrow.

She glanced at her watch; it was nearly noon. *I've got to get ready for dinner.* She frowned at the thought of seeing her mother and Howard and toyed with the idea of running off with Sam somewhere, ice-skating or sledding.

* * *

Elaine and Howard bought a new pre-lit Christmas tree and decorated it with quaint holiday figurines and ornaments that Falco remembered from her childhood. She was feeling pangs of inadequacy after her mother and Howard had showered Sam with presents. Jeffery scolded them for their overindulgence, but Sam was bouncing off the walls. "Sorry I couldn't get that game you wanted, Sam. But I'll have my friend see if he can get it," Falco told him.

She took a sip of red wine and thought about Chris in Indianapolis. Jeffery was shooting her dirty looks. She excused herself and closed herself up in the guest bathroom.

"A three-eyed monster, that's what I am," she said to the mirror as she squinted under a blast of fluorescent light. "I need to eat something. I've already had too much wine."

Jeffery, Sam, Elaine, and Howard were stuffing armfuls of wrapping paper, ribbon, bows, and gift boxes into a large trash bag. She heard the rustle of the paper and Sam running around with the open bag, talking loudly. She leaned against the sink and felt a swell of emotions. *Yes, I know I've been busy, out of touch*, she thought, *but no one has said anything about my fucking promotion, the training—where the hell I've been over the past month! I guess none of that matters. I could be locked up in a psych ward for all they care. They sure as hell treat me as if I were some…some oddity, a family member no one wants to talk about.* She leaned into the mirror and studied her face. New lines had appeared around her eyes and forehead; they were much more visible in the glaring light. She blew her nose, looked for some lipstick in her mother's vanity, then took a deep breath and opened the bathroom door.

Elaine was in the kitchen making a clatter with dishes and silverware. Falco wandered in. "Need some help, Mom?"

Elaine swung around as if startled. She gave her daughter a curious look, thought for a moment, then pointed to the stack of dishes and utensils. "You can set the table, dear. That was always your job when you were little, remember?" She smiled and bent down to look into the oven.

Falco sighed and started to set the table. Howard came in with the half case of wine she had gotten them. "You know, dear, I don't know much about wine, but these look really good!" He put his arm around her.

"Well, I got some help picking them out. I'm hardly an expert myself."

"We *love* Cabernet Sauvignon," Howard said, patronizing her.

"Nothing like a nice Cab on a sleepless summer night," she muttered under her breath.

"Huh?" Howard said.

Falco looked at him as if she had awoken from a dream. She smiled. "Nothing, Howard. Nothing."

Sam came over and pulled her away from the table. "You promised to tell me all about the FBI Academy, Mom."

"I know, Sam, but I don't think anyone else here wants to hear about it, so why don't we wait 'til after dinner, okay? Then we can talk."

Sam gave her an odd look as a cold silence fell over the kitchen. He frowned with confusion then sped out of the room and sat in front of the TV.

"He thinks the world of you," Howard said quietly.

"Yeah. Too bad no one else does," she muttered as she wandered into the living room.

Jeffery ignored her as he stared at the football game on TV. Falco sighed, found her coat, and went outside to the front porch. She lit a cigarette and sat on the concrete steps. It was cold, and she had forgotten her scarf and gloves at home. It didn't matter.

CHAPTER 152

"Hi, Andie. How are you today?" asked Alan as he looked at the bandages on her hands. Andie didn't respond as she slid the drawing she was working on under her bed. "I guess you need some more drawing paper," he prodded, trying to get her to say something.

Andie nodded as if not wanting to talk. Her head and shoulder jerked in one quick movement as she avoided his gaze.

"Listen, Andie. I want you to pay attention to what I'm going to say. I want to make a deal with you," he said. "You know the drawings we've been working through together? Well, you've worked really hard sorting through the images and memories. I'd like to give you a reward for your hard work."

Andie glanced up and gave him a suspicious look.

"We have three more drawings to go through today. If we can get through them, I'd like to give you a weekend out of here, a weekend at home."

Andie stared at Alan in disbelief. "Home?"

"Yes, a weekend at home. Michael will stay with you, but yes."

Andie sat up straight, and her face brightened. "Yes, yes," she said eagerly. "I want to go home. I want to see Leo and Curry."

Alan nodded then sat on the bed. "You're going to get some help with the remaining drawings we go through today. I've invited someone to be here with you."

Andie gave him a curious look. "Who?"

"You remember Detective Falco. Monica Falco?"

She looked away then stared at Alan. "Detective Falco?" she asked slowly.

"Yes, Detective Falco. I've asked her to come today."

Andie shook her head as she processed the information. She chewed nervously at her thumbnail and stared off. Alan watched an uneasiness washed over her.

* * *

The hospital was quiet. Margaret had the day off, as did most of the clerical staff. Falco took a deep breath as she followed the lighted numbers of the elevator up to the sixth floor. She gripped her keys and walked quickly down a dimly lit corridor to Alan's office. His door was ajar; she pushed it gently and spotted Alan at his desk on the phone. He waved and motioned her in. Anxiety filled her as she smelled the familiar scents of his office: leather, furniture polish, and the faint hint of Margaret's perfume.

Alan walked around his desk as the phone cord knocked over a cup of pens. He took Falco's coat and draped it over the chair next to his desk. He noted the tension in her face.

"Look, Bill, if Karen Jennings says it's a go, then we'll agree to it. We'll bundle the drawings up and ship them to her via messenger. It's that simple… No, the original ones she saw aren't available. They were destroyed… Yes, by the artist. No, we don't have them anymore. Andie tore them up. The others no one would want, believe me." Alan hung up as Falco tried to calm herself. "Lawyers," he said breathlessly.

He came around the desk and knelt in front of her. "I'm really grateful you're here," he said, gazing at her tenderly. They kissed just as Michael entered then stopped. Seeing them, he spun around and left the room. Alan straightened up, "Michael? I just got off the phone with Bill Kucer. It's a done deal with Kat."

Falco gave him a confused look. "What's going on with Kat?"

Alan sighed. "You don't even want to know."

Michael entered looking a little embarrassed. "Happy holidays, Detective," he said, giving her a hug and a kiss on the cheek. "You're a sight for sore eyes." He had a look of sadness on his face; Falco couldn't tell if it was because he missed her or if it had something to do with Andie.

Alan let out a deep breath. "It's two o'clock," he said. "How do you want to work this?" Michael shrugged. "Okay, we'll go into one of the therapy rooms on the ninth floor. I'll bring the drawings, and you can go get Andie. Bring Donald Franklin if you need to." He turned to Falco. "Are you okay with this?"

"I'll admit I'm a little scared."

He opened his office door as they filed out and headed to the elevators. Alan had the three drawings in his hand. A tiny Christmas tree greeted them as the elevator doors opened to the ninth floor. A haggard-looking nurse with Christmas ornaments as earrings frowned as she saw the three. "Happy holidays, Doctor," she said.

Alan nodded with a smile. He guided Falco to a dark hallway where they turned left into a small area of conference rooms. Michael walked quickly ahead and went in the other direction.

The door opened with a click as Alan swiped his ID. He arranged four chairs in a circle and moved a table to the far end of the room, wedging it in a corner. "Wish we had a bigger space," he said. He placed the drawings face-down on the seat of one of the chairs and took a deep breath. "You okay?" he asked Falco.

"Yeah, sure."

Michael appeared at the window of the therapy room door. "I called Donald. Andie doesn't want to come."

Alan looked down.

"I thought you made a deal with her," Michael said.

Alan scowled. "I did. So much for that."

Michael looked down the hall and saw Donald Franklin, the nursing attendant, enter Andie's room. "I'd better go help. Andie doesn't like him."

"Don't get her all excited!" Alan cautioned as Michael headed down the hall. Alan turned then quickly followed Michael.

Falco's anxiety wasn't easing up. She tried to take deep breaths, but it didn't help. She picked up the three drawings and glanced at each one. A cold chill came over her as she saw obvious references to the shooting and McCaffery's death. "Jesus," she whispered, remembering that day.

Down the hallway she heard a woman's voice pleading and the shuffle of feet. "No, I don't want to. No, please," Andie said as she tried to twist herself away from Michael.

Donald looked for his cue as Andie resisted them. Then Falco heard Alan's voice grow louder. She stared at the floor, bracing herself. "Shit."

She heard a booming voice as Andie's pleas grew louder. "Put me down. Alan, tell him to put me down. Fuck you, Franklin!"

Falco got up suddenly as Alan pulled the door open, looking flustered. She saw a flurry of brown hair and fists as Donald set Andie on the floor just outside the therapy room. Andie punched him hard in the stomach, but the large man hardly flinched.

"Okay. Come on, Andie. Let's go," Michael said from behind Donald. He walked around the man and took Andie's arm and pulled her into the room. Her hair covered her face; her sweater was loose and pulled out of shape. She looked angry.

"Take it easy," Michael said firmly, taking her shoulders and setting her on the loveseat near the door. Andie promptly pulled her knees up, wrapped her arms around her legs, and buried her face. "I don't want this," Andie said, her eyes darting about.

Falco sat quietly, wondering who this person was. Andie had grown quite thin, her hair had gotten long, and wild and streaks of gray were every-where. Her hands trembled as her head twitched uncontrollably. "Fuck *you*," she jeered, not looking up from under the mass of hair.

Alan glanced at Falco and quietly shut the door. He knelt in front of Andie and said, "Remember our deal, Andie." Andie said nothing.

Michael sat next to her on the loveseat and took the drawings from the floor and set them on his lap. "Andie, I know this isn't going to be easy, but as Alan said, the worst is over. We just need to talk about these."

"I shouldn't have given them up!" she yelled, shaking her fist at the two men.

Michael shifted away, not wanting to get hit. "Andie, you *gave* these to us. And remember the drawing on the floor? We thought you drew them as a way out, as a path toward healing *yourself*."

"How do you know what *I* want? *I* want to get out of here! That's what *I* want!" Andie said into her chest as she cradled her head with her arms.

Michael glared at her then looked at the drawings. He was growing frustrated. Alan moved closer, motioning to Michael to switch places. Then softly a hand touched Alan's arm. It was Falco gently pulling him out of the way. Michael moved out of the seat as she quietly sat next to Andie. She waited a moment as Andie sat motionless. Michael quietly put the drawings on the floor next to her.

"Hey, Andie," came Falco's voice.

Andie jerked as if struck by lightning. She wrapped her head tighter with her arms as she wheezed.

"Andie, it's Monica. You remember me, don't you? Detective Falco?" Andie picked up her head and put her hand over her face, then nodded slowly. "I haven't seen you in a long time. It would be nice if I could see your face. Then maybe we can talk."

Andie rubbed her forehead from under the mass of hair then pulled the hair out of her eyes. Her expression was angry and scared. She hid her face in her hands again and mumbled something indiscernible.

Falco waited and watched. "I'm here to help you go through these drawings, to help you remember what happened that day. You know what day I'm talking about, don't you?"

Andie stiffened.

"We were both there together, right? It was raining, and—"

"I *remember* the rain. I *remember* you were there!" Andie said with a cry. A shudder of emotion ran through her as the twitch persisted. Her breathing grew faster and labored as she whispered, "Bang, bang, bang."

"It was early evening and getting dark. Detective Ballard and I found you at the top of a concrete embankment. Do you remember what he, what Brian McCaff—"

Andie's feet hit the floor as she grabbed the drawings from Falco's lap, turned, and clutched them to her chest. She sank to the floor and put her head down. "It hurts. It hurts," she moaned, rocking herself. "The nails, the wires... It's getting worse, getting worse. He's here. He's here right now!" Andie gripped the drawings as her eyes caught the images of barbed wire and blue lights of the top drawing. They held her gaze, and she quieted. "It's so cold, so cold," she whispered as her body trembled.

Falco knelt next to her. "I know it's cold. I know you're scared and wet and you're hurt so badly, but you've got to stay with me, Andie. We got through it once. You can do it again…with me."

"No, no, I'm dizzy. There's so much pain. I'm bleeding. The blood is everywhere. I'm so scared!" Andie gripped her left arm as phantom pains shot through her. She grasped the top drawing and pulled the center of the paper into a crumpled ball. "His eyes…his eyes are staring. He's here… He's here right now!"

Falco lightly gripped Andie's arm. "Listen to me, Andie. He's not here. Brian McCaffery isn't *anywhere* in this room. He's never going to hurt you again. Do you understand?" Falco was trembling.

Andie stopped breathing for a moment as the top drawing fell to the floor. The decapitated heads from the next drawing stared up at the two of them. Andie glanced briefly at the images, the streaks of blood, the hands, the guns. She dodged away and ran to the door, pulling frantically at the handle. Falco ran to her as Andie pounded it with her fists.

"Please! I don't want to. Please. Please! I can't! Let me out!"

Falco put her arm around her and rubbed her shoulders. "I know this is hard, Andie, but we've got to talk about it," she said softly. "You're stronger than you think."

Andie shook her head as she sobbed into her hands. She shrunk to the floor and wept, covering her face with the drawing. Falco sat next to her and watched. She gently pulled the drawing from Andie's hands and smoothed it on the floor. She eyed Andie then said, "There are two heads in this drawing, Andie—the man with the green eyes and the other with the brown eyes. Where are the rest of their bodies?"

Andie gave her a riveting glance. "I…I don't know what happened to them."

Falco glanced at Alan and Michael. "Remember, I was there, Andie. Come on. *Try* to remember."

She settled onto the floor next to Andie and turned the drawing so Andie could see it. Andie swallowed hard and stared at the images. She began to shake and twitch; her hands balled up into fists. She got to her knees and pounded the paper where the images of the handgun and the green-eyed man were drawn. "You! *You! You!*" Andie screamed with each punch. "You can't hurt me. You can't hurt me. You're dead. Dead. You're dead!" She pressed her face into the drawing and screamed into it. "I hate you. I hate you. And now you're dead!" She gasped for breath as Falco let her scream, her hand steady on her back.

Alan and Michael waited. Andie was wheezing and trembling.

For a moment the three considered the possibility that Andie didn't remember the shooting, that somehow she just knew McCaffery was dead. Falco looked at Alan and Michael. Alan nodded for her to continue.

"Look at this. What does this cross mean, Andie? Why is it colored red?"

Andie looked at her in horror, as if Falco knew her secret, then she looked away. Her head and neck twitched, and her face contorted. As her right hand gripped her ear, she whispered, "Bang, bang!"

She stared at the images and the truth they represented. Suddenly a sense of calm washed over her, as if the drawing itself had released the answer, the truth. Her eyes glazed over as her head dropped. "Oh, oh. I know. I know."

She lowered herself to the floor. She made eye contact with Falco first then Alan and Michael. "I shot him," she said quietly to the floor. "I shot him." She looked up at Falco. Her head twitched again as her body wavered, weak from her own words. "I shot him…in the chest, then I shot him again. She sniffed then looked up at the ceiling and said in a high voice. "He looked so surprised, like it was funny or something, then his eyes went black as death." Andie smiled and laughed deep inside herself, then stared off. She then looked down again at the drawing. Tears flooded her face. She bent over the paper then touched the image of the other severed head. The paper was blotchy from her tears. She paused and stared at it, touching the surface lightly and running her finger over the face of the image. "My dad's dead too," she said softly. "I did it. I shot him too. He hurt my Mom. Now he's dead too." She smiled knowingly.

Andie's words jolted Falco. She hadn't realized it, but her hands were clenched under her chin as if she had been praying. She steadied herself on the floor then looked at Michael and Alan. They were frozen, stunned.

Andie's body crumpled over the wrinkled drawing. Her eyes bulged as she wheezed and shivered. "I'm sorry, I…I just couldn't hang on," she said to the floor. She took another breath then grew silent as her body went limp. The remnants of the three drawings were crumpled and torn. The final draw-ing lay untouched on the floor near the loveseat.

* * *

Falco found herself alone in the dimly lit hallway. Michael and Alan made sure Andie was all right and took her back to her room. Andie was shaky, but Alan felt the session had gone well considering the trauma of the memories.

The two joined Falco and walked from the elevator toward Alan's office. They entered hearing the rumble of traffic and the steady whistle of the wind around the building. Michael sat heavily in one of the leather chairs and put his face in his hands. Falco wandered to the window and looked out absently. Andie's words echoed in her head.

CHAPTER 153

It was nearly eight p.m. by the time Falco returned home. She was drained and still shaken by the session. Alan had offered to buy her and Michael dinner, but she declined, saying she wasn't hungry and needed to get home. He could tell she was upset and promised to call her later.

Falco refused to consider that Andie had taken her father's life. *She killed McCaffery in self-defense, but she's no murderer*, she thought. Her mind raced a mile a minute. *I need to calm down. I just need to calm down.*

The cold glass of Chardonnay chilled her, but somehow it cleared her head. An idea came to her as she finished the rest of her glass. She pulled on her coat and jumped into her car and headed south toward the expressway.

The twenty-third district was quiet for the day after Christmas. Domestic violence was the typical crime around the holidays, she thought, not much else. Tim Strickland met her as she climbed up the stairs. "Hey, Detective, aren't you supposed to be on vacation or something?"

Falco buzzed past him, not saying a word. She pulled out her desk chair and turned on her computer. On her desk was a stack of holiday cards and a few tiny presents. She pushed them out of the way and wiggled her mouse. The page took a minute to load. Her heart sped; she almost heard it beating inside her head. *I've got to know. I've got to know.*

The database came up and prompted her password. She typed it in as a flash of colors and text whirled before her. She typed Andie's full name. *I don't know her birthdate. Maybe I can guess. Fuck. I don't know her father's first name either.* Suddenly she realized this search would be more difficult than she'd thought. "Let's just go with what we know," she said softly, squinting at the screen. "Okay…"

Name: Andrea Fulbright

Birthplace: Chicago, Illinois

Birthdate: 1960

Father's name: ?

Mother's name: ?

Offense: murder/suicide/unknown

Year: 1988

Falco hit the search key on the screen. A series of documents came up, including full-text articles from the *Chicago Tribune*, *Sun-Times*, and *Wall Street Journal*. She printed them then hit the link to the FBI's National Crime Database. Two hits appeared using Falco's criteria. Her heart sank. "Damn it," she whispered. She clicked on the links as her eyes sped through the entries. She sighed with relief. Andie's name appeared on two gay and lesbian databases. She shook her head in disbelief. "Republicans," she hissed.

She scanned the five documents she printed and looked for police reports or names of CPD personnel she might know who had investigated the case—all dead ends. She turned to the two articles about Andie's father's death; his name was Douglas Andrew Fulbright, II. She returned to the search screen and typed his full name at the prompt. Except for the articles she already had found, no police reports or other information suggested that Douglas Fulbright's death was due to anything other than suicide. She breathed a huge sigh of relief. *Andie must have made it up*, she thought. She put on her coat and headed out of the building.

By the time she got home, Alan had called twice. She dragged off her coat and dialed his number as she poured herself another glass of wine.

"Hi, Alan," she said.

"Where have you been?"

"The twenty-third district, I had to look into what Andie said about her father."

"What did you find out?"

"I couldn't find a thing. Would she make up a thing like that?"

Alan sighed. "Possibly. That was a startling revelation, but where it came from, I don't know." His voice sounded tired. "But you didn't *find* anything, right?" he asked again, needing reassurance. "Because if I missed that after all these years, I may as well find another line of work," he said half seriously.

"No, Alan. I did a search on her father's name and Andie's. I used her birthdate and the year of her father's death. Some documents came up, but they were mostly obituaries and articles about her father's life. Andie's name came up on two LGBT databases, ones the FBI considered 'subversive.'"

Alan laughed. "Well, I'm relieved on many accounts."

* * *

While Andie recovered quickly from the trauma of the last session, her overall emotional state was still tenuous. Alan knew he couldn't offer her the weekend home just yet but was optimistic that she'd be ready in a few weeks.

The last drawing disappeared with Andie. She stashed it under her bed and requested more books from the library. Michael brought a CD player and a box of recorded music, mostly Beethoven and Mozart.

Falco spent New Year's Eve with Jeffery and Sam. They played Trivial Pursuit and ate pizza. Jeffery won both games as usual. *It's all that useless stuff that clogs his brain and makes him such a stubborn asshole in the real world*, Falco thought as she shot him an annoyed look. She drove home soon after midnight. Sam was fast asleep on the sofa and Jeffery was still holding some crazy grudge.

"So, back to Quantico. When's your flight, Monica?" Alan asked. It was Tuesday night.

"Nine-thirty tomorrow morning."

"Can I drive you?"

"No, I can take the train or a taxi."

"But I have something to give you, so I'd like to drive you, if that's okay."

She felt a bit uneasy all of a sudden. "Well, okay. I'll need to leave pretty early, though."

"Not a problem. I'm staying downtown for a conference anyway. I'll just take a little detour and drive you—you know, see you off."

"Okay. How about seven?"

"Great."

CHAPTER 154

Falco stood on the porch, keeping an eye out for Alan's Volvo. She was shaking from the cold and a rising sense of anxiety about leaving again. She had resisted buying another pack of cigarettes and found her gloves in her pocket instead of her lighter. "All the better," she whispered. Alan's car appeared exactly at seven in the driveway. She dragged her rolling suitcase behind her as he jumped out to open the trunk.

"Curbside service with a smile," he said, smiling broadly.

Falco looked a bit sad. Alan eyed her closely then kissed her on the forehead.

"Listen, I'm going to take surface streets 'cause the expressway is backed up, okay?" He glanced at the rearview mirror and put the car in reverse.

"Sure, whatever works. How's Andie?"

"She's doing better. In fact she surprised both Michael and me. Her twitch has all but disappeared, and the noises in her right ear, which I attributed to the shooting, have diminished too."

"And her admission about her father?"

"Well, that's another issue. We may never know about that," Alan said, glancing at her. "We may just have to leave that one alone. Plus you found no evidence of a suspicious death in your databases. I'd call it a dead issue."

Falco nodded. "I guess, but why would she...?"

"For another time, I think. Andie still has a lot to sort through," he said thoughtfully.

Before long the silver Volvo was approaching the terminal for United Airlines. Falco pulled her coat closed and put on her gloves. "I appreciate the ride, Alan."

He pulled behind a parked taxi as the two jumped out of the car. Alan heaved her suitcase out of the trunk and wheeled it next to her. "See you soon, Detective?"

"Yes. Two weeks," she said, giving him a quick kiss and a longer hug.

"You take care of yourself. You know I'll miss you."

"I'll miss you too, Alan. I know you'll keep me posted on Andie."

"Oh, yeah. Hey, wait a sec." He patted his chest pocket of his coat then did the same to his hip pockets. "I've got something for you." He opened the rear passenger seat of his car and pulled out a sealed manila envelope and handed it to her. "It's from Andie."

Falco gave him a blank look. She glanced at the envelope then slid it into the zippered compartment of her suitcase.

"Have a good flight," Alan said softly.

Falco nodded and smiled then turned toward the terminal. She waved as Alan got into his car, jutted out around the parked cab, and headed toward the expressway. The porter immediately grabbed her suitcase, set it on a gurney, and scanned her boarding pass. She glanced back at her bag as she ducked into the busy terminal and looked for her boarding gate.

* * *

Snow threatened Falco's departure, but she didn't really care. A flood of emotions had consumed her well before she found a seat far away from everyone in the waiting area. She felt irritable and sad, dizzy and acutely alert. "I could use a cigarette," she said under her breath.

She pulled out her cell phone to call Sam to say goodbye, but the phone immediately went to voicemail. She started to leave a message, but her voice caught and she quickly hung up. "I love you Sammy. I'll be home in a few weeks for good. Then we'll catch up, I promise," she said into the silence. Quickly she pulled a tissue from her purse and pinched the tears from her eyes. "Don't start. Don't start or you won't be able to stop."

On the plane she ran through the memories of the last week: Christmas dinner at her mother's, Jeffery's nasty attitude, Andie's session with the drawings, and her disturbing admission about her father. Her eyes filled with tears as she recalled that day at the station. In her mind she saw Andie standing next to her desk with Ballard's gift and her sweater in her arms. So many months had passed, and the memory of that day, of Andie's face, had grown foggy and disjointed.

Her thoughts turned to Tuesday as she remembered Andie's pleas and screams. She wished she had something by which to remember her—some strand of hair, perhaps something so fleeting as a tear to hold close until she saw her again. She wished she had studied Andie more closely, taken some picture of her in her mind's eye. She wished she would once again know her as she had that past July.

Richmond loomed as dark clouds parted and revealed rooftops, trees, and traffic below. "Ladies and gentlemen, we'd like to welcome you to Richmond, Virginia. Currently it's twenty-six degrees and rainy. We hope you enjoyed your flight. Thank you for flying United Airlines."

A strange familiarity swept over Falco as she slid out of the taxi and walked through the hotel lobby. Richmond and Quantico were no longer a strange and hostile place, but one of comfort and exhilaration—a place that brought back her old self, her identity as a law enforcement professional and as a woman. She entered her hotel room and unzipped her suitcase. then started to hang her clothes in the closet. Her hand felt something firm inside the suitcase. She flipped the bag over, unzipped the outer compartment, and pulled out the manila envelope. She stared at it, looking at one side then the other. She tore off the flap and pulled out a folded piece of paper. She bit her lip as she eyed it then carefully unfolded it. It was the final drawing of the set, the drawing that didn't seem to fit, it was the faceless angel.

Falco scanned it as her heart quickened. The angel now had a face, it was Falco's. She was clad in armor over a flowing robe and holding bolts of lightning. The angel floated through a stormy sky over a field that resembled barbed wire. Andie had drawn her portrait, a superhuman portrait. She realized she was the missing image at the end of the maze. The final piece was Falco saving Andie, breathing life back into her. Falco was stunned. Her eyes studied the image then she glanced at the bottom of the drawing. Written in navy blue pencil were the words:

You saved me, Monica.

I love you.

—Andie

Later that day, Chris Sommers called after her from across the street. "Happy New Year, lady!"

Falco smiled almost shyly. Chris waved and bolted across the street. "You got some R&R, Falco!" Falco was grinning as if she wanted to say something. Chris squinted at her and said, "You look great! But....something's different about you."

Falco gulped down a smile.

Chris stepped back and grinned. "I think something's happened, and from the look on your face, I think it's a good thing."

"Yeah," Falco smiled and blushed. "It's a really good thing."

A brutal arctic wind blew past them as Falco linked her arm to Chris's and pulled her close. They walked together, talking. Neither one noticed the cold.